WORKS OF HERMAN MELVILLE

"Both jaws, like enormous shears, bit the craft completely
in twain."

Works of Herman Melville

~~~~~~~~~~~~~~~~~~~~~~~~~~~~~~~~

MOBY DICK or THE WHALE

BARTLEBY

BENITO CERENO

THE PARADISE OF BACHELORS
AND THE TARTARUS OF MAIDS

BILLY BUDD, SAILOR

AVENEL BOOKS
NEW YORK

First published in 1987 by Avenel Books,
distributed by Crown Publishers, Inc.,
225 Park Avenue South, New York, New York 10003.

Printed and Bound in the United States of America

Library of Congress Cataloging-in-Publication Data
Melville, Herman, 1819-1891.
    Works of Herman Melville.
    Contents: Moby Dick or The whale—Bartleby—
Benito Cereno—[etc.]
    I. Title.
PS2382   1987   813′.3   87-14445
ISBN 0-517-65084-3

h g f e d c b a

CONTENTS

FOREWORD

~~~~~~

HERMAN MELVILLE'S professional writing career spanned a brief eleven years. Between the ages of twenty-five and thirty-six, he published nine novels and a collection of short fiction. Then, bitter and defeated, abandoned by the critics who had praised his early work and no longer able to support his family by his writing, he retired to a private life of travel and, later, a twenty-year stint as a customs house inspector on the New York City docks. At the time of his death in 1891, a faded if not totally forgotten star in the literary heavens, Melville merited an obituary in the *New York Times*. That the *Times* eulogized him as "Henry Melville" is an irony the writer no doubt would have appreciated.

Melville's route to becoming a writer was as twisted and hopscotched as the *Pequod*'s quest for *Moby Dick*. Born in New York City in 1819 into a family whose circumstances promised a comfortable middle-class upbringing and education, young Melville received his first dose of the harsh realities of life at the age of sixteen. His father, whose health and sanity had evaporated under the strain of disastrous financial fortune, died, thus forcing Herman and his brother, Gansvoort, to leave school and help support their debt-ridden family.

For the next four years Melville served as a bank clerk, a farm hand, an assistant in the family's cap and fur store, and an elementary school teacher. Finding none of these occupations to his liking, and perhaps already succumbing to a restless and wandering nature, Melville signed on as a sailor on a summer voyage to Liverpool and back. While the experience did not seem to make a critical impression on Melville, it would provide the background for his novel *Redburn*.

Once home again, Melville made another stab at teaching but with no more success than before. And after an aborted trip to Illinois to visit his Uncle Thomas, the old restlessness returned and he went back to the sea—this time for four years.

If his record as a sailor was far from exemplary, Melville's travels did provide the raw material for much of his fiction. In January of 1841, he sailed from Massachusetts on the whaler *Acushnet* and deserted eighteen months later on the Marquesas Islands. After living as a beachcomber for several months among the cannibals of the Taipi Valley, he shipped aboard an Australian whaler, the *Lucy Ann,* and promptly joined a mutiny by some of the crew, which landed him in a British stockade on Tahiti. The prison was little more than a shack and Melville escaped to sign on the Nantucket whaler *Charles & Henry* as a boat steerer and harpooneer, and served without incident until his discharge. After another extended period of odd jobs and beachcombing, Melville shipped as an ordinary seaman on the American naval vessel the *United States* and returned to his family in October of 1844. From these adventures and misadventures, Melville gleaned enough raw material for his novels *Typee, Omoo, Mardi, Moby Dick,* and *White-Jacket.*

Melville spent the next winter back home in Lansingburgh, New York, enthralling his mother and sisters with elaborately told tales of adventure on the high seas and among pagan races. Out of these fanciful renderings came his first book, *Typee,* and its sequel, *Omoo.* Melville soon found himself a literary success both in the United States and in England. He moved to New York City to continue his career and in 1847 married Elizabeth Shaw, daughter of the Chief Justice of Massachusetts, Lemuel Shaw.

Still flush with his initial success, Melville published *Mardi,* a romance that was experimental in form and content. It was an immediate disaster with critics and general readers alike.

Stung by this rebuke, no longer wishing to be known as a writer of simple sea stories, yet feeling the pinch of a growing family, Melville rebounded, pounding out his next two novels, *Redburn* and *White-Jacket,* in a remarkable five months. The critics were delighted with his return to the traditional form that had first won him success, although Melville himself remained ambivalent, feeling an author's pride for his work and yet bitter about the restraints placed on his artistic freedom. "What I feel most moved to write, that is banned—it will not pay," he wrote to his friend and neighbor Nathaniel Hawthorne. "Yet, altogether, write the *other* way I cannot. So the product is a final hash, and all my books are botches."

Melville's next "botch" was his masterpiece, *Moby Dick, or the Whale.* And while *Moby Dick* was neither critically acclaimed nor commercially successful, Melville clearly wrote the book *he* wanted to write.

Completed in eighteen months of feverish writing and published in 1851 when Melville was thirty-one years old, *Moby Dick* to this day stands as a landmark in American literature. This sprawling epic is part sea adventure, part whaling textbook, part journey into the uncharted depths of human obsession, and part exposé of man's need to question the boundaries of his existence and do battle, however hopelessly, against an unreasoning and unyielding Nature. And Melville, by not yielding to the advice of the literary establishment and the pressures of his economic needs, explored the complexities of man's tenuous place in a hostile world and produced a classic that has withstood the most meticulous academic analysis. Scholars from every political, economic, religious, cultural, and social point of view have taken a stab at *Moby Dick*'s darker message. The whale and the ship that pursues it have been interpreted as representations of God, the devil, capitalism, communism, the wilderness, the imagination, the Id, good and evil. There is no definitive answer, of course. But that these questions still persist, more than 130 years after the book's publication, proves that Melville had hit upon a vein running right to the core of western civilization, and was able to mine his claim so dynamically and dramatically that the book remains rich and vibrant for each succeeding generation of readers.

The three shorter works of fiction also collected here were written between the years 1853 and 1856, published first in *Putnam's Magazine*, and later collected in book form under the title *The Piazza Tales*. "Bartleby," "Benito Cereno," and "The Paradise of Bachelors and the Tartarus of Maids" all exemplify Melville's talent for bringing two opposing forces into conflict to illuminate the deeper, unanswerable questions that confront us in daily life.

The elderly, pragmatic narrator of "Bartleby" meets his nemesis in the form of a mysterious, quiet young scrivener named Bartleby. Relegated to a tiny cubicle in a lawyer's offices where his only outlet to the world is a window facing the blank wall of the building next door, Bartleby withdraws more and more into himself until all requests from his employer elicit a polite, "I would prefer not to." The lawyer, discovering that Bartleby is actually living in the office, attempts to help. But since he is not a spiritual man he cannot understand what ails his employee, and all of his efforts fail. Finally, in an astounding reversal of power, the lawyer, refusing to have an unwanted employee removed by force, moves to a different building. But even then he can never be fully rid of Bartleby, as expressed in his final lament, "Ah, Bartleby! Ah, humanity!"

The employer/employee relationship is taken to its most extreme in "Benito Cereno." This story was based on an actual slave uprising aboard a ship and was described in the writings of Captain Amasa Delano, although Melville liberally reworked the facts to suit his purpose. The *San Dominick* is described as a floating hearse carrying aboard it the dying social evil of slavery. But slavery as a moral question is not Melville's sole concern. He also investigates the interdependent roles of slave and master. Where does one end and the other begin? The line is by no means clear. The realization that the people Benito Cereno had always thought of as tamed animals proved capable of organizing, plotting, and successfully defeating their captors, destroys the young Spaniard. On the other hand, there is Benito's opposite, the painfully innocent Captain Delano, so preoccupied with trivial social amenities and so secure in his smug superiority that he completely fails to realize what is happening aboard the *San Dominick*. It is one of the great ironies of the story that Delano's innocence saves his life, for if he had expressed the least inkling that he was aware of what was happening aboard the ship, he would surely have been killed.

"The Paradise of Bachelors and the Tartarus of Maids" offers the most obvious of Melville's clashes of opposites but, again, there is another layer beneath the surface. While the young gentlemen of the tale enjoy ease and prosperous living, their world is ultimately barren and self-defeating. Nothing is produced; all is consumed. Yet even in the story's dreariest and most sorrowful scene there is a sense of hope, renewal, potential.

Billy Budd, Sailor was completed a few months before Melville's death, but not published until 1924. It was also based on an actual incident that took place aboard an American naval vessel. Melville switches the scene to an English ship, taking advantage of the series of mutinies that plagued the Royal Navy during its war with France following the French Revolution. Melville's message that in times of peril it is necessary, if tragic, to sacrifice innocence in order to preserve the prevailing order is poignantly brought forth in this tale of the beautiful young sailor who falls prey to the evil Claggart and pays with his life.

Even if we were to put aside all the myth and literary treasure hunt that has accompanied Melville's life and work, we would still be left with Melville's true gift—language. Melville is, first and foremost, a storyteller. When we read Melville, we hear a distinctive voice, confident and reassuring, drawing us onward through every turn of plot or allusion. When naming the great storytellers of literature—Twain, Conrad, Faulkner—Melville, too, must be mentioned. Whether we are immersed in the Shakespearian rantings of Ahab in the final pursuit, the Hawthorne-inspired inner debate revealed in Starbuck's soliloquy, or the peaceful insights of Ishmael adrift among a pod of whales, we can feel the magnificent power of Melville's language. Whether we are enjoying the burlesque of the lawyer's office help in "Bartleby," the tragic vision of the *San Dominick* in "Benito Cereno," the stark contrast in tone between "The Paradise of Bachelors and the Tartarus of Maids," or the beautifully haunting hanging scene in *Billy Budd*, we know we are in the hands of a master.

There is no question that Melville could have continued to prosper from his early success simply by imitating it. He could have produced one simple sea adventure after another, established himself within the social circles of his day, a comfortable living for his family, and, having published nothing memorable, would have been completely forgotten after his death. Of course, the world would not have had *Moby Dick*, or "Bartleby," or any of Melville's self-described "botches." Melville wrestled with the promise of easy success and, fortunately for the world, preferred instead to follow a different course—one charted on a piece of paper glued to the inside cover of the writing box in which the manuscript for *Billy Budd* was found. It read: "Follow the dreams of thy youth." It is apparent from the works reprinted in this collection that Melville chose to do exactly that. And whether you are about to encounter Melville for the first time or whether you are paying a visit to an old friend, you must agree that, despite the hardships he encountered keeping to his own course, Melville most certainly made the right choice.

PHILIP J. MADANS

Brooklyn, New York
1987

EDITORIAL NOTE

The editions that were chosen for this collection are, in all cases, early ones. The modern reader may be surprised to discover old-fashioned styles of punctuation and spelling, but these have been kept in order to retain the flavor and authenticity of the originals.

MOBY DICK or THE WHALE

CONTENTS

ETYMOLOGY

(SUPPLIED BY A LATE CONSUMPTIVE USHER
TO A GRAMMAR SCHOOL.)

The pale Usher—threadbare in coat, heart, body, and brain; I see him now. He was ever dusting his old lexicons and grammars, with a queer handkerchief, mockingly embellished with all the gay flags of all the known nations of the world. He loved to dust his old grammars; it somehow mildly reminded him of his mortality.

'While you take in hand to school others, and to teach them by what name a whale-fish is to be called in our tongue, leaving out, through ignorance, the letter H, which almost alone maketh up the signification of the word, you deliver that which is not true.'

HACKLUYT.

'WHALE. * * * Sw. and Dan. hval. This animal is named from roundness or rolling; for in Dan. hvalt is arched or vaulted.'

WEBSTER'S DICTIONARY.

'WHALE. * * * It is more immediately from the Dut. and Ger. Wallen; A.S. Walw-ian, to roll, to wallow.'

RICHARDSON'S DICTIONARY.

חן,	*Hebrew.*
χητος,	*Greek.*
CETUS,	*Latin.*
WHŒL,	*Angle-Saxon.*
HVALT,	*Danish.*
WAL,	*Dutch.*
HWAL,	*Swedish.*
WHALE,	*Icelandic.*
WHALE,	*English.*
BALEINE,	*French.*
BALLENA,	*Spanish.*
PEKEE-NUEE-NUEE,	*Fegee.*
PEHEE-NUEE-NUEE,	*Erromangoan.*

EXTRACTS

(SUPPLIED BY A SUB-SUB-LIBRARIAN.)

It will be seen that this mere painstaking burrower and grubworm of a poor devil of a Sub-Sub appears to have gone through the long Vaticans and street-stalls of the earth, picking up whatever random allusions to whales he could anyways find in any book whatsoever, sacred or profane. Therefore you must not, in every case at least, take the higgledy-piggledy whale statements, however authentic, in these extracts, for veritable gospel cetology. Far from it. As touching the ancient authors generally, as well as the poets here appearing, these extracts are solely valuable or entertaining, as affording a glancing bird's eye view of what has been promiscuously said, thought, fancied, and sung of Leviathan, by many nations and generations, including our own.

So fare thee well, poor devil of a Sub-Sub, whose commentator I am. Thou belongest to that hopeless, sallow tribe which no wine of this world will ever warm; and for whom even Pale Sherry would be too rosy-strong; but with whom one sometimes loves to sit, and feel poor-devilish, too; and grow convivial upon tears; and say to them bluntly, with full eyes and empty glasses, and in not altogether unpleasant sadness—Give it up, Sub-Subs! For by how much the more pains ye take to please the world, by so much the more shall ye for ever go thankless! Would that I could clear out Hampton Court and the Tuileries for ye! But gulp down your tears and hie aloft to the royal-mast with your hearts; for your friends who have gone before are clearing out the seven-storied heavens, and making refugees of long-pampered Gabriel, Michael, and Raphael, against your coming. Here ye strike but splintered hearts together—there, ye shall strike unsplinterable glasses!

'And God created great whales.'
GENESIS.

'Leviathan maketh a path to shine after him;
One would think the deep to be hoary.'
JOB.

'Now the Lord had prepared a great fish to swallow up Jonah.'
JONAH.

'There go the ships; there is that Leviathan whom thou has made to play therein.' PSALMS.

'In that day, the Lord with his sore, and great, and strong sword, shall punish Leviathan the piercing serpent, even Leviathan that crooked serpent; and he shall slay the dragon that is in the sea.'

ISAIAH.

'And what thing soever besides cometh within the chaos of this monster's mouth, be it beast, boat, or stone, down it goes all incontinently that foul great swallow of his, and perisheth in the bottomless gulf of his paunch.'   HOLLAND'S PLUTARCH'S MORALS.

'The Indian Sea breedeth the most and the biggest fishes that are: among which the Whales and Whirlpooles called Balæne, take up as much in length as four acres or arpens of land.'

HOLLAND'S PLINY.

'Scarcely had we proceeded two days on the sea, when about sunrise a great many Whales and other monsters of the sea, appeared. Among the former, one was of a most monstrous size. * * This came towards us, open-mouthed, raising the waves on all sides, and beating the sea before him into a foam.'   TOOKE'S LUCIAN. 'THE TRUE HISTORY.'

'He visited this country also with a view of catching horse-whales, which had bones of very great value for their teeth, of which he brought some to the king. * * * The best whales were catched in his own country, of which some were forty-eight, some fifty yards long. He said that he was one of six who had killed sixty in two days.'

OTHER OR OCTHER'S VERBAL NARRATIVE TAKEN
DOWN FROM HIS MOUTH BY KING ALFRED. A.D.
890.

'And whereas all the other things, whether beast or vessel, that enter into the dreadful gulf of this monster's (whale's) mouth, are immediately lost and swallowed up, the sea-gudgeon retires into it in great security, and there sleeps.'   MONTAIGNE.—APOLOGY FOR RAIMOND SEBOND.

'Let us fly, let us fly! Old Nick take me if it is not Leviathan described by the noble prophet Moses in the life of patient Job.'

RABELAIS.

'This whale's liver was two cart-loads.'

STOWE'S ANNALS.

'The great Leviathan that maketh the seas to seethe like a boiling pan.'   LORD BACON'S VERSION OF THE PSALMS.

'Touching that monstrous bulk of the whale or ork we have received nothing certain. They grow exceeding fat, insomuch that an incredible quantity of oil will be extracted out of one whale.'

IBID 'HISTORY OF LIFE AND DEATH.'

'The sovereignest thing on earth is parmacetti for an inward bruise.'

KING HENRY.

'Very like a whale.'   HAMLET.

*'Which to secure, no skill of leach's art
Mote him availle, but to returne againe
To his wound's worker, that with lowly dart,
Dinting his breast, had bred his restless paine,
Like as the wounded whale to shore flies thro' the maine.'*

THE FAIRIE QUEEN.

'Immense as whales, the motion of whose vast bodies can in a peaceful calm trouble the ocean till it boil.'   SIR WILLIAM DAVENANT. PREFACE TO GONDIBERT.

'What spermacetti is, men might justly doubt, since the learned Hosmannus in his work of thirty years, saith plainly, Nescio quid sit.*'*

SIR T. BROWNE. OF SPERMA CETI AND THE SPERMA CETI WHALE. VIDE HIS V.E.

*'Like Spencer's Talus with his modern flail
He threatens ruin with his ponderous tail.*

* * *

*Their fixed jav'lins in his side he wears,
And on his back a grove of pikes appears.'*

WALLER'S BATTLE OF THE SUMMER ISLANDS.

'By art is created that great Leviathan, called a Commonwealth or State—(in Latin, Civitas) which is but an artificial man.'

OPENING SENTENCE OF HOBBES'S LEVIATHAN.

'Silly Mansoul swallowed it without chewing, as if it had been a sprat in the mouth of a whale.'   HOLY WAR.

*'That sea beast
Leviathan, which God of all his works
Created hugest that swim the ocean stream.'*

PARADISE LOST.

—————— 'There Leviathan,
Hugest of living creatures, in the deep
Stretched like a promontory sleeps or swims,
And seems a moving land; and at his gills
Draws in, and at his breath spouts out a sea.'
                    IBID.

'The mighty whales which swim in a sea of water, and have a sea
of oil swimming in them.'   FULLER'S PROFANE AND HOLY STATE.

'So close behind some promontory lie
The huge Leviathans to attend their prey,
And give no chace, but swallow in the fry,
Which through their gaping jaws mistake the way.'
                    DRYDEN'S ANNUS MIRABILIS.

'While the whale is floating at the stern of the ship, they cut off his
head, and tow it with a boat as near the shore as it will come; but it
will be aground in twelve or thirteen feet water.'
                    THOMAS EDGE'S TEN VOYAGES TO SPITZBERGEN,
                    IN PURCHASS.

'In their way they saw many whales sporting in the ocean, and in
wantonness fuzzing up the water through their pipes and vents, which
nature has placed on their shoulders.' SIR T. HERBERT'S VOYAGES INTO ASIA AND
                    AFRICA. HARRIS COLL.

'Here they saw such huge troops of whales, that they were forced to
proceed with a great deal of caution for fear they should run their ship
upon them.'
                    SCHOUTEN'S SIXTH CIRCUMNAVIGATION.

'We set sail from the Elbe, wind N.E. in the ship called The Jonas-
in-the-Whale. * * *
Some say the whale can't open his mouth, but that is a fable. * * *
They frequently climb up the masts to see whether they can see a
whale, for the first discoverer has a ducat for his pains. * * *
I was told of a whale taken near Shetland, that had above a barrel
of herrings in his belly. * * *
One of our harpooneers told me that he caught once a whale in
Spitzbergen that was white all over.' A VOYAGE TO GREENLAND, A.D. 1671. HARRIS
                    COLL.

'Several whales have come in upon this coast (Fife). Anno 1652, one eighty feet in length of the whale-bone kind came in, which, (as I was informed) besides a vast quantity of oil, did afford 500 weight of baleen. The jaws of it stand for a gate in the garden of Pitferren.'

SIBBALD'S FIFE AND KINROSS.

'Myself have agreed to try whether I can master and kill this Sperma-ceti whale, for I could never hear of any of that sort that was killed by any man, such is his fierceness and swiftness.'

RICHARD STRAFFORD'S LETTER FROM THE BER-
MUDAS. PHIL. TRANS. A.D. 1668.

*'Whales in the sea
God's voice obey.'*

N.E. PRIMER.

'We saw also abundance of large whales, there being more in those southern seas, as I may say, by a hundred to one; than we have to the northward of us.' CAPTAIN COWLEY'S VOYAGE ROUND THE GLOBE.
A.D. 1729.

* * * * * *'and the breath of the whale is frequently attended with such an insupportable smell, as to bring on a disorder of the brain.'*

ULLOA'S SOUTH AMERICA.

*'To fifty chosen sylphs of special note,
We trust the important charge, the petticoat.
Oft have we known that seven-fold fence to fail,
Tho' stiff with hoops and armed with ribs of whale.'*

RAPE OF THE LOCK.

'If we compare land animals in respect to magnitude, with those that take up their abode in the deep, we shall find they will appear con-temptible in the comparison. The whale is doubtless the largest animal in creation.' GOLDSMITH, NAT. HIS.

'If you should write a fable for little fishes, you would make them speak like great whales.' GOLDSMITH TO JOHNSON.

'In the afternoon we saw what was supposed to be a rock, but it was found to be a dead whale, which some Asiatics had killed, and were then towing ashore. They seemed to endeavor to conceal themselves behind the whale, in order to avoid being seen by us.'

COOK'S VOYAGES.

'The larger whales, they seldom venture to attack. They stand in so great dread of some of them, that when out at sea they are afraid to mention even their names, and carry dung, lime-stone, juniper-wood, and some other articles of the same nature in their boats, in order to terrify and prevent their too near approach.'

UNO VON TROIL'S LETTERS ON BANKS'S AND
SOLANDER'S VOYAGE TO ICELAND IN 1772.

'The Spermacetti Whale found by the Nantuckois, is an active, fierce animal, and requires vast address and boldness in the fishermen.'

THOMAS JEFFERSON'S WHALE MEMORIAL TO THE
FRENCH MINISTER IN 1778.

'And pray, sir, what in the world is equal to it?'

EDMUND BURKE'S REFERENCE IN PARLIAMENT
TO THE NANTUCKET WHALE-FISHERY.

'Spain—a great whale stranded on the shores of Europe.'

EDMUND BURKE. (SOMEWHERE.)

'A tenth branch of the king's ordinary revenue, said to be grounded on the consideration of his guarding and protecting the seas from pirates and robbers, is the right to royal fish, which are whale and sturgeon. And these, when either thrown ashore or caught near the coast, are the property of the king.'   BLACKSTONE.

'Soon to the sport of death the crews repair:
Rodmond unerring o'er his head suspends
The barbed steel, and every turn attends.'

FALCONER'S SHIPWRECK.

'Bright shone the roofs, the domes, the spires,
   And rockets blew self driven,
To hang their momentary fire
   Around the vault of heaven.

'So fire with water to compare,
   The ocean serves on high,
Up-spouted by a whale in air,
   To express unwieldy joy.'

COWPER. ON THE QUEEN'S VISIT TO LONDON.

'Ten or fifteen gallons of blood are thrown out of the heart at a stroke, with immense velocity.'   JOHN HUNTER'S ACCOUNT OF THE DISSECTION
OF A WHALE. (A SMALL SIZED ONE.)

'The aorta of a whale is larger in the bore than the main pipe of the water-works at London Bridge, and the water roaring in its passage through that pipe is inferior in impetus and velocity to the blood gushing from the whale's heart.'   PALEY'S THEOLOGY.

'The whale is a mammiferous animal without hind feet.'
                                                BARON CUVIER.

'In 40 degrees south, we saw Spermacetti Whales, but did not take any till the first of May, the sea being then covered with them.'
                      COLNETT'S VOYAGE FOR THE PURPOSE OF EX-
                      TENDING THE SPERMACETTI WHALE FISHERY.

'In the free element beneath me swam,
Floundered and dived, in play, in chace, in battle,
Fishes of every color, form, and kind;
Which language cannot paint, and mariner
Had never seen; from dread Leviathan
To insect millions peopling every wave:
Gather'd in shoals immense, like floating islands,
Led by mysterious instincts through that waste
And trackless region, though on every side
Assaulted by voracious enemies,
Whales, sharks, and monsters, arm'd in front or jaw.
With swords, saws, spiral horns, or hooked fangs.'
                      MONTGOMERY'S WORLD BEFORE THE FLOOD.

'Io! Pæan! Io! sing,
To the finny people's king.
Not a mightier whale than this
In the vast Atlantic is;
Not a fatter fish than he,
Flounders round the Polar Sea.'
                      CHARLES LAMB'S TRIUMPH OF THE WHALE.

'In the year 1690 some persons were on a high hill observing the whales spouting and sporting with each other, when one observed; there— pointing to the sea—is a green pasture where our children's grand-children will go for bread.'   OBED MACY'S HISTORY OF NANTUCKET.

'I built a cottage for Susan and myself and made a gateway in the form of a Gothic Arch, by setting up a whale's jaw bones.'
                      HAWTHORNE'S TWICE TOLD TALES.

'*She came to bespeak a monument for her first love, who had been killed by a whale in the Pacific ocean, no less than forty years ago.*'
IBID.

'*No, Sir, 'tis a Right Whale,*' *answered Tom; 'I saw his spout; he threw up a pair of as pretty rainbows as a Christian would wish to look at. He's a raal oil-butt, that fellow!*' COOPER'S PILOT.

'*The papers were brought in, and we saw in the Berlin Gazette that whales had been introduced on the stage there.*'
ECKERMANN'S CONVERSATIONS WITH GOETHE.

'*My God! Mr Chace, what is the matter?*' *I answered, 'we have been stove by a whale.*' 'NARRATIVE OF THE SHIPWRECK OF THE WHALE SHIP ESSEX OF NANTUCKET, WHICH WAS ATTACKED AND FINALLY DESTROYED BY A LARGE SPERM WHALE IN THE PACIFIC OCEAN.' BY OWEN CHACE OF NANTUCKET, FIRST MATE OF THE SAID VESSEL. NEW YORK. 1821.

'*A mariner sat in the shrouds one night,*
The wind was piping free;
Now bright, now dimmed, was the moonlight pale,
And the phospher gleamed in the wake of the whale,
As it floundered in the sea.'
ELIZABETH OAKES SMITH.

'*The quantity of line withdrawn from the different boats engaged in the capture of this one whale, amounted altogether to 10,440 yards or nearly six English miles.*' * * *
'*Sometimes the whale shakes its tremendous tail in the air, which, cracking like a whip, resounds to the distance of three or four miles.*'
SCORESBY.

'*Mad with the agonies he endures from these fresh attacks, the infuriated Sperm Whale rolls over and over; he rears his enormous head, and with wide expanded jaws snaps at everything around him; he rushes at the boats with his head; they are propelled before him with vast swiftness, and sometimes utterly destroyed.*
* * * *It is a matter of great astonishment that the consideration of the habits of so interesting, and, in a commercial point of view, of so important an animal (as the Sperm Whale) should have been so entirely neglected, or should have excited so little curiosity among the numerous, and many of them competent observers, that of late years must have*

*possessed the most abundant and the most convenient opportunities of
witnessing their habitudes.'* THOMAS BEALE'S HISTORY OF THE SPERM WHALE,
1839.

'The Cachalot' (Sperm Whale) 'is not only better armed than the
True Whale' (Greenland or Right Whale) 'in possessing a formidable
weapon at either extremity of its body, but also more frequently displays
a disposition to employ these weapons offensively, and in a manner at
once so artful, bold, and mischievous, as to lead to its being regarded
as the most dangerous to attack of all the known species of the whale
tribe.' FREDERICK DEBELL BENNETT'S WHALING VOY-
AGE ROUND THE GLOBE. 1840.

October 13. 'There she blows,' was sung out from the mast-head.
'Where away?' demanded the captain.
'Three points off the lee bow, sir.'
'Raise up your wheel. Steady!'
'Steady, sir.'
'Mast-head ahoy! Do you see that whale now?'
'Ay ay, sir! A shoal of Sperm Whales! There she blows! There she
breaches!'
'Sing out! sing out every time!'
'Ay ay, sir! There she blows! there—there—thar she blows—bowes—
bo-o-o-s!'
'How far off?'
'Two miles and a half.'
'Thunder and lightning! so near! Call all hands!'
J. ROSS BROWNE'S ETCHINGS OF A WHALING
CRUISE. 1846.

'The Whale-ship Globe, on board of which vessel occurred the horrid
transactions we are about to relate, belonged to the island of Nantucket.'
'NARRATIVE OF THE GLOBE MUTINY,' BY LAY
AND HUSSEY SURVIVORS. A.D. 1828.

'Being once pursued by a whale which he had wounded, he parried
the assault for some time with a lance; but the furious monster at length
rushed on the boat; himself and comrades only being preserved by
leaping into the water when they saw the onset was inevitable.'
MISSIONARY JOURNAL OF TYERMAN AND
BENNETT.

'Nantucket itself,' said Mr Webster, 'is a very striking and peculiar
portion of the National interest. There is a population of eight or nine

thousand persons, living here in the sea, adding largely every year to the National wealth by the boldest and most persevering industry.'

REPORT OF DANIEL WEBSTER'S SPEECH IN THE
U.S. SENATE, ON THE APPLICATION FOR THE
ERECTION OF A BREAKWATER AT NANTUCKET.
1828.

'The whale fell directly over him, and probably killed him in a moment.'

'THE WHALE AND HIS CAPTORS, OR THE
WHALEMAN'S ADVENTURES AND THE WHALE'S
BIOGRAPHY, GATHERED ON THE HOMEWARD
CRUISE OF THE COMMODORE PREBLE.' BY REV.
HENRY T. CHEEVER.

'If you make the least damn bit of noise,' replied Samuel, 'I will send you to hell.'

LIFE OF SAMUEL COMSTOCK (THE MUTINEER),
BY HIS BROTHER, WILLIAM COMSTOCK ANOTHER
VERSION OF THE WHALE-SHIP GLOBE NARRATIVE.

'The voyages of the Dutch and English to the Northern Ocean, in order, if possible, to discover a passage through it to India, though they failed of their main object, laid open the haunts of the whale.'

MCCULLOCH'S COMMERCIAL DICTIONARY.

'These things are reciprocal; the ball rebounds, only to bound forward again; for now in laying open the haunts of the whale, the whalemen seem to have indirectly hit upon new clews to that same mystic North-West Passage.'

FROM 'SOMETHING' UNPUBLISHED.

'It is impossible to meet a whale-ship on the ocean without being struck by her mere appearance. The vessel under short sail, with look-outs at the mast-heads, eagerly scanning the wide expanse around them, has a totally different air from those engaged in a regular voyage.'

CURRENTS AND WHALING. U.S. EX. EX.

'Pedestrians in the vicinity of London and elsewhere may recollect having seen large curved bones set upright in the earth, either to form arches over gateways, or entrances to alcoves, and they may perhaps have been told that these were the ribs of whales.'

TALES OF A WHALE VOYAGER TO THE ARCTIC
OCEAN.

'It was not till the boats returned from the pursuit of these whales, that the whites saw their ship in bloody possession of the savages enrolled among the crew.'

NEWSPAPER ACCOUNT OF THE TAKING AND RE-
TAKING OF THE WHALE-SHIP HOBOMACK.

'It is generally well known that out of the crews of Whaling vessels
(American) few ever return in the ships on board of which they departed.'
CRUISE IN A WHALE BOAT.

'Suddenly a mighty mass emerged from the water, and shot up
perpendicularly into the air. It was the whale.'
MIRIAM COFFIN OR THE WHALE FISHERMAN.

'The Whale is harpooned to be sure; but bethink you, how you would
manage a powerful unbroken colt, with the mere appliance of a rope
tied to the root of his tail.'   A CHAPTER ON WHALING IN RIBS AND TRUCKS.

'On one occasion I saw two of these monsters (whales) probably male
and female, slowly swimming, one after the other, within less than a
stone's throw of the shore' (Terra Del Fuego), 'over which the beech tree
extended its branches.'   DARWIN'S VOYAGE OF A NATURALIST.

' "Stern all!" exclaimed the mate, as upon turning his head, he saw
the distended jaws of a large Sperm Whale close to the head of the
boat, threatening it with instant destruction;—"Stern all, for your lives!" '
WHARTON THE WHALE KILLER.

'So be cheery, my lads, let your hearts never fail,
While the bold harpooneer is striking the whale!'
NANTUCKET SONG.

'Oh, the rare old Whale, mid storm and gale
     In his ocean home will be
A giant in might, where might is right,
     And King of the boundless sea.'
WHALE SONG.

1

LOOMINGS

CALL me Ishmael. Some years ago—never mind how long precisely—having little or no money in my purse, and nothing particular to interest me on shore, I thought I would sail about a little and see the watery part of the world. It is a way I have of driving off the spleen, and regulating the circulation. Whenever I find myself growing grim about the mouth; whenever it is a damp, drizzly November in my soul; whenever I find myself involuntarily pausing before coffin warehouses, and bringing up the rear of every funeral I meet; and especially whenever my hypos get such an upper hand of me, that it requires a strong moral principle to prevent me from deliberately stepping into the street, and methodically knocking people's hats off—then, I account it high time to get to sea as soon as I can. This is my substitute for pistol and ball. With a philosophical flourish Cato throws himself upon his sword; I quietly take to the ship. There is nothing surprising in this. If they but knew it, almost all men in their degree, some time or other, cherish very nearly the same feelings towards the ocean with me.

There now is your insular city of the Manhattoes, belted round by wharves as Indian isles by coral reefs—commerce surrounds it with her surf. Right and left, the streets take you waterward. Its extreme down-town is the Battery, where that noble mole is washed by waves, and cooled by breezes, which a few hours previous were out of sight of land. Look at the crowds of water-gazers there.

Circumambulate the city of a dreamy Sabbath afternoon. Go from Corlears Hook to Coenties Slip, and from thence, by Whitehall, northward. What do you see?—Posted like silent sentinels all around the town, stand thousands upon thousands of mortal men fixed in ocean reveries. Some leaning against the spiles; some seated upon the pier-heads; some looking over the bulwarks of ships from China; some high aloft in the rigging, as if striving to get a still better seaward peep. But these are all landsmen; of week days pent up in lath and plaster—tied to counters, nailed to benches, clinched to desks. How then is this? Are the green fields gone? What do they here?

But look! here come more crowds, pacing straight for the water, and seemingly bound for a dive. Strange! Nothing will content them but the extremest limit of the land; loitering under the shady lee of yonder warehouses will not suffice. No. They must get just as nigh the water as they possibly can without falling in. And there they stand—miles of them—leagues. Inlanders all, they come from lanes and alleys, streets and avenues—north, east, south, and west. Yet here they all unite. Tell me, does the magnetic virtue in the needles of the compasses of all those ships attract them thither?

Once more. Say, you are in the country; in some high land of lakes. Take almost any path you please, and ten to one it carries you down in a dale, and leaves you there by a pool in the stream. There is magic in it. Let the most absentminded of men be plunged in his deepest reveries—stand that man on his legs, set his feet a-going, and he will infallibly lead you to water, if water there be in all that region. Should you ever be athirst in the great American desert, try this experiment, if your caravan happen to be supplied with a metaphysical professor. Yes, as every one knows, meditation and water are wedded for ever.

But here is an artist. He desires to paint you the dreamiest, shadiest, quietest, most enchanting bit of romantic landscape in all the valley of the Saco. What is the chief element he employs? There stand his trees, each with a hollow trunk, as if a hermit and a crucifix were within; and here sleeps his meadow, and there sleep his cattle; and up from yonder cottage goes a sleepy smoke. Deep into distant woodlands winds a mazy way, reaching to overlapping spurs of mountains bathed in their hill-side blue. But though the picture lies thus tranced, and though this pine-tree shakes down its sighs like leaves upon this shepherd's head, yet all were vain, unless the shepherd's eye were fixed upon the magic stream before him. Go visit the Prairies in June, when for scores on scores of miles you wade knee-deep among Tiger-lilies—what is the one charm wanting?—Water—there is not a drop of water there! Were Niagara but a cataract of sand, would you travel your thousand miles to see it? Why did the poor poet of Tennessee, upon suddenly receiving two handfuls of silver, deliberate whether to buy him a coat, which he sadly needed, or invest his money in a pedestrian trip to Rockaway Beach? Why is almost every robust healthy boy with a robust healthy soul in him, at some time or other crazy to go to sea? Why upon your first voyage as a passenger, did you yourself feel such a mystical vibration, when first told that you and your ship were now out of sight of land? Why did the old Persians hold the sea holy? Why did the Greeks give it a separate deity, and own brother of Jove? Surely all this is not without meaning. And still deeper the meaning of that story of Narcissus, who because he could not grasp the tormenting, mild image he saw in the fountain, plunged into it and was drowned. But that same image, we ourselves see in all rivers and oceans. It is the image of the ungraspable phantom of life; and this is the key to it all.

Now, when I say that I am in the habit of going to sea whenever I begin to grow hazy about the eyes, and begin to be over conscious of my lungs, I do not mean to have it inferred that I ever go to sea as a passenger. For to go as a passenger you must needs have a purse, and a purse is but a rag unless you have something in it. Besides, passengers get sea-sick—grow quarrelsome—don't sleep of nights—do not enjoy themselves much, as a general thing;— no, I never go as a passenger; nor, though I am something of a salt, do I ever go to sea as a Commodore, or a Captain, or a Cook. I abandon the glory and distinction of such offices to those who like them. For my part, I abominate all honorable respectable toils, trials, and tribulations of every kind whatsoever. It is quite as much as I can do to take care of myself, without taking care of ships, barques, brigs, schooners, and what not. And as for going as cook,—though I confess there is considerable glory in that, a cook being a sort of officer on ship-board—yet, somehow, I never fancied broiling fowls;—though once broiled, judiciously buttered, and judgmatically salted and peppered, there is no one who will speak more respectfully, not to say reverentially, of a broiled fowl than I will. It is out of the idolatrous dotings of the old Egyptians upon broiled ibis and roasted river horse, that you see the mummies of those creatures in their huge bakehouses the pyramids.

No, when I go to sea, I go as a simple sailor, right before the mast, plumb down into the forecastle, aloft there to the royal mast-head. True, they rather order me about some, and make me jump from spar to spar, like a grasshopper in a May meadow. And at first, this sort of thing is unpleasant enough. It touches one's sense of honor, particularly if you come of an old established family in the land, the Van Rensselaers, or Randolphs, or Hardicanutes. And more than all, if just previous to putting your hand into the tar-pot, you have been lording it as a country schoolmaster, making the tallest boys stand in awe of you. The transition is a keen one, I assure you, from a schoolmaster to a sailor, and requires a strong decoction of Seneca and the Stoics to enable you to grin and bear it. But even this wears off in time.

What of it, if some old hunks of a sea-captain orders me to get a broom and sweep down the decks? What does that indignity amount to, weighed, I mean, in the scales of the New Testament? Do you think the archangel Gabriel thinks anything the less of me, because I promptly and respectfully obey that old hunks in that particular instance? Who aint a slave? Tell me that. Well, then, however the old sea-captains may order me about—however they may thump and punch me about, I have the satisfaction of knowing that it is all right; that everybody else is one way or other served in much the same way—either in a physical or metaphysical point of view, that is; and so the universal thump is passed round, and all hands should rub each other's shoulderblades, and be content.

Again, I always go to sea as a sailor, because they make a point of paying me for my trouble, whereas they never pay passengers a single penny that I ever heard of. On the contrary, passengers themselves must pay. And there is all the difference in the world between paying and being paid. The act of paying is perhaps the most uncomfortable infliction that the two orchard thieves entailed upon us. But *being paid*,—what will compare with it? The urbane activity with which a man receives money is really marvellous, considering that we so earnestly believe money to be the root of all earthly ills, and on no account can a monied man enter heaven. Ah! how cheerfully we consign ourselves to perdition!

Finally, I always go to sea as a sailor, because of the wholesome exercise and pure air of the forecastle deck. For as in this world, head winds are far more prevalent than winds from astern (that is, if you never violate the Pythagorean maxim), so for the most part the Commodore on the quarter-deck gets his atmosphere at second hand from the sailors on the forecastle. He thinks he breathes it first; but not so. In much the same way do the commonalty lead their leaders in many other things, at the same time that the leaders little suspect it. But wherefore it was that after having repeatedly smelt the sea as a merchant sailor, I should now take it into my head to go on a whaling voyage; this the invisible police officer of the Fates, who has the constant surveillance of me, and secretly dogs me, and influences me in some unaccountable way—he can better answer than any one else. And, doubtless, my going on this whaling voyage, formed part of the grand programme of Providence that was drawn up a long time ago. It came in as a sort of brief interlude and solo between more extensive performances. I take it that this part of the bill must have run something like this:

*Grand Contested Election for the Presidency of the
United States.*

WHALING VOYAGE BY ONE ISHMAEL.

BLOODY BATTLE IN AFFGHANISTAN.

Though I cannot tell why it was exactly that those stage managers, the Fates, put me down for this shabby part of a whaling voyage, when others were set down for magnificent parts in high tragedies, and short and easy parts in genteel comedies, and jolly parts in farces—though I cannot tell why this was exactly; yet, now that I recall all the circumstances, I think I can see a little into the springs and motives which being cunningly presented to me under various disguises, induced me to set about performing the part I did, besides cajoling me into the delusion that it was a choice resulting from my own unbiased freewill and discriminating judgment.

Chief among these motives was the overwhelming idea of the great whale himself. Such a portentous and mysterious monster roused all my curiosity. Then the wild and distant seas where he rolled his island bulk; the undeliverable, nameless perils of the whale; these, with all the attending marvels of a thousand Patagonian sights and sounds, helped to sway me to my wish. With other men, perhaps, such things would not have been inducements; but as for me, I am tormented with an everlasting itch for things remote. I love to sail forbidden seas, and land on barbarous coasts. Not ignoring what is good, I am quick to perceive a horror, and could still be social with it—would they let me—since it is but well to be on friendly terms with all the inmates of the place one lodges in.

By reason of these things, then, the whaling voyage was welcome; the great flood-gates of the wonder-world swung open, and in the wild conceits that swayed me to my purpose, two and two there floated into my inmost soul, endless processions of the whale, and, mid most of them all, one grand hooded phantom, like a snow hill in the air.

2
THE CARPET-BAG

I stuffed a shirt or two into my old carpet-bag, tucked it under my arm, and started for Cape Horn and the Pacific. Quitting the good city of old Manhatto, I duly arrived in New Bedford. It was on a Saturday night in December. Much was I disappointed upon learning that the little packet for Nantucket had already sailed, and that no way of reaching that place would offer, till the following Monday.

As most young candidates for the pains and penalties of whaling stop at this same New Bedford, thence to embark on their voyage, it may as well be related that I, for one, had no idea of so doing. For my mind was made up to sail in no other than a Nantucket craft, because there was a fine, boisterous something about everything connected with that famous old island, which amazingly pleased me. Besides though New Bedford has of late been gradually monopolizing the business of whaling, and though in this matter poor old Nantucket is now much behind her, yet Nantucket was her great original—the Tyre of this Carthage;—the place where the first dead American whale was stranded. Where else but from Nantucket did those aboriginal whalemen, the Red-Men, first sally out in canoes to give chase to the Leviathan? And where but from Nantucket, too, did that first adventurous little sloop put forth, partly laden with imported cobble-stones—so goes the story—to throw at the whales, in order to discover when they were nigh enough to risk a harpoon from the bowsprit?

Now having a night, a day, and still another night following before me in New Bedford, ere I could embark for my destined port, it became a matter of concernment where I was to eat and sleep meanwhile. It was a very dubious-looking, nay, a very dark and dismal night, bitingly cold and cheerless. I knew no one in the place. With anxious grapnels I had sounded my pocket, and only brought up a few pieces of silver,—So, wherever you go, Ishmael, said I to myself, as I stood in the middle of a dreary street shouldering my bag, and comparing the gloom towards the north with the darkness towards the south—wherever in your wisdom you may conclude to lodge for the night, my dear Ishmael, be sure to inquire the price, and don't be too particular.

With halting steps I paced the streets, and passed the sign of 'The Crossed Harpoons'—but it looked too expensive and jolly there. Further on, from the bright red windows of the 'Sword-Fish Inn', there came such fervent rays, that it seemed to have melted the packed snow and ice from before the house, for everywhere else the congealed frost lay ten inches thick in a hard, asphaltic pavement,—rather weary for me, when I struck my foot against the flinty projections, because from hard, remorseless service the soles of my boots were in a most miserable plight. Too expensive and jolly, again thought I, pausing one moment to watch the broad glare in the street, and hear the sounds of the tinkling glasses within. But go on, Ishmael, said I at last; don't you hear? get away from before the door; your patched boots are stopping the way. So on I went. I now by instinct followed the streets that took me waterward, for there, doubtless, were the cheapest, if not the cheeriest inns.

Such dreary streets! blocks of blackness, not houses, on either hand, and here and there a candle, like a candle moving about in a tomb. At this hour of the night, of the last day of the week, that quarter of the town proved all but deserted. But presently I came to a smoky light proceeding from a low, wide building, the door of which stood invitingly open. It had a careless look, as if it were meant for the uses of the public; so, entering, the first thing I did was to stumble over an ash-box in the porch. Ha! thought I, ha, as the flying particles almost choked me, are these ashes from that destroyed city, Gomorrah? But 'The Crossed Harpoons', and 'The Sword-Fish'?—this, then, must needs be the sign of 'The Trap'. However, I picked myself up and hearing a loud voice within, pushed on and opened a second, interior door.

It seemed the great Black Parliament sitting in Tophet. A hundred black faces turned round in their rows to peer; and beyond, a black Angel of Doom was beating a book in a pulpit. It was a negro church; and the preacher's text was about the blackness of darkness, and the weeping and wailing and teeth-gnashing there. Ha, Ishmael, muttered I, backing out, Wretched entertainment at the sign of 'The Trap!'

Moving on, I at last came to a dim sort of out-hanging light not far from the docks, and heard a forlorn creaking in the air; and looking up, saw a swinging sign over the door with a white painting upon it, faintly representing a tall straight jet of misty spray, and these words underneath—'The Spouter-Inn:—Peter Coffin.'

Coffin?—Spouter?—Rather ominous in that particular connexion, thought I. But it is a common name in Nantucket, they say, and I suppose this Peter here is an emigrant from there. As the light looked so dim, and the place, for the time, looked quiet enough, and the dilapidated little wooden house itself looked as if it might have been carted here from the ruins of some burnt district, and as the swinging sign had a poverty-stricken sort of creak to it, I thought that here was the very spot for cheap lodgings, and the best of pea coffee.

It was a queer sort of place—a gable-ended old house, one side palsied as it were, and leaning over sadly. It stood on a sharp bleak corner, where that tempestuous wind Euroclydon kept up a worse howling than ever it did about poor Paul's tossed craft. Euroclydon, nevertheless, is a mighty pleasant zephyr to any one in-doors, with his feet on the hob quietly toasting for bed. 'In judging of that tempestuous wind called Euroclydon,' says an old writer—of whose works I possess the only copy extant—'it maketh a marvellous difference, whether thou lookest out at it from a glass window where the frost is all on the outside, or whether thou observest it from that sashless window, where the frost is on both sides, and of which the wight Death is the only glazier.' True enough, thought I, as this passage occurred to my mind—old black-letter, thou reasonest well. Yes, these eyes are windows, and this body of mine is the house. What a pity they didn't stop up the chinks and the crannies though, and thrust in a little lint here and there. But it's too late to make any improvements now. The universe is finished; the copestone is on, and the chips were carted off a million years ago. Poor Lazarus there, chattering his teeth against the curbstone for his pillow, and shaking off his tatters with his shiverings, he might plug up both ears with rags, and put a corn-cob into his mouth, and yet that would not keep out the tempestuous Euroclydon. Euroclydon! says old Dives, in his red silken wrapper (he had a redder one afterwards)—pooh, pooh! What a fine frosty night; how Orion glitters; what northern lights! Let them talk of their oriental summer climes of everlasting conservatories; give me the privilege of making my own summer with my own coals.

But what thinks Lazarus? Can he warm his blue hands by holding them up to the grand northern lights? Would not Lazarus rather be in Sumatra than here? Would he not far rather lay him down lengthwise along the line of the equator; yea, ye gods! go down to the fiery pit itself, in order to keep out this frost?

Now, that Lazarus should lie stranded there on the curbstone before the door of Dives, this is more wonderful than that an iceberg should be moored to one of the Moluccas. Yet Dives himself, he too lives like a Czar in an ice palace made of frozen sighs, and being a president of a temperance society, he only drinks the tepid tears of orphans.

But no more of this blubbering now, we are going a-whaling, and there is plenty of that yet to come. Let us scrape the ice from our frosted feet, and see what sort of a place this 'Spouter' may be.

3
THE SPOUTER-INN

ENTERING that gable-ended Spouter-Inn, you found yourself in a wide, low, straggling entry with old-fashioned wainscots, reminding one of the bulwarks of some condemned old craft. On one side hung a very large oil-painting so thoroughly be-smoked, and every way defaced, that in the unequal cross-lights by which you viewed it, it was only by diligent study and a series of systematic visits to it, and careful inquiry of the neighbors, that you could any way arrive at an understanding of its purpose. Such unaccountable masses of shades and shadows, that at first you almost thought some ambitious young artist, in the time of the New England hags, had endeavored to delineate chaos bewitched. But by dint of much and earnest contemplation, and oft repeated ponderings, and especially by throwing open the little window towards the back of the entry, you at last come to the conclusion that such an idea, however wild, might not be altogether unwarranted.

But what most puzzled and confounded you was a long, limber, portentous, black mass of something hovering in the centre of the picture over three blue, dim, perpendicular lines floating in a nameless yeast. A boggy, soggy, squitchy picture truly, enough to drive a nervous man distracted. Yet was there a sort of indefinite, half-attained, unimaginable sublimity about it that fairly froze you to it, till you involuntarily took an oath with yourself to find out what that marvellous painting meant. Ever and anon a bright, but, alas, deceptive idea would dart you through.—It's the Black Sea in a midnight gale.—It's the unnatural combat of the four primal elements.—It's a blasted heath.—It's a Hyperborean winter scene.—It's the breaking-up of the ice-bound stream of Time. But at last all these fancies yielded to that one portentous something in the picture's midst. *That* once found out, and all the rest were plain. But stop; does it not bear a faint resemblance to a gigantic fish? even the great leviathan himself?

In fact, the artist's design seemed this: a final theory of my own, partly based upon the aggregated opinions of many aged persons with whom I conversed upon the subject. The picture represents a Cape-Horner in a great hurricane; the half-foundered ship weltering there with its three dismantled masts alone visible; and an exasperated whale, purposing to spring clean over the craft, is in the enormous act of impaling himself upon the three mast-heads.

The opposite wall of this entry was hung all over with a heathenish array of monstrous clubs and spears. Some were thickly set with glittering teeth resembling ivory saws; others were tufted with knots of human hair; and one was sickle-shaped, with a vast handle sweeping round like the segment made in the new-mown grass by a long-armed mower. You shuddered as you gazed, and wondered what monstrous cannibal and savage could ever have gone a death-harvesting with such a hacking, horrifying implement. Mixed with these were rusty old whaling lances and harpoons all broken and deformed. Some were storied weapons. With this once long lance, now wildly elbowed, fifty years ago did Nathan Swain kill fifteen whales between a sunrise and a sunset. And that harpoon—so like a corkscrew now—was flung in Javan seas, and run away with by a whale, years afterward slain off the Cape of Blanco. The original iron entered nigh the tail, and, like a restless needle sojourning in the body of a man, travelled full forty feet, and at last was found imbedded in the hump.

Crossing this dusky entry, and on through yon low-arched way—cut through what in old times must have been a great central chimney with fire-places all round—you enter the public room. A still duskier place is this, with such low ponderous beams above, and such old wrinkled planks beneath, that you would almost fancy you trod some old craft's cockpits, especially of such a howling night, when this corner-anchored old ark rocked so furiously. On one side stood a long, low, shelf-like table covered with cracked glass cases, filled with dusty rarities gathered from this wide world's remotest nooks. Projecting from the further angle of the room stands a dark-looking den—the bar—a rude attempt at a right whale's head. Be that how it may, there stands the vast arched bone of the whale's jaw, so wide, a coach might almost drive beneath it. Within are shabby shelves, ranged round with old decanters, bottles, flasks; and in those jaws of swift destruction, like another cursed Jonah (by which name indeed they called him), bustles a little withered old man, who, for their money, dearly sells the sailors deliriums and death.

Abominable are the tumblers into which he pours his poison. Though true cylinders without—within, the villanous green goggling glasses deceitfully tapered downwards to a cheating bottom. Parallel meridians rudely pecked into the glass, surround these footpads' goblets. Fill to *this* mark, and your charge is but a penny; to *this* a penny more; and so on to the full glass—the Cape Horn measure, which you may gulph down for a shilling.

Upon entering the place I found a number of young seamen gathered about a table, examining by a dim light divers specimens of *skrimshander*. I sought the landlord, and telling him I desired to be accommodated with a room, received for answer that his house was full—not a bed unoccupied. 'But avast,' he added, tapping his forehead, 'you haint no objections to sharing a harpooneer's blanket, have ye? I s'pose you are goin' a whalin', so you'd better get used to that sort of thing.'

I told him that I never liked to sleep two in a bed; that if I should ever do so, it would depend upon who the harpooneer might be, and that if he (the landlord) really had no other place for me, and the harpooneer was not decidedly objectionable, why rather than wander further about a strange town on so bitter a night, I would put up with the half of any decent man's blanket.

'I thought so. All right; take a seat. Supper?—you want supper? Supper'll be ready directly.'

I sat down on an old wooden settle, carved all over like a bench on the Battery. At one end a ruminating tar was still further adorning it with his jack-knife, stooping over and diligently working away at the space between his legs. He was trying his hand at a ship under full sail, but he didn't make much headway, I thought.

At last some four or five of us were summoned to our meal in an adjoining room. It was cold as Iceland—no fire at all—the landlord said he couldn't afford it. Nothing but two dismal tallow candles, each in a winding sheet. We were fain to button up our monkey jackets, and hold to our lips cups of scalding tea with our half frozen fingers. But the fare was of the most substantial kind—not only meat and potatoes, but dumplings; good heavens! dumplings for supper! One young fellow in a green box coat, addressed himself to these dumplings in a most direful manner.

'My boy,' said the landlord, 'you'll have the nightmare to a dead sartainty.'

'Landlord,' I whispered, 'that aint the harpooneer, is it?'

'Oh, no,' said he, looking a sort of diabolically funny, 'the harpooneer is a dark complexioned chap. He never eats dumplings, he don't—he eats nothing but steaks, and likes 'em rare.'

'The devil he does,' says I. 'Where is that harpooneer? Is he here?'

'He'll be here afore long,' was the answer.

I could not help it, but I began to feel suspicious of this 'dark complexioned' harpooneer. At any rate, I made up my mind that if it so turned out that we should sleep together, he must undress and get into bed before I did.

Supper over, the company went back to the bar-room, when, knowing not what else to do with myself, I resolved to spend the rest of the evening as a looker on.

Presently a rioting noise was heard without. Starting up, the landlord cried, 'That's the Grampus's crew. I seed her reported in the offing this morning; a three years' voyage, and a full ship. Hurrah, boys; now we'll have the latest news from the Feegees.'

A tramping of sea boots was heard in the entry; the door was flung open, and in rolled a wild set of mariners enough. Enveloped in their shaggy watch coats, and with their heads muffled in woollen comforters, all bedarned and ragged, and their beards stiff with icicles, they seemed an eruption of bears from Labrador. They had just landed from their boat, and this was the first house they entered. No wonder, then, that they made a straight wake for the whale's mouth—the bar—when the wrinkled little old Jonah, there officiating, soon poured them out brimmers all round. One complained of a bad cold in his head, upon which Jonah mixed him a pitch-like potion of gin and molasses, which he swore was a sovereign cure for all colds and catarrhs whatsoever, never mind of how long standing, or whether caught off the coast of Labrador, or on the weather side of an ice-island.

The liquor soon mounted into their heads, as it generally does even with the arrantest topers newly landed from sea, and they began capering about most obstreperously.

I observed, however, that one of them held somewhat aloof, and though he seemed desirous not to spoil the hilarity of his shipmates by his own sober face, yet upon the whole he refrained from making as much noise as the rest. This man interested me at once; and since the sea-gods had ordained that he should soon become my shipmate (though but a sleeping-partner one, so far as this narrative is concerned), I will here venture upon a little description of him. He stood full six feet in height, with noble shoulders, and a chest like a coffer-dam. I have seldom seen such brawn in a man. His face was deeply brown and burnt, making his white teeth dazzling by the contrast; while in the deep shadows of his eyes floated some reminiscences that did not seem to give him much joy. His voice at once announced that he was a Southerner, and from his fine stature, I thought he must be one of those tall mountaineers from the Alleganian Ridge in Virginia. When the revelry of his companions had mounted to its height, this man slipped away unobserved, and I saw no more of him till he became my comrade on the sea. In a few minutes, however, he was missed by his shipmates, and being, it seems, for some reason a huge favorite with them, they raised a cry of 'Bulkington! Bulkington! where's Bulkington?' and darted out of the house in pursuit of him.

It was now about nine o'clock, and the room seeming almost supernaturally quiet after these orgies, I began to congratulate myself upon a little plan that had occurred to me just previous to the entrance of the seamen.

No man prefers to sleep two in a bed. In fact, you would a good deal rather not sleep with your own brother. I don't know how it is, but people like to be private when they are sleeping. And when it comes to sleeping with an unknown stranger, in a strange inn, in a strange town, and that stranger a harpooneer, then your objections indefinitely multiply. Nor was there any earthly reason why I as a sailor should sleep two in a bed, more than anybody else; for sailors no more sleep two in a bed at sea, than bachelor Kings do ashore. To be sure they all sleep together in one apartment, but you have your own hammock, and cover yourself with your own blanket, and sleep in your own skin.

The more I pondered over this harpooneer, the more I abominated the thought of sleeping with him. It was fair to presume that being a harpooneer, his linen or woollen, as the case might be, would not be of the tidiest, certainly none of the finest. I began to twitch all over. Besides, it was getting late, and any decent harpooneer ought to be home and going bedwards. Suppose now, he should tumble in upon me at midnight—how could I tell from what vile hole he had been coming?

'Landlord! I've changed my mind about that harpooneer.—I shan't sleep with him. I'll try the bench here.'

'Just as you please; I'm sorry I cant spare ye a tablecloth for a mattress, and it's a plaguy rough board here'—feeling of the knots and notches. 'But wait a bit, Skrimshander; I've got a carpenter's plane there in the bar—wait, I say, and I'll make ye snug enough.' So saying he procured the plane; and with his old silk handkerchief first dusting the bench, vigorously set to planing away at my bed, the while grinning like an ape. The shavings flew right and left; till at last the plane-iron came bump against an indestructible knot. The landlord was near spraining his wrist, and I told him for heaven's sake to quit—the bed was soft enough to suit me, and I did not know how all the planing in the world could make eider down of a pine plank. So gathering up the shavings with another grin, and throwing them into the great stove in the middle of the room, he went about his business, and left me in a brown study.

I now took the measure of the bench, and found that it was a foot too short; but that could be mended with a chair. But it was a foot too narrow, and the other bench in the room was about four inches higher than the planed one—so there was no yoking them. I then placed the first bench lengthwise along the only clear space against the wall, leaving a little interval between, for my back to settle down in. But I soon found that there came such a draught of cold air over me from under the sill of the window, that this plan would never do at all, especially as another current from the rickety door met the one from the window, and both together formed a series of small whirlwinds in the immediate vicinity of the spot where I had thought to spend the night.

The devil fetch that harpooneer, thought I, but stop, couldn't I steal a march on him—bolt his door inside, and jump into his bed, not to be wakened by the most violent knockings? It seemed no bad idea; but upon second thoughts I dismissed it. For who could tell but what the next morning, so soon as I popped out of the room, the harpooneer might be standing in the entry, all ready to knock me down!

Still, looking around me again, and seeing no possible chance of spending a sufferable night unless in some other person's bed, I began to think that after all I might be cherishing unwarrantable prejudices against this unknown harpooneer. Thinks I, I'll wait awhile; he must be dropping in before long. I'll have a good look at him then, and perhaps we may become jolly good bedfellows after all—there's no telling.

But though the other boarders kept coming in by ones, twos, and threes, and going to bed, yet no sign of my harpooneer.

'Landlord!' said I, 'what sort of a chap is he—does he always keep such late hours?' It was now hard upon twelve o'clock.

The landlord chuckled again with his lean chuckle, and seemed to be mightily tickled at something beyond my comprehension. 'No,' he answered, 'generally he's an airley bird—airley to bed

and airley to rise—yes, he's the bird what catches the worm.—
But tonight he went out a peddling, you see, and I don't see what
on airth keeps him so late, unless, may be, he can't sell his head.'

'Can't sell his head?—What sort of a bamboozling story is this
you are telling me?' getting into a towering rage. 'Do you pretend
to say, landlord, that this harpooneer is actually engaged this
blessed Saturday night, or rather Sunday morning, in peddling his
head around this town?'

'That's precisely it,' said the landlord, 'and I told him he couldn't
sell it here, the market's overstocked.'

'With what?' shouted I.

'With heads to be sure; ain't there too many heads in the world?'

'I tell you what it is, landlord,' said I, quite calmly, 'you'd better
stop spinning that yarn to me—I'm not green.'

'May be not,' taking out a stick and whittling a toothpick, 'but
I rayther guess you'll be done *brown* if that ere harpooneer hears
you a slanderin' his head.'

'I'll break it for him,' said I, now flying into a passion again
at this unaccountable farrago of the landlord's.

'It's broke a'ready,' said he.

'Broke,' said I—'*broke*, do you mean?'

'Sartain, and that's the very reason he can't sell it, I guess.'

'Landlord,' said I, going up to him as cool as Mt. Hecla in a
snow storm,—'landlord, stop whittling. You and I must understand
one another, and that too without delay. I come to your house
and want a bed; you tell me you can only give me half a one;
that the other half belongs to a certain harpooneer. And about
this harpooneer, whom I have not yet seen, you persist in telling
me the most mystifying and exasperating stories, tending to beget
in me an uncomfortable feeling towards the man whom you design
for my bedfellow—a sort of connexion, landlord, which is an
intimate and confidential one in the highest degree. I now demand
of you to speak out and tell me who and what this harpooneer
is, and whether I shall be in all respects safe to spend the night
with him. And in the first place, you will be so good as to unsay
that story about selling his head, which if true I take to be good
evidence that this harpooneer is stark mad, and I've no idea of
sleeping with a madman; and you, sir, *you* I mean, landlord, *you*,
sir, by trying to induce me to do so knowingly, would thereby
render yourself liable to a criminal prosecution.'

'Wall,' said the landlord, fetching a long breath, 'that's a purty
long sarmon for a chap that rips a little now and then. But be
easy, be easy, this here harpooneer I have been tellin' you of has

just arrived from the south seas, where he bought up a lot of 'balmed New Zealand heads (great curios, you know), and he's sold all on 'em but one, and that one he's trying to sell tonight, cause to-morrow's Sunday, and it would not do to be sellin' human heads about the streets when folks is goin' to churches. He wanted to, last Sunday, but I stopped him just as he was goin' out of the door with four heads strung on a string, for all the airth like a string of inions.'

This account cleared up the otherwise unaccountable mystery, and showed that the landlord, after all, had had no idea of fooling me—but at the same time what could I think of a harpooneer who stayed out of a Saturday night clean into the holy Sabbath, engaged in such a cannibal business as selling the heads of dead idolators?

'Depend upon it, landlord, that harpooneer is a dangerous man.'

'He pays reg'lar,' was the rejoinder. 'But come, it's getting dreadful late, you had better be turning flukes—it's a nice bed: Sal and me slept in that ere bed the night we were spliced. There's plenty room for two to kick about in that bed; it's an almighty big bed that. Why, afore we give it up, Sal used to put our Sam and little Johnny in the foot of it. But I got a dreaming and sprawling about one night, and somehow, Sam got pitched on the floor, and came near breaking his arm. Arter that, Sal said it wouldn't do. Come along here, I'll give ye a glim in a jiffy;' and so saying he lighted a candle and held it towards me, offering to lead the way. But I stood irresolute; when looking at a clock in the corner, he exclaimed, 'I vum it's Sunday—you won't see that harpooneer tonight; he's come to anchor somewhere—come along then; *do* come; *won't* ye come?'

I considered the matter a moment, and then up stairs we went, and I was ushered into a small room, cold as a clam, and furnished, sure enough, with a prodigious bed, almost big enough indeed for any four harpooneers to sleep abreast.

'There,' said the landlord, placing the candle on a crazy old sea chest that did double duty as a wash-stand and centre table; 'there, make yourself comfortable now, and good night to ye.' I turned round from eyeing the bed, but he had disappeared.

Folding back the counterpane, I stooped over the bed. Though none of the most elegant, it yet stood the scrutiny tolerably well. I then glanced round the room; and besides the bedstead and centre table, could see no other furniture belonging to the place, but a rude shelf, the four walls, and a papered fireboard representing a man striking a whale. Of things not properly belonging to the room, there was a hammock lashed up, and thrown upon the floor in one corner; also a large seaman's bag, containing the harpooneers' wardrobe, no doubt in lieu of a land trunk. Likewise, there was a parcel of outlandish bone fish hooks on the shelf over the fire-place, and a tall harpoon standing at the head of the bed.

But what is this on the chest? I took it up, and held it close to the light, and felt it, and smelt it, and tried every way possible to arrive at some satisfactory conclusion concerning it. I can compare it to nothing but a large door mat, ornamented at the edges with little tinkling tags something like the stained porcupine quills round an Indian moccasin. There was a hole or slit in the middle of this mat, as you see the same in South American ponchos. But could it be possible that any sober harpooneer would get into a door mat, and parade the streets of any Christian town in that sort of guise? I put it on, to try it, and it weighed me down like a hamper, being uncommonly shaggy and thick, and I thought a little damp, as though this mysterious harpooneer had been wearing it of a rainy day. I went up in it to a bit of glass stuck against the wall, and I never saw such a sight in my life. I tore myself out of it in such a hurry that I gave myself a kink in the neck.

I sat down on the side of the bed, and commenced thinking about this head-peddling harpooneer, and his door mat. After thinking some time on the bed-side, I got up and took off my monkey jacket, and then stood in the middle of the room thinking. I then took off my coat, and thought a little more in my shirt sleeves. But beginning to feel very cold now, half undressed as I was, and remembering what the landlord said about the harpooneer's not coming home at all that night, it being so very late, I made no more ado, but jumped out of my pantaloons and boots, and then blowing out the light tumbled into bed, and commended myself to the care of heaven.

Whether that mattress was stuffed with corn-cobs or broken crockery, there is no telling, but I rolled about a good deal, and could not sleep for a long time. At last I slid off into a light doze, and had pretty nearly made a good offing towards the land of Nod, when I heard a heavy footfall in the passage, and saw a glimmer of light come into the room from under the door.

Lord save me, thinks I, that must be the harpooneer, the infernal head-peddler. But I lay perfectly still, and resolved not to say a word till spoken to. Holding a light in one hand, and that identical New Zealand head in the other, the stranger entered the room, and without looking towards the bed, placed his candle a good

way off from me on the floor in one corner, and then began
working away at the knotted cords of the large bag I before spoke
of as being in the room. I was all eagerness to see his face, but
he kept it averted for some time while employed in unlacing the
bag's mouth. This accomplished, however, he turned round—
when, good heavens! what a sight! Such a face! It was of a dark,
purplish, yellow color, here and there stuck over with large, blackish
looking squares. Yes, it's just as I thought, he's a terrible bedfellow;
he's been in a fight, got dreadfully cut, and here he is, just from
the surgeon. But at that moment he chanced to turn his face so
towards the light, that I plainly saw they could not be sticking-
plasters at all, those black squares on his cheeks. They were stains
of some sort or other. At first I knew not what to make of this;
but soon an inkling of the truth occurred to me. I remembered
a story of a white man—a whaleman too—who, falling among
the cannibals, had been tattooed by them. I concluded that this
harpooneer, in the course of his distant voyages, must have met
with a similar adventure. And what is it, thought I, after all! It's
only his outside; a man can be honest in any sort of skin. But
then, what to make of his unearthly complexion, that part of it,
I mean, lying round about, and completely independent of the
squares of tattooing. To be sure, it might be nothing but a good
coat of tropical tanning; but I never heard of a hot sun's tanning
a white man into a purplish yellow one. However, I had never
been in the South Seas; and perhaps the sun there produced these
extraordinary effects upon the skin. Now, while all these ideas
were passing through me like lightning, this harpooneer never
noticed me at all. But, after some difficulty having opened his
bag, he commenced fumbling in it, and presently pulled out a
sort of tomahawk, and a seal-skin wallet with the hair on. Placing
these on the old chest in the middle of the room, he then took
the New Zealand head—a ghastly thing enough—and crammed
it down into the bag. He now took off his hat—a new beaver
hat, when I came nigh singing out with fresh surprise. There was
no hair on his head—none to speak of at least—nothing but a
small scalp-knot twisted up on his forehead. His bald purplish
head now looked for all the world like a mildewed skull. Had
not the stranger stood between me and the door, I would have
bolted out of it quicker than ever I bolted a dinner.

Even as it was, I thought something of slipping out of the
window, but it was the second floor back. I am no coward, but
what to make of this head-peddling purple rascal altogether passed
my comprehension. Ignorance is the parent of fear, and being

completely nonplussed and confounded about the stranger, I confess I was now as much afraid of him as if it was the devil himself
who had thus broken into my room at the dead of night. In fact,
I was so afraid of him that I was not game enough just then to
address him, and demand a satisfactory answer concerning what
seemed inexplicable in him.

Meanwhile, he continued the business of undressing, and at last
showed his chest and arms. As I live, these covered parts of him
were checkered with the same squares as his face; his back, too,
was all over the same dark squares; he seemed to have been in
a Thirty Years' War, and just escaped from it with a sticking-
plaster shirt. Still more, his very legs were marked, as if a parcel
of dark green frogs were running up the trunks of young palms.
It was now quite plain that he must be some abominable savage
or other shipped aboard of a whaleman in the South Seas, and
so landed in this Christian country. I quaked to think of it. A
peddler of heads too—perhaps the heads of his own brothers. He
might take a fancy to mine—heavens! look at that tomahawk!

But there was no time for shuddering, for now the savage went
about something that completely fascinated my attention, and
convinced me that he must indeed be a heathen. Going to his
heavy grego, or wrapall, or dreadnaught, which he had previously
hung on a chair, he fumbled in the pockets, and produced at
length a curious deformed image with a hunch on its back, and
exactly the colour of a three days' old Congo baby. Remembering
the embalmed head, at first I almost thought that this black
manikin was a real baby preserved in some similar manner. But
seeing that it was not at all limber, and that it glistened a good
deal like polished ebony, I concluded that it must be nothing but
a wooden idol, which indeed it proved to be. For now the savage
goes up to the empty fire-place, and removing the papered fire-
board, sets up this little hunchbacked image, like a tenpin, between
the andirons. The chimney jambs and all the bricks inside were
very sooty, so that I thought this fire-place made a very appropriate
little shrine or chapel for his Congo idol.

I now screwed my eyes hard towards the half hidden image,
feeling but ill at ease meantime—to see what was next to follow.
First he takes about a double handful of shavings out of his grego
pocket, and places them carefully before the idol; then laying a
bit of ship biscuit on top and applying the flame from the lamp,
he kindled the shavings into a sacrificial blaze. Presently, after
many hasty snatches into the fire, and still hastier withdrawals of
his fingers (whereby he seemed to be scorching them badly), he

at last succeeded in drawing out the biscuit; then blowing off the heat and ashes a little, he made a polite offer of it to the little negro. But the little devil did not seem to fancy such dry sort of fare at all; he never moved his lips. All these strange antics were accompanied by still stranger guttural noises from the devotee, who seemed to be praying in a sing-song or else singing some pagan psalmody or other, during which his face twitched about in the most unnatural manner. At last extinguishing the fire, he took the idol up very unceremoniously, and bagged it again in his grego pocket as carelessly as if he were a sportsman bagging a dead woodcock.

All these queer proceedings increased my uncomfortableness, and seeing him now exhibiting strong symptoms of concluding his business operations, and jumping into bed with me, I thought it was high time, now or never, before the light was put out, to break the spell in which I had so long been bound.

But the interval I spent in deliberating what to say, was a fatal one. Taking up his tomahawk from the table, he examined the head of it for an instant, and then holding it to the light, with his mouth at the handle, he puffed out great clouds of tobacco smoke. The next moment the light was extinguished, and this wild cannibal, tomahawk between his teeth, sprang into bed with me. I sang out, I could not help it now; and giving a sudden grunt of astonishment he began feeling me.

Stammering out something, I knew not what, I rolled away from him against the wall, and then conjured him, whoever or whatever he might be, to keep quiet, and let me get up and light the lamp again. But his guttural responses satisfied me at once that he but ill comprehended my meaning.

'Who-e debel you?'—he at last said—'you no speak-e, dam-me, I kill-e.' And so saying the lighted tomahawk began flourishing about me in the dark.

'Landlord, for God's sake, Peter Coffin!' shouted I. 'Landlord! Watch! Coffin! Angels! save me!'

'Speak-e! tell-ee me whoo-ee be, or dam-me, I kill-e!' again growled the cannibal, while his horrid flourishings of the tomahawk scattered the hot tobacco ashes about me till I thought my linen would get on fire. But thank heaven, at that moment the landlord came into the room light in hand, and leaping from the bed I ran up to him.

'Don't be afraid now,' said he, grinning again. 'Queequeg here wouldn't harm a hair of your head.'

'Stop your grinning,' shouted I, 'and why didn't you tell me that that infernal harpooneer was a cannibal?'

'I thought ye know'd it;—didn't I tell ye, he was a peddlin' heads around town?—but turn flukes again and go to sleep. Queequeg, look here—you sabbee me, I sabbee you—this man sleepe you—you sabbee?'—

'Me sabbee plenty'—grunted Queequeg, puffing away at his pipe and sitting up in bed.

'You gettee in,' he added, motioning to me with his tomahawk, and throwing the clothes to one side. He really did this in not only a civil but a really kind and charitable way. I stood looking at him a moment. For all his tattooings he was on the whole a clean, comely looking cannibal. What's all this fuss I have been making about, thought I to myself—the man's a human being just as I am: he has just as much reason to fear me, as I have to be afraid of him. Better sleep with a sober cannibal than a drunken Christian.

'Landlord,' said I, 'tell him to stash his tomahawk there, or pipe, or whatever you call it; tell him to stop smoking, in short, and I will turn in with him. But I don't fancy having a man smoking in bed with me. It's dangerous. Besides, I ain't insured.'

This being told to Queequeg, he at once complied, and again politely motioned me to get into bed—rolling over to one side as much as to say—I wont touch a leg of ye.

'Good night, landlord,' said I, 'you may go.'

I turned in, and never slept better in my life.

4

THE COUNTERPANE

Upon waking next morning about daylight, I found Queequeg's arm thrown over me in the most loving and affectionate manner. You had almost thought I had been his wife. The counterpane was of patchwork, full of odd little parti-colored squares and triangles; and this arm of his tattooed all over with an interminable Cretan labyrinth of a figure, no two parts of which were of one precise shade—owing I suppose to his keeping his arm at sea unmethodically in sun and shade, his shirt sleeves irregularly rolled up at various times—this same arm of his, I say, looked for all the world like a strip of that same patchwork quilt. Indeed, partly lying on it as the arm did when I first awoke, I could hardly tell

it from the quilt, they so blended their hues together; and it was
only by the sense of weight and pressure that I could tell that
Queequeg was hugging me.

My sensations were strange. Let me try to explain them. When
I was a child, I well remember a somewhat similar circumstance
that befell me; whether it was a reality or a dream, I never could
entirely settle. The circumstance was this. I had been cutting up
some caper or other—I think it was trying to crawl up the chimney,
as I had seen a little sweep do a few days previous; and my
stepmother who, somehow or other, was all the time whipping
me, or sending me to bed supperless,—my mother dragged me
by the legs out of the chimney and packed me off to bed, though
it was only two o'clock in the afternoon of the 21st June, the
longest day in the year in our hemisphere. I felt dreadfully. But
there was no help for it, so up stairs I went to my little room in
the third floor, undressed myself as slowly as possible so as to kill
time, and with a bitter sigh got between the sheets.

I lay there dismally calculating that sixteen entire hours must
elapse before I could hope for a resurrection. Sixteen hours in
bed! the small of my back ached to think of it. And it was so
light too; the sun shining in at the window, and a great rattling
of coaches in the streets, and the sound of gay voices all over the
house. I felt worse and worse—at last I got up, dressed, and softly
going down in my stockinged feet, sought out my stepmother,
and suddenly threw myself at her feet, beseeching her as a particular
favor to give me a good slippering for my misbehavior; anything
indeed but condemning me to lie abed such an unendurable length
of time. But she was the best and most conscientious of step-
mothers, and back I had to go to my room. For several hours I
lay there broad awake, feeling a great deal worse than I have ever
done since, even from the greatest subsequent misfortunes. At last
I must have fallen into a troubled nightmare of a doze; and slowly
waking from it—half steeped in dreams—I opened my eyes, and
the before sun-lit room was now wrapped in outer darkness.
Instantly I felt a shock running through all my frame; nothing
was to be seen, and nothing was to be heard; but a supernatural
hand seemed placed in mine. My arm hung over the counterpane,
and the nameless, unimaginable, silent form or phantom, to which
the hand belonged, seemed closely seated by my bedside. For what
seemed ages piled on ages, I lay there, frozen with the most awful
fears, not daring to drag away my hand; yet ever thinking that if
I could but stir it one single inch, the horrid spell would be broken.
I knew not how this consciousness at last glided away from me;

but waking in the morning, I shudderingly remembered it all, and for days and weeks and months afterwards I lost myself in confounding attempts to explain the mystery. Nay, to this very hour, I often puzzle myself with it.

Now, take away the awful fear, and my sensations at feeling the supernatural hand in mine were very similar, in their strangeness, to those which I experienced on waking up and seeing Queequeg's pagan arm thrown round me. But at length all the past night's events soberly recurred, one by one, in fixed reality, and then I lay only alive to the comical predicament. For though I tried to move his arm—unlock his bridegroom clasp—yet, sleeping as he was, he still hugged me tightly, as though naught but death should part us twain. I now strove to rouse him—'Queequeg!'—but his only answer was a snore. I then rolled over, my neck feeling as if it were in a horse-collar; and suddenly felt a slight scratch. Throwing aside the counterpane, there lay the tomahawk sleeping by the savage's side, as if it were a hatchet-faced baby. A pretty pickle, truly, thought I; abed here in a strange house in the broad day, with a cannibal and a tomahawk! 'Queequeg!—in the name of goodness, Queequeg, wake!' At length, by dint of much wriggling, and loud and incessant expostulations upon the unbecomingness of his hugging a fellow male in that matrimonial sort of style, I succeeded in extracting a grunt; and presently, he drew back his arm, shook himself all over like a Newfoundland dog just from the water, and sat up in bed, stiff as a pike-staff, looking at me, and rubbing his eyes as if he did not altogether remember how I came to be there, though a dim consciousness of knowing something about me seemed slowly dawning over him. Meanwhile, I lay quietly eyeing him, having no serious misgivings now, and bent upon narrowly observing so curious a creature. When, at last, his mind seemed made up touching the character of his bedfellow, and he became, as it were, reconciled to the fact; he jumped out upon the floor, and by certain signs and sounds gave me to understand that, if it pleased me, he would dress first and then leave me to dress afterwards, having the whole apartment to myself. Thinks I, Queequeg, under the circumstances, this is a very civilized overture; but, the truth is, these savages have an innate sense of delicacy, say what you will; it is marvellous how essentially polite they are. I pay this particular compliment to Queequeg, because he treated me with so much civility and consideration, while I was guilty of great rudeness; staring at him from the bed, and watching all his toilette motions; for the time my curiosity getting the better of my breeding.

Nevertheless, a man like Queequeg you don't see every day, he and his ways were well worth unusual regarding.

He commenced dressing at top by donning his beaver hat, a very tall one, by the by, and then—still minus his trowsers—he hunted up his boots. What under the heavens he did it for, I cannot tell, but his next movement was to crush himself—boots in hand, and hat on—under the bed; when, from sundry violent graspings and strainings, I inferred he was hard at work booting himself; though by no law of propriety that I ever heard of, is any man required to be private when putting on his boots. But Queequeg, do you see, was a creature in the transition state—neither caterpillar nor butterfly. He was just enough civilized to show off his outlandishness in the strangest possible manner. His education was not yet completed. He was an undergraduate. If he had not been a small degree civilized, he very probably would not have troubled himself with boots at all; but then, if he had not been still a savage, he never would have dreamt of getting under the bed to put them on. At last, he emerged with his hat very much dented and crushed down over his eyes, and began creaking and limping about the room, as if, not being much accustomed to boots, his pair of damp, wrinkled cowhide ones—probably not made to order either—rather pinched and tormented him at the first go off of a bitter cold morning.

Seeing, now, that there were no curtains to the window, and that the street being very narrow, the house opposite commanded a plain view into the room, and observing more and more the indecorous figure that Queequeg made, staving about with little else but his hat and boots on; I begged him as well as I could, to accelerate his toilet somewhat, and particularly to get into his pantaloons as soon as possible. He complied, and then proceeded to wash himself. At that time in the morning any Christian would have washed his face; but Queequeg, to my amazement, contented himself with restricting his ablutions to his chest, arms, and hands. He then donned his waistcoat, and taking up a piece of hard soap on the wash-stand centre-table, dipped it into water and commenced lathering his face. I was watching to see where he kept his razor, when lo and behold, he takes the harpoon from the bed corner, slips out the long wooden stock, unsheathes the head, whets it a little on his boot, and striding up to the bit of mirror against the wall, begins a vigorous scraping, or rather harpooning of his cheeks. Thinks I, Queequeg, this is using Rogers's best cutlery with a vengeance. Afterwards I wondered the less at this operation when I came to know of what fine steel the head of a harpoon is made, and how exceedingly sharp the long straight edges are always kept.

The rest of his toilet was soon achieved, and he proudly marched out of the room, wrapped up in his great pilot monkey jacket, and sporting his harpoon like a marshal's baton.

5
BREAKFAST

I QUICKLY followed suit, and descending into the bar-room accosted the grinning landlord very pleasantly. I cherished no malice towards him, though he had been skylarking with me not a little in the matter of my bedfellow.

However, a good laugh is a mighty good thing, and rather too scarce a good thing; the more's the pity. So, if any one man, in his own proper person, afford stuff for a good joke to anybody, let him not be backward, but let him cheerfully allow himself to spend and be spent in that way. And the man that has anything bountifully laughable about him, be sure there is more in that man than you perhaps think for.

The bar-room was now full of the boarders who had been dropping in the night previous, and whom I had not as yet had a good look at. They were nearly all whalemen; chief mates, and second mates, and third mates, and sea carpenters, and sea coopers, and sea blacksmiths, and harpooneers, and ship keepers; a brown and brawny company, with bosky beards; an unshorn, shaggy set, all wearing monkey jackets for morning gowns.

You could pretty plainly tell how long each one had been ashore. This young fellow's healthy cheek is like a suntoasted pear in hue, and would seem to smell almost as musky; he cannot have been three days landed from his Indian voyage. That man next him looks a few shades lighter; you might say a touch of satin wood is in him. In the complexion of a third still lingers a tropic tawn, but slightly bleached withal; *he* doubtless has tarried whole weeks ashore. But who could show a cheek like Queequeg? which, barred with various tints, seemed like the Andes' western slope, to show forth in one array, contrasting climates, zone by zone.

'Grub, ho!' now cried the landlord, flinging open a door, and in we went to breakfast.

They say that men who have seen the world, thereby become quite at ease in manner, quite self-possessed in company. Not always, though: Ledyard, the great New Englander traveller, and Mungo Park, the Scotch one; of all men, they possessed the least assurance in the parlor. But perhaps the mere crossing of Siberia in a sledge drawn by dogs as Ledyard did, or the taking a long solitary walk on an empty stomach, in the negro heart of Africa, which was the sum of poor Mungo's performances—this kind of travel, I say, may not be the very best mode of attaining a high social polish. Still, for the most part, that sort of thing is to be had anywhere.

These reflections just here are occasioned by the circumstance that after we were all seated at the table, and I was preparing to hear some good stories about whaling; to my no small surprise, nearly every man maintained a profound silence. And not only that, but they looked embarrassed. Yes, here were a set of sea-dogs, many of whom without the slightest bashfulness had boarded great whales on the high seas—entire strangers to them—and duelled them dead without winking; and yet, here they sat at a social breakfast table—all of the same calling, all of kindred tastes—looking round as sheepishly at each other as though they had never been out of sight of some sheepfold among the Green Mountains. A curious sight; these bashful bears, these timid warrior whalemen!

But as for Queequeg—why, Queequeg sat there among them—at the head of the table, too, it so chanced; as cool as an icicle. To be sure I cannot say much for his breeding. His greatest admirer could not have cordially justified his bringing his harpoon into breakfast with him, and using it there without ceremony; reaching over the table with it, to the imminent jeopardy of many heads, and grappling the beefsteaks towards him. But *that* was certainly very coolly done by him, and every one knows that in most people's estimation, to do anything coolly is to do it genteelly.

We will not speak of all Queequeg's peculiarities here; how he eschewed coffee and hot rolls, and applied his undivided attention to beefsteaks, done rare. Enough, that when breakfast was over he withdrew like the rest into the public room, lighted his tom-ahawk-pipe, and was sitting there quietly digesting and smoking with his inseparable hat on, when I sallied out for a stroll.

6

THE STREET

IF I had been astonished at first catching a glimpse of so outlandish an individual as Queequeg circulating among the polite society of a civilized town, that astonishment soon departed upon taking my first daylight stroll through the streets of New Bedford.

In thoroughfares nigh the docks, any considerable seaport will frequently offer to view the queerest looking nondescripts from foreign parts. Even in Broadway and Chestnut streets, Mediterranean mariners will sometimes jostle the affrighted ladies. Regent Street is not unknown to Lascars and Malays; and at Bombay, in the Apollo Green, live Yankees have often scared the natives. But New Bedford beats all Water Street and Wapping. In these last-mentioned haunts you see only sailors; but in New Bedford, actual cannibals stand chatting at street corners; savages outright; many of whom yet carry on their bones unholy flesh. It makes a stranger stare.

But, besides the Feegeeans, Tongatabooans, Erromanggoans, Pannangians, and Brighggians, and, besides the wild specimens of the whaling-craft which unheeded reel about the streets, you will see other sights still more curious, certainly more comical. There weekly arrive in this town scores of green Vermonters and New Hampshire men, all athirst for gain and glory in the fishery. They are mostly young, of stalwart frames; fellows who have felled forests, and now seek to drop the axe and snatch the whale-lance. Many are as green as the Green Mountains whence they came. In some things you would think them but a few hours old. Look there! that chap strutting round the corner. He wears a beaver hat and swallow-tailed coat, girdled with a sailor-belt and sheath-knife. Here comes another with a sou'-wester and a bombazine cloak.

No town-bred dandy will compare with a country-bred one— I mean a downright bumpkin dandy—a fellow that, in the dog-days, will mow his two acres in buckskin gloves for fear of tanning his hands. Now when a country dandy like this takes it into his head to make a distinguished reputation, and joins the great whale-fishery, you should see the comical things he does upon reaching the seaport. In bespeaking his sea-outfit, he orders bell-buttons to his waistcoats; straps to his canvas trowsers. Ah, poor Hay-Seed! how bitterly will burst those straps in the first howling gale, when thou art driven, straps, buttons, and all, down the throat of the tempest.

But think not that this famous town has only harpooneers, cannibals, and bumpkins to show her visitors. Not at all. Still New Bedford is a queer place. Had it not been for us whalemen, that tract of land would this day perhaps have been in as howling condition as the coast of Labrador. As it is, parts of her back country are enough to frighten one, they look so bony. The town itself is perhaps the dearest place to live in, in all New England. It is a land of oil, true enough: but not like Canaan; a land, also, of corn and wine. The streets do not run with milk; nor in the spring-time do they pave them with fresh eggs. Yet, in spite of this, nowhere in all America will you find more patrician-like houses, parks and gardens more opulent, than in New Bedford. Whence came they? how planted upon this once scraggy scoria of a country?

Go and gaze upon the iron emblematical harpoons round yonder lofty mansion, and your question will be answered. Yes; all these brave houses and flowery gardens came from the Atlantic, Pacific, and Indian oceans. One and all, they were harpooned and dragged up hither from the bottom of the sea. Can Herr Alexander perform a feat like that?

In New Bedford, fathers, they say, give whales for dowers to their daughters, and portion off their nieces with a few porpoises a-piece. You must go to New Bedford to see a brilliant wedding; for, they say, they have reservoirs of oil in every house, and every night recklessly burn their lengths in spermaceti candles.

In summer time, the town is sweet to see; full of fine maples— long avenues of green and gold. And in August, high in air, the beautiful and bountiful horse-chestnuts, candelabra-wise, proffer the passer-by their tapering upright cones of congregated blossoms. So omnipotent is art; which in many a district of New Bedford has superinduced bright terraces of flowers upon the barren refuse rocks thrown aside at creation's final day.

And the women of New Bedford, they bloom like their own red roses. But roses only bloom in summer; whereas the fine carnation of their cheeks is perennial as sunlight in the seventh heavens. Elsewhere match that bloom of theirs, ye cannot, save in Salem, where they tell me the young girls breathe such musk, their sailor sweethearts smell them miles off shore, as though they were drawing nigh the odorous Moluccas instead of the Puritanic sands.

7

THE CHAPEL

IN this same New Bedford there stands a Whaleman's Chapel, and few are the moody fishermen, shortly bound for the Indian Ocean or Pacific, who fail to make a Sunday visit to the spot. I am sure that I did not.

Returning from my first morning stroll, I again sallied out upon this special errand. The sky had changed from clear, sunny cold, to driving sleet and mist. Wrapping myself in my shaggy jacket of the cloth called bearskin, I fought my way against the stubborn storm. Entering, I found a small scattered congregation of sailors, and sailors' wives and widows. A muffled silence reigned, only broken at times by the shrieks of the storm. Each silent worshipper seemed purposely sitting apart from the other, as if each silent grief were insular and incommunicable. The chaplain had not yet arrived; and there these silent islands of men and women sat steadfastly eyeing several marble tablets, with black borders, masoned into the wall on either side the pulpit. Three of them ran something like the following, but I do not pretend to quote:

SACRED TO THE MEMORY OF

JOHN TALBOT,

WHO, AT THE AGE OF EIGHTEEN, WAS LOST OVERBOARD,

NEAR THE ISLE OF DESOLATION, OFF PATAGONIA,

NOVEMBER 1ST, 1836.

THIS TABLET IS ERECTED TO HIS MEMORY

BY HIS SISTER.

SACRED TO THE MEMORY OF

ROBERT LONG, WILLIS ELLERY, NATHAN COLEMAN,

WALTER CANNY, SETH MACY, AND SAMUEL GLEIG,

FORMING ONE OF THE BOATS' CREWS OF

THE SHIP ELIZA,

WHO WERE TOWED OUT OF SIGHT BY A WHALE,

ON THE OFF-SHORE GROUND IN THE PACIFIC,

DECEMBER 31ST, 1839.

THIS MARBLE IS HERE PLACED BY THEIR SURVIVING

SHIPMATES.

SACRED TO THE MEMORY OF

THE LATE

CAPTAIN EZEKIEL HARDY,

WHO IN THE BOWS OF HIS BOAT WAS KILLED BY A

SPERM WHALE ON THE COAST OF JAPAN,

AUGUST 3D, 1833.

THIS TABLET IS ERECTED TO HIS MEMORY BY

HIS WIDOW.

Shaking off the sleet from my ice-glazed hat and jacket, I seated myself near the door, and turning sideways was surprised to see Queequeg near me. Affected by the solemnity of the scene, there was a wondering gaze of incredulous curiosity in his countenance. This savage was the only person present who seemed to notice my entrance; because he was the only one who could not read, and, therefore, was not reading those frigid inscriptions on the wall. Whether any of the relatives of the seamen whose names appeared there were now among the congregation, I knew not; but so many are the unrecorded accidents in the fishery, and so plainly did several women present wear the countenance if not

the trappings of some unceasing grief, that I feel sure that here
before me were assembled those, in whose unhealing hearts the
sight of those bleak tablets sympathetically caused the old wounds
to bleed afresh.

Oh! ye whose dead lie buried beneath the green grass; who
standing among flowers can say—here, *here* lies my beloved, ye
know not the desolation that broods in bosoms like these. What
bitter blanks in those black-bordered marbles which cover no
ashes! What despair in those immovable inscriptions! What deadly
voids and unbidden infidelities in the lines that seem to gnaw
upon all Faith, and refuse resurrections to the beings who have
placelessly perished without a grave. As well might those tablets
stand in the cave of Elephanta as here.

In what census of living creatures, the dead of mankind are
included; why it is that a universal proverb says of them, that
they tell no tales, though containing more secrets than the Goodwin
Sands; how it is that to his name who yesterday departed for the
other world, we prefix so significant and infidel a word, and yet
do not thus entitle him, if he but embarks for the remotest Indies
of this living earth; why the Life Insurance Companies pay death-
forfeitures upon immortals; in what eternal, unstirring paralysis,
and deadly, hopeless trance, yet lies antique Adam who died sixty
round centuries ago; how it is that we still refuse to be comforted
for those who we nevertheless maintain are dwelling in unspeakable
bliss; why all the living so strive to hush all the dead; wherefore
but the rumor of a knocking in a tomb will terrify a whole city.
All these things are not without their meanings.

But Faith, like a jackal, feeds among the tombs, and even from
these dead doubts she gathers her most vital hope.

It needs scarcely to be told, with what feelings, on the eve of
a Nantucket voyage, I regarded those marble tablets, and by the
murky light of that darkened, doleful day read the fate of the
whalemen who had gone before me. Yes, Ishmael, the same fate
may be thine. But somehow I grew merry again. Delightful inducements to embark, fine chance for promotion, it seems—aye,
a stove boat will make me an immortal by brevet. Yes, there is
death in this business of whaling—a speechlessly quick chaotic
bundling of a man into Eternity. But what then? Methinks we
have hugely mistaken this matter of Life and Death. Methinks
that what they call my shadow here on earth is my true substance.
Methinks that in looking at things spiritual, we are too much like
oysters observing the sun through the water, and thinking that
thick water the thinnest of air. Methinks my body is but the lees

of my better being. In fact take my body who will, take it I say,
it is not me. And therefore three cheers for Nantucket; and come
a stove boat and stove body when they will, for stave my soul,
Jove himself cannot.

8
THE PULPIT

I had not been seated very long ere a man of a certain venerable
robustness entered; immediately as the storm-pelted door flew back
upon admitting him, a quick regardful eyeing of him by all the
congregation, sufficiently attested that this fine old man was the
chaplain. Yes, it was the famous Father Mapple, so called by the
whalemen, among whom he was a very great favorite. He had
been a sailor and a harpooneer in his youth, but for many years
past had dedicated his life to the ministry. At the time I now
write of, Father Mapple was in the hardy winter of a healthy old
age; that sort of old age which seems merging into a second
flowering youth, for among all the fissures of his wrinkles, there
shone certain mild gleams of a newly developing bloom—the
spring verdure peeping forth even beneath February's snow. No
one having previously heard his history, could for the first time
behold Father Mapple without the utmost interest, because there
were certain engrafted clerical peculiarities about him, imputable
to that adventurous maritime life he had led. When he entered I
observed that he carried no umbrella, and certainly had not come
in his carriage, for his tarpaulin hat ran down with melting sleet,
and his great pilot cloth jacket seemed almost to drag him to the
floor with the weight of the water it had absorbed. However, hat
and coat and overshoes were one by one removed, and hung up
in a little space in an adjacent corner; when, arrayed in a decent
suit, he quietly approached the pulpit.
  Like most old fashioned pulpits, it was a very lofty one, and
since a regular stairs to such a height would, by its long angle
with the floor, seriously contract the already small area of the
chapel, the architect, it seemed, had acted upon the hint of Father
Mapple, and finished the pulpit without a stairs, substituting a
perpendicular side ladder, like those used in mounting a ship from
a boat at sea. The wife of a whaling captain had provided the
chapel with a handsome pair of red worsted man-ropes for this

ladder, which, being itself nicely headed, and stained with a mahogany color, the whole contrivance, considering what manner of chapel it was, seemed by no means in bad taste. Halting for an instant at the foot of the ladder, and with both hands grasping the ornamental knobs of the man-ropes, Father Mapple cast a look upwards, and then with a truly sailor-like but still reverential dexterity, hand over hand, mounted the steps as if ascending the main-top of his vessel.

The perpendicular parts of this side ladder, as is usually the case with swinging ones, were of cloth-covered rope, only the rounds were of wood, so that at every step there was a joint. At my first glimpse of the pulpit, it had not escaped me that however convenient for a ship, these joints in the present instance seemed unnecessary. For I was not prepared to see Father Mapple after gaining the height, slowly turn round, and stooping over the pulpit, deliberately drag up the ladder step by step, till the whole was deposited within, leaving him impregnable in his little Quebec.

I pondered some time without fully comprehending the reason for this. Father Mapple enjoyed such a wide reputation for sincerity and sanctity, that I could not suspect him of courting notoriety by any mere tricks of the stage. No, thought I, there must be some sober reason for this thing; furthermore, it must symbolize something unseen. Can it be, then, that by that act of physical isolation, he signifies his spiritual withdrawal for the time, from all outward worldly ties and connexions? Yes, for replenished with the meat and wine of the word, to the faithful man of God, this pulpit, I see, is a self-containing strong-hold—a lofty Ehrenbreitstein, with a perennial well of water within the walls.

But the side ladder was not the only strange feature of the place, borrowed from the chaplain's former sea-farings. Between the marble cenotaphs on either hand of the pulpit, the wall which formed its back was adorned with a large painting representing a gallant ship beating against a terrible storm off a lee coast of black rocks and snowy breakers. But high above the flying scud and dark-rolling clouds, there floated a little isle of sunlight, from which beamed forth an angel's face; and this bright face shed a distinct spot of radiance upon the ship's tossed deck, something like that silver plate now inserted into the Victory's plank where Nelson fell. 'Ah, noble ship,' the angel seemed to say, 'beat on, beat on, thou noble ship, and bear a hardy helm; for lo! the sun is breaking through; the clouds are rolling off—serenest azure is at hand.'

Nor was the pulpit itself without a trace of the same sea-taste that had achieved the ladder and the picture. Its panelled front was in the likeness of a ship's bluff bows, and the Holy Bible rested on a projecting piece of scroll work, fashioned after a ship's fiddle-headed beak.

What could be more full of meaning?—for the pulpit is ever this earth's foremost part; all the rest comes in its rear; the pulpit leads the world. From thence it is the storm of God's quick wrath is first descried, and the bow must bear the earliest brunt. From thence it is the God of breezes fair or foul is first invoked for favorable winds. Yes, the world's a ship on its passage out, and not a voyage complete; and the pulpit is its prow.

9

THE SERMON

FATHER MAPPLE rose, and in a mild voice of unassuming authority ordered the scattered people to condense. 'Starboard gangway, there! side away to larboard—larboard gangway to starboard! Midships! midships!'

There was a low rumbling of heavy sea-boots among the benches, and a still slighter shuffling of women's shoes, and all was quiet again, and every eye on the preacher.

He paused a little; then kneeling in the pulpit's bows, folded his large brown hands across his chest, uplifted his closed eyes, and offered a prayer so deeply devout that he seemed kneeling and praying at the bottom of the sea.

This ended, in prolonged solemn tones, like the continual tolling of a bell in a ship that is foundering at sea in a fog—in such tones he commenced reading the following hymn; but changing his manner towards the concluding stanzas, burst forth with a pealing exultation and joy—

> The ribs and terrors in the whale,
>   Arched over me a dismal gloom,
> While all God's sun-lit waves rolled by,
>   And lift me deepening down to doom.
>
> I saw the opening maw of hell,
>   With endless pains and sorrows there;
> Which none but they that feel can tell—
>   Oh, I was plunging to despair.

In black distress, I called my God,
    When I could scarce believe him mine,
He bowed his ear to my complaints—
    No more the whale did me confine.

With speed he flew to my relief,
    As on a radiant dolphin borne;
Awful, yet bright, as lightning shone
    The face of my Deliverer God.

My song for ever shall record
    That terrible, that joyful hour;
I give the glory to my God,
    His all the mercy and the power.

Nearly all joined in singing this hymn, which swelled high above the howling of the storm. A brief pause ensued; the preacher slowly turned over the leaves of the Bible, and at last, folding his hand down upon the proper page, said: 'Beloved shipmates, clinch the last verse of the first chapter of Jonah—"And God had prepared a great fish to swallow up Jonah."

'Shipmates, this book, containing only four chapters—four yarns—is one of the smallest strands in the mighty cable of the Scriptures. Yet what depths of the soul does Jonah's deep sea-line sound! what a pregnant lesson to us is this prophet! What a noble thing is that canticle in the fish's belly! How billow-like and boisterously grand! We feel the floods surging over us; we sound with him to the kelpy bottom of the waters; sea-weed and all the slime of the sea is about us! But *what* is this lesson that the book of Jonah teaches? Shipmates, it is a two-stranded lesson; a lesson to us all as sinful men, and a lesson to me as a pilot of the living God. As sinful men, it is a lesson to us all, because it is a story of the sin, hard-heartedness, suddenly awakened fears, the swift punishment, repentance, prayers, and finally the deliverance and joy of Jonah. As with all sinners among men, the sin of this son of Amittai was in his wilful disobedience of the command of God—never mind now what that command was, or how conveyed—which he found a hard command. But all the things that God would have us do are hard for us to do—remember that—and hence, he oftener commands us than endeavors to persuade. And if we obey God, we must disobey ourselves; and it is in this disobeying ourselves, wherein the hardness of obeying God consists.

'With this sin of disobedience in him, Jonah still further flouts at God, by seeking to flee from Him. He thinks that a ship made by men, will carry him into countries where God does not reign,

but only the Captains of this earth. He skulks about the wharves
of Joppa, and seeks a ship that's bound for Tarshish. There lurks,
perhaps, a hitherto unheeded meaning here. By all accounts Tarshish could have been no other city than the modern Cadiz. That's
the opinion of learned men. And where is Cadiz, shipmates? Cadiz
is in Spain; as far by water, from Joppa, as Jonah could possibly
have sailed in those ancient days, when the Atlantic was an almost
unknown sea. Because Joppa, the modern Jaffa, shipmates, is on
the most easterly coast of the Mediterranean, the Syrian; and
Tarshish or Cadiz more than two thousand miles to the westward
from that, just outside the Straits of Gibraltar. See ye not then,
shipmates, that Jonah sought to flee world-wide from God? Miserable man! Oh! most contemptible and worthy of all scorn; with
slouched hat and guilty eye, skulking from his God; prowling
among the shipping like a vile burglar hastening to cross the sea.
So disordered, self-condemning is his look, that had there been
policemen in those days, Jonah, on the mere suspicion of something wrong, had been arrested ere he touched a deck. How plainly
he's a fugitive! no baggage, not a hat-box, valise, or carpet-bag,—
no friends accompany him to the wharf with their adieux. At last,
after much dodging search, he finds the Tarshish ship receiving
the last items of her cargo; and as he steps on board to see its
Captain in the cabin, all the sailors for the moment desist from
hoisting in the goods, to mark the stranger's evil eye. Jonah sees
this; but in vain he tries to look all ease and confidence; in vain
essays his wretched smile. Strong intuitions of the man assure the
mariners he can be no innocent. In their gamesome but still
serious way, one whispers to the other—"Jack, he's robbed a
widow;" or, "Joe, do you mark him; he's a bigamist;" or, "Harry
lad, I guess he's the adulterer that broke jail in old Gomorrah,
or belike, one of the missing murderers from Sodom." Another
runs to read the bill that's stuck against the spile upon the wharf
to which the ship is moored, offering five hundred gold coins for
the apprehension of a parricide, and containing a description of
his person. He reads, and looks from Jonah to the bill; while all
his sympathetic shipmates now crowd round Jonah, prepared to
lay their hands upon him. Frighted Jonah trembles, and summoning all his boldness to his face, only looks so much the more
a coward. He will not confess himself suspected; but that itself is
strong suspicion. So he makes the best of it; and when the sailors
find him not to be the man that is advertised, they let him pass,
and he descends into the cabin.

  ' "Who's there?" cries the Captain at his busy desk, hurriedly

making out his papers for the Customs—"Who's there?" Oh! how
that harmless question mangles Jonah! For the instant he almost
turns to flee again. But he rallies. "I seek a passage in this ship
to Tarshish; how soon sail ye, sir?" Thus far the busy Captain
had not looked up to Jonah, though the man now stands before
him; but no sooner does he hear that hollow voice, than he darts
a scrutinizing glance. "We sail with the next coming tide," at last
he slowly answered, still intently eyeing him. "No sooner, sir?"—
"Soon enough for any honest man that goes a passenger." Ha!
Jonah, that's another stab. But he swiftly calls away the Captain
from that scent. "I'll sail with ye,"—he says,—"the passage money,
how much is that?—I'll pay now." For it is particularly written,
shipmates, as if it were a thing not to be overlooked in this history,
"that he paid the fare thereof" ere the craft did sail. And taken
with the context, this is full of meaning.

'Now Jonah's Captain, shipmates, was one whose discernment
detects crime in any, but whose cupidity exposes it only in the
penniless. In this world, shipmates, sin that pays its way can travel
freely, and without a passport; whereas Virtue, if a pauper, is
stopped at all frontiers. So Jonah's Captain prepares to test the
length of Jonah's purse, ere he judge him openly. He charges him
thrice the usual sum; and it's assented to. Then the Captain knows
that Jonah is a fugitive; but at the same time resolves to help a
flight that paves its rear with gold. Yet when Jonah fairly takes
out his purse, prudent suspicions still molest the Captain. He rings
every coin to find a counterfeit. Not a forger, any way, he mutters;
and Jonah is put down for his passage. "Point out my state-room,
Sir," says Jonah now, "I'm travel-weary; I need sleep." "Thou
look'st like it," says the Captain, "there's thy room." Jonah enters,
and would lock the door, but the lock contains no key. Hearing
him foolishly fumbling there, the Captain laughs lowly to himself,
and mutters something about the doors of convicts' cells being
never allowed to be locked within. All dressed and dusty as he
is, Jonah throws himself into his berth, and finds the little state-
room ceiling almost resting on his forehead. The air is close, and
Jonah gasps. Then, in that contracted hole, sunk, too, beneath
the ship's water-line, Jonah feels the heralding presentiment of
that stifling hour, when the whale shall hold him in the smallest
of his bowel's wards.

'Screwed at its axis against the side, a swinging lamp slightly
oscillates in Jonah's room; and the ship, heeling over towards the
wharf with the weight of the last bales received, the lamp, flame
and all, though in slight motion, still maintains a permanent

obliquity with reference to the room; though, in truth, infallibly
straight itself, it but made obvious the false, lying levels among
which it hung. The lamp alarms and frightens Jonah; as lying in
his berth his tormented eyes roll round the place, and this thus
far successful fugitive finds no refuge for his restless glance. But
that contradiction in the lamp more and more appals him. The
floor, the ceiling, and the side, are all awry. "Oh! so my conscience
hangs in me!" he groans, "straight upward, so it burns; but the
chambers of my soul are all in crookedness!"

'Like one who after a night of drunken revelry hies to his bed,
still reeling, but with conscience yet pricking him, as the plungings
of the Roman race-horse but so much the more strike his steel
tags into him; as one who in that miserable plight still turns and
turns in giddy anguish, praying God for annihilation until the fit
be passed; and at last amid the whirl of woe he feels, a deep
stupor steals over him, as over the man who bleeds to death, for
conscience is the wound, and there's naught to staunch it; so,
after sore wrestlings in his berth, Jonah's prodigy of ponderous
misery drags him drowning down to sleep.

'And now the time of tide has come; the ship casts off her
cables; and from the deserted wharf the uncheered ship for Tarshish, all careening, glides to sea. That ship, my friends, was the
first of recorded smugglers! the contraband was Jonah. But the
sea rebels; he will not bear the wicked burden. A dreadful storm
comes on, the ship is like to break. But now when the boatswain
calls all hands to lighten her; when boxes, bales, and jars are
clattering overboard; when the wind is shrieking, and the men are
yelling, and every plank thunders with trampling feet right over
Jonah's head; in all this raging tumult, Jonah sleeps his hideous
sleep. He sees no black sky and raging sea, feels not the reeling
timbers, and little hears he or heeds he the far rush of the mighty
whale, which even now with open mouth is cleaving the seas after
him. Aye, shipmates, Jonah was gone down into the sides of the
ship—a berth in the cabin as I have taken it, and was fast asleep.
But the frightened master comes to him, and shrieks in his dead
ear, "What meanest thou, O sleeper! arise!" Startled from his
lethargy by that direful cry, Jonah staggers to his feet, and stumbling
to the deck, grasps a shroud, to look out upon the sea. But at
that moment he is sprung upon by a panther billow leaping over
the bulwarks. Wave after wave thus leaps into the ship, and finding
no speedy vent runs roaring fore and aft, till the mariners come
nigh to drowning while yet afloat. And ever, as the white moon
shows her afrighted face from the steep gullies in the blackness

overhead, aghast Jonah sees the rearing bowsprit pointing high upward, but soon beat downward again towards the tormented deep.

'Terrors upon terrors run shouting through his soul. In all his cringing attitudes, the God-fugitive is now too plainly known. The sailors mark him; more and more certain grow their suspicions of him, and at last, fully to test the truth, by referring the whole matter to high Heaven, they fall to casting lots, to see for whose cause this great tempest was upon them. The lot is Jonah's; that discovered, then how furiously they mob him with their questions. "What is thine occupation? Whence comest thou? Thy country? What people?" But mark now, my shipmates, the behavior of poor Jonah. The eager mariners but ask him who he is, and where from; whereas, they not only receive an answer to those questions, but likewise another answer to a question not put by them, but the unsolicited answer is forced from Jonah by the hard hand of God that is upon him.

' "I am a Hebrew," he cries—and then—"I fear the Lord the God of Heaven who hath made the sea and the dry land!" Fear him, O Jonah? Aye, well mightest thou fear the Lord God *then*! Straightway, he now goes on to make a full confession; whereupon the mariners become more and more appalled, but still are pitiful. For when Jonah, not yet supplicating God for mercy, since he but too well knew the darkness of his deserts,—when wretched Jonah cries out to them to take him and cast him forth into the sea, for he knew that for *his* sake this great tempest was upon them; they mercifully turn from him, and seek by other means to save the ship. But all in vain; the indignant gale howls louder; then, with one hand raised invokingly to God, with the other they not unreluctantly lay hold of Jonah.

'And now behold Jonah taken up as an anchor and dropped into the sea; when instantly an oily calmness floats out from the east, and the sea is still, as Jonah carries down the gale with him, leaving smooth water behind. He goes down in the whirling heart of such a masterless commotion that he scarce heeds the moment when he drops seething into the yawning jaws awaiting him; and the whale shoots-to all his ivory teeth, like so many white bolts, upon his prison. Then Jonah prayed unto the Lord out of the fish's belly. But observe his prayer, and learn a weighty lesson. For sinful as he is, Jonah does not weep and wail for direct deliverance. He feels that his dreadful punishment is just. He leaves all his deliverance to God, contenting himself with this, that spite of all his pains and pangs, he will still look towards

His holy temple. And here, shipmates, is true and faithful repentance; not clamorous for pardon, but grateful for punishment. And how pleasing to God was this conduct in Jonah, is shown in the eventual deliverance of him from the sea and the whale. Shipmates, I do not place Jonah before you to be copied for his sin but I do place him before you as a model for repentance. Sin not; but if you do, take heed to repent of it like Jonah.'

While he was speaking these words, the howling of the shrieking, slanting storm without seemed to add new power to the preacher, who, when describing Jonah's sea-storm, seemed tossed by a storm himself. His deep chest heaved as with a ground-swell; his tossed arms seemed the warring elements at work; and the thunders that rolled away from off his swarthy brow, and the light leaping from his eye, made all his simple hearers look on him with a quick fear that was strange to them.

There now came a lull in his look, as he silently turned over the leaves of the Book once more; and, at last, standing motionless, with closed eyes, for the moment, seemed communing with God and himself.

But again he leaned over towards the people, and bowing his head lowly, with an aspect of the deepest yet manliest humility, he spake these words:

'Shipmates, God has laid but one hand upon you; both his hands press upon me. I have read ye by what murky light may be mine the lesson that Jonah teaches to all sinners; and therefore to ye, and still more to me, for I am a greater sinner than ye. And now how gladly would I come down from this mast-head and sit on the hatches there where you sit, and listen as you listen, while some one of you reads *me* that other and more awful lesson which Jonah teaches to *me*, as a pilot of the living God. How being an anointed pilot-prophet, or speaker of true things, and bidden by the Lord to sound those unwelcome truths in the ears of a wicked Nineveh, Jonah, appalled at the hostility he should raise, fled from his mission, and sought to escape his duty and his God by taking ship at Joppa. But God is everywhere; Tarshish he never reached. As we have seen, God came upon him in the whale, and swallowed him down to living gulfs of doom, and with swift slantings tore him along "into the midst of the seas," where the eddying depths sucked him ten thousand fathoms down, and "the weeds were wrapped about his head," and all the watery world of woe bowled over him. Yet even then beyond the reach of any plummet—"out of the belly of hell"—when the whale grounded upon the ocean's utmost bones, even then, God heard the engulphed, repenting prophet when he cried. Then God spake unto the fish; and from the shuddering cold and blackness of the sea, the whale came breeching up towards the warm and pleasant sun, and all the delights of air and earth; and "vomited out Jonah upon the dry land;" when the word of the Lord came a second time; and Jonah, bruised and beaten—his ears, like two sea-shells, still multitudinously murmuring of the ocean—Jonah did the Almighty's bidding. And what was that, shipmates? To preach the Truth to the face of Falsehood! That was it!

'This, shipmates, this is that other lesson; and woe to that pilot of the living God who slights it. Woe to him whom this world charms from Gospel duty! Woe to him who seeks to pour oil upon the waters when God has brewed them into a gale! Woe to him who seeks to please rather than to appal! Woe to him whose good name is more to him than goodness! Woe to him who, in this world, courts not dishonor! Woe to him who would not be true, even though to be false were salvation! Yea, woe to him who, as the great Pilot Paul has it, while preaching to others is himself a castaway!'

He drooped and fell away from himself for a moment; then lifting his face to them again, showed a deep joy in his eyes, as he cried out with a heavenly enthusiasm,—'But oh! shipmates! on the starboard hand of every woe, there is a sure delight; and higher the top of that delight, than the bottom of the woe is deep. Is not the main-truck higher than the kelson is low? Delight is to him—a far, far upward, and inward delight—who against the proud gods and commodores of this earth, ever stands forth his own inexorable self. Delight is to him whose strong arms yet support him, when the ship of this base treacherous world has gone down beneath him. Delight is to him, who gives no quarter in the truth, and kills, burns, and destroys all sin though he pluck it out from under the robes of Senators and Judges. Delight,— top-gallant delight is to him, who acknowledges no law or lord, but the Lord his God, and is only a patriot to heaven. Delight is to him, whom all the waves of the billows of the seas of the boisterous mob can never shake from this sure Keel of the Ages. And eternal delight and deliciousness will be his, who coming to lay him down, can say with his final breath—O Father!—chiefly known to me by Thy rod—mortal or immortal, here I die. I have striven to be Thine, more than to be this world's, or mine own. Yet this is nothing; I leave eternity to Thee; for what is man that he should live out the lifetime of his God?'

He said no more, but slowly waving a benediction, covered his face with his hands, and so remained kneeling, till all the people had departed, and he was left alone in the place.

10
A BOSOM FRIEND

RETURNING to the Spouter-Inn from the Chapel, I found Queequeg there quite alone; he having left the Chapel before the benediction some time. He was sitting on a bench before the fire, with his feet on the stove hearth, and in one hand was holding close up to his face that little negro idol of his; peering hard into its face, and with a jack-knife gently whittling away at its nose, meanwhile humming to himself in his heathenish way.

But being now interrupted, he put up the image; and pretty soon, going to the table, took up a large book there, and placing it on his lap began counting the pages with deliberate regularity; at every fiftieth page—as I fancied—stopping a moment, looking vacantly around him, and giving utterance to a long-drawn gurgling whistle of astonishment. He would then begin again at the next fifty; seeming to commence at number one each time, as though he could not count more than fifty, and it was only by such a large number of fifties being found together, that his astonishment at the multitude of pages was excited.

With much interest I sat watching him. Savage though he was, and hideously marred about the face—at least to my taste—his countenance yet had a something in it which was by no means disagreeable. You cannot hide the soul. Through all his unearthly tattooings, I thought I saw the traces of a simple honest heart; and in his large, deep eyes, fiery black and bold, there seemed tokens of a spirit that would dare a thousand devils. And besides all this, there was a certain lofty bearing about the Pagan, which even his uncouthness could not altogether maim. He looked like a man who had never cringed and never had had a creditor. Whether it was, too, that his head being shaved, his forehead was drawn out in freer and brighter relief, and looked more expansive than it otherwise would, this I will not venture to decide; but certain it was his head was phrenologically an excellent one. It may seem ridiculous, but it reminded me of General Washington's head, as seen in the popular busts of him. It had the same long regularly graded retreating slope from above the brows, which were likewise very projecting, like two long promontories thickly wooded on top. Queequeg was George Washington cannibalistically developed.

Whilst I was thus closely scanning him, half-pretending meanwhile to be looking out at the storm from the casement, he never heeded my presence, never troubled himself with so much as a single glance; but appeared wholly occupied with counting the pages of the marvellous book. Considering how sociably we had been sleeping together the night previous, and especially considering the affectionate arm I had found thrown over me upon waking in the morning, I thought this indifference of his very strange. But savages are strange beings; at times you do not know exactly how to take them. At first they are overawing; their calm self-collectedness of simplicity seems a Socratic wisdom. I had noticed also that Queequeg never consorted at all, or but very little, with the other seamen in the inn. He made no advances whatever; appeared to have no desire to enlarge the circle of his acquaintances. All this struck me as mighty singular; yet, upon second thoughts, there was something almost sublime in it. Here was a man some twenty thousand miles from home, by the way of Cape Horn, that is—which was the only way he could get there—thrown among people as strange to him as though he were in the planet Jupiter; and yet he seemed entirely at his ease; preserving the utmost serenity; content with his own companionship; always equal to himself. Surely this was a touch of fine philosophy; though no doubt he had never heard there was such a thing as that. But, perhaps, to be true philosophers, we mortals should not be conscious of so living or so striving. So soon as I hear that such or such a man gives himself out for a philosopher, I conclude that, like the dyspeptic old woman, he must have 'broken his digester.'

As I sat there in that now lonely room; the fire burning low, in that mild stage when, after its first intensity has warmed the air, it then only glows to be looked at; the evening shades and phantoms gathering round the casements, and peering in upon us silent, solitary twain; the storm booming without in solemn swells; I began to be sensible of strange feelings. I felt a melting in me. No more my splintered heart and maddened hand were turned against the wolfish world. This soothing savage had redeemed it. There he sat, his very indifference speaking a nature in which there lurked no civilized hypocrisies and bland deceits. Wild he was; a very sight of sights to see; yet I began to feel myself mysteriously drawn towards him. And those same things that would have repelled most others, they were the very magnets that thus drew me. I'll try a pagan friend, thought I, since Christian kindness has proved but hollow courtesy. I drew my bench near him, and made some friendly signs and hints, doing my best to talk with him meanwhile. At first he little noticed these advances; but presently, upon my referring to his last night's hospitalities, he made out to ask me whether we were again to be bedfellows. I told him yes; whereat I thought he looked pleased, perhaps a little complimented.

We then turned over the book together, and I endeavored to explain to him the purpose of the printing, and the meaning of the few pictures that were in it. Thus I soon engaged his interest; and from that we went to jabbering the best we could about the various outer sights to be seen in this famous town. Soon I proposed a social smoke; and, producing his pouch and tomahawk, he quietly offered me a puff. And then we sat exchanging puffs from that wild pipe of his, and keeping it regularly passing between us.

If there yet lurked any ice of indifference towards me in the Pagan's breast, this pleasant, genial smoke we had, soon thawed it out, and left us cronies. He seemed to take to me quite as naturally and unbiddenly as I to him; and when our smoke was over, he pressed his forehead against mine, clasped me round the waist, and said that henceforth we were married; meaning, in his country's phrase, that we were bosom friends; he would gladly die for me, if need should be. In a countryman, this sudden flame of friendship would have seemed far too premature, a thing to be much distrusted; but in this simple savage those old rules would not apply.

After supper, and another social chat and smoke, we went to our room together. He made me a present of his embalmed head; took out his enormous tobacco wallet, and groping under the tobacco, drew out some thirty dollars in silver; then spreading them on the table, and mechanically dividing them into two equal portions, pushed one of them towards me, and said it was mine. I was going to remonstrate; but he silenced me by pouring them into my trowsers' pockets. I let them stay. He then went about his evening prayers, took out his idol, and removed the paper fireboard. By certain signs and symptoms, I thought he seemed anxious for me to join him; but well knowing what was to follow, I deliberated a moment whether, in case he invited me, I would comply or otherwise.

I was a good Christian; born and bred in the bosom of the infallible Presbyterian Church. How then could I unite with this wild idolator in worshipping his piece of wood? But what is worship? thought I. Do you suppose now, Ishmael, that the magnanimous God of heaven and earth—pagans and all included—can possibly be jealous of an insignificant bit of black wood? Impossible! But what is worship?—to do the will of God—*that* is worship. And what is the will of God?—to do to my fellow man what I would have my fellow man to do to me—*that* is the will of God. Now, Queequeg is my fellow man. And what do I wish that this Queequeg would do to me? Why, unite with me in my particular Presbyterian form of worship. Consequently, I must then unite with him in his; ergo, I must turn idolator. So I kindled the shavings; helped prop up the innocent little idol; offered him burnt biscuit with Queequeg; salamed before him twice or thrice; kissed his nose; and that done, we undressed and went to bed, at peace with our own consciences and all the world. But we did not go to sleep without some little chat.

How it is I know not; but there is no place like a bed for confidential disclosures between friends. Man and wife, they say, there open the very bottom of their souls to each other; and some old couples often lie and chat over old times till nearly morning. Thus, then, in our hearts' honeymoon, lay I and Queequeg—a cosy, loving pair.

11
NIGHTGOWN

WE had lain thus in bed, chatting and napping at short intervals, and Queequeg now and then affectionately throwing his brown tattooed legs over mine, and then drawing them back; so entirely sociable and free and easy were we; when, at last, by reason of our confabulations, what little nappishness remained in us altogether departed, and we felt like getting up again, though daybreak was yet some way down the future.

Yes, we became very wakeful; so much so that our recumbent position began to grow wearisome, and by little and little we found ourselves sitting up; the clothes well tucked around us, leaning against the head-board with our four knees drawn up close together, and our two noses bending over them, as if our knee-pans were warming-pans. We felt very nice and snug, the more so since it was so chilly out of doors; indeed out of bed-clothes too, seeing that there was no fire in the room. The more so, I say, because truly to enjoy bodily warmth, some small part of you must be cold, for there is no quality in this world that is not what it is merely by contrast. Nothing exists in itself. If you flatter yourself that you are all over comfortable, and have been so a long time, then you cannot be said to be comfortable any more. But if, like Queequeg and me in the bed, the tip of your nose or the crown of your head be slightly chilled, why then, indeed, in the general consciousness you feel most delightfully and unmistakably warm. For this reason a sleeping apartment should never be furnished with a fire, which is one of the luxurious discomforts of the rich. For the height of this sort of deliciousness is to have nothing but the blanket between you and your snugness and the cold of the outer air. Then there you lie like the one warm spark in the heart of an arctic crystal.

We had been sitting in this crouching manner for some time, when all at once I thought I would open my eyes; for when between sheets, whether by day or by night, and whether asleep or awake, I have a way of always keeping my eyes shut, in order the more to concentrate the snugness of being in bed. Because no man can ever feel his own identity aright except his eyes be closed; as if darkness were indeed the proper element of our essences, though light be more congenial to our clayey part. Upon opening my eyes then, and coming out of my own pleasant and self-created darkness into the imposed and coarse outer gloom of the unilluminated twelve-o'clock-at-night, I experienced a disagreeable revulsion. Nor did I at all object to the hint from Queequeg that perhaps it were best to strike a light, seeing that we were so wide awake; and besides he felt a strong desire to have a few quiet puffs from his Tomahawk. Be it said, that though I had felt such a strong repugnance to his smoking in the bed the night before, yet see how elastic our stiff prejudices grow when love once comes to bend them. For now I liked nothing better than to have Queequeg smoking by me, even in bed, because he seemed to be full of such serene household joy then. I no more felt unduly concerned for the landlord's policy of insurance. I was only alive to the condensed confidential comfortableness of sharing a pipe and a blanket with a real friend. With our shaggy jackets drawn about our shoulders, we now passed the Tomahawk from one to the other, till slowly there grew over us a blue hanging tester of smoke, illuminated by the flame of the new-lit lamp.

Whether it was that this undulating tester rolled the savage away to far distant scenes, I know not, but he now spoke of his native island; and, eager to hear his history, I begged him to go on and tell it. He gladly complied. Though at the time I but ill comprehended not a few of his words, yet subsequent disclosures, when I had become more familiar with his broken phraseology, now enable me to present the whole story such as it may prove in the mere skeleton I give.

12

BIOGRAPHICAL

QUEEQUEG was a native of Kokovoko, an island far away to the West and South. It is not down in any map; true places never are.

When a new-hatched savage running wild about his native woodlands in a grass clout, followed by the nibbling goats, as if he were a green sapling; even then, in Queequeg's ambitious soul, lurked a strong desire to see something more of Christendom than a specimen whaler or two. His father was a High Chief, a King; his uncle a High Priest; and on the maternal side he boasted aunts who were the wives of unconquerable warriors. There was excellent blood in his veins—royal stuff; though sadly vitiated, I fear, by the cannibal propensity he nourished in his untutored youth.

A Sag Harbor ship visited his father's bay, and Queequeg sought a passage to Christian lands. But the ship, having her full complement of seamen, spurned his suit; and not all the King his father's influence could prevail. But Queequeg vowed a vow. Alone in his canoe, he paddled off to a distant strait, which he knew the ship must pass through when she quitted the island. On one side was a coral reef; on the other a low tongue of land, covered with mangrove thickets that grew out into the water. Hiding his canoe, still afloat, among these thickets, with its prow seaward, he sat down in the stern, paddle low in hand; and when the ship was gliding by, like a flash he darted out; gained her side; with one backward dash of his foot capsized and sank his canoe; climbed up the chains; and throwing himself at full length upon the deck, grappled a ring-bolt there, and swore not to let it go, though hacked in pieces.

In vain the captain threatened to throw him overboard; suspended a cutlass over his naked wrists; Queequeg was the son of a King, and Queequeg budged not. Struck by his desperate dauntlessness, and his wild desire to visit Christendom, the captain at last relented, and told him he might make himself at home. But this fine young savage—this sea Prince of Wales, never saw the captain's cabin. They put him down among the sailors, and made a whaleman of him. But like Czar Peter content to toil in the shipyards of foreign cities, Queequeg disdained no seeming ignominy, if thereby he might happily gain the power of enlightening his untutored countrymen. For at bottom—so he told me—he was actuated by a profound desire to learn among the Christians, the arts whereby to make his people still happier than they were; and more than that, still better than they were. But, alas! the practices of whalemen soon convinced him that even Christians could be both miserable and wicked; infinitely more so, than all his father's heathens. Arrived at last in old Sag Harbor; and seeing what the sailors did there; and then going on to Nantucket, and seeing how they spent their wages in *that* place also, poor Queequeg gave it up for lost. Thought he, it's a wicked world in all meridians; I'll die a pagan.

And thus an old idolator at heart, he yet lived among these Christians, wore their clothes, and tried to talk their gibberish. Hence the queer ways about him, though now some time from home.

By hints, I asked him whether he did not propose going back, and having a coronation; since he might now consider his father dead and gone, he being very old and feeble at the last accounts. He answered no, not yet; and added that he was fearful Christianity, or rather Christians, had unfitted him for ascending the pure and undefiled throne of thirty pagan Kings before him. But by and by, he said, he would return,—as soon as he felt himself baptized again. For the nonce, however, he proposed to sail about, and sow his wild oats in all four oceans. They had made a harpooneer of him, and that barbed iron was in lieu of a sceptre now.

I asked him what might be his immediate purpose, touching his future movements. He answered, to go to sea again, in his own vocation. Upon this, I told him that whaling was my own design, and informed him of my intention to sail out of Nantucket, as being the most promising port for an adventurous whaleman to embark from. He at once resolved to accompany me to that island, ship aboard the same vessel, get into the same watch, the same boat, the same mess with me, in short to share my every hap; with both my hands in his, boldly dip into the Potluck of both worlds. To all this I joyously assented; for besides the affection I now felt for Queequeg, he was an experienced harpooneer, and as such, could not fail to be of great usefulness to one, who, like me, was wholly ignorant of the mysteries of whaling, though well acquainted with the sea, as known to merchant seamen.

His story being ended with his pipe's last dying puff, Queequeg embraced me, pressed his forehead against mine, and blowing out the light, we rolled over from each other, this way and that, and very soon were sleeping.

13

WHEELBARROW

NEXT morning, Monday, after disposing of the embalmed head to a barber, for a block, I settled my own and comrade's bill; using, however, my comrade's money. The grinning landlord, as well as the boarders, seemed amazingly tickled at the sudden friendship which had sprung up between me and Queequeg—especially as Peter Coffin's cock and bull stories about him had previously so much alarmed me concerning the very person whom I now companied with.

We borrowed a wheelbarrow, and embarking our things, including my own poor carpet-bag, and Queequeg's canvas sack and hammock, away we went down to the 'Moss,' the little Nantucket packet schooner moored at the wharf. As we were going along the people stared; not at Queequeg so much—for they were used to seeing cannibals like him in their streets,—but at seeing him and me upon such confidential terms. But we heeded them not, going along wheeling the barrow by turns, and Queequeg now and then stopping to adjust the sheath on his harpoon barbs. I asked him why he carried such a troublesome thing with him ashore, and whether all whaling ships did not find their own harpoons. To this, in substance, he replied, that though what I hinted was true enough, yet he had a particular affection for his own harpoon, because it was of assured stuff, well tried in many a mortal combat, and deeply intimate with the hearts of whales. In short, like many inland reapers and mowers, who go into the farmers' meadows armed with their own scythes—though in no wise obliged to furnish them—even so Queequeg, for his own private reasons, preferred his own harpoon.

Shifting the barrow from my hand to his, he told me a funny story about the first wheelbarrow he had ever seen. It was in Sag

Harbor. The owners of his ship, it seems, had lent him one, in which to carry his heavy chest to his boarding house. Not to seem ignorant about the thing—though in truth he was entirely so, concerning the precise way in which to manage the barrow—Queequeg puts his chest upon it; lashes it fast; and then shoulders the barrow and marches up the wharf. 'Why,' said I, 'Queequeg, you might have known better than that, one would think. Didn't the people laugh?'

Upon this, he told me another story. The people of his island of Kokovoko, it seems, at their wedding feasts express the fragrant water of young cocoanuts into a large stained calabash like a punchbowl; and this punchbowl always forms the great central ornament on the braided mat where the feast is held. Now a certain grand merchant ship once touched at Kokovoko, and its commander—from all accounts, a very stately punctilious gentleman, at least for a sea captain—this commander was invited to the wedding feast of Queequeg's sister, a pretty young princess just turned of ten. Well; when all the wedding guests were assembled at the bride's bamboo cottage, this Captain marches in, and being assigned the post of honor, placed himself over against the punchbowl, and between the High Priest and his majesty the King, Queequeg's father. Grace being said,—for those people have their grace as well as we—though Queequeg told me that unlike us, who at such times look downwards to our platters, they, on the contrary, copying the ducks, glance upwards to the great Giver of all feasts—Grace, I say, being said, the High Priest opens the banquet by the immemorial ceremony of the island; that is, dipping his consecrated and consecrating fingers into the bowl before the blessed beverage circulates. Seeing himself placed next the Priest, and noting the ceremony, and thinking himself—being Captain of a ship—as having plain precedence over a mere island King, especially in the King's own house—the Captain coolly proceeds to wash his hands in the punch bowl;—taking it I suppose for a huge fingerglass. 'Now,' said Queequeg, 'what you tink now?—Didn't our people laugh?'

At last, passage paid, and luggage safe, we stood on board the schooner. Hoisting sail, it glided down the Acushnet river. On one side, New Bedford rose in terraces of streets, their ice-covered trees all glittering in the clear, cold air. Huge hills and mountains of casks on casks were piled upon her wharves, and side by side the world-wandering whale ships lay silent and safely moored at last; while from others came a sound of carpenters and coopers, with blended noises of fires and forges to melt the pitch, all betokening that new cruises were on the start; that one most perilous and long voyage ended, only begins a second; and a second ended, only begins a third, and so on, for ever and for aye. Such is the endlessness, yea, the intolerableness of all earthly effort.

Gaining the more open water, the bracing breeze waxed fresh; the little Moss tossed the quick foam from her bows, as a young colt his snortings. How I snuffed that Tartar air!—how I spurned that turnpike earth!—that common highway all over dented with the marks of slavish heels and hoofs; and turned me to admire the magnanimity of the sea which will permit no records.

At the same foam-fountain, Queequeg seemed to drink and reel with me. His dusky nostrils swelled apart; he showed his filed and pointed teeth. On, on we flew, and our offing gained, the Moss did homage to the blast; ducked and dived her bows as a slave before the Sultan. Sideways leaning, we sideways darted; every ropeyarn tingling like a wire; the two tall masts buckling like Indian canes in land tornadoes. So full of this reeling scene were we, as we stood by the plunging bowsprit, that for some time we did not notice the jeering glances of the passengers, a lubber-like assembly, who marvelled that two fellow beings should be so companionable; as though a white man were anything more dignified than a whitewashed negro. But there were some boobies and bumpkins there, who, by their intense greenness, must have come from the heart and centre of all verdure. Queequeg caught one of these young saplings mimicking him behind his back. I thought the bumpkin's hour of doom was come. Dropping his harpoon, the brawny savage caught him in his arms, and by an almost miraculous dexterity and strength, sent him high up bodily into the air; then slightly tapping his stern in mid-somerset, the fellow landed with bursting lungs upon his feet, while Queequeg, turning his back upon him, lighted his tomahawk pipe and passed it to me for a puff.

'Capting! Capting!' yelled the bumpkin, running towards that officer; 'Capting, Capting, here's the devil.'

'Hallo, *you* sir,' cried the Captain, a gaunt rib of the sea, stalking up to Queequeg, 'what in thunder do you mean by that? Don't you know you might have killed that chap?'

'What him say?' said Queequeg, as he mildly turned to me.

'He say,' said I, 'that you came near kill-e that man there,' pointing to the still shivering greenhorn.

'Kill-e,' cried Queequeg, twisting his tattooed face into an unearthly expression of disdain, 'ah! him bery small-e fish-e; Queequeg no kill-e so small-e fish-e; Queequeg kill-e big whale!'

'Look you,' roared the Captain, 'I'll kill-e *you*, you cannibal, if you try any more of your tricks aboard here; so mind your eye.'

But it so happened just then, that it was high time for the Captain to mind his own eye. The prodigious strain upon the main-sail had parted the weather-sheet, and the tremendous boom was now flying from side to side, completely sweeping the entire after part of the deck. The poor fellow whom Queequeg had handled so roughly, was swept overboard; all hands were in a panic; and to attempt snatching at the boom to stay it, seemed madness. It flew from right to left, and back again, almost in one ticking of a watch, and every instant seemed on the point of snapping into splinters. Nothing was done, and nothing seemed capable of being done; those on deck rushed towards the bows, and stood eyeing the boom as if it were the lower jaw of an exasperated whale. In the midst of this consternation, Queequeg dropped deftly to his knees, and crawling under the path of the boom, whipped hold of a rope, secured one end to the bulwarks, and then flinging the other like a lasso, caught it round the boom as it swept over his head, and at the next jerk, the spar was that way trapped, and all was safe. The schooner was run into the wind, and while the hands were clearing away the stern boat, Queequeg, stripped to the waist, darted from the side with a long living arc of a leap. For three minutes or more he was seen swimming like a dog, throwing his long arms straight out before him, and by turns revealing his brawny shoulders through the freezing foam. I looked at the grand and glorious fellow, but saw no one to be saved. The greenhorn had gone down. Shooting himself perpendicularly from the water, Queequeg now took an instant's glance around him, and seeming to see just how matters were, dived down and disappeared. A few minutes more, and he rose again, one arm still striking out, and with the other dragging a lifeless form. The boat soon picked them up. The poor bumpkin was restored. All hands voted Queequeg a noble trump; the captain begged his pardon. From that hour I clove to Queequeg like a barnacle; yea, till poor Queequeg took his last long dive.

Was there ever such unconsciousness? He did not seem to think that he at all deserved a medal from the Humane and Magnanimous Societies. He only asked for water—fresh water—something to wipe the brine off; that done, he put on dry clothes, lighted his pipe, and leaning against the bulwarks, and mildly eyeing those around him, seemed to be saying to himself—'It's a mutual, joint-stock world, in all meridians. We cannibals must help these Christians.'

14
NANTUCKET

NOTHING more happened on the passage worthy the mentioning; so, after a fine run, we safely arrived in Nantucket.

Nantucket! Take out your map and look at it. See what a real corner of the world it occupies; how it stands there, away off shore, more lonely than the Eddystone lighthouse. Look at it—a mere hillock, and elbow of sand; all beach, without a background. There is more sand there than you would use in twenty years as a substitute for blotting paper. Some gamesome wights will tell you that they have to plant weeds there, they don't grow naturally; that they import Canada thistles; that they have to send beyond seas for a spile to stop a leak in an oil cask; that pieces of wood in Nantucket are carried about like bits of the true cross in Rome; that people there plant toadstools before their houses, to get under the shade in summer time; that one blade of grass makes an oasis, three blades in a day's walk a prairie; that they wear quicksand shoes, something like Laplander snowshoes; that they are so shut up, belted about, every way inclosed, surrounded, and made an utter island of by the ocean, that to their very chairs and tables small clams will sometimes be found adhering, as to the backs of sea turtles. But these extravaganzas only show that Nantucket is no Illinois.

Look now at the wondrous traditional story of how this island was settled by the red-men. Thus goes the legend. In olden times an eagle swooped down upon the New England coast, and carried off an infant Indian in his talons. With loud lament the parents saw their child borne out of sight over the wide waters. They resolved to follow in the same direction. Setting out in their canoes, after a perilous passage they discovered the island, and there they found an empty ivory casket,—the poor little Indian's skeleton.

What wonder, then, that these Nantucketers, born on a beach, should take to the sea for a livelihood! They first caught crabs and quohogs in the sand; grown bolder, they waded out with nets for mackerel; more experienced, they pushed off in boats and captured cod; and at last, launching a navy of great ships on the sea, explored this watery world; put an incessant belt of circumnavigations round it; peeped in at Behring's Straits; and in all seasons and all oceans declared everlasting war with the mightiest animated mass that has survived the flood; most monstrous and most mountainous! That Himmalehan, salt-sea Mastodon, clothed with such portentousness of unconscious power, that his very panics are more to be dreaded than his most fearless and malicious assaults!

And thus have these naked Nantucketers, these sea hermits, issuing from their ant-hill in the sea, overrun and conquered the watery world like so many Alexanders; parcelling out among them the Atlantic, Pacific, and Indian oceans, as the three pirate powers did Poland. Let America add Mexico to Texas, and pile Cuba upon Canada; let the English overswarm all India, and hang out their blazing banner from the sun; two thirds of this terraqueous globe are the Nantucketer's. For the sea is his; he owns it, as Emperors own empires; other seamen having but a right of way through it. Merchant ships are but extension bridges; armed ones but floating forts; even pirates and privateers, though following the sea as highwaymen the road, they but plunder other ships, other fragments of the land like themselves, without seeking to draw their living from the bottomless deep itself. The Nantucketer, he alone resides and riots on the sea; he alone, in Bible language, goes down to it in ships; to and fro ploughing it as his own special plantation. *There* is his home; *there* lies his business, which a Noah's flood would not interrupt, though it overwhelmed all the millions in China. He lives on the sea, as prairie cocks in the prairie; he hides among the waves, he climbs them as chamois hunters climb the Alps. For years he knows not the land; so that when he comes to it at last, it smells like another world, more strangely than the moon would to an Earthsman. With the landless gull, that at sunset folds her wings and is rocked to sleep between billows; so at nightfall, the Nantucketer, out of sight of land, furls his sails, and lays him to his rest, while under his very pillow rush herds of walruses and whales.

15

CHOWDER

It was quite late in the evening when the little Moss came snugly to anchor, and Queequeg and I went ashore; so we could attend to no business that day, at least none but a supper and a bed. The landlord of the Spouter-Inn had recommended us to his

cousin Hosea Hussey of the Try Pots, whom he asserted to be
the proprietor of one of the best kept hotels in all Nantucket, and
moreover he had assured us that cousin Hosea, as he called him,
was famous for his chowders. In short, he plainly hinted that we
could not possibly do better than try pot-luck at the Try Pots.
But the directions he had given us about keeping a yellow warehouse on our starboard hand till we opened a white church to
the larboard, and then keeping that on the larboard hand till we
made a corner three points to the starboard, and that done, then
ask the first man we met where the place was: these crooked
directions of his very much puzzled us at first, especially as, at
the outset, Queequeg insisted that the yellow warehouse—our first
point of departure—must be left on the larboard hand, whereas
I had understood Peter Coffin to say it was on the starboard.
However, by dint of beating about a little in the dark, and now
and then knocking up a peaceable inhabitant to inquire the way,
we at last came to something which there was no mistaking.

Two enormous wooden pots painted black, and suspended by
asses' ears, swung from the cross-trees of an old top-mast, planted
in front of an old doorway. The horns of the cross-trees were
sawed off on the other side, so that this old top-mast looked not
a little like a gallows. Perhaps I was over sensitive to such impressions at the time, but I could not help staring at this gallows with
a vague misgiving. A sort of crick was in my neck as I gazed up
to the two remaining horns; yes, *two* of them, one for Queequeg,
and one for me. It's ominous, thinks I. A Coffin my Innkeeper
upon landing in my first whaling port, tombstones staring at me
in the whalemen's chapel; and here a gallows! and a pair of
prodigious black pots too! Are these last throwing out oblique
hints touching Tophet?

I was called from these reflections by the sight of a freckled
woman with yellow hair and a yellow gown, standing in the porch
of the inn, under a dull red lamp swinging there, that looked
much like an injured eye, and carrying on a brisk scolding with
a man in a purple woollen shirt.

'Get along with ye,' said she to the man, 'or I'll be combing
ye!'

'Come on, Queequeg,' said I, 'all right. There's Mrs Hussey.'

And so it turned out; Mr Hosea Hussey being from home, but
leaving Mrs Hussey entirely competent to attend to all his affairs.
Upon making known our desires for a supper and a bed, Mrs
Hussey, postponing further scolding for the present, ushered us
into a little room, and seating us at a table spread with the relics

of a recently concluded repast, turned round to us and said—
'Clam or Cod?'

'What's that about Cods, ma'am?' said I, with much politeness.
'Clam or Cod?' she repeated.

'A clam for supper? a cold clam; is *that* what you mean, Mrs
Hussey?' says I; 'but that's a rather cold and clammy reception
in the winter time, ain't it, Mrs Hussey?'

But being in a great hurry to resume scolding the man in the
purple shirt, who was waiting for it in the entry, and seeming to
hear nothing but the word 'clam,' Mrs Hussey hurried towards
an open door leading to the kitchen, and bawling out 'clam for
two,' disappeared.

'Queequeg,' said I, 'do you think that we can make out a supper
for us both on one clam?'

However, a warm savory steam from the kitchen served to belie
the apparently cheerless prospect before us. But when that smoking
chowder came in, the mystery was delightfully explained. Oh,
sweet friends! hearken to me. It was made of small juicy clams,
scarcely bigger than hazel nuts, mixed with pounded ship biscuit,
and salted pork cut up into little flakes; the whole enriched with
butter, and plentifully seasoned with pepper and salt. Our appetites
being sharpened by the frosty voyage, and in particular, Queequeg
seeing his favorite fishing food before him, and the chowder being
surpassingly excellent, we despatched it with great expedition: when
leaning back a moment and bethinking me of Mrs Hussey's clam
and cod announcement, I thought I would try a little experiment.
Stepping to the kitchen door, I uttered the word 'cod' with great
emphasis, and resumed my seat. In a few moments the savory
steam came forth again, but with a different flavor, and in good
time a fine cod-chowder was placed before us.

We resumed business; and while plying our spoons in the bowl,
thinks I to myself, I wonder now if this here has any effect on
the head? What's that stultifying saying about chowder-headed
people? 'But look, Queequeg, ain't that a live eel in your bowl?
Where's your harpoon?'

Fishiest of all fishy places was the Try Pots, which well deserved
its name; for the pots there were always boiling chowders. Chowder
for breakfast, and chowder for dinner, and chowder for supper,
till you began to look for fish-bones coming through your clothes.
The area before the house was paved with clam-shells. Mrs Hussey
wore a polished necklace of codfish vertebrae; and Hosea Hussey
had his account books bound in superior old shark-skin. There
was a fishy flavor to the milk, too, which I could not at all account

for, till one morning happening to take a stroll along the beach among some fishermen's boats, I saw Hosea's brindled cow feeding on fish remnants, and marching along the sand with each foot in a cod's decapitated head, looking very slip-shod, I assure ye.

Supper concluded, we received a lamp, and directions from Mrs Hussey concerning the nearest way to bed; but, as Queequeg was about to precede me up the stairs, the lady reached forth her arm, and demanded his harpoon; she allowed no harpoon in her chambers. 'Why not?' said I; 'every true whaleman sleeps with his harpoon—but why not?' 'Because it's dangerous,' says she. 'Ever since young Stiggs coming from that unfort'nt v'y'ge of his, when he was gone four years and a half, with only three barrels of *ile,* was found dead in my first floor back, with his harpoon in his side; ever since then I allow no boarders to take sich dangerous weepons in their rooms a-night. So, Mr Queequeg' (for she had learned his name), 'I will just take this here iron, and keep it for you till morning. But the chowder; clam or cod tomorrow for breakfast, men?'

'Both,' says I; 'and let's have a couple of smoked herring by way of variety.'

16
THE SHIP

IN bed we concocted our plans for the morrow. But to my surprise and no small concern, Queequeg now gave me to understand, that he had been diligently consulting Yojo—the name of his black little god—and Yojo had told him two or three times over, and strongly insisted upon it everyway, that instead of our going together among the whaling-fleet in harbor, and in concert selecting our craft; instead of this, I say, Yojo earnestly enjoined that the selection of the ship should rest wholly with me, inasmuch as Yojo purposed befriending us; and, in order to do so, had already pitched upon a vessel, which, if left to myself, I, Ishmael, should infallibly light upon, for all the world as though it had turned out by chance; and in that vessel I must immediately ship myself, for the present irrespective of Queequeg.

I have forgotten to mention that, in many things, Queequeg placed great confidence in the excellence of Yojo's judgment and surprising forecast of things; and cherished Yojo with considerable esteem, as a rather good sort of god, who perhaps meant well enough upon the whole, but in all cases did not succeed in his benevolent designs.

Now, this plan of Queequeg's, or rather Yojo's, touching the selection of our craft; I did not like that plan at all. I had not a little relied upon Queequeg's sagacity to point out the whaler best fitted to carry us and our fortunes securely. But as all my remonstrances produced no effect upon Queequeg, I was obliged to acquiesce; and accordingly prepared to set about this business with a determined rushing sort of energy and vigor, that should quickly settle that trifling little affair. Next morning early, leaving Queequeg shut up with Yojo in our little bedroom—for it seemed that it was some sort of Lent or Ramadan, or day of fasting, humiliation, and prayer with Queequeg and Yojo that day; *how* it was I never could find out, for, though I applied myself to it several times, I never could master his liturgies and XXXIX Articles—leaving Queequeg, then, fasting on his tomahawk pipe, and Yojo warming himself at his sacrificial fire of shavings, I sallied out among the shipping. After much prolonged sauntering and many random inquiries, I learnt that there were three ships up for three-years' voyages—The Devil-Dam, the Tit-bit, and the Pequod. *Devil-Dam*, I do not know the origin of; *Tit-bit* is obvious; *Pequod*, you will no doubt remember, was the name of a celebrated tribe of Massachusetts Indians, now extinct as the ancient Medes. I peered and pryed about the Devil-Dam; from her, hopped over to the Tit-bit; and, finally, going on board the Pequod, looked around her for a moment, and then decided that this was the very ship for us.

You may have seen many a quaint craft in your day, for aught I know;—squared-toed luggers; mountainous Japanese junks; butter-box galliots, and what not; but take my word for it, you never saw such a rare old craft as this same rare old Pequod. She was a ship of the old school, rather small if anything; with an old fashioned claw-footed look about her. Long seasoned and weather-stained in the typhoons and calms of all four oceans, her old hull's complexion was darkened like a French grenadier's, who has alike fought in Egypt and Siberia. Her venerable bows looked bearded. Her masts—cut somewhere on the coast of Japan, where her original ones were lost overboard in a gale—her masts stood stiffly up like the spines of the three old kings of Cologne. Her ancient decks were worn and wrinkled, like the pilgrim-worshipped flag-stone in Canterbury Cathedral where Beckett bled. But to all these her old antiquities, were added new and marvellous features, pertaining to the wild business that for more than half a century she had followed. Old Captain Peleg, many years her chief-mate, before he commanded another vessel of his own, and now a retired seaman, and one of the principal owners of the Pequod,—this old Peleg, during the term of his chiefmateship, had built upon her original grotesqueness, and inlaid it, all over, with a quaintness both of material and device, unmatched by anything except it be Thorkill-Hake's carved buckler or bedstead. She was apparelled like any barbaric Ethiopian emperor, his neck heavy with pendants of polished ivory. She was a thing of trophies. A cannibal of a craft, tricking herself forth in the chased bones of her enemies. All round, her unpannelled, open bulwarks were garnished like one continuous jaw, with the long sharp teeth of the sperm whale, inserted there for pins, to fasten her old hempen thews and tendons to. Those thews ran not through base blocks of land wood, but deftly travelled over sheaves of sea-ivory. Scorning a turnstile wheel at her reverend helm, she sported there a tiller; and that tiller was in one mass, curiously carved from the long narrow lower jaw of her hereditary foe. The helmsman who steered by that tiller in a tempest, felt like the Tartar, when he holds back his fiery steed by clutching its jaw. A noble craft, but somehow a most melancholy! All noble things are touched with that.

Now when I looked about the quarter-deck, for some one having authority, in order to propose myself as a candidate for the voyage, at first I saw nobody; but I could not well overlook a strange sort of tent, or rather wigwam, pitched a little behind the main-mast. It seemed only a temporary erection used in port. It was of a conical shape, some ten feet high; consisting of the long, huge slabs of limber black bone taken from the middle and highest part of the jaws of the right-whale. Planted with their broad ends on the deck, a circle of these slabs laced together, mutually sloped towards each other, and at the apex united in a tufted point, where the loose hairy fibres waved to and fro like the topknot on some old Pottowottamie Sachem's head. A triangular opening faced towards the bows of the ship, so that the insider commanded a complete view forward.

And half concealed in this queer tenement, I at length found one who by his aspect seemed to have authority; and who, it being noon, and the ship's work suspended, was now enjoying respite from the burden of command. He was seated on an old-fashioned oaken chair, wriggling all over with curious carving; and the bottom of which was formed of a stout interlacing of the same elastic stuff of which the wigwam was constructed.

There was nothing so very particular, perhaps, about the appearance of the elderly man I saw; he was brown and brawny, like most old seamen, and heavily rolled up in blue pilot-cloth, cut in the Quaker style; only there was a fine and almost microscopic net-work of the minutest wrinkles interlacing round his eyes, which must have arisen from his continual sailings in many hard gales, and always looking to windward;—for this causes the muscles about the eyes to become pursed together. Such eye-wrinkles are very effectual in a scowl.

'Is this the Captain of the Pequod?' said I, advancing to the door of the tent.

'Supposing it be the Captain of the Pequod, what dost thou want of him?' he demanded.

'I was thinking of shipping.'

'Thou wast, wast thou? I see thou art no Nantucketer—ever been in a stove boat?'

'No, Sir, I never have.'

'Dost know nothing at all about whaling, I dare say—eh?'

'Nothing, Sir; but I have no doubt I shall soon learn. I've been several voyages in the merchant service, and I think that—'

'Marchant service be damned. Talk not that lingo to me. Dost see that leg?—I'll take that leg away from thy stern, if ever thou talkest of the marchant service to me again. Marchant service indeed! I suppose now ye feel considerable proud of having served in those marchant ships. But flukes! man, what makes thee want to go a whaling, eh?—it looks a little suspicious, don't it, eh?—Hast not been a pirate, hast thou?—Didst not rob thy last Captain, didst thou?—Dost not think of murdering the officers when thou gettest to sea?'

I protested my innocence of these things. I saw that under the mask of these half humorous innuendoes, this old seaman, as an insulated Quakerish Nantucketer, was full of his insular prejudices, and rather distrustful of all aliens, unless they hailed from Cape Cod or the Vineyard.

'But what takes thee a-whaling? I want to know that before I think of shipping ye.'

'Well, sir, I want to see what whaling is. I want to see the world.'

'Want to see what whaling is, eh? Have ye clapped eye on Captain Ahab?'

'Who is Captain Ahab, sir?'

'Aye, aye, I thought so. Captain Ahab is the Captain of this ship.'

'I am mistaken then. I thought I was speaking to the Captain himself.'

'Thou art speaking to Captain Peleg—that's who ye are speaking to, young man. It belongs to me and Captain Bildad to see the Pequod fitted out for the voyage, and supplied with all her needs, including crew. We are part owners and agents. But as I was going to say, if thou wantest to know what whaling is, as thou tellest ye do, I can put ye in a way of finding it out before ye bind yourself to it, past backing out. Clap eye on Captain Ahab, young man, and thou wilt find that he has only one leg.'

'What do you mean, sir? Was the other one lost by a whale?'

'Lost by a whale! Young man, come nearer to me: it was devoured, chewed up, crunched by the monstrousest parmacetty that ever chipped a boat!—ah, ah!'

I was a little alarmed by his energy, perhaps also a little touched at the hearty grief in his concluding exclamation, but said as calmly as I could, 'What you say is no doubt true enough, sir; but how could I know there was any peculiar ferocity in that particular whale, though indeed I might have inferred as much from the simple fact of the accident.'

'Look ye now, young man, thy lungs are a sort of soft, d'ye see; thou dost not talk shark a bit. *Sure,* ye've been to sea before now; sure of that?'

'Sir,' said I, 'I thought I told you that I had been four voyages in the merchant—'

'Hard down out of that! Mind what I said about the marchant service—don't aggravate me—I won't have it. But let us understand each other. I have given thee a hint about what whaling is; do ye yet feel inclined for it?'

'I do, sir.'

'Very good. Now, art thou the man to pitch a harpoon down a live whale's throat, and then jump after it? Answer, quick!'

'I am, sir, if it should be positively indispensable to do so; not to be got rid of, that is; which I don't take to be the fact.'

'Good again. Now then, thou not only wantest to go a-whaling, to find out by experience what whaling is, but ye also want to go in order to see the world? Was not that what ye said? I thought so. Well then, just step forward there, and take a peep over the weather-bow, and then back to me and tell me what ye see there.'

For a moment I stood a little puzzled by this curious request, not knowing exactly how to take it, whether humorously or in earnest. But concentrating all his crow's feet into one scowl, Captain Peleg started me on the errand.

Going forward and glancing over the weather bow, I perceived that the ship swinging to her anchor with the flood-tide, was now obliquely pointing towards the open ocean. The prospect was unlimited, but exceedingly monotonous and forbidding; not the slightest variety that I could see.

'Well, what's the report?' said Peleg when I came back; 'what did ye see?'

'Not much,' I replied—'nothing but water; considerable horizon though, and there's a squall coming up, I think.'

'Well, what dost thou think then of seeing the world? Do ye wish to go round Cape Horn to see any more of it, eh? Can't ye see the world where you stand?'

I was a little staggered, but go a-whaling I must, and I would; and the Pequod was as good a ship as any—I thought the best—and all this I now repeated to Peleg. Seeing me so determined, he expressed his willingness to ship me.

'And thou mayest as well sign the papers right off,' he added—'come along with ye.' And so saying, he led the way below deck into the cabin.

Seated on the transom was what seemed to me a most uncommon and surprising figure. It turned out to be Captain Bildad, who along with Captain Peleg was one of the largest owners of the vessel; the other shares, as is sometimes the case in these ports, being held by a crowd of old annuitants; widows, fatherless children, and chancery wards; each owning about the value of a timber head, or a foot of plank, or a nail or two in the ship. People in Nantucket invest their money in whaling vessels, the same way that you do yours in approved state stocks bringing in good interest.

Now, Bildad, like Peleg, and indeed many other Nantucketers, was a Quaker, the island having been originally settled by that sect; and to this day its inhabitants in general retain in an uncommon measure the peculiarities of the Quaker, only variously and anomalously modified by things altogether alien and heterogeneous. For some of these same Quakers are the most sanguinary of all sailors and whalehunters. They are fighting Quakers; they are Quakers with a vengeance.

So that there are instances among them of men, who, named with Scripture names—a singularly common fashion on the island—and in childhood naturally imbibing the stately dramatic *thee* and *thou* of the Quaker idiom; still, from the audacious, daring, and boundless adventure of their subsequent lives, strangely blend with these unoutgrown peculiarities, a thousand bold dashes of character, not unworthy a Scandinavian sea-king, or a poetical

Pagan Roman. And when these things unite in a man of greatly
superior natural force, with a globular brain and a ponderous
heart; who has also by the stillness and seclusion of many long
night-watches in the remotest waters, and beneath constellations
never seen here at the north, been led to think untraditionally
and independently; receiving all nature's sweet or savage impressions fresh from her own virgin voluntary and confiding breast,
and thereby chiefly, but with some help from occidental advantages,
to learn a bold and nervous lofty language—that man makes one
in a whole nation's census—a mighty pageant creature, formed
for noble tragedies. Nor will it at all detract from him, dramatically
regarded, if either by birth or other circumstances, he have what
seems a half wilful over-ruling morbidness at the bottom of his
nature. For all men tragically great are made so through a certain
morbidness. Be sure of this, O young ambition, all mortal greatness
is but disease. But, as yet we have not to do with such an one,
but with quite another; and still a man, who, if indeed peculiar,
it only results again from another phase of the Quaker, modified
by individual circumstances.

Like Captain Peleg, Captain Bildad was a well-to-do, retired
whaleman. But unlike Captain Peleg—who cared not a rush for
what are called serious things, and indeed deemed those self-same
serious things the veriest of all trifles—Captain Bildad had not
only been originally educated according to the strictest sect of
Nantucket Quakerism, but all his subsequent ocean life, and the
sight of many unclad, lovely island creatures, round the Horn—
all that had not moved this native born Quaker one single jot,
had not so much as altered one angle of his vest. Still, for all this
immutableness, was there some lack of common consistency about
worthy Captain Bildad. Though refusing, from conscientious scruples, to bear arms against land invaders, yet himself had illimitably
invaded the Atlantic and Pacific; and though a sworn foe to human
bloodshed, yet had he in his straight-bodied coat, spilled tuns
upon tuns of leviathan gore. How now in the contemplative
evening of his days, the pious Bildad reconciled these things in
the reminiscence, I do not know; but it did not seem to concern
him much, and very probably he had long since come to the sage
and sensible conclusion that a man's religion is one thing, and
this practical world quite another. This world pays dividends.
Rising from a little cabin-boy in short clothes of the drabbest
drab, to a harpooneer in a broad shad-bellied waistcoat; from that
becoming boat-header, chief-mate, and captain, and finally a ship-
owner; Bildad, as I hinted before, had concluded his adventurous

career by wholly retiring from active life at the goodly age of
sixty, and dedicating his remaining days to the quiet receiving of
his well-earned income.

Now Bildad, I am sorry to say, had the reputation of being an
incorrigible old hunks, and in his sea-going days, a bitter, hard
task-master. They told me in Nantucket, though it certainly seems
a curious story, that when he sailed the old Categut whaleman,
his crew, upon arriving home, were mostly all carried ashore to
the hospital, sore exhausted and worn out. For a pious man,
especially for a Quaker, he was certainly rather hard-hearted, to
say the least. He never used to swear, though, at his men, they
said; but somehow he got an inordinate quantity of cruel, un-
mitigated hard work out of them. When Bildad was a chief-mate,
to have his drab-colored eye intently looking at you, made you
feel completely nervous, till you could clutch something—a hammer or a marling-spike, and go to work like mad, at something
or other, never mind what. Indolence and idleness perished from
before him. His own person was the exact embodiment of his
utilitarian character. On his long, gaunt body, he carried no spare
flesh, no superfluous beard, his chin having a soft, economical
nap to it, like the worn nap of his broad-brimmed hat.

Such, then, was the person that I saw seated on the transom
when I followed Captain Peleg down into the cabin. The space
between the decks was small; and there, bolt-upright, sat old Bildad,
who always sat so, and never leaned, and this to save his coat
tails. His broad-brim was placed beside him; his legs were stiffly
crossed; his drab vesture was buttoned up to his chin; and spectacles
on nose, he seemed absorbed in reading from a ponderous volume.

'Bildad,' cried Captain Peleg, 'at it again, Bildad, eh? Ye have
been studying those Scriptures, now, for the last thirty years, to
my certain knowledge. How far ye got, Bildad?'

As if long habituated to such profane talk from his old shipmate,
Bildad, without noticing his present irreverence, quietly looked
up, and seeing me, glanced again inquiringly towards Peleg.

'He says he's our man, Bildad,' said Peleg, 'he wants to ship.'

'Dost thee?' said Bildad, in a hollow tone, and turning round
to me.

'I *dost*,' said I unconsciously, he was so intense a Quaker.

'What do ye think of him, Bildad?' said Peleg.

'He'll do,' said Bildad, eyeing me, and then went on spelling
away at his book in a mumbling tone quite audible.

I thought him the queerest old Quaker I ever saw, especially as
Peleg, his friend and old shipmate, seemed such a blusterer. But

I said nothing, only looking round me sharply. Peleg now threw open a chest, and drawing forth the ship's articles, placed pen and ink before him, and seated himself at a little table. I began to think it was high time to settle with myself at what terms I would be willing to engage for the voyage. I was already aware that in the whaling business they paid no wages; but all hands, including the captain, received certain shares of the profits called *lays*, and that these lays were proportioned to the degree of importance pertaining to the respective duties of the ship's company. I was also aware that being a green hand at whaling, my own lay would not be very large; but considering that I was used to the sea, could steer a ship, splice a rope, and all that, I made no doubt that from all I had heard I should be offered at least the 275th lay—that is, the 275th part of the clear net proceeds of the voyage, whatever that might eventually amount to. And though the 275th lay was what they call a rather *long lay*, yet it was better than nothing; and if we had a lucky voyage, might pretty nearly pay for the clothing I would wear out on it, not to speak of my three years' beef and board, for which I would not have to pay one stiver.

It might be thought that this was a poor way to accumulate a princely fortune—and so it was, a very poor way indeed. But I am one of those that never take on about princely fortunes, and am quite content if the world is ready to board and lodge me, while I am putting up at this grim sign of the Thunder Cloud. Upon the whole, I thought that the 275th lay would be about the fair thing, but would not have been surprised had I been offered the 200th, considering I was of a broad-shouldered make.

But one thing, nevertheless, that made me a little distrustful about receiving a generous share of the profits was this: Ashore, I had heard something of both Captain Peleg and his unaccountable old crony Bildad; how that they being the principal proprietors of the Pequod, therefore the other and more inconsiderable and scattered owners, left nearly the whole management of the ship's affairs to these two. And I did not know but what the stingy old Bildad might have a mighty deal to say about shipping hands, especially as I now found him on board the Pequod, quite at home there in the cabin, and reading his Bible as if at his own fireside. Now while Peleg was vainly trying to mend a pen with his jack-knife, old Bildad, to my no small surprise, considering that he was such an interested party in these proceedings; Bildad never heeded us, but went on mumbling to himself out of his book, ' "*Lay* not up for yourselves treasures upon earth, where moth—" '

'Well, Captain Bildad,' interrupted Peleg, 'what d'ye say, what lay shall we give this young man?'

'Thou knowest best,' was the sepulchral reply, 'the seven hundred and seventy-seventh wouldn't be too much, would it?—"where moth and rust do corrupt, but *lay*—" '

Lay, indeed, thought I, and such a lay! the seven hundred and seventy-seventh! Well, old Bildad, you are determined that I, for one, shall not *lay* up many *lays* here below, where moth and rust do corrupt. It was an exceedingly *long lay* that, indeed; and though from the magnitude of the figure it might at first deceive a landsman, yet the slightest consideration will show that though seven hundred and seventy-seven is a pretty large number, yet, when you come to make a *teenth* of it, you will then see, I say, that the seven hundred and seventy-seventh part of a farthing is a good deal less than seven hundred and seventy-seven gold doubloons; and so I thought at the time.

'Why, blast your eyes, Bildad,' cried Peleg, 'thou dost not want to swindle this young man! he must have more than that.'

'Seven hundred and seventy-seventh,' again said Bildad, without lifting his eyes; and then went on mumbling—' "for where your treasure is, there will your heart be also." '

'I am going to put him down for the three hundredth,' said Peleg, 'do ye hear that, Bildad! The three hundredth lay, I say.'

Bildad laid down his book, and turning solemnly towards him said, 'Captain Peleg, thou hast a generous heart; but thou must consider the duty thou owest to the other owners of this ship— widows and orphans, many of them—and that if we too abundantly reward the labors of this young man, we may be taking the bread from those widows and those orphans. The seven hundred and seventy-seventh lay, Captain Peleg.'

'Thou Bildad!' roared Peleg, starting up and clattering about the cabin. 'Blast ye, Captain Bildad, if I had followed thy advice in these matters, I would afore now had a conscience to lug about that would be heavy enough to founder the largest ship that ever sailed round Cape Horn.'

'Captain Peleg,' said Bildad steadily, 'thy conscience may be drawing ten inches of water, or ten fathoms, I can't tell; but as thou art still an impenitent man, Captain Peleg, I greatly fear lest thy conscience be but a leaky one; and will in the end sink thee foundering down to the fiery pit, Captain Peleg.'

'Fiery pit! fiery pit! ye insult me, man; past all natural bearing,

ye insult me. It's an all-fired outrage to tell any human creature
that he's bound to hell. Flukes and flames! Bildad, say that again
to me, and start my soul-bolts, but I'll—I'll—yes, I'll swallow a
live goat with all his hair and horns on. Out of the cabin, ye
canting, drab-colored son of a wooden gun—a straight wake with
ye!'

As he thundered out this he made a rush at Bildad, but with
a marvellous oblique, sliding celerity, Bildad for that time eluded
him.

Alarmed at this terrible outburst between the two principal and
responsible owners of the ship, and feeling half a mind to give
up all idea of sailing in a vessel so questionably owned and
temporarily commanded, I stepped aside from the door to give
egress to Bildad, who, I made no doubt, was all eagerness to
vanish from before the awakened wrath of Peleg. But to my
astonishment, he sat down again on the transom very quietly, and
seemed to have not the slightest intention of withdrawing. He
seemed quite used to impenitent Peleg and his ways. As for Peleg,
after letting off his rage as he had, there seemed no more left in
him, and he, too, sat down like a lamb, though he twitched a
little as if still nervously agitated. 'Whew!' he whistled at last—
'the squall's gone off to leeward, I think. Bildad, thou used to be
good at sharpening a lance, mend that pen, will ye. My jack-knife
here needs the grindstone. That's he; thank ye, Bildad. Now then,
my young man, Ishmael's thy name, didn't ye say? Well then,
down ye go here, Ishmael, for the three hundredth lay.'

'Captain Peleg,' said I, 'I have a friend with me who wants to
ship too—shall I bring him down tomorrow?'

'To be sure,' said Peleg. 'Fetch him along, and we'll look at
him.'

'What lay does *he* want?' groaned Bildad, glancing up from the
book in which he had again been burying himself.

'Oh! never thee mind about that, Bildad,' said Peleg. 'Has he
ever whaled it any?' turning to me.

'Killed more whales than I can count, Captain Peleg.'

'Well, bring him along then.'

And, after signing the papers, off I went; nothing doubting but
that I had done a good morning's work, and that the Pequod was
the identical ship that Yojo had provided to carry Queequeg and
me round the Cape.

But I had not proceeded far, when I began to bethink me that
the captain with whom I was to sail yet remained unseen by me;
though, indeed, in many cases, a whale-ship will be completely

fitted out, and receive all her crew on board, ere the captain makes himself visible by arriving to take command; for sometimes these voyages are so prolonged, and the shore intervals at home so exceedingly brief, that if the captain have a family, or any absorbing concernment of that sort, he does not trouble himself much about his ship in port, but leaves her to the owners till all is ready for sea. However, it is always as well to have a look at him before irrevocably committing yourself into his hands. Turning back I accosted Captain Peleg, inquiring where Captain Ahab was to be found.

'And what dost thou want of Captain Ahab? It's all right enough; thou art shipped.'

'Yes, but I should like to see him.'

'But I don't think thou wilt be able to at present. I don't know exactly what's the matter with him; but he keeps close inside the house; a sort of sick, and yet he don't look so. In fact, he ain't sick; but no, he isn't well either. Any how, young man, he won't always see me, so I don't suppose he will thee. He's a queer man, Captain Ahab—so some think—but a good one. Oh, thou'lt like him well enough; no fear, no fear. He's a grand, ungodly, god-like man, Captain Ahab; doesn't speak much; but, when he does speak, then you may well listen. Mark ye, be forewarned; Ahab's above the common; Ahab's been in colleges, as well as 'mong the cannibals; been used to deeper wonders than the waves; fixed his fiery lance in mightier, stranger foes than whales. His lance! aye, the keenest and the surest that out of all our isle! Oh! he ain't Captain Bildad; no, and he ain't Captain Peleg; *he's Ahab*, boy; and Ahab of old, thou knowest, was a crowned king!'

'And a very vile one. When that wicked king was slain, the dogs, did they not lick his blood?'

'Come hither to me—hither, hither,' said Peleg, with a significance in his eye that almost startled me. 'Look ye, lad; never say that on board the Pequod. Never say it anywhere. Captain Ahab did not name himself. 'Twas a foolish, ignorant whim of his crazy, widowed mother, who died when he was only a twelvemonth old. And yet the old squaw Tistig, at Gayhead, said that the name would somehow prove prophetic. And, perhaps, other fools like her may tell thee the same. I wish to warn thee. It's a lie. I know Captain Ahab well; I've sailed with him as mate years ago; I know what he is—a good man—not a pious, good man, like Bildad, but a swearing good man—something like me—only there's a good deal more of him. Aye, aye, I know that he was never very jolly; and I know that on the passage home, he was a little out of his mind for a spell; but it was the sharp shooting pains in his bleeding stump that brought that about, as any one might see. I know, too, that ever since he lost his leg last voyage by that accursed whale, he's been a kind of moody—desperate moody, and savage sometimes; but that will all pass off. And once for all, let me tell thee and assure thee, young man, it's better to sail with a moody good captain than a laughing bad one. So good-bye to thee—and wrong not Captain Ahab, because he happens to have a wicked name. Besides, my boy, he has a wife—not three voyages wedded—a sweet, resigned girl. Think of that; by that sweet girl that old man has a child: hold ye then there can be any utter, hopeless harm in Ahab? No, no, my lad; stricken, blasted, if he be, Ahab has his humanities!'

As I walked away, I was full of thoughtfulness; what had been incidentally revealed to me of Captain Ahab, filled me with a certain wild vagueness of painfulness concerning him. And some-how, at the time, I felt a sympathy and a sorrow for him, but for I don't know what, unless it was the cruel loss of his leg. And yet I also felt a strange awe of him; but that sort of awe, which I cannot at all describe, was not exactly awe; I do not know what it was. But I felt it; and it did not disincline me towards him; though I felt impatience at what seemed like mystery in him, so imperfectly as he was known to me then. However, my thoughts were at length carried in other directions, so that for the present dark Ahab slipped my mind.

17

THE RAMADAN

As Queequeg's Ramadan, or Fasting and Humiliation, was to continue all day, I did not choose to disturb him till towards night-fall; for I cherish the greatest respect towards everybody's religious obligations, never mind how comical, and could not find it in my heart to undervalue even a congregation of ants wor-shipping a toad-stool; or those other creatures in certain parts of our earth, who with a degree of footmanism quite unprecedented in other planets, bow down before the torso of a deceased landed proprietor merely on account of the inordinate possessions yet owned and rented in his name.

I say, we good Presbyterian Christians should be charitable in these things, and not fancy ourselves so vastly superior to other mortals, pagans and what not, because of their half-crazy conceits on these subjects. There was Queequeg, now, certainly entertaining the most absurd notions about Yojo and his Ramadan;—but what of that? Queequeg thought he knew what he was about, I suppose; he seemed to be content; and there let him rest. All our arguing with him would not avail; let him be, I say: and Heaven have mercy on us all—Presbyterians and Pagans alike—for we are all somehow dreadfully cracked about the head, and sadly need mending.

Towards evening, when I felt assured that all his performances and rituals must be over, I went up to his room and knocked at the door; but no answer. I tried to open it, but it was fastened inside. 'Queequeg,' said I softly through the key-hole:—all silent. 'I say, Queequeg! why don't you speak? It's I—Ishmael.' But all remained still as before. I began to grow alarmed. I had allowed him such abundant time; I thought he might have had an apoplectic fit. I looked through the key-hole; but the door opening into an odd corner of the room, the key-hole prospect was but a crooked and sinister one. I could only see part of the footboard of the bed and a line of the wall, but nothing more. I was surprised to behold resting against the wall the wooden shaft of Queequeg's harpoon, which the landlady the evening previous had taken from him, before our mounting to the chamber. That's strange, thought I; but at any rate, since the harpoon stands yonder, and he seldom or never goes abroad without it, therefore he must be inside here, and no possible mistake.

'Queequeg!—Queequeg!'—all still. Something must have happened. Apoplexy! I tried to burst open the door; but it stubbornly resisted. Running down stairs, I quickly stated my suspicions to the first person I met—the chambermaid. 'La! La!' she cried, 'I thought something must be the matter. I went to make the bed after breakfast, and the door was locked; and not a mouse to be heard; and it's been just so silent ever since. But I thought, may be, you had both gone off and locked your baggage in for safe keeping. La! La, ma'am!—Mistress! murder! Mrs Hussey! apoplexy!'—and with these cries, she ran towards the kitchen, I following.

Mrs Hussey soon appeared, with a mustard-pot in one hand and a vinegar-cruet in the other, having just broken away from the occupation of attending to the castors, and scolding her little black boy meantime.

'Wood-house!' cried I, 'which way to it? Run for God's sake, and fetch something to pry open the door—the axe!—the axe!—

he's had a stroke; depend upon it!'—and so saying I was un-methodically rushing up stairs again emptyhanded, when Mrs Hussey interposed the mustard-pot and vinegar-cruet, and the entire castor of her countenance.

'What's the matter with you, young man?'

'Get the axe! For God's sake, run for the doctor, some one, while I pry it open!'

'Look here,' said the landlady, quickly putting down the vinegar-cruet, so as to have one hand free; 'look here; are you talking about prying open any of my doors?'—and with that she seized my arm. 'What's the matter with you? What's the matter with you, shipmate?'

In as calm, but rapid a manner as possible, I gave her to understand the whole case. Unconsciously clapping the vinegar-cruet to one side of her nose, she ruminated for an instant; then exclaimed—'No! I haven't seen it since I put it there.' Running to a little closet under the landing of the stairs, she glanced in, and returning, told me that Queequeg's harpoon was missing. 'He's killed himself,' she cried. 'It's unfort'nate Stiggs done over again—there goes another counterpane—God pity his poor mother!—it will be the ruin of my house. Has the poor lad a sister? Where's that girl?—there, Betty, go to Snarles the Painter, and tell him to paint me a sign, with—"no suicides permitted here, and no smoking in the parlor;"—might as well kill both birds at once. Kill? The Lord be merciful to his ghost! What's that noise there? You, young man, avast there!'

And running up after me, she caught me as I was again trying to force open the door.

'I won't allow it; I won't have my premises spoiled. Go for the locksmith, there's one about a mile from here. But avast!' putting her hand in her side-pocket, 'here's a key that'll fit, I guess; let's see.' And with that, she turned it in the lock; but, alas! Queequeg's supplemental bolt remained unwithdrawn within.

'Have to burst it open,' said I, and was running down the entry a little, for a good start, when the landlady caught at me, again vowing I should not break down her premises; but I tore from her, and with a sudden bodily rush dashed myself full against the mark.

With a prodigious noise the door flew open, and the knob slamming against the wall, sent the plaster to the ceiling; and there, good heavens! there sat Queequeg, altogether cool and self-collected; right in the middle of the room; squatting on his hams, and holding Yojo on top of his head. He looked neither one way nor the other way, but sat like a carved image with scarce a sign of active life.

'Queequeg,' said I, going up to him, 'Queequeg, what's the matter with you?'

'He hain't been a sittin' so all day, has he?' said the landlady.

But all we said, not a word could we drag out of him; I almost felt like pushing him over, so as to change his position, for it was almost intolerable, it seemed so painfully and unnaturally constrained; especially, as in all probability he had been sitting so for upwards of eight or ten hours, going too without his regular meals.

'Mrs Hussey,' said I, 'he's *alive* at all events; so leave us, if you please, and I will see to this strange affair myself.'

Closing the door upon the landlady, I endeavored to prevail upon Queequeg to take a chair; but in vain. There he sat; and all I could do—for all my polite arts and blandishments—he would not move a peg, nor say a single word, nor even look at me, nor notice my presence in any the slightest way.

I wonder, thought I, if this can possibly be a part of his Ramadan; do they fast on their hams that way in his native island? It must be so; yes, it's part of his creed, I suppose; well, then, let him rest; he'll get up sooner or later, no doubt. It can't last for ever, thank God, and his Ramadan only comes once a year; and I don't believe it's very punctual then.

I went down to supper. After sitting a long time listening to the long stories of some sailors who had just come from a plum-pudding voyage, as they called it (that is, a short whaling-voyage in a schooner or brig, confined to the north of the line, in the Atlantic Ocean only); after listening to these plum-puddingers till nearly eleven o'clock, I went up stairs to go to bed, feeling quite sure by this time Queequeg must certainly have brought his Ramadan to a termination. But no; there he was just where I had left him; he had not stirred an inch. I began to grow vexed with him; it seemed so downright senseless and insane to be sitting there all day and half the night on his hams in a cold room, holding a piece of wood on his head.

'For heaven's sake, Queequeg, get up and shake yourself; get up and have some supper. You'll starve; you'll kill yourself, Queequeg.' But not a word did he reply.

Despairing of him, therefore, I determined to go to bed and to sleep; and no doubt, before a great while, he would follow me. But previous to turning in, I took my heavy bearskin jacket, and threw it over him, as it promised to be a very cold night; and he had nothing but his ordinary round jacket on. For some time, do all I would, I could not get into the faintest doze. I had blown out the candle; and the mere thought of Queequeg—not four feet off—sitting there in that uneasy position, stark alone in the cold and dark; this made me really wretched. Think of it; sleeping all night in the same room with a wide awake pagan on his hams in this dreary, unaccountable Ramadan!

But somehow I dropped off at last, and knew nothing more till break of day; when, looking over the bedside, there squatted Queequeg, as if he had been screwed down to the floor. But as soon as the first glimpse of sun entered the window, up he got, with stiff and grating joints, but with a cheerful look; limped towards me where I lay; pressed his forehead again against mine; and said his Ramadan was over.

Now, as I before hinted, I have no objection to any person's religion, be it what it may, so long as that person does not kill or insult any other person, because that other person don't believe it also. But when a man's religion becomes really frantic; when it is a positive torment to him; and, in fine, makes this earth of ours an uncomfortable inn to lodge in; then I think it high time to take that individual aside and argue the point with him.

And just so I now did with Queequeg. 'Queequeg,' said I, 'get into bed now, and lie and listen to me.' I then went on, beginning with the rise and progress of the primitive religions, and coming down to the various religions of the present time, during which time I labored to show Queequeg that all these Lents, Ramadans, and prolonged ham-squattings in cold, cheerless rooms were stark nonsense; bad for the health; useless for the soul; opposed, in short, to the obvious laws of Hygiene and common sense. I told him, too, that he being in other things such an extremely sensible and sagacious savage, it pained me, very badly pained me, to see him now so deplorably foolish about this ridiculous Ramadan of his. Besides, argued I, fasting makes the body cave in; hence the spirit caves in; and all thoughts born of a fast must necessarily be half-starved. This is the reason why most dyspeptic religionists cherish such melancholy notions about their hereafters. In one word, Queequeg, said I, rather digressively; hell is an idea first born on an undigested apple-dumpling; and since then perpetuated through the hereditary dyspepsias nurtured by Ramadans.

I then asked Queequeg whether he himself was ever troubled with dyspepsia; expressing the idea very plainly, so that he could take it in. He said no; only upon one memorable occasion. It was after a great feast given by his father the king, on the gaining of a great battle wherein fifty of the enemy had been killed by about two o'clock in the afternoon, and all cooked and eaten that very evening.

'No more, Queequeg,' said I, shuddering; 'that will do;' for I knew the inferences without his further hinting them. I had seen a sailor who had visited that very island, and he told me that it was the custom, when a great battle had been gained there, to barbecue all the slain in the yard or garden of the victor; and then, one by one, they were placed in great wooden trenchers, and garnished round like a pilau, with breadfruit and cocoanuts; and with some parsley in their mouths, were sent round with the victor's compliments to all his friends, just as though these presents were so many Christmas turkeys.

After all, I do not think that my remarks about religion made much impression upon Queequeg. Because, in the first place, he somehow seemed dull of hearing on that important subject, unless considered from his own point of view; and, in the second place, he did not more than one third understand me, couch my ideas simply as I would; and, finally, he no doubt thought he knew a good deal more about the true religion than I did. He looked at me with a sort of condescending concern and compassion, as though he thought it a great pity that such a sensible young man should be so hopelessly lost to evangelical pagan piety.

At last we rose and dressed; and Queequeg, taking a prodigiously hearty breakfast of chowders of all sorts, so that the landlady should not make much profit by reason of his Ramadan, we sallied out to board the Pequod, sauntering along, and picking our teeth with halibut bones.

18

HIS MARK

As we were walking down the end of the wharf towards the ship, Queequeg carrying his harpoon, Captain Peleg in his gruff voice loudly hailed us from his wigwam, saying he had not suspected my friend was a cannibal, and furthermore announcing that he let no cannibals on board that craft, unless they previously produced their papers.

'What do you mean by that, Captain Peleg!' said I, now jumping on the bulwarks, and leaving my comrade standing on the wharf.

'I mean,' he replied, 'he must show his papers.'

'Yea,' said Captain Bildad in his hollow voice, sticking his head from behind Peleg's, out of the wigwam. 'He must show that he's converted. Son of darkness,' he added, turning to Queequeg, 'art thou at present in communion with any Christian church?'

'Why,' said I, 'he's a member of the First Congregational Church.' Here be it said, that many tattooed savages sailing in Nantucket ships at last come to be converted into the churches.

'First Congregational Church,' cried Bildad, 'what! that worships in Deacon Deuteronomy Coleman's meetinghouse?' and so saying, taking out his spectacles, he rubbed them with his great yellow bandana handkerchief, and putting them on very carefully, came out of the wigwam, and leaning stiffly over the bulwarks, took a good long look at Queequeg.

'How long hath he been a member?' he then said, turning to me; 'not very long, I rather guess, young man.'

'No,' said Peleg, 'and he hasn't been baptized right either, or it would have washed some of that devil's blue off his face.'

'Do tell, now,' cried Bildad, 'is this Philistine a regular member of Deacon Deuteronomy's meeting? I never saw him going there, and I pass it every Lord's day.'

'I don't know anything about Deacon Deuteronomy or his meeting,' said I, 'all I know is, that Queequeg here is a born member of the First Congregational Church. He is a deacon himself, Queequeg is.'

'Young man,' said Bildad sternly, 'thou art skylarking with me— explain thyself, thou young Hittite. What church dost thee mean? answer me.'

Finding myself thus hard pushed, I replied, 'I mean, sir, the same ancient Catholic Church to which you and I, and Captain Peleg there, and Queequeg here, and all of us, and every mother's son and soul of us belong; the great and everlasting First Congregation of this whole worshipping world; we all belong to that; only some of us cherish some queer crotchets noways touching the grand belief; in *that* we all join hands.'

'Splice, thou mean'st *splice* hands,' cried Peleg, drawing nearer. 'Young man, you'd better ship for a missionary, instead of a fore-mast hand; I never heard a better sermon. Deacon Deuteronomy— why Father Mapple himself couldn't beat it, and he's reckoned something. Come aboard, come aboard; never mind about the papers. I say, tell Quohog there—what's that you call him? tell Quohog to step along. By the great anchor, what a harpoon he's got there! looks like good stuff that; and he handles it about right. I say, Quohog, or whatever your name is, did you ever stand in the head of a whale-boat? did you ever strike a fish?'

Without saying a word, Queequeg, in his wild sort of way, jumped upon the bulwarks, from thence into the bows of one of the whale-boats hanging to the side; and then bracing his left knee, and poising his harpoon, cried out in some such way as this:—

'Cap'ain, you see him small drop tar on water dere? You see him? well, spose him one whale eye, well, den!' and taking sharp aim at it, he darted the iron right over old Bildad's broad brim, clean across the ship's decks, and struck the glistening tar spot out of sight.

'Now,' said Queequeg, quietly hauling in the line, 'spos-ee him whale-e eye; why, dad whale dead.'

'Quick, Bildad,' said Peleg, to his partner, who, aghast at the close vicinity of the flying harpoon, had retreated towards the cabin gangway. 'Quick, I say, you Bildad, and get the ship's papers. We must have Hedgehog there, I mean Quohog, in one of our boats. Look ye, Quohog, we'll give ye the ninetieth lay, and that's more than ever was given a harpooneer yet out of Nantucket.'

So down we went into the cabin, and to my great joy Queequeg was soon enrolled among the same ship's company to which I myself belonged.

When all preliminaries were over and Peleg had got everything ready for signing, he turned to me and said, 'I guess, Quohog there don't know how to write, does he? I say, Quohog, blast ye! dost thou sign thy name or make thy mark?'

But at this question, Queequeg, who had twice or thrice before taken part in similar ceremonies, looked no ways abashed; but taking the offered pen, copied upon the paper, in the proper place, an exact counterpart of a queer round figure which was tattooed upon his arm; so that through Captain Peleg's obstinate mistake touching his appellative, it stood something like this:—

Quohog.

his ∞ mark.

Meanwhile Captain Bildad sat earnestly and steadfastly eyeing Queequeg, and at last rising solemnly and fumbling in the huge pockets of his broad-skirted drab coat, took out a bundle of tracts, and selecting one entitled 'The Latter Day Coming; or No Time to Lose,' placed it in Queequeg's hands, and then grasping them and the book with both his, looked earnestly into his eyes, and said, 'Son of darkness, I must do my duty by thee; I am part owner of this ship, and feel concerned for the souls of all its crew; if thou still clingest to thy Pagan ways, which I sadly fear, I beseech thee, remain not for aye a Belial bondsman. Spurn the idol Bell, and the hideous dragon; turn from the wrath to come; mind thine eye, I say; oh! goodness gracious! steer clear of the fiery pit!'

Something of the salt sea yet lingered in old Bildad's language, heterogeneously mixed with Scriptural and domestic phrases.

'Avast there, avast there, Bildad, avast now spoiling our harpooneer,' cried Peleg. 'Pious harpooneers never make good voyagers—it takes the shark out of 'em; no harpooneer is worth a straw who aint pretty sharkish. There was young Nat Swaine, once the bravest boat-header out of all Nantucket and the Vineyard; he joined the meeting, and never came to good. He got so frightened about his plaguy soul, that he shrinked and sheered away from whales, for fear of after-claps in case he got stove and went to Davy Jones.'

'Peleg! Peleg!' said Bildad, lifting his eyes and hands, 'thou thyself, as I myself, hast seen many a perilous time; thou knowest, Peleg, what it is to have the fear of death; how, then, can'st thou prate in this ungodly guise. Thou beliest thine own heart, Peleg. Tell me, when this same Pequod here had her three masts overboard in that typhoon off Japan, that same voyage when thou went mate with Captain Ahab, did'st thou not think of Death and the Judgment then?'

'Hear him, hear him now,' cried Peleg, marching across the cabin, and thrusting his hands far down into his pockets,—'hear him, all of ye. Think of that! When every moment we thought the ship would sink! Death and the Judgment then? What? With all three masts making such an everlasting thundering against the side; and every sea breaking over us, fore and aft. Think of Death and the Judgment then? No! no time to think about Death then. Life was what Captain Ahab and I was thinking of; and how to save all hands—how to rig jury-masts—how to get into the nearest port; that was what I was thinking of.'

Bildad said no more, but buttoning up his coat, stalked on deck, where we followed him. There he stood, very quietly overlooking some sail-makers who were mending a top-sail in the waist. Now and then he stooped to pick up a patch, or save an end of the tarred twine, which otherwise might have been wasted.

19
THE PROPHET

'SHIPMATES, have ye shipped in that ship?'

Queequeg and I had just left the Pequod, and were sauntering away from the water, for the moment each occupied with his own thoughts, when the above words were put to us by a stranger, who, pausing before us, levelled his massive forefinger at the vessel in question. He was but shabbily apparelled in faded jacket and patched trowsers; a rag of a black handkerchief investing his neck. A confluent small-pox had in all directions flowed over his face, and left it like the complicated ribbed bed of a torrent, when the rushing waters have been dried up.

'Have ye shipped in her?' he repeated.

'You mean the ship Pequod, I suppose,' said I, trying to gain a little more time for an uninterrupted look at him.

'Aye, the Pequod—that ship there,' he said, drawing back his whole arm, and then rapidly shoving it straight out from him, with the fixed bayonet of his pointed finger darted full at the object.

'Yes,' said I, 'we have just signed the articles.'

'Anything down there about your souls?'

'About what?'

'Oh, perhaps you hav'n't got any,' he said quickly. 'No matter though, I know many chaps that hav'n't got any,—good luck to 'em; and they are all the better off for it. A soul's a sort of a fifth wheel to a wagon.'

'What are you jabbering about, shipmate?' said I.

'*He's* got enough, though, to make up for all deficiencies of that sort in other chaps,' abruptly said the stranger, placing a nervous emphasis upon the word *he*.

'Queequeg,' said I, 'let's go; this fellow has broken loose from somewhere; he's talking about something and somebody we don't know.'

'Stop!' cried the stranger. 'Ye said true—ye hav'n't seen Old Thunder yet, have ye?'

'Who's Old Thunder?' said I, again riveted with the insane earnestness of his manner.

'Captain Ahab.'

'What! the captain of our ship, the Pequod?'

'Aye, among some of us old sailor chaps, he goes by that name. Ye hav'n't seen him yet, have ye?'

'No, we hav'n't. He's sick they say, but is getting better, and will be all right again before long.'

'All right again before long!' laughed the stranger, with a solemnly derisive sort of laugh. 'Look ye; when Captain Ahab is all right, then this left arm of mine will be all right, not before.'

'What do you know about him?'

'What did they *tell* you about him? Say that!'

'They didn't tell much of anything about him; only I've heard that he's a good whale-hunter, and a good captain to his crew.'

'That's true, that's true—yes, both true enough. But you must jump when he gives an order. Step and growl; growl and go— that's the word with Captain Ahab. But nothing about that thing that happened to him off Cape Horn, long ago, when he lay like dead for three days and nights; nothing about that deadly skrimmage with the Spaniard afore the altar in Santa?—heard nothing about that, eh? Nothing about the silver calabash he spat into? And nothing about his losing his leg last voyage, according to the prophecy? Didn't ye hear a word about them matters and something more, eh? No, I don't think ye did; how could ye? Who knows it? Not all Nantucket, I guess. But hows'ever, mayhap, ye've heard tell about the leg, and how he lost it; aye, ye have heard of that, I dare say. Oh yes, *that* every one knows a'most— I mean they know he's only one leg; and that a parmacetti took the other off.'

'My friend,' said I, 'what all this gibberish of yours is about, I don't know, and I don't much care; for it seems to me that you must be a little damaged in the head. But if you are speaking of Captain Ahab, of that ship there, the Pequod, then let me tell, that I know all about the loss of his leg.'

'*All* about it, eh—sure you do?—all?'

'Pretty sure.'

With finger pointed and eye levelled at the Pequod, the beggar-like stranger stood a moment, as if in a troubled reverie; then starting a little, turned and said:—'Ye've shipped, have ye? Names down on the papers? Well, well, what's signed, is signed; and what's to be, will be; and then again, perhaps it wont be, after all. Any how, it's all fixed and arranged a'ready, and some sailors or other must go with him, I suppose; as well these as any other men, God pity 'em! Morning to ye, shipmates, morning; the ineffable heavens bless ye; I'm sorry I stopped ye.'

'Look here, friend,' said I, 'if you have anything important to tell us, out with it; but if you are only trying to bamboozle us, you are mistaken in your game; that's all I have to say.'

'And it's said very well, and I like to hear a chap talk up that way; you are just the man for him—the likes of ye. Morning to ye, shipmates, morning! Oh! when ye get there, tell 'em I've concluded not to make one of 'em.'

'Ah, my dear fellow, you can't fool us that way—you can't fool us. It is the easiest thing in the world for a man to look as if he had a great secret in him.'

'Morning to ye, shipmates, morning.'

'Morning it is,' said I. 'Come along, Queequeg, let's leave this crazy man. But stop, tell me your name, will you?'

'Elijah.'

Elijah! thought I, and we walked away, both commenting, after each other's fashion, upon this ragged old sailor; and agreed that he was nothing but a humbug, trying to be a bugbear. But we had not gone perhaps above a hundred yards, when chancing to turn a corner, and looking back as I did so, who should be seen but Elijah following us, though at a distance. Somehow, the sight of him struck me so, that I said nothing to Queequeg of his being behind, but passed on with my comrade, anxious to see whether the stranger would turn the same corner that we did. He did; and then it seemed to me that he was dogging us, but with what intent I could not for the life of me imagine. This circumstance, coupled with his ambiguous, half-hinting, half-revealing, shrouded sort of talk, now begat in me all kinds of vague wonderments and half-apprehensions, and all connected with the Pequod; and Captain Ahab; and the leg he had lost; and the Cape Horn fit; and the silver calabash; and what Captain Peleg had said of him, when I left the ship the day previous; and the prediction of the squaw Tistig; and the voyage we had bound ourselves to sail; and a hundred other shadowy things.

I was resolved to satisfy myself whether this ragged Elijah was really dogging us or not, and with that intent crossed the way with Queequeg, and on that side of it retraced our steps. But Elijah passed on, without seeming to notice us. This relieved me; and once more, and finally as it seemed to me, I pronounced him in my heart, a humbug.

20
ALL ASTIR

A day or two passed, and there was great activity aboard the Pequod. Not only were the old sails being mended, but new sails were coming on board, and bolts of canvas, and coils of rigging; in short, everything betokened that the ship's preparations were hurrying to a close. Captain Peleg seldom or never went ashore, but sat in his wigwam keeping a sharp look-out upon the hands; Bildad did all the purchasing and providing at the stores; and the men employed in the hold and on the rigging were working till long after night-fall.

On the day following Queequeg's signing the articles, word was given at all the inns where the ship's company were stopping, that their chests must be on board before night, for there was no telling how soon the vessel might be sailing. So Queequeg and I got down our traps, resolving, however, to sleep ashore till the last. But it seems they always give very long notice in these cases, and the ship did not sail for several days. But no wonder; there was a good deal to be done, and there is no telling how many things to be thought of, before the Pequod was fully equipped.

Every one knows what a multitude of things—beds, saucepans, knives and forks, shovels and tongs, napkins, nutcrackers, and what not, are indispensable to the business of housekeeping. Just so with whaling, which necessitates a three-years' housekeeping upon the wide ocean, far from all grocers, costermongers, doctors, bakers, and bankers. And though this also holds true of merchant vessels, yet not by any means to the same extent as with whalemen. For besides the great length of the whaling voyage, the numerous articles peculiar to the prosecution of the fishery, and the impossibility of replacing them at the remote harbors usually frequented, it must be remembered, that of all ships, whaling vessels are the most exposed to accidents of all kinds, and especially to the destruction and loss of the very things upon which the success of the voyage most depends. Hence, the spare boats, spare spars, and spare lines and harpoons, and spare everythings, almost, but a spare Captain and duplicate ship.

At the period of our arrival at the Island, the heaviest stowage of the Pequod had been almost completed; comprising her beef, bread, water, fuel, and iron hoops and staves. But, as before hinted, for some time there was a continual fetching and carrying on board of divers odds and ends of things, both large and small.

Chief among those who did this fetching and carrying was Captain Bildad's sister, a lean old lady of a most determined and indefatigable spirit, but withal very kindhearted, who seemed resolved that, if *she* could help it, nothing should be found wanting in the Pequod, after once fairly getting to sea. At one time she would come on board with a jar of pickles for the steward's pantry; another time with a bunch of quills for the chief mate's desk, where he kept his log; a third time with a roll of flannel for the small of some one's rheumatic back. Never did any woman better deserve her name, which was Charity—Aunt Charity, as everybody called her. And like a sister of charity did this charitable Aunt Charity bustle about hither and thither, ready to turn her hand and heart to anything that promised to yield safety, comfort, and consolation to all on board a ship in which her beloved brother Bildad was concerned, and in which she herself owned a score or two of well-saved dollars.

But it was startling to see this excellent hearted Quakeress coming on board, as she did the last day, with a long oilladle in one hand, and a still longer whaling lance in the other. Nor was Bildad himself nor Captain Peleg at all backward. As for Bildad, he carried about with him a long list of the articles needed, and at every fresh arrival, down went his mark opposite that article upon the paper. Every once and a while Peleg came hobbling out of his whalebone den, roaring at the men down the hatchways, roaring up to the riggers at the mast-head, and then concluded by roaring back into his wigwam.

During these days of preparation, Queequeg and I often visited the craft, and as often I asked about Captain Ahab, and how he was, and when he was going to come on board his ship. To these questions they would answer, that he was getting better and better, and was expected aboard every day; meantime, the two Captains, Peleg and Bildad, could attend to everything necessary to fit the vessel for the voyage. If I had been downright honest with myself, I would have seen very plainly in my heart that I did but half fancy being committed this way to so long a voyage, without once laying my eyes on the man who was to be the absolute dictator of it, so soon as the ship sailed out upon the open sea. But when a man suspects any wrong, it sometimes happens that if he be already involved in the matter, he insensibly strives to cover up his suspicions even from himself. And much this way it was with me. I said nothing, and tried to think nothing.

At last it was given out that some time next day the ship would certainly sail. So next morning, Queequeg and I took a very early start.

21
GOING ABOARD

IT was nearly six o'clock, but only grey imperfect misty dawn, when we drew nigh the wharf.

'There are some sailors running ahead there, if I see right,' said I to Queequeg, 'it can't be shadows; she's off by sunrise, I guess; come on!'

'Avast!' cried a voice, whose owner at the same time coming close behind us, laid a hand upon both our shoulders, and then insinuating himself between us, stood stooping forward a little, in the uncertain twilight, strangely peering from Queequeg to me. It was Elijah.

'Going aboard?'

'Hands off, will you,' said I.

'Lookee here,' said Queequeg, shaking himself, 'go 'way!'

'Aint going aboard, then?'

'Yes, we are,' said I, 'but what business is that of yours? Do you know, Mr Elijah, that I consider you a little impertinent?'

'No, no, no; I wasn't aware of that,' said Elijah, slowly and wonderingly looking from me to Queequeg, with the most unaccountable glances.

'Elijah,' said I, 'you will oblige my friend and me by withdrawing. We are going to the Indian and Pacific Oceans, and would prefer not to be detained.'

'Ye be, be ye? Coming back afore breakfast?'

'He's cracked, Queequeg,' said I, 'come on.'

'Holloa!' cried stationary Elijah, hailing us when we had removed a few paces.

'Never mind him,' said I, 'Queequeg, come on.'

But he stole up to us again, and suddenly clapping his hand on my shoulder, said—'Did ye see anything looking like men going towards that ship a while ago?'

Struck by this plain matter-of-fact question, I answered, saying,

'Yes, I thought I did see four or five men; but it was too dim to be sure.'

'Very dim, very dim,' said Elijah. 'Morning to ye.'

Once more we quitted him; but once more he came softly after us; and touching my shoulder again, said, 'See if you can find 'em now, will ye?'

'Find who?'

'Morning to ye! morning to ye!' he rejoined, again moving off. 'Oh! I was going to warn ye against—but never mind, never mind—it's all one, all in the family too;—sharp frost this morning, ain't it? Good bye to ye. Shan't see ye again very soon, I guess; unless it's before the Grand Jury.' And with these cracked words he finally departed, leaving me, for the moment, in no small wonderment at his frantic impudence.

At last, stepping on board the Pequod, we found everything in profound quiet, not a soul moving. The cabin entrance was locked within; the hatches were all on, and lumbered with coils of rigging. Going forward to the forecastle, we found the slide of the scuttle open. Seeing a light, we went down, and found only an old rigger there, wrapped in a tattered pea-jacket. He was thrown at whole length upon two chests, his face downwards and inclosed in his folded arms. The profoundest slumber slept upon him.

'Those sailors we saw, Queequeg, where can they have gone to?' said I, looking dubiously at the sleeper. But it seemed that, when on the wharf, Queequeg had not at all noticed what I now alluded to; hence I would have thought myself to have been optically deceived in that matter, were it not for Elijah's otherwise inexplicable question. But I beat the thing down; and again marking the sleeper, jocularly hinted to Queequeg that perhaps we had best sit up with the body; telling him to establish himself accordingly. He put his hand upon the sleeper's rear, as though feeling if it was soft enough; and then, without more ado, sat quietly down there.

'Gracious! Queequeg, don't sit there,' said I.

'Oh! perry dood seat,' said Queequeg, 'my country way; won't hurt him face.'

'Face!' said I, 'call that his face? very benevolent countenance then; but how hard he breathes, he's heaving himself; get off, Queequeg, you are heavy, it's grinding the face of the poor. Get off, Queequeg! Look, he'll twitch you off soon. I wonder he don't wake.'

Queequeg removed himself to just beyond the head of the sleeper, and lighted his tomahawk pipe. I sat at the feet. We kept the pipe passing over the sleeper, from one to the other. Meanwhile, upon questioning him, in his broken fashion, Queequeg gave me to understand that, in his land, owing to the absence of settees and sofas of all sorts, the king, chiefs, and great people generally, were in the custom of fattening some of the lower orders for ottomans; and to furnish a house comfortably in that respect, you had only to buy up eight or ten lazy fellows, and lay them round in the piers and alcoves. Besides, it was very convenient on an excursion; much better than those garden-chairs which are convertible into walking-sticks; upon occasion, a chief calling his attendant, and desiring him to make a settee of himself under a spreading tree, perhaps in some damp marshy place.

While narrating these things, every time Queequeg received the tomahawk from me, he flourished the hatchetside of it over the sleeper's head.

'What's that for, Queequeg?'

'Perry easy, kill-e; oh! perry easy!'

He was going on with some wild reminiscences about his tomahawk-pipe, which, it seemed, had in its two uses both brained his foes and soothed his soul, when we were directly attracted to the sleeping rigger. The strong vapor now completely filling the contracted hole, it began to tell upon him. He breathed with a sort of muffledness; then seemed troubled in the nose; then revolved over once or twice; then sat up and rubbed his eyes.

'Holloa!' he breathed at last, 'who be ye smokers?'

'Shipped men,' answered I, 'when does she sail?'

'Aye, aye, ye are going in her, be ye? She sails to-day. The Captain came aboard last night.'

'What Captain?—Ahab?'

'Who but him indeed?'

I was going to ask him some further questions concerning Ahab, when we heard a noise on deck.

'Halloa! Starbuck's astir,' said the rigger. 'He's a lively chief mate, that; good man, and a pious; but all alive now, I must turn to.' And so saying he went on deck, and we followed.

It was now clear sunrise. Soon the crew came on board in twos and threes; the riggers bestirred themselves; the mates were actively engaged; and several of the shore people were busy in bringing various last things on board. Meanwhile Captain Ahab remained invisibly enshrined within his cabin.

22
MERRY CHRISTMAS

AT length, towards noon, upon the final dismissal of the ship's riggers, and after the Pequod had been hauled out from the wharf, and after the ever-thoughtful Charity had come off in a whaleboat, with her last gift—a night-cap for Stubb, the second mate, her brother-in-law, and a spare Bible for the steward—after all this, the two captains, Peleg and Bildad, issued from the cabin, and turning to the chief mate, Peleg said:

'Now, Mr Starbuck, are you sure everything is right? Captain Ahab is all ready—just spoke to him—nothing more to be got from shore, eh? Well, call all hands, then. Muster 'em aft here— blast 'em!'

'No need of profane words, however great the hurry, Peleg,' said Bildad, 'but away with thee, friend Starbuck, and do our bidding.'

How now! Here upon the very point of starting for the voyage, Captain Peleg and Captain Bildad were going it with a high hand on the quarter-deck, just as if they were to be joint-commanders at sea, as well as to all appearances in port. And, as for Captain Ahab, no sign of him was yet to be seen; only, they said he was in the cabin. But then, the idea was, that his presence was by no means necessary in getting the ship under weigh, and steering her well out to sea. Indeed, as that was not at all his proper business, but the pilot's; and as he was not yet completely recovered—so they said—therefore, Captain Ahab stayed below. And all this seemed natural enough; especially as in the merchant service many captains never show themselves on deck for a considerable time after heaving up the anchor, but remain over the cabin table, having a farewell merry-making with their shore friends, before they quit the ship for good with the pilot.

But there was not much chance to think over the matter, for Captain Peleg was now all alive. He seemed to do most of the talking and commanding, and not Bildad.

'Aft here, ye sons of bachelors,' he cried, as the sailors lingered at the main-mast. 'Mr Starbuck, drive 'em aft.'

'Strike the tent there!'—was the next order. As I hinted before, this whalebone marquee was never pitched except in port; and on board the Pequod, for thirty years, the order to strike the tent was well known to be the next thing to heaving up the anchor.

'Man the capstan! Blood and thunder!—jump!'—was the next command, and the crew sprang for the handspikes.

Now, in getting under weigh, the station generally occupied by the pilot is the forward part of the ship. And here Bildad, who, with Peleg, be it known, in addition to his other offices, was one of the licensed pilots of the port—he being suspected to have got himself made a pilot in order to save the Nantucket pilot-fee to all the ships he was concerned in, for he never piloted any other craft—Bildad, I say, might now be seen actively engaged in looking over the bows for the approaching anchor, and at intervals singing what seemed a dismal stave of psalmody, to cheer the hands at the windlass, who roared forth some sort of a chorus about the girls in Booble Alley, with hearty good will. Nevertheless, not three days previous, Bildad had told them that no profane songs would be allowed on board the Pequod, particularly in getting under weigh; and Charity, his sister, had placed a small choice copy of Watts in each seaman's berth.

Meantime, overseeing the other part of the ship, Captain Peleg ripped and swore astern in the most frightful manner. I almost thought he would sink the ship before the anchor could be got up; involuntarily I paused on my handspike, and told Queequeg to do the same, thinking of the perils we both ran, in starting on the voyage with such a devil for a pilot. I was comforting myself, however with the thought that in pious Bildad might be found some salvation, spite of his seven hundred and seventy-seventh lay; when I felt a sudden sharp poke in my rear, and turning round, was horrified at the apparition of Captain Peleg in the act of withdrawing his leg from my immediate vicinity. That was my first kick.

'Is that the way they heave in the marchant service?' he roared. 'Spring, thou sheep-head; spring, and break thy back-bone! Why don't ye spring, I say, all of ye—spring! Quohag! spring, thou chap with the red whiskers; spring there, Scotch-cap; spring, thou green pants. Spring, I say, all of ye, and spring your eyes out!' And so saying, he moved along the windlass, here and there using his leg very freely, while imperturbable Bildad kept leading off with his psalmody. Thinks I, Captain Peleg must have been drinking something to-day.

At last the anchor was up, the sails were set, and off we glided. It was a short, cold Christmas; and as the short northern day merged into night, we found ourselves almost broad upon the

wintry ocean, whose freezing spray cased us in ice, as in polished
armor. The long rows of teeth on the bulwarks glistened in the
moonlight; and like the white ivory tusks of some huge elephant,
vast curving icicles depended from the bows.

Lank Bildad, as pilot, headed the first watch, and ever and
anon, as the old craft deep dived into the green seas, and sent
the shivering frost all over her, and the winds howled, and the
cordage rang, his steady notes were heard,—

> 'Sweet fields beyond the swelling flood,
>   Stand dressed in living green.
> So to the Jews old Canaan stood,
>   While Jordan rolled between.'

Never did those sweet words sound more sweetly to me than
then. They were full of hope and fruition. Spite of this frigid
winter night in the boisterous Atlantic, spite of my wet feet and
wetter jacket, there was yet, it then seemed to me, many a pleasant
haven in store; and meads and glades so eternally vernal, that the
grass shot up by the spring, untrodden, unwilted, remains at
midsummer.

At last we gained such an offing, that the two pilots were needed
no longer. The stout sail-boat that had accompanied us began
ranging alongside.

It was curious and not unpleasing, how Peleg and Bildad were
affected at this juncture, especially Captain Bildad. For loath to
depart, yet; very loath to leave, for good, a ship bound on so long
and perilous a voyage—beyond both stormy Capes; a ship in
which some thousands of his hard earned dollars were invested;
a ship, in which an old shipmate sailed as captain; a man almost
as old as he, once more starting to encounter all the terrors of
the pitiless jaw; loath to say good-bye to a thing so every way
brimful of every interest to him,—poor old Bildad lingered long;
paced the deck with anxious strides; ran down into the cabin to
speak another farewell word there; again came on deck, and looked
to windward; looked towards the wide and endless waters, only
bounded by the far-off unseen Eastern Continents; looked towards
the land; looked aloft; looked right and left; looked everywhere
and nowhere; and at last, mechanically coiling a rope upon its
pin, convulsively grasped stout Peleg by the hand, and holding
up a lantern, for a moment stood gazing heroically in his face,
as much as to say, 'Nevertheless, friend Peleg, I can stand it; yes,
I can.'

As for Peleg himself, he took it more like a philosopher; but for all his philosophy, there was a tear twinkling in his eye, when the lantern came too near. And he, too, did not a little run from cabin to deck—now a word below, and now a word with Starbuck, the chief mate.

But, at last, he turned to his comrade, with a final sort of look about him,—'Captain Bildad—come, old shipmate, we must go. Back the main-yard there! Boat ahoy! Stand by to come close alongside, now! Careful, careful!—come, Bildad, boy—say your last. Luck to ye, Starbuck—luck to ye, Mr Stubb—luck to ye, Mr Flask—good-bye, and good luck to ye all—and this day three years I'll have a hot supper smoking for ye in old Nantucket. Hurrah and away!'

'God bless ye, and have ye in His holy keeping, men,' murmured old Bildad, almost incoherently. 'I hope ye'll have fine weather now, so that Captain Ahab may soon be moving among ye—a pleasant sun is all he needs, and ye'll have plenty of them in the tropic voyage ye go. Be careful in the hunt, ye mates. Don't stave the boats needlessly, ye harpooneers; good white cedar plank is raised full three per cent. within the year. Don't forget your prayers, either. Mr Starbuck, mind that cooper don't waste the spare staves. Oh! the sail-needles are in the green locker! Don't whale it too much a' Lord's days, men; but don't miss a fair chance either, that's rejecting Heaven's good gifts. Have an eye to the molasses tierce, Mr Stubb; it was a little leaky, I thought. If ye touch at the islands, Mr Flask, beware of fornication. Good-bye, good-bye! Don't keep that cheese too long down in the hold, Mr Starbuck; it'll spoil. Be careful with the butter—twenty cents the pound it was, and mind ye, if—'

'Come, come, Captain Bildad; stop palavering,—away!' and with that, Peleg hurried him over the side, and both dropt into the boat.

Ship and boat diverged; the cold, damp night breeze blew between; a screaming gull flew overhead; the two hulls wildly rolled; we gave three heavy-hearted cheers, and blindly plunged like fate into the lone Atlantic.

23
THE LEE SHORE

SOME chapters back, one Bulkington was spoken of, a tall, new-landed mariner, encountered in New Bedford at the inn.

When on that shivering winter's night, the Pequod thrust her vindictive bows into the cold malicious waves, who should I see standing at her helm but Bulkington! I looked with sympathetic awe and fearfulness upon the man, who in mid-winter just landed from a four years' dangerous voyage, could so unrestingly push off again for still another tempestuous term. The land seemed scorching to his feet. Wonderfullest things are ever the unmentionable; deep memories yield no epitaphs; this six-inch chapter is the stoneless grave of Bulkington. Let me only say that it fared with him as with the storm-tossed ship, that miserably drives along the leeward land. The port would fain give succor; the port is pitiful; in the port is safety, comfort, hearthstone, supper, warm blankets, friends, all that's kind to our mortalities. But in that gale, the port, the land, is that ship's direst jeopardy; she must fly all hospitality; one touch of land, though it but graze the keel, would make her shudder through and through. With all her might she crowds all sail off shore; in so doing, fights 'gainst the very winds that fain would blow her homeward; seeks all the lashed sea's landlessness again; for refuge's sake forlornly rushing into peril; her only friend her bitterest foe!

Know ye, now, Bulkington? Glimpses do ye seem to see of that mortally intolerable truth; that all deep, earnest thinking is but the intrepid effort of the soul to keep the open independence of her sea; while the wildest winds of heaven and earth conspire to cast her on the treacherous, slavish shore?

But as in landlessness alone resides the highest truth, shoreless, indefinite as God—so, better is it to perish in that howling infinite, than be ingloriously dashed upon the lee, even if that were safety! For worm-like, then, oh! who would craven crawl to land! Terrors of the terrible! is all this agony so vain? Take heart, take heart, O Bulkington! Bear thee grimly, demigod! Up from the spray of thy oceanperishing—straight up, leaps thy apotheosis!

110

24
THE ADVOCATE

As Queequeg and I are now fairly embarked in this business of whaling; and as this business of whaling has somehow come to be regarded among landsmen as a rather unpoetical and disreputable pursuit; therefore, I am all anxiety to convince ye, ye landsmen, of the injustice hereby done to us hunters of whales.

In the first place, it may be deemed almost superfluous to establish the fact, that among people at large, the business of whaling is not accounted on a level with what are called the liberal professions. If a stranger were introduced into any miscellaneous metropolitan society, it would but slightly advance the general opinion of his merits, were he presented to the company as a harpooneer, say; and if in emulation of the naval officers he should append the initials S.W.F. (Sperm Whale Fishery) to his visiting card, such a procedure would be deemed pre-eminently presuming and ridiculous.

Doubtless one leading reason why the world declines honoring us whalemen, is this: they think that, at best, our vocation amounts to a butchering sort of business; and that when actively engaged therein, we are surrounded by all manner of defilements. Butchers we are, that is true. But butchers, also, and butchers of the bloodiest badge have been all Martial Commanders whom the world invariably delights to honor. And as for the matter of the alleged uncleanliness of our business, ye shall soon be initiated into certain facts hitherto pretty generally unknown, and which, upon the whole, will triumphantly plant the sperm whaleship at least among the cleanliest things of this tidy earth. But even granting the charge in question to be true; what disordered slippery decks of a whaleship are comparable to the unspeakable carrion of those battlefields from which so many soldiers return to drink in all ladies' plaudits? And if the idea of peril so much enhances the popular conceit of the soldier's profession; let me assure ye that many a veteran who has freely marched up to a battery, would quickly recoil at the apparition of the sperm whale's vast tail, fanning into eddies the air over his head. For what are the comprehensible terrors of man compared with the interlinked terrors and wonders of God!

But, though the world scouts at us whale hunters, yet does it unwittingly pay us the profoundest homage; yea an all-abounding adoration! for almost all the tapers, lamps, and candles that burn round the globe, burn, as before so many shrines, to our glory!

But look at this matter in other lights; weigh it in all sorts of scales; see what we whalemen are, and have been.

Why did the Dutch in DeWitt's time have admirals of their whaling fleets? Why did Louis XVI of France, at his own personal expense, fit out whaling ships from Dunkirk, and politely invite to that town some score or two of families from our own island of Nantucket? Why did Britain between the years 1750 and 1788 pay to her whalemen in bounties upwards of £1,000,000? And lastly, how comes it that we whalemen of America now outnumber all the rest of the banded whalemen in the world; sail a navy of upwards of seven hundred vessels; manned by eighteen thousand men; yearly consuming 4,000,000 of dollars; the ship's worth, at the time of sailing, $20,000,000; and every year importing into our harbors a well reaped harvest of $7,000,000. How comes all this, if there be not something puissant in whaling?

But this is not the half; look again.

I freely assert, that the cosmopolite philosopher cannot, for his life, point out one single peaceful influence, which within the last sixty years has operated more potentially upon the whole broad world, taken in one aggregate, than the high and mighty business of whaling. One way and another, it has begotten events so remarkable in themselves, and so continuously momentous in their sequential issues, that whaling may well be regarded as that Egyptian mother, who bore offspring themselves pregnant from her womb. It would be a hopeless, endless task to catalogue all these things. Let a handful suffice. For many years past the whaleship has been the pioneer in ferreting out the remotest and least known parts of the earth. She has explored seas and archipelagoes which had no chart, where no Cook or Vancouver had ever sailed. If American and European men-of-war now peacefully ride in once savage harbors, let them fire salutes to the honor and the glory of the whale-ship, which originally showed them the way, and first interpreted between them and the savages. They may celebrate as they will the heroes of Exploring Expeditions, your Cookes, your Krusensterns; but I say that scores of anonymous Captains have sailed out of Nantucket, that were as great, and greater than your Cooke and your Krusenstern. For in their succorless empty-handedness, they, in the heathenish sharked waters, and by the beaches of unrecorded, javelin islands, battled with virgin wonders and terrors that Cooke with all his marines and muskets would not willingly have dared. All that is made such a flourish of in the old South Sea Voyages, those things were but the life-time commonplaces of our heroic Nantucketers. Often, adventures which Vancouver dedicates three chapters to, these men accounted unworthy of being set down in the ship's common log. Ah, the world! Oh, the world!

Until the whale fishery rounded Cape Horn, no commerce but colonial, scarcely any intercourse but colonial, was carried on between Europe and the long line of the opulent Spanish provinces on the Pacific coast. It was the whalemen who first broke through the jealous policy of the Spanish crown, touching those colonies; and, if space permitted, it might be distinctly shown how from those whalemen at last eventuated the liberation of Peru, Chili, and Bolivia from the yoke of Old Spain, and the establishment of the eternal democracy in those parts.

That great America on the other side of the sphere, Australia, was given to the enlightened world by the whalemen. After its first blunder-born discovery by a Dutchman, all other ships long shunned those shores as pestiferously barbarous; but the whale-ship touched there. The whale-ship is the true mother of that now mighty colony. Moreover, in the infancy of the first Australian settlement, the emigrants were several times saved from starvation by the benevolent biscuit of the whale-ship luckily dropping an anchor in their waters. The uncounted isles of all Polynesia confess the same truth, and do commercial homage to the whale-ship, that cleared the way for the missionary and the merchant, and in many cases carried the primitive missionaries to their first destinations. If that double-bolted land, Japan, is ever to become hospitable, it is the whale-ship alone to whom the credit will be due; for already she is on the threshold.

But if, in the face of all this, you still declare that whaling has no aesthetically noble associations connected with it, then am I ready to shiver fifty lances with you there, and unhorse you with a split helmet every time.

The whale has no famous author, and whaling no famous chronicler, you will say.

The whale no famous author, and whaling no famous chronicler? Who wrote the first account of our Leviathan? Who but mighty Job! And who composed the first narrative of a whaling voyage? Who, but no less a prince than Alfred the Great, who, with his own royal pen, took down the words from Other, the Norwegian whale-hunter of those times! And who pronounced our glowing eulogy in Parliament? Who, but Edmund Burke!

True enough, but then whalemen themselves are poor devils; they have no good blood in their veins.

No good blood in their veins? They have something better than royal blood there. The grandmother of Benjamin Franklin was Mary Morrel; afterwards, by marriage, Mary Folger, one of the old settlers of Nantucket, and the ancestress to a long line of Folgers and harpooneers—all kith and kin to noble Benjamin— this day darting the barbed iron from one side of the world to the other.

Good again; but then all confess that somehow whaling is not respectable.

Whaling not respectable? Whaling is imperial! By old English statutory law, the whale is declared 'a royal fish.' *

Oh, that's only nominal! The whale himself has never figured in any grand imposing way.

The whale never figured in any grand imposing way? In one of the mighty triumphs given to a Roman general upon his entering the world's capital, the bones of a whale, brought all the way from the Syrian coast, were the most conspicuous object in the cymballed procession.*

Grant it, since you cite it; but, say what you will, there is no real dignity in whaling.

No dignity in whaling? The dignity of our calling the very heavens attest. Cetus is a constellation in the South! No more! Drive down your hat in presence of the Czar, and take it off to Queequeg! No more! I know a man that, in his lifetime, has taken three hundred and fifty whales. I account that man more honorable than that great captain of antiquity who boasted of taking as many walled towns.

And, as for me, if, by any possibility, there be any as yet undiscovered prime thing in me; if I shall ever deserve any real repute in that small but high hushed world which I might not be unreasonably ambitious of; if hereafter I shall do anything that, upon the whole, a man might rather have done than to have left undone; if, at my death, my executors, or more properly my creditors, find any precious MSS. in my desk, then here I prospectively ascribe all the honor and the glory to whaling; for a whale-ship was my Yale College and my Harvard.

---

* See subsequent chapters for something more on this head.

25
POSTSCRIPT

IN behalf of the dignity of whaling, I would fain advance naught but substantiated facts. But after embattling his facts, an advocate who should wholly suppress a not unreasonable surmise, which might tell eloquently upon his cause—such an advocate, would he not be blameworthy?

It is well known that at the coronation of kings and queens, even modern ones, a certain curious process of seasoning them for their functions is gone through. There is a saltcellar of state, so called, and there may be a caster of state. How they use the salt, precisely—who knows? Certain I am, however, that a king's head is solemnly oiled at his coronation, even as a head of salad. Can it be, though, that they anoint it with a view of making its interior run well, as they anoint machinery? Much might be ruminated here, concerning the essential dignity of this regal process, because in common life we esteem but meanly and contemptibly a fellow who anoints his hair, and palpably smells of that anointing. In truth, a mature man who uses hair-oil, unless medicinally, that man has probably got a quoggy spot in him somewhere. As a general rule, he can't amount to much in his totality.

But the only thing to be considered here, is this—what kind of oil is used at coronations? Certainly it cannot be olive oil, nor macassar oil, nor castor oil, nor bear's oil, nor train oil, nor cod-liver oil. What then can it possibly be, but sperm oil in its unmanufactured, unpolluted state, the sweetest of all oils?

Think of that, ye loyal Britons! we whalemen supply your kings and queens with coronation stuff!

26
KNIGHTS AND SQUIRES

THE chief mate of the Pequod was Starbuck, a native of Nantucket, and a Quaker by descent. He was a long, earnest man, and though born on an icy coast, seemed well adapted to endure hot latitudes, his flesh being hard as twice-baked biscuit. Transported to the Indies, his live blood would not spoil like bottled ale. He must have been born in some time of general drought and famine, or upon one of those fast days for which his state is famous. Only some thirty arid summers had he seen; those summers had dried up all his physical superfluousness. But this, his thinness, so to speak, seemed no more the token of wasting anxieties and cares, than it seemed the indication of any bodily blight. It was merely the condensation of the man. He was by no means ill-looking; quite the contrary. His pure tight skin was an excellent fit; and closely wrapped up in it, and embalmed with inner health and strength, like a revivified Egyptian, this Starbuck seemed prepared to endure for long ages to come, and to endure always, as now; for be it Polar snow or torrid sun, like a patent chronometer, his interior vitality was warranted to do well in all climates. Looking into his eyes, you seemed to see there the yet lingering images of those thousand-fold perils he had calmly confronted through life. A staid, steadfast man, whose life for the most part was a telling pantomime of action, and not a tame chapter of sounds. Yet, for all his hardy sobriety and fortitude, there were certain qualities in him which at times affected, and in some cases seemed well nigh to overbalance all the rest. Uncommonly conscientious for a seaman, and endued with a deep natural reverence, the wild watery loneliness of his life did therefore strongly incline him to superstition; but to that sort of superstition, which in some organizations seems rather to spring, somehow, from intelligence than from ignorance. Outward portents and inward presentiments were his. And if at times these things bent the welded iron of his soul, much more did his far-away domestic memories of his young Cape wife and child, tend to bend him still more from the original ruggedness of his nature, and open him still further to those latent influences which, in some honest-hearted men, restrain the gush of dare-devil daring, so often evinced by others in the more perilous vicissitudes of the fishery. 'I will have no man in my boat,' said Starbuck, 'who is not afraid of a whale.' By this, he seemed to mean, not only that the most reliable and useful courage was that which arises from the fair estimation of the encountered peril, but that an utterly fearless man is a far more dangerous comrade than a coward.

'Aye, aye,' said Stubb, the second mate, 'Starbuck, there, is as careful a man as you'll find anywhere in this fishery.' But we shall ere long see what that word 'careful' precisely means when used by a man like Stubb, or almost any other whale hunter.

Starbuck was no crusader after perils; in him courage was not a sentiment; but a thing simply useful to him, and always at hand upon all mortally practical occasions. Besides, he thought, perhaps, that in this business of whaling, courage was one of the great staple outfits of the ship, like her beef and her bread, and not to be foolishly wasted. Wherefore he had no fancy for lowering for whales after sun-down; nor for persisting in fighting a fish that too much persisted in fighting him. For, thought Starbuck, I am here in this critical ocean to kill whales for my living, and not to be killed by them for theirs; and that hundreds of men had been so killed Starbuck well knew. What doom was his own father's? Where, in the bottomless deeps, could he find the torn limbs of his brother?

With memories like these in him, and, moreover, given to a certain superstitiousness, as has been said; the courage of this Starbuck which could, nevertheless, still flourish, must indeed have been extreme. But it was not in reasonable nature that a man so organized, and with such terrible experiences and remembrances as he had; it was not in nature that these things should fail in latently engendering an element in him, which, under suitable circumstances, would break out from its confinement, and burn all his courage up. And brave as he might be, it was that sort of bravery chiefly, visible in some intrepid men, which, while generally abiding firm in the conflict with seas, or winds, or whales, or any of the ordinary irrational horrors of the world, yet cannot withstand those more terrific, because more spiritual terrors, which sometimes menace you from the concentrating brow of an enraged and mighty man.

But were the coming narrative to reveal, in any instance, the complete abasement of poor Starbuck's fortitude, scarce might I have the heart to write it; for it is a thing most sorrowful, nay shocking, to expose the fall of valor in the soul. Men may seem detestable as joint stock-companies and nations; knaves, fools, and murderers there may be; men may have mean and meagre faces; but man, in the ideal, is so noble and so sparkling, such a grand and glowing creature, that over any ignominious blemish in him all his fellows should run to throw their costliest robes. That immaculate manliness we feel within ourselves, so far within us, that it remains intact though all the outer character seem gone; bleeds with keenest anguish at the undraped spectacle of a valor-ruined man. Nor can piety itself, at such a shameful sight, completely stifle her upbraidings against the permitting stars. But this august dignity I treat of, is not the dignity of kings and robes, but that abounding dignity which has no robed investiture. Thou shalt see it shining in the arm that wields a pick or drives a spike; that democratic dignity which, on all hands, radiates without end from God; Himself! The great God absolute! The centre and circumference of all democracy! His omnipresence, our divine equality!

If, then, to meanest mariners, and renegades and castaways, I shall hereafter ascribe high qualities, though dark; weave round them tragic graces; if even the most mournful, perchance the most abased, among them all, shall at times lift himself to the exalted mounts; if I shall touch that workman's arm with some ethereal light; if I shall spread a rainbow over his disastrous set of sun; then against all mortal critics bear me out in it, thou just Spirit of Equality, which hast spread one royal mantle of humanity over all my kind! Bear me out in it, thou great democratic God! who didst not refuse to the swart convict, Bunyan, the pale, poetic pearl; Thou who didst clothe with doubly hammered leaves of finest gold, the stumped and paupered arm of old Cervantes; Thou who didst pick up Andrew Jackson from the pebbles; who didst hurl him upon a war-horse; who didst thunder him higher than a throne! Thou who, in all Thy mighty, earthly marchings, ever cullest Thy selectest champions from the kingly commons; bear me out in it, O God!

27

KNIGHTS AND SQUIRES

STUBB was the second mate. He was a native of Cape Cod; and hence, according to local usage, was called a Cape-Codman. A happy-go-lucky; neither craven nor valiant; taking perils as they came with an indifferent air; and while engaged in the most imminent crisis of the chase, toiling away, calm and collected as a journeyman joiner engaged for the year. Good-humored, easy, and careless, he presided over his whale-boat as if the most deadly encounter were but a dinner, and his crew all invited guests. He was as particular about the comfortable arrangement of his part of the boat, as an old stage-driver is about the snugness of his box. When close to the whale, in the very death-lock of the fight, he handled his unpitying lance coolly and off-handedly, as a whistling tinker his hammer. He would hum over his old rigadig tunes while flank and flank with the most exasperated monster. Long usage had, for this Stubb, converted the jaws of death into an easy chair. What he thought of death itself, there is no telling. Whether he ever thought of it at all, might be a question; but, if he ever did chance to cast his mind that way after a comfortable dinner, no doubt, like a good sailor, he took it to be a sort of call of the watch to tumble aloft, and bestir themselves there, about something which he would find out when he obeyed the order, and not sooner.

What, perhaps, with other things, made Stubb such an easy-going, unfearing man, so cheerily trudging off with the burden of life in a world full of grave peddlers, all bowed to the ground with their packs; what helped to bring about that almost impious good-humor of his; that thing must have been his pipe. For, like his nose, his short, black little pipe was one of the regular features of his face. You would almost as soon have expected him to turn out of his bunk without his nose as without his pipe. He kept a whole row of pipes there ready loaded, stuck in a rack, within easy reach of his hand; and, whenever he turned in, he smoked them all out in succession, lighting one from the other to the end of the chapter; then loading them again to be in readiness anew. For, when Stubb dressed, instead of first putting his legs into his trowsers, he put his pipe into his mouth.

I say this continual smoking must have been one cause, at least, of his peculiar disposition; for every one knows that this earthly air, whether ashore or afloat, is terribly infected with the nameless miseries of the numberless mortals who have died exhaling it; and as in time of the cholera, some people go about with a camphorated handkerchief to their mouths; so, likewise, against all mortal tribulations, Stubb's tobacco smoke might have operated as a sort of disinfecting agent.

The third mate was Flask, a native of Tisbury, in Martha's Vineyard. A short, stout, ruddy young fellow, very pugnacious concerning whales, who somehow seemed to think that the great Leviathans had personally and hereditarily affronted him; and therefore it was a sort of point of honor with him, to destroy them whenever encountered. So utterly lost was he to all sense of reverence for the many marvels of their majestic bulk and mystic ways; and so dead to anything like an apprehension of any possible danger from encountering them; that in his poor opinion, the wondrous whale was but a species of magnified mouse, or at least water-rat, requiring only a little circumvention and some small application of time and trouble in order to kill and boil. This ignorant, unconscious fearlessness of his made him a little waggish in the matter of whales; he followed these fish for the fun of it; and a three years' voyage round Cape Horn was only a jolly joke that lasted that length of time. As a carpenter's nails are divided into wrought nails and cut nails; so mankind may be similarly divided. Little Flask was one of the wrought ones; made to clinch tight and last long. They called him King-Post on board of the Pequod; because, in form, he could be well likened to the short, square timber known by that name in Arctic whalers; and which by the means of many radiating side timbers inserted into it, serves to brace the ship against the icy concussions of those battering seas.

Now these three mates—Starbuck, Stubb, and Flask, were momentous men. They it was who by universal prescription commanded three of the Pequod's boats as headsmen. In that grand order of battle in which Captain Ahab would probably marshal his forces to descend on the whales, these three headsmen were as captains of companies. Or, being armed with their long keen whaling spears, they were as a picked trio of lancers; even as the harpooneers were flingers of javelins.

And since in this famous fishery, each mate or headsman, like a Gothic Knight of old, is always accompanied by his boat-steerer or harpooneer, who in certain conjunctures provides him with a fresh lance, when the former one has been badly twisted, or elbowed in the assault; and moreover, as there generally subsists between the two, a close intimacy and friendliness; it is therefore but meet, that in this place we set down who the Pequod's harpooneers were, and to what headsman each of them belonged.

First of all was Queequeg, whom Starbuck, the chief mate, had selected for his squire. But Queequeg is already known.

Next was Tashtego, an unmixed Indian from Gay Head, the most westerly promontory of Martha's Vineyard, where there still exists the last remnant of a village of red men, which has long supplied the neighboring island of Nantucket with many of her most daring harpooneers. In the fishery, they usually go by the generic name of Gay-Headers. Tashtego's long, lean, sable hair, his high cheek bones, and black rounding eyes—for an Indian, Oriental in their largeness, but Antarctic in their glittering expression—all this sufficiently proclaimed him an inheritor of the unvitiated blood of those proud warrior hunters, who, in quest of the great New England moose, had scoured, bow in hand, the aboriginal forests of the main. But no longer snuffing in the trail of the wild beasts of the woodland, Tashtego now hunted in the wake of the great whales of the sea; the unerring harpoon of the son fitly replacing the infallible arrow of the sires. To look at the tawny brawn of his lithe snaky limbs, you would almost have credited the superstitions of some of the earlier Puritans, and half believed this wild Indian to be a son of the Prince of the Powers of the Air. Tashtego was Stubb the second mate's squire.

Third among the harpooneers was Daggoo, a gigantic, coal-black negro-savage, with a lion-like tread—an Ahasuerus to behold. Suspended from his ears were two golden hoops, so large that the sailors called them ring-bolts, and would talk of securing the top-sail halyards to them. In his youth Daggoo had voluntarily shipped on board of a whaler, lying in a lonely bay on his native coast. And never having been anywhere in the world but in Africa, Nantucket, and the pagan harbors most frequented by whalemen; and having now led for many years the bold life of the fishery in the ships of owners uncommonly heedful of what manner of men they shipped; Daggoo retained all his barbaric virtues, and erect as a giraffe, moved about the decks in all the pomp of six feet five in his socks. There was a corporeal humility in looking up at him; and a white man standing before him seemed a white flag come to beg truce of a fortress. Curious to tell, this imperial negro, Ahasuerus Daggoo, was the Squire of little Flask, who looked like a chess-man beside him. As for the residue of the Pequod's company, be it said, that at the present day not one in two of the many thousand men before the mast employed in the American whale fishery, are Americans born, though pretty nearly all the officers are. Herein it is the same with the American whale fishery as with the American army and military and merchant navies, and the engineering forces employed in the construction of the American Canals and Railroads. The same, I say, because in all these cases the native American liberally provides the brains, the rest of the world as generously supplying the muscles. No small number of these whaling seamen belong to the Azores, where the outward bound Nantucket whalers frequently touch to augment their crews from the hardy peasants of those rocky shores. In like manner, the Greenland whalers sailing out of Hull or London, put in at the Shetland Islands, to receive the full complement of their crew. Upon the passage homewards, they drop them there again. How it is, there is no telling, but Islanders seem to make the best whalemen. They were nearly all Islanders in the Pequod, _Isolatoes_ too, I call such, not acknowledging the common continent of men, but each _Isolato_ living on a separate continent of his own. Yet now, federated along one keel, what a set these Isolatoes were! An Anacharsis Clootz deputation from all the isles of the sea, and all the ends of the earth, accompanying Old Ahab in the Pequod to lay the world's grievances before that bar from which not very many of them ever come back. Black Little Pip—he never did—oh, no! he went before. Poor Alabama boy! On the grim Pequod's forecastle, ye shall ere long see him, beating his tambourine; prelusive of the eternal time, when sent for, to the great quarter-deck on high, he was bid strike in with angels, and beat his tambourine in glory; called a coward here, hailed a hero there!

28
AHAB

FOR several days after leaving Nantucket, nothing above hatches was seen of Captain Ahab. The mates regularly relieved each other at the watches, and for aught that could be seen to the contrary, they seemed to be the only commanders of the ship; only they sometimes issued from the cabin with orders so sudden and peremptory, that after all it was plain they but commanded vicariously. Yes, their supreme lord and dictator was there, though hitherto unseen by any eyes not permitted to penetrate into the now sacred retreat of the cabin.

Every time I ascended to the deck from my watches below, I instantly gazed aft to mark if any strange face were visible; for my first vague disquietude touching the unknown captain, now in the seclusion of the sea, became almost a perturbation. This was strangely heightened at times by the ragged Elijah's diabolical incoherences uninvitedly recurring to me, with a subtle energy I could not have before conceived of. But poorly could I withstand them, much as in other moods I was almost ready to smile at the solemn whimsicalities of that outlandish prophet of the wharves. But whatever it was of apprehensiveness or uneasiness—to call it so—which I felt, yet whenever I came to look about me in the ship, it seemed against all warranty to cherish such emotions. For though the harpooneers, with the great body of the crew, were a far more barbaric, heathenish, and motley set than any of the tame merchant-ship companies which my previous experiences had made me acquainted with, still I ascribed this—and rightly ascribed it—to the fierce uniqueness of the very nature of that wild Scandinavian vocation in which I had so abandonedly embarked. But it was especially the aspect of the three chief officers of the ship, the mates, which was most forcibly calculated to allay these colorless misgivings, and induce confidence and cheerfulness in every presentment of the voyage. Three better, more likely sea-officers and men, each in his own different way, could not readily be found, and they were every one of them Americans; a Nantucketer, a Vineyarder, a Cape man. Now, it being Christmas when the ship shot from out her harbor, for a space we had biting Polar weather, though all the time running away from it to the southward; and by every degree and minute of latitude which we sailed, gradually leaving that merciless winter, and all its intolerable weather behind us. It was one of those less lowering, but still grey and gloomy enough mornings of the transition, when with a fair wind the ship was rushing through the water with a vindictive sort of leaping and melancholy rapidity, that as I mounted to the deck at the call of the forenoon watch, so soon as I levelled my glance towards the taffrail, foreboding shivers ran over me. Reality outran apprehension; Captain Ahab stood upon his quarterdeck.

There seemed no sign of common bodily illness about him, nor of the recovery from any. He looked like a man cut away from the stake, when the fire has overrunningly wasted all the limbs without consuming them, or taking away one particle from their compacted aged robustness. His whole high, broad form, seemed made of solid bronze, and shaped in an unalterable mould, like Cellini's cast Perseus. Threading its way out from among his grey hairs, and continuing right down one side of his tawny scorched face and neck, till it disappeared in his clothing, you saw a slender rod-like mark, lividly whitish. It resembled that perpendicular seam sometimes made in the straight, lofty trunk of a great tree, when the upper lightning tearingly darts down it, and without wrenching a single twig, peels and grooves out the bark from top to bottom, ere running off into the soil, leaving the tree still greenly alive, but branded. Whether that mark was born with him, or whether it was the scar left by some desperate wound, no one could certainly say. By some tacit consent, throughout the voyage little or no allusion was made to it, especially by the mates. But once Tashtego's senior, an old Gay-Head Indian among the crew, superstitiously asserted that not till he was full forty years old did Ahab become that way branded, and then it came upon him, not in the fury of any mortal fray, but in an elemental strife at sea. Yet, this wild hint seemed inferentially negatived, by what a grey

Manxman insinuated, an old sepulchral man, who, having never
before sailed out of Nantucket, had never ere this laid eye upon
wild Ahab. Nevertheless, the old sea-traditions, the immemorial
credulities, popularly invested this old Manxman with preternatural
powers of discernment. So that no white sailor seriously contra-
dicted him when he said that if ever Captain Ahab should be
tranquilly laid out—which might hardly come to pass, so he
muttered—then, whoever should do that last office for the dead,
would find a birth-mark on him from crown to sole.

So powerfully did the whole grim aspect of Ahab affect me,
and the livid brand which streaked it, that for the first few moments
I hardly noted that not a little of this overbearing grimness was
owing to the barbaric white leg upon which he partly stood. It
had previously come to me that this ivory leg had at sea been
fashioned from the polished bone of the sperm whale's jaw. 'Aye,
he was dismasted off Japan,' said the old Gay-Head Indian once;
'but like his dismasted craft, he shipped another mast without
coming home for it. He has a quiver of 'em.'

I was struck with the singular posture he maintained. Upon
each side of the Pequod's quarter deck, and pretty close to the
mizen shrouds, there was an auger hole, bored about half an inch
or so, into the plank. His bone leg steadied in that hole; one arm
elevated, and holding by a shroud; Captain Ahab stood erect,
looking straight out beyond the ship's ever-pitching prow. There
was an infinity of firmest fortitude, a determinate, unsurrenderable
wilfulness, in the fixed and fearless, forward dedication of that
glance. Not a word he spoke; nor did his officers say aught to
him; though by all their minutest gestures and expressions, they
plainly showed the uneasy, if not painful, consciousness of being
under a troubled master-eye. And not only that, but moody stricken
Ahab stood before them with a crucifixion in his face; in all the
nameless regal overbearing dignity of some mighty woe.

Ere long, from his first visit in the air, he withdrew into his
cabin. But after that morning, he was every day visible to the
crew; either standing in his pivot-hole, or seated upon an ivory
stool he had; or heavily walking the deck. As the sky grew less
gloomy; indeed, began to grow a little genial, he became still less
and less a recluse; as if, when the ship had sailed from home,
nothing but the dead wintry bleakness of the sea had then kept
him so secluded. And, by and by, it came to pass, that he was
almost continually in the air; but, as yet, for all that he said, or
perceptibly did, on the at last sunny deck, he seemed as unnecessary
there as another mast. But the Pequod was only making a passage

now; not regularly cruising; nearly all whaling preparatives needing supervision the mates were fully competent to, so that there was little or nothing, out of himself, to employ or excite Ahab, now; and thus chase away, for that one interval, the clouds that layer upon layer were piled upon his brow, as ever all clouds choose the loftiest peaks to pile themselves upon.

Nevertheless, ere long, the warm, warbling persuasiveness of the pleasant, holiday weather we came to, seemed gradually to charm him from his mood. For, as when the red-cheeked, dancing girls, April and May, trip home to the wintry, misanthropic woods; even the barest, ruggedest, most thunder-cloven old oak will at least send forth some few green sprouts, to welcome such glad-hearted visitants; so Ahab did, in the end, a little respond to the playful allurings of that girlish air. More than once did he put forth the faint blossom of a look, which, in any other man, would have soon flowered out in a smile.

29
ENTER AHAB; TO HIM, STUBB

SOME days elapsed, and ice and icebergs all astern, the Pequod now went rolling through the bright Quito spring, which, at sea, almost perpetually reigns on the threshold of the eternal August of the Tropic. The warmly cool, clear, ringing, perfumed, over-flowing, redundant days, were as crystal goblets of Persian sherbet, heaped up—flaked up, with rose-water snow. The starred and stately nights seemed haughty dames in jewelled velvets, nursing at home in lonely pride, the memory of their absent conquering Earls, the golden helmeted suns! For sleeping man, 'twas hard to choose between such winsome days and such seducing nights. But all the witcheries of that unwaning weather did not merely lend new spells and potencies to the outward world. Inward they turned upon the soul, especially when the still mild hours of eve came on; then, memory shot her crystals as the clear ice most forms of noiseless twilights. And all these subtle agencies, more and more they wrought on Ahab's texture.

Old age is always wakeful; as if, the longer linked with life, the less man has to do with aught that looks like death. Among sea-commanders, the old greybeards will oftenest leave their berths to visit the night-cloaked deck. It was so with Ahab; only that now, of late, he seemed so much to live in the open air, that truly speaking, his visits were more to the cabin, than from the cabin to the planks. 'It feels like going down into one's tomb,'—he would mutter to himself,—'for an old captain like me to be descending this narrow scuttle, to go to my grave-dug berth.'

So, almost every twenty-four hours, when the watches of the night were set, and the band on deck sentinelled the slumbers of the band below; and when if a rope was to be hauled upon the forecastle, the sailors flung it not rudely down, as by day, but with some cautiousness dropt it to its place, for fear of disturbing their slumbering shipmates; when this sort of steady quietude would begin to prevail, habitually, the silent steersman would watch the cabinscuttle; and ere long the old man would emerge, gripping at the iron banister, to help his crippled way. Some considerating touch of humanity was in him; for at times like these, he usually abstained from patrolling the quarter-deck; because to his wearied mates, seeking repose within six inches of his ivory heel, such would have been the reverberating crack and din of that bony step, that their dreams would have been of the crunching teeth of sharks. But once, the mood was on him too deep for common regardings; and as with heavy, lumber-like pace he was measuring the ship from taffrail to mainmast, Stubb, the odd second mate, came up from below, and with a certain unassured, deprecating humorousness, hinted that if Captain Ahab was pleased to walk the planks, then, no one could say nay; but there might be some way of muffling the noise; hinting something indistinctly and hesitatingly about a globe of tow, and the insertion into it, of the ivory heel. Ah! Stubb, thou did'st not know Ahab then.

'Am I a cannon-ball, Stubb,' said Ahab, 'that thou wouldst wad me that fashion? But go thy ways; I had forgot. Below to thy nighty grave; where such as ye sleep between shrouds, to use ye to the filling one at last.—Down, dog, and kennel!'

Starting at the unforeseen concluding exclamation of the so suddenly scornful old man, Stubb was speechless a moment; then said excitedly, 'I am not used to be spoken to that way, sir; I do but less than half like it, sir.'

'Avast!' gritted Ahab between his set teeth, and violently moving away, as if to avoid some passionate temptation.

'No, sir; not yet,' said Stubb, emboldened, 'I will not tamely be called a dog, sir.'

'Then be called ten times a donkey, and a mule, and an ass, and begone, or I'll clear the world of thee!'

As he said this, Ahab advanced upon him with such overbearing terrors in his aspect, that Stubb involuntarily retreated.

'I was never served so before without giving a hard blow for it,' muttered Stubb, as he found himself descending the cabin-scuttle. 'It's very queer. Stop, Stubb; somehow, now, I don't well know whether to go back and strike him, or—what's that?—down here on my knees and pray for him? Yes, that was the thought coming up in me; but it would be the first time I ever *did* pray. It's queer; very queer; and he's queer too; aye, take him fore and aft, he's about the queerest old man Stubb ever sailed with. How he flashed at me!—his eyes like powder-pans! is he mad? Anyway there's something on his mind, as sure as there must be something on a deck when it cracks. He aint in his bed now, either, more than three hours out of the twenty-four; and he don't sleep then. Didn't that Dough-Boy, the steward, tell me that of a morning he always finds the old man's hammock clothes all rumpled and tumbled, and the sheets down at the foot, and the coverlid almost tied into knots, and the pillow a sort of frightful hot, as though a baked brick had been on it? A hot old man! I guess he's got what some folks ashore call a conscience; it's a kind of Tic-Dolly-row they say—worse nor a toothache. Well, well; I don't know what it is, but the Lord keep me from catching it. He's full of riddles; I wonder what he goes into the after hold for, every night, as Dough-Boy tells me he suspects; what's that for, I should like to know? Who's made appointments with him in the hold? Ain't that queer, now? But there's no telling, it's the old game—Here goes for a snooze. Damn me, it's worth a fellow's while to be born into the world, if only to fall right asleep. And now that I think of it, that's about the first thing babies do, and that's a sort of queer, too. Damn me, but all things are queer, come to think of 'em. But that's against my principles. Think not, is my eleventh commandment; and sleep when you can, is my twelfth—So here goes again. But how's that? didn't he call me a dog? blazes! he called me ten times a donkey, and piled a lot of jackasses on top of *that!* He might as well have kicked me, and done with it. Maybe he *did* kick me, and I didn't observe it, I was so taken all aback with his brow, somehow. It flashed like a bleached bone. What the devil's the matter with me? I don't stand right on my legs. Coming afoul of that old man has a sort of turned me wrong side out. By the Lord, I must have been dreaming, though—How? how? how?—but the only way's to stash it; so here goes to hammock again; and in the morning, I'll see how this plaguey juggling thinks over by day-light.'

30
THE PIPE

WHEN Stubb had departed, Ahab stood for a while leaning over the bulwarks; and then, as had been usual with him of late, calling a sailor of the watch, he sent him below for his ivory stool, and also his pipe. Lighting the pipe at the binnacle lamp and planting the stool on the weather side of the deck, he sat and smoked.

In old Norse times, the thrones of the sea-loving Danish kings were fabricated, saith tradition, of the tusks of the narwhale. How could one look at Ahab then, seated on that tripod of bones, without bethinking him of the royalty it symbolized? For a Khan of the plank, and a king of the sea, and a great lord of Leviathans was Ahab.

Some moments passed, during which the thick vapor came from his mouth in quick and constant puffs, which blew back again into his face. 'How now,' he soliloquized at last, withdrawing the tube, 'this smoking no longer soothes. Oh, my pipe! hard must it go with me if thy charm be gone! Here have I been unconsciously toiling, not pleasuring,—aye, and ignorantly smoking to windward all the while; to windward, and with such nervous whiffs, as if, like the dying whale, my final jets were the strongest and fullest of trouble. What business have I with this pipe? This thing that is meant for sereneness, to send up mild white vapors among mild white hairs, not among torn iron-grey locks like mine. I'll smoke no more—'

He tossed the still lighted pipe into the sea. The fire hissed in the waves; the same instant the ship shot by the bubble the sinking pipe made. With slouched hat, Ahab lurchingly paced the planks.

31
QUEEN MAB

NEXT morning Stubb accosted Flask.

'Such a queer dream, King-Post, I never had. You know the old man's ivory leg, well I dreamed he kicked me with it; and

when I tried to kick back, upon my soul, my little man, I kicked
my leg right off! And then, presto! Ahab seemed a pyramid, and
I, like a blazing fool, kept kicking at it. But what was still more
curious, Flask—you know how curious all dreams are—through
all this rage that I was in, I somehow seemed to be thinking to
myself, that after all, it was not much of an insult, that kick from
Ahab. "Why," thinks I, "what's the row! It's not a real leg, only
a false leg." And there's a mighty difference between a living
thump and a dead thump. That's what makes a blow from the
hand, Flask, fifty times more savage to bear than a blow from a
cane. The living member—that makes the living insult, my little
man. And thinks I to myself all the while, mind, while I was
stubbing my silly toes against that cursed pryamid—so confound-
edly contradictory was it all, all the while, I say, I was thinking
to myself, "what's his leg now, but a cane—a whalebone cane.
Yes," thinks I, "it was only a playful cudgelling—in fact, only a
whaleboning that he gave me—not a base kick. Besides," thinks
I, "look at it once; why, the end of it—the foot part—what a
small sort of end it is; whereas, if a broad footed farmer kicked
me, *there's* a devilish broad insult. But this insult is whittled down
to a point only." But now comes the greatest joke of the dream,
Flask. While I was battering away at the pyramid, a sort of badger-
haired old merman, with a hump on his back, takes me by the
shoulders, and slews me round. "What are you 'bout?" says he.
'Slid! man, but I was frightened. Such a phiz! But, somehow, next
moment I was over the fright. "What am I about?" says I at last.
"And what business is that of yours, I should like to know, Mr
Humpback? Do *you* want a kick?" By the lord, Flask, I had no
sooner said that, than he turned round his stern to me, bent over,
and dragging up a lot of seaweed he had for a clout—what do
you think, I saw?—why thunder alive, man, his stern was stuck
full of marlinspikes, with the points out. Says I, on second thoughts,
"I guess I won't kick you, old fellow." "Wise Stubb," said he,
"wise Stubb;" and kept muttering it all the time, a sort of eating
of his own gums like a chimney hag. Seeing he wasn't going to
stop saying over his "wise Stubb, wise Stubb," I thought I might
as well fall to kicking the pyramid again. But I had only just
lifted my foot for it, when he roared out, "Stop that kicking!"
"Halloa," says, I, "what's the matter now, old fellow?" "Look ye
here," says he; "let's argue the insult. Captain Ahab kicked ye,
didn't he?" "Yes, he did," says I—"right *here* it was." "Very
good," says he—"he used his ivory leg, didn't he?" "Yes, he did,"
says I. "Well then," says he, "wise Stubb, what have you to

complain of? Didn't he kick with right good will? it wasn't a common pitch pine leg he kicked with, was it? No, you were kicked by a great man, and with a beautiful ivory leg, Stubb. It's an honor; I consider it an honor. Listen, wise Stubb. In old England the greatest lords think it great glory to be slapped by a queen, and made garter-knights of; but, be *your* boast, Stubb, that ye were kicked by old Ahab, and made a wise man of. Remember what I say; *be* kicked by him; account his kicks honors; and on no account kick back; for you can't help yourself, wise Stubb. Don't you see that pyramid?" With that, he all of a sudden seemed somehow, in some queer fashion, to swim off into the air. I snored; rolled over; and there I was in my hammock! Now, what do you think of that dream, Flask?'

'I don't know; it seems a sort of foolish to me, tho'.'

'May be; may be. But it's made a wise man of me, Flask. D'ye see Ahab standing there, sideways looking over the stern? Well, the best thing you can do, Flask, is to let that old man alone; never speak quick to him, whatever he says. Halloa! what's that he shouts? Hark!'

'Mast-head, there! Look sharp, all of ye! There are whales hereabouts! If ye see a white one, split your lungs for him!'

'What d'ye think of that now, Flask? ain't there a small drop of something queer about that, eh? A white whale—did ye mark that, man? Look ye—there's something special in the wind. Stand by for it, Flask. Ahab has that that's bloody on his mind. But, mum; he comes this way.'

32

CETOLOGY

ALREADY we are boldly launched upon the deep; but soon we shall be lost in its unshored, harborless immensities. Ere that come to pass; ere the Pequod's weedy hull rolls side by side with the barnacled hulls of the leviathan; at the outset it is but well to attend to a matter almost indispensable to a thorough appreciative understanding of the more special leviathanic revelations and allusions of all sorts which are to follow.

It is some systematized exhibition of the whale in his broad genera, that I would now fain put before you. Yet is it no easy task. The classification of the constituents of a chaos, nothing less is here essayed. Listen to what the best and latest authorities have laid down.

'No branch of Zoology is so much involved as that which is entitled Cetology,' says Captain Scoresby, A.D. 1820.

'It is not my intention, were it in my power, to enter into the inquiry as to the true method of dividing the cetacea into groups and families. * * * Utter confusion exists among the historians of this animal' (sperm whale), says Surgeon Beale, A.D. 1839.

'Unfitness to pursue our research in the unfathomable waters.' 'Impenetrable veil covering our knowledge of the cetacea.' 'A field strewn with thorns.' 'All these incomplete indications but serve to torture us naturalists.'

Thus speak of the whale, the great Cuvier, and John Hunter, and Lesson, those lights of zoology and anatomy. Nevertheless, though of real knowledge there be little, yet of books there are a plenty; and so in some small degree, with cetology, or the science of whales. Many are the men, small and great, old and new, landsmen and seamen, who have at large or in little, written of the whale. Run over a few:—The Authors of the Bible; Aristotle; Pliny; Aldrovandi; Sir Thomas Browne; Gesner; Ray; Linnæus; Rondeletius; Willoughby; Green; Artedi; Sibbald; Brisson; Marten; Lacépède; Bonneterre; Desmarest; Baron Cuvier; Frederick Cuvier; John Hunter; Owen; Scoresby; Beale; Bennett; J. Ross Browne; the Author of Miriam Coffin; Olmstead; and the Rev. T. Cheever. But to what ultimate generalizing purpose all these have written, the above cited extracts will show.

Of the names in this list of whale authors, only those following Owen ever saw living whales; and but one of them was a real professional harpooneer and whaleman. I mean Captain Scoresby. On the separate subject of the Greenland or right-whale, he is the best existing authority. But Scoresby knew nothing and says nothing of the great sperm whale, compared with which the Greenland whale is almost unworthy mentioning. And here be it said, that the Greenland whale is an usurper upon the throne of the seas. He is not even by any means the largest of the whales. Yet, owing to the long priority of his claims, and the profound ignorance which, till some seventy years back, invested the then fabulous or utterly unknown sperm-whale, and which ignorance to this present day still reigns in all but some few scientific retreats and whale-ports; this usurpation has been every way complete. Reference to nearly all the leviathanic allusions in the great poets of past days, will satisfy you that the Greenland whale, without one rival, was to them the monarch of the seas. But the time has at last come for a new proclamation. This is Charing Cross; hear ye! good people all,—the Greenland whale is deposed,—the great sperm whale now reigneth!

There are only two books in being which at all pretend to put the living sperm whale before you, and at the same time, in the remotest degree succeed in the attempt. Those books are Beale's and Bennett's; both in their time surgeons to English South-Sea whale-ships, and both exact and reliable men. The original matter touching the sperm whale to be found in their volumes is necessarily small; but so far as it goes, it is of excellent quality, though mostly confined to scientific description. As yet, however, the sperm whale, scientific or poetic, lives not complete in any literature. Far above all other hunted whales, his is an unwritten life.

Now the various species of whales need some sort of popular comprehensive classification, if only an easy outline one for the present, hereafter to be filled in all its departments by subsequent laborers. As no better man advances to take this matter in hand, I hereupon offer my own poor endeavors. I promise nothing complete; because any human thing supposed to be complete, must for that very reason infallibly be faulty. I shall not pretend to a minute anatomical description of the various species, or—in this place at least—to much of any description. My object here is simply to project the draught of a systematization of cetology. I am the architect, not the builder.

But it is a ponderous task; no ordinary letter-sorter in the Post-office is equal to it. To grope down into the bottom of the sea after them; to have one's hands among the unspeakable foundations, ribs, and very pelvis of the world; this is a fearful thing. What am I that I should essay to hook the nose of this leviathan! The awful tauntings in Job might well appal me. 'Will he' (the leviathan) 'make a covenant with thee? Behold the hope of him is vain!' But I have swam through libraries and sailed through oceans; I have had to do with whales with these visible hands; I am in earnest; and I will try. There are some preliminaries to settle.

First: The uncertain, unsettled condition of this science of Cetology is in the very vestibule attested by the fact, that in some quarters it still remains a moot point whether a whale be a fish. In his System of Nature, A.D. 1776, Linnæus declares, 'I hereby separate the whales from the fish.' But of my own knowledge, I know that down to the year 1850, sharks and shad, alewives and herring, against Linnæus's express edict, were still found dividing the possession of the same seas with the Leviathan.

The grounds upon which Linnæus would fain have banished the whales from the waters, he states as follows: 'On account of their warm bilocular heart, their lungs, their movable eyelids, their hollow ears, penem intrantem feminam mammis lactantem,' and finally, 'ex lege naturae jure meritoque.' I submitted all this to my friends Simeon Macey and Charley Coffin, of Nantucket, both messmates of mine in a certain voyage, and they united in the opinion that the reasons set forth were altogether insufficient. Charley profanely hinted they were humbug.

Be it known that, waiving all argument, I take the good old fashioned ground that the whale is a fish, and call upon holy Jonah to back me. This fundamental thing settled, the next point is, in what internal respect does the whale differ from other fish. Above, Linnæus has given you those items. But in brief, they are these: lungs and warm blood; whereas, all other fish are lungless and cold blooded.

Next: how shall we define the whale, by his obvious externals, so as conspicuously to label him for all time to come? To be short, then, a whale is *a spouting fish with a horizontal tail*. There you have him. However contracted, that definition is the result of expanded meditation. A walrus spouts much like a whale, but the walrus is not a fish, because he is amphibious. But the last term of the definition is still more cogent, as coupled with the first. Almost any one must have noticed that all the fish fimiliar to landsmen have not a flat, but a vertical, or up-and-down tail. Whereas, among spouting fish the tail, though it may be similarly shaped, invariably assumes a horizontal position.

By the above definition of what a whale is, I do by no means exclude from the leviathanic brotherhood any sea creature hitherto identified with the whale by the best informed Nantucketers; nor, on the other hand, link with it any fish hitherto authoritatively regarded as alien.* Hence, all the smaller, spouting, and horizontal tailed fish must be included in this ground-plan of Cetology. Now, then, come the grand divisions of the entire whale host.

First: According to magnitude I divide the whales into three

---

* I am aware that down to the present time, the fish styled Lamatins and Dugongs (Pig-fish and Sow-fish of the Coffins of Nantucket) are included by many naturalists among the whales. But as these pig-fish are a nosy, contemptible set, mostly lurking in the mouths of rivers, and feeding on wet hay, and especially as they do not spout, I deny their credentials as whales; and have presented them with their passports to quit the Kingdom of Cetology.

primary BOOKS (subdivisible into CHAPTERS), and these shall comprehend them all, both small and large.

I. The FOLIO WHALE; II. the OCTAVO WHALE; III. the DUO-DECIMO WHALE.

As the type of the FOLIO I present the *Sperm Whale*; of the OCTAVO, the *Grampus*; of the DUODECIMO, the *Porpoise*.

FOLIOS. Among these I here include the following chapters:— I. The *Sperm Whale*; II. the *Right Whale*; III. the *Fin Back Whale*; IV. the *Hump-backed Whale*; V. the *Razor Back Whale*; VI. the *Sulphur Bottom Whale*.

BOOK I. (*Folio*), CHAPTER I. (*Sperm Whale*).—This whale, among the English of old vaguely known as the Trumpa whale, and the Physeter whale, and the Anvil Headed whale, is the present Cachalot of the French, and the Pottsfich of the Germans, and the Macrocephalus of the Long Words. He is, without doubt, the largest inhabitant of the globe; the most formidable of all whales to encounter; the most majestic in aspect; and lastly, by far the most valuable in commerce; he being the only creature from which that valuable substance, spermaceti, is obtained. All his peculiarities will, in many other places, be enlarged upon. It is chiefly with his name that I now have to do. Philologically considered, it is absurd. Some centuries ago, when the Sperm whale was almost wholly unknown in his own proper individuality, and when his oil was only accidentally obtained from the stranded fish; in those days spermaceti, it would seem, was popularly supposed to be derived from a creature identical with the one then known in England as the Greenland or Right Whale. It was the idea also, that this same spermaceti was that quickening humor of the Greenland Whale which the first syllable of the word literally expresses. In those times, also, spermaceti was exceedingly scarce, not being used for light, but only as an ointment and medicament. It was only to be had from the druggists as you nowadays buy an ounce of rhubarb. When, as I opine, in the course of time, the true nature of spermaceti became known, its original name was still retained by the dealers; no doubt to enhance its value by a notion so strangely significant of its scarcity. And so the appellation must at last have come to be bestowed upon the whale from which this spermaceti was really derived.

BOOK I. (*Folio*), CHAPTER II. (*Right Whale*).—In one respect this is the most venerable of the leviathans, being the one first regularly hunted by man. It yields the article commonly known as whalebone or baleen; and the oil specially known as 'whale oil', an inferior article in commerce. Among the fishermen, he is indiscriminately designated by all the following titles: The Whale; the Greenland Whale; the Black Whale; the Great Whale; the True Whale; the Right Whale. There is a deal of obscurity concerning the identity of the species thus multitudinously baptized. What then is the whale, which I include in the second species of my Folios? It is the Great Mysticetus of the English naturalists; the Greenland Whale of the English whalemen; the Baliene Ordinaire of the French whalemen; the Growlands Walfish of the Swedes. It is the whale which for more than two centuries past has been hunted by the Dutch and English in the Arctic seas; it is the whale which the American fishermen have long pursued in the Indian ocean, on the Brazil Banks, on the Nor' West Coast, and various other parts of the world, designated by them Right Whale Cruising Grounds.

Some pretend to see a difference between the Greenland whale of the English and the right whale of the Americans. But they precisely agree in all their grand features; nor has there yet been presented a single determinate fact upon which to ground a radical distinction. It is by endless subdivisions based upon the most inconclusive differences, that some departments of natural history become so repellingly intricate. The right whale will be elsewhere treated of at some length, with reference to elucidating the sperm whale.

BOOK I. (*Folio*), CHAPTER III. (*Fin-Back*).—Under this head I reckon a monster which, by the various names of Fin-Back, Tall-Spout, and Long-John, has been seen almost in every sea and is commonly the whale whose distant jet is so often descried by passengers crossing the Atlantic, in the New York packet-tracks. In the length he attains, and in his baleen, the Fin-back resembles the right whale, but is of a less portly girth, and a lighter color, approaching to olive. His great lips present a cable-like aspect, formed by the intertwisting, slanting folds of large wrinkles. His grand distinguishing feature, the fin, from which he derives his name, is often a conspicuous object. This fin is some three or four feet long, growing vertically from the hinder part of the back, of an angular shape, and with a very sharp pointed end. Even if not the slightest other part of the creature be visible, this isolated fin will, at times, be seen plainly projecting from the surface. When the sea is moderately calm, and slightly marked with spherical ripples, and this gnomon-like fin stands up and casts shadows upon the wrinkled surface, it may well be supposed that the watery circle surrounding it somewhat resembles a dial, with its style and wavy hour-lines graved on it. On that Ahaz-dial the shadow often goes back. The Fin-Back is not gregarious. He seems a whale-hater, as some men are man-haters. Very shy; always going solitary; unexpectedly rising to the surface in the remotest and most sullen waters; his straight and single lofty jet rising like a tall misanthropic spear upon a barren plain; gifted with such wondrous power and velocity in swimming, as to defy all present pursuit from man; this leviathan seems the banished and unconquerable Cain of his race, bearing for his mark that style upon his back. From having the baleen in his mouth, the Fin-Back is sometimes included with the right whale, among a theoretic species denominated *Whalebone whales*, that is, whales with baleen. Of these so called Whalebone whales, there would seem to be several varieties, most of which, however, are little known. Broad-nosed whales and beaked whales; pike-headed whales; bunched whales; under-jawed whales and ros-trated whales, are the fishermen's names for a few sorts.

In connexion with this appellative of 'Whalebone whales,' it is of great importance to mention, that however such a nomenclature may be convenient in facilitating allusions to some kind of whales, yet it is in vain to attempt a clear classification of the Leviathan, founded upon either his baleen, or hump, or fin, or teeth; not-withstanding that those marked parts or features very obviously seem better adapted to afford the basis for a regular system of Cetology than any other detached bodily distinctions, which the whale, in his kinds, presents. How then? The baleen, hump, back-fin, and teeth; these are things whose peculiarities are indiscrim-inately dispersed among all sorts of whales, without any regard to what may be the nature of their structure in other and more essential particulars. Thus, the sperm whale and the humpbacked whale, each has a hump; but there the similitude ceases. Then, this same humpbacked whale and the Greenland whale, each of these has baleen; but there again the similitude ceases. And it is just the same with the other parts above mentioned. In various sorts of whales, they form such irregular combinations; or, in the case of any one of them detached, such an irregular isolation; as utterly to defy all general methodization formed upon such a basis. On this rock every one of the whale-naturalists has split.

But it may possibly be conceived that, in the internal parts of the whale, in his anatomy—there, at least, we shall be able to hit the right classification. Nay; what thing, for example, is there in the Greenland whale's anatomy more striking than his baleen? Yet we have seen that by his baleen it is impossible correctly to classify the Greenland whale. And if you descend into the bowels of the various leviathans, why there you will not find distinctions a fiftieth part as available to the systematizer as those external ones already enumerated. What then remains? nothing but to take hold of the whales bodily, in their entire liberal volume, and boldly sort them that way. And this is the Bibliographical system here adopted; and it is the only one that can possibly succeed, for it alone is practicable. To proceed.

BOOK I. (*Folio*), CHAPTER IV. (*Hump Back*).—This whale is often seen on the northern American coast. He has been frequently captured there, and towed into harbor. He has a great pack on him like a peddler; or you might call him the Elephant and Castle whale. At any rate, the popular name for him does not sufficiently distinguish him, since the sperm whale also has a hump, though a smaller one. His oil is not very valuable. He has baleen. He is the most gamesome and light-hearted of all the whales, making more gay foam and white water generally than any other of them.

BOOK I. (*Folio*), CHAPTER V. (*Razor Back*).—Of this whale little is known but his name. I have seen him at a distance off Cape Horn. Of a retiring nature, he eludes both hunters and philosophers. Though no coward, he has never yet shown any part of him but his back, which rises in a long sharp ridge. Let him go. I know little more of him, nor does anybody else.

BOOK I. (*Folio*), CHAPTER VI. (*Sulphur Bottom*).—Another re-tiring gentleman, with a brimstone belly, doubtless got by scraping along the Tartarian tiles in some of his profounder divings. He is seldom seen; at least I have never seen him except in the remoter southern seas, and then always at too great a distance to study his countenance. He is never chased; he would run away with rope-walks of line. Prodigies are told of him. Adieu, Sulphur Bottom! I can say nothing more that is true of ye, nor can the oldest Nantucketer.

Thus ends BOOK I (*Folio*), and now begins BOOK II. (*Octavo*).

OCTAVOES.* These embrace the whales of middling magnitude, among which at present may be numbered:—I., the *Grampus*; II., the *Black Fish*; III., the *Narwhale*; IV., the *Thrasher*; V., the *Killer*.

BOOK II. (*Octavo*), CHAPTER I. (*Grampus*).—Though this fish, whose loud sonorous breathing, or rather blowing, has furnished a proverb to landsmen, is so well known a denizen of the deep,

---

* Why this book of whales is not denominated the Quarto is very plain. Because, while the whales of this order, though smaller than those of the former order, nevertheless retain a proportionate likeness to them in figure, yet the bookbinder's Quarto volume in its diminished form does not preserve the shape of the Folio volume, but the Octavo volume does.

yet is he not popularly classed among whales. But possessing all the grand distinctive features of the leviathan, most naturalists have recognised him for one. He is of moderate octavo size, varying from fifteen to twenty-five feet in length, and of corresponding dimensions round the waist. He swims in herds; he is never regularly hunted, though his oil is considerable in quantity, and pretty good for light. By some fishermen his approach is regarded as premonitory of the advance of the great sperm whale.

BOOK II. (*Octavo*). CHAPTER II. (*Black Fish*).—I give the popular fishermen's names for all these fish, for generally they are the best. Where any name happens to be vague or inexpressive, I shall say so, and suggest another. I do so now, touching the Black Fish, so called, because blackness is the rule among almost all whales. So, call him the Hyena Whale, if you please. His voracity is well known, and from the circumstance that the inner angles of his lips are curved upwards, he carries an everlasting Mephistophelean grin on his face. This whale averages some sixteen or eighteen feet in length. He is found in almost all latitudes. He has a peculiar way of showing his dorsal hooked fin in swimming, which looks something like a Roman nose. When not more profitably employed, the sperm whale hunters sometimes capture the Hyena whale, to keep up the supply of cheap oil for domestic employment—as some frugal housekeepers, in the absence of company, and quite alone by themselves, burn unsavory tallow instead of odorous wax. Though their blubber is very thin, some of these whales will yield you upwards of thirty gallons of oil.

BOOK II. (*Octavo*), CHAPTER III. (*Narwhale*), that is, *Nostril whale*.—Another instance of a curiously named whale, so named I suppose from his peculiar horn being originally mistaken for a peaked nose. The creature is some sixteen feet in length, while its horn averages five feet, though some exceed ten, and even attain to fifteen feet. Strictly speaking, this horn is but a lengthened tusk, growing out from the jaw in a line a little depressed from the horizontal. But it is only found on the sinister side, which has an ill effect, giving its owner something analogous to the aspect of a clumsy left-handed man. What precise purpose this ivory horn or lance answers, it would be hard to say. It does not seem to be used like the blade of the sword-fish and bill-fish; though some sailors tell me that the Narwhale employs it for a rake in turning over the bottom of the sea for food. Charley Coffin said it was used for an ice-piercer; for the Narwhale, rising to the surface of the Polar Sea, and finding it sheeted with ice, thrusts his horn up, and so breaks through. But you cannot prove either of these surmises to be correct. My own opinion is, that however this one-sided horn may really be used by the Narwhale—however that may be—it would certainly be very convenient to him for a folder in reading pamphlets. The Narwhale I have heard called the Tusked whale, the Horned whale, and the Unicorn whale. He is certainly a curious example of the Unicornism to be found in almost every kingdom of animated nature. From certain cloistered old authors I have gathered that this same sea-unicorn's horn was in ancient days regarded as the great antidote against poison, and as such, preparations of it brought immense prices. It was also distilled to a volatile salts for fainting ladies, the same way that the horns of the male deer are manufactured into hartshorn. Originally it was in itself accounted an object of great curiosity. Black Letter tells me that Sir Martin Frobisher on his return from that voyage, when Queen Bess did gallantly wave her jewelled hand to him from a window of Greenwich Palace, as his bold ship sailed down the Thames; 'when Sir Martin returned from that voyage,' saith Black Letter, 'on bended knees he presented to her highness a prodigious long horn of the Narwhale, which for a long period after hung in the castle at Windsor.' An Irish author avers that the Earl of Leicester, on bended knees, did likewise present to her highness another horn, pertaining to a land beast of the unicorn nature.

The Narwhale has a very picturesque, leopard-like look, being of a milk-white ground color, dotted with round and oblong spots of black. His oil is very superior, clear and fine; but there is little of it, and he is seldom hunted. He is mostly found in the circumpolar seas.

BOOK II. (*Octavo*), CHAPTER IV. (*Killer*).—Of this whale little is precisely known to the Nantucketer, and nothing at all to the professed naturalist. From what I have seen of him at a distance, I should say that he was about the bigness of a grampus. He is very savage—a sort of Feegee fish. He sometimes takes the great Folio whales by the lip, and hangs there like a leech, till the mighty brute is worried to death. The Killer is never hunted. I never heard what sort of oil he has. Exception might be taken to the name bestowed upon this whale, on the ground of its indistinctness. For we are all killers, on land and on sea; Bonapartes and Sharks included.

BOOK II. (*Octavo*), CHAPTER V. (*Thrasher*).—This gentleman is famous for his tail, which he uses for a ferule in thrashing his foes. He mounts the Folio whale's back, and as he swims, he works his passage by flogging him; as some schoolmasters get along

in the world by a similar process. Still less is known of the Thrasher
than of the Killer. Both are outlaws, even in the lawless seas.

Thus ends BOOK II. (*Octavo*), and begins BOOK III. (*Duodecimo*).

DUODECIMOES.—These include the smaller whales. I. The
Huzza Porpoise. II. The Algerine Porpoise. III. The Mealy-mouthed
Porpoise.

To those who have not chanced specially to study the subject,
it may possibly seem strange, that fishes not commonly exceeding
four or five feet should be marshalled among WHALES—a word,
which, in the popular sense, always conveys an idea of hugeness.
But the creatures set down above as Duodecimoes are infallibly
whales, by the terms of my definition of what a whale is—i.e. a
spouting fish, with a horizontal tail.

BOOK III. (*Duodecimo*), CHAPTER I. (*Huzza Porpoise*).—This
is the common porpoise found almost all over the globe. The
name is of my own bestowal; for there are more than one sort
of porpoises, and something must be done to distinguish them. I
call him thus, because he always swims in hilarious shoals, which
upon the broad sea keep tossing themselves to heaven like caps
in a Fourth-of-July crowd. Their appearance is generally hailed
with delight by the mariner. Full of fine spirits, they invariably
come from the breezy billows to windward. They are the lads that
always live before the wind. They are accounted a lucky omen.
If you yourself can withstand three cheers at beholding these
vivacious fish, then heaven help ye; the spirit of godly gamesomeness is not in ye. A well-fed, plump Huzza Porpoise will
yield you one good gallon of good oil. But the fine and delicate
fluid extracted from his jaws is exceedingly valuable. It is in request
among jewellers and watchmakers. Sailors put it on their hones.
Porpoise meat is good eating, you know. It may never have
occurred to you that a porpoise spouts. Indeed, his spout is so
small that it is not very readily discernible. But the next time you
have a chance, watch him; and you will then see the great Sperm
whale himself in miniature.

BOOK III. (*Duodecimo*), CHAPTER II. (*Algerine Porpoise*).—A
pirate. Very savage. He is only found, I think, in the Pacific. He
is somewhat larger than the Huzza Porpoise, but much of the
same general make. Provoke him, and he will buckle to a shark.
I have lowered for him many times, but never yet saw him
captured.

BOOK III. (*Duodecimo*), CHAPTER III. (*Mealy-mouthed Porpoise*).—The largest kind of Porpoise; and only found in the Pacific,

so far as it is known. The only English name, by which he has
hitherto been designated, is that of the fishers—Right-Whale Porpoise, from the circumstance that he is chiefly found in the vicinity
of that Folio. In shape, he differs in some degree from the Huzza
Porpoise, being of a less rotund and jolly girth; indeed, he is of
quite a neat and gentleman-like figure. He has no fins on his back
(most other porpoises have), he has a lovely tail, and sentimental
Indian eyes of a hazel hue. But his mealy-mouth spoils all. Though
his entire back down to his side fins is of a deep sable, yet a
boundary line, distinct as the mark in a ship's hull, called the
'bright waist,' that line streaks him from stem to stern, with two
separate colors, black above and white below. The white comprises
part of his head, and the whole of his mouth, which makes him
look as if he had just escaped from a felonious visit to a meal-
bag. A most mean and mealy aspect! His oil is much like that
of the common porpoise.

Beyond the DUODECIMO, this system does not proceed, inasmuch as the Porpoise is the smallest of the whales. Above, you
have all the Leviathans of note. But there are a rabble of uncertain,
fugitive, half-fabulous whales, which, as an American whaleman,
I know by reputation, but not personally. I shall enumerate them
by their forecastle appellations; for possibly such a list may be
valuable to future investigators, who may complete what I have
here but begun. If any of the following whales, shall hereafter be
caught and marked, then he can readily be incorporated into this
System, according to his Folio, Octavo, or Duodecimo magnitude:—The Bottle-Nose Whale; the Junk Whale; the Pudding-
Headed Whale; the Cape Whale; the Leading Whale; the Cannon
Whale; the Scragg Whale; the Coppered Whale; the Elephant
Whale; the Iceberg Whale; the Quog Whale; the Blue Whale; &c.
From Icelandic, Dutch and old English authorities, there might
be quoted other lists of uncertain whales, blessed with all manner
of uncouth names. But I omit them as altogether obsolete; and
can hardly help suspecting them for mere sounds, full of Levi-
athanism, but signifying nothing.

Finally: It was stated at the outset, that this system would not
be here, and at once, perfected. You cannot but plainly see that
I have kept my word. But I now leave my cetological System
standing thus unfinished, even as the great Cathedral of Cologne
was left, with the crane still standing upon the top of the uncom-
pleted tower. For small erections may be finished by their first

architects; grand ones, true ones, ever leave the copestone to posterity. God keep me from ever completing anything. This whole book is but a draught—nay, but the draught of a draught. Oh, Time, Strength, Cash, and Patience!

33
THE SPECKSYNDER

CONCERNING the officers of the whale-craft, this seems as good a place as any to set down a little domestic peculiarity on shipboard, arising from the existence of the harpooneer class of officers, a class unknown of course in any other marine than the whale-fleet.

The large importance attached to the harpooneer's vocation is evinced by the fact, that originally in the old Dutch Fishery, two centuries and more ago, the command of a whale ship was not wholly lodged in the person now called the captain, but was divided between him and an officer called the Specksynder. Literally this word means Fat-Cutter; usage, however, in time made it equivalent to Chief Harpooneer. In those days, the captain's authority was restricted to the navigation and general management of the vessel: while over the whale-hunting department and all its concerns, the Specksynder or Chief Harpooneer reigned supreme. In the British Greenland Fishery, under the corrupted title of Specksioneer, this old Dutch official is still retained, but his former dignity is sadly abridged. At present he ranks simply as senior Harpooneer; and as such, is but one of the captain's more inferior subalterns. Nevertheless, as upon the good conduct of the harpooneers the success of a whaling voyage largely depends, and since in the American Fishery he is not only an important officer in the boat, but under certain circumstances (night watches on a whaling ground) the command of the ship's deck is also his; therefore the grand political maxim of the sea demands, that he should nominally live apart from the men before the mast, and be in some way distinguished as their professional superior; though always, by them, familiarly regarded as their social equal.

Now, the grand distinction drawn between officer and man at sea, is this—the first lives aft, the last forward. Hence, in whale-ships and merchantmen alike, the mates have their quarters with the captain; and so, too, in most of the American whalers the harpooneers are lodged in the after part of the ship. That is to say, they take their meals in the captain's cabin, and sleep in a place indirectly communicating with it.

Though the long period of a Southern whaling voyage (by far the longest of all voyages now or ever made by man), the peculiar perils of it, and the community of interest prevailing among a company, all of whom, high or low, depend for their profits, not upon fixed wages, but upon their common luck, together with their common vigilance, intrepidity, and hard work; though all these things do in some cases tend to beget a less rigorous discipline than in merchantmen generally; yet, never mind how much like an old Mesopotamian family these whalemen may, in some primitive instances, live together; for all that, the punctilious externals, at least, of the quarter-deck are seldom materially relaxed, and in no instance done away. Indeed, many are the Nantucket ships in which you will see the skipper parading his quarter-deck with an elated grandeur not surpassed in any military navy; nay, extorting almost as much homage as if he wore the imperial purple, and not the shabbiest of pilot-cloth.

And though of all men the moody captain of the Pequod was the least given to that sort of shallowest assumption; and though the only homage he ever exacted, was implicit, instantaneous obedience; though he required no man to remove the shoes from his feet ere stepping upon the quarter-deck; and though there were times when, owing to peculiar circumstances connected with events hereafter to be detailed, he addressed them in unusual terms, whether of condescension or *in terrorem*, or otherwise; yet even Captain Ahab was by no means unobservant of the paramount forms and usages of the sea.

Nor, perhaps, will it fail to be eventually perceived, that behind those forms and usages, as it were, he sometimes masked himself; incidentally making use of them for other and more private ends than they were legitimately intended to subserve. That certain sultanism of his brain, which had otherwise in a good degree remained unmanifested; through those forms that same sultanism became incarnate in an irresistible dictatorship. For be a man's intellectual superiority what it will, it can never assume the practical, available supremacy over other men, without the aid of some sort of external arts and entrenchments, always, in themselves, more or less paltry and base. This it is, that for ever keeps God's true princes of the Empire from the world's hustings; and leaves the highest honors that this air can give, to those men who become famous more through their infinite inferiority to the choice hidden handful of the Divine Inert, than through their undoubted superiority over the dead level of the mass. Such large virtue lurks in these small things when extreme political superstitions invest them, that in some royal instances even to idiot imbecility they have imparted potency. But when, as in the case of Nicholas the Czar, the ringed crown of geographical empire encircles an imperial brain; then, the plebeian herds crouch abased before the tremendous centralization. Nor, will the tragic dramatist who would depict mortal indomitableness in its fullest sweep and direst swing, ever forget a hint, incidentally so important in his art, as the one now alluded to.

But Ahab, my Captain, still moves before me in all his Nantucket grimness and shagginess; and in this episode touching Emperors and Kings, I must not conceal that I have only to do with a poor old whale-hunter like him; and, therefore, all outward majestical trappings and housings are denied me. Oh, Ahab! what shall be grand in thee, it must needs be plucked at from the skies, and dived for in the deep, and featured in the unbodied air!

34
THE CABIN-TABLE

IT is noon; and Dough-Boy, the steward, thrusting his pale loaf-of-bread face from the cabin-scuttle, announces dinner to his lord and master; who, sitting in the lee quarter-boat, has just been taking an observation of the sun; and is now mutely reckoning the latitude on the smooth, medallion-shaped tablet, reserved for that daily purpose on the upper part of his ivory leg. From his complete inattention to the tidings, you would think that moody Ahab had not heard his menial. But presently, catching hold of the mizen shrouds, he swings himself to the deck, and in an even, unexhilarated voice, saying, 'Dinner, Mr Starbuck,' disappears into the cabin.

When the last echo of his sultan's step has died away, and Starbuck, the first Emir, has every reason to suppose that he is seated, then Starbuck rouses from his quietude, takes a few turns along the planks, and, after a grave peep into the binnacle, says, with some touch of pleasantness, 'Dinner, Mr Stubb,' and descends the scuttle. The second Emir lounges about the rigging awhile, and then slightly shaking the main brace, to see whether it be all right with that important rope, he likewise takes up the old burden, and with a rapid 'Dinner, Mr Flask,' follows after his predecessors.

But the third Emir, now seeing himself all alone on the quarter-deck, seems to feel relieved from some curious restraint; for, tipping all sorts of knowing winks in all sorts of directions, and kicking off his shoes, he strikes into a sharp but noiseless squall of a hornpipe right over the Grand Turk's head; and then, by a dexterous sleight, pitching his cap into the mizen-top for a shelf, he goes down rollicking, so far at least as he remains visible from the deck, reversing all other processions, by bringing up the rear with music. But ere stepping into the cabin doorway below, he pauses, ships a new face altogether, and, then, independent, hilarious little Flask enters King Ahab's presence, in the character of Abjectus, or the Slave.

It is not the least among the strange things bred by the intense artificialness of sea-usages, that while in the open air of the deck some officers will, upon provocation, bear themselves boldly and defyingly enough towards their commander; yet, ten to one, let those very officers the next moment go down to their customary dinner in that same commander's cabin, and straightway their inoffensive, not to say deprecatory and humble air towards him, as he sits at the head of the table; this is marvellous, sometimes most comical. Wherefore this difference? A problem? Perhaps not. To have been Belshazzar, King of Babylon; and to have been Belshazzar, not haughtily but courteously, therein certainly must have been some touch of mundane grandeur. But he who in the rightly regal and intelligent spirit presides over his own private dinner-table of invited guests, that man's unchallenged power and dominion of individual influence for the time; that man's royalty of state transcends Belshazzar's, for Belshazzar was not the greatest. Who has but once dined his friends, has tasted what it is to be Cæsar. It is a witchery of social czarship which there is no withstanding. Now, if to this consideration you superadd the official supremacy of a ship-master, then, by inference, you will derive the cause of that peculiarity of sea-life just mentioned.

Over his ivory-inlaid table, Ahab presided like a mute, maned sea-lion on the white coral beach, surrounded by his warlike but still deferential cubs. In his own proper turn, each officer waited to be served. They were as little children before Ahab; and yet, in Ahab, there seemed not to lurk the smallest social arrogance. With one mind, their intent eyes all fastened upon the old man's knife, as he carved the chief dish before him. I do not suppose that for the world they would have profaned that moment with the slightest observation, even upon so neutral a topic as the weather. No! And when reaching out his knife and fork, between which the slice of beef was locked, Ahab thereby motioned Starbuck's plate towards him, the mate received his meat as though receiving alms; and cut it tenderly; and a little started if, perchance, the knife grazed against the plate; and chewed it noiselessly; and swallowed it, not without circumspection. For, like the Coronation banquet at Frankfort, where the German Emperor profoundly dines with the seven Imperial Electors, so these cabin meals were somehow solemn meals, eaten in awful silence; and yet at table old Ahab forbade not conversation; only he himself was dumb. What a relief it was to choking Stubb, when a rat made a sudden racket in the hold below. And poor little Flask, he was the youngest son, and little boy of this weary family party. His were the shinbones of the saline beef; his would have been the drumsticks. For Flask to have presumed to help himself, this must have seemed to him tantamount to larceny in the first degree. Had he helped himself at that table, doubtless, never more would he have been able to hold his head up in this honest world; nevertheless, strange to say, Ahab never forbade him. And had Flask helped himself, the chances were Ahab had never so much as noticed it. Least of all, did Flask presume to help himself to butter. Whether he thought the owners of the ship denied it to him, on account of its clotting his clear, sunny complexion; or whether he deemed that, on so long a voyage in such marketless waters, butter was at a premium, and therefore was not for him, a subaltern; however it was, Flask, alas! was a butterless man!

Another thing. Flask was the last person down at the dinner, and Flask is the first man up. Consider! For hereby Flask's dinner was badly jammed in point of time. Starbuck and Stubb both had the start of him; and yet they also have the privilege of lounging in the rear. If Stubb even, who is but a peg higher than Flask, happens to have but a small appetite, and soon shows symptoms of concluding his repast, then Flask must bestir himself, he will not get more than three mouthfuls that day; for it is against holy usage for Stubb to precede Flask to the deck. Therefore it was that Flask once admitted in private, that ever since he had arisen to the dignity of an officer, from that moment he had never known what it was to be otherwise than hungry, more or less. For what he ate did not so much relieve his hunger, as keep it immortal in him. Peace and satisfaction, thought Flask, have for ever departed from my stomach. I am an officer; but, how I wish I could fist a bit of old-fashioned beef in the forecastle, as I used to when I was before the mast. There's the fruits of promotion now; there's the vanity of glory: there's the insanity of life! Besides, if it were so that any mere sailor of the Pequod had a grudge against Flask in Flask's official capacity, all that sailor had to do, in order to obtain ample vengeance, was to go aft at dinner-time, and get a peep at Flask through the cabin sky-light, sitting silly and dumfoundered before awful Ahab.

Now, Ahab and his three mates formed what may be called the first table in the Pequod's cabin. After their departure, taking place in inverted order to their arrival, the canvas cloth was cleared, or rather was restored to some hurried order by the pallid steward. And then the three harpooneers were bidden to the feast, they being its residuary legatees. They made a sort of temporary servants' hall of the high and mighty cabin.

In strange contrast to the hardly tolerable constraint and name-less invisible domineerings of the captain's table, was the entire care-free license and ease, the almost frantic democracy of those inferior fellows the harpooneers. While their masters, the mates, seemed afraid of the sound of the hinges of their own jaws, the harpooneers chewed their food with such a relish that there was a report to it. They dined like lords; they filled their bellies like Indian ships all day loading with spices. Such portentous appetites had Queequeg and Tashtego, that to fill out the vacancies made by the previous repast, often the pale Dough-Boy was fain to bring on a great baron of salt-junk, seemingly quarried out of the solid ox. And if he were not lively about it, if he did not go with a nimble hop-skip-and-jump, then Tashtego had an ungentlemanly way of accelerating him by darting a fork at his back, harpoonwise. And once Daggoo, seized with a sudden humor, assisted Dough-Boy's memory by snatching him up bodily, and thrusting his head into a great empty wooden trencher, while Tashtego, knife in hand, began laying out the circle preliminary to scalping him. He was naturally a very nervous, shuddering sort of little fellow, this bread-faced steward; the progeny of a bankrupt baker and a hospital nurse. And what with the standing spectacle of the black terrific Ahab, and the periodical tumultuous visitations of these three savages, Dough-Boy's whole life was one continual lip-quiver. Commonly, after seeing the harpooneers furnished with all things they demanded, he would escape from their clutches into his little pantry adjoining, and fearfully peep out at them through the blinds of its door, till all was over.

It was a sight to see Queequeg seated over against Tashtego, opposing his filed teeth to the Indian's: crosswise to them, Daggoo seated on the floor, for a bench would have brought his hearse-plumed head to the low carlines; at every motion of his colossal limbs, making the low cabin framework to shake, as when an African elephant goes passenger in a ship. But for all this, the great negro was wonderfully abstemious, not to say dainty. It seemed hardly possible that by such comparatively small mouthfuls he could keep up the vitality diffused through so broad, baronial, and superb a person. But, doubtless, this noble savage fed strong and drank deep of the abounding element of air; and through his dilated nostrils snuffed in the sublime life of the worlds. Not by beef or by bread, are giants made or nourished. But Queequeg, he had a mortal, barbaric smack of the lip in eating—an ugly sound enough—so much so, that the trembling Dough-Boy almost looked to see whether any marks of teeth lurked in his own lean arms. And when he would hear Tashtego singing out for him to produce himself, that his bones might be picked, the simple-witted Steward all but shattered the crockery hanging round him in the pantry, by his sudden fits of the palsy. Nor did the whetstones which the harpooneers carried in their pockets, for their lances and other weapons; and with which whetstones, at dinner, they would ostentatiously sharpen their knives; that grating sound did not at all tend to tranquillize poor Dough-Boy. How could he forget that in his Island days, Queequeg, for one, must certainly have been guilty of some murderous, convivial indiscretions. Alas! Dough-Boy! hard fares the white waiter who waits upon cannibals. Not a napkin should he carry on his arm, but a buckler. In good time, though, to his great delight, the three salt-sea warriors would rise and depart; to his credulous, fable-mongering ears, all their martial bones jingling in them at every step, like Moorish scimetars in scabbards.

But, though these barbarians dined in the cabin, and nominally lived there; still, being anything but sedentary in their habits, they were scarcely ever in it except at meal-times, and just before sleeping-time, when they passed through it to their own peculiar quarters.

In this one matter, Ahab seemed no exception to most American whale captains, who, as a set, rather incline to the opinion that by rights the ship's cabin belongs to them; and that it is by courtesy alone that anybody else is, at any time, permitted there. So that, in real truth, the mates and harpooneers of the Pequod might more properly be said to have lived out of the cabin than in it. For when they did enter it, it was something as a street-door enters a house; turning inwards for a moment, only to be turned out the next; and, as a permanent thing, residing in the open air. Nor did they lose much hereby; in the cabin was no companionship; socially, Ahab was inaccessible. Though nominally included in the census of Christendom, he was still an alien to it. He lived in the world, as the last of the Grisly Bears lived in settled Missouri. And as when Spring and Summer had departed, that wild Logan of the woods, burying himself in the hollow of a tree, lived out the winter there, sucking his own paws; so, in his inclement, howling old age, Ahab's soul, shut up in the caved trunk of his body, there fed upon the sullen paws of its gloom!

35
THE MAST-HEAD

IT was during the more pleasant weather, that in due rotation with the other seamen my first mast-head came round.

In most American whalemen the mast-heads are manned almost simultaneously with the vessel's leaving her port; even though she may have fifteen thousand miles, and more, to sail ere reaching her proper cruising ground. And if, after a three, four, or five years' voyage she is drawing nigh home with anything empty in her—say, an empty vial even—then, her mast-heads are kept manned to the last; and not till her skysail poles sail in among the spires of the port, does she altogether relinquish the hope of capturing one whale more.

Now, as the business of standing mast-heads, ashore or afloat, is a very ancient and interesting one, let us in some measure expatiate here. I take it, that the earliest standers of mast-heads were the old Egyptians; because, in all my researches, I find none prior to them. For though their progenitors, the builders of Babel, must doubtless, by their tower, have intended to rear the loftiest mast-head in all Asia, or Africa either; yet (ere the final truck was put to it) as that great stone mast of theirs may be said to have gone by the board, in the dread gale of God's wrath; therefore, we cannot give these Babel builders priority over the Egyptians. And that the Egyptians were a nation of mast-head standers, is an assertion based upon the general belief among archæologists, that the first pyramids were founded for astronomical purposes: a theory singularly supported by the peculiar stair-like formation of all four sides of those edifices; whereby, with prodigious long

upliftings of their legs, those old astronomers were wont to mount
to the apex, and sing out for new stars; even as the look-outs of
a modern ship sing out for a sail, or a whale just bearing in sight.
In Saint Stylites, the famous Christian hermit of old times, who
built him a lofty stone pillar in the desert and spent the whole
latter portion of his life on its summit, hoisting his food from the
ground with a tackle; in him we have a remarkable instance of
a dauntless stander-of-mast-heads; who was not to be driven from
his place by fogs or frosts, rain, hail, or sleet; but valiantly facing
everything out to the last, literally died at his post. Of modern
standers-of-mast-heads we have but a lifeless set; mere stone, iron,
and bronze men; who, though well capable of facing out a stiff
gale, are still entirely incompetent to the business of singing out
upon discovering any strange sight. There is Napoleon; who, upon
the top of the column of Vendome, stands with arms folded, some
one hundred and fifty feet in the air; careless, now, who rules the
decks below; whether Louis Philippe, Louis Blanc, or Louis the
Devil. Great Washington, too, stands high aloft on his towering
main-mast in Baltimore, and like one of Hercules' pillars, his
column marks that point of human grandeur beyond which few
mortals will go. Admiral Nelson, also, on a capstan of gun-metal,
stands his mast-head in Trafalgar Square; and even when most
obscured by that London smoke, token is yet given that a hidden
hero is there; for where there is smoke, must be fire. But neither
great Washington, nor Napoleon, nor Nelson, will answer a single
hail from below, however madly invoked to befriend by their
counsels the distracted decks upon which they gaze; however, it
may be surmised, that their spirits penetrate through the thick
haze of the future, and descry what shoals and what rocks must
be shunned.

It may seem unwarrantable to couple in any respect the mast-
head standers of the land with those of the sea; but that in truth
it is not so, is plainly evinced by an item for which Obed Macy,
the sole historian of Nantucket, stands accountable. The worthy
Obed tells us, that in the early times of the whale fishery, ere
ships were regularly launched in pursuit of the game, the people
of that island erected lofty spars along the sea-coast, to which the
look-outs ascended by means of nailed cleats, something as fowls
go upstairs in a hen-house. A few years ago this same plan was
adopted by the Bay whalemen of New Zealand, who, upon descrying the game, gave notice to the ready-manned boats nigh the
beach. But this custom has now become obsolete; turn we then
to the one proper mast-head, that of a whale-ship at sea.

The three mast-heads are kept manned from sun-rise to sun-set; the seamen taking their regular turns (as at the helm), and relieving each other every two hours. In the serene weather of the tropics it is exceedingly pleasant—the mast-head; nay, to a dreamy meditative man it is delightful. There you stand, a hundred feet above the silent decks, striding along the deep, as if the masts were gigantic stilts, while beneath you and between your legs, as it were, swim the hugest monsters of the sea, even as ships once sailed between the boots of the famous Colossus at old Rhodes. There you stand, lost in the infinite series of the sea, with nothing ruffled but the waves. The tranced ship indolently rolls; the drowsy trade winds blow; everything resolves you into languor. For the most part, in this tropic whaling life, a sublime uneventfulness invests you; you hear no news; read no gazettes; extras with startling accounts of commonplaces never delude you into unnecessary excitements; you hear of no domestic afflictions; bankrupt securities; fall of stocks; are never troubled with the thought of what you shall have for dinner—for all your meals for three years and more are snugly stowed in casks, and your bill of fare is immutable.

In one of those southern whalemen, on a long three or four years' voyage, as often happens, the sum of the various hours you spend at the mast-head would amount to several entire months. And it is much to be deplored that the place to which you devote so considerable a portion of the whole term of your natural life, should be so sadly destitute of anything approaching to a cosy inhabitiveness, or adapted to breed a comfortable localness of feeling, such as pertains to a bed, a hammock, a hearse, a sentry box, a pulpit, a coach, or any other of those small and snug contrivances in which men temporarily isolate themselves. Your most usual point of perch is the head of the t' gallant-mast, where you stand upon two thin parallel sticks (almost peculiar to whale-men) called the t' gallant cross-trees. Here, tossed about by the sea, the beginner feels about as cosy as he would standing on a bull's horns. To be sure, in coolish weather you may carry your house aloft with you, in the shape of a watch-coat; but properly speaking the thickest watch-coat is no more of a house than the unclad body; for as the soul is glued inside of its fleshly tabernacle, and cannot freely move about in it, nor even move out of it, without running great risk of perishing (like an ignorant pilgrim crossing the snowy Alps in winter); so a watch-coat is not so much of a house as it is a mere envelope, or additional skin encasing you. You cannot put a shelf or chest of drawers in your body, and no more can you make a convenient closet of your watch-coat.

Concerning all this, it is much to be deplored that the mast-heads of a southern whale ship are unprovided with those enviable little tents or pulpits, called *crow's-nests*, in which the lookouts of a Greenland whaler are protected from the inclement weather of the frozen seas. In the fireside narrative of Captain Sleet, entitled 'A Voyage among the Icebergs, in quest of the Greenland Whale, and incidentally for the re-discovery of the Lost Icelandic Colonies of Old Greenland;' in this admirable volume, all standers of mast-heads are furnished with a charmingly circumstantial account of the then recently invented *crow's-nest* of the Glacier, which was the name of Captain Sleet's good craft. He called it the *Sleet's crow's-nest*, in honor of himself; he being the original inventor and patentee, and free from all ridiculous false delicacy, and holding that if we call our own children after our own names (we fathers being the original inventors and patentees), so likewise should we denominate after ourselves any other apparatus we may beget. In shape, the Sleet's crow's-nest is something like a large tierce or pipe; it is open above, however, where it is furnished with a movable side-screen to keep to windward of your head in a hard gale. Being fixed on the summit of the mast, you ascend into it through a little trap-hatch in the bottom. On the after side, or side next the stern of the ship, is a comfortable seat, with a locker underneath for umbrellas, comforters, and coats. In front is a leather rack, in which to keep your speaking trumpet, pipe, telescope, and other nautical conveniences. When Captain Sleet in person stood his mast-head in this crow's nest of his, he tells us that he always had a rifle with him (also fixed in the rack), together with a powder flask and shot, for the purpose of popping off the stray narwhales, or vagrant sea unicorns infesting those waters; for you cannot successfully shoot at them from the deck owing to the resistance of the water, but to shoot down upon them is a very different thing. Now, it was plainly a labor of love for Captain Sleet to describe, as he does, all the little detailed conveniences of his crow's-nest; but though he so enlarges upon many of these, and though he treats us to a very scientific account of his experiments in this crow's-nest, with a small compass he kept there for the purpose of counteracting the errors resulting from what is called the 'local attraction' of all binnacle magnets; an error ascribable to the horizontal vicinity of the iron in the ship's planks, and in the Glacier's case, perhaps, to there having been so many broken-down black-smiths among her crew; I say, that though the Captain is very discreet and scientific here, yet, for all his learned 'binnacle deviations,' 'azimuth compass observations,' and 'approximate errors,' he knows very well, Captain Sleet, that he was not so much immersed in those profound magnetic meditations, as to fail being attracted occasionally towards that well replenished little case-bottle, so nicely tucked in on one side of his crow's nest, within easy reach of his hand. Though, upon the whole, I greatly admire and even love the brave, the honest, and learned Captain; yet I take it very ill of him that he should so utterly ignore that case-bottle, seeing what a faithful friend and comforter it must have been, while with mittened fingers and hooded head he was studying the mathematics aloft there in that bird's nest within three or four perches of the pole.

But if we Southern whale-fishers are not so snugly housed aloft as Captain Sleet and his Greenland-men were; yet that disadvantage is greatly counterbalanced by the widely contrasting serenity of those seductive seas in which we South fishers mostly float. For one, I used to lounge up the rigging very leisurely, resting in the top to have a chat with Queequeg, or any one else off duty whom I might find there; then ascending a little way further, and throwing a lazy leg over the top-sail yard, take a preliminary view of the watery pastures, and so at last mount to my ultimate destination.

Let me make a clean breast of it here, and frankly admit that I kept but sorry guard. With the problem of the universe revolving in me, how could I—being left completely to myself at such a thought-engendering altitude,—how could I but lightly hold my obligations to observe all whale-ships' standing orders, 'Keep your weather eye open, and sing out every time.'

And let me in this place movingly admonish you, ye shipowners of Nantucket! Beware of enlisting in your vigilant fisheries any lad with lean brow and hollow eye; given to unseasonable meditativeness; and who offers to ship with the Phædon instead of Bowditch in his head. Beware of such an one, I say: your whales must be seen before they can be killed; and this sunken-eyed young Platonist will tow you ten wakes round the world, and never make you one pint of sperm the richer. Nor are these monitions at all unneeded. For nowadays, the whale-fishery furnishes an asylum for many romantic, melancholy, and absent-minded young men, disgusted with the carking cares of earth, and seeking sentiment in tar and blubber. Childe Harold not unfrequently perches himself upon the mast-head of some luckless disappointed whale-ship, and in moody phrase ejaculates:—

'Roll on, thou deep and dark blue ocean, roll!
Ten thousand blubber-hunters sweep over thee in vain.'

Very often do the captains of such ships take those absent-minded young philosophers to task, upbraiding them with not feeling sufficient 'interest' in the voyage; half-hinting that they are so hopelessly lost to all honorable ambition, as that in their secret souls they would rather not see whales than otherwise. But all in vain; those young Platonists have a notion that their vision is imperfect; they are short-sighted; what use, then, to strain the visual nerve? They have left their opera-glasses at home.

'Why, thou monkey,' said a harpooneer to one of these lads, 'we've been cruising now hard upon three years, and thou hast not raised a whale yet. Whales are scarce as hen's teeth whenever thou art up here.' Perhaps they were; or perhaps there might have been shoals of them in the far horizon; but lulled into such an opium-like listlessness of vacant, unconscious reverie is this absent-minded youth by the blending cadence of waves with thoughts, that at last he loses his identity; takes the mystic ocean at his feet for the visible image of that deep, blue, bottomless soul, pervading mankind and nature; and every strange, half-seen, gliding, beautiful thing that eludes him; every dimly-discovered, uprising fin of some undiscernible form, seems to him the embodiment of those elusive thoughts that only people the soul by continually flitting through it. In this enchanted mood, thy spirit ebbs away to whence it came; becomes diffused through time and space; like Cranmer's sprinkled Pantheistic ashes, forming at last a part of every shore the round globe over.

There is no life in thee, now, except that rocking life imparted by a gently rolling ship; by her, borrowed from the sea; by the sea, from the inscrutable tides of God. But while this sleep, this dream is on ye, move your foot or hand an inch; slip your hold at all; and your identity comes back in horror. Over Descartian vortices you hover. And perhaps, at mid-day, in the fairest weather, with one half-throttled shriek you drop through that transparent air into the summer sea, no more to rise for ever. Heed it well, ye Pantheists!

36
THE QUARTER-DECK

(*Enter Ahab: Then, all.*)

It was not a great while after the affair of the pipe, that one morning shortly after breakfast, Ahab, as was his wont, ascended the cabin-gangway to the deck. There most sea-captains usually walk at that hour, as country gentlemen, after the same meal, take a few turns in the garden.

Soon his steady, ivory stride was heard, as to and fro he paced his old rounds, upon planks so familiar to his tread, that they were all over dented, like geological stones, with the peculiar mark of his walk. Did you fixedly gaze, too, upon that ribbed and dented brow; there also, you would see still stranger foot-prints—the foot-prints of his one unsleeping, ever-pacing thought.

But on the occasion in question, those dents looked deeper, even as his nervous step that morning left a deeper mark. And, so full of his thought was Ahab, that at every uniform turn that he made, now at the main-mast and now at the binnacle, you could almost see that thought turn in him as he turned, and pace in him as he paced; so completely possessing him, indeed, that it all but seemed the inward mould of every outer movement.

'D'ye mark him, Flask?' whispered Stubb; 'the chick that's in him pecks the shell. 'Twill soon be out.'

The hours wore on;—Ahab now shut up within his cabin; anon, pacing the deck, with the same intense bigotry of purpose in his aspect.

It drew near the close of day. Suddenly he came to a halt by the bulwarks, and inserting his bone leg in the auger-hole there, and with one hand grasping a shroud, he ordered Starbuck to send everybody aft.

'Sir!' said the mate, astonished at an order seldom or never given on ship-board except in some extraordinary case.

'Send everybody aft,' repeated Ahab. 'Mast-heads, there! come down!'

When the entire ship's company were assembled, and with curious and not wholly unapprehensive faces, were eyeing him, for he looked not unlike the weather horizon when a storm is coming up, Ahab, after rapidly glancing over the bulwarks, and then darting his eyes among the crew, started from his standpoint; and as though not a soul were nigh him resumed his heavy turns upon the deck. With bent head and half-slouched hat he continued to pace, unmindful of the wondering whispering among the men; till Stubb cautiously whispered to Flask, that Ahab must have summoned them there for the purpose of witnessing a pedestrian feat. But this did not last long. Vehemently pausing, he cried:—

'What do ye do when ye see a whale, men?'

'Sing out for him!' was the impulsive rejoinder from a score of clubbed voices.

'Good!' cried Ahab, with a wild approval in his tones; observing the hearty animation into which his unexpected question had so magnetically thrown them.

'And what do ye next, men?'

'Lower away, and after him!'

'And what tune is it ye pull to, men?'

'A dead whale or a stove boat!'

More and more strangely and fiercely glad and approving, grew the countenance of the old man at every shout; while the mariners began to gaze curiously at each other, as if marvelling how it was that they themselves became so excited at such seemingly purposeless questions.

But, they were all eagerness again, as Ahab, now half-revolving in his pivot-hole, with one hand reaching high up a shroud, and tightly, almost convulsively grasping it, addressed them thus:—

'All ye mast-headers have before now heard me give orders about a white whale. Look ye! d'ye see this Spanish ounce of gold?'—holding up a broad bright coin to the sun—'it is a sixteen dollar piece, men. D'ye see it? Mr Starbuck, hand me yon top-maul.'

While the mate was getting the hammer, Ahab, without speaking, was slowly rubbing the gold piece against the skirts of his jacket, as if to heighten its lustre, and without using any words was meanwhile lowly humming to himself, producing a sound so strangely muffled and inarticulate that it seemed the mechanical humming of the wheels of his vitality in him.

Receiving the top-maul from Starbuck, he advanced towards the main-mast with the hammer uplifted in one hand, exhibiting the gold with the other, and with a high raised voice exclaiming: 'Whosoever of ye raises me a white-headed whale with a wrinkled brow and a crooked jaw; whosoever of ye raises me that white-headed whale, with three holes punctured in his starboard fluke—

look ye, whosoever of ye raises me that same white whale, he shall have this gold ounce, my boys!'

'Huzza! huzza!' cried the seamen, as with swinging tarpaulins they hailed the act of nailing the gold to the mast.

'It's a white whale, I say,' resumed Ahab, as he threw down the top-maul; 'a white whale. Skin your eyes for him, men; look sharp for white water; if ye see but a bubble, sing out.'

All this while Tashtego, Daggoo, and Queequeg had looked on with even more intense interest and surprise than the rest, and at the mention of the wrinkled brow and crooked jaw they had started as if each was separately touched by some specific recollection.

'Captain Ahab,' said Tashtego, 'that white whale must be the same that some call Moby Dick.'

'Moby Dick?' shouted Ahab. 'Do ye know the white whale then, Tash?'

'Does he fan-tail a little curious, sir, before he goes down?' said the Gay-Header deliberately.

'And has he a curious spout, too,' said Daggoo, 'very bushy, even for a parmacetty, and mighty quick, Captain Ahab?'

'And he have one, two, tree—oh! good many iron in him hide, too, Captain,' cried Queequeg disjointedly, 'all twisketee be-twisk, like him—him—' faltering hard for a word, and screwing his hand round and round as though uncorking a bottle—'like him— him—'

'Corkscrew!' cried Ahab, 'aye, Queequeg, the harpoons lie all twisted and wrenched in him; aye, Daggoo, his spout is a big one, like a whole shock of wheat, and white as a pile of our Nantucket wool after the great annual sheep-shearing; aye, Tashtego, and he fan-tails like a split jib in a squall. Death and devils! men, it is Moby Dick ye have seen—Moby Dick—Moby Dick!'

'Captain Ahab,' said Starbuck, who, with Stubb and Flask, had thus far been eyeing his superior with increasing surprise, but at last seemed struck with a thought which somewhat explained all the wonder. 'Captain Ahab, I have heard of Moby Dick—but it was not Moby Dick that took off thy leg?'

'Who told thee that?' cried Ahab; then pausing, 'Aye, Starbuck; aye, my hearties all round; it was Moby Dick that dismasted me; Moby Dick that brought me to this dead stump I stand on now. Aye, aye,' he shouted with a terrific, loud, animal sob, like that of a heart-stricken moose; 'Aye, aye! it was that accursed white whale that razeed me; made a poor pegging lubber of me for ever and a day!' Then tossing both arms, with measureless imprecations he shouted out: 'Aye, aye! and I'll chase him round Good Hope, and round the Horn, and round the Norway Maelstrom, and round perdition's flames before I give him up. And this is what ye have shipped for, men! to chase that white whale on both sides of land, and over all sides of earth, till he spouts black blood and rolls fin out. What say ye, men, will ye splice hands on it, now? I think ye do look brave.'

'Aye, aye!' shouted the harpooneers and seamen, running closer to the excited old man: 'A sharp eye for the White Whale; a sharp lance for Moby Dick!'

'God bless ye,' he seemed to half sob and half shout. 'God bless ye, men. Steward! go draw the great measure of grog. But what's this long face about, Mr Starbuck; wilt thou not chase the white whale? art not game for Moby Dick?'

'I am game for his crooked jaw, and for the jaws of Death too, Captain Ahab, if it fairly comes in the way of the business we follow; but I came here to hunt whales, not my commander's vengeance. How many barrels will thy vengeance yield thee even if thou gettest it, Captain Ahab? it will not fetch thee much in our Nantucket market.'

'Nantucket market! Hoot! But come closer, Starbuck; thou requirest a little lower layer. If money's to be the measurer, man, and the accountants have computed their great counting-house the globe, by girdling it with guineas, one to every three parts of an inch; then, let me tell thee, that my vengeance will fetch a great premium *here*!'

'He smites his chest,' whispered Stubb, 'what's that for? methinks it rings most vast, but hollow.'

'Vengeance on a dumb brute!' cried Starbuck, 'that simply smote thee from blindest instinct! Madness! To be enraged with a dumb thing, Captain Ahab, seems blasphemous.'

'Hark ye yet again,—the little lower layer. All visible objects, man, are but as pasteboard masks. But in each event—in the living act, the undoubted deed—there, some unknown but still reasoning thing puts forth the mouldings of its features from behind the unreasoning mask. If man will strike, strike through the mask! How can the prisoner reach outside except by thrusting through the wall? To me, the white whale is that wall, shoved near to me. Sometimes I think there's naught beyond. But 'tis enough. He tasks me; he heaps me; I see in him outrageous strength, with an inscrutable malice sinewing it. That inscrutable thing is chiefly what I hate; and be the white whale agent, or be the white whale principal, I will wreak that hate upon him. Talk not to me of blasphemy, man; I'd strike the sun if it insulted me. For could the sun do that, then could I do the other; since there is ever a sort of fair play herein, jealousy presiding over all creations. But not my master, man, is even that fair play. Who's over me? Truth hath no confines. Take off thine eye! more intolerable than fiends' glarings is a doltish stare! So, so; thou reddenest and palest; my heat has melted thee to anger-glow. But look ye, Starbuck, what is said in heat, that thing unsays itself. There are men from whom warm words are small indignity. I meant not to incense thee. Let it go. Look! see yonder Turkish cheeks of spotted tawn—living, breathing pictures painted by the sun. The Pagan leopards—the unrecking and unworshipping things, that live; and seek, and give no reasons for the torrid life they feel! The crew, man, the crew! Are they not one and all with Ahab, in this matter of the whale? See Stubb! he laughs! See yonder Chilian! he snorts to think of it Stand up amid the general hurricane, thy one tost sapling cannot, Starbuck! And what is it? Reckon it. 'Tis but to help strike a fin; no wondrous feat for Starbuck. What is it more? From this one poor hunt, then, the best lance out of all Nantucket, surely he will not hang back, when every foremast-hand has clutched a whetstone? Ah! constrainings seize thee; I see! the billow lifts thee! Speak, but speak!—Aye, aye! thy silence, then, *that* voices thee. (*Aside*) Something shot from my dilated nostrils, he has inhaled it in his lungs. Starbuck now is mine; cannot oppose me now, without rebellion.'

'God keep me!—keep us all!' murmured Starbuck, lowly.

But in his joy at the enchanted, tacit acquiescence of the mate, Ahab did not hear his foreboding invocation; nor yet the low laugh from the hold; nor yet the presaging vibrations of the winds in the cordage; nor yet the hollow flap of the sails against the masts, as for a moment their hearts sank in. For again Starbuck's downcast eyes lighted up with the stubbornness of life; the subterranean laugh died away; the winds blew on; the sails filled out; the ship heaved and rolled as before. Ah, ye admonitions and warnings! why stay ye not when ye come? But rather are ye predictions than warnings, ye shadows! Yet not so much predictions from without, as verifications of the foregoing things within. For with little external to constrain us, the innermost necessities in our being, these still drive us on.

'The measure! the measure!' cried Ahab.

Receiving the brimming pewter, and turning to the harpooneers, he ordered them to produce their weapons. Then ranging them before him near the capstan, with their harpoons in their hands, while his three mates stood at his side with their lances, and the rest of the ship's company formed a circle round the group; he stood for an instant searchingly eyeing every man of his crew. But those wild eyes met his, as the bloodshot eyes of the prairie wolves meet the eye of their leader, ere he rushes on at their head in the trail of the bison; but, alas! only to fall into the hidden snare of the Indian.

'Drink and pass!' he cried, handing the heavy charged flagon to the nearest seaman. 'The crew alone now drink. Round with it, round! Short draughts—long swallows, men; 'tis hot as Satan's hoof. So, so; it goes round excellently. It spiralizes in ye; forks out at the serpent-snapping eye. Well done; almost drained. That way it went, this way it comes. Hand it me—here's a hollow! Men, ye seem the years; so brimming life is gulped and gone. Steward, refill!

'Attend now, my braves. I have mustered ye all round this capstan; and ye mates, flank me with your lances; and ye harpooneers, stand there with your irons; and ye, stout mariners, ring me in, that I may in some sort revive a noble custom of my fishermen fathers before me. O men, you will yet see that—Ha! boy, come back? bad pennies come not sooner. Hand it me. Why, now, this pewter had run brimming again, wert not thou St. Vitus' imp—away, thou ague!

'Advance, ye mates! Cross your lances full before me. Well done! Let me touch the axis.' So saying, with extended arm, he grasped the three level, radiating lances at their crossed centre; while so doing, suddenly and nervously twitched them; meanwhile, glancing intently from Starbuck to Stubb; from Stubb to Flask. It seemed as though, by some nameless, interior volition, he would fain have shocked into them the same fiery emotion accumulated within the Leyden jar of his own magnetic life. The three mates quailed before his strong, sustained, and mystic aspect. Stubb and Flask looked sideways from him; the honest eye of Starbuck fell downright.

'In vain!' cried Ahab; 'but, maybe, 'tis well. For did ye three but once take the full-forced shock, then mine own electric thing, *that* had perhaps expired from out me. Perchance, too, it would have dropped ye dead. Perchance ye need it not. Down lances! And now, ye mates, I do appoint ye three cup-bearers to my three pagan kinsmen there—yon three most honorable gentlemen and noblemen, my valiant harpooneers. Disdain the task? What, when the great Pope washes the feet of beggars, using his tiara for ewer? Oh, my sweet cardinals! your own condescension, *that* shall bend ye to it. I do not order ye; ye will it. Cut your seizings and draw the poles, ye harpooneers!'

Silently obeying the order, the three harpooneers now stood with the detached iron part of their harpoons, some three feet long, held, barbs up, before him.

'Stab me not with that keen steel! Cant them; cant them over! know ye not the goblet end? Turn up the socket! So, so; now, ye cup bearers, advance. The irons! take them; hold them while I fill!' Forthwith, slowly going from one officer to the other, he brimmed the harpoon sockets with the fiery waters from the pewter.

'Now, three to three, ye stand. Commend the murderous chalices! Bestow them, ye who are now made parties to this indissoluble league. Ha! Starbuck! but the deed is done! Yon ratifying sun now waits to sit upon it. Drink, ye harpooneers! drink and swear, ye men that man the deathful whaleboat's bow—Death to Moby Dick! God hunt us all, if we do not hunt Moby Dick to his death!' The long, barbed steel goblets were lifted; and to cries and maledictions against the white whale, the spirits were simultaneously quaffed down with a hiss. Starbuck paled, and turned, and shivered. Once more, and finally, the replenished pewter went the rounds among the frantic crew; when, waving his free hand to them, they all dispersed; and Ahab retired within his cabin.

37

SUNSET

The cabin; by the stern windows; Ahab sitting alone, and gazing out.

I leave a white and turbid wake; pale waters, paler cheeks, where'er I sail. The envious billows sidelong swell to whelm my track; let them; but first I pass.

Yonder, by the ever-brimming goblet's rim, the warm waves blush like wine. The gold brow plumbs the blue. The diver sun— slow dived from noon,—goes down; my soul mounts up! she wearies with her endless hill. Is, then, the crown too heavy that I wear? this Iron Crown of Lombardy. Yet is it bright with many a gem; I, the wearer, see not its far flashings; but darkly feel that I wear that, that dazzlingly confounds. 'Tis iron—that I know—not gold. 'Tis split, too—that I feel; the jagged edge galls me so, my brain seems to beat against the solid metal; aye, steel skull, mine; the sort that needs no helmet in the most brain-battering fight!

Dry heat upon my brow? Oh! time was, when as the sunrise nobly spurred me, so the sunset soothed. No more. This lovely light, it lights not me; all loveliness is anguish to me, since I can ne'er enjoy. Gifted with the high perception, I lack the low, enjoying power; damned, most subtly and most malignantly! damned in the midst of Paradise! Good night—good night! (*waving his hand, he moves from the window.*)

'Twas not so hard a task. I thought to find one stubborn, at the least; but my one cogged circle fits into all their various wheels, and they revolve. Or, if you will, like so many ant-hills of powder, they all stand before me; and I their match. Oh, hard! that to fire others, the match itself must needs be wasting! What I've dared, I've willed; and what I've willed, I'll do! They think me mad—Starbuck does; but I'm demoniac, I am madness maddened! That wild madness that's only calm to comprehend itself! The prophecy was that I should be dismembered; and—Aye! I lost this leg. I now prophesy that I will dismember my dismemberer. Now, then, be the prophet and the fulfiller one. That's more than ye, ye great gods, ever were. I laugh and hoot at ye, ye cricket-players, ye pugilists, ye deaf Burkes and blinded Bendigoes! I will not say as schoolboys do to bullies,—Take some one of your own size; don't pommel *me*! No, ye've knocked me down, and I am up again; but *ye* have run and hidden. Come forth from behind your cotton bags! I have no long gun to reach ye. Come, Ahab's compliments to ye; come and see if ye can swerve me. Swerve me? ye cannot swerve me, else ye swerve yourselves! man has ye there. Swerve me? The path to my fixed purpose is laid with iron rails, whereon my soul is grooved to run. Over unsounded gorges, through the rifled hearts of mountains, under torrents' beds, unerringly I rush! Naught's an obstacle, naught's an angle to the iron way!

38

DUSK

By the Mainmast; Starbuck leaning against it.

MY soul is more than matched; she's overmanned; and by a madman! Insufferable sting, that sanity should ground arms on such a field! But he drilled deep down, and blasted all my reason out of me! I think I see his impious end; but feel that I must help him to it. Will I, nill I, the ineffable thing has tied me to him; tows me with a cable I have no knife to cut. Horrible old man! Who's over him, he cries;—aye, he would be a democrat to all above; look, how he lords it over all below! Oh! I plainly see my miserable office,—to obey, rebelling; and worse yet, to hate with touch of pity! For in his eyes I read some lurid woe would shrivel me up, had I it. Yet is there hope. Time and tide flow wide. The hated whale has the round watery world to swim in, as the small gold-fish has its glassy globe. His heaven-insulting purpose, God may wedge aside. I would up heart, were it not like lead. But my whole clock's run down; my heart the all-controlling weight, I have no key to life again.

A burst of revelry from the forecastle.

Oh, God! to sail with such a heathen crew that have small touch of human mothers in them! Whelped somewhere by the sharkish sea. The white whale is their demigorgon. Hark! the infernal orgies! that revelry is forward! mark the unfaltering silence aft! Methinks it pictures life. Foremost through the sparkling sea shoots on the gay, embattled, bantering bow, but only to drag dark Ahab after it, where he broods within his sternward cabin, builded over the dead water of the wake, and further on, hunted by its wolfish gurglings. The long howl thrills me through! Peace! ye revellers, and set the watch! Oh, life! 'tis in an hour like this, with soul beat down and held to knowledge,—as wild, untutored things are forced to feed—Oh, life! 'tis now that I do feel the latent horror in thee! but 'tis not me! that horror's out of me! and with the soft feeling of the human in me, yet will I try to fight ye, ye grim, phantom futures! Stand by me, hold me, bind me, O ye blessed influences!

39
FIRST NIGHT-WATCH

FORE-TOP (*Stubb solus, and mending a brace.*)

HA! ha! ha! ha! hem! clear my throat!—I've been thinking over it ever since, and that ha-ha's the final consequence. Why so? Because a laugh's the wisest, easiest answer to all that's queer; and come what will, one comfort's always left—that unfailing comfort is, it's all predestinated. I heard not all his talk with

Starbuck; but to my poor eye Starbuck then looked something as I the other evening felt. Be sure the old Mogul has fixed him, too. I twigged it, knew it; had had the gift, might readily have prophesied it—for when I clapped my eye upon his skull I saw it. Well, Stubb, *wise* Stubb—that's my title—well, Stubb, what of it, Stubb? Here's a carcase. I know not all that may be coming, but be it what it will, I'll go to it laughing. Such a waggish leering as lurks in all your horribles! I feel funny. Fa, la! lirra, skirra! What's my juicy little pear at home doing now? Crying its eyes out?—Giving a party to the last arrived harpooneers, I dare say, gay as a frigate's pennant, and so am I—fa, la! lirra, skirra! Oh—

> We'll drink to-night with hearts as light,
>   To love, as gay and fleeting
> As bubbles that swim, on the beaker's brim,
>   And break on the lips while meeting.

A brave stave that—who calls? Mr Starbuck? Aye, aye, sir— (*Aside*) he's my superior, he has his too, if I'm not mistaken.— Aye, aye, sir, just through with this job—coming.

40

MIDNIGHT, FORECASTLE

HARPOONEERS AND SAILORS
(*Foresail rises and discovers the watch standing, lounging, leaning, and lying in various attitudes, all singing in chorus.*)
> Farewell and adieu to you, Spanish ladies!
> Farewell and adieu to you, ladies of Spain!
> Our captain's commanded—

1ST NANTUCKET SAILOR

Oh, boys, don't be sentimental; it's bad for the digestion! Take a tonic, follow me! (*Sings, and all follow.*)
> Our captain stood upon the deck,
>   A spy-glass in his hand,
> A viewing of those gallant whales
>   That blew at every strand.
> Oh, your tubs in your boats, my boys,
>   And by your braces stand,
> And we'll have one of those fine whales,
>   Hand, boys, over hand!
> So, be cheery, my lads! may your hearts never fail!
> While the bold harpooneer is striking the whale!

MATE'S VOICE FROM THE QUARTER-DECK

Eight bells there, forward!

2D NANTUCKET SAILOR

Avast the chorus! Eight bells there! d'ye hear, bell-boy? Strike the bell eight, thou Pip! thou blackling! and let me call the watch. I've the sort of mouth for that—the hogs-head mouth. So, so, (*thrusts his head down the scuttle,*) Star-bo-l-e-e-n-s, a-h-o-y! Eight bells there below! Tumble up!

DUTCH SAILOR

Grand snoozing to-night, maty; fat night for that. I mark this in our old Mogul's wine; it's quite as deadening to some as filliping to others. We sing; they sleep—aye, lie down there, like ground-tier butts. At 'em again! There, take this copper-pump, and hail 'em through it. Tell 'em to avast dreaming of their lasses. Tell 'em it's the resurrection; they must kiss their last, and come to judgment. That's the way—*that's* it; thy throat ain't spoiled with eating Amsterdam butter.

FRENCH SAILOR

Hist, boys! let's have a jig or two before we ride to anchor in Blanket Bay. What say ye? There comes the other watch. Stand by all legs! Pip! little Pip! hurrah with your tambourine!

PIP (*Sulky and sleepy.*)

Don't know where it is.

FRENCH SAILOR

Beat thy belly, then, and wag thy ears. Jig it, men, I say; merry's the word; hurrah! Damn me, won't you dance? Form, now, Indian-file, and gallop into the double-shuffle? Throw yourselves! Legs! legs!

ICELAND SAILOR

I don't like your floor, maty; it's too springy to my taste. I'm used to ice-floors. I'm sorry to throw cold water on the subject; but excuse me.

MALTESE SAILOR

Me too; where's your girls? Who but a fool would take his left hand by his right, and say to himself, how d'ye do? Partners! I must have partners!

SICILIAN SAILOR

Aye; girls and a green!—then I'll hop with ye; yea, turn grass-hopper!

LONG-ISLAND SAILOR

Well, well, ye sulkies, there's plenty more of us. Hoe corn when you may, say I. All legs go to harvest soon. Ah! here comes the music; now for it!

AZORE SAILOR

(*Ascending, and pitching the tambourine up the scuttle.*)

Here you are, Pip; and there's the windlass-bitts; up you mount! Now, boys!

(*The half of them dance to the tambourine; some go below; some sleep or lie among the coils of rigging. Oaths a-plenty.*)

AZORE SAILOR (*Dancing.*)

Go it, Pip! Bang it, bell-boy! Rig it, dig it, stig it, quig it, bell-boy! Make fire-flies; break the jinglers!

PIP

Jinglers, you say?—there goes another, dropped off, I pound it so.

CHINA SAILOR

Rattle thy teeth, then, and pound away; make a pagoda of thyself.

FRENCH SAILOR

Merry-mad! Hold up thy hoop, Pip, till I jump through it! Split jibs! tear yourselves!

TASHTEGO (*Quietly smoking.*)

That's a white man; he calls that fun: humph; I save my sweat.

OLD MANX SAILOR

I wonder whether those jolly lads bethink them of what they are dancing over. I'll dance over your grave, I will—that's the bitterest threat of your night-women, that beat head-winds round corners. O Christ! to think of the green navies and the green-skulled crews! Well, well; belike, the whole world's a ball, as you scholars have it; and so 'tis right to make one ball-room of it. Dance on, lads, you're young; I was once.

3D NANTUCKET SAILOR

Spell oh!—whew! this is worse than pulling after whales in a calm—give us a whiff, Tash.

(*They cease dancing, and gather in clusters. Meantime the sky darkens— the wind rises.*)

LASCAR SAILOR

By Brahma! boys, it'll be douse sail soon. The sky-born, high-tide Ganges turned to wind! Thou showest thy black brow, Seeva!

MALTESE SAILOR (*Reclining and shaking his cap.*)

It's the waves'—the snow-caps' turn to jig it now. They'll shake their tassels soon. Now would all the waves were women, then I'd go drown, and chassce with them evermore! There's naught so sweet on earth—heaven may not match it!—as those swift glances of warm, wild bosoms in the dance, when the over-arboring arms hide such ripe, bursting grapes.

SICILIAN SAILOR (*Reclining.*)

Tell me not of it! Hark ye, lad—fleet interlacings of the limbs—lithe swayings—coyings—flutterings! lip! heart! hip! all graze: unceasing touch and go! not taste, observe ye, else come satiety. Eh, Pagan? (*Nudging.*)

TAHITAN SAILOR (*Reclining on a mat.*)

Hail, holy nakedness of our dancing girls!—the Heeva-Heeva! Ah! low veiled, high palmed Tahiti! I still rest me on thy mat, but the soft soil has slid! I saw thee woven in the wood, my mat! green the first day I brought ye thence; now worn and wilted quite. Ah me!—not thou nor can I bear the change! How then, if so be transplanted to yon sky? Hear I the roaring streams from Pirohitee's peak of spears, when they leap down the crags and drown the villages?—The blast! the blast! Up, spine, and meet it! (*Leaps to his feet.*)

PORTUGUESE SAILOR

How the sea rolls swashing 'gainst the side! Stand by for reefing, hearties! the winds are just crossing swords, pell-mell they'll go lunging presently.

DANISH SAILOR

Crack, crack, old ship! so long as thou crackest, thou holdest! Well done! The mate there holds ye to it stiffly. He's no more afraid than the isle fort at Cattegat, put there to fight the Baltic with storm-lashed guns, on which the sea-salt cakes!

4TH NANTUCKET SAILOR

He has his orders, mind ye that. I heard old Ahab tell him he must always kill a squall, something as they burst a water-spout with a pistol—fire your ship right into it!

ENGLISH SAILOR

Blood! but that old man's a grand old cove! We are the lads to hunt him up his whale!

ALL

Aye! aye!

OLD MANX SAILOR

How the three pines shake! Pines are the hardest sort of tree to live when shifted to any other soil, and here there's none but the crew's cursed clay. Steady, helmsman! steady. This is the sort of weather when brave hearts snap ashore, and keeled hulls split at sea. Our captain has his birthmark; look yonder, boys, there's another in the sky—lurid-like, ye see, all else pitch black.

DAGGOO

What of that? Who's afraid of black's afraid of me! I'm quarried out of it!

SPANISH SAILOR

(*Aside.*) He wants to bully, ah!—the old grudge makes me touchy. (*Advancing.*) Aye, harpooneer, thy race is the undeniable dark side of mankind—devilish dark at that. No offence.

DAGGOO (*grimly*)

None.

ST. JAGO'S SAILOR

That Spaniard's mad or drunk. But that can't be, or else in his one case our old Mogul's fire-waters are somewhat long in working.

5TH NANTUCKET SAILOR

What's that I saw—lightning? Yes.

SPANISH SAILOR

No; Daggoo showing his teeth.

DAGGOO (*springing*)

Swallow thine, mannikin! White skin, white liver!

SPANISH SAILOR (*meeting him*)

Knife thee heartily! big frame, small spirit!

ALL

A row! a row! a row!

TASHTEGO (*with a whiff*)

A row a'low, and a row aloft—Gods and men—both brawlers! Humph!

BELFAST SAILOR

A row! arrah a row! The Virgin be blessed, a row! Plunge in with ye!

ENGLISH SAILOR

Fair play! Snatch the Spaniard's knife! A ring, a ring!

OLD MANX SAILOR

Ready formed. There! the ringed horizon. In that ring Cain struck Abel. Sweet work, right work! No? Why then, God, mad'st thou the ring?

MATE'S VOICE FROM THE QUARTER DECK

Hands by the halyards! in top-gallant sails! Stand by to reef topsails!

ALL

The squall! the squall! jump, my jollies! (*They scatter.*)

PIP (*shrinking under the windlass*)

Jollies? Lord help such jollies! Crish, crash! there goes the jib-stay! Blang-whang! God! Duck lower, Pip, here comes the royal yard! It's worse than being in the whirled woods, the last day of the year! Who'd go climbing after chestnuts now? But there they go, all cursing, and here I don't. Fine prospects to 'em; they're on the road to heaven. Hold on hard! Jimmini, what a squall! But those chaps there are worse yet—they are your white squalls, they. White squalls? white whale, shirr! shirr! Here have I heard all their chat just now, and the white whale—shirr! shirr!—but spoken of once! and only this evening—it makes me jingle all over like my tambourine—that anaconda of an old man swore 'em in to hunt him! Oh, thou big white God aloft there somewhere in yon darkness, have mercy on this small black boy down here; preserve him from all men that have no bowels to feel fear!

41
MOBY DICK

I, Ishmael, was one of that crew; my shouts had gone up with the rest; my oath had been welded with theirs; and stronger I shouted, and more did I hammer and clinch my oath, because of the dread in my soul. A wild, mystical, sympathetical feeling was in me; Ahab's quenchless feud seemed mine. With greedy ears I learned the history of that murderous monster against whom I and all the others had taken our oaths of violence and revenge.

For some time past, though at intervals only, the unaccompanied, secluded White Whale had haunted those uncivilized seas mostly frequented by the Sperm Whale fishermen. But not all of them knew of his existence; only a few of them, comparatively, had knowingly seen him; while the number who as yet had actually and knowingly given battle to him, was small indeed. For, owing to the large number of whale-cruisers; the disorderly way they were sprinkled over the entire watery circumference, many of them adventurously pushing their quest along solitary latitudes, so as seldom or never for a whole twelvemonth or more on a stretch, to encounter a single news-telling sail of any sort; the inordinate length of each separate voyage; the irregularity of the times of sailing from home; all these, with other circumstances, direct and indirect, long obstructed the spread through the whole world-wide whaling-fleet of the special individualizing tidings concerning Moby Dick. It was hardly to be doubted, that several vessels reported to have encountered, at such or such a time, or on such or such a meridian, a Sperm Whale of uncommon magnitude and malignity, which whale, after doing great mischief to his assailants, had completely escaped them; to some minds it was not an unfair presumption, I say, that the whale in question must have been no other than Moby Dick. Yet as of late the Sperm Whale fishery had been marked by various and not infrequent instances of great ferocity, cunning, and malice in the monster attacked; therefore it was, that those who by accident ignorantly gave battle to Moby Dick; such hunters, perhaps, for the most part, were content to ascribe the peculiar terror he bred, more, as it were, to the perils of the Sperm Whale fishery at large, than to the individual cause. In that way, mostly, the disastrous encounter between Ahab and the whale had hitherto been popularly regarded.

And as for those who, previously hearing of the White Whale, by chance caught sight of him; in the beginning of the thing they had every one of them, almost, as boldly and fearlessly lowered for him, as for any other whale of that species. But at length, such calamities did ensue in these assaults—not restricted to sprained wrists and ankles, broken limbs, or devouring amputations—but fatal to the last degree of fatality; those repeated disastrous repulses, all accumulating and piling their terrors upon Moby Dick; those things had gone far to shake the fortitude of many brave hunters, to whom the story of the White Whale had eventually come.

Nor did wild rumors of all sorts fail to exaggerate, and still the more horrify the true histories of these deadly encounters. For not only do fabulous rumors naturally grow out of the very body of all surprising terrible events,—as the smitten tree gives birth to its fungi; but, in maritime life, far more than in that of terra firma, wild rumors abound, wherever there is any adequate reality for them to cling to. And as the sea surpasses the land in this matter, so the whale fishery surpasses every other sort of maritime life, in the wonderfulness and fearfulness of the rumors which sometimes circulate there. For not only are whalemen as a body unexempt from that ignorance and superstitiousness hereditary to all sailors; but of all sailors, they are by all odds the most directly brought into contact with whatever is appallingly astonishing in the sea; face to face they not only eye its greatest marvels, but, hand to jaw, give battle to them. Alone, in such remotest waters, that though you sailed a thousand miles, and passed a thousand shores, you would not come to any chiselled hearthstone, or aught hospitable beneath that part of the sun; in such latitudes and longitudes, pursuing too such a calling as he does, the whaleman is wrapped by influences all tending to make his fancy pregnant with many a mighty birth.

No wonder, then, that ever gathering volume from the mere transit over the widest watery spaces, the outblown rumors of the White Whale did in the end incorporate with themselves all manner of morbid hints, and half-formed fœtal suggestions of supernatural agencies, which eventually invested Moby Dick with new terrors unborrowed from anything that visibly appears. So that in many cases such a panic did he finally strike, that few who by those rumors, at least, had heard of the White Whale, few of those hunters were willing to encounter the perils of his jaw.

But there were still other and more vital practical influences at work. Not even at the present day has the original prestige of the

Sperm Whale, as fearfully distinguished from all other species of
the leviathan, died out of the minds of the whalemen as a body.
There are those this day among them, who, though intelligent and
courageous enough in offering battle to the Greenland or Right
whale, would perhaps—either from professional inexperience, or
incompetency, or timidity, decline a contest with the Sperm Whale;
at any rate, there are plenty of whalemen, especially among those
whaling nations not sailing under the American flag, who have
never hostilely encountered the Sperm Whale, but whose sole
knowledge of the leviathan is restricted to the ignoble monster
primitively pursued in the North; seated on their hatches, these
men will hearken with a childish fire-side interest and awe, to the
wild, strange tales of Southern whaling. Nor is the preeminent
tremendousness of the great Sperm Whale anywhere more feelingly
comprehended, than on board of those prows which stem him.

And as if the now tested reality of his might had in former
legendary times thrown its shadow before it; we find some book
naturalists—Olassen and Povelson—declaring the Sperm Whale
not only to be a consternation to every other creature in the sea,
but also to be so incredibly ferocious as continually to be athirst
for human blood. Nor even down to so late a time as Cuvier's,
were these or almost similar impressions effaced. For in his Natural
History, the Baron himself affirms that at sight of the Sperm
Whale, all fish (sharks included) are 'struck with the most lively
terrors,' and 'often in the precipitancy of their flight dash themselves against the rocks with such violence as to cause instantaneous
death.' And however the general experiences in the fishery may
amend such reports as these; yet in their full terribleness, even to
the bloodthirsty item of Povelson, the superstitious belief in them
is, in some vicissitudes of their vocation, revived in the minds of
the hunters.

So that overawed by the rumors and portents concerning him,
not a few of the fishermen recalled, in reference to Moby Dick,
the earlier days of the Sperm Whale fishery, when it was oftentimes
hard to induce long practised Right whalemen to embark in the
perils of this new and daring warfare; such men protesting that
although other leviathans might be hopefully pursued, yet to chase
and point lance at such an apparition as the Sperm Whale was
not for mortal man. That to attempt it, would be inevitably to
be torn into a quick eternity. On this head, there are some
remarkable documents that may be consulted.

Nevertheless, some there were, who even in the face of these
things were ready to give chase to Moby Dick; and a still greater

number who, chancing only to hear of him distantly and vaguely, without the specific details of any certain calamity, and without superstitious accompaniments, were sufficiently hardy not to flee from the battle if offered.

One of the wild suggestings referred to, as at last coming to be linked with the White Whale in the minds of the superstitiously inclined, was the unearthly conceit that Moby Dick was ubiquitous; that he had actually been encountered in opposite latitudes at one and the same instant of time.

Nor, credulous as such minds must have been, was this conceit altogether without some faint show of superstitious probability. For as the secrets of the currents in the seas have never yet been divulged, even to the most erudite research; so the hidden ways of the Sperm Whale when beneath the surface remain, in great part, unaccountable to his pursuers; and from time to time have originated the most curious and contradictory speculations regarding them, especially concerning the mystic modes whereby, after sounding to a great depth, he transports himself with such vast swiftness to the most widely distant points.

It is a thing well known to both American and English whale-ships, and as well a thing placed upon authoritative record years ago by Scoresby, that some whales have been captured far north in the Pacific, in whose bodies have been found the barbs of harpoons darted in the Greenland seas. Nor is it to be gainsaid, that in some of these instances it has been declared that the interval of time between the two assaults could not have exceeded very many days. Hence, by inference, it has been believed by some whalemen, that the Nor' West Passage, so long a problem to man, was never a problem to the whale. So that here, in the real living experience of living men, the prodigies related in old times of the inland Strello mountain in Portugal (near whose top there was said to be a lake in which the wrecks of ships floated up to the surface); and that still more wonderful story of the Arethusa fountain near Syracuse (whose waters were believed to have come from the Holy Land by an underground passage); these fabulous narrations are almost fully equalled by the realities of the whaleman.

Forced into familiarity, then, with such prodigies as these; and knowing that after repeated, intrepid assaults, the White Whale had escaped alive; it cannot be much matter of surprise that some whalemen should go still further in their superstitions; declaring Moby Dick not only ubiquitous, but immortal (for immortality is but ubiquity in time); that though groves of spears should be planted in his flanks, he would still swim away unharmed; or if indeed he should ever be made to spout thick blood, such a sight would be but a ghastly deception; for again in unensanguined billows hundreds of leagues away, his unsullied jet would once more be seen.

But even stripped of these supernatural surmisings, there was enough in the earthly make and incontestable character of the monster to strike the imagination with unwonted power. For, it was not so much his uncommon bulk that so much distinguished him from other sperm whales, but, as was elsewhere thrown out— a peculiar snow-white wrinkled forehead, and a high, pyramidical white hump. These were his prominent features; the tokens whereby, even in the limitless, uncharted seas, he revealed his identity, at a long distance, to those who knew him.

The rest of his body was so streaked, and spotted, and marbled with the same shrouded hue, that, in the end, he had gained his distinctive appellation of the White Whale; a name, indeed, literally justified by his vivid aspect, when seen gliding at high noon through a dark blue sea, leaving a milky-way wake of creamy foam, all spangled with golden gleamings.

Nor was it his unwonted magnitude, nor his remarkable hue, nor yet his deformed lower jaw, that so much invested the whale with natural terror, as that unexampled, intelligent malignity which, according to specific accounts, he had over and over again evinced in his assaults. More than all, his treacherous retreats struck more of dismay than perhaps aught else. For, when swimming before his exulting pursuers, with every apparent symptom of alarm, he had several times been known to turn round suddenly, and, bearing down upon them, either stave their boats to splinters, or drive them back in consternation to their ship.

Already several fatalities had attended his chase. But though similar disasters, however little bruited ashore, were by no means unusual in the fishery; yet, in most instances, such seemed the White Whale's infernal aforethought of ferocity, that every dis- membering or death that he caused, was not wholly regarded as having been inflicted by an unintelligent agent.

Judge, then, to what pitches of inflamed, distracted fury the minds of his more desperate hunters were impelled, when amid the chips of chewed boats, and the sinking limbs of torn comrades, they swam out of the white curds of the whale's direful wrath into the serene, exasperating sunlight, that smiled on, as if at a birth or a bridal.

His three boats stove around him, and oars and men both

whirling in the eddies; one captain, seizing the line-knife from his broken prow, had dashed at the whale, as an Arkansas duellist at his foe, blindly seeking with a six inch blade to reach the fathom-deep life of the whale. That captain was Ahab. And then it was, that suddenly sweeping his sickle shaped lower jaw beneath him, Moby Dick had reaped away Ahab's leg, as a mower a blade of grass in the field. No turbaned Turk, no hired Venetian, or Malay, could have smote him with more seeming malice. Small reason was there to doubt, then, that ever since that almost fatal encounter, Ahab had cherished a wild vindictiveness against the whale, all the more fell for that in his frantic morbidness he at last came to identify with him, not only all his bodily woes, but all his intellectual and spiritual exasperations. The White Whale swam before him as the monomaniac incarnation of all those malicious agencies which some deep men feel eating in them, till they are left living on with half a heart and half a lung. That intangible malignity which has been from the beginning; to whose dominion even the modern Christians ascribe one-half of the worlds; which the ancient Ophites of the east reverenced in their statue devil,— Ahab did not fall down and worship it like them; but deliriously transferring its idea to the abhorred white whale, he pitted himself, all mutilated, against it. All that most maddens and torments; all that stirs up the lees of things; all truth with malice in it; all that cracks the sinews and cakes the brain; all the subtle demonisms of life and thought; all evil, to crazy Ahab, were visibly personified, and made practically assailable in Moby Dick. He piled upon the whale's white hump the sum of all the general rage and hate felt by his whole race from Adam down; and then, as if his chest had been a mortar, he burst his hot heart's shell upon it.

It is not probable that this monomania in him took its instant rise at the precise time of his bodily dismemberment. Then, in darting at the monster, knife in hand, he had but given loose to a sudden, passionate, corporal animosity; and when he received the stroke that tore him, he probably but felt the agonizing bodily laceration, but nothing more. Yet, when by this collision forced to turn towards home, and for long months of days and weeks, Ahab and anguish lay stretched together in one hammock, round-ing in mid winter that dreary, howling Patagonian Cape; then it was, that his torn body and gashed soul bled into one another; and so interfusing, made him mad. That it was only then, on the homeward voyage, after the encounter, that the final monomania seized him, seems all but certain from the fact that, at intervals during the passage, he was a raving lunatic; and, though unlimbed of a leg, yet such vital strength yet lurked in his Egyptian chest, and was moreover intensified by his delirium, that his mates were forced to lace him fast, even there, as he sailed, raving in his hammock. In a straitjacket, he swung to the mad rockings of the gales. And, when running into more sufferable latitudes, the ship, with mild stun'sails spread, floated across the tranquil tropics, and, to all appearances, the old man's delirium seemed left behind him with the Cape Horn swells, and he came forth from his dark den into the blessed light and air; even then, when he bore that firm, collected front, however pale, and issued his calm orders once again; and his mates thanked God the direful madness was now gone; even then, Ahab, in his hidden self, raved on. Human madness is oftentimes a cunning and most feline thing. When you think it fled, it may have but become transfigured into some still subtler form. Ahab's full lunacy subsided not, but deepeningly contracted; like the unabated Hudson, when that noble Northman flows narrowly, but unfathomably through the Highland gorge. But, as in his narrow-flowing monomania, not one jot of Ahab's broad madness had been left behind; so in that broad madness, not one jot of his great natural intellect had perished. That before living agent, now became the living instrument. If such a furious trope may stand, his special lunacy stormed his general sanity, and carried it, and turned all its concentred cannon upon its own mad mark; so that far from having lost his strength, Ahab, to that one end, did now possess a thousand fold more potency than ever he had sanely brought to bear upon any one reasonable object.

This is much; yet Ahab's larger, darker, deeper part remains unhinted. But vain to popularize profundities, and all truth is profound. Winding far down from within the very heart of this spiked Hotel de Cluny where we here stand—however grand and wonderful, now quit it;—and take your way, ye nobler, sadder souls, to those vast Roman halls of Thermes; where far beneath the fantastic towers of man's upper earth, his root of grandeur, his whole awful essence sits in bearded state; an antique buried beneath antiquities, and throned on torsoes! So with a broken throne, the great gods mock that captive king; so like a Caryatid, he patient sits, upholding on his frozen brow the piled entablatures of ages. Wind ye down there, ye prouder, sadder souls! question that proud, sad king! A family likeness! aye, he did beget ye, ye young exiled royalties; and from your grim sire only will the old State-secret come.

Now, in his heart, Ahab had some glimpse of this, namely: all my means are sane, my motive and my object mad. Yet without power to kill, or change, or shun the fact; he likewise knew that to mankind he did long dissemble; in some sort, did still. But that thing of his dissembling, was only subject to his perceptibility, not to his will determinate. Nevertheless, so well did he succeed in that dissembling, that when with ivory leg he stepped ashore at last, no Nantucketer thought him otherwise than but naturally grieved, and that to the quick, with the terrible casualty which had overtaken him.

The report of his undeniable delirium at sea was likewise popularly ascribed to a kindred cause. And so too, all the added moodiness which always afterwards, to the very day of sailing in the Pequod on the present voyage, sat brooding on his brow. Nor is it so very unlikely, that far from distrusting his fitness for another whaling voyage, on account of such dark symptoms, the calculating people of that prudent isle were inclined to harbor the conceit, that for those very reasons he was all the better qualified and set on edge, for a pursuit so full of rage and wildness as the bloody hunt of whales. Gnawed within and scorched without, with the infixed, unrelenting fangs of some incurable idea; such an one, could he be found, would seem the very man to dart his iron and lift his lance against the most appalling of all brutes. Or, if for any reason thought to be corporeally incapacitated for that, yet such an one would seem superlatively competent to cheer and howl on his underlings to the attack. But be all this as it may, certain it is, that with the mad secret of his unabated rage bolted up and keyed in him, Ahab had purposely sailed upon the present voyage with the one only and all-engrossing object of hunting the White Whale. Had any one of his old acquaintances on shore but half dreamed of what was lurking in him then, how soon would their aghast and righteous souls have wrenched the ship from such a fiendish man! They were bent on profitable cruises, the profit to be counted down in dollars from the mint. He was intent on an audacious, immitigable, and supernatural revenge.

Here, then, was this grey-headed, ungodly old man, chasing with curses a Job's whale round the world, at the head of a crew, too, chiefly made up of mongrel renegades, and castaways, and cannibals—morally enfeebled also, by the incompetence of mere unaided virtue or right-mindedness in Starbuck, the invulnerable jollity of indifference and recklessness in Stubb, and the pervading mediocrity in Flask. Such a crew, so officered, seemed specially picked and packed by some infernal fatality to help him to his monomaniac revenge. How it was that they so aboundingly re-

sponded to the old man's ire—by what evil magic their souls were
possessed, that at times his hate seemed almost theirs; the White
Whale as much their insufferable foe as his; how all this came to
be—what the White Whale was to them, or how to their unconscious understandings, also, in some dim, unsuspected way, he
might have seemed the gliding great demon of the seas of life,—
all this to explain, would be to dive deeper than Ishmael can go.
The subterranean miner that works in us all, how can one tell
whither leads his shaft by the ever shifting, muffled sound of his
pick? Who does not feel the irresistible arm drag? What skiff in
tow of a seventy-four can stand still? For one, I gave myself up
to the abandonment of the time and the place; but while yet all
a-rush to encounter the whale, could see naught in that brute but
the deadliest ill.

42
THE WHITENESS OF THE WHALE

WHAT the white whale was to Ahab, has been hinted; what, at
times, he was to me, as yet remains unsaid.

Aside from those more obvious considerations touching Moby
Dick, which could not but occasionally awaken in any man's soul
some alarm, there was another thought, or rather vague, nameless
horror concerning him, which at times by its intensity completely
overpowered all the rest; and yet so mystical and well nigh ineffable
was it, that I almost despair of putting it in a comprehensible
form. It was the whiteness of the whale that above all things
appalled me. But how can I hope to explain myself here; and yet,
in some dim, random way, explain myself I must, else all these
chapters might be naught.

Though in many natural objects, whiteness refiningly enhances
beauty, as if imparting some special virtue of its own, as in marbles,
japonicas, and pearls; and though various nations have in some
way recognised a certain royal pre-eminence in this hue; even the
barbaric, grand old kings of Pegu placing the title 'Lord of the
White Elephants' above all other magniloquent ascriptions of
dominion; and the modern kings of Siam unfurling the same
snow-white quadruped in the royal standard; and the Hanoverian
flag bearing the one figure of a snow-white charger; and the great

Austrian Empire, Cæsarian heir to overlording Rome, having for the imperial color the same imperial hue; and though this pre-eminence in it applies to the human race itself, giving the white man ideal mastership over every dusky tribe; and though, besides all this, whiteness has been even made significant of gladness, for among the Romans a white stone marked a joyful day; and though in other mortal sympathies and symbolizings, this same hue is made the emblem of many touching, noble things—the innocence of brides, the benignity of age; though among the Red Men of America the giving of the white belt of wampum was the deepest pledge of honor; though in many climes, whiteness typifies the majesty of Justice in the ermine of the Judge, and contributes to the daily state of kings and queens drawn by milk-white steeds; though even in the higher mysteries of the most august religions it has been made the symbol of the divine spotlessness and power; by the Persian fire worshippers, the white forked flame being held the holiest on the altar; and in the Greek mythologies, Great Jove himself being made incarnate in a snow-white bull; and though to the noble Iroquois, the midwinter sacrifice of the sacred White Dog was by far the holiest festival of their theology, that spotless, faithful creature being held the purest envoy they could send to the Great Spirit with the annual tidings of their own fidelity; and though directly from the Latin word for white, all Christian priests derive the name of one part of their sacred vesture, the alb or tunic, worn beneath the cassock; and though among the holy pomps of the Romish faith, white is specially employed in the celebration of the Passion of our Lord; though in the Vision of St. John, white robes are given to the redeemed, and the four-and-twenty elders stand clothed in white before the great white throne, and the Holy One that sitteth there white like wool; yet for all these accumulated associations, with whatever is sweet, and honorable, and sublime, there yet lurks an elusive something in the innermost idea of this hue, which strikes more of panic to the soul than that redness which affrights in blood.

This elusive quality it is, which causes the thought of whiteness, when divorced from more kindly associations, and coupled with any object terrible in itself, to heighten that terror to the furthest bounds. Witness the white bear of the poles, and the white shark of the tropics; what but their smooth, flaky whiteness makes them the transcendent horrors they are! That ghastly whiteness it is which imparts such an abhorrent mildness, even more loathsome than terrific, to the dumb gloating of their aspect. So that not the fierce-fanged tiger in his heraldic coat can so stagger courage as the white-shrouded bear or shark.*

Bethink thee of the albatross: whence come those clouds of spiritual wonderment and pale dread, in which that white phantom sails in all imaginations? Not Coleridge first threw that spell; but God's great, unflattering laureate, Nature.†

* With reference to the Polar bear, it may possibly be urged by him who would fain go still deeper into this matter, that it is not the whiteness, separately regarded, which heightens the intolerable hideousness of that brute; for, analysed, that heightened hideousness, it might be said, only arises from the circumstances, that the irresponsible ferociousness of the creature stands invested in the fleece of celestial innocence and love; and hence, by bringing together two such opposite emotions in our minds, the Polar bear frightens us with so unnatural a contrast. But even assuming all this to be true; yet, were it not for the whiteness, you would not have that intensified terror.

As for the white shark, the white gliding ghostliness of repose in that creature, when beheld in his ordinary moods, strangely tallies with the same quality in the Polar quadruped. This peculiarity is most vividly hit by the French in the name they bestow upon that fish. The Romish mass for the dead begins with 'Requiem eternam' (eternal rest), whence *Requiem* denominating the mass itself, and any other funereal music. Now, in allusion to the white, silent stillness of death in this shark, and the mild deadliness of his habits, the French call him *Requin.*

† I remember the first albatross I ever saw. It was during a prolonged gale, in waters hard upon the Antarctic seas. From my forenoon watch below, I ascended to the overclouded deck; and there, dashed upon the main hatches, I saw a regal, feathery thing of unspotted whiteness, and with a hooked, Roman bill sublime. At intervals, it arched forth its vast archangel wings, as if to embrace some holy ark. Wondrous flutterings and throbbings shook it. Though bodily unharmed, it uttered cries, as some king's ghost in supernatural distress. Through its inexpressible, strange eyes, methought I peeped to secrets which took hold of God. As Abraham before the angels, I bowed myself; the white thing was so white, its wings so wide, and in those for ever exiled waters, I had lost the miserable warping memories of traditions and of towns. Long I gazed at that prodigy of plumage. I cannot tell, can only hint, the things that darted through me then. But at last I awoke; and turning, asked a sailor what bird was this. A goney, he replied. Goney! I never had heard that name before; is it conceivable that this glorious thing is utterly unknown to men ashore! never! But some time after, I learned that goney was some seaman's name for albatross. So that by no possibility could Coleridge's wild Rhyme have had aught to do with those mystical impressions which were mine, when I saw that bird upon our deck. For neither had I then read the Rhyme, nor knew the bird to be an albatross. Yet, in saying this, I do but indirectly burnish a little brighter the noble merit of the poem and the poet.

I assert, then, that in the wondrous bodily whiteness of the bird chiefly lurks the secret of the spell; a truth the more evinced in this, that by a solecism of terms there are birds called grey albatrosses; and these I have frequently seen, but never with such emotions as when I beheld the Antarctic fowl.

But how had the mystic thing been caught? Whisper it not, and I will tell; with a treacherous hook and line, as the fowl floated on the sea. At last the Captain made a postman of it; tying a lettered, leathern tally round its neck, with the ship's time and place; and then letting it escape. But I doubt not, that leathern tally, meant for man,

Most famous in our Western annals and Indian traditions is that of the White Steed of the Prairies; a magnificent milk-white charger, large-eyed, small-headed, bluff-chested, and with the dignity of a thousand monarchs in his lofty, overscorning carriage. He was the elected Xerxes of vast herds of wild horses, whose pastures in those days were only fenced by the Rocky Mountains and the Alleghanies. At their flaming head he westward trooped it like that chosen star which every evening leads on the hosts of light. The flashing cascade of his mane, the curving comet of his tail, invested him with housings more resplendent than gold and silver-beaters could have furnished him. A most imperial and archangelical apparition of that unfallen, western world, which to the eyes of the old trappers and hunters revived the glories of those primeval times when Adam walked majestic as a god, bluff-bowed and fearless as this mighty steed. Whether marching amid his aides and marshals in the van of countless cohorts that endlessly streamed it over the plains, like an Ohio; or whether with his circumambient subjects browsing all around at the horizon, the White Steed gallopingly reviewed them with warm nostrils reddening through his cool milkiness; in whatever aspect he presented himself, always to the bravest Indians he was the object of trembling reverence and awe. Nor can it be questioned from what stands on legendary record of this noble horse, that it was his spiritual whiteness chiefly, which so clothed him with divineness; and that this divineness had that in it which, though commanding worship, at the same time enforced a certain nameless terror.

But there are other instances where this whiteness loses all that accessory and strange glory which invests it in the White Steed and Albatross.

What is it that in the Albino man so peculiarly repels and often shocks the eye, as that sometimes he is loathed by his own kith and kin! It is that whiteness which invests him, a thing expressed by the name he bears. The Albino is as well made as other men—has no substantive deformity—and yet this mere aspect of all-pervading whiteness makes him more strangely hideous than the ugliest abortion. Why should this be so?

Nor, in quite other aspects, does Nature in her least palpable but not the less malicious agencies, fail to enlist among her forces this crowning attribute of the terrible. From its snowy aspect, the

was taken off in Heaven, when the white fowl flew to join the wing-folding, the invoking, and adoring cherubim!

gauntleted ghost of the Southern Seas has been denominated the White Squall. Nor, in some historic instances, has the art of human malice omitted so potent an auxiliary. How wildly it heightens the effect of that passage in Froissart, when, masked in the snowy symbol of their faction, the desperate White Hoods of Ghent murder their bailiff in the market-place!

Nor, in some things, does the common, hereditary experience of all mankind fail to bear witness to the supernaturalism of this hue. It cannot well be doubted, that the one visible quality in the aspect of the dead which most appals the gazer, is the marble pallor lingering there; as if indeed that pallor were as much like the badge of consternation in the other world, as of mortal trepidation here. And from that pallor of the dead, we borrow the expressive hue of the shroud in which we wrap them. Nor even in our superstitions do we fail to throw the same snowy mantle round our phantoms; all ghosts rising in a milk-white fog—Yea, while these terrors seize us, let us add, that even the king of terrors, when personified by the evangelist, rides on his pallid horse.

Therefore, in his other moods, symbolise whatever grand or gracious thing he will by whiteness, no man can deny that in its profoundest idealized significance it calls up a peculiar apparition to the soul.

But though without dissent this point be fixed, how is mortal man to account for it? To analyse it, would seem impossible. Can we, then, by the citation of some of those instances wherein this thing of whiteness—though for the time either wholly or in great part stripped of all direct associations calculated to impart to it aught fearful, but, nevertheless, is found to exert over us the same sorcery, however modified;—can we thus hope to light upon some chance clue to conduct us to the hidden cause we seek?

Let us try. But in a matter like this, subtlety appeals to subtlety, and without imagination no man can follow another into these halls. And though, doubtless, some at least of the imaginative impressions about to be presented may have been shared by most men, yet few perhaps were entirely conscious of them at the time, and therefore may not be able to recall them now.

Why to the man of untutored ideality, who happens to be but loosely acquainted with the peculiar character of the day, does the bare mention of Whitsuntide marshal in the fancy such long, dreary, speechless processions of slow-pacing pilgrims, down-cast and hooded with new-fallen snow? Or, to the unread, unsophisticated Protestant of the Middle American States, why does the passing mention of a White Friar or a White Nun, evoke such an eyeless statue in the soul?

Or what is there apart from the traditions of dungeoned warriors and kings (which will not wholly account for it) that makes the White Tower of London tell so much more strongly on the imagination of an untravelled American, than those other storied structures, its neighbors—the Byward Tower, or even the Bloody? And those sublimer towers, the White Mountains of New Hampshire, whence, in peculiar moods, comes that gigantic ghostliness over the soul at the bare mention of that name, while the thought of Virginia's Blue Ridge is full of a soft, dewy, distant dreaminess? Or why, irrespective of all latitudes and longitudes, does the name of the White Sea exert such a spectralness over the fancy, while that of the Yellow Sea lulls us with mortal thoughts of long lacquered mild afternoons on the waves, followed by the gaudiest and yet sleepiest of sunsets? Or, to choose a wholly unsubstantial instance, purely addressed to the fancy, why, in reading the old fairy tales of Central Europe, does 'the tall pale man' of the Hartz forests, whose changeless pallor unrustlingly glides through the green of the groves—why is this phantom more terrible than all the whooping imps of the Blocksburg?

Nor is it, altogether, the remembrance of her cathedral-toppling earthquakes; nor the stampedoes of her frantic seas; nor the tearlessness of arid skies that never rain; nor the sight of her wide field of leaning spires, wrenched cope-stones, and crosses all adroop (like canted yards of anchored fleets); and her suburban avenues of house-walls lying over upon each other, as a tossed pack of cards;—it is not these things alone which make tearless Lima, the strangest, saddest city thou can'st see. For Lima has taken the white veil; and there is a higher horror in this whiteness of her woe. Old as Pizarro, this whiteness keeps her ruins for ever new; admits not the cheerful greenness of complete decay; spreads over her broken ramparts the rigid pallor of an apoplexy that fixes its own distortions.

I know that, to the common apprehension, this phenomenon of whiteness is not confessed to be the prime agent in exaggerating the terror of objects otherwise terrible; nor to the unimaginative mind is there aught of terror in those appearances whose awfulness to another mind almost solely consists in this one phenomenon, especially when exhibited under any form at all approaching to muteness or universality. What I mean by these two statements may perhaps be respectively elucidated by the following examples.

First: The mariner, when drawing nigh the coasts of foreign

lands, if by night he hear the roar of breakers, starts to vigilance, and feels just enough of trepidation to sharpen all his faculties; but under precisely similar circumstances, let him be called from his hammock to view his ship sailing through a midnight sea of milky whiteness—as if from encircling headlands shoals of combed white bears were swimming round him, then he feels a silent, superstitious dread; the shrouded phantom of the whitened waters is horrible to him as a real ghost; in vain the lead assures him he is still off soundings; heart and helm they both go down; he never rests till blue water is under him again. Yet where is the mariner who will tell thee, 'Sir, it was not so much the fear of striking hidden rocks, as the fear of that hideous whiteness that so stirred me'?

Second: To the native Indian of Peru, the continual sight of the snow-howdahed Andes conveys naught of dread, except, perhaps, in the mere fancying of the eternal frosted desolateness reigning at such vast altitudes, and the natural conceit of what a fearfulness it would be to lose oneself in such inhuman solitudes. Much the same is it with the back-woodsman of the West, who with comparative indifference views an unbounded prairie sheeted with driven snow, no shadow of tree or twig to break the fixed trance of whiteness. Not so the sailor, beholding the scenery of the Antarctic seas; where at times, by some infernal trick of legerdemain in the powers of frost and air, he, shivering and half ship-wrecked, instead of rainbows speaking hope and solace to his misery, views what seems a boundless church-yard grinning upon him with its lean ice monuments and splintered crosses.

But thou sayest, methinks this white-lead chapter about whiteness is but a white flag hung out from a craven soul; thou surrenderest to a hypo, Ishmael.

Tell me, why this strong young colt, foaled in some peaceful valley of Vermont, far removed from all beasts of prey—why is it that upon the sunniest day, if you but shake a fresh buffalo robe behind him, so that he cannot even see it, but only smells its wild animal muskiness—why will he start, snort, and with bursting eyes paw the ground in phrensies of affright? There is no remembrance in him of any gorings of wild creatures in his green northern home, so that the strange muskiness he smells cannot recall to him anything associated with the experience of former perils; for what knows he, this New England colt, of the black bisons of distant Oregon?

No: but here thou beholdest even in a dumb brute, the instinct of the knowledge of the demonism in the world. Though thousands of miles from Oregon, still when he smells that savage musk, the rending, goring bison herds are as present as to the deserted wild foal of the prairies, which this instant they may be trampling into dust.

Thus, then, the muffled rollings of a milky sea; the bleak rustlings of the festooned frosts of mountains; the desolate shiftings of the windrowed snows of prairies; all these, to Ishmael, are as the shaking of that buffalo robe to the frightened colt!

Though neither knows where lie the nameless things of which the mystic sign gives forth such hints; yet with me, as with the colt, somewhere those things must exist. Though in many of its aspects this visible world seems formed in love, the invisible spheres were formed in fright.

But not yet have we solved the incantation of this whiteness, and learned why it appeals with such power to the soul; and more strange and far more portentous—why, as we have seen, it is at once the most meaning symbol of spiritual things, nay, the very veil of the Christian's Deity; and yet should be as it is, the intensifying agent in things the most appalling to mankind.

Is it that by its indefiniteness it shadows forth the heartless voids and immensities of the universe, and thus stabs us from behind with the thought of annihilation, when beholding the white depths of the milky way? Or is it, that as in essence whiteness is not so much a color as the visible absence of color, and at the same time the concrete of all colors; is it for these reasons that there is such a dumb blankness, full of meaning, in a wide landscape of snows—a colorless, all-color of atheism from which we shrink? And when we consider that other theory of the natural philosophers, that all other earthly hues—every stately or lovely emblazoning—the sweet tinges of sunset skies and woods; yea, and the gilded velvets of butterflies, and the butterfly cheeks of young girls; all these are but subtile deceits, not actually inherent in substances, but only laid on from without; so that all deified Nature absolutely paints like the harlot, whose allurements cover nothing but the charnel-house within; and when we proceed further, and consider that the mystical cosmetic which produces every one of her hues, the great principle of light, for ever remains white or colorless in itself, and if operating without medium upon matter, would touch all objects, even tulips and roses, with its own blank tinge—pondering all this, the palsied universe lies before us a leper; and like wilful travellers in Lapland, who refuse to wear colored and coloring glasses upon their eyes, so the wretched infidel gazes himself blind at the monumental white shroud that wraps all the prospect around him. And of all these things the Albino whale was the symbol. Wonder ye then at the fiery hunt?

43
HARK!

'HIST! Did you hear that noise, Cabaco?'

It was the middle-watch: a fair moonlight; the seamen were standing in a cordon, extending from one of the fresh-water butts in the waist, to the scuttle-butt near the taffrail. In this manner, they passed the buckets to fill the scuttle-butt. Standing, for the most part, on the hallowed precincts of the quarter-deck, they were careful not to speak or rustle their feet. From hand to hand, the buckets went in the deepest silence, only broken by the occasional flap of a sail, and the steady hum of the unceasingly advancing keel.

It was in the midst of this repose, that Archy, one of the cordon, whose post was near the after-hatches, whispered to his neighbor, a Cholo, the words above.

'Hist! did you hear that noise, Cabaco?'

'Take the bucket, will ye, Archy? what noise d'ye mean?'

'There it is again—under the hatches—don't you hear it—a cough—it sounded like a cough.'

'Cough be damned! Pass along that return bucket.'

'There again—there it is!—it sounds like two or three sleepers turning over, now!'

'Caramba! have done, shipmate, will ye? It's the three soaked biscuits ye eat for supper turning over inside of ye—nothing else. Look to the bucket!'

'Say what ye will, shipmate; I've sharp ears.'

'Aye, you are the chap, ain't ye, that heard the hum of the old Quakeress's knitting-needles fifty miles at sea from Nantucket; you're the chap.'

'Grin away; we'll see what turns up. Hark ye, Cabaco, there is somebody down in the after-hold that has not yet been seen on deck; and I suspect our old Mogul knows something of it too. I heard Stubb tell Flask, one morning watch, that there was something of that sort in the wind.'

'Tish! the bucket!'

44

THE CHART

HAD you followed Captain Ahab down into his cabin after the squall that took place on the night succeeding that wild ratification of his purpose with his crew, you would have seen him go to a locker in the transom, and bringing out a large wrinkled roll of yellowish sea charts, spread them before him on his screwed-down table. Then seating himself before it, you would have seen him intently study the various lines and shadings which there met his eye; and with slow but steady pencil trace additional courses over spaces that before were blank. At intervals, he would refer to piles of old log-books beside him, wherein were set down the seasons and places in which, on various former voyages of various ships, sperm whales had been captured or seen.

While thus employed, the heavy pewter lamp suspended in chains over his head, continually rocked with the motion of the ship, and for ever threw shifting gleams and shadows of lines upon his wrinkled brow, till it almost seemed that while he himself was marking out lines and courses on the wrinkled charts, some invisible pencil was also tracing lines and courses upon the deeply marked chart of his forehead.

But it was not this night in particular that, in the solitude of his cabin, Ahab thus pondered over his charts. Almost every night they were brought out; almost every night some pencil marks were effaced, and others were substituted. For with the charts of all four oceans before him, Ahab was threading a maze of currents and eddies, with a view to the more certain accomplishment of that monomaniac thought of his soul.

Now, to any one not fully acquainted with the ways of the leviathans, it might seem an absurdly hopeless task thus to seek out one solitary creature in the unhooped oceans of this planet. But not so did it seem to Ahab, who knew the sets of all tides and currents; and thereby calculating the driftings of the sperm whale's food; and, also, calling to mind the regular, ascertained seasons for hunting him in particular latitudes; could arrive at reasonable surmises, almost approaching to certainties, concerning the timeliest day to be upon this or that ground in search of his prey.

So assured, indeed, is the fact concerning the periodicalness of
the sperm whale's resorting to given waters, that many hunters
believe that, could he be closely observed and studied throughout
the world; were the logs for one voyage of the entire whale fleet
carefully collated, then the migrations of the sperm whale would
be found to correspond in invariability to those of the herring-
shoals or the flights of swallows. On this hint, attempts have been
made to construct elaborate migratory charts of the sperm whale.*

Besides, when making a passage from one feeding-ground to
another, the sperm whales, guided by some infallible instinct—
say, rather, secret intelligence from the Deity—mostly swim in
veins, as they are called; containing their way along a given ocean-
line with such undeviating exactitude, that no ship ever sailed her
course, by any chart, with one tithe of such marvellous precision.
Though, in these cases, the direction taken by any one whale be
straight as a surveyor's parallel, and though the line of advance
be strictly confined to its own unavoidable, straight wake, yet the
arbitrary *vein* in which at these times he is said to swim, generally
embraces some few miles in width (more or less, as the vein is
presumed to expand or contract); but never exceeds the visual
sweep from the whale-ship's mast-heads, when circumspectly gliding along this magic zone. The sum is, that at particular seasons
within that breadth and along that path, migrating whales may
with great confidence be looked for.

And hence not only at substantiated times, upon well known
separate feeding-grounds, could Ahab hope to encounter his prey;
but in crossing the widest expanses of water between those grounds
he could, by his art, so place and time himself on his way, as
even then not to be wholly without prospect of a meeting.

There was a circumstance which at first sight seemed to entangle
his delirious but still methodical scheme. But not so in the reality,
perhaps. Though the gregarious sperm whales have their regular
seasons for particular grounds, yet in general you cannot conclude
that the herds which haunted such and such a latitude or longitude

---

* Since the above was written, the statement is happily borne out by an official circular,
issued by Lieutenant Maury, of the National Observatory, Washington, April 16th, 1851.
By that circular, it appears that precisely such a chart is in course of completion; and
portions of it are presented in the circular. 'This chart divides the ocean into districts
of five degrees of latitude by five degrees of longitude; perpendicularly through each of
which districts are twelve columns for the twelve months; and horizontally through each
of which districts are three lines; one to show the number of days that have been spent
in each month in every district, and the two others to show the number of days in
which whales, sperm or right, have been seen.'

this year, say, will turn out to be identically the same with those that were found there the preceding season; though there are peculiar and unquestionable instances where the contrary of this has proved true. In general, the same remark, only within a less wide limit, applies to the solitaries and hermits among the matured, aged sperm whales. So that though Moby Dick had in a former year been seen, for example, on what is called the Seychelle ground in the Indian ocean, or Volcano Bay on the Japanese Coast; yet it did not follow, that were the Pequod to visit either of those spots at any subsequent corresponding season, she would infallibly encounter him there. So, too, with some other feeding grounds, where he had at times revealed himself. But all these seemed only his casual stopping-places and ocean-inns, so to speak, not his places of prolonged abode. And where Ahab's chances of accomplishing his object have hitherto been spoken of, allusion has only been made to whatever wayside, antecedent, extra prospects were his, ere a particular set time or place were attained, when all possibilities would become probabilities, and, as Ahab fondly thought, every possibility the next thing to a certainty. That particular set time and place were conjoined in the one technical phrase—the Season-on-the-Line. For there and then, for several consecutive years, Moby Dick had been periodically descried, lingering in those waters for awhile, as the sun, in its annual round, loiters for a predicted interval in any one sign of the Zodiac. There it was, too, that most of the deadly encounters with the white whale had taken place; there the waves were storied with his deeds; there also was that tragic spot where the monomaniac old man had found the awful motive to his vengeance. But in the cautious comprehensiveness and unloitering vigilance with which Ahab threw his brooding soul into this unfaltering hunt, he would not permit himself to rest all his hopes upon the one crowning fact above mentioned, however flattering it might be to those hopes; nor in the sleeplessness of his vow could he so tranquillize his unquiet heart as to postpone all intervening quest.

Now, the Pequod had sailed from Nantucket at the very beginning of the Season-on-the-Line. No possible endeavor then could enable her commander to make the great passage southwards, double Cape Horn, and then running down sixty degrees of latitude arrive in the equatorial Pacific in time to cruise there. Therefore, he must wait for the next ensuing season. Yet the premature hour of the Pequod's sailing had, perhaps, been covertly selected by Ahab, with a view to this very complexion of things. Because, an interval of three hundred and sixty-five days and nights was before him; an interval which, instead of impatiently enduring ashore, he would spend in a miscellaneous hunt; if by chance the White Whale, spending his vacation in seas far remote from his periodical feeding-grounds, should turn up his wrinkled brow off the Persian Gulf, or in the Bengal Bay, or China Seas, or in any other waters haunted by his race. So that Monsoons, Pampas, Nor-Westers, Harmattans, Trades; any wind but the Levanter and Simoom, might blow Moby Dick into the devious zig-zag world-circle of the Pequod's circumnavigating wake.

But granting all this; yet, regarded discreetly and coolly, seems it not but a mad idea, this; that in the broad boundless ocean, one solitary whale, even if encountered, should be thought capable of individual recognition from his hunter, even as a white-bearded Mufti in the thronged thoroughfares of Constantinople? Yes. For the peculiar snow-white brow of Moby Dick, and his snow-white hump, could not but be unmistakable. And have I not tallied the whale, Ahab would mutter to himself, as after poring over his charts till long after midnight he would throw himself back in reveries—tallied him, and shall he escape? His broad fins are bored, and scalloped out like a lost sheep's ear! And here, his mad mind would run on in a breathless race; till a weariness and faintness of pondering came over him; and in the open air of the deck he would seek to recover his strength. Ah, God! what trances of torments does that man endure who is consumed with one unachieved revengeful desire. He sleeps with clenched hands; and wakes with his own bloody nails in his palms.

Often, when forced from his hammock by exhausting and intolerably vivid dreams of the night, which, resuming his own intense thoughts through the day, carried them on amid a clashing of phrensies, and whirled them round and round in his blazing brain, till the very throbbing of his life-spot became insufferable anguish; and when, as was sometimes the case, these spiritual throes in him heaved his being up from its base, and a chasm seemed opening in him, from which forked flames and lightnings shot up, and accursed fiends beckoned him to leap down among them; when this hell in himself yawned beneath him, a wild cry would be heard through the ship; and with glaring eyes Ahab would burst from his state room, as though escaping from a bed that was on fire. Yet these, perhaps, instead of being the unsuppressable symptoms of some latent weakness, or fright at his own resolve, were but the plainest tokens of its intensity. For, at such times, crazy Ahab, the scheming, unappeasedly steadfast hunter

of the white whale; this Ahab that had gone to his hammock, was
not the agent that so caused him to burst from it in horror again.
The latter was the eternal, living principle or soul in him; and in
sleep, being for the time dissociated from the characterizing mind,
which at other times employed it for its outer vehicle or agent,
it spontaneously sought escape from the scorching contiguity of
the frantic thing, of which, for the time, it was no longer an
integral. But as the mind does not exist unless leagued with the
soul, therefore it must have been that, in Ahab's case, yielding
up all his thoughts and fancies to his one supreme purpose; that
purpose, by its own sheer inveteracy of will, forced itself against
gods and devils into a kind of self-assumed, independent being of
its own. Nay, could grimly live and burn, while the common
vitality to which it was conjoined, fled horror-stricken from the
unbidden and unfathered birth. Therefore, the tormented spirit
that glared out of bodily eyes, when what seemed Ahab rushed
from his room, was for the time but a vacated thing, a formless
somnambulistic being, a ray of living light, to be sure, but without
an object to color, and therefore a blankness in itself. God help
thee, old man, thy thoughts have created a creature in thee; and
he whose intense thinking thus makes him a Prometheus; a vulture
feeds upon that heart for ever; that vulture the very creature he
creates.

45

THE AFFIDAVIT

So far as what there may be of a narrative in this book; and,
indeed, as indirectly touching one or two very interesting and
curious particulars in the habits of sperm whales, the foregoing
chapter, in its earlier part, is as important a one as will be found
in this volume; but the leading matter of it requires to be still
further and more familiarly enlarged upon, in order to be adequately understood, and moreover to take away any incredulity
which a profound ignorance of the entire subject may induce in
some minds, as to the natural verity of the main points of this
affair.

I care not to perform this part of my task methodically; but
shall be content to produce the desired impression by separate
citations of items, practically or reliably known to me as a whale-

man; and from these citations, I take it—the conclusion aimed at will naturally follow of itself.

First: I have personally known three instances where a whale, after receiving a harpoon, has effected a complete escape; and, after an interval (in one instance of three years), has been again struck by the same hand, and slain; when the two irons, both marked by the same private cypher, have been taken from the body. In the instance where three years intervened between the flinging of the two harpoons; and I think it may have been something more than that; the man who darted them happening, in the interval, to go in a trading ship on a voyage to Africa, went ashore there, joined a discovery party, and penetrated far into the interior, where he travelled for a period of nearly two years, often endangered by serpents, savages, tigers, poisonous miasmas, with all the other common perils incident to wandering in the heart of unknown regions. Meanwhile, the whale he had struck must also have been on its travels; no doubt it had thrice circumnavigated the globe, brushing with its flanks all the coasts of Africa; but to no purpose. This man and this whale again came together, and the one vanquished the other. I say I, myself, have known three instances similar to this; that is in two of them I saw the whales struck; and, upon the second attack, saw the two irons with the respective marks cut in them, afterwards taken from the dead fish. In the three-year instance, it so fell out that I was in the boat both times, first and last, and the last time distinctly recognized a peculiar sort of huge mole under the whale's eye, which I had observed there three years previous. I say three years, but I am pretty sure it was more than that. Here are three instances, then, which I personally know the truth of; but I have heard of many other instances from persons whose veracity in the matter there is no good ground to impeach.

Secondly: It is well known in the Sperm Whale Fishery, however ignorant the world ashore may be of it, that there have been several memorable historical instances where a particular whale in the ocean has been at distant times and places popularly cognisable. Why such a whale became thus marked was not altogether and originally owing to his bodily peculiarities as distinguished from other whales; for however peculiar in that respect any chance whale may be, they soon put an end to his peculiarities by killing him, and boiling him down into a peculiarly valuable oil. No: the reason was this: that from the fatal experiences of the fishery there hung a terrible prestige of perilousness about such a whale as there did about Rinaldo Rinaldini, insomuch that most fishermen were content to recognise him by merely touching their tarpaulins when he would be discovered lounging by them on the sea, without seeking to cultivate a more intimate acquaintance. Like some poor devils ashore that happen to know an irascible great man, they make distant unobtrusive salutations to him in the street, lest if they pursued the acquaintance further, they might receive a summary thump for their presumption.

But not only did each of these famous whales enjoy great individual celebrity—nay, you may call it an ocean-wide renown; not only was he famous in life and now is immortal in forecastle stories after death, but he was admitted into all the rights, privileges, and distinctions of a name; had as much a name indeed as Cambyses or Cæsar. Was it not so, O Timor Tom! thou famed leviathan, scarred like an iceberg, who so long did'st lurk in the Oriental straits of that name, whose spout was oft seen from the palmy beach of Ombay? Was it not so, O New Zealand Jack! thou terror of all cruisers that crossed their wakes in the vicinity of the Tattoo Land? Was it not so, O Morquan! King of Japan, whose lofty jet they say at times assumed the semblance of a snow-white cross against the sky? Was it not so, O Don Miguel! thou Chilian whale, marked like an old tortoise with mystic hieroglyphics upon the back! In plain prose, here are four whales as well known to the students of Cetacean History as Marius or Sylla to the classic scholar.

But this is not all. New Zealand Tom and Don Miguel, after at various times creating great havoc among the boats of different vessels, were finally gone in quest of, systematically hunted out, chased and killed by valiant whaling captains, who heaved up their anchors with that express object as much in view, as in setting out through the Narragansett Woods, Captain Butler of old had it in his mind to capture that notorious murderous savage Annawon, the headmost warrior of the Indian King Philip.

I do not know where I can find a better place than just here, to make mention of one or two other things, which to me seem important, as in printed form establishing in all respects the reasonableness of the whole story of the White Whale, more especially the catastrophe. For this is one of those disheartening instances where truth requires full as much bolstering as error. So ignorant are most landsmen of some of the plainest and most palpable wonders of the world, that without some hints touching the plain facts, historical and otherwise, of the fishery, they might scout at Moby Dick as a monstrous fable, or still worse and more detestable, a hideous and intolerable allegory.

First: Though most men have some vague flitting ideas of the general perils of the grand fishery, yet they have nothing like a fixed, vivid conception of those perils, and the frequency with which they recur. One reason perhaps is, that not one in fifty of the actual disasters and deaths by casualties in the fishery, ever finds a public record at home, however transient and immediately forgotten that record. Do you suppose that that poor fellow there, who this moment perhaps caught by the whale-line off the coast of New Guinea, is being carried down to the bottom of the sea by the sounding leviathan—do you suppose that that poor fellow's name will appear in the newspaper obituary you will read to-morrow at your breakfast? No: because the mails are very irregular between here and New Guinea. In fact, did you ever hear what might be called regular news direct or indirect from New Guinea? Yet I tell you that upon one particular voyage which I made to the Pacific, among many others, we spoke thirty different ships, every one of which had had a death by a whale, some of them more than one, and three that had each lost a boat's crew. For God's sake, be economical with your lamps and candles! not a gallon you burn, but at least one drop of man's blood was spilled for it.

Secondly: People ashore have indeed some indefinite idea that a whale is an enormous creature of enormous power; but I have ever found that when narrating to them some specific example of this two-fold enormousness, they have significantly complimented me upon my facetiousness; when, I declare upon my soul, I had no more idea of being facetious than Moses, when he wrote the history of the plagues of Egypt.

But fortunately the special point I here seek can be established upon testimony entirely independent of my own. That point is this: The Sperm Whale is in some cases sufficiently powerful, knowing, and judiciously malicious, as with direct aforethought to stave in, utterly destroy, and sink a large ship; and what is more, the Sperm Whale *has* done it.

First: in the year 1820 the ship Essex, Captain Pollard, of Nantucket, was cruising in the Pacific Ocean. One day she saw spouts, lowered her boats, and gave chase to a shoal of sperm whales. Ere long, several of the whales were wounded; when, suddenly, a very large whale escaping from the boats, issued from the shoal, and bore directly down upon the ship. Dashing his forehead against her hull, he so stove her in, that in less than 'ten minutes' she settled down and fell over. Not a surviving plank of her has been seen since. After the severest exposure, part of the crew reached the land in their boats. Being returned home at last, Captain Pollard once more sailed for the Pacific in command of another ship, but the gods shipwrecked him again upon unknown rocks and breakers; for the second time his ship was utterly lost, and forthwith forswearing the sea, he has never tempted it since. At this day Captain Pollard is a resident of Nantucket. I have seen Owen Chace, who was chief mate of the Essex at the time of the tragedy; I have read his plain and faithful narrative; I have conversed with his son; and all this within a few miles of the scene of the catastrophe.*

Secondly: The ship Union, also of Nantucket, was in the year 1807 totally lost off the Azores by a similar onset, but the authentic particulars of this catastrophe I have never chanced to encounter, though from the whale hunters I have now and then heard casual allusions to it.

Thirdly: Some eighteen or twenty years ago Commodore J—— then commanding an American sloop-of-war of the first class, happened to be dining with a party of whaling captains, on board a Nantucket ship in the harbor of Oahu, Sandwich Islands. Conversation turning upon whales, the Commodore was pleased to be sceptical touching the amazing strength ascribed to them by the professional gentlemen present. He peremptorily denied for example, that any whale could so smite his stout sloop-of-war as to cause her to leak so much as a thimbleful. Very good; but

---

* The following are extracts from Chace's narrative: 'Every fact seemed to warrant me in concluding that it was anything but chance which directed his operations; he made two several attacks upon the ship, at a short interval between them, both of which, according to their direction were calculated to do us the most injury, by being made ahead, and thereby combining the speed of the two objects for the shock; to effect which, the exact manœuvres which he made were necessary. His aspect was most horrible, and such as indicated resentment and fury. He came directly from the shoal which we had just before entered, and in which we had struck three of his companions, as if fired with revenge for their sufferings.' Again: 'At all events, the whole circumstances taken together, all happening before my own eyes, and producing, at the time, impressions in my mind of decided, calculating mischief, on the part of the whale (many of which impressions I cannot now recall), induce me to be satisfied that I am correct in my opinion.'

Here are his reflections some time after quitting the ship, during a black night in an open boat, when almost despairing of reaching any hospitable shore. 'The dark ocean and swelling waters were nothing; the fears of being swallowed up by some dreadful tempest, or dashed upon hidden rocks, with all the other ordinary subjects of fearful contemplation, seemed scarcely entitled to a moment's thought; the dismal looking wreck, and *the horrid aspect and revenge of the whale*, wholly engrossed my reflections, until day again made its appearance.'

In another place—p. 45,—he speaks of *'the mysterious and mortal attack of the animal.'*

there is more coming. Some weeks after, the Commodore set sail in this impregnable craft for Valparaiso. But he was stopped on the way by a portly sperm whale, that begged a few moments' confidential business with him. That business consisted in fetching the Commodore's craft such a thwack, that with all his pumps going he made straight for the nearest port to heave down and repair. I am not superstitious, but I consider the Commodore's interview with that whale as providential. Was not Saul of Tarsus converted from unbelief by a similar fright? I tell you, the sperm whale will stand no nonsense.

I will now refer you to Langsdorff's Voyages for a little circumstance in point, peculiarly interesting to the writer hereof. Langsdorff, you must know by the way, was attached to the Russian Admiral Krusenstern's famous Discovery Expedition in the beginning of the present century. Captain Langsdorff thus begins his seventeenth chapter.

'By the thirteenth of May our ship was ready to sail, and the next day we were out in the open sea, on our way to Ochotsh. The weather was very clear and fine, but so intolerably cold that we were obliged to keep on our fur clothing. For some days we had very little wind; it was not till the nineteenth that a brisk gale from the northwest sprang up. An uncommon large whale, the body of which was larger than the ship itself, lay almost at the surface of the water, but was not perceived by any one on board till the moment when the ship, which was in full sail, was almost upon him, so that it was impossible to prevent its striking against him. We were thus placed in the most imminent danger, as this gigantic creature, setting up its back, raised the ship three feet at least out of the water. The masts reeled, and the sails fell altogether, while we who were below all sprang instantly upon the deck, concluding that we had struck upon some rock; instead of this we saw the monster sailing off with the utmost gravity and solemnity. Captain D'Wolf applied immediately to the pumps to examine whether or not the vessel had received any damage from the shock, but we found that very happily it had escaped entirely uninjured.'

Now, the Captain D'Wolf here alluded to as commanding the ship in question, is a New Englander, who, after a long life of unusual adventures as a sea-captain, this day resides in the village of Dorchester near Boston. I have the honor of being a nephew of his. I have particularly questioned him concerning this passage in Langsdorff. He substantiates every word. The ship, however, was by no means a large one: a Russian craft built on the Siberian coast, and purchased by my uncle after bartering away the vessel in which he sailed from home.

In that up and down manly book of old-fashioned adventure, so full, too, of honest wonders—the voyage of Lionel Wafer, one of ancient Dampier's old chums—I found a little matter set down so like that just quoted from Langsdorff, that I cannot forbear inserting it here for a corroborative example, if such be needed.

Lionel, it seems, was on his way to 'John Ferdinando,' as he calls the modern Juan Fernandes. 'In our way thither,' he says, 'about four o'clock in the morning, when we were about one hundred and fifty leagues from the Main of America, our ship felt a terrible shock, which put our men in such consternation that they could hardly tell where they were or what to think; but every one began to prepare for death. And, indeed, the shock was so sudden and violent, that we took it for granted the ship had struck against a rock; but when the amazement was a little over, we cast the lead, and sounded, but found no ground. * * * * The suddenness of the shock made the guns leap in their carriages, and several of the men were shaken out of their hammocks. Captain Davis, who lay with his head on a gun, was thrown out of his cabin!' Lionel then goes on to impute the shock to an earthquake, and seems to substantiate the imputation by stating that a great earthquake, somewhere about that time, did actually do great mischief along the Spanish land. But I should not much wonder if, in the darkness of that early hour of the morning, the shock was after all caused by an unseen whale vertically bumping the hull from beneath.

I might proceed with several more examples, one way or another known to me, of the great power and malice at times of the sperm whale. In more than one instance, he has been known, not only to chase the assailing boats back to their ships, but to pursue the ship itself, and long withstand all the lances hurled at him from its decks. The English ship Pusie Hall can tell a story on that head; and, as for his strength, let me say, that there have been examples where the lines attached to a running sperm whale have, in a calm, been transferred to the ship, and secured there; the whale towing her great hull through the water, as a horse walks off with a cart. Again, it is very often observed that, if the sperm whale, once struck, is allowed time to rally, he then acts, not so often with blind rage, as with wilful, deliberate designs of destruction to his pursuers; nor is it without conveying some eloquent indication of his character, that upon being attacked he will frequently open his mouth, and retain it in that dread expansion for several consecutive minutes. But I must be content with only one more and a concluding illustration; a remarkable and most significant one, by which you will not fail to see, that not only is the most marvellous event in this book corroborated by plain facts of the present day, but that these marvels (like all marvels) are mere repetitions of the ages; so that for the millionth time we say amen with Solomon—Verily there is nothing new under the sun.

In the sixth Christian century lived Procopius, a Christian magistrate of Constantinople, in the days when Justinian was Emperor and Belisarius general. As many know, he wrote the history of his own times, a work every way of uncommon value. By the best authorities, he has always been considered a most trustworthy and unexaggerating historian, except in some one or two particulars, not at all affecting the matter presently to be mentioned.

Now, in this history of his, Procopius mentions that, during the term of his prefecture at Constantinople, a great sea-monster was captured in the neighboring Propontis, or Sea of Marmora, after having destroyed vessels at intervals in those waters for a period of more than fifty years. A fact thus set down in substantial history cannot easily be gainsaid. Nor is there any reason it should be. Of what precise species this sea-monster was, is not mentioned. But as he destroyed ships, as well as for other reasons, he must have been a whale; and I am strongly inclined to think a sperm whale. And I will tell you why. For a long time I fancied that the sperm whale had been always unknown in the Mediterranean and the deep waters connecting with it. Even now I am certain that those seas are not, and perhaps never can be, in the present constitution of things, a place for his habitual gregarious resort. But further investigations have recently proved to me, that in modern times there have been isolated instances of the presence of the sperm whale in the Mediterranean. I am told, on good authority, that on the Barbary coast, a Commodore Davis of the British navy found the skeleton of a sperm whale. Now, as a vessel of war readily passes through the Dardanelles, hence a sperm whale could, by the same route, pass out of the Mediterranean into the Propontis.

In the Propontis, as far as I can learn, none of that peculiar substance called *brit* is to be found, the aliment of the right whale. But I have every reason to believe that the food of the sperm whale—squid or cuttle-fish—lurks at the bottom of that sea, because large creatures, but by no means the largest of that sort, have been found at its surface. If, then, you properly put these statements together, and reason upon them a bit, you will clearly perceive that, according to all human reasoning, Procopius's sea-monster, that for half a century stove the ships of a Roman Emperor, must in all probability have been a sperm whale.

46

SURMISES

THOUGH, consumed with the hot fire of his purpose, Ahab in all his thoughts and actions ever had in view the ultimate capture of Moby Dick; though he seemed ready to sacrifice all mortal interests to that one passion; nevertheless it may have been that he was by nature and long habituation far too wedded to a fiery whale-man's way, altogether to abandon the collateral prosecution of the voyage. Or at least if this were otherwise, there were not wanting other motives much more influential with him. It would be refining too much, perhaps, even considering his monomania, to hint that his vindictiveness towards the White Whale might have possibly extended itself in some degree to all sperm whales, and that the more monsters he slew by so much the more he multiplied the chances that each subsequently encountered whale would prove to be the hated one he hunted. But if such an hypothesis be indeed exceptionable, there were still additional considerations which, though not so strictly according with the wildness of his ruling passion, yet were by no means incapable of swaying him.

To accomplish his object Ahab must use tools; and of all tools used in the shadow of the moon, men are most apt to get out of order. He knew, for example, that however magnetic his as-cendency in some respects was over Starbuck, yet that ascendency did not cover the complete spiritual man any more than mere corporeal superiority involves intellectual mastership; for to the purely spiritual, the intellectual but stands in a sort of corporeal relation. Starbuck's body and Starbuck's coerced will were Ahab's, so long as Ahab kept his magnet at Starbuck's brain; still he knew that for all this the chief mate, in his soul, abhorred his captain's quest, and could he, would joyfully disintegrate himself from it, or even frustrate it. It might be that a long interval would elapse ere the White Whale was seen. During that long interval Starbuck would ever be apt to fall into open relapses of rebellion against his captain's leadership, unless some ordinary, prudential, circumstantial influences were brought to bear upon him. Not only that, but the subtle insanity of Ahab respecting Moby Dick was noways more significantly manifested than in his superlative sense and shrewdness in foreseeing that, for the present, the hunt should in some way be stripped of that strange imaginative impiousness which naturally invested it; that the full terror of the voyage must be kept withdrawn into the obscure background (for few men's courage is proof against protracted meditation unrelieved by action); that when they stood their long night watches, his officers and men must have some nearer things to think of than Moby Dick. For however eagerly and impetuously the savage crew had hailed the announcement of his quest; yet all sailors of all sorts are more or less capricious and unreliable—they live in the varying outer weather, and they inhale its fickleness—and when retained for any object remote and blank in the pursuit, however promissory of life and passion in the end, it is above all things requisite that temporary interests and employments should intervene and hold them healthily suspended for the final dash.

Nor was Ahab unmindful of another thing. In times of strong emotion mankind disdain all base considerations; but such times are evanescent. The permanent constitutional condition of the manufactured man, thought Ahab, is sordidness. Granting that the White Whale fully incites the hearts of this my savage crew, and playing round their savageness even breeds a certain generous knight-errantism in them, still, while for the love of it they give chase to Moby Dick, they must also have food for their more common, daily appetites. For even the high lifted and chivalric Crusaders of old times were not content to traverse two thousand miles of land to fight for their holy sepulchre, without committing burglaries, picking pockets, and gaining other pious perquisites by the way. Had they been strictly held to their one final and romantic object—that final and romantic object, too many would have turned from in disgust. I will not strip these men, thought Ahab, of all hopes of cash—aye, cash. They may scorn cash now; but let some months go by, and no perspective promise of it to them, and then this same quiescent cash all at once mutinying in them, this same cash would soon cashier Ahab.

Nor was there wanting still another precautionary motive more related to Ahab personally. Having impulsively, it is probable, and perhaps somewhat prematurely revealed the prime but private purpose of the Pequod's voyage, Ahab was now entirely conscious that, in so doing, he had indirectly laid himself open to the unanswerable charge of usurpation; and with perfect impunity, both moral and legal, his crew if so disposed, and to that end competent, could refuse all further obedience to him, and even violently wrest from him the command. From even the barely hinted imputation of usurpation, and the possible consequences of such a suppressed impression gaining ground, Ahab must of course have been most anxious to protect himself. That protection could only consist in his own predominating brain and heart and hand, backed by a heedful, closely calculating attention to every minute atmospheric influence which it was possible for his crew to be subjected to.

For all these reasons then, and others perhaps too analytic to be verbally developed here, Ahab plainly saw that he must still in a good degree continue true to the natural, nominal purpose of the Pequod's voyage; observe all customary usages; and not only that, but force himself to evince all his well known passionate interest in the general pursuit of his profession.

Be all this as it may, his voice was now often heard hailing the three mast-heads and admonishing them to keep a bright look-out, and not omit reporting even a porpoise. This vigilance was not long without reward.

47

THE MAT- MAKER

It was a cloudy, sultry afternoon; the seamen were lazily lounging about the decks, or vacantly gazing over into the lead-colored water. Queequeg and I were mildly employed weaving what is called a sword-mat, for an additional lashing to our boat. So still and subdued and yet somehow preluding was all the scene, and such an incantation of revery lurked in the air, that each silent sailor seemed resolved into his own invisible self.

I was the attendant or page of Queequeg, while busy at the mat. As I kept passing and repassing the filling or woof of marline between the long yarns of the warp, using my own hand for the shuttle, and as Queequeg, standing sideways, ever and anon slid his heavy oaken sword between the threads, and idly looking off upon the water, carelessly and unthinkingly drove home every yarn: I say so strange a dreaminess did there then reign all over the ship and all over the sea, only broken by the intermitting dull sound of the sword, that it seemed as if this were the Loom of Time, and I myself were a shuttle mechanically weaving and weaving away at the Fates. There lay the fixed threads of the warp subject to but one single, ever returning, unchanging vibration, and that vibration merely enough to admit of the crosswise interblending of other threads with its own. This warp seemed necessity; and here, thought I, with my own hand I ply my own shuttle and weave my own destiny into these unalterable threads. Meantime, Queequeg's impulsive, indifferent sword, sometimes hitting the woof slantingly, or crookedly, or strongly, or weakly, as the case might be; and by this difference in the concluding blow producing a corresponding contrast in the final aspect of the completed fabric; this savage's sword, thought I, which thus finally shapes and fashions both warp and woof; this easy, indifferent sword must be chance—aye, chance, free will, and necessity—no wise incompatible—all interweavingly working together. The straight warp of necessity, not to be swerved from its ultimate course— its every alternating vibration, indeed, only tending to that; free will still free to ply her shuttle between given threads; and chance, though restrained in its play within the right lines of necessity, and sideways in its motions directed by free will, though thus prescribed to by both, chance by turns rules either, and has the last featuring blow at events.

Thus we were weaving and weaving away when I started at a sound so strange, long drawn, and musically wild and unearthly, that the ball of free will dropped from my hand, and I stood gazing up at the clouds whence that voice dropped like a wing. High aloft in the cross-trees was that mad Gay-Header, Tashtego. His body was reaching eagerly forward, his hand stretched out like a wand, and at brief sudden intervals he continued his cries. To be sure the same sound was that very moment perhaps being heard all over the seas, from hundreds of whalemen's look-outs perched as high in the air; but from few of those lungs could that accustomed old cry have derived such a marvellous cadence as from Tashtego the Indian's.

As he stood hovering over you half suspended in air, so wildly and eagerly peering towards the horizon, you would have thought him some prophet or seer beholding the shadows of Fate, and by those wild cries announcing their coming.

'There she blows! there! there! there! she blows! she blows!'
'Where-away?'

'On the lee-beam, about two miles off! a school of them!'

Instantly all was commotion.

The Sperm Whale blows as a clock ticks, with the same un-deviating and reliable uniformity. And thereby whalemen distin-guish this fish from other tribes of his genus.

'There go flukes!' was now the cry from Tashtego; and the whales disappeared.

'Quick, steward!' cried Ahab. 'Time! time!'

Dough-Boy hurried below, glanced at the watch, and reported the exact minute to Ahab.

The ship was now kept away from the wind, and she went gently rolling before it. Tashtego reporting that the whales had gone down heading to leeward, we confidently looked to see them again directly in advance of our bows. For that singular craft at times evinced by the Sperm Whale when, sounding with his head in one direction, he nevertheless, while concealed beneath the surface, mills round, and swiftly swims off in the opposite quarter—this deceitfulness of his could not now be in action; for there was no reason to suppose that the fish seen by Tashtego had been in any way alarmed, or indeed knew at all of our vicinity. One of the men selected for shipkeepers—that is, those not appointed to the boats, by this time relieved the Indian at the main-mast head. The sailors at the fore and mizzen had come down; the line tubs were fixed in their places; the cranes were thrust out; the mainyard was backed, and the three boats swung over the sea like three samphire baskets over high cliffs. Outside of the bulwarks their eager crews with one hand clung to the rail, while one foot was expectantly poised on the gunwale. So look the long line of man-of-war's men about to throw themselves on board an enemy's ship.

But at this critical instant a sudden exclamation was heard that took every eye from the whale. With a start all glared at dark Ahab, who was surrounded by five dusky phantoms that seemed fresh formed out of air.

48

THE FIRST LOWERING

THE phantoms, for so they then seemed, were flitting on the other side of the deck, and, with a noiseless celerity, were casting loose the tackles and bands of the boat which swung there. This boat had always been deemed one of the spare boats, though technically called the captain's, on account of its hanging from the starboard quarter. The figure that now stood by its bows was tall and swart, with one white tooth evilly protuding from its steel-like lips. A rumpled Chinese jacket of black cotton funereally invested him, with wide black trowsers of the same dark stuff. But strangely crowning this ebonness was a glistening white plaited turban, the living hair braided and coiled round and round upon his head. Less swart in aspect, the companions of this figure were of that vivid, tiger-yellow complexion peculiar to some of the aboriginal natives of the Manillas;—a race notorious for a certain diabolism of subtilty, and by some honest white mariners supposed to be the paid spies and secret confidential agents on the water of the devil, their lord, whose counting-room they suppose to be elsewhere.

While yet the wondering ship's company were gazing upon these strangers, Ahab cried out to the white-turbaned old man at their head, 'All ready there, Fedallah?'

'Ready,' was the half-hissed reply.

'Lower away then; d'ye hear?' shouting across the deck. 'Lower away there, I say.'

Such was the thunder of his voice, that spite of their amazement the men sprang over the rail; the sheaves whirled round in the blocks; with a wallow, the three boats dropped into the sea; while, with a dexterous, off-handed daring, unknown in any other vocation, the sailors, goat-like, leaped down the rolling ship's side into the tossed boats below.

Hardly had they pulled out from under the ship's lee, when a fourth keel, coming from the windward side, pulled round under the stern, and showed the five strangers rowing Ahab, who, standing erect in the stern, loudly hailed Starbuck, Stubb, and Flask, to spread themselves widely, so as to cover a large expanse of water. But with all their eyes again riveted upon the swart Fedallah and his crew, the inmates of the other boats obeyed not the command.

'Captain Ahab?—' said Starbuck.

'Spread yourselves,' cried Ahab; 'give way, all four boats. Thou, Flask, pull out more to leeward!'

'Aye, aye, sir,' cheerily cried little King-Post, sweeping round his great steering oar. 'Lay back!' addressing his crew. 'There!—there!—there again! There she blows right ahead, boys!—lay back!—Never heed yonder yellow boys, Archy.'

'Oh, I don't mind 'em, sir,' said Archy; 'I knew it all before now. Didn't I hear 'em in the hold? And didn't I tell Cabaco here of it? What say ye, Cabaco? They are stowaways, Mr Flask.'

'Pull, pull, my fine hearts-alive; pull, my children; pull, my little ones,' drawlingly and soothingly sighed Stubb to his crew, some of whom still showed signs of uneasiness. 'Why don't you break your backbones, my boys? What is it you stare at? Those chaps in yonder boat? Tut! They are only five more hands come to help us—never mind from where—the more the merrier. Pull, then, do pull; never mind the brimstone—devils are good fellows enough. So, so; there you are now; that's the stroke for a thousand pounds; that's the stroke to sweep the stakes! Hurrah for the gold cup of sperm oil, my heroes! Three cheers, men—all hearts alive! Easy, easy; don't be in a hurry—don't be in a hurry. Why don't you snap your oars, you rascals? Bite something, you dogs! So, so, so, then;—softly, softly! That's it—that's it! long and strong. Give way there, give way! The devil fetch ye, ye ragamuffin rapscallions; ye are all asleep. Stop snoring, ye sleepers, and pull. Pull, will ye? pull, can't ye? pull, won't ye? Why in the name of gudgeons and ginger cakes don't ye pull? pull and break something! pull, and start your eyes out! Here!' whipping out the sharp knife from his girdle; 'every mother's son of ye draw his knife, and pull with the blade between his teeth. That's it—that's it. Now ye do something; that looks like it, my steel-bits. Start her—start her, my silver-spoons! Start her, marling-spikes!'

Stubb's exordium to his crew is given here at large, because he had rather a peculiar way of talking to them in general, and especially in inculcating the religion of rowing. But you must not suppose from this specimen of his sermonizings that he ever flew into downright passions with his congregation. Not at all; and therein consisted his chief peculiarity. He would say the most terrific things to his crew, in a tone so strangely compounded of fun and fury, and the fury seemed so calculated merely as a spice to the fun, that no oarsman could hear such queer invocations without pulling for dear life, and yet pulling for the mere joke of the thing. Besides he all the time looked so easy and indolent himself, so loungingly managed his steering-oar, and so broadly gaped—open-mouthed at times—that the mere sight of such a yawning commander, by sheer force of contrast, acted like a charm upon the crew. Then again, Stubb was one of those odd sort of humorists, whose jollity is sometimes so curiously ambiguous, as to put all inferiors on their guard in the matter of obeying them.

In obedience to a sign from Ahab, Starbuck was now pulling obliquely across Stubb's bow; and when for a minute or so the two boats were pretty near to each other, Stubb hailed the mate.

'Mr Starbuck! larboard boat there, ahoy! a word with ye, sir, if ye please!'

'Halloa!' returned Starbuck, turning round not a single inch as he spoke; earnestly but whisperingly urging his crew; his face set like a flint from Stubb's.

'What think ye of those yellow boys, sir!'

'Smuggled on board, somehow, before the ship sailed. (Strong, strong, boys!)' in a whisper to his crew, then speaking out loud again: 'A sad business, Mr Stubb! (seethe her, seethe her, my lads!) but never mind, Mr Stubb, all for the best. Let all your crew pull strong, come what will. (Spring, my men, spring!) There's hogsheads of sperm ahead, Mr Stubb, and that's what ye came for. (Pull, my boys!) Sperm, sperm's the play! This at least is duty; duty and profit hand in hand!'

'Aye, aye, I thought as much,' soliloquized Stubb, when the boats diverged, 'as soon as I clapt eye on 'em, I thought so. Aye, and that's what he went into the after hold for, so often, as Dough-Boy long suspected. They were hidden down there. The White Whale's at the bottom of it. Well, well, so be it! Can't be helped! All right! Give way, men! It ain't the White Whale to-day! Give way!'

Now the advent of these outlandish strangers at such a critical instant as the lowering of the boats from the deck, this had not unreasonably awakened a sort of superstitious amazement in some of the ship's company; but Archy's fancied discovery having some time previous got abroad among them, though indeed not credited then, this had in some small measure prepared them for the event. It took off the extreme edge of their wonder; and so what with all this and Stubb's confident way of accounting for their appearance, they were for the time freed from superstitious surmisings; though the affair still left abundant room for all manner of wild conjectures as to dark Ahab's precise agency in the matter from the beginning. For me, I silently recalled the mysterious shadows I had seen creeping on board the Pequod during the dim Nantucket dawn, as well as the enigmatical hintings of the unaccountable Elijah.

Meantime, Ahab, out of hearing of his officers, having sided the furthest to windward, was still ranging ahead of the other boats; a circumstance bespeaking how potent a crew was pulling him. Those tiger yellow creatures of his seemed all steel and whalebone; like five trip-hammers they rose and fell with regular strokes of strength, which periodically started the boat along the water like a horizontal burst boiler out of a Mississippi steamer. As for Fedallah, who was seen pulling the harpooneer oar, he had thrown aside his black jacket, and displayed his naked chest with the whole part of his body above the gunwale, clearly cut against the alternating depressions of the watery horizon; while at the other end of the boat Ahab, with one arm, like a fencer's, thrown half backward into the air, as if to counterbalance any tendency to trip; Ahab was seen steadily managing his steering oar as in a thousand boat lowerings ere the White Whale had torn him. All at once the out-stretched arm gave a peculiar motion and then remained fixed, while the boat's five oars were seen simultaneously peaked. Boat and crew sat motionless on the sea. Instantly the three spread boats in the rear paused on their way. The whales had irregularly settled bodily down into the blue, thus giving no distantly discernible token of the movement, though from his closer vicinity Ahab had observed it.

'Every man look out along his oar!' cried Starbuck. 'Thou, Queequeg, stand up!'

Nimbly springing up on the triangular raised box in the bow, the savage stood erect there, and with intensely eager eyes gazed off towards the spot where the chase had last been descried. Likewise upon the extreme stern of the boat where it was also triangularly platformed level with the gunwale, Starbuck himself was seen coolly and adroitly balancing himself to the jerking tossings of his chip of a craft, and silently eyeing the vast blue eye of the sea.

Not very far distant Flask's boat was also lying breathlessly still; its commander recklessly standing upon the top of the loggerhead, a stout sort of post rooted in the keel, and rising some two feet above the level of the stern platform. It is used for catching turns with the whale line. Its top is not more spacious than the palm of a man's hand, and standing upon such a base as that, Flask seemed perched at the mast-head of some ship which had sunk to all but her trucks. But little King-Post was small and short, and at the same time little King-Post was full of a large and tall ambition, so that this loggerhead stand-point of his did by no means satisfy King-Post.

'I can't see three seas off; tip us up an oar there, and let me on to that.'

Upon this, Daggoo, with either hand upon the gunwale to steady his way, swiftly slid aft, and then erecting himself volunteered his lofty shoulders for a pedestal.

'Good a mast-head as any, sir. Will you mount?'

'That I will, and thank ye very much, my fine fellow; only I wish you fifty feet taller.'

Whereupon planting his feet firmly against two opposite planks of the boat, the gigantic negro, stooping a little, presented his flat palm to Flask's foot, and then putting Flask's hand on his hearse-plumed head and bidding him spring as he himself should toss, with one dexterous fling landed the little man high and dry on his shoulders. And here was Flask now standing, Daggoo with one lifted arm furnishing him with a breast-band to lean against and steady himself by.

At any time it is a strange sight to the tyro to see with what wondrous habitude of unconscious skill the whaleman will maintain an erect posture in his boat, even when pitched about by the most riotously perverse and cross-running seas. Still more strange to see him giddily perched upon the loggerhead itself, under such circumstances. But the sight of little Flask mounted upon gigantic Daggoo was yet more curious; for sustaining himself with a cool, indifferent, easy, unthought of, barbaric majesty, the noble negro to every roll of the sea harmoniously rolled his fine form. On his broad back, flaxen-haired Flask seemed a snow-flake. The bearer looked nobler than the rider. Though, truly, vivacious, tumultuous, ostentatious little Flask would now and then stamp with impatience; but not one added heave did he thereby give to the negro's lordly chest. So have I seen Passion and Vanity stamping the living magnanimous earth, but the earth did not alter her tides and her seasons for that.

Meanwhile Stubb, the second mate, betrayed no such far-gazing solicitudes. The whales might have made one of their regular soundings, not a temporary dive from mere fright; and if that were the case, Stubb, as his wont in such cases, it seems, was resolved to solace the languishing interval with his pipe. He withdrew it from his hatband, where he always wore it aslant like a feather. He loaded it, and rammed home the loading with his thumb-end; but hardly had he ignited his match across the rough sand-paper of his hand, when Tashtego, his harpooneer, whose eyes had been setting to windward like two fixed stars, suddenly dropped like light from his erect attitude to his seat, crying out in a quick phrensy of hurry, 'Down, down all, and give way!—there they are!'

To a landsman, no whale, nor any sign of a herring, would have been visible at that moment; nothing but a troubled bit of greenish white water, and thin scattered puffs of vapor hovering over it, and suffusingly blowing off to leeward, like the confused scud from white rolling billows. The air around suddenly vibrated and tingled, as it were, like the air over intensely heated plates of iron. Beneath this atmospheric waving and curling, and partially beneath a thin layer of water, also, the whales were swimming. Seen in advance of all the other indications, the puffs of vapor they spouted, seemed their forerunning couriers and detached flying outriders.

All four boats were now in keen pursuit of that one spot of troubled water and air. But it bade far to outstrip them; it flew on and on, as a mass of interblending bubbles borne down a rapid stream from the hills.

'Pull, pull, my good boys,' said Starbuck, in the lowest possible but intensest concentrated whisper to his men; while the sharp fixed glance from his eyes, darted straight ahead of the bow, almost seemed as two visible needles in two unerring binnacle compasses. He did not say much to his crew, though, nor did his crew say anything to him. Only the silence of the boat was at intervals startlingly pierced by one of his peculiar whispers, now harsh with command, now soft with entreaty.

How different the loud little King-Post. 'Sing out and say something, my hearties. Roar and pull, my thunderbolts! Beach me, beach me on their black backs, boys; only do that for me, and I'll sign over to you my Martha's Vineyard plantation, boys; including wife and children, boys. Lay me on—lay me on! O Lord, Lord! but I shall go stark, staring mad: See! see that white water!' And so shouting, he pulled his hat from his head, and stamped up and down on it; then picking it up, flirted it far off upon the sea; and finally fell to rearing and plunging in the boat's stern like a crazed colt from the prairie.

'Look at that chap now,' philosophically drawled Stubb, who, with his unlighted short pipe, mechanically retained between his teeth, at a short distance, followed after—'He's got fits, that Flask has. Fits? yes, give him fits—that's the very word—pitch fits into 'em. Merrily, merrily, hearts-alive. Pudding for supper, you know;— merry's the word. Pull, babes—pull, sucklings—pull, all. But what the devil are you hurrying about? Softly, softly, and steadily, my men. Only pull, and keep pulling; nothing more. Crack all your backbones, and bite your knives in two—that's all. Take it easy— why don't ye take it easy, I say, and burst all your livers and lungs!'

But what it was that inscrutable Ahab said to that tiger-yellow crew of his—these were words best omitted here; for you live under the blessed light of the evangelical land. Only the infidel sharks in the audacious seas may give ear to such words, when, with tornado brow, and eyes of red murder, and foam-glued lips, Ahab leaped after his prey.

Meanwhile, all the boats tore on. The repeated specific allusions of Flask to 'that whale,' as he called the fictitious monster which he declared to be incessantly tantalizing his boat's bow with its tail—these allusions of his were at times so vivid and life-like, that they would cause some one or two of his men to snatch a fearful look over the shoulder. But this was against all rule; for the oarsmen must put out their eyes, and ram a skewer through their necks; usage pronouncing that they must have no organs but ears, and no limbs but arms, in these critical moments.

It was a sight full of quick wonder and awe! The vast swells of the omnipotent sea; the surging, hollow roar they made, as they rolled along the eight gunwales, like gigantic bowls in a boundless bowling-green; the brief suspended agony of the boat, as it would tip for an instant on the knife-like edge of the sharper waves, that almost seemed threatening to cut it in two; the sudden profound dip into the watery glens and hollows; the keen spurrings and goadings to gain the top of the opposite hill; the headlong, sled-like slide down its other side;—all these, with the cries of the headsmen and harpooneers, and the shuddering gasps of the oars-men, with the wondrous sight of the ivory Pequod bearing down upon her boats with outstretched sails, like a wild hen after her screaming brood;—all this was thrilling. Not the raw recruit, marching from the bosom of his wife into the fever heat of his first battle; not the dead man's ghost encountering the first un-known phantom in the other world;—neither of these can feel stranger and stronger emotions than that man does, who for the first time finds himself pulling into the charmed, churned circle of the hunted sperm whale.

The dancing white water made by the chase was now becoming more and more visible, owing to the increasing darkness of the dun cloud-shadows flung upon the sea. The jets of vapor no longer blended, but tilted everywhere to right and left; the whales seemed separating their wakes. The boats were pulled more apart; Starbuck giving chase to three whales running dead to leeward. Our sail was now set, and, with the still rising wind, we rushed along; the boat going with such madness through the water, that the lee oars could scarcely be worked rapidly enough to escape being torn from the row-locks.

Soon we were running through a suffusing wide veil of mist; neither ship nor boat to be seen.

'Give way, men,' whispered Starbuck, drawing still further aft the sheet of his sail; 'there is time to kill a fish yet before the squall comes. There's white water again!—close to! Spring!'

Soon after, two cries in quick succession on each side of us denoted that the other boats had got fast; but hardly were they overheard, when with a lightning-like hurtling whisper Starbuck said: 'Stand up!' and Queequeg, harpoon in hand, sprang to his feet.

Though not one of the oarsmen was then facing the life and death peril so close to them ahead, yet with their eyes on the intense countenance of the mate in the stern of the boat, they knew that the imminent instant had come; they heard, too, an enormous wallowing sound as of fifty elephants stirring in their litter. Meanwhile the boat was still booming through the mist, the waves curling and hissing around us like the erected crests of enraged serpents.

'That's him hump. *There, there*, give it to him!' whispered Starbuck.

A short rushing sound leaped out of the boat; it was the darted iron of Queequeg. Then all in one welded commotion came an invisible push from astern, while forward the boat seemed striking on a ledge; the sail collapsed and exploded; a gush of scalding vapor shot up near by; something rolled and tumbled like an earthquake beneath us. The whole crew were half suffocated as they were tossed helter-skelter into the white curdling cream of the squall. Squall, whale, and harpoon had all blended together; and the whale, merely grazed by the iron, escaped.

Though completely swamped, the boat was nearly unharmed. Swimming round it we picked up the floating oars, and lashing them across the gunwale, tumbled back to our places. There we sat up to our knees in the sea, the water covering every rib and plank, so that to our downward gazing eyes the suspended craft seemed a coral boat grown up to us from the bottom of the ocean.

The wind increased to a howl; the waves dashed their bucklers together; the whole squall roared, forked, and crackled around us like a white fire upon the prairie, in which, unconsumed, we were burning; immortal in these jaws of death! In vain we hailed the other boats; as well roar to the live coals down the chimney of a flaming furnace as hail those boats in that storm. Meanwhile the driving scud, rack, and mist, grew darker with the shadows of night; no sign of the ship could be seen. The rising sea forbade all attempts to bale out the boat. The oars were useless as propellers, performing now the office of life-preservers. So, cutting the lashing of the waterproof match keg, after many failures Starbuck contrived to ignite the lamp in the lantern; then stretching it on a waif pole, handed it to Queequeg as the standard-bearer of this forlorn hope. There, then, he sat, holding up that imbecile candle in the heart of that almighty forlornness. There, then, he sat, the sign and symbol of a man without faith, hopelessly holding up hope in the midst of despair.

Wet, drenched through, and shivering cold, despairing of ship or boat, we lifted up our eyes as the dawn came on. The mist still spread over the sea, the empty lantern lay crushed in the bottom of the boat. Suddenly Queequeg started to his feet, hollowing his hand to his ear. We all heard a faint creaking, as of ropes and yards hitherto muffled by the storm. The sound came nearer and nearer; the thick mists were dimly parted by a huge, vague form. Affrighted, we all sprang into the sea as the ship at last loomed into view, bearing right down upon us within a distance of not much more than its length.

Floating on the waves we saw the abandoned boat, as for one instant it tossed and gaped beneath the ship's bows like a chip at the base of a cataract; and then the vast hull rolled over it, and it was seen no more till it came up weltering astern. Again we swam for it, were dashed against it by the seas, and were at last taken up and safely landed on board. Ere the squall came close to, the other boats had cut loose from their fish and returned to the ship in good time. The ship had given us up, but was still cruising, if haply it might light upon some token of our perishing,— an oar or a lance pole.

49

THE HYENA

THERE are certain queer times and occasions in this strange mixed affair we call life when a man takes this whole universe for a vast practical joke, though the wit thereof he but dimly discerns, and more than suspects that the joke is at nobody's expense but his own. However, nothing dispirits, and nothing seems worth while disputing. He bolts down all events, all creeds, and beliefs, and persuasions, all hard things visible and invisible, never mind how knobby; as an ostrich of potent digestion gobbles down bullets and gun flints. And as for small difficulties and worryings, prospects of sudden disaster, peril of life and limb; all these, and death itself, seem to him only sly, good-natured hits, and jolly punches in the side bestowed by the unseen and unaccountable old joker. That odd sort of wayward mood I am speaking of, comes over a man only in some time of extreme tribulation; it comes in the very midst of his earnestness, so that what just before might have seemed to him a thing most momentous, now seems but a part of the general joke. There is nothing like the perils of whaling to breed this free and easy sort of genial, desperado philosophy; and with it I now regarded this whole voyage of the Pequod, and the great White Whale its object.

'Queequeg,' said I, when they had dragged me, the last man, to the deck, and I was still shaking myself in my jacket to fling off the water; 'Queequeg, my fine friend, does this sort of thing often happen?' Without much emotion, though soaked through just like me, he gave me to understand that such things did often happen.

'Mr Stubb,' said I, turning to that worthy, who, buttoned up in his oil-jacket, was now calmly smoking his pipe in the rain; 'Mr Stubb, I think I have heard you say that of all whalemen you ever met, our chief mate, Mr Starbuck, is by far the most careful and prudent. I suppose then, that going plump on a flying whale with your sail set in a foggy squall is the height of a whaleman's discretion?'

'Certain. I've lowered for whales from a leaking ship in a gale off Cape Horn.'

'Mr Flask,' said I, turning to little King-Post, who was standing close by; 'you are experienced in these things, and I am not. Will you tell me whether it is an unalterable law in this fishery, Mr Flask, for an oarsman to break his own back pulling himself back-foremost into death's jaws?'

'Can't you twist that smaller?' said Flask. 'Yes, that's the law. I should like to see a boat's crew backing water up to a whale face foremost. Ha, ha! the whale would give them squint for squint, mind that!'

Here then, from three impartial witnesses, I had a deliberate statement of the entire case. Considering, therefore, that squalls and capsizings in the water and consequent bivouacks on the deep, were matters of common occurrence in this kind of life; considering that at the superlatively critical instant of going on to the whale I must resign my life into the hands of him who steered the boat—oftentimes a fellow who at that very moment is in his impetuousness upon the point of scuttling the craft with his own frantic stampings; considering that the particular disaster to our own particular boat was chiefly to be imputed to Starbuck's driving on to his whale almost in the teeth of a squall, and considering that Starbuck, notwithstanding, was famous for his great heedfulness in the fishery; considering that I belonged to this uncommonly prudent Starbuck's boat; and finally considering in what a devil's chase I was implicated, touching the White Whale: taking all things together, I say, I thought I might as well go below and make a rough draft of my will. 'Queequeg,' said I, 'come along, you shall be my lawyer, executor, and legatee.'

It may seem strange that of all men sailors should be tinkering at their last wills and testaments, but there are no people in the world more fond of that diversion. This was the fourth time in my nautical life that I had done the same thing. After the ceremony was concluded upon the present occasion, I felt all the easier; a stone was rolled away from my heart. Besides, all the days I should now live would be as good as the days that Lazarus lived after his resurrection; a supplementary clean gain of so many months or weeks as the case might be. I survived myself; my death and burial were locked up in my chest. I looked round me tranquilly and contentedly, like a quiet ghost with a clean conscience sitting inside the bars of a snug family vault.

Now then, thought I, unconsciously rolling up the sleeves of my frock, here goes for a cool, collected dive at death and destruction, and the devil fetch the hindmost.

50

AHAB'S BOAT AND CREW. FEDALLAH

'WHO would have thought it, Flask!' cried Stubb; 'if I had but one leg you would not catch me in a boat, unless maybe to stop the plug-hole with my timber toe. Oh! he's a wonderful old man!'

'I don't think it so strange, after all, on that account,' said Flask. 'If his leg were off at the hip, now, it would be a different thing. That would disable him; but he has one knee, and a good part of the other left, you know.'

'I don't know that, my little man; I never yet saw him kneel.'

Among whale-wise people it has often been argued whether,

considering the paramount importance of his life to the success
of the voyage, it is right for a whaling captain to jeopardize that
life in the active perils of the chase. So Tamerlane's soldiers often
argued with tears in their eyes, whether that invaluable life of his
ought to be carried into the thickest of the fight.

But with Ahab the question assumed a modified aspect. Considering that with two legs man is but a hobbling wight in all
times of danger; considering that the pursuit of whales is always
under great and extraordinary difficulties; that every individual
moment, indeed, then comprises a peril; under these circumstances
is it wise for any maimed man to enter a whale-boat in the hunt?
As a general thing, the joint-owners of the Pequod must have
plainly thought not.

Ahab well knew that although his friends at home would think
little of his entering a boat in certain comparatively harmless
vicissitudes of the chase, for the sake of being near the scene of
action and giving his orders in person, yet for Captain Ahab to
have a boat actually apportioned to him as a regular headsman
in the hunt—above all for Captain Ahab to be supplied with five
extra men, as that same boat's crew, he well knew that such
generous conceits never entered the heads of the owners of the
Pequod. Therefore he had not solicited a boat's crew from them,
nor had he in any way hinted his desires on that head. Nevertheless
he had taken private measures of his own touching all that matter.
Until Archy's published discovery, the sailors had little foreseen
it, though to be sure when, after being a little while out of port,
all hands had concluded the customary business of fitting the
whaleboats for service; when some time after this Ahab was now
and then found bestirring himself in the matter of making thole-
pins with his own hands for what was thought to be one of the
spare boats, and even solicitously cutting the small wooden skewers,
which when the line is running out are pinned over the groove
in the bow: when all this was observed in him, and particularly
his solicitude in having an extra coat of sheathing in the bottom
of the boat, as if to make it better withstand the pointed pressure
of his ivory limb; and also the anxiety he evinced in exactly
shaping the thigh board, or clumsy cleat, as it is sometimes called,
the horizontal piece in the boat's bow for bracing the knee against
in darting or stabbing at the whale; when it was observed how
often he stood up in that boat with his solitary knee fixed in the
semi-circular depression in the cleat, and with the carpenter's
chisel gouged out a little here and straightened it a little there;
all these things, I say, had awakened much interest and curiosity

at the time. But almost everybody supposed that this particular preparative heedfulness in Ahab must only be with a view to the ultimate chase of Moby Dick; for he had already revealed his intention to hunt that mortal monster in person. But such a supposition did by no means involve the remotest suspicion as to any boat's crew being assigned to that boat.

Now, with the subordinate phantoms, what wonder remained soon waned away; for in a whaler wonders soon wane. Besides, now and then such unaccountable odds and ends of strange nations come up from the unknown nooks and ash-holes of the earth to man these floating outlaws of whalers; and the ships themselves often pick up such queer castaway creatures found tossing about the open sea on planks, bits of wreck, oars, whaleboats, canoes, blown-off Japanese junks, and what not; that Beelzebub himself might climb up the side and step down into the cabin to chat with the captain, and it would not create any unsubduable excitement in the forecastle.

But be all this as it may, certain it is that while the subordinate phantoms soon found their place among the crew, though still as it were somehow distinct from them, yet that hair-turbaned Fedallah remained a muffled mystery to the last. Whence he came in a mannerly world like this, by what sort of unaccountable tie he soon evinced himself to be linked with Ahab's peculiar fortunes; nay, so far as to have some sort of half-hinted influence; Heaven knows, but it might have been even authority over him; all this none knew. But one cannot sustain an indifferent air concerning Fedallah. He was such a creature as civilized, domestic people in the temperate zone only see in their dreams, and that but dimly; but the like of whom now and then glide among the unchanging Asiatic communities, especially the Oriental isles to the east of the continent—those insulated, immemorial, unalterable countries, which even in these modern days still preserve much of the ghostly aboriginalness of earth's primal generations, when the memory of the first man was a distinct recollection, and all men his descendants, unknowing whence he came, eyed each other as real phantoms, and asked of the sun and the moon why they were created and to what end; when though, according to Genesis, the angels indeed consorted with the daughters of men, the devils also, add the uncanonical Rabbins, indulged in mundane amours.

51
THE SPIRIT-SPOUT

DAYS, weeks passed, and under easy sail, the ivory Pequod had slowly swept across four several cruising-grounds; that off the Azores; off the Cape de Verdes; on the Plate (so called), being off the mouth of the Rio de la Plata; and the Carrol Ground, an unstaked, watery locality, southerly from St Helena.

It was while gliding through these latter waters that one serene and moonlight night, when all the waves rolled by like scrolls of silver, and, by their soft, suffusing seethings, made what seemed a silvery silence, not a solitude: on such a silent night a silvery jet was seen far in advance of the white bubbles at the bow. Lit up by the moon, it looked celestial; seemed some plumed and glittering god uprising from the sea. Fedallah first descried this jet. For of these moonlight nights, it was his wont to mount to the main-mast head, and stand a look-out there, with the same precision as if it had been day. And yet, though herds of whales were seen by night, not one whaleman in a hundred would venture a lowering for them. You may think with what emotions, then, the seamen beheld this old Oriental perched aloft at such unusual hours; his turban and the moon, companions in one sky. But when, after spending his uniform interval there for several successive nights without uttering a single sound; when, after all this silence, his unearthly voice was heard announcing that silvery, moon-lit jet, every reclining mariner started to his feet as if some winged spirit had lighted in the rigging, and hailed the mortal crew. 'There she blows!' Had the trump of judgment blown, they could not have quivered more; yet still they felt no terror; rather pleasure. For though it was a most unwonted hour, yet so impressive was the cry, and so deliriously exciting, that almost every soul on board instinctively desired a lowering.

Walking the deck with quick, side-lunging strides, Ahab commanded the t'gallant sails and royals to be set, and every stunsail spread. The best man in the ship must take the helm. Then, with every mast-head manned, the piled-up craft rolled down before the wind. The strange, upheaving, lifting tendency of the taffrail breeze filling the hollows of so many sails, made the buoyant, hovering deck to feel like air beneath the feet; while still she rushed along, as if two antagonistic influences were struggling in her—one to mount direct to heaven, the other to drive yawingly to some horizontal goal. And had you watched Ahab's face that night, you would have thought that in him also two different things were warring. While his one live leg made lively echoes along the deck, every stroke of his dead limb sounded like a coffin-tap. On life and death this old man walked. But though the ship so swiftly sped, and though from every eye, like arrows, the eager glances shot, yet the silvery jet was no more seen that night. Every sailor swore he saw it once, but not a second time.

This midnight-spout had almost grown a forgotten thing, when, some days after, lo! at the same silent hour, it was again announced: again it was descried by all; but upon making sail to overtake it, once more it disappeared as if it had never been. And so it served us night after night, till no one heeded it but to wonder at it. Mysteriously jetted into the clear moonlight, or starlight, as the case might be; disappearing again for one whole day, or two days, or three; and somehow seeming at every distinct repetition to be advancing still further and further in our van, this solitary jet seemed for ever alluring us on.

Nor with the immemorial superstition of their race, and in accordance with the preternaturalness, as it seemed, which in many things invested the Pequod, were there wanting some of the seamen who swore that whenever and wherever descried; at however remote times, or in however far apart latitudes and longitudes, that unnearable spout was cast by one self-same whale; and that whale, Moby Dick. For a time, there reigned, too, a sense of peculiar dread at this flitting apparition, as if it were treacherously beckoning us on and on, in order that the monster might turn round upon us, and rend us at last in the remotest and most savage seas.

These temporary apprehensions, so vague but so awful, derived a wondrous potency from the contrasting serenity of the weather, in which, beneath all its blue blandness, some thought there lurked a devilish charm, as for days and days we voyaged along, through seas so wearily, lonesomely mild, that all space, in repugnance to our vengeful errand, seemed vacating itself of life before our urn-like prow.

But, at last, when turning to the eastward, the Cape winds began howling around us, and we rose and fell upon the long, troubled seas that are there; when the ivory-tusked Pequod sharply bowed to the blast, and gored the dark waves in her madness, till, like showers of silver chips, the foam-flakes flew over her bulwarks;

then all this desolate vacuity of life went away, but gave place to sights more dismal than before.

Close to our bows, strange forms in the water darted hither and thither before us; while thick in our rear flew the inscrutable sea-ravens. And every morning, perched on our stays, rows of these birds were seen; and spite of our hootings, for a long time obstinately clung to the hemp, as though they deemed our ship some drifting, uninhabited craft; a thing appointed to desolation, and therefore fit roosting-place for their homeless selves. And heaved and heaved, still unrestingly heaved the black sea, as if its vast tides were a conscience; and the great mundane soul were in anguish and remorse for the long sin and suffering it had bred.

Cape of Good Hope, do they call ye? Rather Cape Tormentoso, as called of yore; for long allured by the perfidious silences that before had attended us, we found ourselves launched into this tormented sea, where guilty beings transformed into those fowls and these fish, seemed condemned to swim on everlastingly without any haven in store, or beat that black air without any horizon. But calm, snow-white, and unvarying; still directing its fountain of feathers to the sky; still beckoning us on from before, the solitary jet would at times be descried.

During all this blackness of the elements, Ahab, though assuming for the time the almost continual command of the drenched and dangerous deck, manifested the gloomiest reserve; and more seldom than ever addressed his mates. In tempestuous times like these, after everything above and aloft has been secured, nothing more can be done but passively to wait the issue of the gale. Then Captain and crew become practical fatalists. So, with his ivory leg inserted into its accustomed hole, and with one hand firmly grasping a shroud, Ahab for hours and hours would stand gazing dead to windward, while an occasional squall of sleet or snow would all but congeal his very eyelashes together. Meantime, the crew driven from the forward part of the ship by the perilous seas that burstingly broke over its bows, stood in a line along the bulwarks in the waist; and the better to guard against the leaping waves, each man had slipped himself into a sort of bowline secured to the rail, in which he swung as in a loosened belt. Few or no words were spoken; and the silent ship, as if manned by painted sailors in wax, day after day tore on through all the swift madness and gladness of the demoniac waves. By night the same muteness of humanity before the shrieks of the ocean prevailed; still in silence the men swung in the bowlines; still wordless Ahab stood up to the blast. Even when wearied nature seemed demanding repose he would not seek that repose in his hammock. Never could Starbuck forget the old man's aspect, when one night going down into the cabin to mark how the barometer stood, he saw him with closed eyes sitting straight in his floor-screwed chair; the rain and half-melted sleet of the storm from which he had some time before emerged, still slowly dripping from the unremoved hat and coat. On the table beside him lay unrolled one of those charts of tides and currents which have previously been spoken of. His lantern swung from his tightly clenched hand. Though the body was erect, the head was thrown back so that the closed eyes were pointed towards the needle of the tell-tale that swung from a beam in the ceiling.*

Terrible old man! thought Starbuck with a shudder, sleeping in this gale, still thou steadfastly eyest thy purpose.

52
THE ALBATROSS

SOUTH-EASTWARD from the Cape, off the distant Crozetts, a good cruising ground for Right Whalemen, a sail loomed ahead, the Goney (Albatross) by name. As she slowly drew nigh, from my lofty perch at the fore-mast-head, I had a good view of that sight so remarkable to a tyro in the far ocean fisheries—a whaler at sea, and long absent from home.

As if the waves had been fullers, this craft was bleached like the skeleton of a stranded walrus. All down her sides, this spectral appearance was traced with long channels of reddened rust, while all her spars and her rigging were like the thick branches of trees furred over with hoar-frost. Only her lower sails were set. A wild sight it was to see her long-bearded look-outs at those three mast-heads. They seemed clad in the skin of beasts, so torn and bepatched the raiment that had survived nearly four years of cruising. Standing in iron hoops nailed to the mast, they swayed and swung over a fathomless sea; and though, when the ship slowly glided close under our stern, we six men in the air came so nigh to each other that we might almost have leaped from the

---

* The cabin-compass is called the tell-tale, because without going to the compass at the helm, the Captain, while below, can inform himself of the course of the ship.

mast-heads of one ship to those of the other; yet, those forlorn-looking fishermen, mildly eyeing us as they passed, said not one word to our own look-outs, while the quarter-deck hail was being heard from below.

'Ship ahoy! Have ye seen the White Whale?'

But as the strange captain, leaning over the pallid bulwarks, was in the act of putting his trumpet to his mouth, it somehow fell from his hand into the sea; and the wind now rising amain, he in vain strove to make himself heard without it. Meantime his ship was still increasing the distance between. While in various silent ways the seamen of the Pequod were evincing their observance of this ominous incident at the first mere mention of the White Whale's name to another ship, Ahab for a moment paused; it almost seemed as though he would have lowered a boat to board the stranger, had not the threatening wind forbade. But taking advantage of his windward position, he again seized his trumpet, and knowing by her aspect that the stranger vessel was a Nantucketer and shortly bound home, he loudly hailed—'Ahoy there! This is the Pequod, bound round the world! Tell them to address all future letters to the Pacific ocean! and this time three years, if I am not at home, tell them to address them to—'

At that moment the two wakes were fairly crossed, and instantly, then, in accordance with their singular ways, shoals of small harmless fish, that for some days before had been placidly swimming by our side, darted away with what seemed shuddering fins, and ranged themselves fore and aft with the stranger's flanks. Though in the course of his continual voyagings Ahab must often before have noticed a similar sight, yet, to any monomaniac man, the veriest trifles capriciously carry meanings.

'Swim away from me, do ye?' murmured Ahab, gazing over into the water. There seemed but little in the words, but the tone conveyed more of deep helpless sadness than the insane old man had ever before evinced. But turning to the steersman, who thus far had been holding the ship in the wind to diminish her headway, he cried out in his old lion voice,—'Up helm! Keep her off round the world!'

Round the world! There is much in that sound to inspire proud feelings; but whereto does all that circumnavigation conduct? Only through numberless perils to the very point whence we started, where those that we left behind secure, were all the time before us.

Were this world an endless plain, and by sailing eastward we could for ever reach new distances, and discover sights more sweet and strange than any Cyclades or Islands of King Solomon, then there were promise in the voyage. But in pursuit of those far mysteries we dream of, or in tormented chase of that demon phantom that, some time or other, swims before all human hearts; while chasing such over this round globe, they either lead us on in barren mazes or midway leave us whelmed.

53
THE GAM

THE ostensible reason why Ahab did not go on aboard of the whaler we had spoken was this: the wind and seas betokened storms. But even had this not been the case, he would not after all, perhaps, have boarded her—judging by his subsequent conduct on similar occasions—if so it had been that, by the process of hailing, he had obtained a negative answer to the question he put. For, as it eventually turned out, he cared not to consort, even for five minutes, with any stranger captain, except he could contribute some of that information he so absorbingly sought. But all this might remain inadequately estimated, were not something said here of the peculiar usages of whaling-vessels when meeting each other in foreign seas, and especially on a common cruising-ground.

If two strangers crossing the Pine Barrens in New York State, or the equally desolate Salisbury Plain in England; if casually encountering each other in such inhospitable wilds, these twain, for the life of them, cannot well avoid a mutual salutation; and stopping for a moment to interchange the news; and, perhaps, sitting down for a while and resting in concert: then, how much more natural that upon the illimitable Pine Barrens and Salisbury Plains of the sea, two whaling vessels descrying each other at the ends of the earth—off lone Fanning's Island, or the far away King's Mills; how much more natural, I say, that under such circumstances these ships should not only interchange hails, but come into still closer, more friendly and sociable contact. And especially would this seem to be a matter of course, in the case of vessels owned in one seaport, and whose captains, officers, and not a few of the men are personally known to each other: and consequently, have all sorts of dear domestic things to talk about.

For the long absent ship, the outward-bounder, perhaps, has letters on board; at any rate, she will be sure to let her have some

papers of a date a year or two later than the last one on her
blurred and thumb-worn files. And in return for that courtesy,
the outward-bound ship would receive the latest whaling intelligence from the cruising-ground to which she may be destined, a
thing of the utmost importance to her. And in degree, all this
will hold true concerning whaling vessels crossing each other's
track on the cruising-ground itself, even though they are equally
long absent from home. For one of them may have received a
transfer of letters from some third, and now far remote vessel;
and some of those letters may be for the people of the ship she
now meets. Besides, they would exchange the whaling news, and
have an agreeable chat. For not only would they meet with all
the sympathies of sailors, but likewise with all the peculiar con-
genialities arising from a common pursuit and mutually shared
privations and perils.

Nor would difference of country make any very essential difference; that is, so long as both parties speak one language, as is
the case with Americans and English. Though, to be sure, from
the small number of English whalers, such meetings do not very
often occur, and when they do occur there is too apt to be a sort
of shyness between them; for your Englishman is rather reserved,
and your Yankee, he does not fancy that sort of thing in anybody
but himself. Besides, the English whalers sometimes affect a kind
of metropolitan superiority over the American whalers; regarding
the long, lean Nantucketer, with his nondescript provincialisms,
as a sort of sea-peasant. But where this superiority in the English
whalemen does really consist, it would be hard to say, seeing that
the Yankees in one day, collectively, kill more whales than all
the English, collectively, in ten years. But this is a harmless little
foible in the English whalehunters, which the Nantucketer does
not take much to heart; probably, because he knows that he has
a few foibles himself.

So, then, we see that of all ships separately sailing the sea, the
whalers have most reason to be sociable—and they are so. Whereas,
some merchant ships crossing each other's wake in the Mid-
Atlantic, will oftentimes pass on without so much as a single word
of recognition, mutually cutting each other on the high seas, like
a brace of dandies in Broadway; and all the time indulging, perhaps,
in finical criticism upon each other's rig. As for Men-of-War, when
they chance to meet at sea, they first go through such a string of
silly bowings and scrapings, such a ducking of ensigns, that there
does not seem to be much right-down hearty good-will and brotherly love about it at all. As touching Slave-ships meeting, why,

they are in such a prodigious hurry, they run away from each other as soon as possible. And as for Pirates, when they chance to cross each other's cross-bones, the first hail is—'How many skulls?'—the same way that whalers hail—'How many barrels?' And that question once answered, pirates straightway steer apart, for they are infernal villains on both sides, and don't like to see overmuch of each other's villainous likenesses.

But look at the godly, honest, unostentatious, hospitable, sociable, free-and-easy whaler! What does the whaler do when she meets another whaler in any sort of decent weather? She has a '*Gam*,' a thing so utterly unknown to all other ships that they never heard of the name even; and if by chance they should hear of it, they only grin at it, and repeat gamesome stuff about 'spouters' and 'blubber-boilers,' and such like pretty exclamations. Why it is that all Merchant-seamen, and also all Pirates and Man-of-War's men, and Slave-ship sailors, cherish such a scornful feeling towards Whale-ships; this is a question it would be hard to answer. Because, in the case of pirates, say, I should like to know whether that profession of theirs has any peculiar glory about it. It sometimes ends in uncommon elevation, indeed; but only at the gallows. And besides, when a man is elevated in that odd fashion, he has no proper foundation for his superior altitude. Hence, I conclude, that in boasting himself to be high lifted above a whaleman, in that assertion the pirate has no solid basis to stand on.

But what is a *Gam*? You might wear out your index-finger running up and down the columns of dictionaries, and never find the word. Dr Johnson never attained to that erudition; Noah Webster's ark does not hold it. Nevertheless, this same expressive word has now for many years been in constant use among some fifteen thousand true born Yankees. Certainly, it needs a definition, and should be incorporated into the Lexicon. With that view, let me learnedly define it.

GAM. NOUN—*A social meeting of two (or more) Whaleships, generally on a cruising-ground; when, after exchanging hails, they exchange visits by boats' crews: the two captains remaining, for the time, on board of one ship, and the two chief mates on the other.*

There is another little item about Gamming which must not be forgotten here. All professions have their own little peculiarities of detail; so has the whale fishery. In a pirate, man-of-war, or slave ship, when the captain is rowed anywhere in his boat, he always sits in the stern sheets on a comfortable, sometimes cushioned seat there, and often steers himself with a pretty little milliner's tiller decorated with gay cords and ribbons. But the whale-boat has no seat astern, no sofa of that sort whatever, and no tiller at all. High times indeed, if whaling captains were wheeled about the water on castors like gouty old aldermen in patent chairs. And as for a tiller, the whale-boat never admits of any such effeminacy; and therefore as in gamming a complete boat's crew must leave the ship, and hence as the boat steerer or harpooneer is of the number, that subordinate is the steersman upon the occasion, and the captain, having no place to sit in, is pulled off to his visit all standing like a pine tree. And often you will notice that being conscious of the eyes of the whole visible world resting on him from the sides of the two ships, this standing captain is all alive to the importance of sustaining his dignity by maintaining his legs. Nor is this any very easy matter; for in his rear is the immense projecting steering oar hitting him now and then in the small of his back, the after-oar reciprocating by rapping his knees in front. He is thus completely wedged before and behind, and can only expand himself sideways by settling down on his stretched legs; but a sudden, violent pitch of the boat will often go far to topple him, because length of foundation is nothing without corresponding breadth. Merely make a spread angle of two poles, and you cannot stand them up. Then, again, it would never do in plain sight of the world's riveted eyes, it would never do, I say, for this straddling captain to be seen steadying himself the slightest particle by catching hold of anything with his hands; indeed, as token of his entire, buoyant self-command, he generally carries his hands in his trowsers' pockets; but perhaps being generally very large, heavy hands, he carries them there for ballast. Nevertheless there have occurred instances, well authenticated ones too, where the captain has been known for an uncommonly critical moment or two, in a sudden squall say—to seize hold of the nearest oarsman's hair, and hold on there like grim death.

54

THE TOWN-HO'S STORY

(As told at the Golden Inn.)

The Cape of Good Hope, and all the watery region round about there, is much like some noted four corners of a great highway, where you meet more travellers than in any other part.

It was not very long after speaking the Goney that another

homeward-bound whaleman, the Town-Ho,* was encountered. She was manned almost wholly by Polynesians. In the short gam that ensued she gave us strong news of Moby Dick. To some the general interest in the White Whale was now wildly heightened by a circumstance of the Town-Ho's story, which seemed obscurely to involve with the whale a certain wondrous, inverted visitation of one of those so called judgments of God which at times are said to overtake some men. This latter circumstance, with its own particular accompaniments, forming what may be called the secret part of the tragedy about to be narrated, never reached the ears of Captain Ahab or his mates. For that secret part of the story was unknown to the captain of the Town-Ho himself. It was the private property of three confederate white seamen of that ship, one of whom, it seems, communicated it to Tashtego with Romish injunctions of secresy, but the following night Tashtego rambled in his sleep, and revealed so much of it in that way, that when he was awakened he could not well withhold the rest. Nevertheless, so potent an influence did this thing have on those seamen in the Pequod who came to the full knowledge of it, and by such a strange delicacy, to call it so, were they governed in this matter, that they kept the secret among themselves so that it never transpired abaft the Pequod's main-mast. Interweaving in its proper place this darker thread with the story as publicly narrated on the ship, the whole of this strange affair I now proceed to put on lasting record.

For my humor's sake, I shall preserve the style in which I once narrated it at Lima, to a lounging circle of my Spanish friends, one saint's eve, smoking upon the thick-gilt tiled piazza of the Golden Inn. Of those fine cavaliers, the young Dons, Pedro and Sebastian, were on the closer terms with me; and hence the interluding questions they occasionally put, and which are duly answered at the time.

'Some two years prior to my first learning the events which I am about rehearsing to you, gentlemen, the Town-Ho, Sperm Whaler of Nantucket, was cruising in your Pacific here, not very many days' sail westward from the eaves of this good Golden Inn. She was somewhere to the northward of the Line. One morning upon handling the pumps, according to daily usage, it was observed that she made more water in her hold than common. They

---

* The ancient whale-cry upon first sighting a whale from the mast-head, still used by whalemen in hunting the famous Gallipagos terrapin.

supposed a sword-fish had stabbed her, gentlemen. But the captain, having some unusual reason for believing that rare good luck awaited him in those latitudes; and therefore being very averse to quit them, and the leak not being then considered at all dangerous, though, indeed, they could not find it after searching the hold as low down as was possible in the rather heavy weather, the ship still continued her cruisings, the mariners working at the pumps at wide and easy intervals; but no good luck came; more days went by, and not only was the leak yet undiscovered, but it sensibly increased. So much so, that now taking some alarm, the captain, making all sail, stood away for the nearest harbor among the islands, there to have his hull hove out and repaired.

'Though no small passage was before her, yet, if the commonest chance favored, he did not at all fear that his ship would founder by the way, because his pumps were of the best, and being periodically relieved at them, those six-and-thirty men of his could easily keep the ship free; never mind if the leak should double on her. In truth, well nigh the whole of this passage being attended by very prosperous breezes, the Town-Ho had all but certainly arrived in perfect safety at her port without the occurrence of the least fatality, had it not been for the brutal overbearing of Radney, the mate, a Vineyarder, and the bitterly provoked vengeance of Steelkilt, a Lakeman and desperado from Buffalo.'

'Lakeman!—Buffalo! Pray, what is a Lakeman, and where is Buffalo?' said Don Sebastian, rising in his swinging mat of grass.

'On the eastern shore of our Lake Erie, Don; but—I crave your courtesy—may be, you shall soon hear further of all that. Now, gentlemen, in square-sail brigs and three-masted ship, well nigh as large and stout as any that ever sailed out of your old Callao to far Manilla; this Lakeman, in the land-locked heart of our America, had yet been nurtured by all those agrarian freebooting impressions popularly connected with the open ocean. For in their interflowing aggregate, those grand fresh-water seas of ours,—Erie, and Ontario, and Huron, and Superior, and Michigan,—possess an ocean-like expansiveness, with many of the ocean's noblest traits; with many of its rimmed varieties of races and of climes. They contain round archipelagoes of romantic isles, even as the Polynesian waters do; in large part, are shored by two great contrasting nations, as the Atlantic is; they furnish long maritime approaches to our numerous territorial colonies from the East, dotted all round their banks; here and there are frowned upon by batteries, and by the goat-like craggy guns of lofty Mackinaw; they have heard the fleet thunderings of naval victories; at intervals, they yield their beaches to wild barbarians, whose red painted faces flash from out their peltry wigwams; for leagues and leagues are flanked by ancient and unentered forests, where the gaunt pines stand like serried lines of kings in Gothic genealogies; those same woods harboring wild Afric beasts of prey, and silken creatures whose exported furs give robes to Tartar Emperors; they mirror the paved capitals of Buffalo and Cleveland, as well as Winnebago villages; they float alike the full-rigged merchant ship, the armed cruiser of the State, the steamer, and the beech canoe; they are swept by Borean and dismasting blasts as direful as any that lash the salted wave; they know what shipwrecks are, for out of sight of land, however inland, they have drowned full many a midnight ship with all its shrieking crew.

'Thus, gentlemen, though an inlander, Steelkilt was wild-ocean born, and wild-ocean nurtured; as much of an audacious mariner as any. And for Radney, though in his infancy he may have laid him down on the lone Nantucket beach, to nurse at his maternal sea; though in after life he had long followed our austere Atlantic and your contemplative Pacific; yet was he quite as vengeful and full of social quarrel as the backwoods seamen, fresh from the latitudes of buck-horn handled Bowie-knives. Yet was this Nantucketer a man with some good-hearted traits; and this Lakeman, a mariner, who though a sort of devil indeed, might yet by inflexible firmness, only tempered by that common decency of human recognition which is the meanest slave's right; thus treated, this Steelkilt had long been retained harmless and docile. At all events, he had proved so thus far; but Radney was doomed and made mad, and Steelkilt—but, gentlemen, you shall hear.

'It was not more than a day or two at the furthest after pointing her prow for her island haven, that the Town-Ho's leak seemed again increasing, but only so as to require an hour or more at the pumps every day. You must know that in a settled and civilized ocean like our Atlantic, for example, some skippers think little of pumping their whole way across it; though of a still, sleepy night, should the officer of the deck happen to forget his duty in that respect, the probability would be that he and his shipmates would never again remember it, on account of all hands gently subsiding to the bottom. Nor in the solitary and savage seas far from you to the westward, gentlemen, is it altogether unusual for ships to keep clanging at their pump-handles in full chorus even for a voyage of considerable length; that is, if it lie along a tolerably accessible coast, or if any other reasonable retreat is afforded them. It is only when a leaky vessel is in some very out of the way part

of those waters, some really landless latitude, that her captain
begins to feel a little anxious.

'Much this way had it been with the Town-Ho; so when her
leak was found gaining once more, there was in truth some small
concern manifested by several of her company; especially by
Radney the mate. He commanded the upper sails to be well
hoisted, sheeted home anew, and every way expanded to the breeze.
Now this Radney, I suppose, was as little of a coward, and as
little inclined to any sort of nervous apprehensiveness touching
his own person as any fearless, unthinking creature on land or
on sea that you can conveniently imagine, gentlemen. Therefore
when he betrayed this solicitude about the safety of the ship, some
of the seamen declared that it was only on account of his being
a part owner in her. So when they were working that evening at
the pumps, there was on this head no small gamesomeness slily
going on among them, as they stood with their feet continually
overflowed by the rippling clear water; clear as any mountain
spring, gentlemen—that bubbling from the pumps ran across the
deck, and poured itself out in steady spouts at the lee scupper-
holes.

'Now, as you well know, it is not seldom the case in this
conventional world of ours—watery or otherwise; that when a
person placed in command over his fellow-men finds one of them
to be very significantly his superior in general pride of manhood,
straightway against that man he conceives an unconquerable dislike
and bitterness; and if he have a chance he will pull down and
pulverise that subaltern's tower, and make a little heap of dust of
it. Be this conceit of mine as it may, gentlemen, at all events
Steelkilt was a tall and noble animal with a head like a Roman,
and a flowing golden beard like the tasseled housings of your last
viceroy's snorting charger; and a brain, and a heart, and a soul
in him, gentlemen, which had made Steelkilt Charlemagne, had
he been born son to Charlemagne's father. But Radney, the mate,
was ugly as a mule; yet as hardy, as stubborn, as malicious. He
did not love Steelkilt, and Steelkilt knew it.

'Espying the mate drawing near as he was toiling at the pump
with the rest, the Lakeman affected not to notice him, but unawed,
went on with his gay banterings.

' "Aye, aye, my merry lads, it's a lively leak this; hold a cannikin,
one of ye, and let's have a taste. By the Lord, it's worth bottling!
I tell ye what, men, old Rad's investment must go for it! he had
best cut away his part of the hull and tow it home. The fact is,
boys, that sword-fish only began the job; he's come back again

with a gang of ship-carpenters, saw-fish, and file-fish, and what not; and the whole posse of 'em are now hard at work cutting and slashing at the bottom; making improvements, I suppose. If old Rad were here now, I'd tell him to jump overboard and scatter 'em. They're playing the devil with his estate, I can tell him. But he's a simple old soul,—Rad, and a beauty too. Boys, they say the rest of his property is invested in looking-glasses. I wonder if he'd give a poor devil like me the model of his nose."

' "Damn your eyes! what's that pump stopping for?" roared Radney, pretending not to have heard the sailor's talk. "Thunder away at it!"

' "Aye, aye, sir," said Steelkilt, merry as a cricket. "Lively, boys, lively, now!" And with that the pump clanged like fifty fire-engines; the men tossed their hats off to it, and ere long that peculiar gasping of the lungs was heard which denotes the fullest tension of life's utmost energies.

'Quitting the pump at last, with the rest of his band, the Lakeman went forward all panting, and sat himself down on the windlass; his face fiery red, his eyes bloodshot, and wiping the profuse sweat from his brow. Now what cozening fiend it was, gentlemen, that possessed Radney to meddle with such a man in that corporeally exasperated state, I know not; but so it happened. Intolerably striding along the deck, the mate commanded him to get a broom and sweep down the planks, and also a shovel, and remove some offensive matters consequent upon allowing a pig to run at large.

'Now, gentlemen, sweeping a ship's deck at sea is a piece of household work which in all times but raging gales is regularly attended to every evening; it has been known to be done in the case of ships actually foundering at the time. Such, gentlemen, is the inflexibility of sea-usages and the instinctive love of neatness in seamen; some of whom would not willingly drown without first washing their faces. But in all vessels this broom business is the prescriptive province of the boys, if boys there be aboard. Besides, it was the stronger men in the Town-Ho that had been divided into gangs, taking turns at the pumps; and being the most athletic seaman of them all, Steelkilt had been regularly assigned captain of one of the gangs; consequently he should have been freed from any trivial business not connected with truly nautical duties, such being the case with his comrades. I mention all these particulars so that you may understand exactly how this affair stood between the two men.

'But there was more than this: the order about the shovel was almost as plainly meant to sting and insult Steelkilt, as though

Radney had spat in his face. Any man who has gone sailor in a
whale-ship will understand this; and all this and doubtless much
more, the Lakeman fully comprehended when the mate uttered
his command. But as he sat still for a moment, and as he steadfastly
looked into the mate's malignant eye and perceived the stacks of
powder-casks heaped up in him and the slow-match silently burning along towards them; as he instinctively saw all this, that strange
forbearance and unwillingness to stir up the deeper passionateness
in any already ireful being—a repugnance most felt, when felt at
all, by really valiant men even when aggrieved—this nameless
phantom feeling, gentlemen, stole over Steelkilt.

'Therefore, in his ordinary tone, only a little broken by the
bodily exhaustion he was temporarily in, he answered him saying
that sweeping the deck was not his businss, and he would not do
it. And then, without at all alluding to the shovel, he pointed to
three lads as the customary sweepers; who, not being billeted at
the pumps, had done little or nothing all day. To this, Radney
replied with an oath, in a most domineering and outrageous
manner unconditionally reiterating his command; meanwhile advancing upon the still seated Lakeman, with an uplifted cooper's
club hammer which he had snatched from a cask near by.

'Heated and irritated as he was by his spasmodic toil at the
pumps, for all his first nameless feeling of forbearance the sweating
Steelkilt could but ill brook this bearing in the mate; but somehow
still smothering the conflagration within him, without speaking he
remained doggedly rooted to his seat, till at last the incensed
Radney shook the hammer within a few inches of his face, furiously
commanding him to do his bidding.

'Steelkilt rose, and slowly retreating round the windlass, steadily
followed by the mate with his menacing hammer, deliberately
repeated his intention not to obey. Seeing, however, that his
forbearance had not the slightest effect, by an awful and unspeakable intimation with his twisted hand he warned off the foolish
and infatuated man; but it was to no purpose. And in this way
the two went once slowly round the windlass; when, resolved at
last no longer to retreat, bethinking him that he had now forborne
as much as comported with his humor, the Lakeman paused on
the hatches and thus spoke to the officer:

' "Mr Radney, I will not obey you. Take that hammer away,
or look to yourself." But the predestinated mate coming still closer
to him, where the Lakeman stood fixed, now shook the heavy
hammer within an inch of his teeth; meanwhile repeating a string
of insufferable maledictions. Retreating not the thousandth part

of an inch; stabbing him in the eye with the unflinching poniard of his glance, Steelkilt, clenching his right hand behind him and creepingly drawing it back, told his persecutor that if the hammer but grazed his cheek he (Steelkilt) would murder him. But, gentlemen, the fool had been branded for the slaughter by the gods. Immediately the hammer touched the cheek; the next instant the lower jaw of the mate was stove in his head; he fell on the hatch spouting blood like a whale.

'Ere the cry could go aft Steelkilt was shaking one of the backstays leading far aloft to where two of his comrades were standing their mast-heads. They were both Canallers.'

'Canallers!' cried Don Pedro. 'We have seen many whale-ships in our harbors, but never heard of your Canallers. Pardon: who and what are they?'

'Canallers, Don, are the boatmen belonging to our grand Erie Canal. You must have heard of it.'

'Nay, Senor; hereabouts in this dull, warm, most lazy, and hereditary land, we know but little of your vigorous North.'

'Aye? Well then, Don, refill my cup. Your chicha's very fine; and ere proceeding further I will tell ye what our Canallers are; for such information may throw side-light upon my story.

'For three hundred and sixty miles, gentlemen, through the entire breadth of the state of New York; through numerous populous cities and most thriving villages; through long, dismal, uninhabited swamps, and affluent, cultivated fields, unrivalled for fertility; by billiard-room and bar-room; through the holy-of-holies of great forests; on Roman arches over Indian rivers; through sun and shade; by happy hearts or broken; through all the wide contrasting scenery of those noble Mohawk counties; and especially, by rows of snow-white chapels, whose spires stand almost like milestones, flows one continual stream of Venetianly corrupt and often lawless life. There's your true Ashantee, gentlemen; there howl your pagans; where you ever find them, next door to you; under the long-flung shadow, and the snug patronizing lee of churches. For by some curious fatality, as it is often noted of your metropolitan freebooters that they ever encamp around the halls of justice, so sinners, gentlemen, most abound in holiest vicinities.'

'Is that a friar passing?' said Don Pedro, looking downwards into the crowded plaza, with humorous concern.

'Well for our northern friend, Dame Isabella's Inquisition wanes in Lima,' laughed Don Sebastian, 'Proceed, Senor.'

'A moment! Pardon!' cried another of the company. 'In the

name of all us Limeese, I but desire to express to you, sir sailor,
that we have by no means overlooked your delicacy in not substituting present Lima for distant Venice in your currupt comparison. Oh! do not bow and look surprised; you know the proverb
all along this coast—"Corrupt as Lima." It but bears out your
saying, too; churches more plentiful than billiard-tables, and for
ever open—and "Corrupt as Lima." So, too, Venice; I have been
there; the holy city of the blessed evangelist, St Mark!—St Dominic,
purge it! Your cup! Thanks: here I refill; now, you pour out again.'

'Freely depicted in his own vocation, gentlemen, the Canaller
would make a fine dramatic hero, so abundantly and picturesquely
wicked is he. Like Mark Antony, for days and days along his
green-turfed, flowery Nile, he indolently floats, openly toying with
his red-cheeked Cleopatra, ripening his apricot thigh upon the
sunny deck. But ashore, all this effeminacy is dashed. The brigandish guise which the Canaller so proudly sports; his slouched
and gaily-ribboned hat betoken his grand features. A terror to the
smiling innocence of the villages through which he floats; his swart
visage and bold swagger are not unshunned in cities. Once a
vagabond on his own canal, I have received good turns from one
of these Canallers; I thank him heartily; would fain be not ungrateful; but it is often one of the prime redeeming qualities of
your man of violence, that at times he has as stiff an arm to back
a poor stranger in a strait, as to plunder a wealthy one. In sum,
gentlemen, what the wildness of this canal life is, is emphatically
evinced by this; that our wild whale-fishery contains so many of
its most finished graduates, and that scarce any race of mankind,
except Sydney men, are so much distrusted by our whaling captains. Nor does it at all diminish the curiousness of this matter,
that to many thousands of our rural boys and young men born
along its line, the probationary life of the Grand Canal furnishes
the sole transition between quietly reaping in a Christian corn-
field, and recklessly ploughing the waters of the most barbaric
seas.'

'I see! I see!' impetuously exclaimed Don Pedro, spilling his
chicha upon his silvery ruffles. 'No need to travel! The world's
one Lima. I had thought, now, that at your temperate North the
generations were cold and holy as the hills.—But the story.'

'I left off, gentlemen, where the Lakeman shook the backstay.
Hardly had he done so, when he was surrounded by the three
junior mates and the four harpooneers, who all crowded him to
the deck. But sliding down the ropes like baleful comets, the two
Canallers rushed into the uproar, and sought to drag their man

out of it towards the forecastle. Others of the sailors joined with
them in this attempt, and a twisted turmoil ensued; while standing
out of harm's way, the valiant captain danced up and down with
a whale-pike, calling upon his officers to manhandle that atrocious
scoundrel, and smoke him along to the quarter-deck. At intervals,
he ran close up to the revolving border of the confusion, and
prying into the heart of it with his pike, sought to prick out the
object of his resentment. But Steelkilt and his desperadoes were
too much for them all; they succeeded in gaining the forecastle
deck, where, hastily slewing about three or four large casks in a
line with the windlass, these sea-Parisians entrenched themselves
behind the barricade.'

' "Come out of that, ye pirates!" roared the captain, now menacing them with a pistol in each hand, just brought to him by
the steward. "Come out of that, ye cut-throats!"

'Steelkilt leaped on the barricade, and striding up and down
there, defied the worst the pistols could do; but gave the captain
to understand distinctly, that his (Steelkilt's) death would be the
signal for a murderous mutiny on the part of all hands. Fearing
in his heart lest this might prove but too true, the captain a little
desisted, but still commanded the insurgents instantly to return
to their duty.

' "Will you promise not to touch us, if we do?" demanded their
ringleader.

' "Turn to! turn to!—I make no promise;—to your duty! Do
you want to sink the ship, by knocking off at a time like this?
Turn to!" and he once more raised a pistol.

' "Sink the ship?" cried Steelkilt. "Aye, let her sink. Not a man
of us turns to, unless you swear not to raise a rope-yarn against
us. What say ye, men?" turning to his comrades. A fierce cheer
was their response.

'The Lakeman now patrolled the barricade, all the while keeping
his eye on the Captain, and jerking out such sentences as these:—
"It's not our fault; we didn't want it; I told him to take his
hammer away; it was boys' business; he might have known me
before this; I told him not to prick the buffalo; I believe I have
broken a finger here against his cursed jaw; ain't those mincing
knives down in the forecastle there, men? look to those handspikes,
my hearties. Captain, by God, look to yourself; say the word;
don't be a fool; forget it all; we are ready to turn to; treat us
decently, and we're your men; but we won't be flogged."

' "Turn to! I make no promises, turn to, I say!"

' "Look ye, now," cried the Lakeman, flinging out his arm

towards him, "there are a few of us here (and I am one of them) who have shipped for the cruise, d'ye see; now as you well know, sir, we can claim our discharge as soon as the anchor is down; so we don't want a row; it's not our interest; we want to be peaceable; we are ready to work, but we won't be flogged."

' "Turn to!" roared the Captain.

'Steelkilt glanced round him a moment, and then said:—"I tell you what it is now, Captain, rather than kill ye, and be hung for such a shabby rascal, we won't lift a hand against ye unless ye attack us; but till you say the word about not flogging us, we don't do a hand's turn."

' "Down into the forecastle then, down with ye, I'll keep ye there till ye're sick of it. Down ye go."

' "Shall we?" cried the ringleader to his men. Most of them were against it; but at length, in obedience to Steelkilt, they preceded him down into their dark den, growlingly disappearing, like bears into a cave.

'As the Lakeman's bare head was just level with the planks, the Captain and his posse leaped the barricade, and rapidly drawing over the slide of the scuttle, planted their group of hands upon it, and loudly called for the steward to bring the heavy brass padlock belonging to the companionway. Then opening the slide a little, the Captain whispered something down the crack, closed it, and turned the key upon them—ten in number—leaving on deck some twenty or more, who thus far had remained neutral.

'All night a wide-awake watch was kept by all the officers, forward and aft, especially about the forecastle scuttle and fore hatchway; at which last place it was feared the insurgents might emerge, after breaking through the bulkhead below. But the hours of darkness passed in peace; the men who still remained at their duty toiling hard at the pumps, whose clinking and clanking at intervals through the dreary night dismally resounded through the ship.

'At sunrise the Captain went forward, and knocking on the deck, summoned the prisoners to work; but with a yell they refused. Water was then lowered down to them, and a couple of handfuls of biscuit were tossed after it; when again turning the key upon them and pocketing it, the Captain returned to the quarter-deck. Twice every day for three days this was repeated; but on the fourth morning a confused wrangling, and then scuffling was heard, as the customary summons was delivered; and suddenly four men burst up from the forecastle, saying they were ready to turn to. The fetid closeness of the air, and a famishing diet, united perhaps

to some fears of ultimate retribution, had constrained them to
surrender at discretion. Emboldened by this, the Captain reiterated
his demand to the rest, but Steelkilt shouted up to him a terrific
hint to stop his babbling and betake himself where he belonged.
On the fifth morning three others of the mutineers bolted up into
the air from the desperate arms below that sought to restrain
them. Only three were left.

' "Better turn to, now?" said the Captain with a heartless jeer.

' "Shut us up again, will ye!" cried Steelkilt.

' "Oh! certainly," said the Captain, and the key clicked.

'It was at this point, gentlemen, that enraged by the defection
of seven of his former associates, and stung by the mocking voice
that had last hailed him, and maddened by his long entombment
in a place as black as the bowels of despair; it was then that
Steelkilt proposed to the two Canallers, thus far apparently of one
mind with him, to burst out of their hole at the next summoning
of the garrison; and armed with their keen mincing knives (long,
crescentic, heavy implements with a handle at each end) run
amuck from the bowsprit to the taffrail; and if by any devilishness
of desperation possible, seize the ship. For himself, he would do
this, he said, whether they joined him or not. That was the last
night he should spend in that den. But the scheme met with no
opposition on the part of the other two; they swore they were
ready for that, or for any other mad thing, for anything in short
but a surrender. And what was more, they each insisted upon
being the first man on deck, when the time to make the rush
should come. But to this their leader as fiercely objected, reserving
that priority for himself; particularly as his two comrades would
not yield, the one to the other, in the matter; and both of them
could not be first, for the ladder would but admit one man at a
time. And here, gentlemen, the foul play of these miscreants must
come out.

'Upon hearing the frantic project of their leader, each in his
own separate soul had suddenly lighted, it would seem, upon the
same piece of treachery, namely: to be foremost in breaking out,
in order to be the first of the three, though the last of the ten,
to surrender; and thereby secure whatever small chance of pardon
such conduct might merit. But when Steelkilt made known his
determination still to lead them to the last, they in some way, by
some subtle chemistry of villainy, mixed their before secret treach-
eries together; and when their leader fell into a doze, verbally
opened their souls to each other in three sentences; and bound

the sleeper with cords, and gagged him with cords; and shrieked out for the Captain at midnight.

'Thinking murder at hand, and smelling in the dark for the blood, he and all his armed mates and harpooneers rushed for the forecastle. In a few minutes the scuttle was opened, and, bound hand and foot, the still struggling ringleader was shoved up into the air by his perfidious allies, who at once claimed the honor of securing a man who had been fully ripe for murder. But all three were collared, and dragged along the deck like dead cattle; and, side by side, were seized up into the mizen rigging, like three quarters of meat, and there they hung till morning. "Damn ye," cried the Captain, pacing to and fro before them, "the vultures would not touch ye, ye villains!"

'At sunrise he summoned all hands; and separating those who had rebelled from those who had taken no part in the mutiny, he told the former that he had a good mind to flog them all round—thought, upon the whole, he would do so—he ought to—justice demanded it; but for the present, considering their timely surrender, he would let them go with a reprimand, which he accordingly administered in the vernacular.

' "But as for you, ye carrion rogues," turning to the three men in the rigging—"for you, I mean to mince ye up for the try-pots;" and, seizing a rope, he applied it with all his might to the backs of the two traitors, till they yelled no more, but lifelessly hung their heads sideways, as the two crucified thieves are drawn.

' "My wrist is sprained with ye!" he cried, at last; "but there is still rope enough left for you, my fine bantam, that wouldn't give up. Take that gag from his mouth, and let us hear what he can say for himself."

'For a moment the exhausted mutineer made a tremulous motion of his cramped jaws, and then painfully twisting round his head, said in a sort of hiss, "What I say is this—and mind it well—if you flog me, I murder you!"

' "Say ye so? then see how ye frighten me"—and the Captain drew off with the rope to strike.

' "Best not," hissed the Lakeman.

' "But I must,"—and the rope was once more drawn back for the stroke.

'Steelkilt here hissed out something, inaudible to all but the Captain; who, to the amazement of all hands, started back, paced the deck rapidly two or three times, and then suddenly throwing down his rope, said, "I won't do it—let him go—cut him down: d'ye hear?"

'But as the junior mates were hurrying to execute the order, a pale man, with a bandaged head, arrested them—Radney the chief mate. Ever since the blow, he had lain in his berth; but that morning, hearing the tumult on the deck, he had crept out, and thus far had watched the whole scene. Such was the state of his mouth, that he could hardly speak; but mumbling something about *his* being willing and able to do what the captain dared not attempt, he snatched the rope and advanced to his pinioned foe.

' "You are a coward!" hissed the Lakeman.

' "So I am, but take that." The mate was in the very act of striking, when another hiss stayed his uplifted arm. He paused: and then pausing no more, made good his word, spite of Steelkilt's threat, whatever that might have been. The three men were then cut down, all hands were turned to, and, sullenly worked by the moody seamen, the iron pumps clanged as before.

'Just after dark that day, when one watch had retired below, a clamor was heard in the forecastle; and the two trembling traitors running up, besieged the cabin door, saying they durst not consort with the crew. Entreaties, cuffs, and kicks could not drive them back, so at their own instance they were put down in the ship's run for salvation. Still, no sign of mutiny reappeared among the rest. On the contrary, it seemed, that mainly at Steelkilt's instigation, they had resolved to maintain the strictest peacefulness, obey all orders to the last, and, when the ship reached port, desert her in a body. But in order to insure the speediest end to the voyage, they all agreed to another thing—namely, not to sing out for whales, in case any should be discovered. For, spite of her leak, and spite of all her other perils, the Town-Ho still maintained her mast-heads, and her captain was just as willing to lower for a fish that moment, as on the day his craft first struck the cruising ground; and Radney the mate was quite as ready to change his berth for a boat, and with his bandaged mouth seek to gag in death the vital jaw of the whale.

'But though the Lakeman had induced the seamen to adopt this sort of passiveness in their conduct, he kept his own counsel (at least till all was over) concerning his own proper and private revenge upon the man who had stung him in the ventricles of his heart. He was in Radney the chief mate's watch; and as if the infatuated man sought to run more than half way to meet his doom, after the scene at the rigging, he insisted, against the express counsel of the captain, upon resuming the head of his watch at night. Upon this, and one or two other circumstances, Steelkilt systematically built the plan of his revenge.

'During the night, Radney had an unseamanlike way of sitting on the bulwarks of the quarter-deck, and leaning his arm upon the gunwale of the boat which was hoisted up there, a little above the ship's side. In this attitude, it was well known, he sometimes dozed. There was a considerable vacancy between the boat and the ship, and down between this was the sea. Steelkilt calculated his time, and found that his next trick at the helm would come round at two o'clock, in the morning of the third day from that in which he had been betrayed. At his leisure, he employed the interval in braiding something very carefully in his watches below.

' "What are you making there?" said a shipmate.

' "What do you think? what does it look like?"

' "Like a lanyard for your bag; but it's an odd one, seems to me."

' "Yes, rather oddish," said the Lakeman, holding it at arm's length before him; "but I think it will answer. Shipmate, I haven't enough twine,—have you any?"

'But there was none in the forecastle.'

' "Then I must get some from old Rad;" and he rose to go aft.

' "You don't mean to go a begging to *him*!" said a sailor.

' "Why not? Do you think he won't do me a turn, when it's to help himself in the end, shipmate?" and going to the mate, he looked at him quietly, and asked him for some twine to mend his hammock. It was given him—neither twine nor lanyard were seen again; but the next night an iron ball, closely netted, partly rolled from the pocket of the Lakeman's monkey jacket, as he was tucking the coat into his hammock for a pillow. Twenty-four hours after, his trick at the silent helm—nigh to the man who was apt to doze over the grave always ready dug to the seaman's hand—that fatal hour was then to come; and in the fore-ordaining soul of Steelkilt, the mate was already stark and stretched as a corpse, with his forehead crushed in.

'But, gentlemen, a fool saved the would-be murderer from the bloody deed he had planned. Yet complete revenge he had, and without being the avenger. For by a mysterious fatality, Heaven itself seemed to step in to take out of his hands into its own the damning thing he would have done.

'It was just between daybreak and sunrise of the morning of the second day, when they were washing down the decks, that a stupid Teneriffe man, drawing water in the main-chains, all at once shouted out, "There she rolls! there she rolls! Jesu! what a whale!" It was Moby Dick.'

'Moby Dick!' cried Don Sebastian; 'St Dominic! Sir sailor, but do whales have christenings? Whom call you Moby Dick?'

'A very white, and famous, and most deadly immortal monster, Don;—but that would be too long a story.'

'How how?' cried all the young Spaniards, crowding.

'Nay, Dons, Dons—nay, nay! I cannot rehearse that now. Let me get more into the air, Sirs.'

'The chicha; the chicha;' cried Don Pedro; 'our vigorous friend looks faint;—fill up his empty glass!'

'No need, gentlemen; one moment, and I proceed.—Now, gentlemen, so suddenly perceiving the snowy whale within fifty yards of the ship—forgetful of the compact among the crew—in the excitement of the moment, the Teneriffe man had instinctively and involuntarily lifted his voice for the monster, though for some little time past it had been plainly beheld from the three sullen mast-heads. All was now a phrensy. "The White Whale—the White Whale!" was the cry from captain, mates, and harpooneers, who, undeterred by fearful rumors, were all anxious to capture so famous and precious a fish; while the dogged crew eyed askance, and with curses, the appalling beauty of the vast milky mass, that lit up by a horizontal spangling sun, shifted and glistened like a living opal in the blue morning sea. Gentlemen, a strange fatality pervades the whole career of these events, as if verily mapped out before the world itself was charted. The mutineer was the bowsman of the mate, and when fast to a fish, it was his duty to sit next him, while Radney stood up with his lance in the prow, and haul in or slacken the line, at the word of command. Moreover, when the four boats were lowered, the mate's got the start; and none howled more fiercely with delight than did Steelkilt, as he strained at his oar. After a stiff pull, their harpooneer got fast, and, spear in hand, Radney sprang to the bow. He was always a furious man, it seems, in a boat. And now his bandaged cry was, to beach him on the whale's topmost back. Nothing loath, his bowsman hauled him up and up, through a blinding foam that blent two whitenesses together; till of a sudden the boat struck as against a sunken ledge, and keeling over, spilled out the standing mate. That instant, as he fell on the whale's slippery back, the boat righted, and was dashed aside by the swell, while Radney was tossed over into the sea, on the other flank of the whale. He struck out through the spray, and, for an instant, was dimly seen through that veil, wildly seeking to remove himself from the eye of Moby Dick. But the whale rushed round in a sudden maelstrom; seized the swimmer between his jaws; and rearing high up with him, plunged headlong again, and went down.

'Meantime, at the first tap of the boat's bottom, the Lakeman had slackened the line, so as to drop astern from the whirlpool; calmly looking on, he thought his own thoughts. But a sudden, terrific, downward jerking of the boat, quickly brought his knife to the line. He cut it; and the whale was free. But, at some distance, Moby Dick rose again, with some tatters of Radney's red woollen shirt, caught in the teeth that had destroyed him. All four boats gave chase again; but the whale eluded them, and finally wholly disappeared.

'In good time, the Town-Ho reached her port—a savage, solitary place—where no civilized creature resided. There, headed by the Lakeman, all but five or six of the foremastmen deliberately deserted among the palms; eventually, as it turned out, seizing a large double war-canoe of the savages, and setting sail for some other harbor.

'The ship's company being reduced to but a handful, the captain called upon the Islanders to assist him in the laborious business of heaving down the ship to stop the leak. But to such unresting vigilance over their dangerous allies was this small band of whites necessitated, both by night and by day, and so extreme was the hard work they underwent, that upon the vessel being ready again for sea, they were in such a weakened condition that the captain durst not put off with them in so heavy a vessel. After taking counsel with his officers, he anchored the ship as far off shore as possible; loaded and ran out his two cannon from the bows; stacked his muskets on the poop; and warning the Islanders not to approach the ship at their peril, took one man with him, and setting the sail of his best whaleboat, steered straight before the wind for Tahiti, five hundred miles distant, to procure a reinforcement to his crew.

'On the fourth day of the sail, a large canoe was descried, which seemed to have touched at a low isle of corals. He steered away from it; but the savage craft bore down on him; and soon the voice of Steelkilt hailed him to heave to, or he would run him under water. The captain presented a pistol. With one foot on each prow of the yoked war-canoes, the Lakeman laughed him to scorn; assuring him that if the pistol so much as clicked in the lock, he would bury him in bubbles and foam.

' "What do you want of me?" cried the captain.

' "Where are you bound? and for what are you bound?" demanded Steelkilt; "no lies."

' "I am bound to Tahiti for more men."

' "Very good. Let me board you a moment—I come in peace."

With that he leaped from the canoe, swam to the boat; and climbing the gunwale, stood face to face with the captain.

' "Cross your arms, sir; throw back your head. Now, repeat after me. As soon as Steelkilt leaves me, I swear to beach this boat on yonder island, and remain there six days. If I do not, may lightning strike me!"

' "A pretty scholar," laughed the Lakeman. "Adios, Senor!" and leaping into the sea, he swam back to his comrades.

'Watching the boat till it was fairly beached, and drawn up to the roots of the cocoa-nut trees, Steelkilt made sail again, and in due time arrived at Tahiti, his own place of destination. There, luck befriended him; two ships were about to sail for France, and were providentially in want of precisely that number of men which the sailor headed. They embarked; and so for ever got the start of their former captain, had he been at all minded to work them legal retribution.

'Some ten days after the French ships sailed, the whaleboat arrived, and the captain was forced to enlist some of the more civilized Tahitians, who had been somewhat used to the sea. Chartering a small native schooner, he returned with them to his vessel; and finding all right there, again resumed his cruisings.

'Where Steelkilt now is, gentlemen, none know; but upon the island of Nantucket, the widow of Radney still turns to the sea which refuses to give up its dead; still in dreams sees the awful white whale that destroyed him.'   * * *

'Are you through?' said Don Sebastian, quietly.

'I am, Don.'

'Then I entreat you, tell me if to the best of your own convictions, this your story is in substance really true? It is so passing wonderful! Did you get it from an unquestionable source? Bear with me if I seem to press.'

'Also bear with all of us, sir sailor; for we all join in Don Sebastian's suit,' cried the company, with exceeding interest.

'Is there a copy of the Holy Evangelists in the Golden Inn, gentlemen?'

'Nay,' said Don Sebastian; 'but I know a worthy priest near by, who will quickly procure one for me. I go for it; but are you well advised? this may grow too serious.'

'Will you be so good as to bring the priest also, Don?'

'Though there are no Auto-da-Fés in Lima now,' said one of the company to another; 'I fear our sailor friend runs risk of the archiepiscopacy. Let us withdraw more out of the moonlight. I see no need of this.'

'Excuse me for running after you, Don Sebastian; but may I also beg that you will be particular in procuring the largest sized Evangelist you can.'

'This is the priest, he brings you the Evangelists,' said Don Sebastian, gravely, returning with a tall and solemn figure.

'Let me remove my hat. Now, venerable priest, further into the light, and hold the Holy Book before me that I may touch it.'

'So help me Heaven, and on my honor, the story I have told ye, gentlemen, is in substance and its great items, true. I know it to be true; it happened on this ball; I trod the ship; I knew the crew; I have seen and talked with Steelkilt since the death of Radney.'

55
OF THE MONSTROUS PICTURES
OF WHALES

I shall ere long paint to you as well as one can without canvas, something like the true form of the whale as he actually appears to the eye of the whaleman when in his own absolute body the whale is moored alongside the whaleship so that he can be fairly stepped upon there. It may be worth while, therefore, previously to advert to those curious imaginary portraits of him which even down to the present day confidently challenge the faith of the landsman. It is time to set the world right in this matter, by proving such pictures of the whale all wrong.

It may be that the primal source of all those pictorial delusions will be found among the oldest Hindoo, Egyptian, and Grecian sculptures. For ever since those inventive but unscrupulous times when on the marble panellings of temples, the pedestals of statues, and on shields, medallions, cups, and coins, the dolphin was drawn in scales of chain-armor like Saladin's, and a helmeted head like St George's; ever since then has some thing of the same sort of license prevailed, not only in most popular pictures of the whale, but in many scientific presentations of him.

Now, by all odds, the most ancient extant portrait anyways

purporting to be the whale's, is to be found in the famous cavern-pagoda of Elephanta, in India. The Brahmins maintain that in the almost endless sculptures of that immemorial pagoda, all the trades and pursuits, every conceivable avocation of man, were prefigured ages before any of them actually came into being. No wonder then, that in some sort our noble profession of whaling should have been there shadowed forth. The Hindoo whale referred to, occurs in a separate department of the wall, depicting the incarnation of Vishnu in the form of leviathan, learnedly known as the Matse Avatar. But though this sculpture is half man and half whale, so as only to give the tail of the latter, yet that small section of him is all wrong. It looks more like the tapering tail of an anaconda, than the broad palms of the true whale's majestic flukes.

But go to the old Galleries, and look now at a great Christian painter's portrait of this fish; for he succeeds no better than the antediluvian Hindoo. It is Guido's picture of Perseus rescuing Andromeda from the sea-monster or whale. Where did Guido get the model of such a strange creature as that? Nor does Hogarth, in painting the same scene in his own 'Perseus Descending,' make out one whit better. The huge corpulence of that Hogarthian monster undulates on the surface, scarcely drawing one inch of water. It has a sort of howdah on its back, and its distended tusked mouth into which the billows are rolling, might be taken for the Traitors' Gate leading from the Thames by water into the Tower. Then, there are the Prodromus whales of old Scotch Sibbald, and Jonah's whale, as depicted in the prints of old Bibles and the cuts of old primers. What shall be said of these? As for the book-binder's whale winding like a vine-stalk round the stock of a descending anchor—as stamped and gilded on the backs and title-pages of many books both old and new—that is a very picturesque but purely fabulous creature, imitated, I take it, from the like figures on antique vases. Though universally denominated a dolphin, I nevertheless call this book-binder's fish an attempt at a whale; because it was so intended when the device was first introduced. It was introduced by an old Italian publisher some-where about the 15th century, during the Revival of Learning; and in those days, and even down to a comparatively late period, dolphins were popularly supposed to be a species of the Leviathan.

In the vignettes and other embellishments of some ancient books you will at times meet with very curious touches at the whale, where all manner of spouts, jets d'eau, hot springs and cold, Saratoga and Baden-Baden, come bubbling up from his unexhausted brain. In the title-page of the original edition of the 'Advancement of Learning' you will find some curious whales.

But quitting all these unprofessional attempts, let us glance at those pictures of leviathan purporting to be sober, scientific delineations, by those who know. In old Harris's collection of voyages there are some plates of whales extracted from a Dutch book of voyages, A.D. 1671, entitled 'A Whaling Voyage to Spitzbergen in the ship Jonas in the Whale, Peter Peterson of Friesland, master.' In one of those plates the whales, like great rafts of logs, are represented lying among ice-isles, with white bears running over their living backs. In another plate, the prodigious blunder is made of representing the whale with perpendicular flukes.

Then again, there is an imposing quarto, written by one Captain Colnett, a Post Captain in the English navy, entitled 'A Voyage round Cape Horn into the South Seas, for the purpose of extending the Spermaceti Whale Fisheries.' In this book is an outline purporting to be a 'Picture of a Physeter or Spermaceti whale, drawn by scale from one killed on the coast of Mexico, August, 1793, and hoisted on deck.' I doubt not the captain had this veracious picture taken for the benefit of his marines. To mention but one thing about it, let me say that it has an eye which applied, according to the accompanying scale, to a full grown sperm whale, would make the eye of that whale a bow-window some five feet long. Ah, my gallant captain, why did ye not give us Jonah looking out of that eye!

Nor are the most conscientious compilations of Natural History for the benefit of the young and tender, free from the same heinousness of mistake. Look at that popular work 'Goldsmith's Animated Nature.' In the abridged London edition of 1807, there are plates of an alleged 'whale' and a 'narwhale.' I do not wish to seem inelegant, but this unsightly whale looks much like an amputated sow; and, as for the narwhale, one glimpse at it is enough to amaze one, that in this nineteenth century such a hippogriff could be palmed for genuine upon any intelligent public of school-boys.

Then, again, in 1825, Bernard Germain, Count de Lacépède, a great naturalist, published a scientific systemized whale book, wherein are several pictures of the different species of the Leviathan. All these are not only incorrect, but the picture of the Mysticetus or Greenland whale (that is to say, the Right whale), even Scoresby, a long experienced man as touching that species, declares not to have its counterpart in nature.

But the placing of the cap-sheaf to all this blundering business was reserved for the scientific Frederick Cuvier, brother to the famous Baron. In 1836 he published a Natural History of Whales, in which he gives what he calls a picture of the Sperm Whale. Before showing that picture to any Nantucketer, you had best provide for your summary retreat from Nantucket. In a word, Frederick Cuvier's Sperm Whale is not a Sperm Whale, but a squash. Of course, he never had the benefit of a whaling voyage (such men seldom have), but whence he derived that picture, who can tell? Perhaps he got it as his scientific predecessor in the same field, Desmarest, got one of his authentic abortions; that is, from a Chinese drawing. And what sort of lively lads with the pencil those Chinese are, many queer cups and saucers inform us.

As for the sign-painters' whales seen in the streets hanging over the shops of oil-dealers, what shall be said of them? They are generally Richard III whales, with dromedary humps, and very savage; breakfasting on three or four sailor tarts, that is whaleboats full of mariners: their deformities floundering in seas of blood and blue paint.

But these manifold mistakes in depicting the whale are not so very surprising after all. Consider! Most of the scientific drawings have been taken from the stranded fish; and these are about as correct as a drawing of a wrecked ship, with broken back, would correctly represent the noble animal itself in all its undashed pride of hull and spars. Though elephants have stood for their full-lengths, the living Leviathan has never yet fairly floated himself for his portrait. The living whale, in his full majesty and significance, is only to be seen at sea in unfathomable waters; and afloat the vask bulk of him is out of sight, like a launched line-of-battle ship; and out of that element it is a thing eternally impossible for mortal man to hoist him bodily into the air, so as to preserve all his mighty swells and undulations. And, not to speak of the highly presumable difference of contour between a young sucking whale and a full-grown Platonian Leviathan; yet, even in the case of one of those young sucking whales hoisted to a ship's deck, such is then the outlandish, eel-like, limbered, varying shape of him, that his precise expression the devil himself could not catch.

But it may be fancied, that from the naked skeleton of the stranded whale, accurate hints may be derived touching his true form. Not at all. For it is one of the more curious things about this Leviathan, that his skeleton gives very little idea of his general shape. Though Jeremy Bentham's skeleton, which hangs for candelabra in the library of one of his executors, correctly conveys the idea of a burly-browed utilitarian old gentleman, with all

Jeremy's other leading personal characteristics; yet nothing of this kind could be inferred from any leviathan's articulated bones. In fact, as the great Hunter says, the mere skeleton of the whale bears the same relation to the fully invested and padded animal as the insect does to the chrysalis that so roundingly envelopes it. This peculiarity is strikingly evinced in the head, as in some part of this book will be incidentally shown. It is also very curiously displayed in the side fin, the bones of which almost exactly answer to the bones of the human hand, minus only the thumb. This fin has four regular bone-fingers, the index, middle, ring, and little finger. But all these are permanently lodged in their fleshy covering, as the human fingers in an artificial covering. 'However recklessly the whale may sometimes serve us,' said humorous Stubb one day, 'he can never be truly said to handle us without mittens.'

For all these reasons, then, any way you may look at it, you must needs conclude that the great Leviathan is that one creature in the world which must remain unpainted to the last. True, one portrait may hit the mark much nearer than another, but none can hit it with any very considerable degree of exactness. So there is no earthly way of finding out precisely what the whale really looks like. And the only mode in which you can derive even a tolerable idea of his living contour, is by going a whaling yourself; but by so doing, you run no small risk of being eternally stove and sunk by him. Wherefore, it seems to me you had best not be too fastidious in your curiosity touching this Leviathan.

56

OF THE LESS ERRONEOUS PICTURES OF WHALES, AND THE TRUE PICTURES OF WHALING SCENES

IN connexion with the monstrous pictures of whales, I am strongly tempted here to enter upon those still more monstrous stories of them which are to be found in certain books, both ancient and modern, especially in Pliny, Purchas, Hackluyt, Harris, Cuvier, &c. But I pass that matter by.

I know of only four published outlines of the great Sperm Whale; Colnett's, Huggins's, Frederick Cuvier's, and Beale's. In the previous chapter Colnett and Cuvier have been referred to. Huggins's is far better than theirs; but, by great odds, Beale's is the best. All Beale's drawings of this whale are good, excepting the middle figure in the picture of three whales in various attitudes, capping his second chapter. His frontispiece, boats attacking Sperm Whales, though no doubt calculated to excite the civil scepticism of some parlor men, is admirably correct and life-like in its general effect. Some of the Sperm Whale drawings in J. Ross Browne are pretty correct in contour; but they are wretchedly engraved. That is not his fault though.

Of the Right Whale, the best outline pictures are in Scoresby; but they are drawn on too small a scale to convey a desirable impression. He has but one picture of whaling scenes, and this is a sad deficiency, because it is by such pictures only, when at all well done, that you can derive anything like a truthful idea of the living whale as seen by his living hunters.

But, taken for all in all, by far the finest, though in some details not the most correct, presentations of whales and whaling scenes to be anywhere found, are two large French engravings, well executed, and taken from paintings by one Garnery. Respectively, they represent attacks on the Sperm and Right Whale. In the first engraving a noble Sperm Whale is depicted in full majesty of might, just risen beneath the boat from the profundities of the ocean, and bearing high in the air upon his back the terrific wreck of the stoven planks. The prow of the boat is partially unbroken, and is drawn just balancing upon the monster's spine; and standing in that prow, for that one single incomputable flash of time, you behold an oarsman, half shrouded by the incensed boiling spout of the whale, and in the act of leaping, as if from a precipice. The action of the whole thing is wonderfully good and true. The half-emptied line-tub floats on the whitened sea; the wooden poles of the spilled harpoons obliquely bob in it; the heads of the swimming crew are scattered about the whale in contrasting expressions of affright; while in the black stormy distance the ship is bearing down upon the scene. Serious fault might be found with the anatomical details of this whale, but let that pass; since, for the life of me, I could not draw so good a one.

In the second engraving, the boat is in the act of drawing alongside the barnacled flank of a large running Right Whale, that rolls his black weedy bulk in the sea like some mossy rock-slide from the Patagonian cliffs. His jets are erect, full, and black like soot; so that from so abounding a smoke in the chimney, you would think there must be a brave supper cooking in the great bowels below. Sea fowls are pecking at the small crabs, shell-fish, and other sea candies and maccaroni, which the Right Whale sometimes carries on his pestilent back. And all the while the thick-lipped leviathan is rushing through the deep, leaving tons of tumultuous white curds in his wake, and causing the slight boat to rock in the swells like a skiff caught nigh the paddle-wheels of an ocean steamer. Thus, the foreground is all raging commotion; but behind, in admirable artistic contrast, is the glassy level of a sea becalmed, the drooping unstarched sails of the powerless ship, and the inert mass of a dead whale, a conquered fortress, with the flag of capture lazily hanging from the whale-pole inserted into his spout-hole.

Who Garnery the painter is, or was, I know not. But my life for it he was either practically conversant with his subject, or else marvellously tutored by some experienced whaleman. The French are the lads for painting action. Go and gaze upon all the paintings of Europe, and where will you find such a gallery of living and breathing commotion on canvas, as in that triumphal hall at Versailles; where the beholder fights his way, pell-mell, through the consecutive great battles of France; where every sword seems a flash of the Northern Lights, and the successive armed kings and Emperors dash by, like a charge of crowned centaurs? Not wholly unworthy of a place in that gallery, are these sea battle-pieces of Garnery.

The natural aptitude of the French for seizing the picturesqueness of things seems to be peculiarly evinced in what paintings and engravings they have of their whaling scenes. With not one tenth of England's experience in the fishery, and not the thousandth part of that of the Americans, they have nevertheless furnished both nations with the only finished sketches at all capable of conveying the real spirit of the whale hunt. For the most part, the English and American whale draughtsmen seem entirely content with presenting the mechanical outline of things, such as the vacant profile of the whale; which, so far as picturesqueness of effect is concerned, is about tantamount to sketching the profile of a pyramid. Even Scoresby, the justly renowned Right whaleman, after giving us a stiff full length of the Greenland whale, and three or four delicate miniatures of narwhales and porpoises, treats us to a series of classical engravings of boat hooks, chopping knives, and grapnels; and with the microscopic diligence of a Leuwenhoeck submits to the inspection of a shivering world ninety-six facsimiles of magnified Arctic snow crystals. I mean no disparagement to the excellent voyager (I honor him for a veteran), but in so important a matter it was certainly an oversight not to have procured for every crystal a sworn affidavit taken before a Greenland Justice of the Peace.

In addition to those fine engravings from Garnery, there are two other French engravings worthy of note, by some one who subscribes himself 'H. Durand.' One of them, though not precisely adapted to our present purpose, nevertheless deserves mention on other accounts. It is a quiet noon-scene among the isles of the Pacific; a French whaler anchored, inshore, in a calm, and lazily taking water on board; the loosened sails of the ship, and the long leaves of the palms in the background, both drooping together in the breezeless air. The effect is very fine, when considered with reference to its presenting the hardy fishermen under one of their few aspects of oriental repose. The other engraving is quite a different affair: the ship hove-to upon the open sea, and in the very heart of the Leviathanic life, with a Right Whale alongside; the vessel (in the act of cutting-in) hove over to the monster as if to a quay; and a boat, hurriedly pushing off from this scene of activity, is about giving chase to whales in the distance. The harpoons and lances lie levelled for use; three oarsmen are just setting the mast in its hole; while from a sudden roll of the sea, the little craft stands half-erect out of the water, like a rearing horse. From the ship, the smoke of the torments of the boiling whale is going up like the smoke over a village of smithies; and to windward, a black cloud, rising up with earnest of squalls and rains, seems to quicken the activity of the excited seamen.

57

OF WHALES IN PAINT; IN TEETH; IN WOOD; IN SHEET-IRON; IN STONE; IN MOUNTAINS; IN STARS

On Tower-hill, as you go down to the London docks, you may have seen a crippled beggar (or *kedger*, as the sailors say) holding a painted board before him, representing the tragic scene in which he lost his leg. There are three whales and three boats; and one of the boats (presumed to contain the missing leg in all its original integrity) is being crunched by the jaws of the foremost whale.

Any time these ten years, they tell me, has that man held up that picture, and exhibited that stump to an incredulous world. But the time of his justification has now come. His three whales are as good whales as were ever published in Wapping, at any rate; and his stump as unquestionable a stump as any you will find in the western clearings. But, though for ever mounted on that stump, never a stump-speech does the poor whaleman make; but, with downcast eyes, stands ruefully contemplating his own amputation.

Throughout the Pacific, and also in Nantucket, and New Bedford, and Sag Harbor, you will come across lively sketches of whales and whaling-scenes, graven by the fishermen themselves on Sperm Whale-teeth, or ladies' busks wrought out of the Right Whale-bone, and other like skrimshander articles, as the whalemen call the numerous little ingenious contrivances they elaborately carve out of the rough material, in their hours of ocean leisure. Some of them have little boxes of dentistical-looking implements, specially intended for the skrimshandering business. But, in general, they toil with their jack-knives alone; and, with that almost omnipotent tool of the sailor, they will turn you out anything you please, in the way of a mariner's fancy.

Long exile from Christendom and civilization inevitably restores a man to that condition in which God placed him, i.e. what is called savagery. Your true whale-hunter is as much a savage as an Iroquois. I myself am a savage, owning no allegiance but to the King of the Cannibals; and ready at any moment to rebel against him.

Now, one of the peculiar characteristics of the savage in his domestic hours, is his wonderful patience of industry. An ancient Hawaiian war-club or spear-paddle, in its full multiplicity and elaboration of carving, is as great a trophy of human perseverance as a Latin lexicon. For, with but a bit of broken sea-shell or a shark's tooth, that miraculous intricacy of wooden net-work has been achieved; and it has cost steady years of steady application.

As with the Hawaiian savage, so with the white sailor-savage. With the same marvellous patience, and with the same single shark's tooth, of his one poor jack-knife, he will carve you a bit of bone sculpture, not quite as workmanlike, but as close packed in its maziness of design, as the Greek savage, Achilles's shield; and full of barbaric spirit and suggestiveness, as the prints of that fine old Dutch savage, Albert Durer.

Wooden whales, or whales cut in profile out of the small dark slabs of the noble South Sea war-wood, are frequently met with

in the forecastles of American whalers. Some of them are done
with much accuracy.

At some gable-roofed country houses you will see brass whales
hung by the tail for knockers to the road-side door. When the
porter is sleepy, the anvil-headed whale would be best. But these
knocking whales are seldom remarkable as faithful essays. On the
spires of some old-fashioned churches you will see sheet-iron whales
placed there for weathercocks; but they are so elevated, and besides
that are to all intents and purposes so labelled with 'Hands off!'
you cannot examine them closely enough to decide upon their
merit.

In bony, ribby regions of the earth, where at the base of high
broken cliffs masses of rock lie strewn in fantastic groupings upon
the plain, you will often discover images of the petrified forms of
the Leviathan partly merged in grass, which of a windy day breaks
against them in a surf of green surges.

Then, again, in mountainous countries where the traveller is
continually girdled by amphitheatrical heights; here and there from
some lucky point of view you will catch passing glimpses of the
profiles of whales defined along the undulating ridges. But you
must be a thorough whaleman, to see these sights; and not only
that, but if you wish to return to such a sight again, you must
be sure and take the exact intersecting latitude and longitude of
your first standpoint, else so chance-like are such observations of
the hills, that your precise, previous stand-point would require a
laborious re-discovery; like the Solomon islands, which still remain
incognita, though once high-ruffed Mendanna trod them and old
Figuera chronicled them.

Nor when expandingly lifted by your subject, can you fail to
trace out great whales in the starry heavens, and boats in pursuit
of them; as when long filled with thoughts of war the Eastern
nations saw armies locked in battle among the clouds. Thus at
the North have I chased Leviathan round and round the Pole
with the revolutions of the bright points that first defined him to
me. And beneath the effulgent Antarctic skies I have boarded the
Argo-Navis, and joined the chase against the starry Cetus far
beyond the utmost stretch of Hydrus and the Flying Fish.

With a frigate's anchors for my bridle-bits and fasces of harpoons
for spurs, would I could mount that whale and leap the topmost
skies, to see whether the fabled heavens with all their countless
tents really lie encamped beyond my mortal sight!

58

BRIT

STEERING north-eastward from the Crozetts, we fell in with vast meadows of brit, the minute, yellow substance, upon which the Right Whale largely feeds. For leagues and leagues it undulated round us, so that we seemed to be sailing through boundless fields of ripe and golden wheat.

On the second day, numbers of Right Whales were seen, who, secure from the attack of a Sperm Whaler like the Pequod, with open jaws sluggishly swam through the brit, which, adhering to the fringing fibres of that wondrous Venetian blind in their mouths, was in that manner separated from the water that escaped at the lip.

As morning mowers, who side by side slowly and seethingly advance their scythes through the long wet grass of marshy meads; even so these monsters swam, making a strange, grassy, cutting sound; and leaving behind them endless swaths of blue upon the yellow sea.*

But it was only the sound they made as they parted the brit which at all reminded one of mowers. Seen from the mast-heads, especially when they paused and were stationary for a while, their vast black forms looked more like lifeless masses of rock than anything else. And as in the great hunting countries of India, the stranger at a distance will sometimes pass on the plains recumbent elephants without knowing them to be such, taking them for bare, blackened elevations of the soil; even so, often, with him, who for the first time beholds this species of the leviathans of the sea. And even when recognized at last, their immense magnitude renders it very hard really to believe that such bulky masses of overgrowth can possibly be instinct, in all parts, with the same sort of life that lives in a dog or a horse.

Indeed, in other respects, you can hardly regard any creatures

* That part of the sea known among whalemen as the 'Brazil Banks' does not bear that name as the Banks of Newfoundland do, because of there being shallows and soundings there, but because of this remarkable meadow-like appearance, caused by the vast drifts of brit continually floating in those latitudes, where the Right Whale is often chased.

of the deep with the same feelings that you do those of the shore. For though some old naturalists have maintained that all creatures of the land are of their kind in the sea; and though taking a broad general view of the thing, this may very well be; yet coming to specialities, where, for example, does the ocean furnish any fish that in disposition answers to the sagacious kindness of the dog? The accursed shark alone can in any generic respect be said to bear comparative analogy to him.

But though, to landsmen in general, the native inhabitants of the seas have ever been regarded with emotions unspeakably unsocial and repelling; though we know the sea to be an everlasting terra incognita, so that Columbus sailed over numberless unknown worlds to discover his one superficial western one; though, by vast odds, the most terrific of all mortal disasters have immemorially and indiscriminately befallen tens and hundreds of thousands of those who have gone upon the waters; though but a moment's consideration will teach, that however baby man may brag of his science and skill, and however much, in a flattering future, that science and skill may augment; yet for ever and for ever, to the crack of doom, the sea will insult and murder him, and pulverize the stateliest, stiffest frigate he can make; nevertheless, by the continual repetition of these very impressions, man has lost that sense of the full awfulness of the sea which aboriginally belongs to it.

The first boat we read of, floated on an ocean, that with Portuguese vengeance had whelmed a whole world without leaving so much as a widow. That same ocean rolls now; that same ocean destroyed the wrecked ships of last year. Yea, foolish mortals, Noah's flood is not yet subsided; two thirds of the fair world it yet covers.

Wherein differ the sea and the land, that a miracle upon one is not a miracle upon the other? Preternatural terrors rested upon the Hebrews, when under the feet of Korah and his company the live ground opened and swallowed them up for ever; yet not a modern sun ever sets, but in precisely the same manner the live sea swallows up ships and crews.

But not only is the sea such a foe to man who is an alien to it, but it is also a fiend to its own offspring; worse than the Persian host who murdered his own guests; sparing not the creatures which itself hath spawned. Like a savage tigress that tossing in the jungle overlays her own cubs, so the sea dashes even the mightiest whales against the rocks, and leaves them there side by side with the split wrecks of ships. No mercy, no power but its own controls it.

Panting and snorting like a mad battle steed that has lost its rider, the masterless ocean overruns the globe.

Consider the subtleness of the sea; how its most dreaded creatures glide under water, unapparent for the most part, and treacherously hidden beneath the loveliest tints of azure. Consider also the devilish brilliance and beauty of many of its most remorseless tribes, as the dainty embellished shape of many species of sharks. Consider, once more, the universal cannibalism of the sea; all whose creatures prey upon each other, carrying on eternal war since the world began.

Consider all this; and then turn to this green, gentle, and most docile earth; consider them both, the sea and the land; and do you not find a strange analogy to something in yourself? For as this appalling ocean surrounds the verdant land, so in the soul of man there lies one insular Tahiti, full of peace and joy, but encompassed by all the horrors of the half known life. God keep thee! Push not off from that isle, thou canst never return!

59

SQUID

SLOWLY wading through the meadows of brit, the Pequod still held on her way north-eastward towards the island of Java; a gentle air impelling her keel, so that in the surrounding serenity her three tall tapering masts mildly waved to that languid breeze, as three mild palms on a plain. And still, at wide intervals in the silvery night, the lonely, alluring jet would be seen.

But one transparent blue morning, when a stillness almost preternatural spread over the sea, however unattended with any stagnant calm; when the long burnished sun-glade on the waters seemed a golden finger laid across them, enjoining some secrecy; when the slippered waves whispered together as they softly ran on; in this profound hush of the visible sphere a strange spectre was seen by Daggoo from the main-mast-head.

In the distance, a great white mass lazily rose, and rising higher and higher, and disentangling itself from the azure, at last gleamed before our prow like a snow-slide, new slid from the hills. Thus glistening for a moment, as slowly it subsided, and sank. Then once more arose, and silently gleamed. It seemed not a whale; and yet is this Moby Dick? thought Daggoo. Again the phantom went down, but on reappearing once more, with a stiletto-like cry that startled every man from his nod, the negro yelled out— 'There! there again! there she breaches! right ahead! The White Whale, the White Whale!'

Upon this, the seamen rushed to the yard-arms, as in swarming-time the bees rush to the boughs. Bare-headed in the sultry sun, Ahab stood on the bowsprit, and with one hand pushed far behind in readiness to wave his orders to the helmsman, cast his eager glance in the direction indicated aloft by the outstretched motionless arm of Daggoo.

Whether the flitting attendance of the one still and solitary jet had gradually worked upon Ahab, so that he was now prepared to connect the ideas of mildness and repose with the first sight of the particular whale he pursued; however this was, or whether his eagerness betrayed him; whichever way it might have been, no sooner did he distinctly perceive the white mass, than with a quick intensity he instantly gave orders for lowering.

The four boats were soon on the water; Ahab's in advance, and all swiftly pulling towards their prey. Soon it went down, and while, with oars suspended, we were awaiting its reappearance, lo! in the same spot where it sank, once more it slowly rose. Almost forgetting for the moment all thoughts of Moby Dick, we now gazed at the most wondrous phenomenon which the secret seas have hitherto revealed to mankind. A vast pulpy mass, furlongs in length and breadth, of a glancing cream-color, lay floating on the water, innumerable long arms radiating from its centre, and curling and twisting like a nest of anacondas, as if blindly to clutch at any hapless object within reach. No perceptible face or front did it have; no conceivable token of either sensation or instinct; but undulated there on the billows, an unearthly, formless, chance-like apparition of life.

As with a low sucking sound it slowly disappeared again, Starbuck still gazing at the agitated waters where it had sunk, with a wild voice exlaimed—'Almost rather had I seen Moby Dick and fought him, than to have seen thee, thou white ghost!'

'What was it, Sir?' said Flask.

'The great live squid, which, they say, few whale-ships ever beheld, and returned to their ports to tell of it.'

But Ahab said nothing; turning his boat, he sailed back to the vessel; the rest as silently following.

Whatever superstitions the sperm whalemen in general have connected with the sight of this object, certain it is, that a glimpse of it being so very unusual, that circumstance has gone far to invest it with portentousness. So rarely is it beheld, that though one and all of them declare it to be the largest animated thing in the ocean, yet very few of them have any but the most vague ideas concerning its true nature and form; notwithstanding, they believe it to furnish to the sperm whale his only food. For though other species of whales find their food above water, and may be seen by man in the act of feeding, the spermaccti whale obtains his whole food in unknown zones below the surface; and only by inference is it that any one can tell of what, precisely, that food consists. At times, when closely pursued, he will disgorge what are supposed to be the detached arms of the squid; some of them thus exhibited exceeding twenty and thirty feet in length. They fancy that the monster to which these arms belonged ordinarily clings by them to the bed of the ocean; and that the sperm whale, unlike other species, is supplied with teeth in order to attack and tear it.

There seems some ground to imagine that the great Kraken of Bishop Pontoppodan may ultimately resolve itself into Squid. The manner in which the Bishop describes it, as alternately rising and sinking, with some other particulars he narrates, in all this the two correspond. But much abatement is necessary with respect to the incredible bulk he assigns it.

By some naturalists who have vaguely heard rumors of the mysterious creature, here spoken of, it is included among the class of cuttle-fish, to which, indeed, in certain external respects it would seem to belong, but only as the Anak of the tribe.

60

THE LINE

WITH reference to the whaling scene shortly to be described, as well as for the better understanding of all similar scenes elsewhere presented, I have here to speak of the magical, sometimes horrible whale-line.

The line originally used in the fishery was of the best hemp, slightly vapored with tar, not impregnated with it, as in the case of ordinary ropes; for while tar, as ordinarily used, makes the hemp more pliable to the rope-maker, and also renders the rope itself more convenient to the sailor for common ship use; yet, not only would the ordinary quantity too much stiffen the whale-line for the close coiling to which it must be subjected; but as most seamen are beginning to learn, tar in general by no means adds to the rope's durability or strength, however much it may give it compactness and gloss.

Of late years the Manilla rope has in the American fishery almost entirely superseded hemp as a material for whale-lines; for, though not so durable as hemp, it is stronger, and far more soft and elastic; and I will add (since there is an aesthetics in all things), is much more handsome and becoming to the boat, than hemp. Hemp is a dusky, dark fellow, a sort of Indian; but Manilla is as a golden-haired Circassian to behold.

The whale line is only two thirds of an inch in thickness. At first sight, you would not think it so strong as it really is. By experiment its one and fifty yarns will each suspend a weight of one hundred and twenty pounds; so that the whole rope will bear a strain nearly equal to three tons. In length, the common sperm whale-line measures something over two hundred fathoms. Towards the stern of the boat it is spirally coiled away in the tub, not like the worm-pipe of a still though, but so as to form one round, cheese-shaped mass of densely bedded 'sheaves', or layers of concentric spiralizations, without any hollow but the 'heart', or minute vertical tube formed at the axis of the cheese. As the least tangle or kink in the coiling would, in running out, infallibly take somebody's arm, leg, or entire body off, the utmost precaution is used in stowing the line in its tub. Some harpooneers will consume almost an entire morning in this business, carrying the line high aloft and then reeving it downwards through a block towards the tub, so as in the act of coiling to free it from all possible wrinkles and twists.

In the English boats two tubs are used instead of one; the same line being continuously coiled in both tubs. There is some advantage in this; because these twin-tubs being so small they fit more readily into the boat, and do not strain it so much; whereas, the American tub, nearly three feet in diameter and of proportionate depth, makes a rather bulky freight for a craft whose planks are but one half-inch in thickness; for the bottom of the whale-boat is like critical ice, which will bear up a considerable distributed weight, but not very much of a concentrated one. When the painted canvas cover is clapped on the American line-tub, the boat looks as if it were pulling off with a prodigious great wedding-cake to present to the whales.

Both ends of the line are exposed; the lower end terminating in an eye-splice or loop coming up from the bottom against the

side of the tub, and hanging over its edge completely disengaged
from everything. This arrangement of the lower end is necessary
on two accounts. First: In order to facilitate the fastening to it of
an additional line from a neighboring boat, in case the stricken
whale should sound so deep as to threaten to carry off the entire
line originally attached to the harpoon. In these instances, the
whale of course is shifted like a mug of ale, as it were, from the
one boat to the other; though the first boat always hovers at hand
to assist its consort. Second: This arrangement is indispensable
for common safety's sake; for were the lower end of the line in
any way attached to the boat, and were the whale then to run
the line out to the end almost in a single, smoking minute as he
sometimes does, he would not stop there, for the doomed boat
would infallibly be dragged down after him into the profundity
of the sea; and in that case no town-crier would ever find her
again.

Before lowering the boat for the chase, the upper end of the
line is taken aft from the tub, and passing round the loggerhead
there, is again carried forward the entire length of the boat, resting
crosswise upon the loom or handle of every man's oar, so that it
jogs against his wrist in rowing; and also passing between the men,
as they alternately sit at the opposite gunwales, to the leaded
chocks or grooves in the extreme pointed prow of the boat, where
a wooden pin or skewer the size of a common quill, prevents it
from slipping out. From the chocks it hangs in a slight festoon
over the bows, and is then passed inside the boat again; and some
ten or twenty fathoms (called box-line) being coiled upon the box
in the bows, it continues its way to the gunwale still a little further
aft, and is then attached to the short-warp—rope which is immediately connected with the harpoon; but previous to that connexion, the short-warp goes through sundry mystifications too
tedious to detail.

Thus the whale-line folds the whole boat in its complicated
coils, twisting and writhing around it in almost every direction.
All the oarsmen are involved in its perilous contortions; so that
to the timid eye of the landsman, they seem as Indian jugglers,
with the deadliest snakes sportively festooning their limbs. Nor
can any son of mortal woman, for the first time, seat himself
amid those hempen intricacies, and while straining his utmost at
the oar, bethink him that at any unknown instant the harpoon
may be darted, and all these horrible contortions be put in play
like ringed lightnings; he cannot be thus circumstanced without
a shudder that makes the very marrow in his bones to quiver in

him like a shaken jelly. Yet habit—strange thing! what cannot habit accomplish?—Gayer sallies, more merry mirth, better jokes, and brighter repartees, you never heard over your mahogany, than you will hear over the half-inch white cedar of the whale-boat, when thus hung in hangman's nooses; and, like the six burghers of Calais before King Edward, the six men composing the crew pull into the jaws of death, with a halter around every neck, as you may say.

Perhaps a very little thought will now enable you to account for those repeated whaling disasters—some few of which are casually chronicled—of this man or that man being taken out of the boat by the line, and lost. For, when the line is darting out, to be seated then in the boat, is like being seated in the midst of the manifold whizzings of a steam-engine in full play, when every flying beam, and shaft, and wheel, is grazing you. It is worse; for you cannot sit motionless in the heart of these perils, because the boat is rocking like a cradle, and you are pitched one way and the other, without the slightest warning; and only by a certain self-adjusting buoyancy and simultaneousness of volition and action, can you escape being made a Mazeppa of, and run away with where the all-seeing sun himself could never pierce you out.

Again: as the profound calm which only apparently precedes and prophesies of the storm, is perhaps more awful than the storm itself; for, indeed, the calm is but the wrapper and envelope of the storm; and contains it in itself, as the seemingly harmless rifle holds the fatal powder, and the ball, and the explosion; so the graceful repose of the line, as it silently serpentines about the oarsmen before being brought into actual play—this is a thing which carries more of true terror than any other aspect of this dangerous affair. But why say more? All men live enveloped in whale-lines. All are born with halters round their necks; but it is only when caught in the swift, sudden turn of death, that mortals realize the silent, subtle, ever-present perils of life. And if you be a philosopher, though seated in the whale-boat, you would not at heart feel one whit more of terror, than though seated before your evening fire with a poker, and not a harpoon, by your side.

61

STUBB KILLS A WHALE

IF to Starbuck the apparition of the Squid was a thing of portents, to Queequeg it was quite a different object.

'When you see him 'quid,' said the savage, honing his harpoon in the bow of his hoisted boat, 'then you quick see him 'parm whale.'

The next day was exceedingly still and sultry, and with nothing special to engage them, the Pequod's crew could hardly resist the spell of sleep induced by such a vacant sea. For this part of the Indian Ocean through which we then were voyaging is not what whalemen call a lively ground; that is, it affords fewer glimpses of porpoises, dolphins, flying-fish, and other vivacious denizens of more stirring waters, than those off the Rio de la Plata, or the in-shore ground off Peru.

It was my turn to stand at the foremast-head; and with my shoulders leaning against the slackened royal shrouds, to and fro I idly swayed in what seemed an enchanted air. No resolution could withstand it; in that dreamy mood losing all consciousness, at last my soul went out of my body; though my body still continued to sway as a pendulum will, long after the power which first moved it is withdrawn.

Ere forgetfulness altogether came over me, I had noticed that the seamen at the main and mizen mast-heads were already drowsy. So that at last all three of us lifelessly swung from the spars, and for every swing that we made there was a nod from below from the slumbering helmsman. The waves, too, nodded their indolent crests; and across the wide trance of the sea, east nodded to west, and the sun over all.

Suddenly bubbles seemed bursting beneath my closed eyes; like vices my hands grasped the shrouds; some invisible, gracious agency preserved me; with a shock I came back to life. And lo! close under our lee, not forty fathoms off, a gigantic Sperm Whale lay rolling in the water like the capsized hull of a frigate, his broad, glossy back, of an Ethiopian hue, glistening in the sun's rays like a mirror. But lazily undulating in the trough of the sea, and ever and anon tranquilly spouting his vapory jet, the whale looked like a portly burgher smoking his pipe of a warm afternoon. But that pipe, poor whale, was thy last. As if struck by some enchanter's wand, the sleepy ship and every sleeper in it all at once started into wakefulness; and more than a score of voices from all parts of the vessel, simultaneously with the three notes from aloft, shouted forth the accustomed cry, as the great fish slowly and regularly spouted the sparkling brine into the air.

'Clear away the boats! Luff!' cried Ahab. And obeying his own order, he dashed the helm down before the helmsman could handle the spokes.

The sudden exclamations of the crew must have alarmed the whale; and ere the boats were down, majestically turning, he swam away to the leeward, but with such a steady tranquillity, and making so few ripples as he swam, that thinking after all he might not as yet be alarmed, Ahab gave orders that not an oar should be used, and no man must speak but in whispers. So seated like Ontario Indians on the gunwales of the boats, we swiftly but silently paddled along; the calm not admitting of the noiseless sails being set. Presently, as we thus glided in chase, the monster perpendicularly flitted his tail forty feet into the air, and then sank out of sight like a tower swallowed up.

'There go flukes!' was the cry, an announcement immediately followed by Stubb's producing his match and igniting his pipe, for now a respite was granted. After the full interval of his sounding had elapsed, the whale rose again, and being now in advance of the smoker's boat, and much nearer to it than to any of the others, Stubb counted upon the honor of the capture. It was obvious, now, that the whale had at length become aware of his pursuers. All silence of cautiousness was therefore no longer of use. Paddles were dropped, and oars came loudly into play. And still puffing at his pipe, Stubb cheered on his crew to the assault.

Yes, a mighty change had come over the fish. All alive to his jeopardy, he was going 'head out'; that part obliquely projecting from the mad yeast which he brewed.*

'Start her, start her, my men! Don't hurry yourselves; take plenty of time—but start her; start her like thunder-claps, that's all,' cried

---

* It will be seen in some other place of what a very light substance the entire interior of the sperm whale's enormous head consists. Though apparently the most massive, it is by far the most buoyant part about him. So that with ease he elevates it in the air, and invariably does so when going at his utmost speed. Besides, such is the breadth of the upper part of the front of his head, and such the tapering cut-water formation of the lower part, that by obliquely elevating his head, he thereby may be said to transform himself from a bluff-bowed sluggish galliot into a sharp-pointed New York pilot-boat.

Stubb, spluttering out the smoke as he spoke. 'Start her, now; give 'em the long and strong stroke, Tashtego. Start her, Tash, my boy—start her, all; but keep cool, keep cool—cucumbers is the word—easy, easy—only start her like grim death and grinning devils, and raise the buried dead perpendicular out of their graves, boys—that's all. Start her!'

'Woo-hoo! Wa-hee!' screamed the Gay-Header in reply, raising some old war-whoop to the skies; as every oarsman in the strained boat involuntarily bounced forward with the one tremendous leading stroke which the eager Indian gave.

But his wild screams were answered by others quite as wild. 'Kee-hee! Kee-hee!' yelled Daggoo, straining forwards and backwards on his seat, like a pacing tiger in his cage.

'Ka-la! Koo-loo!' howled Queequeg, as if smacking his lips over a mouthful of Grenadier's steak. And thus with oars and yells the keels cut the sea. Meanwhile, Stubb retaining his place in the van, still encouraged his men to the onset, all the while puffing the smoke from his mouth. Like desperadoes they tugged and they strained, till the welcome cry was heard—'Stand up, Tashtego!— give it to him!' The harpoon was hurled. 'Stern all!' The oarsmen backed water; the same moment something went hot and hissing along every one of their wrists. It was the magical line. An instant before, Stubb had swiftly caught two additional turns with it round the loggerhead, whence, by reason of its increased rapid circlings, a hempen blue smoke now jetted up and mingled with the steady fumes from his pipe. As the line passed round and round the loggerhead; so also, just before reaching that point, it blisteringly passed through and through both of Stubb's hands, from which the hand-cloths, or squares of quilted canvas sometimes worn at these times, had accidentally dropped. It was like holding an enemy's sharp two-edged sword by the blade, and that enemy all the time striving to wrest it out of your clutch.

'Wet the line! wet the line!' cried Stubb to the tub oarsman (him seated by the tub) who, snatching off his hat, dashed the sea-water into it.* More turns were taken, so that the line began holding its place. The boat now flew through the boiling water like a shark all fins. Stubb and Tashtego here changed places—

---

* Partly to show the indispensableness of this act, it may here be stated, that, in the old Dutch fishery, a mop was used to dash the running line with water; in many other ships, a wooden piggin, or bailer, is set apart for that purpose. Your hat, however, is the most convenient.

stem for stern—a staggering business truly in that rocking commotion.

From the vibrating line extending the entire length of the upper part of the boat, and from its now being more tight than a harpstring, you would have thought the craft had two keels—one cleaving the water, the other the air—as the boat churned on through both opposing elements at once. A continual cascade played at the bows; a ceaseless whirling eddy in her wake; and, at the slightest motion from within, even but of a little finger, the vibrating, cracking craft canted over her spasmodic gunwale into the sea. Thus they rushed; each man with might and main clinging to his seat, to prevent being tossed to the foam; and the tall form of Tashtego at the steering oar crouching almost double, in order to bring down his centre of gravity. Whole Atlantics and Pacifics seemed passed as they shot on their way, till at length the whale somewhat slackened his flight.

'Haul in—haul in!' cried Stubb to the bowsman; and, facing round towards the whale, all hands began pulling the boat up to him, while yet the boat was being towed on. Soon ranging up by his flank, Stubb, firmly planting his knee in the clumsy cleat, darted dart after dart into the flying fish; at the word of command, the boat alternately sterning out of the way of the whale's horrible wallow, and then ranging up for another fling.

The red tide now poured from all sides of the monster like brooks down a hill. His tormented body rolled not in brine but in blood, which bubbled and seethed for furlongs behind in their wake. The slanting sun playing upon this crimson pond in the sea, sent back its reflection into every face, so that they all glowed to each other like red men. And all the while, jet after jet of white smoke was agonizingly shot from the spiracle of the whale, and vehement puff after puff from the mouth of the excited headsman; as at every dart, hauling in upon his crooked lance (by the line attached to it), Stubb straightened it again and again, by a few rapid blows against the gunwale, then again and again sent it into the whale.

'Pull up—pull up!' he now cried to the bowsman, as the waning whale relaxed in his wrath. 'Pull up—close to!' and the boat ranged along the fish's flank. When reaching far over the bow, Stubb slowly churned his long sharp lance into the fish, and kept it there, carefully churning and churning, as if cautiously seeking to feel after some gold watch that the whale might have swallowed, and which he was fearful of breaking ere he could hook it out. But that gold watch he sought was the innermost life of the fish.

And now it is struck; for, starting from his trance into that unspeakable thing called his 'flurry,' the monster horribly wallowed in his blood, overwrapped himself in impenetrable, mad, boiling spray, so that the imperilled craft, instantly dropping astern, had much ado blindly to struggle out from that phrensied twilight into the clear air of the day.

And now abating in his flurry, the whale once more rolled out into view; surging from side to side; spasmodically dilating and contracting his spout-hole, with sharp, cracking, agonized respirations. At last, gush after gush of clotted red gore, as if it had been the purple lees of red wine, shot into the frighted air; and falling back again, ran dripping down his motionless flanks into the sea. His heart had burst!

'He's dead, Mr Stubb,' said Tashtego.

'Yes; both pipes smoked out!' and withdrawing his own from his mouth, Stubb scattered the dead ashes over the water; and, for a moment, stood thoughtfully eyeing the vast corpse he had made.

62
THE DART

A word concerning an incident in the last chapter.

According to the invariable usage of the fishery, the whale-boat pushes off from the ship, with the headsman or whale-killer as temporary steersman, and the harpooneer or whale-fastener pulling the foremost oar, the one known as the harpooneer-oar. Now it needs a strong, nervous arm to strike the first iron into the fish; for often, in what is called a long dart, the heavy implement has to be flung to the distance of twenty or thirty feet. But however prolonged and exhausting the chase, the harpooneer is expected to pull his oar meanwhile to the uttermost; indeed, he is expected to set an example of superhuman activity to the rest, not only by incredible rowing, but by repeated loud and intrepid exclamations; and what it is to keep shouting at the top of one's compass, while all the other muscles are strained and half started— what that is none know but those who have tried it. For one, I cannot bawl very heartily and work very recklessly at one and the same time. In this straining, bawling state, then, with his back to the fish, all at once the exhausted harpooneer hears the exciting cry—'Stand up, and give it to him!' He now has to drop and secure his oar, turn round on his centre half way, seize his harpoon from the crotch, and with what little strength may remain, he essays to pitch it somehow into the whale. No wonder, taking the whole fleet of whalemen in a body, that out of fifty fair chances for a dart, not five are successful; no wonder that so many hapless harpooneers are madly cursed and disrated; no wonder that some of them actually burst their blood-vessels in the boat; no wonder that some sperm whalemen are absent four years with four barrels; no wonder that to many ship owners, whaling is but a losing concern; for it is the harpooneer that makes the voyage, and if you take the breath out of his body how can you expect to find it there when most wanted!

Again, if the dart be successful, then at the second critical instant, that is, when the whale starts to run, the boat-header and harpooneer likewise start to running fore and aft, to the imminent jeopardy of themselves and every one else. It is then they change places; and the headsman, the chief officer of the little craft, takes his proper station in the bows of the boat.

Now, I care not who maintains the contrary, but all this is both foolish and unnecessary. The headsman should stay in the bows from first to last; he should both dart the harpoon and the lance, and no rowing whatever should be expected of him, except under circumstances obvious to any fisherman. I know that this would sometimes involve a slight loss of speed in the chase; but long experience in various whalemen of more than one nation has convinced me that in the vast majority of failures in the fishery, it has not by any means been so much the speed of the whale as the before described exhaustion of the harpooneer that has caused them.

To insure the greatest efficiency in the dart, the harpooneers of this world must start to their feet from out of idleness, and not from out of toil.

63

THE CROTCH

OUT of the trunk, the branches grow; out of them, the twigs. So, in productive subjects, grow the chapters.

The crotch alluded to on a previous page deserves independent mention. It is a notched stick of a peculiar form, some two feet in length, which is perpendicularly inserted into the starboard gunwale near the bow, for the purpose of furnishing a rest for the wooden extremity of the harpoon, whose other naked, barbed end slopingly projects from the prow. Thereby the weapon is instantly at hand to its hurler, who snatches it up as readily from its rest as a backwoodsman swings his rifle from the wall. It is customary to have two harpoons reposing in the crotch, respectively called the first and second irons.

But these two harpoons, each by its own cord, are both connected with the line; the object being this: to dart them both, if possible, one instantly after the other into the same whale; so that if, in the coming drag, one should draw out, the other may still retain a hold. It is a doubling of the chances. But it very often happens that owing to the instantaneous, violent, convulsive running of the whale upon receiving the first iron, it becomes impossible for the harpooneer, however lightning-like in his movements, to pitch the second iron into him. Nevertheless, as the second iron is already connected with the line, and the line is running, hence that weapon must, at all events, be anticipatingly tossed out of the boat, somehow and somewhere; else the most terrible jeopardy would involve all hands. Tumbled into the water, it accordingly is in such cases; the spare coils of box line (mentioned in a preceding chapter) making this feat, in most instances, prudently practicable. But this critical act is not always unattended with the saddest and most fatal casualties.

Furthermore: you must know that when the second iron is thrown overboard, it thenceforth becomes a dangling, sharp-edged terror, skittishly curvetting about both boat and whale, entangling the lines, or cutting them, and making a prodigious sensation in all directions. Nor, in general, is it possible to secure it again until the whale is fairly captured and a corpse.

Consider, now, how it must be in the case of four boats all engaging one unusually strong, active, and knowing whale; when owing to these qualities in him, as well as to the thousand concurring accidents of such an audacious enterprise, eight or ten loose second irons may be simultaneously dangling about him. For, of course, each boat is supplied with several harpoons to bend on to the line should the first one be ineffectually darted without recovery. All these particulars are faithfully narrated here, as they will not fail to elucidate several most important, however intricate passages, in scenes hereafter to be painted.

64

STUBB'S SUPPER

STUBB'S whale had been killed some distance from the ship. It was a calm; so, forming a tandem of three boats, we commenced the slow business of towing the trophy to the Pequod. And now, as we eighteen men with our thirty-six arms, and one hundred and eighty thumbs and fingers, slowly toiled hour after hour upon that inert, sluggish corpse in the sea; and it seemed hardly to budge at all, except at long intervals; good evidence was hereby furnished of the enormousness of the mass we moved. For, upon the great canal of Hang-Ho, or whatever they call it, in China, four or five laborers on the foot-path will draw a bulky freighted junk at the rate of a mile an hour; but this grand argosy we towed heavily forged along, as if laden with pig-lead in bulk.

Darkness came on; but three lights up and down in the Pequod's main-rigging dimly guided our way; till drawing nearer we saw Ahab dropping one of several more lanterns over the bulwarks. Vacantly eyeing the heaving whale for a moment, he issued the usual orders for securing it for the night, and then handing his lantern to a seaman, went his way into the cabin, and did not come forward again until morning.

Though, in overseeing the pursuit of this whale, Captain Ahab had evinced his customary activity, to call it so; yet now that the creature was dead, some vague dissatisfaction, or impatience, or despair, seemed working in him; as if the sight of that dead body reminded him that Moby Dick was yet to be slain; and though a thousand other whales were brought to his ship, all that would not one jot advance his grand, monomaniac object. Very soon you would have thought from the sound on the Pequod's decks, that all hands were preparing to cast anchor in the deep; for heavy chains are being dragged along the deck, and thrust rattling out of the port-holes. But by those clanking links, the vast corpse itself, not the ship, is to be moored. Tied by the head to the stern, and by the tail to the bows, the whale now lies with its black hull close to the vessel's, and seen through the darkness of the night, which obscured the spars and rigging aloft, the two—ship and whale, seemed yoked together like colossal bullocks, whereof one reclines while the other remains standing.*

If moody Ahab was now all quiescence, at least so far as could be known on deck, Stubb, his second mate, flushed with conquest, betrayed an unusual but still good-natured excitement. Such an unwonted bustle was he in that the staid Starbuck, his official superior, quietly resigned to him for the time the sole management of affairs. One small, helping cause of all this liveliness in Stubb, was soon made strangely manifest. Stubb was a high liver; he was somewhat intemperately fond of the whale as a flavorish thing to his palate.

'A steak, a steak, ere I sleep! You, Daggoo! overboard you go, and cut me one from his small!'

Here be it known, that though these wild fishermen do not, as a general thing, and according to the great military maxim, make the enemy defray the current expenses of the war (at least before realizing the proceeds of the voyage), yet now and then you find some of these Nantucketers who have a genuine relish for that particular part of the Sperm Whale designated by Stubb; comprising the tapering extremity of the body.

About midnight that steak was cut and cooked; and lighted by two lanterns of sperm oil, Stubb stoutly stood up to his spermaceti supper at the capstan-head, as if that capstan were a sideboard. Nor was Stubb the only banqueter on whale's flesh that night. Mingling their mumblings with his own mastication, thousands on thousands of sharks, swarming round the dead leviathan, smackingly feasted on its fatness. The few sleepers below in their bunks were often startled by the sharp slapping of their tails against the hull, within a few inches of the sleepers' hearts. Peering over the side you could just see them (as before you heard them) wallowing in the sullen, black waters, and turning over on their backs as they scooped out huge globular pieces of the whale of the bigness of a human head. This particular feat of the shark seems all but

---

* A little item may as well be related here. The strongest and most reliable hold which the ship has upon the whale when moored alongside, is by the flukes or tail; and as from its greater density that part is relatively heavier than any other (excepting the side-fins), its flexibility even in death, causes it to sink low beneath the surface; so that with the hand you cannot get at it from the boat, in order to put the chain round it. But this difficulty is ingeniously overcome: a small, strong line is prepared with a wooden float at its outer end, and a weight in its middle, while the other end is secured to the ship. By adroit management the wooden float is made to rise on the other side of the mass, so that now having girdled the whale, the chain is readily made to follow suit; and being slipped along the body, is at last locked fast round the smallest part of the tail, at the point of junction with its broad flukes or lobes.

miraculous. How, at such an apparently unassailable surface, they contrive to gouge out such symmetrical mouthfuls, remains a part of the universal problem of all things. The mark they thus leave on the whale, may best be likened to the hollow made by a carpenter in countersinking for a screw.

Though amid all the smoking horror and diabolism of a sea-fight, sharks will be seen longingly gazing up to the ship's decks, like hungry dogs round a table where red meat is being carved, ready to bolt down every killed man that is tossed to them; and though, while the valiant butchers over the deck-table are thus cannibally carving each other's live meat with carving-knives all gilded and tasselled, the sharks, also, with their jewel-hilted mouths, are quarrelsomely carving away under the table at the dead meat; and though, were you to turn the whole affair upside down, it would still be pretty much the same thing, that is to say, a shocking sharkish business enough for all parties; and though sharks also are the invariable outriders of all slave ships crossing the Atlantic, systematically trotting alongside, to be handy in case a parcel is to be carried anywhere, or a dead slave to be decently buried; and though one or two other like instances might be set down, touching the set terms, places, and occasions, when sharks do most socially congregate, and most hilariously feast; yet is there no conceivable time or occasion when you will find them in such countless numbers, and in gayer or more jovial spirits, then around a dead sperm whale, moored by night to a whale-ship at sea. If you have never seen that sight, then suspend your decision about the propriety of devil-worship, and the expediency of conciliating the devil.

But, as yet, Stubb heeded not the mumblings of the banquet that was going on so nigh him, no more than the sharks heeded the smacking of his own epicurean lips.

'Cook, cook!—where's that old Fleece?' he cried at length, widening his legs still further, as if to form a more secure base for his supper; and, at the same time, darting his fork into the dish, as if stabbing with his lance; 'cook, you cook!—sail this way, cook!'

The old black, not in any very high glee at having been previously roused from his warm hammock at a most unseasonable hour, came shambling along from his galley, for, like many old blacks, there was something the matter with his knee-pans, which he did not keep well scoured like his other pans; this old Fleece, as they called him, came shuffling and limping along, assisting his step with his tongs, which, after a clumsy fashion, were made of straightened iron hoops; this old Ebony floundered along, and in obedience to the word of command, came to a dead stop on the opposite side of Stubb's sideboard; when, with both hands folded before him, and resting on his two-legged cane, he bowed his arched back still further over, at the same time sideways inclining his head, so as to bring his best ear into play.

'Cook,' said Stubb, rapidly lifting a rather reddish morsel to his mouth, 'don't you think this steak is rather overdone? You've been beating this steak too much, cook; it's too tender. Don't I always say that to be good, a whale-steak must be tough? There are those sharks now over the side, don't you see they prefer it tough and rare? What a shindy they are kicking up! Cook, go and talk to 'em; tell 'em they are welcome to help themselves civilly, and in moderation, but they must keep quiet. Blast me, if I can hear my own voice. Away, cook, and deliver my message. Here, take this lantern,' snatching one from his sideboard; 'now then, go and preach to 'em!'

Sullenly taking the offered lantern, old Fleece limped across the deck to the bulwarks; and then, with one hand dropping his light low over the sea, so as to get a good view of his congregation, with the other hand he solemnly flourished his tongs, and leaning far over the side in a mumbling voice began addressing the sharks, while Stubb, softly crawling behind, overheard all that was said.

'Fellow-critters: I'se ordered here to say dat you must stop dat dam noise dare. You hear? Stop dat dam smackin' ob de lip! Massa Stubb say dat you can fill your dam bellies up to de hatchings, but by Gor! you must stop dat dam racket!'

'Cook,' here interposed Stubb, accompanying the word with a sudden slap on the shoulder,—'Cook! why, damn your eyes, you mustn't swear that way when you're preaching. That's no way to convert sinners, Cook!'

'Who dat? Den preach to him yourself,' sullenly turning to go.

'No, Cook; go on, go on.'

'Well, den, Belubed fellow-critters:'—

'Right!' exclaimed Stubb, approvingly, 'coax 'em to it; try that,' and Fleece continued.

'Dough you is all sharks, and by natur wery woracious, yet I zay to you, fellow-critters, dat dat woraciousness—'top dat dam slappin' ob de tail! How you tink to hear, 'spose you keep up such a dam slappin' and bitin' dare?'

'Cook,' cried Stubb, collaring him, 'I wont have that swearing. Talk to 'em gentlemanly.'

Once more the sermon proceeded.

'Your woraciousness, fellow-critters, I don't blame ye so much for; dat is natur, and can't be helped; but to gobern dat wicked natur, dat is de pint. You is sharks, sartin; but if you gobern de shark in you, why den you be angel; for all angel is not'ing more dan de shark well goberned. Now, look here, bred'ren, just try wonst to be cibil, a helping yourselbs from dat whale. Don't be tearin' de blubber out your neighbour's mout, I say. Is not one shark dood right as toder to dat whale? And, by Gor, none on you has de right to dat whale; dat whale belong to some one else. I know some o' you has berry brig mout, brigger dan oders; but den de brig mouts sometimes has de small bellies; so dat de brigness ob de mout is not to swaller wid, but to bite off de blubber for de small fry ob sharks, dat can't get into de scrouge to help demselves.'

'Well done, old Fleece!' cried Stubb, 'that's Christianity; go on.'

'No use goin' on; de dam willains will keep a scrougin' and slappin' each oder, Massa Stubb; dey don't hear one word; no use a-preachin' to such dam g'uttons as you call 'em, till dare bellies is full, and dare bellies is bottomless; and when dey do get 'em full, dey wont hear you den; for den dey sink in de sea, go fast to sleep on de coral, and can't hear not'ing at all, no more, for eber and eber.'

'Upon my soul, I am about of the same opinion; so give the benediction, Fleece, and I'll away to my supper.'

Upon this, Fleece, holding both hands over the fishy mob, raised his shrill voice, and cried—

'Cussed fellow-critters! Kick up de damndest row as ever you can; fill your dam' bellies till dey bust—and den die.'

'Now, cook,' said Stubb, resuming his supper at the capstan; 'Stand just where you stood before, there, over against me, and pay particular attention.'

'All 'dention,' said Fleece, again stooping over upon his tongs in the desired position.

'Well,' said Stubb, helping himself freely meanwhile; 'I shall now go back to the subject of this steak. In the first place, how old are you, cook?'

'What dat do wid de 'teak,' said the old black, testily.

'Silence! How old are you, cook?'

' 'Bout ninety, dey say,' he gloomily muttered.

'And have you lived in this world hard upon one hundred years, cook, and don't know yet how to cook a whale-steak?' rapidly bolting another mouthful at the last word, so that that morsel seemed a continuation of the question. 'Where were you born, cook?'

' 'Hind de hatchway, in ferry-boat, goin' ober de Roanoke.'

'Born in a ferry-boat! That's queer, too. But I want to know what country you were born in, cook?'

'Didn't I say de Roanoke country?' he cried, sharply.

'No, you didn't, cook; but I'll tell you what I'm coming to, cook. You must go home and be born over again; you don't know how to cook a whale-steak yet.'

'Bress my soul, if I cook 'noder one,' he growled, angrily, turning round to depart.

'Come back, cook;—here, hand me those tongs;—now take that bit of steak there, and tell me if you think that steak cooked as it should be? Take it, I say'—holding the tongs towards him— 'take it, and taste it.'

Faintly smacking his withered lips over it for a moment, the old negro muttered, 'Best cooked 'teak I eber taste; joosy, berry joosy.'

'Cook,' said Stubb, squaring himself once more; 'do you belong to the church?'

'Passed one once in Cape-Down,' said the old man sullenly.

'And you have once in your life passed a holy church in Cape-Town, where you doubtless overheard a holy parson addressing his hearers as his beloved fellow-creatures, have you, cook! And yet you come here, and tell me such a dreadful lie as you did just now, eh?' said Stubb. 'Where do you expect to go to, cook?'

'Go to bed berry soon,' he mumbled, half-turning as he spoke.

'Avast! heave to! I mean when you die, cook. It's an awful question. Now what's your answer?'

'When dis old brack man dies,' said the negro slowly, changing his whole air and demeanor, 'he hisself won't go nowhere; but some bressed angel will come and fetch him.'

'Fetch him? How? In a coach and four, as they fetched Elijah? And fetch him where?'

'Up dere,' said Fleece, holding his tongs straight over his head, and keeping it there very solemnly.

'So, then, you expect to go up into our main-top, do you, cook, when you are dead? But don't you know the higher you climb, the colder it gets? Main-top, eh?'

'Didn't say dat 'tall,' said Fleece, again in the sulks.

'You said up there, didn't you? and now look yourself, and see where your tongs are pointing. But, perhaps you expect to get into heaven by crawling through the lubber's hole, cook; but, no, no, cook, you don't get there, except you go the regular way, round by the rigging. It's a ticklish business, but must be done, or else it's no go. But none of us are in heaven yet. Drop your tongs, cook, and hear my orders. Do ye hear? Hold your hat in one hand, and clap t'other a'top of your heart, when I'm giving my orders, cook. What! that your heart, there?—that's your gizzard! Aloft! aloft!—that's it—now you have it. Hold it there now, and pay attention.'

'All 'dention,' said the old black, with both hands placed as desired, vainly wriggling his grizzled head, as if to get both ears in front at one and the same time.

'Well then, cook, you see this whale-steak of yours was so very bad, that I have put it out of sight as soon as possible; you see that, don't you? Well, for the future, when you cook another whale-steak for my private table here, the capstan, I'll tell you what to do so as not to spoil it by overdoing. Hold the steak in one hand, and show a live coal to it with the other; that done, dish it; d'ye hear? And now tomorrow, cook, when we are cutting in the fish, be sure you stand by to get the tips of his fins; have them put in pickle. As for the ends of the flukes, have them soused, cook. There, now ye may go.'

But Fleece had hardly got three paces off, when he was recalled.

'Cook, give me cutlets for supper to-morrow night in the mid-watch. D'ye hear? away you sail, then.—Halloa! stop! make a bow before you go.—Avast heaving again! Whaleballs for breakfast—don't forget.'

'Wish, by gor! whale eat him, 'stead of him eat whale. I'm bressed if he ain't more of shark dan Massa Shark hisself,' muttered the old man, limping away; with which sage ejaculation he went to his hammock.

65

THE WHALE AS A DISH

THAT mortal man should feed upon the creature that feeds his lamp, and, like Stubb, eat him by his own light, as you may say; this seems so outlandish a thing that one must needs go a little into the history and philosophy of it.

It is upon record, that three centuries ago the tongue of the Right Whale was esteemed a great delicacy in France, and commanded large prices there. Also, that in Henry VIIIth's time, a certain cook of the court obtained a handsome reward for inventing an admirable sauce to be eaten with barbacued porpoises, which, you remember, are a species of whale. Porpoises, indeed, are to this day considered fine eating. The meat is made into balls about the size of billiard balls, and being well seasoned and spiced might be taken for turtle-balls or veal balls. The old monks of Dunfermline were very fond of them. They had a great porpoise grant from the crown.

The fact is, that among his hunters at least, the whale would by all hands be considered a noble dish, were there not so much of him; but when you come to sit down before a meat-pie nearly one hundred feet long, it takes away your appetite. Only the most unprejudiced of men like Stubb, nowadays partake of cooked whales; but the Esquimaux are not so fastidious. We all know how they live upon whales, and have rare old vintages of prime old train oil. Zogranda, one of their most famous doctors, recommends strips of blubber for infants, as being exceedingly juicy and nourishing. And this reminds me that certain Englishmen, who long ago were accidentally left in Greenland by a whaling vessel—that these men actually lived for several months on the mouldy scraps of whales which had been left ashore after trying out the blubber. Among the Dutch whalemen these scraps are called 'fritters'; which, indeed, they greatly resemble, being brown and crisp, and smelling something like old Amsterdam housewives' dough-nuts or oly-cooks, when fresh. They have such an eatable look that the most self-denying stranger can hardly keep his hands off.

But what further depreciates the whale as a civilized dish, is his exceeding richness. He is the great prize ox of the sea, too fat to be delicately good. Look at his hump, which would be as fine eating as the buffalo's (which is esteemed a rare dish), were it not such a solid pyramid of fat. But the spermaceti itself, how bland and creamy that is; like the transparent, half-jellied, white meat of a cocoanut in the third month of its growth, yet far too rich to supply a substitute for butter. Nevertheless, many whalemen have a method of absorbing it into some other substance, and then partaking of it. In the long try watches of the night it is a common thing for the seamen to dip their ship-biscuit into the huge oil-pots and let them fry there awhile. Many a good supper have I thus made.

In the case of a small Sperm Whale the brains are accounted a fine dish. The casket of the skull is broken into with an axe, and the two plump, whitish lobes being withdrawn (precisely resembling two large puddings), they are then mixed with flour, and cooked into a most delectable mess, in flavor somewhat resembling calves' heads, which is quite a dish among some epicures; and every one knows that some young bucks among the epicures, by continually dining upon calves' brains, by and by get to have a little brains of their own, so as to be able to tell a calf's head from their own heads; which, indeed, requires uncommon discrimination. And that is the reason why a young buck with an intelligent looking calf's head before him, is somehow one of the saddest sights you can see. The head looks a sort of reproachfully at him, with an 'Et tu Brute!' expression.

It is not, perhaps, entirely because the whale is so excessively unctuous that landsmen seem to regard the eating of him with abhorrence; that appears to result, in some way, from the consideration before mentioned: i.e. that a man should eat a newly murdered thing of the sea, and eat it too by its own light. But no doubt the first man that ever murdered an ox was regarded as a murderer; perhaps he was hung; and if he had been put on his trial by oxen, he certainly would have been; and he certainly deserved it if any murderer does. Go to the meat-market of a Saturday night and see the crowds of live bipeds staring up at the long rows of dead quadrupeds. Does not that sight take a tooth out of the cannibal's jaw? Cannibals? who is not a cannibal? I tell you it will be more tolerable for the Fejee that salted down a lean missionary in his cellar against a coming famine; it will be more tolerable for that provident Fejee, I say, in the day of judgment, than for thee, civilized and enlightened gourmand, who nailest geese to the ground and feastest on their bloated livers in thy paté-de-foie-gras.

But Stubb, he eats the whale by its own light, does he? and that is adding insult to injury, is it? Look at your knife-handle, there, my civilized and enlightened gourmand dining off that roast beef, what is that handle made of?—what but the bones of the brother of the very ox you are eating? And what do you pick your teeth with, after devouring that fat goose? With a feather of the same fowl. And with what quill did the Secretary of the Society for the Suppression of Cruelty to Ganders formally indite his circulars? It is only within the last month or two that that society passed a resolution to patronize nothing but steel pens.

66
THE SHARK MASSACRE

WHEN in the Southern Fishery, a captured Sperm Whale, after long and weary toil, is brought alongside late at night, it is not, as a general thing at least, customary to proceed at once to the business of cutting him in. For that business is an exceedingly laborious one; is not very soon completed; and requires all hands to set about it. Therefore, the common usage is to take in all sail; lash the helm a'lee; and then send every one below to his hammock till daylight, with the reservation that, until that time, anchor-watches shall be kept; that is, two and two, for an hour each couple, the crew in rotation shall mount the deck to see that all goes well.

But sometimes, especially upon the Line in the Pacific, this plan will not answer at all; because such incalculable host of sharks gather round the moored carcase, that were he left so for six hours, say, on a stretch, little more than the skeleton would be visible by morning. In most other parts of the ocean, however, where these fish do not so largely abound, their wondrous voracity can be at times considerably diminished, by vigorously stirring them up with sharp whaling-spades, a procedure notwithstanding, which, in some instances, only seems to tickle them into still greater activity. But it was not thus in the present case with the Pequod's sharks; though, to be sure, any man unaccustomed to such sights, to have looked over her side that night, would have almost thought the whole round sea was one huge cheese, and those sharks the maggots in it.

Nevertheless, upon Stubb setting the anchor-watch after his supper was concluded; and when, accordingly, Queequeg and a forecastle seaman came on deck, no small excitement was created among the sharks; for immediately suspending the cutting stages over the side, and lowering three lanterns, so that they cast long gleams of light over the turbid sea, these two mariners, darting their long whaling-spades, kept up an incessant murdering of the sharks,* by striking the keen steel deep into their skulls, seemingly

---

* The whaling-spade used for cutting-in is made of the very best steel; is about the

their only vital part. But in the foamy confusion of their mixed and struggling hosts, the marksmen could not always hit their marks; and this brought about new revelations of the incredible ferocity of the foe. They viciously snapped, not only at each other's disembowelments, but like flexible bows, bent round, and bit their own; till those entrails seemed swallowed over and over again by the same mouth, to be oppositely voided by the gaping wound. Nor was this all. It was unsafe to meddle with the corpses and ghosts of these creatures. A sort of generic or Pantheistic vitality seemed to lurk in their very joints and bones, after what might be called the individual life had departed. Killed and hoisted on deck for the sake of his skin, one of these sharks almost took poor Queequeg's hand off, when he tried to shut down the dead lid of his murderous jaw.

'Queequeg no care what god made him shark,' said the savage, agonizingly lifting his hand up and down; 'wedder Fejee god or Nantucket god; but de god wat made shark must be one dam Ingin.'

67

CUTTING IN

IT was a Saturday night, and such a Sabbath as followed! Ex officio professors of Sabbath breaking are all whalemen. The ivory Pequod was turned into what seemed a shamble; every sailor a butcher. You would have thought we were offering up ten thousand red oxen to the sea gods.

In the first place, the enormous cutting tackles, among other ponderous things comprising a cluster of blocks generally painted green, and which no single man can possibly lift—this vast bunch of grapes was swayed up to the main-top and firmly lashed to the lower mast-head, the strongest point anywhere above a ship's deck. The end of the hawser-like rope winding through these intricacies, was then conducted to the windlass, and the huge lower

---

bigness of a man's spread hand; and in general shape, corresponds to the garden implement after which it is named; only its sides are perfectly flat, and its upper end considerably narrower than the lower. This weapon is always kept as sharp as possible; and when being used is occasionally honed, just like a razor. In its socket, a stiff pole, from twenty to thirty feet long, is inserted for a handle.

block of the tackles was swung over the whale; to this block the
great blubber hook, weighing some one hundred pounds, was
attached. And now suspended in stages over the side, Starbuck
and Stubb, the mates, armed with their long spades, began cutting
a hole in the body for the insertion of the hook just above the
nearest of the two side-fins. This done, a broad, semicircular line
is cut round the hole, the hook is inserted, and the main body
of the crew striking up a wild chorus, now commence heaving in
one dense crowd at the windlass. When instantly, the entire ship
careens over on her side; every bolt in her starts like the nail-
heads of an old house in frosty weather; she trembles, quivers,
and nods her frighted mast-heads to the sky. More and more she
leans over to the whale, while every gasping heave of the windlass
is answered by a helping heave from the billows; till at last, a
swift, startling snap is heard; with a great swash the ship rolls
upwards and backwards from the whale, and the triumphant tackle
rises into sight dragging after it the disengaged semicircular end
of the first strip of blubber. Now as the blubber envelopes the
whale precisely as the rind does an orange, so is it stripped off
from the body precisely as an orange is sometimes stripped by
spiralizing it. For the strain constantly kept up by the windlass
continually keeps the whale rolling over and over in the water,
and as the blubber in one strip uniformly peels off along the line
called the 'scarf', simultaneously cut by the spades of Starbuck
and Stubb, the mates; and just as fast as it is thus peeled off, and
indeed by that very act itself, it is all the time being hoisted higher
and higher aloft till its upper end grazes the main-top; the men
at the windlass then cease heaving, and for a moment or two the
prodigious blood-dripping mass sways to and fro as if let down
from the sky, and every one present must take good heed to dodge
it when it swings, else it may box his ears and pitch him headlong
overboard.

One of the attending harpooneers now advances with a long,
keen weapon called a boarding-sword, and watching his chance
he dexterously slices out a considerable hole in the lower part of
the swaying mass. Into this hole, the end of the second alternating
great tackle is then hooked so as to retain a hold upon the blubber,
in order to prepare for what follows. Whereupon, this accomplished
swordsman, warning all hands to stand off, once more makes a
scientific dash at the mass, and with a few sidelong, desperate,
lunging slicings, severs it completely in twain; so that while the
short lower part is still fast, the long upper strip, called a blanket-
piece, swings clear, and is all ready for lowering. The heavers

forward now resume their song, and while the one tackle is peeling
and hoisting a second strip from the whale, the other is slowly
slackened away, and down goes the first strip through the main
hatchway right beneath, into an unfurnished parlor called the
blubber-room. Into this twilight apartment sundry nimble hands
keep coiling away the long blanket-piece as if it were a great live
mass of plaited serpents. And thus the work proceeds; the two
tackles hoisting and lowering simultaneously; both whale and
windlass heaving, the heavers singing, the blubber-room gentlemen
coiling, the mates scarfing, the ship straining, and all hands swearing occasionally, by way of assuaging the general friction.

68
THE BLANKET

I have given no small attention to that not unvexed subject, the
skin of the whale. I have had controversies about it with experienced whalemen afloat, and learned naturalists ashore. My original opinion remains unchanged; but it is only an opinion.

The question is, what and where is the skin of the whale?
Already you know what his blubber is. That blubber is something
of the consistence of firm, close-grained beef, but tougher, more
elastic and compact, and ranges from eight or ten to twelve and
fifteen inches in thickness.

Now, however preposterous it may at first seem to talk of any
creature's skin as being of that sort of consistence and thickness,
yet in point of fact these are no arguments against such a presumption; because you cannot raise any other dense enveloping
layer from the whale's body but that same blubber; and the
outermost enveloping layer of any animal, if reasonably dense,
what can that be but the skin? True, from the unmarred dead
body of the whale, you may scrape off with your hand an infinitely
thin, transparent substance, somewhat resembling the thinnest
shreds of isinglass, only it is almost as flexible and soft as satin;
that is, previous to being dried, when it not only contracts and
thickens, but becomes rather hard and brittle. I have several such
dried bits, which I use for marks in my whale-books. It is transparent, as I said before; and being laid upon the printed page, I
have sometimes pleased myself with fancying it exerted a magnifying influence. At any rate, it is pleasant to read about whales

through their own spectacles, as you may say. But what I am driving at here is this. That same infinitely thin, isinglass substance, which, I admit, invests the entire body of the whale, is not so much to be regarded as the skin of the creature, as the skin of the skin, so to speak; for it were simply ridiculous to say, that the proper skin of the tremendous whale is thinner and more tender than the skin of a new-born child. But no more of this.

Assuming the blubber to be the skin of the whale; then, when this skin, as in the case of a very large Sperm Whale, will yield the bulk of one hundred barrels of oil; and, when it is considered that, in quantity, or rather weight, that oil, in its expressed state, is only three fourths, and not the entire substance of the coat; some idea may hence be had of the enormousness of that animated mass, a mere part of whose mere integument yields such a lake of liquid as that. Reckoning ten barrels to the ton, you have ten tons for the net weight of only three quarters of the stuff of the whale's skin.

In life, the visible surface of the Sperm Whale is not the least among the many marvels he presents. Almost invariably it is all over obliquely crossed and re-crossed with numberless straight marks in thick array, something like those in the finest Italian line engravings. But these marks do not seem to be impressed upon the isinglass substance above mentioned, but seem to be seen through it, as if they were engraved upon the body itself. Nor is this all. In some instances, to the quick, observant eye, those linear marks, as in a veritable engraving, but afford the ground for far other delineations. These are hieroglyphical; that is, if you call those mysterious cyphers on the walls of pyramids hieroglyphics, then that is the proper word to use in the present connexion. By my retentive memory of the hieroglyphics upon one Sperm Whale in particular, I was much struck with a plate representing the old Indian characters chiselled on the famous hieroglyphic palisades on the banks of the Upper Mississippi. Like those mystic rocks, too, the mystic-marked whale remains undecipherable. This allusion to the Indian rocks reminds me of another thing. Besides all the other phenomena which the exterior of the Sperm Whale presents, he not seldom displays the back, and more especially his flanks, effaced in great part of the regular linear appearance, by reason of numerous rude scratches, altogether of an irregular, random aspect. I should say that those New England rocks on the sea-coast, which Agassiz imagines to bear the marks of violent scraping contact with vast floating icebergs—I should say, that those rocks must not a little resemble the Sperm Whale in this particular. It also seems to me that such scratches in the whale are probably made by hostile contact with other whales; for I have most remarked them in the large, full-grown bulls of the species.

A word or two more concerning this matter of the skin or blubber of the whale. It has already been said, that it is stript from him in long pieces, called blanket-pieces. Like most sea-terms, this one is very happy and significant. For the whale is indeed wrapt up in his blubber as in a real blanket or counterpane; or, still better, an Indian poncho slipt over his head, and skirting his extremity. It is by reason of this cosy blanketing of his body, that the whale is enabled to keep himself comfortable in all weathers, in all seas, times, and tides. What would become of a Greenland whale, say, in those shuddering, icy seas of the North, if unsupplied with his cosy surtout? True, other fish are found exceedingly brisk in those Hyperborean waters; but these, be it observed, are your cold-blooded, lungless fish, whose very bellies are refrigerators; creatures, that warm themselves under the lee of an iceberg, as a traveller in winter would bask before an inn fire, whereas, like man, the whale has lungs and warm blood. Freeze his blood, and he dies. How wonderful is it then—except after explanation—that this great monster, to whom corporeal warmth is as indispensable as it is to man; how wonderful that he should be found at home, immersed to his lips for life in those Arctic waters! where, when seamen fall overboard, they are sometimes found, months afterwards, perpendicularly frozen into the hearts of fields of ice, as a fly is found glued in amber. But more surprising is it to know, as has been proved by experiment, that the blood of a Polar whale is warmer than that of a Borneo negro in summer.

It does seem to me, that herein we see the rare virtue of a strong individual vitality, and the rare virtue of thick walls, and the rare virtue of interior spaciousness. Oh, man! admire and model thyself after the whale! Do thou, too, remain warm among ice. Do thou, too, live in this world without being of it. Be cool at the equator; keep thy blood fluid at the Pole. Like the great dome of St Peter's, and like the great whale, retain, O man! in all seasons a temperature of thine own.

But how easy and how hopeless to teach these fine things! Of erections, how few are domed like St Peter's! of creatures, how few vast as the whale!

69

THE FUNERAL

'HAUL in the chains! Let the carcase go astern!'

The vast tackles have now done their duty. The peeled white body of the beheaded whale flashes like a marble sepulchre; though changed in hue, it has not perceptibly lost anything in bulk. It is still colossal. Slowly it floats more and more away, the water round it torn and splashed by the insatiate sharks, and the air above vexed with rapacious flights of screaming fowls, whose beaks are like so many insulting poniards in the whale. The vast white headless phantom floats further and further from the ship, and every rod that it so floats, what seem square roods of sharks and cubic roods of fowls, augment the murderous din. For hours and hours from the almost stationary ship that hideous sight is seen. Beneath the unclouded and mild azure sky, upon the fair face of the pleasant sea, wafted by the joyous breezes, that great mass of death floats on and on, till lost in infinite perspectives.

There's a most doleful and most mocking funeral! The sea-vultures all in pious mourning, the air-sharks all punctiliously in black or speckled. In life but few of them would have helped the whale, I ween, if peradventure he had needed it; but upon the banquet of his funeral they most piously do pounce. Oh, horrible vulturism of earth! from which not the mightiest whale is free.

Nor is this the end. Desecrated as the body is, a vengeful ghost survives and hovers over it to scare. Espied by some timid man-of-war or blundering discovery-vessel from afar, when the distance obscuring the swarming fowls, nevertheless still shows the white mass floating in the sun, and the white spray heaving high against it; straightway the whale's unharming corpse, with trembling fingers is set down in the log—*shoals, rocks, and breakers hereabouts: beware!* And for years afterwards, perhaps, ships shun the place; leaping over it as silly sheep leap over a vacuum, because their leader originally leaped there when a stick was held. There's your law of precedents; there's your utility of traditions; there's the story of your obstinate survival of old beliefs never bottomed on the earth, and now not even hovering in the air! There's orthodoxy!

Thus, while in life the great whale's body may have been a real terror to his foes, in his death his ghost becomes a powerless panic to a world.

Are you a believer in ghosts, my friend? There are other ghosts than the Cock-Lane one, and far deeper men than Doctor Johnson who believe in them.

70
THE SPHYNX

IT should not have been omitted that previous to completely stripping the body of the leviathan, he was beheaded. Now, the beheading of the Sperm Whale is a scientific anatomical feat, upon which experienced whale surgeons very much pride themselves: and not without reason.

Consider that the whale has nothing that can properly be called a neck; on the contrary, where his head and body seem to join, there, in that very place, is the thickest part of him. Remember, also, that the surgeon must operate from above, some eight or ten feet intervening between him and his subject, and that subject almost hidden in a discolored, rolling, and oftentimes tumultuous and bursting sea. Bear in mind, too, that under these untoward circumstances he has to cut many feet deep in the flesh; and in that subterraneous manner, without so much as getting one single peep into the ever-contracting gash thus made, he must skilfully steer clear of all adjacent, interdicted parts, and exactly divide the spine at a critical point hard by its insertion into the skull. Do you not marvel, then, at Stubb's boast, that he demanded but ten minutes to behead a sperm whale?

When first severed, the head is dropped astern and held there by a cable till the body is stripped. That done, if it belong to a small whale it is hoisted on deck to be deliberately disposed of. But, with a full grown leviathan this is impossible; for the sperm whale's head embraces nearly one third of his entire bulk, and completely to suspend such a burden as that, even by the immense tackles of a whaler, this were as vain a thing as to attempt weighing a Dutch barn in jewellers' scales.

The Pequod's whale being decapitated and the body stripped, the head was hoisted against the ship's side—about half way out of the sea, so that it might yet in great part be buoyed up by its native element. And there with the strained craft steeply leaning

over to it, by reason of the enormous downward drag from the
lower mast-head, and every yard-arm on that side projecting like
a crane over the waves, there, that blood-dripping head hung to
the Pequod's waist like the giant Holofernes's from the girdle of
Judith.

When this last task was accomplished it was noon, and the
seamen went below to their dinner. Silence reigned over the before
tumultuous but now deserted deck. An intense copper calm, like
a universal yellow lotus, was more and more unfolding its noiseless
measureless leaves upon the sea.

A short space elapsed, and up into this noiselessness came Ahab
alone from his cabin. Taking a few turns on the quarter-deck, he
paused to gaze over the side, then slowly getting into the main-
chains he took Stubb's long spade—still remaining there after the
whale's decapitation—and striking it into the lower part of the
half-suspended mass, placed its other end crutch-wise under one
arm, and so stood leaning over with eyes attentively fixed on this
head.

It was a black and hooded head; and hanging there in the midst
of so intense a calm, it seemed the Sphynx's in the desert. 'Speak,
thou vast and venerable head,' muttered Ahab, 'which, though
ungarnished with a beard, yet here and there lookest hoary with
mosses; speak, mighty head, and tell us the secret thing that is in
thee. Of all divers, thou hast dived the deepest. That head upon
which the upper sun now gleams, has moved amid this world's
foundations. Where unrecorded names and navies rust, and untold
hopes and anchors rot; where in her murderous hold this frigate
earth is ballasted with bones of millions of the drowned; there,
in that awful water-land, there was thy most familiar home. Thou
hast been where bell or diver never went; hast slept by many a
sailor's side, where sleepless mothers would give their lives to lay
them down. Thou saw'st the locked lovers when leaping from
their flaming ship; heart to heart they sank beneath the exulting
wave; true to each other, when heaven seemed false to them.
Thou saw'st the murdered mate when tossed by pirates from the
midnight deck; for hours he fell into the deeper midnight of the
insatiate maw; and his murderers still sailed on unharmed—while
swift lightnings shivered the neighboring ship that would have
borne a righteous husband to outstretched, longing arms. O head!
thou hast seen enough to split the planets and make an infidel
of Abraham, and not one syllable is thine!'

'Sail ho!' cried a triumphant voice from the main-mast-head.

'Aye? Well, now, that's cheering,' cried Ahab, suddenly erecting himself, while whole thunder-clouds swept aside from his brow. 'That lively cry upon this deadly calm might almost convert a better man.—Where away?'

'Three points on the starboard bow, sir, and bringing down her breeze to us!'

'Better and better, man. Would now St Paul would come along that way, and to my breezelessness bring his breeze! O Nature, and O soul of man! how far beyond all utterance are your linked analogies! not the smallest atom stirs or lives in matter, but has its cunning duplicate in mind.'

71
THE JEROBOAM'S STORY

HAND in hand, ship and breeze blew on; but the breeze came faster than the ship, and soon the Pequod began to rock.

By and by, through the glass the stranger's boats and manned mast-heads proved her a whale-ship. But as she was so far to windward, and shooting by, apparently making a passage to some other ground, the Pequod could not hope to reach her. So the signal was set to see what response would be made.

Here be it said, that like the vessels of military marines, the ships of the American Whale Fleet have each a private signal; all which signals being collected in a book with the names of the respective vessels attached, every captain is provided with it. Thereby, the whale commanders are enabled to recognise each other upon the ocean, even at considerable distances, and with no small facility.

The Pequod's signal was at last responded to by the stranger's setting her own; which proved the ship to be the Jeroboam of Nantucket. Squaring her yards, she bore down, ranged abeam under the Pequod's lee, and lowered a boat; it soon drew nigh; but, as the side-ladder was being rigged by Starbuck's order to accommodate the visiting captain, the stranger in question waved his hand from his boat's stern in token of that proceeding being entirely unnecessary. It turned out that the Jeroboam had a malignant epidemic on board, and that Mayhew, her captain, was fearful of infecting the Pequod's company. For, though himself and boat's crew remained untainted, and though his ship was half a rifle-shot off, and an incorruptible sea and air rolling and flowing between; yet conscientiously adhering to the timid quarantine of the land, he peremptorily refused to come into direct contact with the Pequod.

But this did by no means prevent all communication. Preserving an interval of some few yards between itself and the ship, the Jeroboam's boat by the occasional use of its oars contrived to keep parallel to the Pequod, as she heavily forged through the sea (for by this time it blew very fresh), with her main-topsail aback; though, indeed, at times by the sudden onset of a large rolling wave, the boat would be pushed some way ahead; but would be soon skilfully brought to her proper bearings again. Subject to this, and other the like interruptions now and then, a conversation was sustained between the two parties; but at intervals not without still another interruption of a very different sort.

Pulling an oar in the Jeroboam's boat, was a man of a singular appearance, even in that wild whaling life where individual notabilities make up all totalities. He was a small, short, youngish man, sprinkled all over his face with freckles, and wearing redundant yellow hair. A long-skirted, cabalistically-cut coat of a faded walnut tinge enveloped him; the overlapping sleeves of which were rolled up on his wrists. A deep, settled, fanatic delirium was in his eyes.

So soon as this figure had been first descried, Stubb had exclaimed—'That's he! that's he!—the long-togged scaramouch the Town-Ho's company told us of!' Stubb here alluded to a strange story told of the Jeroboam, and a certain man among her crew, some time previous when the Pequod spoke the Town-Ho. According to this account and what was subsequently learned, it seemed that the scaramouch in question had gained a wonderful ascendency over almost everybody in the Jeroboam. His story was this:

He had been originally nurtured among the crazy society of Neskyeuna Shakers, where he had been a great prophet; in their cracked, secret meetings having several times descended from heaven by the way of a trap-door, announcing the speedy opening of the seventh vial, which he carried in his vest-pocket; but, which, instead of containing gunpowder, was supposed to be charged with laudanum. A strange, apostolic whim having seized him, he had left Neskyeuna for Nantucket, where, with that cunning peculiar to craziness, he assumed a steady, common sense exterior, and offered himself as a green-hand candidate for the Jeroboam's whaling voyage. They engaged him; but straightway upon the ship's getting out of sight of land, his insanity broke out in a freshet. He announced himself as the archangel Gabriel, and commanded the captain to jump overboard. He published his manifesto, whereby he set himself forth as the deliverer of the isles of the sea and vicar-general of all Oceanica. The unflinching earnestness with which he declared these things;—the dark, daring play of his sleepless, excited imagination, and all the preternatural terrors of real delirium, united to invest this Gabriel in the minds of the majority of the ignorant crew, with an atmosphere of sacredness. Moreover, they were afraid of him. As such a man, however, was not of much practical use in the ship, especially as he refused to work except when he pleased, the incredulous captain would fain have been rid of him; but apprised that that individual's intention was to land him in the first convenient port, the archangel forthwith opened all his seals and vials—devoting the ship and all hands to unconditional perdition, in case this intention was carried out. So strongly did he work upon his disciples among the crew, that at last in a body they went to the captain and told him if Gabriel was sent from the ship, not a man of them would remain. He was therefore forced to relinquish his plan. Nor would they permit Gabriel to be any way maltreated, say or do what he would; so that it came to pass that Gabriel had the complete freedom of the ship. The consequence of all this was, that the archangel cared little or nothing for the captain and mates; and since the epidemic had broken out, he carried a higher hand than ever; declaring that the plague, as he called it, was at his sole command; nor should it be stayed but according to his good pleasure. The sailors, mostly poor devils, cringed, and some of them fawned before him; in obedience to his instructions, sometimes rendering him personal homage, as to a god. Such things may seem incredible; but, however wondrous, they are true. Nor is the history of fanatics half so striking in respect to the measureless self-deception of the fanatic himself, as his measureless power of deceiving and bedevilling so many others. But it is time to return to the Pequod.

'I fear not thy epidemic, man,' said Ahab from the bulwarks, to Captain Mayhew, who stood in the boat's stern; 'come on board.'

But now Gabriel started to his feet.

'Think, think of the fevers, yellow and bilious! Beware of the horrible plague!'

'Gabriel, Gabriel!' cried Captain Mayhew; 'thou must either—' But that instant a headlong wave shot the boat far ahead, and its seethings drowned all speech.

'Hast thou seen the White Whale?' demanded Ahab, when the boat drifted back.

'Think, think of thy whale-boat, stoven and sunk! Beware of the horrible tail!'

'I tell thee again, Gabriel, that—' But again the boat tore ahead as if dragged by fiends. Nothing was said for some moments, while a succession of riotous waves rolled by, which by one of those occasional caprices of the seas were tumbling, not heaving it. Meantime, the hoisted sperm whale's head jogged about very violently, and Gabriel was seen eyeing it with rather more ap-prehensiveness than his archangel nature seemed to warrant.

When this interlude was over, Captain Mayhew began a dark story concerning Moby Dick; not, however, without frequent in-terruptions from Gabriel, whenever his name was mentioned, and the crazy sea that seemed leagued with him.

It seemed that the Jeroboam had not long left home, when upon speaking a whale-ship, her people were reliably apprised of the existence of Moby Dick, and the havoc he had made. Greedily sucking in this intelligence, Gabriel solemnly warned the captain against attacking the White Whale, in case the monster should be seen; in his gibbering insanity, pronouncing the White Whale to be no less a being than the Shaker God incarnated; the Shakers receiving the Bible. But when, some year or two afterwards, Moby Dick was fairly sighted from the mast-heads, Macey, the chief mate, burned with ardor to encounter him; and the captain himself being not unwilling to let him have the opportunity, despite all the archangel's denunciations and forewarnings, Macey succeeded in persuading five men to man his boat. With them he pushed off; and, after much weary pulling, and many perilous, unsuccessful onsets, he at last succeeded in getting one iron fast. Meantime, Gabriel, ascending to the main-royal mast-head, was tossing one arm in frantic gestures, and hurling forth prophecies of speedy doom to the sacrilegious assailants of his divinity. Now, while Macey, the mate, was standing up in his boat's bow, and with all the reckless energy of his tribe was venting his wild exclamations upon the whale, and essaying to get a fair chance for his poised lance, lo! a broad white shadow rose from the sea; by its quick, fanning motion, temporarily taking the breath out of the bodies of the oarsmen. Next instant, the luckless mate, so full of furious life, was smitten bodily into the air, and making a long arc in his descent, fell into the sea at the distance of about fifty yards. Not a chip of the boat was harmed, nor a hair of any oarsman's head; but the mate for ever sank.

(It is well to parenthesize here, that of the fatal accidents in the Sperm-Whale Fishery, this kind is perhaps almost as frequent as any. Sometimes, nothing is injured but the man who is thus annihilated; oftener the boat's bow is knocked off, or the thigh-board, in which the headsman stands, is torn from its place and accompanies the body. But strangest of all is the circumstance, that in more instances than one, when the body has been recovered, not a single mark of violence is discernible; the man being stark dead.)

The whole calamity, with the falling form of Macey, was plainly descried from the ship. Raising a piercing shriek—'The vial; the vial!' Gabriel called off the terror-stricken crew from the further hunting of the whale. This terrible event clothed the archangel with added influence; because his credulous disciples believed that he had specifically fore-announced it, instead of only making a general prophecy, which any one might have done, and so have chanced to hit one of many marks in the wide margin allowed. He became a nameless terror to the ship.

Mayhew having concluded his narration, Ahab put such questions to him, that the stranger captain could not forbear inquiring whether he intended to hunt the White Whale, if opportunity should offer. To which Ahab answered—'Aye.' Straightway, then, Gabriel once more started to his feet, glaring upon the old man, and vehemently exclaimed, with downward pointed finger—'Think, think of the blasphemer—dead, and down there!—beware of the blasphemer's end!'

Ahab stolidly turned aside; then said to Mayhew, 'Captain, I have just bethought me of my letter-bag; there is a letter for one of thy officers, if I mistake not. Starbuck, look over the bag.'

Every whale-ship takes out a goodly number of letters for various ships, whose delivery to the persons to whom they may be addressed, depends upon the mere chance of encountering them in the four oceans. Thus, most letters never reach their mark; and many are only received after attaining an age of two or three years or more.

Soon Starbuck returned with a letter in his hand. It was sorely tumbled, damp, and covered with a dull, spotted, green mould, in consequence of being kept in a dark locker of the cabin. Of such a letter, Death himself might well have been the post-boy.

'Can'st not read it?' cried Ahab. 'Give it me, man. Aye, aye, it's but a dim scrawl;—what's this?' As he was studying it out, Starbuck took a long cutting-spade pole, and with his knife slightly split the end, to insert the letter there, and in that way, hand it to the boat, without its coming any closer to the ship.

Meantime, Ahab holding the letter, muttered, 'Mr Har—yes, Mr Harry—(a woman's pinny hand,—the man's wife, I'll wager)— Aye—Mr Harry Macey, Ship Jeroboam;—why it's Macey, and he's dead!'

'Poor fellow! poor fellow! and from his wife,' sighed Mayhew; 'but let me have it.'

'Nay, keep it thyself,' cried Gabriel to Ahab; 'thou art soon going that way.'

'Curses throttle thee!' yelled Ahab. 'Captain Mayhew, stand by now to receive it;' and taking the fatal missive from Starbuck's hands, he caught it in the slit of the pole, and reached it over towards the boat. But as he did so, the oarsmen expectantly desisted from rowing; the boat drifted a little towards the ship's stern; so that, as if by magic, the letter suddenly ranged along with Gabriel's eager hand. He clutched it in an instant, seized the boat knife, and impaling the letter on it, sent it thus loaded back into the ship. It fell at Ahab's feet. Then Gabriel shrieked out to his comrades to give way with their oars, and in that manner the mutinous boat rapidly shot away from the Pequod.

As, after this interlude, the seamen resumed their work upon the jacket of the whale, many strange things were hinted in reference to this wild affair.

72

THE MONKEY-ROPE

IN tumultuous business of cutting-in and attending to a whale, there is much running backwards and forwards among the crew. Now hands are wanted here, and then again hands are wanted there. There is no staying in any one place; for at one and the same time everything has to be done everywhere. It is much the same with him who endeavors the description of the scene. We must now retrace our way a little. It was mentioned that upon first breaking ground in the whale's back, the blubber-hook was inserted into the original hole there cut by the spades of the mates. But how did so clumsy and weighty a mass as that same hook get fixed in that hole? It was inserted there by my particular friend Queequeg, whose duty it was, as harpooneer, to descend upon the monster's back for the special purpose referred to. But in very

many cases, circumstances require that the harpooneer shall remain
on the whale till the whole flensing or stripping operation is
concluded. The whale, be it observed, lies almost entirely submerged, excepting the immediate parts operated upon. So down
there, some ten feet below the level of the deck, the poor harpooneer flounders about, half on the whale and half in the water,
as the vast mass revolves like a tread-mill beneath him. On the
occasion in question, Queequeg figured in the Highland costume—
a shirt and socks—in which to my eyes, at least, he appeared to
uncommon advantage; and no one had a better chance to observe
him, as will presently be seen.

Being the savage's bowsman, that is, the person who pulled the
bow-oar in his boat (the second one from forward), it was my
cheerful duty to attend upon him while taking that hard-scrabble
scramble upon the dead whale's back. You have seen Italian organ-
boys holding a dancing-ape by a long cord. Just so, from the
ship's steep side, did I hold Queequeg down there in the sea, by
what is technically called in the fishery a monkey-rope, attached
to a strong strip of canvas belted round his waist.

It was a humorously perilous business for both of us. For, before
we proceed further, it must be said that the monkey-rope was fast
at both ends; fast to Queequeg's broad canvas belt, and fast to
my narrow leather one. So that for better or for worse, we two,
for the time, were wedded; and should poor Queequeg sink to
rise no more, then both usage and honor demanded, that instead
of cutting the cord, it should drag me down in his wake. So, then,
an elongated Siamese ligature united us. Queequeg was my own
inseparable twin brother; nor could I any way get rid of the
dangerous liabilities which the hempen bond entailed.

So strongly and metaphysically did I conceive of my situation
then, that while earnestly watching his motions, I seemed distinctly
to perceive that my own individuality was now merged in a joint
stock company of two: that my free will had received a mortal
wound; and that another's mistake or misfortune might plunge
innocent me into unmerited disaster and death. Therefore, I saw
that here was a sort of interregnum in Providence; for its even-
handed equity never could have sanctioned so gross an injustice.
And yet still further pondering—while I jerked him now and then
from between the whale and the ship, which would threaten to
jam him—still further pondering, I say, I saw that this situation
of mine was the precise situation of every mortal that breathes;
only, in most cases, he, one way or other, has this Siamese
connexion with a plurality of other mortals. If your banker breaks,

you snap; if your apothecary by mistake sends you poison in your pills, you die. True, you may say that, by exceeding caution, you may possibly escape these and the multitudinous other evil chances of life. But handle Queequeg's monkey-rope heedfully as I would, sometimes he jerked it so, that I came very near sliding overboard. Nor could I possibly forget that, do what I would, I only had the management of one end of it.*

I have hinted that I would often jerk poor Queequeg from between the whale and the ship—where he would occasionally fall, from the incessant rolling and swaying of both. But this was not the only jamming jeopardy he was exposed to. Unappalled by the massacre made upon them during the night, the sharks now freshly and more keenly allured by the before pent blood which began to flow from the carcase—the rabid creatures swarmed round it like bees in a beehive.

And right in among those sharks was Queequeg; who often pushed them aside with his floundering feet. A thing altogether incredible were it not that attracted by such prey as a dead whale, the otherwise miscellaneously carnivorous shark will seldom touch a man.

Nevertheless, it may well be believed that since they have such a ravenous finger in the pie, it is deemed but wise to look sharp to them. Accordingly, besides the monkey-rope, with which I now and then jerked the poor fellow from too close a vicinity to the maw of what seemed a peculiarly ferocious shark—he was provided with still another protection. Suspended over the side in one of the stages, Tashtego and Daggoo continually flourished over his head a couple of keen whale-spades, wherewith they slaughtered as many sharks as they could reach. This procedure of theirs, to be sure, was very disinterested and benevolent of them. They meant Queequeg's best happiness, I admit; but in their hasty zeal to befriend him, and from the circumstance that both he and the sharks were at times half hidden by the blood-mudded water, those indiscreet spades of theirs would come nearer amputating a leg than a tail. But poor Queequeg, I suppose, straining and gasping there with that great iron hook—poor Queequeg, I suppose,

---

* The monkey-rope is found in all whalers; but it was only in the Pequod that the monkey and his holder were ever tied together. This improvement upon the original usage was introduced by no less a man than Stubb, in order to afford to the imperilled harpooneer the strongest possible guarantee for the faithfulness and vigilance of his monkey-rope holder.

only prayed to his Yojo, and gave up his life into the hands of his gods.

Well, well, my dear comrade and twin-brother, thought I, as I drew in and then slacked off the rope to every swell of the sea—what matters it, after all? Are you not the precious image of each and all of us men in this whaling world? That unsounded ocean you gasp in, is Life; those sharks, your foes; those spades, your friends; and what between sharks and spades you are in a sad pickle and peril, poor lad.

But courage! there is good cheer in store for you, Queequeg. For now, as with blue lips and bloodshot eyes the exhausted savage at last climbs up the chains and stands all dripping and involuntarily trembling over the side; the steward advances, and with a benevolent, consolatory glance hands him—what? Some hot Cogniac? No! hands him, ye gods! hands him a cup of tepid ginger and water!

'Ginger? Do I smell ginger?' suspiciously asked Stubb, coming near. 'Yes, this must be ginger,' peering into the as yet untasted cup. Then standing as if incredulous for a while, he calmly walked towards the astonished steward slowly saying, 'Ginger? ginger? and will you have the goodness to tell me, Mr Dough-Boy, where lies the virtue of ginger? Ginger! is ginger the sort of fuel you use, Dough-Boy, to kindle a fire in this shivering cannibal? Ginger!—what the devil is ginger?—sea-coal?—fire-wood?—lucifer matches?—tinder?—gun-powder?—what the devil is ginger, I say, that you offer this cup to our poor Queequeg here?'

'There is some sneaking Temperance Society movement about this business,' he suddenly added, now approaching Starbuck, who had just come from forward. 'Will you look at that kannakin, sir: smell of it, if you please.' Then watching the mate's countenance, he added: 'The steward, Mr Starbuck, had the face to offer that calomel and jalap to Queequeg, there, this instant off the whale. Is the steward an apothecary, sir? and may I ask whether this is the sort of bellows by which he blows back the breath into a half-drowned man?'

'I trust not,' said Starbuck, 'it is poor stuff enough.'

'Aye, aye, steward,' cried Stubb, 'we'll teach you to drug a harpooneer; none of your apothecary's medicine here; you want to poison us, do ye? You have got out insurances on our lives and want to murder us all, and pocket the proceeds, do ye?'

'It was not me,' cried Dough-Boy, 'it was Aunt Charity that brought the ginger on board; and bade me never give the harpooneers any spirits, but only this ginger-jub—so she called it.'

'Ginger-jub! you gingerly rascal! take that! and run along with ye to the lockers, and get something better. I hope I do no wrong, Mr Starbuck. It is the captain's orders—grog for the harpooneer on a whale.'

'Enough,' replied Starbuck, 'only don't hit him again, but—'

'Oh, I never hurt when I hit, except when I hit a whale or something of that sort; and this fellow's a weazel. What were you about saying, sir?'

'Only this: go down with him, and get what thou wantest thyself.'

When Stubb reappeared, he came with a dark flask in one hand, and a sort of tea-caddy in the other. The first contained strong spirits, and was handed to Queequeg; the second was Aunt Charity's gift, and that was freely given to the waves.

73

STUBB AND FLASK KILL A RIGHT WHALE; AND THEN HAVE A TALK OVER HIM

IT must be borne in mind that all this time we have a Sperm Whale's prodigious head hanging to the Pequod's side. But we must let it continue hanging there a while till we can get a chance to attend to it. For the present other matters press, and the best we can do now for the head, is to pray heaven the tackles may hold.

Now, during the past night and forenoon, the Pequod had gradually drifted into a sea, which, by its occasional patches of yellow brit, gave unusual tokens of the vicinity of Right Whales, a species of the Leviathan that but few supposed to be at this particular time lurking anywhere near. And though all hands commonly disdained the capture of those inferior creatures; and though the Pequod was not commissioned to cruise for them at all, and though she had passed numbers of them near the Crozetts without lowering a boat; yet now that a Sperm Whale had been brought alongside and beheaded, to the surprise of all, the announcement was made that a Right Whale should be captured that day, if opportunity offered.

Nor was this long wanting. Tall spouts were seen to leeward;

and two boats, Stubb's and Flask's, were detached in pursuit.
Pulling further and further away, they at last became almost
invisible to the men at the mast-head. But suddenly in the distance,
they saw a great heap of tumultuous white water, and soon after
news came from aloft that one or both the boats must be fast.
An interval passed and the boats were in plain sight, in the act
of being dragged right towards the ship by the towing whale. So
close did the monster come to the hull, that at first it seemed as
if he meant it malice; but suddenly going down in a maelstrom,
within three rods of the planks, he wholly disappeared from view,
as if diving under the keel. 'Cut, cut!' was the cry from the ship
to the boats, which, for one instant, seemed on the point of being
brought with a deadly dash against the vessel's hide. But having
plenty of line yet in the tubs, and the whale not sounding very
rapidly, they paid out abundance of rope, and at the same time
pulled with all their might so as to get ahead of the ship. For a
few minutes the struggle was intensely critical; for while they still
slacked out the tightened line in one direction, and still plied their
oars in another, the contending strain threatened to take them
under. But it was only a few feet advance they sought to gain.
And they stuck to it till they did gain it; when instantly, a swift
tremor was felt running like lightning along the keel, as the strained
line, scraping beneath the ship, suddenly rose to view under her
bows, snapping and quivering; and so flinging off its drippings,
that the drops fell like bits of broken glass on the water, while
the whale beyond also rose to sight, and once more the boats
were free to fly. But the fagged whale abated his speed, and blindly
altering his course, went round the stern of the ship towing the
two boats after him, so that they performed a complete circuit.

Meantime, they hauled more and more upon their lines, till
close flanking him on both sides, Stubb answered Flask with lance
for lance; and thus round and round the Pequod the battle went,
while the multitudes of sharks that had before swum round the
Sperm Whale's body, rushed to the fresh blood that was spilled,
thirstily drinking at every new gash, as the eager Israelites did at
the new bursting fountains that poured from the smitten rock.

At last his spout grew thick, and with a frightful roll and vomit,
he turned upon his back a corpse.

While the two headsmen were engaged in making fast cords to
his flukes, and in other ways getting the mass in readiness for
towing, some conversation ensued between them.

"I wonder what the old man wants with this lump of foul lard,' said Stubb, not without some disgust at the thought of having to do with so ignoble a leviathan.

'Wants with it?' said Flask, coiling some spare line in the boat's bow, 'did you never hear that the ship which but once has a Sperm Whale's head hoisted on her starboard side, and at the same time a Right Whale's on the larboard; did you never hear, Stubb, that that ship can never afterwards capsize?'

'Why not?'

'I don't know, but I heard that gamboge ghost of a Fedallah saying so, and he seems to know all about ships' charms. But I sometimes think he'll charm the ship to no good at last. I don't half like that chap, Stubb. Did you ever notice how that tusk of his is a sort of carved into a snake's head, Stubb?'

'Sink him! I never look at him at all; but if ever I get a chance of a dark night, and he standing hard by the bulwarks, and no one by; look down there, Flask'—pointing into the sea with a peculiar motion of both hands—'Aye, will I! Flask, I take that Fedallah to be the devil in disguise. Do you believe that cock and bull story about his having been stowed away on board ship? He's the devil, I say. The reason why you don't see his tail, is because he tucks it up out of sight; he carries it coiled away in his pocket, I guess. Blast him! now that I think of it, he's always wanting oakum to stuff into the toes of his boots.'

'He sleeps in his boots, don't he? He hasn't got any hammock; but I've seen him lay of nights in a coil of rigging.'

'No doubt, and it's because of his cursed tail; he coils it down, do ye see, in the eye of the rigging.'

'What's the old man have so much to do with him for?'

'Striking up a swap or a bargain, I suppose.'

'Bargain?—about what?'

'Why, do ye see, the old man is hard bent after that White Whale, and the devil there is trying to come round him, and get him to swap away his silver watch, or his soul, or something of that sort, and then he'll surrender Moby Dick.'

'Pooh! Stubb, you are skylarking; how can Fedallah do that?'

'I don't know, Flask, but the devil is a curious chap, and a wicked one, I tell ye. Why, they say as how he went a sauntering into the old flag-ship once, switching his tail about devilish easy and gentlemanlike, and inquiring if the old governor was at home. Well, he was at home, and asked the devil what he wanted. The devil, switching his hoofs, up and says, "I want John." "What for?" says the old governor. "What business is that of yours," says the devil, getting mad,—"I want to use him." "Take him," says the governor—and by the Lord, Flask, if the devil didn't give John the Asiatic cholera before he got through with him, I'll eat this whale in one mouthful. But look sharp—aint you all ready there? Well, then, pull ahead, and let's get the whale along-side.'

'I think I remember some such story as you were telling,' said Flask, when at last the two boats were slowly advancing with their burden towards the ship, 'but I can't remember where.'

'Three Spaniards? Adventures of those three bloody-minded soldadoes? Did ye read it there, Flask? I guess ye did?'

'No: never saw such a book; heard of it, though. But now, tell me, Stubb, do you suppose that that devil you was speaking of just now, was the same you say is now on board the Pequod?'

'Am I the same man that helped kill this whale? Doesn't the devil live for ever; who ever heard that the devil was dead? Did you ever see any parson a wearing mourning for the devil? And if the devil has a latch-key to get into the admiral's cabin, don't you suppose he can crawl into a port-hole? Tell me that, Mr Flask?'

'How old do you suppose Fedallah is, Stubb?'

'Do you see that mainmast there?' pointing to the ship; 'well, that's the figure one; now take all the hoops in the Pequod's hold, and string 'em along in a row with that mast, for oughts, do you see; well, that wouldn't begin to be Fedallah's age. Nor all the coopers in creation couldn't show hoops enough to make oughts enough.'

'But see here, Stubb, I thought you a little boasted just now, that you meant to give Fedallah a sea-toss, if you got a good chance. Now, if he's so old as all those hoops of yours come to, and if he is going to live for ever, what good will it do to pitch him overboard—tell me that?'

'Give him a good ducking, anyhow.'

'But he'd crawl back.'

'Duck him again; and keep ducking him.'

'Suppose he should take it into his head to duck you, though—yes, and drown you—what then?'

'I should like to see him try it; I'd give him such a pair of black eyes that he wouldn't dare to show his face in the admiral's cabin again for a long while, let alone down in the orlop there, where he lives, and hereabouts on the upper decks where he sneaks so much. Damn the devil, Flask; do you suppose I'm afraid of the devil? Who's afraid of him, except the old governor who daresn't catch him and put him in double-darbies, as he deserves, but lets him go about kidnapping people; aye, and signed a bond

with him, that all the people the devil kidnapped, he'd roast for
him? There's a governor!'

'Do you suppose Fedallah wants to kidnap Captain Ahab?'

'Do I suppose it? You'll know it before long, Flask. But I am
going now to keep a sharp look-out on him; and if I see anything
very suspicious going on, I'll just take him by the nape of his
neck, and say—Look here, Beelzebub, you don't do it! and if he
makes any fuss, by the Lord I'll make a grab into his pocket for
his tail, take it to the capstan, and give him such a wrenching
and heaving, that his tail will come short off at the stump—do
you see; and then, I rather guess when he finds himself docked
in that queer fashion, he'll sneak off without the poor satisfaction
of feeling his tail between his legs.'

'And what will you do with the tail, Stubb?'

'Do with it? Sell it for an ox whip when we get home;—what
else?'

'Now, do you mean what you say, and have been saying all
along, Stubb?'

'Mean or not mean, here we are at the ship.'

The boats were here hailed, to tow the whale on the lar-board
side, where fluke chains and other necessaries were already prepared
for securing him.

'Didn't I tell you so?' said Flask; 'yes, you'll soon see this right
whale's head hoisted up opposite that parmacetti's.'

In good time, Flask's saying proved true. As before, the Pequod
steeply leaned over towards the sperm whale's head, now, by the
counterpoise of both heads, she regained her even keel; though
sorely strained, you may well believe. So, when on one side you
hoist in Locke's head, you go over that way; but now, on the
other side, hoist in Kant's and you come back again; but in very
poor plight. Thus, some minds for ever keep trimming boat. Oh,
ye foolish! throw all these thunder-heads overboard, and then you
will float light and right.

In disposing of the body of a right whale, when brought alongside
the ship, the same preliminary proceedings commonly take place
as in the case of a sperm whale; only, in the latter instance, the
head is cut off whole, but in the former the lips and tongue are
separately removed and hoisted on deck, with all the well known
black bone attached to what is called the crown-piece. But nothing
like this, in the present case, had been done. The carcases of both
whales had dropped astern; and the head-laden ship not a little
resembled a mule carrying a pair of overburdening panniers.

Meantime, Fedallah was calmly eyeing the right whale's head, and ever and anon glancing from the deep wrinkles there to the lines in his own hand. And Ahab chanced so to stand, that the Parsee occupied his shadow; while, if the Parsee's shadow was there at all it seemed only to blend with, and lengthen Ahab's. As the crew toiled on, Laplandish speculations were bandied among them, concerning all these passing things.

74

THE SPERM WHALE'S HEAD— CONTRASTED VIEW

HERE, now, are two great whales, laying their heads together; let us join them, and lay together our own.

Of the grand order of folio leviathans, the Sperm Whale and the Right Whale are by far the most noteworthy. They are the only whales regularly hunted by man. To the Nantucketer, they present the two extremes of all the known varieties of the whale. As the external difference between them is mainly observable in their heads; and as a head of each is this moment hanging from the Pequod's side; and as we may freely go from one to the other, by merely stepping across the deck:—where, I should like to know, will you obtain a better chance to study practical cetology than here?

In the first place, you are struck by the general contrast between these heads. Both are massive enough in all conscience; but there is a certain mathematical symmetry in the Sperm Whale's which the Right Whale's sadly lacks. There is more character in the Sperm Whale's head. As you behold it, you involuntarily yield the immense superiority to him, in point of pervading dignity. In the present instance, too, this dignity is heightened by the pepper and salt color of his head at the summit, giving token of advanced age and large experience. In short, he is what the fishermen technically call a 'grey-headed whale.'

Let us now note what is least dissimilar in these heads—namely, the two most important organs, the eye and the ear. Far back on the side of the head, and low down, near the angle of either whale's jaw, if you narrowly search, you will at last see a lashless eye, which you would fancy to be a young colt's eye; so out of all proportion is it to the magnitude of the head.

Now, from this peculiar sideway position of the whale's eyes, it is plain that he can never see an object which is exactly ahead, no more than he can one exactly astern. In a word, the position of the whale's eyes corresponds to that of a man's ears; and you may fancy, for yourself, how it would fare with you, did you sideways survey objects through your ears. You would find that you could only command some thirty degrees of vision in advance of the straight side-line of sight; and about thirty more behind it. If your bitterest foe were walking straight towards you, with dagger uplifted in broad day, you would not be able to see him, any more than if he were stealing upon you from behind. In a word, you would have two backs, so to speak; but, at the same time, also, two fronts (side fronts): for what is it that makes the front of a man—what, indeed, but his eyes?

Moreover, while in most other animals that I can now think of, the eyes are so planted as imperceptibly to blend their visual power, so as to produce one picture and not two to the brain; the peculiar position of the whale's eyes, effectually divided as they are by many cubic feet of solid head, which towers between them like a great mountain separating two lakes in valleys; this, of course, must wholly separate the impressions which each independent organ imparts. The whale, therefore, must see one distinct picture on this side, and another distinct picture on that side; while all between must be profound darkness and nothingness to him. Man may, in effect, be said to look out on the world from a sentry-box with two joined sashes for his window. But with the whale, these two sashes are separately inserted, making two distinct windows, but sadly impairing the view. This peculiarity of the whale's eyes is a thing always to be borne in mind in the fishery; and to be remembered by the reader in some subsequent scenes.

A curious and most puzzling question might be started concerning this visual matter as touching the Leviathan. But I must be content with a hint. So long as a man's eyes are open in the light, the act of seeing is involuntary; that is, he cannot then help mechanically seeing whatever objects are before him. Nevertheless, any one's experience will teach him, that though he can take in an undiscriminating sweep of things at one glance, it is quite impossible for him, attentively, and completely, to examine any two things—however large or however small—at one and the same instant of time; never mind if they lie side by side and touch each other. But if you now come to separate these two objects,

and surround each by a circle of profound darkness; then, in order
to see one of them, in such a manner as to bring your mind to
bear on it, the other will be utterly excluded from your contemporary consciousness. How is it, then, with the whale? True, both
his eyes, in themselves, must simultaneously act; but is his brain
so much more comprehensive, combining, and subtle than man's,
that he can at the same moment of time attentively examine two
distinct prospects, one on one side of him, and the other in an
exactly opposite direction? If he can, then is it as marvellous a
thing in him, as if a man were able simultaneously to go through
the demonstrations of two distinct problems in Euclid. Nor, strictly
investigated, is there any incongruity in this comparison.

It may be but an idle whim, but it has always seemed to me,
that the extraordinary vacillations of movement displayed by some
whales when beset by three or four boats; the timidity and liability
to queer frights, so common to such whales; I think that all this
indirectly proceeds from the helpless perplexity of volition, in
which their divided and diametrically opposite powers of vision
must involve them.

But the ear of the whale is full as curious as the eye. If you
are an entire stranger to their race, you might hunt over these
two heads for hours, and never discover that organ. The ear has
no external leaf whatever; and into the hole itself you can hardly
insert a quill, so wondrously minute is it. It is lodged a little
behind the eye. With respect to their ears, this important difference
is to be observed between the sperm whale and the right. While
the ear of the former has an external opening, that of the latter
is entirely and evenly covered over with a membrane, so as to be
quite imperceptible from without.

Is it not curious, that so vast a being as the whale should see
the world through so small an eye, and hear the thunder through
an ear which is smaller than a hare's? But if his eyes were broad
as the lens of Herschel's great telescope; and his ears capacious
as the porches of cathedrals; would that make him any longer of
sight, or sharper of hearing? Not at all.—Why then do you try
to 'enlarge' your mind? Subtilize it.

Let us now with whatever levers and steam-engines we have at
hand, cant over the sperm whale's head, so that it may lie bottom
up; then, ascending by a ladder to the summit, have a peep down
the mouth; and were it not that the body is now completely
separated from it, with a lantern we might descend into the great
Kentucky Mammoth Cave of his stomach. But let us hold on
here by this tooth, and look about us where we are. What a really

beautiful and chaste-looking mouth! from floor to ceiling, lined, or rather papered with a glistening white membrane, glossy as bridal satins.

But come out now, and look at this portentous lower jaw, which seems like the long narrow lid of an immense snuff-box, with the hinge at one end, instead of one side. If you pry it up, so as to get it overhead, and expose its rows of teeth, it seems a terrific portcullis; and such, alas! it proves to many a poor wight in the fishery, upon whom these spikes fall with impaling force. But far more terrible is it to behold, when fathoms down in the sea, you see some sulky whale, floating there suspended, with his prodigious jaw, some fifteen feet long, hanging straight down at right-angles with his body, for all the world like a ship's jib-boom. This whale is not dead; he is only dispirited; out of sorts, perhaps; hypochondriac; and so supine, that the hinges of his jaw have relaxed, leaving him there in that ungainly sort of plight, a reproach to all his tribe, who must, no doubt, imprecate lock-jaws upon him.

In most cases this lower jaw—being easily unhinged by a practised artist—is disengaged and hoisted on deck for the purpose of extracting the ivory teeth, and furnishing a supply of that hard white whalebone with which the fishermen fashion all sorts of curious articles, including canes, umbrella-stocks, and handles to riding-whips.

With a long, weary hoist the jaw is dragged on board, as if it were an anchor; and when the proper time comes—some few days after the other work—Queequeg, Daggoo, and Tashtego, being all accomplished dentists, are set to drawing teeth. With a keen cutting-spade, Queequeg lances the gums; then the jaw is lashed down to ringbolts, and a tackle being rigged from aloft, they drag out these teeth, as Michigan oxen drag stumps of old oaks out of wild wood-lands. There are generally forty-two teeth in all; in old whales, much worn down, but undecayed; nor filled after our artificial fashion. The jaw is afterwards sawn into slabs, and piled away like joists for building houses.

75

THE RIGHT WHALE'S HEAD—
CONTRASTED VIEW

CROSSING the deck, let us now have a good long look at the
Right Whale's head.

As in general shape the noble Sperm Whale's head may be
compared to a Roman war-chariot (especially in front, where it
is so broadly rounded); so, at a broad view, the Right Whale's
head bears a rather inelegant resemblance to a gigantic galliot-
toed shoe. Two hundred years ago an old Dutch voyager likened
its shape to that of a shoemaker's last. And in this same last or
shoe, that old woman of the nursery tale, with the swarming brood,
might very comfortably be lodged, she and all her progeny.

But as you come nearer to this great head it begins to assume
different aspects, according to your point of view. If you stand
on its summit and look at these two f-shaped spout-holes, you
would take the whole head for an enormous bass-viol, and these
spiracles, the apertures in its sounding-board. Then, again, if you
fix your eye upon this strange, crested, comb-like incrustation on
the top of the mass—this green, barnacled thing, which the Green-
landers call the 'crown,' and the Southern fishers the 'bonnet' of
the Right Whale; fixing your eyes solely on this, you would take
the head for the trunk of some huge oak, with a bird's nest in
its crotch. At any rate, when you watch those live crabs that nestle
here on this bonnet, such an idea will be almost sure to occur
to you; unless, indeed, your fancy has been fixed by the technical
term 'crown' also bestowed upon it; in which case you will take
great interest in thinking how this mighty monster is actually a
diademed king of the sea, whose green crown has been put together
for him in this marvellous manner. But if this whale be a king,
he is a very sulky looking fellow to grace a diadem. Look at that
hanging lower lip! what a huge sulk and pout is there! a sulk and
pout, by carpenter's measurement, about twenty feet long and five
feet deep; a sulk and pout that will yield you some 500 gallons
of oil and more.

A great pity, now, that this unfortunate whale should be harelipped. The fissure is about a foot across. Probably the mother during an important interval was sailing down the Peruvian coast, when earthquakes caused the beach to gape. Over this lip, as over a slippery threshold, we now slide into the mouth. Upon my word were I at Mackinaw, I should take this to be the inside of an Indian wigwam. Good Lord! is this the road that Jonah went? The roof is about twelve feet high, and runs to a pretty sharp angle, as if there were a regular ridge-pole there; while these ribbed, arched, hairy sides, present us with those wondrous, half vertical, scimetar-shaped slats of whalebone, say three hundred on a side, which depending from the upper part of the head or crown bone, form those Venetian blinds which have elsewhere been cursorily mentioned. The edges of these bones are fringed with hairy fibres, through which the Right Whale strains the water, and in whose intricacies he retains the small fish, when open-mouthed he goes through the seas of brit in feeding time. In the central blinds of bone, as they stand in their natural order, there are certain curious marks, curves, hollows, and ridges, whereby some whalemen calculate the creature's age, as the age of an oak by its circular rings. Though the certainty of this criterion is far from demonstrable, yet it has the savor of analogical probability. At any rate, if we yield to it, we must grant a far greater age to the Right Whale than at first glance will seem reasonable.

In old times, there seem to have prevailed the most curious fancies concerning these blinds. One voyager in Purchas calls them the wondrous 'whiskers' inside of the whale's mouth;* another, 'hogs' bristles;' a third old gentleman in Hackluyt uses the following elegant language: 'There are about two hundred and fifty fins growing on each side of his upper *chop*, which arch over his tongue on each side of his mouth.'

As every one knows, these same 'hogs' bristles', 'fins', 'whiskers', 'blinds', or whatever you please, furnish to the ladies their busks and other stiffening contrivances. But in this particular, the demand has long been on the decline. It was in Queen Anne's time that the bone was in its glory, the farthingale being then all the fashion. And as those ancient dames moved about gaily, though in the jaws of the whale, as you may say; even so, in a shower, with the like thoughtlessness, do we nowadays fly under the same jaws

---

* This reminds us that the Right Whale really has a sort of whisker, or rather a moustache, consisting of a few scattered white hairs on the upper part of the outer end of the lower jaw. Sometimes these tufts impart a rather brigandish expression to his otherwise solemn countenance.

for protection; the umbrella being a tent spread over the same bone.

But now forget all about blinds and whiskers for a moment, and, standing in the Right Whale's mouth, look around you afresh. Seeing all these colonnades of bone so methodically ranged about, would you not think you were inside of the great Haarlem organ, and gazing upon its thousand pipes? For a carpet to the organ we have a rug of the softest Turkey—the tongue, which is glued, as it were, to the floor of the mouth. It is very fat and tender, and apt to tear in pieces in hoisting it on deck. This particular tongue now before us; at a passing glance I should say it was a six-barreler; that is, it will yield you about that amount of oil.

Ere this, you must have plainly seen the truth of what I started with—that the Sperm Whale and the Right Whale have almost entirely different heads. To sum up, then: in the Right Whale's there is no great well of sperm; no ivory teeth at all; no long, slender mandible of a lower jaw, like the Sperm Whale's. Nor in the Sperm Whale are there any of those blinds of bone; no huge lower lip; and scarcely anything of a tongue. Again, the Right Whale has two external spout-holes, the Sperm Whale only one.

Look your last, now, on these venerable hooded heads, while they yet lie together; for one will soon sink, unrecorded, in the sea; the other will not be very long in following.

Can you catch the expression of the Sperm Whale's there? It is the same he died with, only some of the longer wrinkles in the forehead seem now faded away. I think his broad brow to be full of a prairie-like placidity, born of a speculative indifference as to death. But mark the other head's expression. See that amazing lower lip, pressed by accident against the vessel's side, so as firmly to embrace the jaw. Does not this whole head seem to speak of an enormous practical resolution in facing death? This Right Whale I take to have been a Stoic; the Sperm Whale, a Platonian, who might have taken up Spinoza in his latter years.

76

THE BATTERING-RAM

ERE quitting, for the nonce, the Sperm Whale's head, I would have you, as a sensible physiologist, simply—particularly remark its front aspect, in all its compacted collectedness. I would have you investigate it now with the sole view of forming to yourself some unexaggerated, intelligent estimate of whatever battering-ram power may be lodged there. Here is a vital point; for you must either satisfactorily settle this matter with yourself, or for ever remain an infidel as to one of the most appalling, but not the less true events, perhaps anywhere to be found in all recorded history.

You observe that in the ordinary swimming position of the Sperm Whale, the front of his head presents an almost wholly vertical plane to the water; you observe that the lower part of that front slopes considerably backwards, so as to furnish more of a retreat for the long socket which receives the boom-like lower jaw; you observe that the mouth is entirely under the head, much in the same way, indeed, as though your own mouth were entirely under your chin. Moreover you observe that the whale has no external nose; and that what nose he has—his spout hole—is on the top of his head; you observe that his eyes and ears are at the sides of his head, nearly one third of his entire length from the front. Wherefore, you must now have perceived that the Sperm Whale's head is a dead, blind wall, without a single organ or tender prominence of any sort whatsoever. Furthermore, you are now to consider that only in the extreme, lower, backward sloping part of the front of the head, is there the slightest vestige of bone; and not till you get near twenty feet from the forehead do you come to the full cranial development. So that this whole enormous boneless mass is as one wad. Finally, though, as will soon be revealed, its contents partly comprise the most delicate oil; yet, you are now to be apprised of the nature of the substance which so impregnably invests all that apparent effeminacy. In some previous place I have described to you how the blubber wraps the body of the whale, as the rind wraps an orange. Just so with the head; but with this difference: about the head this envelope, though not so thick, is of a boneless toughness, inestimable by any man who has not handled it. The severest pointed harpoon, the sharpest lance darted by the strongest human arm, impotently rebounds from it. It is as though the forehead of the Sperm Whale were paved with horses' hoofs. I do not think that any sensation lurks in it.

Bethink yourself also of another thing. When two large, loaded Indiamen chance to crowd and crush towards each other in the docks, what do the sailors do? They do not suspend between them, at the point of coming contact, any merely hard substance, like iron or wood. No, they hold there a large, round wad of tow and cork, enveloped in the thickest and toughest of ox-hide. That bravely and uninjured takes the jam which would have snapped all their oaken handspikes and iron crowbars. By itself this sufficiently illustrates the obvious fact I drive at. But supplementary to this, it has hypothetically occurred to me, that as ordinary fish possess what is called a swimming bladder in them, capable, at will, of distension or contraction; and as the Sperm Whale, as far as I know, has no such provision in him; considering, too, the otherwise inexplicable manner in which he now depresses his head altogether beneath the surface, and anon swims with it high elevated out of the water; considering the unobstructed elasticity of its envelop; considering the unique interior of his head; it has hypothetically occurred to me, I say, that those mystical lung-celled honeycombs there may possibly have some hitherto unknown and unsuspected connexion with the outer air, so as to be susceptible to atmospheric distension and contraction. If this be so, fancy the irresistibleness of that might, to which the most impalpable and destructive of all elements contributes.

Now, mark. Unerringly impelling this dead, impregnable, uninjurable wall, and this most buoyant thing within; there swims behind it all a mass of tremendous life, only to be adequately estimated as piled wood is—by the cord; and all obedient to one volition, as the smallest insect. So that when I shall hereafter detail to you all the specialties and concentrations of potency everywhere lurking in this expansive monster; when I shall show you some of his more inconsiderable braining feats; I trust you will have renounced all ignorant incredulity, and be ready to abide by this; that though the Sperm Whale stove a passage through the Isthmus of Darien, and mixed the Atlantic with the Pacific, you would not elevate one hair of your eye-brow. For unless you own the whale, you are but a provincial and sentimentalist in Truth. But clear Truth is a thing for salamander giants only to encounter; how small the chances for the provincials then? What befel the weakling youth lifting the dread goddess's veil at Sais?

77

THE GREAT HEIDELBURGH TUN

Now comes the Baling of the Case. But to comprehend it aright, you must know something of the curious internal structure of the thing operated upon.

Regarding the Sperm Whale's head as a solid oblong, you may, on an inclined plane, sideways divide it into two quoins,* whereof the lower is the bony structure, forming the cranium and jaws, and the upper an unctuous mass wholly free from bones; its broad forward end forming the expanded vertical apparent forehead of the whale. At the middle of the forehead horizontally subdivide this upper quoin, and then you have two almost equal parts, which before were naturally divided by an internal wall of a thick tendinous substance.

The lower subdivided part, called the junk, is one immense honeycomb of oil, formed by the crossing and recrossing, into ten thousand infiltrated cells, of tough elastic white fibres throughout its whole extent. The upper part, known as the Case, may be regarded as the great Heidelburgh Tun of the Sperm Whale. And as that famous great tierce is mystically carved in front, so the whale's vast plaited forehead forms innumerable strange devices for the emblematical adornment of his wondrous tun. Moreover, as that of Heidelburgh was always replenished with the most excellent of the wines of the Rhenish valleys, so the tun of the whale contains by far the most precious of all his oily vintages; namely, the highly-prized spermaceti, in its absolutely pure, limpid, and odoriferous state. Nor is this precious substance found unalloyed in any other part of the creature. Though in life it remains perfectly fluid, yet, upon exposure to the air, after death, it soon begins to concrete; sending forth beautiful crystalline shoots, as when the first thin delicate ice is just forming in water. A large whale's case generally yields about five hundred gallons of sperm, though from unavoidable circumstances, considerable of it is spilled, leaks, and dribbles away, or is otherwise irrevocably lost in the ticklish business of securing what you can.

I know not with what fine and costly material the Heidelburgh Tun was coated within, but in superlative richness that coating could not possibly have compared with the silken pearl-colored membrane, like the lining of a fine pelisse, forming the inner surface of the Sperm Whale's case.

It will have been seen that the Heidelburgh Tun of the Sperm Whale embraces the entire length of the entire top of the head; and since—as has been elsewhere set forth—the head embraces

---

* Quoin is not a Euclidean term. It belongs to the pure nautical mathematics. I know not that it has been defined before. A quoin is a solid which differs from a wedge in having its sharp end formed by the steep inclination of one side, instead of the mutual tapering of both sides.

one third of the whole length of the creature, then setting that length down at eighty feet for a good sized whale, you have more than twenty-six feet for the depth of the tun, when it is length-wise hoisted up and down against a ship's side.

As in decapitating the whale, the operator's instrument is brought close to the spot where an entrance is subsequently forced into the spermaceti magazine; he has, therefore, to be uncommonly heedful, lest a careless, untimely stroke should invade the sanctuary and wastingly let out its invaluable contents. It is this decapitated end of the head, also, which is at last elevated out of the water, and retained in that position by the enormous cutting tackles, whose hempen combinations, on one side, make quite a wilderness of ropes in that quarter.

Thus much being said, attend now, I pray you, to that marvellous and—in this particular instance—almost fatal operation whereby the Sperm Whale's great Heidelburgh Tun is tapped.

78
CISTERN AND BUCKETS

NIMBLE as a cat, Tashtego mounts aloft; and without altering his erect posture, runs straight out upon the overhanging main-yard-arm, to the part where it exactly projects over the hoisted Tun. He has carried with him a light tackle called a whip, consisting of only two parts, travelling through a single-sheaved block. Se-curing this block, so that it hangs down from the yard-arm, he swings one end of the rope, till it is caught and firmly held by a hand on deck. Then, hand-over-hand, down the other part, the Indian drops through the air, till dexterously he lands on the summit of the head. There—still high elevated above the rest of the company, to whom he vivaciously cries—he seems some Turkish Muezzin calling the good people to prayers from the top of a tower. A short-handled sharp spade being sent up to him, he diligently searches for the proper place to begin breaking into the Tun. In this business he proceeds very heedfully, like a treasure-hunter in some old house, sounding the walls to find where the gold is masoned in. By the time this cautious search is over, a stout iron-bound bucket, precisely like a well-bucket, has been attached to one end of the whip; while the other end, being stretched across the deck, is there held by two or three alert hands.

These last now hoist the bucket within grasp of the Indian, to whom another person has reached up a very long pole. Inserting this pole into the bucket, Tashtego downward guides the bucket into the Tun, till it entirely disappears; then giving the word to the seamen at the whip, up comes the bucket again, all bubbling like a dairy-maid's pail of new milk. Carefully lowered from its height, the full-freighted vessel is caught by an appointed hand, and quickly emptied into a large tub. Then re-mounting aloft, it again goes through the same round until the deep cistern will yield no more. Towards the end, Tashtego has to ram his long pole harder and harder, and deeper and deeper into the Tun, until some twenty feet of the pole have gone down.

Now, the people of the Pequod had been baling some time in this way; several tubs had been filled with the fragrant sperm; when all at once a queer accident happened. Whether it was that Tashtego, that wild Indian, was so heedless and reckless as to let go for a moment his one-handed hold on the great cabled tackles suspending the head; or whether the place where he stood was so treacherous and oozy; or whether the Evil One himself would have it to fall out so, without stating his particular reasons; how it was exactly, there is no telling now; but, on a sudden, as the eightieth or ninetieth bucket came suckingly up—my God! poor Tashtego—like the twin reciprocating bucket in a veritable well, dropped head-foremost down into this great Tun of Heidelburgh, and with a horrible oily gurgling, went clean out of sight!

'Man overboard!' cried Daggoo, who amid the general consternation first came to his senses. 'Swing the bucket this way!' and putting one foot into it, so as the better to secure his slippery hand-hold on the whip itself, the hoisters ran him high up to the top of the head, almost before Tashtego could have reached its interior bottom. Meantime, there was a terrible tumult. Looking over the side, they saw the before lifeless head throbbing and heaving just below the surface of the sea, as if that moment seized with some momentous idea; whereas it was only the poor Indian unconsciously revealing by those struggles the perilous depth to which he had sunk.

At this instant, while Daggoo, on the summit of the head, was clearing the whip—which had somehow got foul of the great cutting tackles—a sharp cracking noise was heard; and to the unspeakable horror of all, one of the two enormous hooks suspending the head tore out, and with a vast vibration the enormous mass sideways swung, till the drunk ship reeled and shook as if smitten by an iceberg. The one remaining hook, upon which the entire strain now depended, seemed every instant to be on the point of giving way; an event still more likely from the violent motions of the head.

'Come down, come down!' yelled the seamen to Daggoo, but with one hand holding on to the heavy tackles, so that if the head should drop, he would still remain suspended; the negro having cleared the foul line, rammed down the bucket into the now collapsed well, meaning that the buried harpooneer should grasp it, and so be hoisted out.

'In heaven's name, man,' cried Stubb, 'are you ramming home a cartridge there?—Avast! How will that help him; jamming that iron-bound bucket on top of his head? Avast, will ye!'

'Stand clear of the tackle!' cried a voice like the bursting of a rocket.

Almost in the same instant, with a thunder-boom, the enormous mass dropped into the sea, like Niagara's Table-Rock into the whirlpool; the suddenly relieved hull rolled away from it, to far down her glittering copper; and all caught their breath, as half swinging—now over the sailors' heads, and now over the water— Daggoo, through a thick mist of spray, was dimly beheld clinging to the pendulous tackles, while poor, buried-alive Tashtego was sinking utterly down to the bottom of the sea! But hardly had the blinding vapor cleared away, when a naked figure with a boarding-sword in its hand, was for one swift moment seen hovering over the bulwarks. The next, a loud splash announced that my brave Queequeg had dived to the rescue. One packed rush was made to the side, and every eye counted every ripple, as moment followed moment, and no sign of either the sinker or the diver could be seen. Some hands now jumped into a boat alongside, and pushed a little off from the ship.

'Ha! ha!' cried Daggoo, all at once, from his now quiet, swinging perch overhead; and looking further off from the side, we saw an arm thrust upright from the blue waves; a sight strange to see, as an arm thrust forth from the grass over a grave.

'Both! both!—it is both!'—cried Daggoo again with a joyful shout; and soon after, Queequeg was seen boldly striking out with one hand, and with the other clutching the long hair of the Indian. Drawn into the waiting boat, they were quickly brought to the deck; but Tashtego was long in coming to, and Queequeg did not look very brisk.

Now, how had this noble rescue been accomplished? Why, diving after the slowly descending head, Queequeg with his keen sword had made side lunges near its bottom, so as to scuttle a large hole there; then dropping his sword, had thrust his long arm far inwards and upwards, and so hauled out our poor Tash by the head. He averred, that upon first thrusting in for him, a leg was presented; but well knowing that that was not as it ought to be, and might occasion great trouble;—he had thrust back the leg, and by a dexterous heave and toss, had wrought a somerset upon the Indian; so that with the next trial, he came forth in the good old way—head foremost. As for the great head itself, that was doing as well as could be expected.

And thus, through the courage and great skill in obstetrics of Queequeg, the deliverance, or rather, delivery of Tashtego, was successfully accomplished, in the teeth, too, of the most untoward and apparently hopeless impediments; which is a lesson by no means to be forgotten. Midwifery should be taught in the same course with fencing and boxing, riding and rowing.

I know that this queer adventure of the Gay-Header's will be sure to seem incredible to some landsmen, though they themselves may have either seen or heard of some one's falling into a cistern ashore; an accident which not seldom happens, and with much less reason too than the Indian's, considering the exceeding slipperiness of the curb of the Sperm Whale's well.

But, peradventure, it may be sagaciously urged, how is this? We thought the tissued, infiltrated head of the Sperm Whale, was the lightest and most corky part about him; and yet thou makest it sink in an element of a far greater specific gravity than itself. We have thee there. Not at all, but I have ye; for at the time poor Tash fell in, the case had been nearly emptied of its lighter contents, leaving little but the dense tendinous wall of the well—a double welded, hammered substance, as I have before said, much heavier than the sea water, and a lump of which sinks in it like lead almost. But the tendency to rapid sinking in this substance was in the present instance materially counteracted by the other parts of the head remaining undetached from it, so that it sank very slowly and deliberately indeed, affording Queequeg a fair chance for performing his agile obstetrics on the run, as you may say. Yes, it was a running delivery, so it was.

Now, had Tashtego perished in that head, it had been a very precious perishing; smothered in the very whitest and daintiest of fragrant spermaceti; coffined, hearsed, and tombed in the secret inner chamber and sanctum sanctorum of the whale. Only one sweeter end can readily be recalled—the delicious death of an Ohio honey-hunter, who seeking honey in the crotch of a hollow tree, found such exceeding store of it, that leaning too far over, it sucked him in, so that he died embalmed. How many, think ye, have likewise fallen into Plato's honey head, and sweetly perished there?

79

THE PRAIRE

To scan the lines of his face, or feel the bumps on the head of this Leviathan; this is a thing which no Physiognomist or Phrenologist has as yet undertaken. Such an enterprise would seem almost as hopeful as for Lavater to have scrutinized the wrinkles on the Rock of Gibraltar, or for Gall to have mounted a ladder and manipulated the Dome of the Pantheon. Still, in that famous work of his, Lavater not only treats of the various faces of men, but also attentively studies the faces of horses, birds, serpents, and fish; and dwells in detail upon the modifications of expression discernible therein. Nor have Gall and his disciple Spurzheim failed to throw out some hints touching the phrenological characteristics of other beings than man. Therefore, though I am but ill qualified for a pioneer, in the application of these two semi-sciences to the whale, I will do my endeavor. I try all things; I achieve what I can.

Physiognomically regarded, the Sperm Whale is an anomalous creature. He has no proper nose. And since the nose is the central and most conspicuous of the features; and since it perhaps most modifies and finally controls their combined expression; hence it would seem that its entire absence, as an external appendage, must very largely affect the countenance of the whale. For as in landscape gardening, a spire, cupola, monument, or tower of some sort, is deemed almost indispensable to the completion of the scene; so no face can be physiognomically in keeping without the elevated open-work belfry of the nose. Dash the nose from Phidias's marble Jove, and what a sorry remainder! Nevertheless, Leviathan is of so mighty a magnitude, all his proportions are so stately, that the same deficiency which in the sculptured Jove were hideous, in him is no blemish at all. Nay, it is an added grandeur. A nose to the whale would have been impertinent. As on your physiognomical voyage you sail round his vast head in your jolly-boat, your noble conceptions of him are never insulted by the reflection that he has a nose to be pulled. A pestilent conceit, which so often will insist upon obtruding even when beholding the mightiest royal beadle on his throne.

In some particulars, perhaps the most imposing physiognomical view to be had of the Sperm Whale, is that of the full front of his head. This aspect is sublime.

In thought, a fine human brow is like the East when troubled with the morning. In the repose of the pasture, the curled brow of the bull has a touch of the grand in it. Pushing heavy cannon up mountain defiles, the elephant's brow is majestic. Human or animal, the mystical brow is as that great golden seal affixed by the German emperors to their decrees. It signifies—'God: done this day by my hand.' But in most creatures, nay in man himself, very often the brow is but a mere strip of alpine land lying along the snow line. Few are the foreheads which like Shakespeare's or Melancthon's rise so high, and descend so low, that the eyes themselves seem clear, eternal, tideless mountain lakes; and all above them in the forehead's wrinkles, you seem to track the antlered thoughts descending there to drink, as the Highland hunters track the snow prints of the deer. But in the great Sperm Whale, this high and mighty god-like dignity inherent in the brow is so immensely amplified, that gazing on it, in that full front view, you feel the Deity and the dread powers more forcibly than in beholding any other object in living nature. For you see no one point precisely; not one distinct feature is revealed; no nose, eyes, ears, or mouth; no face; he has none, proper; nothing but that one broad firmament of a forehead, pleated with riddles; dumbly lowering with the doom of boats, and ships, and men. Nor, in profile, does this wondrous brow diminish; though that way viewed, its grandeur does not domineer upon you so. In profile, you plainly perceive that horizontal, semi-crescentic depression in the forehead's middle, which, in man, is Lavater's mark of genius.

But how? Genius in the Sperm Whale? Has the Sperm Whale ever written a book, spoken a speech? No, his great genius is declared in his doing nothing particular to prove it. It is moreover declared in his pyramidical silence. And this reminds me that had the great Sperm Whale been known to the young Orient World, he would have been deified by their child-magian thoughts. They deified the crocodile of the Nile, because the crocodile is tongueless; and the Sperm Whale has no tongue, or at least it is so exceedingly small, as to be incapable of protrusion. If hereafter any highly cultured, poetical nation shall lure back to their birth-right, the merry May-day gods of old; and livingly enthrone them again in the now egotistical sky; on the now unhaunted hill; then be sure, exalted to Jove's high seat, the great Sperm Whale shall lord it.

Champollion deciphered the wrinkled granite hieroglyphics. But there is no Champollion to decipher the Egypt of every man's and every being's face. Physiognomy, like every other human science, is but a passing fable. If then, Sir William Jones, who read in thirty languages, could not read the simplest peasant's face in its profounder and more subtle meanings, how may unlettered Ishmael hope to read the awful Chaldee of the Sperm Whale's brow? I but put that brow before you. Read it if you can.

80
THE NUT

IF the Sperm Whale be physiognomically a Sphinx, to the phrenologist his brain seems that geometrical circle which it is impossible to square.

In the full-grown creature the skull will measure at least twenty feet in length. Unhinge the lower jaw, and the side view of this skull is as the side view of a moderately inclined plane resting throughout on a level base. But in life—as we have elsewhere seen—this inclined plane is angularly filled up, and almost squared by the enormous superincumbent mass of the junk and sperm. At the high end the skull forms a crater to bed that part of the mass; while under the long floor of this crater—in another cavity seldom exceeding ten inches in length and as many in depth—reposes the mere handful of this monster's brain. The brain is at least twenty feet from his apparent forehead in life; it is hidden away behind its vast outworks, like the innermost citadel within the amplified fortifications of Quebec. So like a choice casket is it secreted in him, that I have known some whalemen who peremptorily deny that the Sperm Whale has any other brain than that palpable semblance of one formed by the cubic-yards of his sperm magazine. Lying in strange folds, courses, and convolutions, to their apprehensions, it seems more in keeping with the idea of his general might to regard that mystic part of him as the seat of his intelligence.

It is plain, then, that phrenologically the head of this Leviathan, in the creature's living intact state, is an entire delusion. As for his true brain, you can then see no indications of it, nor feel any.

The whale, like all things that are mighty, wears a false brow to the common world.

If you unload his skull of its spermy heaps and then take a rear view of its rear end, which is the high end, you will be struck by its resemblance to the human skull, beheld in the same situation, and from the same point of view. Indeed, place this reversed skull (scaled down to the human magnitude) among a plate of men's skulls, and you would involuntarily confound it with them; and remarking the depressions on one part of its summit, in phrenological phrase you would say—This man had no self-esteem, and no veneration. And by those negations, considered along with the affirmative fact of his prodigious bulk and power, you can best form to yourself the truest, though not the most exhilarating conception of what the most exalted potency is.

But if from the comparative dimensions of the whale's proper brain, you deem it incapable of being adequately charted, then I have another idea for you. If you attentively regard almost any quadruped's spine, you will be struck with the resemblance of its vertebræ to a strung necklace of dwarfed skulls, all bearing rudimental resemblance to the skull proper. It is a German conceit, that the vertebræ are absolutely undeveloped skulls. But the curious external resemblance, I take it the Germans were not the first men to perceive. A foreign friend once pointed it out to me, in the skeleton of a foe he had slain, and with the vertebræ of which he was inlaying, in a sort of basso-relievo, the beaked prow of his canoe. Now, I consider that the phrenologists have omitted an important thing in not pushing their investigations from the cerebellum through the spinal canal. For I believe that much of a man's character will be found betokened in his backbone. I would rather feel your spine than your skull, whoever you are. A thin joint of a spine never yet upheld a full and noble soul. I rejoice in my spine, as in the firm audacious staff of that flag which I fling half out to the world.

Apply this spinal branch of phrenology to the Sperm Whale. His cranial cavity is continuous with the first neck-vertebra; and in that vertebra the bottom of the spinal canal will measure ten inches across, being eight in height, and of a triangular figure with the base downwards. As it passes through the remaining vertebræ the canal tapers in size, but for a considerable distance remains of large capacity. Now, of course, this canal is filled with much the same strangely fibrous substance—the spinal cord—as the brain; and directly communicates with the brain. And what is still more, for many feet after emerging from the brain's cavity, the spinal cord remains of an undecreasing girth, almost equal to that of the brain. Under all these circumstances, would it be unreasonable to survey and map out the whale's spine phrenologically? For, viewed in this light, the wonderful comparative smallness of his brain proper is more than compensated by the wonderful comparative magnitude of his spinal cord.

But leaving this hint to operate as it may with the phrenologists, I would merely assume the spinal theory for a moment, in reference to the Sperm Whale's hump. This august hump, if I mistake not, rises over one of the larger vertebræ, and is, therefore, in some sort, the outer convex mould of it. From its relative situation then, I should call this high hump the organ of firmness or indomitableness in the Sperm Whale. And that the great monster is indomitable, you will yet have reason to know.

81
THE PEQUOD MEETS THE VIRGIN

THE predestinated day arrived, and we duly met the ship Jungfrau, Derick De Deer, master, of Bremen.

At one time the greatest whaling people in the world, the Dutch and Germans are now among the least; but here and there at very wide intervals of latitude and longitude, you still occasionally meet with their flag in the Pacific.

For some reason, the Jungfrau seemed quite eager to pay her respects. While yet some distance from the Pequod, she rounded to, and dropping a boat, her captain was impelled towards us, impatiently standing in the bows instead of the stern.

'What has he in his hand there?' cried Starbuck, pointing to something wavingly held by the German. 'Impossible!—a lamp-feeder!'

'Not that,' said Stubb, 'no, no, it's a coffee-pot, Mr Starbuck; he's coming off to make us our coffee, is the Yarman; don't you see that big tin can there alongside of him?—that's his boiling water. Oh! he's all right, is the Yarman.'

'Go along with you,' cried Flask, 'it's a lamp-feeder and an oil-can. He's out of oil, and has come a-begging.'

However curious it may seem for an oil-ship to be borrowing oil on the whale-ground, and however much it may invertedly contradict the old proverb about carrying coals to Newcastle, yet sometimes such a thing really happens; and in the present case Captain Derick De Deer did indubitably conduct a lamp-feeder as Flask did declare.

As he mounted the deck, Ahab abruptly accosted him, without at all heeding what he had in his hand; but in his broken lingo, the German soon evinced his complete ignorance of the White Whale; immediately turning the conversation to his lamp-feeder and oil-can, with some remarks touching his having to turn into his hammock at night in profound darkness—his last drop of Bremen oil being gone, and not a single flying-fish yet captured to supply the deficiency; concluding by hinting that his ship was indeed what in the Fishery is technically called a *clean* one (that is, an empty one), well deserving the name of Jungfrau or the Virgin.

His necessities supplied, Derick departed; but he had not gained his ship's side, when whales were almost simultaneously raised from the mast-heads of both vessels; and so eager for the chase was Derick, that without pausing to put his oil-can and lamp-feeder aboard, he slewed round his boat and made after the leviathan lamp-feeders.

Now, the game having risen to leeward, he and the other three German boats that soon followed him, had considerably the start of the Pequod's keels. There were eight whales, an average pod. Aware of their danger, they were going all abreast with great speed straight before the wind, rubbing their flanks as closely as so many spans of horses in harness. They left a great, wide wake, as though continually unrolling a great wide parchment upon the sea.

Full in this rapid wake, and many fathoms in the rear, swam a huge, humped old bull, which by his comparatively slow progress, as well as by the unusual yellowish incrustations overgrowing him, seemed afflicted with the jaundice, or some other infirmity. Whether this whale belonged to the pod in advance, seemed questionable; for it is not customary for such venerable leviathans to be at all social. Nevertheless, he stuck to their wake, though indeed their back water must have retarded him, because the white-bone or swell at his broad muzzle was a dashed one, like the swell formed when two hostile currents meet. His spout was short, slow, and laborious; coming forth with a choking sort of gush, and spending itself in torn shreds, followed by strange subterranean commotions in him, which seemed to have egress at his other buried extremity, causing the waters behind him to upbubble.

'Who's got some paregoric?' said Stubb, 'he has the stomach-ache, I'm afraid. Lord, think of having half an acre of stomach-

ache! Adverse winds are holding mad Christmas in him, boys. It's
the first foul wind I ever knew to blow from astern; but look, did
ever whale yaw so before? it must be, he's lost his tiller.'

As an overladen Indiaman bearing down the Hindostan coast
with a deck load of frightened horses, careens, buries, rolls, and
wallows on her way; so did this old whale heave his aged bulk,
and now and then partly turning over on his cumbrous rib-ends,
expose the cause of his devious wake in the unnatural stump of
his starboard fin. Whether he had lost that fin in battle, or had
been born without it, it were hard to say.

'Only wait a bit, old chap, and I'll give ye a sling for that
wounded arm,' cried cruel Flask, pointing to the whale-line near
him.

'Mind he don't sling thee with it,' cried Starbuck. 'Give way,
or the German will have him.'

With one intent all the combined rival boats were pointed for
this one fish, because not only was he the largest, and therefore
the most valuable whale, but he was nearest to them, and the
other whales were going with such great velocity, moreover, as
almost to defy pursuit for the time. At this juncture, the Pequod's
keels had shot by the three German boats last lowered; but from
the great start he had had, Derick's boat still led the chase, though
every moment neared by his foreign rivals. The only thing they
feared, was, that from being already so nigh to his mark, he would
be enabled to dart his iron before they could completely overtake
and pass him. As for Derick, he seemed quite confident that this
would be the case, and occasionally with a deriding gesture shook
his lamp-feeder at the other boats.

'The ungracious and ungrateful dog!' cried Starbuck; 'he mocks
and dares me with the very poor-box I filled for him not five
minutes ago!'—then in his old intense whisper—'give way, grey-
hounds! Dog to it!'

'I tell ye what it is, men'—cried Stubb to his crew—'It's against
my religion to get mad; but I'd like to eat that villainous Yarman—
Pull—wont ye? Are you going to let that rascal beat ye? Do ye
love brandy? A hogshead of brandy, then, to the best man. Come,
why don't some of ye burst a blood-vessel? Who's that been
dropping an anchor over-board—we don't budge an inch—we're
becalmed. Halloo, here's grass growing in the boat's bottom—and
by the Lord, the mast there's budding. This won't do, boys. Look
at that Yarman! The short and long of it is, men, will ye spit fire
or not?'

'Oh! see the suds he makes!' cried Flask, dancing up and down—

'What a hump—Oh, *do* pile on the beef—lays like a log! Oh! my
lads, *do* spring—slap-jacks and quohogs for supper, you know,
my lads—baked clams and muffins—oh, *do, do,* spring—he's a
hundred barreler—don't lose him now—don't, oh, *don't!*—see that
Yarman—Oh! won't ye pull for your duff, my lads—such a sog!
such a sogger! Don't ye love sperm? There goes three thousand
dollars, men!—a bank!—a whole bank! The bank of England!—
Oh, *do, do, do!*—What's that Yarman about now?'

At this moment Derick was in the act of pitching his lamp-
feeder at the advancing boats, and also his oil-can; perhaps with
the double view of retarding his rivals' way, and at the same time
economically accelerating his own by the momentary impetus of
the backward toss.

'The unmannerly Dutch dogger!' cried Stubb. 'Pull now, men,
like fifty thousand line-of-battle-ship loads of red-haired devils.
What d'ye say, Tashtego; are you the man to snap your spine in
two-and-twenty pieces for the honor of old Gay-head? What d'ye
say?'

'I say, pull like god-dam,'—cried the Indian.

Fiercely but evenly, incited by the taunts of the German, the
Pequod's three boats now began ranging almost abreast; and, so
disposed, momentarily neared him. In that fine, loose, chivalrous
attitude of the headsman when drawing near to his prey, the three
mates stood up proudly, occasionally backing the after oarsman
with an exhilarating cry of, 'There she slides, now! Hurrah for
the white-ash breeze! Down with the Yarman! Sail over him!'

But so decided an original start had Derick had, that spite of
all their gallantry, he would have proved the victor in this race,
had not a righteous judgment descended upon him in a crab
which caught the blade of his midship oarsman. While this clumsy
lubber was striving to free his white-ash, and while, in consequence,
Derick's boat was nigh to capsizing, and he thundering away at
his men in a mighty rage;—that was a good time for Starbuck,
Stubb, and Flask. With a shout, they took a mortal start forwards,
and slantingly ranged up on the German's quarter. An instant
more, and all four boats were diagonally in the whale's immediate
wake, while stretching from them, on both sides, was the foaming
swell that he made.

It was a terrific, most pitiable, and maddening sight. The whale
was now going head out, and sending his spout before him in a
continual tormented jet; while his one poor fin beat his side in
an agony of fright. Now to this hand, now to that, he yawed in
his faltering flight, and still at every billow that he broke, he

spasmodically sank in the sea, or sideways rolled towards the sky his one beating fin. So have I seen a bird with clipped wing, making affrighted broken circles in the air, vainly striving to escape the piratical hawks. But the bird has a voice, and with plaintive cries will make known her fear; but the fear of this vast dumb brute of the sea, was chained up and enchanted in him; he had no voice, save that choking respiration through his spiracle, and this made the sight of him unspeakably pitiable; while still, in his amazing bulk, portcullis jaw, and omnipotent tail, there was enough to appal the stoutest man who so pitied.

Seeing now that but a very few moments more would give the Pequod's boats the advantage, and rather than be thus foiled of his game, Derick chose to hazard what to him must have seemed a most unusually long dart, ere the last chance would for ever escape.

But no sooner did his harpooneer stand up for the stroke, than all three tigers—Queequeg, Tashtego, Daggoo—instinctively sprang to their feet, and standing in a diagonal row, simultaneously pointed their barbs; and, darted over the head of the German harpooneer, their three Nantucket irons entered the whale. Blinding vapors of foam and white-fire! The three boats, in the first fury of the whale's headlong rush, bumped the German's aside with such force, that both Derick and his baffled harpooneer were spilled out, and sailed over by the three flying keels.

'Don't be afraid, my butter-boxes,' cried Stubb, casting a passing glance upon them as he shot by; 'ye'll be picked up presently— all right—I saw some sharks astern—St Bernard's dogs, you know— relieve distressed travellers. Hurrah! this is the way to sail now. Every keel a sun-beam! Hurrah!—Here we go like three tin kettles at the tail of a mad cougar! This puts me in mind of fastening to an elephant in a tilbury on a plain—makes the wheel-spokes fly, boys, when you fasten to him that way; and there's danger of being pitched out too, when you strike a hill. Hurrah! this is the way a fellow feels when he's going to Davy Jones—all a rush down an endless inclined plane! Hurrah! this whale carries the everlasting mail!'

But the monster's run was a brief one. Giving a sudden gasp, he tumultuously sounded. With a grating rush, the three lines flew round the loggerheads with such a force as to gouge deep grooves in them; while so fearful were the harpooneers that this rapid sounding would soon exhaust the lines, that using all their dexterous might, they caught repeated smoking turns with the rope to hold on; till at last—owing to the perpendicular strain from the lead-lined chocks of the boats, whence the three ropes went straight down into the blue—the gunwales of the bows were almost even with the water, while the three sterns tilted high in the air. And the whale soon ceasing to sound, for some time they remained in that attitude, fearful of expending more line, though the position was a little ticklish. But though boats have been taken down and lost in this way, yet it is this 'holding on', as it is called; this hooking up by the sharp barbs of his live flesh from the back; this it is that often torments the Leviathan into soon rising again to meet the sharp lance of his foes. Yet not to speak of the peril of the thing, it is to be doubted whether this course is always the best; for it is but reasonable to presume, that the longer the stricken whale stays under water, the more he is exhausted. Because, owing to the enormous surface of him—in a full grown sperm whale something less than 2000 square feet—the pressure of the water is immense. We all know what an astonishing atmospheric weight we ourselves stand up under; even here, aboveground, in the air; how vast, then, the burden of a whale, bearing on his back a column of two hundred fathoms of ocean! It must at least equal the weight of fifty atmospheres. One whaleman has estimated it at the weight of twenty line-of-battle ships, with all their guns, and stores, and men on board.

As the three boats lay there on that gently rolling sea, gazing down into its eternal blue noon; and as not a single groan or cry of any sort, nay, not so much as a ripple or a bubble came up from its depths; what landsman would have thought, that beneath all that silence and placidity, the utmost monster of the seas was writhing and wrenching in agony! Not eight inches of perpendicular rope were visible at the bows. Seems it credible that by three such thin threads the great Leviathan was suspended like the big weight to an eight day clock. Suspended? and to what? To three bits of board. Is this the creature of whom it was once so triumphantly said—'Canst thou fill his skin with barbed irons? or his head with fish-spears? The sword of him that layeth at him cannot hold, the spear, the dart, nor the habergeon: he esteemeth iron as straw; the arrow cannot make him flee; darts are counted as stubble; he laugheth at the shaking of a spear!' This the creature? this he? Oh! that unfulfilments should follow the prophets. For with the strength of a thousand thighs in his tail, Leviathan had run his head under the mountains of the sea, to hide him from the Pequod's fish-spears!

In that sloping afternoon sunlight, the shadows that the three boats sent down beneath the surface, must have been long enough and broad enough to shade half Xerxes' army. Who can tell how appalling to the wounded whale must have been such huge phantoms flitting over his head!

'Stand by, men; he stirs,' cried Starbuck, as the three lines suddenly vibrated in the water, distinctly conducting upwards to them, as by magnetic wires, the life and death throbs of the whale, so that every oarsman felt them in his seat. The next moment, relieved in great part from the downward strain at the bows, the boats gave a sudden bounce upwards, as a small ice-field will, when a dense herd of white bears are scared from it into the sea.

'Haul in! Haul in!' cried Starbuck again; 'he's rising.'

The lines, of which, hardly an instant before, not one hand's breadth could have been gained, were now in long quick coils flung back all dripping into the boats, and soon the whale broke water within two ship's lengths of the hunters.

His motions plainly denoted his extreme exhaustion. In most land animals there are certain valves or flood-gates in many of their veins, whereby when wounded, the blood is in some degree at least instantly shut off in certain directions. Not so with the whale; one of whose peculiarities it is, to have an entire non-valvular structure of the blood vessels, so that when pierced even by so small a point as a harpoon, a deadly drain is at once begun upon his whole arterial system; and when this is heightened by the extraordinary pressure of water at a great distance below the surface, his life may be said to pour from him in incessant streams. Yet so vast is the quantity of blood in him, and so distant and numerous its interior fountains, that he will keep thus bleeding and bleeding for a considerable period; even as in a drought a river will flow, whose source is in the well-springs of far-off and undiscernible hills. Even now, when the boats pulled upon this whale, and perilously drew over his swaying flukes, and the lances were darted into him, they were followed by steady jets from the new made wound, which kept continually playing, while the natural spout-hole in his head was only at intervals, however rapid, sending its affrighted moisture into the air. From this last vent no blood yet came, because no vital part of him had thus far been struck. His life, as they significantly call it, was untouched.

As the boats now more closely surrounded him, the whole upper part of his form, with much of it that is ordinarily submerged, was plainly revealed. His eyes, or rather the places where his eyes had been, were beheld. As strange misgrown masses gather in the knot-holes of the noblest oaks when prostrate, so from the points which the whale's eyes had once occupied, now protruded blind bulbs, horribly pitiable to see. But pity there was none. For all his old age, and his one arm, and his blind eyes, he must die the death and be murdered, in order to light the gay bridals and other merry-makings of men, and also to illuminate the solemn churches that preach unconditional inoffensiveness by all to all. Still rolling in his blood, at last he partially disclosed a strangely discolored bunch or protuberance, the size of a bushel, low down on the flank.

'A nice spot,' cried Flask; 'just let me prick him there once.'

'Avast!' cried Starbuck, 'there's no need of that!'

But humane Starbuck was too late. At the instant of the dart an ulcerous jet shot from this cruel wound, and goaded by it into more than sufferable anguish, the whale now spouting thick blood, with swift fury blindly darted at the craft, bespattering them and their glorying crews all over with showers of gore, capsizing Flask's boat and marring the bows. It was his death stroke. For, by this time, so spent was he by loss of blood, that he helplessly rolled away from the wreck he had made; lay panting on his side, impotently flapped with his stumped fin, then over and over slowly revolved like a waning world; turned up the white secrets of his belly; lay like a log, and died. It was most piteous, that last expiring spout. As when by unseen hands the water is gradually drawn off from some mighty fountain, and with half-stifled melancholy gur-glings the spray-column lowers and lowers to the ground—so the last long dying spout of the whale.

Soon, while the crews were awaiting the arrival of the ship, the body showed symptoms of sinking with all its treasures unrifled. Immediately, by Starbuck's orders, lines were secured to it at different points, so that ere long every boat was a buoy; the sunken whale being suspended a few inches beneath them by the cords. By very heedful management, when the ship drew nigh, the whale was transferred to her side, and was strongly secured there by the stiffest fluke-chains, for it was plain that unless artificially upheld, the body would at once sink to the bottom.

It so chanced that almost upon first cutting into him with the spade, the entire length of a corroded harpoon was found imbedded in his flesh, on the lower part of the bunch before described. But as the stumps of harpoons are frequently found in the dead bodies of captured whales, with the flesh perfectly healed around them, and no prominence of any kind to denote their place; therefore, there must needs have been some other unknown reason in the present case fully to account for the ulceration alluded to. But still more curious was the fact of a lance-head of stone being found in him, not far from the buried iron, the flesh perfectly firm about them. Who had darted that stone lance? And when? It might have been darted by some Nor' West Indian long before America was discovered.

What other marvels might have been rummaged out of this monstrous cabinet there is no telling. But a sudden stop was put to further discoveries, by the ship's being unprecedently dragged over sideways to the sea, owing to the body's immensely increasing tendency to sink. However, Starbuck, who had the ordering of affairs, hung on to it to the last; hung on to it so resolutely, indeed, that when at length the ship would have been capsized, if still persisting in locking arms with the body; then, when the command was given to break clear from it, such was the immovable strain upon the timber-heads to which the fluke-chains and cables were fastened, that it was impossible to cast them off. Meantime everything in the Pequod was aslant. To cross to the other side of the deck was like walking up the steep gabled roof of a house. The ship groaned and gasped. Many of the ivory inlayings of her bulwarks and cabins were started from their places, by the unnatural dislocation. In vain handspikes and crows were brought to bear upon the immovable fluke-chains, to pry them adrift from the timber-heads; and so low had the whale now settled that the submerged ends could not be at all approached, while every moment whole tons of ponderosity seemed added to the sinking bulk, and the ship seemed on the point of going over.

'Hold on, hold on, won't ye?' cried Stubb to the body, 'don't be in such a devil of a hurry to sink! By thunder, men, we must do something or go for it. No use prying there; avast, I say with your handspikes, and run one of ye for a prayer book and a pen-knife, and cut the big chains.'

'Knife? Aye, aye,' cried Queequeg, and seizing the carpenter's heavy hatchet, he leaned out of a porthole, and steel to iron, began slashing at the largest fluke-chains. But a few strokes, full of sparks, were given, when the exceeding strain effected the rest. With a terrific snap, every fastening went adrift; the ship righted, the carcase sank.

Now, this occasional inevitable sinking of the recently killed Sperm Whale is a very curious thing; nor has any fisherman yet adequately accounted for it. Usually the dead Sperm Whale floats with great buoyancy, with its side or belly considerably elevated above the surface. If the only whales that thus sank were old, meagre, and broken-hearted creatures, their pads of lard diminished and all their bones heavy and rheumatic; then you might with some reason assert that this sinking is caused by an uncommon specific gravity in the fish so sinking, consequent upon this absence of buoyant matter in him. But it is not so. For young whales, in the highest health, and swelling with noble aspirations, prematurely cut off in the warm flush and May of life, with all their panting lard about them; even these brawny, buoyant heroes do sometimes sink.

Be it said, however, that the Sperm Whale is far less liable to this accident than any other species. Where one of that sort goes down, twenty Right Whales do. This difference in the species is no doubt imputable in no small degree to the greater quantity of bone in the Right Whale; his Venetian blinds alone sometimes weighing more than a ton; from this incumbrance the Sperm Whale is wholly free. But there are instances where, after the lapse of many hours or several days, the sunken whale again rises, more buoyant than in life. But the reason of this is obvious. Gases are generated in him; he swells to a prodigious magnitude; becomes a sort of animal balloon. A line-of-battle ship could hardly keep him under then. In the Shore Whaling, on soundings, among the Bays of New Zealand, when a Right Whale gives token of sinking, they fasten buoys to him, with plenty of rope; so that when the body has gone down, they know where to look for it when it shall have ascended again.

It was not long after the sinking of the body that a cry was heard from the Pequod's mast-heads, announcing that the Jungfrau was again lowering her boats; though the only spout in sight was that of a Fin-Back, belonging to the species of uncapturable whales, because of its incredible power of swimming. Nevertheless, the Fin-Back's spout is so similar to the Sperm Whale's, that by unskillful fishermen it is often mistaken for it. And consequently Derick and all his host were now in valiant chase of this uncapturable brute. The Virgin crowding all sail, made after her four young keels, and thus they all disappeared far to leeward, still in bold, hopeful chase.

Oh! many are the Fin-Backs, and many are the Dericks, my friend.

82

THE HONOR AND GLORY
OF WHALING

THERE are some enterprises in which a careful disorderliness is the true method.

The more I dive into this matter of whaling, and push my researches up to the very spring-head of it, so much the more am I impressed with its great honorableness and antiquity; and especially when I find so many great demi-gods and heroes, prophets of all sorts, who one way or other have shed distinction upon it, I am transported with the reflection that I myself belong, though but subordinately, to so emblazoned a fraternity.

The gallant Perseus, a son of Jupiter, was the first whaleman; and to the eternal honor of our calling be it said, that the first whale attacked by our brotherhood was not killed with any sordid intent. Those were the knightly days of our profession, when we only bore arms to succor the distressed, and not to fill men's lamp-feeders. Every one knows the fine story of Perseus and Andromeda; how the lovely Andromeda, the daughter of a king, was tied to a rock on the sea-coast, and as Leviathan was in the very act of carrying her off, Perseus, the prince of whalemen, intrepidly advancing, harpooned the monster, and delivered and married the maid. It was an admirable artistic exploit, rarely achieved by the best harpooneers of the present day; inasmuch as this Leviathan was slain at the very first dart. And let no man doubt this Arkite story; for in the ancient Joppa, now Jaffa, on the Syrian coast, in one of the Pagan temples, there stood for many ages the vast skeleton of a whale, which the city's legends and all the inhabitants asserted to be the identical bones of the monster that Perseus slew. When the Romans took Joppa, the same skeleton was carried to Italy in triumph. What seems most singular and suggestively important in this story, is this: it was from Joppa that Jonah set sail.

Akin to the adventure of Perseus and Andromeda—indeed, by some supposed to be indirectly derived from it—is that famous story of St George and the Dragon; which dragon I maintain to

have been a whale; for in many old chronicles whales and dragons
are strangely jumbled together, and often stand for each other.
'Thou art as a lion of the waters, and as a dragon of the sea,'
saith Ezekiel; hereby, plainly meaning a whale; in truth, some
versions of the Bible use that word itself. Besides, it would much
subtract from the glory of the exploit had St George but encountered a crawling reptile of the land, instead of doing battle with
the great monster of the deep. Any man may kill a snake, but
only a Perseus, a St George, a Coffin, have the heart in them to
march boldly up to a whale.

Let not the modern paintings of this scene mislead us; for
though the creature encountered by that valiant whaleman of old
is vaguely represented of a griffin-like shape, and though the battle
is depicted on land and the saint on horseback, yet considering
the great ignorance of those times, when the true form of the
whale was unknown to artists; and considering that as in Perseus'
case, St George's whale might have crawled up out of the sea on
the beach; and considering that the animal ridden by St George
might have been only a large seal, or sea-horse; bearing all this
in mind, it will not appear altogether incompatible with the sacred
legend and the ancientest draughts of the scene, to hold this so-
called dragon no other than the great Leviathan himself. In fact,
placed before the strict and piercing truth, this whole story will
fare like that fish, flesh, and fowl idol of the Philistines, Dragon
by name; who being planted before the ark of Israel, his horse's
head and both the palms of his hands fell off from him, and only
the stump or fishy part of him remained. Thus, then, one of our
own noble stamp, even a whaleman, is the tutelary guardian of
England; and by good rights, we harpooneers of Nantucket should
be enrolled in the most noble order of St George. And therefore,
let not the knights of that honorable company (none of whom,
I venture to say, have ever had to do with a whale like their great
patron), let them never eye a Nantucketer with disdain, since even
in our woollen frocks and tarred trowsers we are much better
entitled to St George's decoration than they.

Whether to admit Hercules among us or not, concerning this
I long remained dubious: for though according to the Greek
mythologies, that antique Crockett and Kit Carson—that brawny
doer of rejoicing good deeds, was swallowed down and thrown
up by a whale; still, whether that strictly makes a whaleman of
him, that might be mooted. It nowhere appears that he ever
actually harpooned his fish, unless, indeed, from the inside. Nevertheless, he may be deemed a sort of involuntary whaleman; at

any rate the whale caught him, if he did not the whale. I claim
him for one of our clan.

But, by the best contradictory authorities, this Grecian story of
Hercules and the whale is considered to be derived from the still
more ancient Hebrew story of Jonah and the whale; and vice
versa; certainly they are very similar. If I claim the demigod then,
why not the prophet?

Nor do heroes, saints, demigods, and prophets alone comprise
the whole roll of our order. Our grand master is still to be named;
for like royal kings of old times, we find the head-waters of our
fraternity in nothing short of the great gods themselves. That
wondrous oriental story is now to be rehearsed from the Shaster,
which gives us the dread Vishnoo, one of the three persons in
the godhead of the Hindoos; gives us this divine Vishnoo himself
for our Lord;—Vishnoo, who, by the first of his ten earthly
incarnations, has for ever set apart and sanctified the whale. When
Brahma, or the God of Gods, saith the Shaster, resolved to recreate
the world after one of its periodical dissolutions, he gave birth to
Vishnoo, to preside over the work; but the Vedas, or mystical
books, whose perusal would seem to have been indispensable to
Vishnoo before beginning the creation, and which therefore must
have contained something in the shape of practical hints to young
architects, these Vedas were lying at the bottom of the waters; so
Vishnoo became incarnate in a whale, and sounding down in him
to the uttermost depths, rescued the sacred volumes. Was not this
Vishnoo a whaleman, then? even as a man who rides a horse is
called a horseman?

Perseus, St George, Hercules, Jonah, and Vishnoo! there's a
member-roll for you! What club but the whaleman's can head off
like that?

83

JONAH HISTORICALLY REGARDED

REFERENCE was made to the historical story of Jonah and the
whale in the preceding chapter. Now some Nantucketers rather
distrust this historical story of Jonah and the whale. But then
there were some sceptical Greeks and Romans, who, standing out
from the orthodox pagans of their times, equally doubted the story
of Hercules and the whale, and Arion and the dolphin; and yet

their doubting those traditions did not make those traditions one whit the less facts, for all that.

One old Sag-Harbor whaleman's chief reason for questioning the Hebrew story was this:—He had one of those quaint old-fashioned Bibles, embellished with curious, unscientific plates; one of which represented Jonah's whale with two spouts in his head— a peculiarity only true with respect to a species of the Leviathan (the Right Whale, and the varieties of that order), concerning which the fishermen have this saying, 'A penny roll would choke him;' his swallow is so very small. But, to this, Bishop Jebb's anticipative answer is ready. It is not necessary, hints the Bishop, that we consider Jonah as tombed in the whale's belly, but as temporarily lodged in some part of his mouth. And this seems reasonable enough in the good Bishop. For truly, the Right Whale's mouth would accommodate a couple of whist-tables, and comfortably seat all the players. Possibly, too, Jonah might have ensconced himself in a hollow tooth; but, on second thoughts, the Right Whale is toothless.

Another reason which Sag-Harbor (he went by that name) urged for his want of faith in this matter of the prophet, was something obscurely in reference to his incarcerated body and the whale's gastric juices. But this objection likewise falls to the ground, because a German exegetist supposes that Jonah must have taken refuge in the floating body of a *dead* whale—even as the French soldiers in the Russian campaign turned their dead horses into tents, and crawled into them. Besides, it has been divined by other continental commentators, that when Jonah was thrown overboard from the Joppa ship, he straightway effected his escape to another vessel near by, some vessel with a whale for a figure-head; and, I would add, possibly called 'The Whale,' as some craft are nowadays christened the 'Shark,' the 'Gull,' the 'Eagle.' Nor have there been wanting learned exegetists who have opined that the whale mentioned in the book of Jonah merely meant a life-preserver—an inflated bag of wind—which the endangered prophet swam to, and so was saved from a watery doom. Poor Sag-Harbor, therefore, seems worsted all round. But he had still another reason for his want of faith. It was this, if I remember right: Jonah was swallowed by the whale in the Mediterranean Sea, and after three days he was vomited up somewhere within three days' journey of Nineveh, a city on the Tigris, very much more than three days' journey across from the nearest point of the Mediterranean coast. How is that?

But was there no other way for the whale to land the prophet within that short distance of Nineveh? Yes. He might have carried him round by the way of the Cape of Good Hope. But not to speak of the passage through the whole length of the Mediterranean, and another passage up the Persian Gulf and Red Sea, such a supposition would involve the complete circumnavigation of all Africa in three days, not to speak of the Tigris waters, near the site of Nineveh, being too shallow for any whale to swim in. Besides, this idea of Jonah's weathering the Cape of Good Hope at so early a day would wrest the honor of the discovery of that great headland from Bartholomew Diaz, its reputed discoverer, and so make modern history a liar.

But all these foolish arguments of old Sag-Harbor only evinced his foolish pride of reason—a thing still more reprehensible in him, seeing that he had but little learning except what he had picked up from the sun and the sea. I say it only shows his foolish, impious pride, and abominable, devilish rebellion against the reverend clergy. For by a Portuguese Catholic priest, this very idea of Jonah's going to Nineveh via the Cape of Good Hope was advanced as a signal magnification of the general miracle. And so it was. Besides, to this day, the highly enlightened Turks devoutly believe in the historical story of Jonah. And some three centuries ago, an English traveller in old Harris's Voyages, speaks of a Turkish Mosque built in honor of Jonah, in which mosque was a miraculous lamp that burnt without any oil.

84

PITCHPOLING

To make them run easily and swiftly, the axles of carriages are anointed; and for much the same purpose, some whalers perform an analogous operation upon their boat; they grease the bottom. Nor is it to be doubted that as such a procedure can do no harm, it may possibly be of no contemptible advantage; considering that oil and water are hostile; that oil is a sliding thing, and that the object in view is to make the boat slide bravely. Queequeg believed strongly in anointing his boat, and one morning not long after the German ship Jungfrau disappeared, took more than customary pains in that occupation; crawling under its bottom, where it hung over the side, and rubbing in the unctuousness as though diligently seeking to insure a crop of hair from the craft's bald keel. He seemed to be working in obedience to some particular presentiment. Nor did it remain unwarranted by the event.

Towards noon whales were raised; but so soon as the ship sailed down to them, they turned and fled with swift precipitancy; a disordered flight, as of Cleopatra's barges from Actium.

Nevertheless, the boats pursued, and Stubb's was foremost. By great exertion, Tashtego at last succeeded in planting one iron; but the stricken whale, without at all sounding, still continued his horizontal flight, with added fleetness. Such unintermitted strainings upon the planted iron must sooner or later inevitably extract it. It became imperative to lance the flying whale, or be content to lose him. But to haul the boat up to his flank was impossible, he swam so fast and furious. What then remained?

Of all the wondrous devices and dexterities, the sleights of hand and countless subtleties, to which the veteran whaleman is so often forced, none exceed that fine manœuvre with the lance called pitchpoling. Small sword, or broad sword, in all its exercises boasts nothing like it. It is only indispensable with an inveterate running whale; its grand fact and feature is the wonderful distance to which the long lance is accurately darted from a violently rocking, jerking boat, under extreme headway. Steel and wood included, the entire spear is some ten or twelve feet in length; the staff is much slighter than that of the harpoon, and also of a lighter material—pine. It is furnished with a small rope called a warp, of considerable length, by which it can be hauled back to the hand after darting.

But before going further, it is important to mention here, that though the harpoon may be pitchpoled in the same way with the lance, yet it is seldom done; and when done, is still less frequently successful, on account of the greater weight and inferior length of the harpoon as compared with the lance, which in effect become serious drawbacks. As a general thing, therefore, you must first get fast to a whale, before any pitchpoling comes into play.

Look now at Stubb, a man who from his humorous, deliberate coolness and equanimity in the direst emergencies, was specially qualified to excel in pitchpoling. Look at him; he stands upright in the tosssed bow of the flying boat; wrapt in fleecy foam, the towing whale is forty feet ahead. Handling the long lance lightly, glancing twice or thrice along its length to see if it be exactly straight, Stubb whistlingly gathers up the coil of the warp in one hand, so as to secure its free end in his grasp, leaving the rest unobstructed. Then holding the lance full before his waistband's middle, he levels it at the whale; when, covering him with it, he steadily depresses the butt-end in his hand, thereby elevating the point till the weapon stands fairly balanced upon his palm, fifteen feet in the air. He minds you somewhat of a juggler, balancing a long staff on his chin. Next moment with a rapid, nameless impulse, in a superb lofty arch the bright steel spans the foaming distance, and quivers in the life spot of the whale. Instead of sparkling water, he now spouts red blood.

'That drove the spigot out of him!' cries Stubb. ' 'Tis July's immortal Fourth; all fountains must run wine to-day! Would now, it were old Orleans whiskey, or old Ohio, or unspeakable old Monongahela! Then, Tashtego, lad, I'd have ye hold a canakin to the jet, and we'd drink round it! Yea, verily, hearts alive, we'd brew choice punch in the spread of his spout-hole there, and from that live punch-bowl quaff the living stuff!'

Again and again to such gamesome talk, the dexterous dart is repeated, the spear returning to its master like a greyhound held in skilful leash. The agonized whale goes into his flurry; the tow-line is slackened, and the pitchpoler dropping astern, folds his hands, and mutely watches the monster die.

85

THE FOUNTAIN

THAT for six thousand years—and no one knows how many millions of ages before—the great whales should have been spouting all over the sea, and sprinkling and mistifying the gardens of the deep, as with so many sprinkling or mistifying pots; and that for some centuries back, thousands of hunters should have been close by the fountain of the whale, watching these sprinklings and spoutings—that all this should be, and yet, that down to this blessed minute (fifteen and a quarter minutes past one o'clock P.M. of this sixteenth day of December, A.D. 1850), it should still remain a problem, whether these spoutings are, after all, really water, or nothing but vapor—this is surely a noteworthy thing.

Let us, then, look at this matter, along with some interesting items contingent. Every one knows that by the peculiar cunning of their gills, the finny tribes in general breathe the air which at all times is combined with the element in which they swim hence, a herring or a cod might live a century, and never once raises its head above the surface. But owing to his marked internal structure which gives him regular lungs, like a human being's, the whale can only live by inhaling the disengaged air in the open atmosphere. Wherefore the necessity for his periodical visits to the upper world. But he cannot in any degree breathe through his mouth, for, in his ordinary attitude, the Sperm Whale's mouth is buried at least eight feet beneath the surface; and what is still more, his windpipe has no connexion with his mouth. No, he breathes through his spiracle alone; and this is on the top of his head.

If I say, that in any creature breathing is only a function indispensable to vitality, inasmuch as it withdraws from the air a certain element, which being subsequently brought into contact with the blood imparts to the blood its vivifying principle, I do not think I shall err; though I may possibly use some superfluous scientific words. Assume it, and it follows that if all the blood in a man could be aerated with one breath, he might then seal up his nostrils and not fetch another for a considerable time. That is to say, he would then live without breathing. Anomalous as it may seem, this is precisely the case with the whale, who systematically lives, by intervals, his full hour and more (when at the bottom) without drawing a single breath, or so much as in any way inhaling a particle of air; for, remember, he has no gills. How is this? Between his ribs and on each side of his spine he is supplied with a remarkable involved Cretan labyrinth of vermicelli-like vessels, which vessels, when he quits the surface, are completely distended with oxygenated blood. So that for an hour or more, a thousand fathoms in the sea, he carries a surplus stock of vitality in him, just as the camel crossing the waterless desert carries a surplus supply of drink for future use in its four supplementary stomachs. The anatomical fact of this labyrinth is indisputable; and that the supposition founded upon it is reasonable and true, seems the more cogent to me, when I consider the otherwise inexplicable obstinacy of that leviathan in *having his spoutings out*, as the fishermen phrase it. This is what I mean. If unmolested, upon rising to the surface, the Sperm Whale will continue there for a period of time exactly uniform with all his other unmolested risings. Say he stays eleven minutes, and jets seventy times, that is, respires seventy breaths; then whenever he rises again, he will be sure to have his seventy breaths over again, to a minute. Now, if after he fetches a few breaths you alarm him, so that he sounds, he will be always dodging up again to make good his regular allowance of air. And not till those seventy breaths are told, will he finally go down to stay out his full term below. Remark, however, that in different individuals these rates are different; but in any one they are alike. Now, why should the whale thus insist upon having his spoutings out, unless it be to replenish his reservoir of air, ere descending for good? How obvious is it, too, that this necessity for the whale's rising exposes him to all the fatal hazards of the chase. For not by hook or by net could this vast leviathan be caught, when sailing a thousand fathoms beneath the sunlight. Not so much thy skill, then, O hunter, as the great necessities, that strike the victory to thee!

In man, breathing is incessantly going on—one breath only serving for two or three pulsations; so that whatever other business he has to attend to, waking or sleeping, breathe he must, or die he will. But the Sperm Whale only breathes about one seventh or Sunday of his time.

It has been said that the whale only breathes through his spouthole; if it could truthfully be added that his spouts are mixed with water, then I opine we should be furnished with the reason why his sense of smell seems obliterated in him; for the only thing about him that at all answers to his nose is that identical spouthole; and being so clogged with two elements, it could not be expected to have the power of smelling. But owing to the mystery of the spout—whether it be water or whether it be vapor—no absolute certainty can as yet be arrived at on this head. Sure it is, nevertheless, that the Sperm Whale has no proper olfactories. But what does he want of them? No roses, no violets, no Cologne-water in the sea.

Furthermore, as his windpipe solely opens into the tube of his spouting canal, and as that long canal—like the grand Erie Canal—is furnished with a sort of locks (that open and shut) for the downward retention of air or the upward exclusion of water, therefore the whale has no voice, unless you insult him by saying, that when he so strangely rumbles, he talks through his nose. But then again, what has the whale to say? Seldom have I known any profound being that had anything to say to this world, unless forced to stammer out something by way of getting a living. Oh! happy that the world is such an excellent listener!

Now, the spouting canal of the Sperm Whale, chiefly intended as it is for the conveyance of air, and for several feet laid along, horizontally, just beneath the upper surface of his head, and a little to one side; this curious canal is very much like a gas-pipe laid down in a city on one side of a street. But the question returns whether this gas-pipe is also a water-pipe; in other words, whether the spout of the Sperm Whale is the mere vapor of the exhaled breath, or whether that exhaled breath is mixed with water taken in at the mouth, and discharged through the spiracle. It is certain that the mouth indirectly communicates with the spouting canal; but it cannot be proved that this is for the purpose of discharging water through the spiracle. Because the greatest necessity for so doing would seem to be, when in feeding he accidentally takes in water. But the Sperm Whale's food is far beneath the surface, and there he cannot spout even if he would. Besides, if you regard him very closely, and time him with your watch, you will find that when unmolested, there is an undeviating rhyme between the periods of his jets and the ordinary periods of respiration.

But why pester one with all this reasoning on the subject? Speak out! You have seen him spout; then declare what the spout is; can you not tell water from air? My dear sir, in this world it is not so easy to settle these plain things. I have ever found your plain things the knottiest of all. And as for this whale spout, you might almost stand in it, and yet be undecided as to what it is precisely.

The central body of it is hidden in the snowy sparkling mist enveloping it; and how can you certainly tell whether any water falls from it, when, always, when you are close enough to a whale to get a close view of his spout, he is in a prodigious commotion, the water cascading all around him. And if at such times you should think that you really perceived drops of moisture in the spout, how do you know that they are not merely condensed from its vapor; or how do you know that they are not those identical drops superficially lodged in the spout-hole fissure, which is countersunk into the summit of the whale's head? For even when tranquilly swimming through the mid-day sea in a calm, with his elevated hump sun-dried as a dromedary's in the desert; even then, the whale always carries a small basin of water on his head, as under a blazing sun you will sometimes see a cavity in a rock filled up with rain.

Nor is it at all prudent for the hunter to be over curious touching the precise nature of the whale spout. It will not do for him to be peering into it, and putting his face in it. You cannot go with your pitcher to this fountain and fill it, and bring it away. For even when coming into slight contact with the outer, vapory shreds of the jet, which will often happen, your skin will feverishly smart, from the acridness of the thing so touching it. And I know one, who coming into still closer contact with the spout, whether with some scientific object in view, or otherwise, I cannot say, the skin peeled off from his cheek and arm. Wherefore, among whalemen, the spout is deemed poisonous; they try to evade it. Another thing; I have heard it said, and I do not much doubt it, that if the jet is fairly spouted into your eyes, it will blind you. The wisest thing the investigator can do then, it seems to me, is to let this deadly spout alone.

Still, we can hypothesize, even if we cannot prove and establish. My hypothesis is this: that the spout is nothing but mist. And besides other reasons, to this conclusion I am impelled, by considerations touching the great inherent dignity and sublimity of the Sperm Whale; I account him no common, shallow being, inasmuch as it is an undisputed fact that he is never found on soundings, or near shores; all other whales sometimes are. He is both ponderous and profound. And I am convinced that from the heads of all ponderous profound beings, such as Plato, Pyrrho, the Devil, Jupiter, Dante, and so on, there always goes up a certain semi-visible steam, while in the act of thinking deep thoughts. While composing a little treatise on Eternity, I had the curiosity to place a mirror before me; and ere long saw reflected there, a curious involved worming and undulation in the atmosphere over my head. The invariable moisture of my hair, while plunged in deep thought, after six cups of hot tea in my thin shingled attic, of an August noon; this seems an additional argument for the above supposition.

And how nobly it raises our conceit of the mighty, misty monster, to behold him solemnly sailing through a calm tropical sea; his vast, mild head overhung by a canopy of vapor, engendered by his incommunicable contemplations, and that vapor—as you will sometimes see it—glorified by a rainbow, as if Heaven itself had put its seal upon his thoughts. For, d'ye see, rainbows do not visit the clear air; they only irradiate vapor. And so, through all the thick mists of the dim doubts in my mind, divine intuitions now and then shoot, enkindling my fog with a heavenly ray. And for this I thank God; for all have doubts; many deny; but doubts or denials, few along with them, have intuitions. Doubts of all things earthly, and intuitions of some things heavenly; this combination makes neither believer nor infidel, but makes a man who regards them both with equal eye.

86
THE TAIL

OTHER poets have warbled the praises of the soft eye of the antelope, and the lovely plumage of the bird that never alights; less celestial, I celebrate a tail.

Reckoning the largest sized Sperm Whale's tail to begin at that point of the trunk where it tapers to about the girth of a man, it comprises upon its upper surface alone, an area of at least fifty square feet. The compact round body of its root expands into two broad, firm, flat palms or flukes, gradually shoaling away to less than an inch in thickness. At the crotch or junction, these flukes slightly overlap, then sideways recede from each other like wings, leaving a wide vacancy between. In no living thing are the lines of beauty more exquisitely defined than in the crescentic borders of these flukes. At its utmost expansion in the full grown whale, the tail will considerably exceed twenty feet across.

The entire member seems a dense webbed bed of welded sinews; but cut into it, and you find that three distinct strata compose it:—upper, middle, and lower. The fibres in the upper and lower layers, are long and horizontal; those of the middle one, very short, and running crosswise between the outside layers. This triune structure, as much as anything else, imparts power to the tail. To the student of old Roman walls, the middle layer will furnish a curious parallel to the thin course of tiles always alternating with the stone in those wonderful relics of the antique, and which undoubtedly contribute so much to the great strength of the masonry.

But as if this vast local power in the tendinous tail were not enough, the whole bulk of the leviathan is knit over with a warp and woof of muscular fibres and filaments, which passing on either side the loins and running down into the flukes, insensibly blend with them, and largely contribute to their might; so that in the tail the confluent measureless force of the whole whale seems concentrated to a point. Could annihilation occur to matter, this were the thing to do it.

Nor does this—its amazing strength, at all tend to cripple the graceful flexion of its motions; where infantileness of ease undulates through a Titanism of power. On the contrary, those motions

derive their most appalling beauty from it. Real strength never
impairs beauty or harmony, but it often bestows it; and in everything imposingly beautiful, strength has much to do with the
magic. Take away the tied tendons that all over seem bursting
from the marble in the carved Hercules, and its charm would be
gone. As devout Eckerman lifted the linen sheet from the naked
corpse of Goethe, he was overwhelmed with the massive chest of
the man, that seemed as a Roman triumphal arch. When Angelo
paints even God the Father in human form, mark what robustness
is there. And whatever they may reveal of the divine love in the
Son, the soft, curled, hermaphroditical Italian pictures, in which
his idea has been most successfully embodied; these pictures, so
destitute as they are of all brawniness, hint nothing of any power,
but the mere negative, feminine one of submission and endurance,
which on all hands it is conceded, form the peculiar practical
virtues of his teachings.

Such is the subtle elasticity of the organ I treat of, that whether
wielded in sport, or in earnest, or in anger, whatever be the mood
it be in, its flexions are invariably marked by exceeding grace.
Therein no fairy's arm can transcend it.

Five great motions are peculiar to it. First, when used as a fin
for progression; Second, when used as a mace in battle; Third, in
sweeping; Fourth, in lobtailing; Fifth, in peaking flukes.

First: Being horizontal in its position, the Leviathan's tail acts
in a different manner from the tails of all other sea creatures. It
never wriggles. In man or fish, wriggling is a sign of inferiority.
To the whale, his tail is the sole means of propulsion. Scroll-wise
coiled forwards beneath the body, and then rapidly sprung backwards, it is this which gives that singular darting, leaping motion
to the monster when furiously swimming. His side-fins only serve
to steer by.

Second: It is a little significant, that while one sperm whale only
fights another sperm whale with his head and jaw, nevertheless,
in his conflicts with man, he chiefly and contemptuously uses his
tail. In striking at a boat, he swiftly curves away his flukes from
it, and the blow is only inflicted by the recoil. If it be made in
the unobstructed air, especially if it descend to its mark, the stroke
is then simply irresistible. No ribs of man or boat can withstand
it. Your only salvation lies in eluding it; but if it comes sideways
through the opposing water, then partly owing to the light buoyancy
of the whale-boat, and the elasticity of its materials, a cracked rib
or a dashed plank or two, a sort of stitch in the side, is generally
the most serious result. These submerged side blows are so often

received in the fishery, that they are accounted mere child's play. Some one strips off a frock, and the hole is stopped.

Third: I cannot demonstrate it, but it seems to me, that in the whale the sense of touch is concentrated in the tail; for in this respect there is a delicacy in it only equalled by the daintiness of the elephant's trunk. This delicacy is chiefly evinced in the action of sweeping, when in maidenly gentleness the whale with a certain soft slowness moves his immense flukes from side to side upon the surface of the sea; and if he feel but a sailor's whisker, woe to that sailor, whiskers and all. What tenderness there is in that preliminary touch! Had this tail any prehensile power, I should straightway bethink me of Darmonodes' elephant that so frequented the flower-market, and with low salutations presented nosegays to damsels, and then caressed their zones. On more accounts than one, a pity it is that the whale does not possess this prehensile virtue in his tail; for I have heard of yet another elephant, that when wounded in the fight, curved round his trunk and extracted the dart.

Fourth: Stealing unawares upon the whale in the fancied security of the middle of solitary seas, you find him unbent from the vast corpulence of his dignity, and kitten-like, he plays on the ocean as if it were a hearth. But still you see his power in his play. The broad palms of his tail are flirted high into the air; then smiting the surface, the thunderous concussion resounds for miles. You would almost think a great gun had been discharged; and if you noticed the light wreath of vapor from the spiracle at his other extremity, you would think that that was the smoke from the touch-hole.

Fifth: As in the ordinary floating posture of the leviathan the flukes lie considerably below the level of his back, they are then completely out of sight beneath the surface; but when he is about to plunge into the deeps, his entire flukes with at least thirty feet of his body are tossed erect in the air, and so remain vibrating a moment, till they downwards shoot out of view. Excepting the sublime *breach*—somewhere else to be described—this peaking of the whale's flukes is perhaps the grandest sight to be seen in all animated nature. Out of the bottomless profundities the gigantic tail seems spasmodically snatching at the highest heaven. So in dreams, have I seen majestic Satan thrusting forth his tormented colossal claw from the flame Baltic of Hell. But in gazing at such scenes, it is all in all what mood you are in; if in the Dantean, the devils will occur to you; if in that of Isaiah, the archangels. Standing at the mast-head of my ship during a sunrise that crimsoned sky and sea, I once saw a large herd of whales in the east, all heading towards the sun, and for a moment vibrating in concert with peaked flukes. As it seemed to me at the time, such a grand embodiment of adoration of the gods was never beheld, even in Persia, the home of the fire worshippers. As Ptolemy Philopater testified of the African elephant, I then testified of the whale, pronouncing him the most devout of all beings. For according to King Juba, the military elephants of antiquity often hailed the morning with their trunks uplifted in the profoundest silence.

The chance comparison in this chapter, between the whale and the elephant, so far as some aspects of the tail of the one and the trunk of the other are concerned, should not tend to place those two opposite organs on an equality, much less the creatures to which they respectively belong. For as the mightiest elephant is but a terrier to Leviathan, so, compared with Leviathan's tail, his trunk is but the stalk of a lily. The most direful blow from the elephant's trunk were as the playful tap of a fan, compared with the measureless crush and crash of the sperm whale's ponderous flukes, which in repeated instances have one after the other hurled entire boats with all their oars and crews into the air, very much as an Indian juggler tosses his balls.*

The more I consider this mighty tail, the more do I deplore my inability to express it. At times there are gestures in it, which, though they would well grace the hand of man, remain wholly inexplicable. In an extensive herd, so remarkable, occasionally, are these mystic gestures, that I have heard hunters who have declared them akin to Free-Mason signs and symbols; that the whale, indeed, by these methods intelligently conversed with the world. Nor are there wanting other motions of the whale in his general body, full of strangeness, and unaccountable to his most experienced assailant. Dissect him how I may, then, I but go skin deep; I know him not, and never will. But if I know not even the tail of this whale, how understand his head? much more, how comprehend his face, when face he has none? Thou shalt see my back parts, my tail, he seems to say, but my face shall not be

---

* Though all comparison in the way of general bulk between the whale and the elephant is preposterous, inasmuch as in that particular the elephant stands in much the same respect to the whale that the dog does to the elephant; nevertheless, there are not wanting some points of curious similitude; among these is the spout. It is well known that the elephant will often draw up water or dust in his trunk, and then elevating it, jet it forth in a stream.

seen. But I cannot completely make out his back parts; and hint what he will about his face, I say again he has no face.

87
THE GRAND ARMADA

THE long and narrow peninsula of Malacca, extending south-eastward from the territories of Birmah, forms the most southerly point of all Asia. In a continuous line from that peninsula stretch the long islands of Sumatra, Java, Bally, and Timor; which, with many others, form a vast mole, or rampart, lengthwise connecting Asia and Australia, and dividing the long unbroken Indian ocean from the thickly studded oriental archipelagoes. This rampart is pierced by several sally-ports for the convenience of ships and whales; conspicuous among which are the straits of Sunda and Malacca. By the straits of Sunda, chiefly, vessels bound to China from the west, emerge into the China seas.

Those narrow straits of Sunda divide Sumatra from Java; and standing midway in that vast rampart of islands, buttressed by that bold green promontory, known to seamen as Java Head; they not a little correspond to the central gateway opening into some vast walled empire: and considering the inexhaustible wealth of spices, and silks, and jewels, and gold, and ivory, with which the thousand islands of that oriental sea are enriched, it seems a significant provision of nature, that such treasures, by the very formation of the land, should at least bear the appearance, however ineffectual, of being guarded from the all-grasping western world. The shores of the Straits of Sunda are unsupplied with those domineering fortresses which guard the entrances to the Mediter-ranean, the Baltic, and the Propontis. Unlike the Danes, these Orientals do not demand the obsequious homage of lowered top-sails from the endless procession of ships before the wind, which for centuries past, by night and by day, have passed between the islands of Sumatra and Java, freighted with the costliest cargoes of the east. But while they freely waive a ceremonial like this, they do by no means renounce their claim to more solid tribute.

Time out of mind the piratical proas of the Malays, lurking among the low shaded coves and islets of Sumatra, have sallied out upon the vessels sailing through the straits, fiercely demanding tribute at the point of their spears. Though by the repeated bloody chastisements, they have received at the hands of European cruisers, the audacity of these corsairs has of late been somewhat repressed; yet, even at the present day, we occasionally hear of English and American vessels, which, in those waters, have been remorselessly boarded and pillaged.

With a fair, fresh wind, the Pequod was now drawing nigh to these straits; Ahab purposing to pass through them into the Javan sea, and thence, cruising northwards, over waters known to be frequented here and there by the Sperm Whale, sweep inshore by the Philippine Islands, and gain the far coast of Japan, in time for the great whaling season there. By these means, the circumnavigating Pequod would sweep almost all the known Sperm Whale cruising grounds of the world, previous to descending upon the Line in the Pacific; where Ahab, though everywhere else foiled in his pursuit, firmly counted upon giving battle to Moby Dick, in the sea he was most known to frequent; and at a season when he might most reasonably be presumed to be haunting it.

But how now? in this zoned quest, does Ahab touch no land? does his crew drink air? Surely, he will stop for water. Nay. For a long time, now, the circus-running sun has raced within his fiery ring, and needs no sustenance but what's in himself. So Ahab. Mark this, too, in the whaler. While other hulls are loaded down with alien stuff, to be transferred to foreign wharves; the world-wandering whale-ship carries no cargo but herself and crew, their weapons and their wants. She has a whole lake's contents bottled in her ample hold. She is ballasted with utilities; not altogether with unusable pig-lead and kentledge. She carries years' water in her. Clear old prime Nantucket water; which, when three years afloat, the Nantucketer, in the Pacific, prefers to drink before the brackish fluid, but yesterday rafted off in casks, from the Peruvian or Indian streams. Hence it is, that, while other ships may have gone to China from New York, and back again, touching at a score of ports, the whale-ship, in all that interval, may not have sighted one grain of soil; her crew having seen no man but floating seamen like themselves. So that did you carry them the news that another flood had come; they would only answer—'Well, boys, here's the ark!'

Now, as many Sperm Whales had been captured off the western coast of Java, in the near vicinity of the Straits of Sunda; indeed, as most of the ground, roundabout, was generally recognized by the fishermen as an excellent spot for cruising; therefore, as the Pequod gained more and more upon Java Head, the look-outs were repeatedly hailed, and admonished to keep wide awake. But

though the green palmy cliffs of the land soon loomed on the
starboard bow, and with delighted nostrils the fresh cinnamon was
snuffed in the air, yet not a single jet was descried. Almost
renouncing all thought of falling in with any game hereabouts,
the ship had well nigh entered the straits, when the customary
cheering cry was heard from aloft, and ere long a spectacle of
singular magnificence saluted us.

But here be it premised, that owing to the unwearied activity
with which of late they have been hunted over all four oceans,
the Sperm Whales, instead of almost invariably sailing in small
detached companies, as in former times, are now frequently met
with in extensive herds, sometimes embracing so great a multiude,
that it would almost seem as if numerous nations of them had
sworn solemn league and covenant for mutual assistance and
protection. To this aggregation of the Sperm Whale into such
immense caravans, may be imputed the circumstance that even
in the best cruising grounds, you may now sometimes sail for
weeks and months together, without being greeted by a single
spout; and then be suddenly saluted by what sometimes seems
thousands on thousands.

Broad on both bows, at the distance of some two or three miles,
and forming a great semicircle, embracing one half of the level
horizon, a continuous chain of whale-jets were up-playing and
sparkling in the noon-day air. Unlike the straight perpendicular
twin-jets of the Right Whale, which, dividing at top, fall over in
two branches, like the cleft drooping boughs of a willow, the single
forward-slanting spout of the Sperm Whale presents a thick curled
bush of white mist, continually rising and falling away to leeward.

Seen from the Pequod's deck, then, as she would rise on a high
hill of the sea, this host of vapory spouts, individually curling up
into the air, and beheld through a blending atmosphere of bluish
haze, showed like the thousand cheerful chimneys of some dense
metropolis, descried of a balmy autumnal morning, by some
horseman on a height.

As marching armies approaching an unfriendly defile in the
mountains, accelerate their march, all eagerness to place that
perilous passage in their rear, and once more expand in comparative security upon the plain; even so did this vast fleet of whales
now seem hurrying forward through the straits; gradually contracting the wings of their semicircle, and swimming on, in one
solid, but still crescentic centre.

Crowding all sail the Pequod pressed after them; the harpooneers
handling their weapons, and loudly cheering from the heads of

their yet suspended boats. If the wind only held, little doubt had they, that chased through these Straits of Sunda, the vast host would only deploy into the Oriental seas to witness the capture of not a few of their number. And who could tell whether, in that congregated caravan, Moby Dick himself might not temporarily be swimming, like the worshipped white-elephant in the coronation procession of the Siamese! So with stun-sail piled on stun-sail, we sailed along, driving these leviathans before us; when, of a sudden, the voice of Tashtego was heard, loudly directing attention to something in our wake.

Corresponding to the crescent in our van, we beheld another in our rear. It seemed formed of detached white vapors, rising and falling something like the spouts of the whales; only they did not so completely come and go; for they constantly hovered, without finally disappearing. Leveling his glass at this sight, Ahab quickly revolved in his pivot-hole, crying, 'Aloft there, and rig whips and buckets to wet the sails;—Malays, sir, and after us!'

As if too long lurking behind the headlands, till the Pequod should fairly have entered the straits, these rascally Asiatics were now in hot pursuit, to make up for their over-cautious delay. But when the swift Pequod, with a fresh leading wind, was herself in hot chase; how very kind of these tawny philanthropists to assist in speeding her on to her own chosen pursuit,—mere riding-whips and rowels to her, that they were. As with glass under arm, Ahab to-and-fro paced the deck; in his forward turn beholding the monsters he chased, and in the after one the bloodthirsty pirates chasing *him*; some such fancy as the above seemed his. And when he glanced upon the green walls of the watery defile in which the ship was then sailing, and bethought him that through that gate lay the route to his vengeance, and beheld, how that through that same gate he was now both chasing and being chased to his deadly end; and not only that, but a herd of remorseless wild pirates and inhuman atheistical devils were infernally cheering him on with their curses;—when all these conceits had passed through his brain, Ahab's brow was left gaunt and ribbed, like the black sand beach after some stormy tide has been gnawing it, without being able to drag the firm thing from its place.

But thoughts like these troubled very few of the reckless crew; and when, after steadily dropping and dropping the pirates astern, the Pequod at last shot by the vivid green Cockatoo Point on the Sumatra side, emerging at last upon the broad waters beyond; then, the harpooneers seemed more to grieve that the swift whales had been gaining upon the ship, than to rejoice that the ship had so victoriously gained upon the Malays. But still driving on in the wake of the whales, at length they seemed abating their speed; gradually the ship neared them; and the wind now dying away, word was passed to spring to the boats. But no sooner did the herd, by some presumed wonderful instinct of the Sperm Whale, become notified of the three keels that were after them,—though as yet a mile in their rear,—than they rallied again, and forming in close ranks and battalions, so that their spouts all looked like flashing lines of stacked bayonets, moved on with redoubled velocity.

Stripped to our shirts and drawers, we sprang to the white-ash, and after several hours' pulling were almost disposed to renounce the chase, when a general pausing commotion among the whales gave animating token that they were now at last under the influence of that strange perplexity of inert irresolution, which, when the fishermen perceive it in the whale, they say he is *gallied*.* The compact martial columns in which they had been hitherto rapidly and steadily swimming, were now broken up in one measureless rout; and like King Porus' elephants in the Indian battle with Alexander, they seemed going mad with consternation. In all directions expanding in vast irregular circles, and aimlessly swimming hither and thither, by their short thick spoutings, they plainly betrayed their distraction of panic. This was still more strangely evinced by those of their number, who, completely paralysed as it were, helplessly floated like water-logged dismantled ships on the sea. Had these leviathans been but a flock of simple sheep, pursued over the pasture by three fierce wolves, they could not possibly have evinced such excessive dismay. But this occasional timidity is characteristic of almost all herding creatures. Though

---

* To *gally*, or *gallow*, is to frighten excessively,—to confound with fright. It is an old Saxon word. It occurs once in Shakespere:—

> 'The wrathful skies
> *Gallow* the very wanderers of the dark,
> And make them keep their caves.'
>
> *Lear*, Act III. sc. ii.

To common land usages, the word is now completely obsolete. When the polite landsman first hears it from the gaunt Nantucketer, he is apt to set it down as one of the whaleman's self-derived savageries. Much the same is it with many other sinewy Saxonisms of this sort, which emigrated to the New-England rocks with the noble brawn of the old English emigrants in the time of the Commonwealth. Thus, some of the best and furthest-descended English words—the etymological Howards and Percys—are now democratised, nay, plebeianised—so to speak—in the New World.

banding together in tens of thousands, the lion-maned buffaloes of the West have fled before a solitary horseman. Witness, too, all human beings, how when herded together in the sheepfold of a theatre's pit, they will, at the slightest alarm of fire, rush helter-skelter for the outlets, crowding, trampling, jamming, and remorselessly dashing each other to death. Best, therefore, withhold any amazement at the strangely gallied whales before us, for there is no folly of the beasts of the earth which is not infinitely outdone by the madness of men.

Though many of the whales, as has been said, were in violent motion, yet it is to be observed that as a whole the herd neither advanced nor retreated, but collectively remained in one place. As is customary in those cases, the boats at once separated, each making for some one lone whale on the outskirts of the shoal. In about three minutes' time, Queequeg's harpoon was flung; the stricken fish darted blinding spray in our faces, and then running away with us like light, steered straight for the heart of the herd. Though such a movement on the part of the whale struck under such circumstances, is in no wise unprecedented; and indeed is almost always more or less anticipated; yet does it present one of the more perilous vicissitudes of the fishery. For as the swift monster drags you deeper and deeper into the frantic shoal, you bid adieu to circumspect life and only exist in a delirious throb.

As, blind and deaf, the whale plunged forward, as if by sheer power of speed to rid himself of the iron leech that had fastened to him; as we thus tore a white gash in the sea, on all sides menaced as we flew, by the crazed creatures to and fro rushing about us; our beset boat was like a ship mobbed by ice-isles in a tempest, and striving to steer through their complicated channels and straits, knowing not at what moment it may be locked in and crushed.

But not a bit daunted, Queequeg steered us manfully; now sheering off from this monster directly across our route in advance; now edging away from that, whose colossal flukes were suspended overhead, while all the time, Starbuck stood up in the bows, lance in hand, pricking out of our way whatever whales he could reach by short darts, for there was no time to make long ones. Nor were the oarsmen quite idle, though their wonted duty was now altogether dispensed with. They chiefly attended to the shouting part of the business. 'Out of the way, Commodore!' cried one, to a great dromedary that of a sudden rose bodily to the surface, and for an instant threatened to swamp us. 'Hard down with your tail, there!' cried a second to another, which, close to our gunwale, seemed calmly cooling himself with his own fan-like extremity.

All whaleboats carry certain curious contrivances, originally invented by the Nantucket Indians, called druggs. Two thick squares of wood of equal size are stoutly clenched together, so that they cross each other's grain at right angles; a line of considerable length is then attached to the middle of this block, and the other end of the line being looped, it can in a moment be fastened to a harpoon. It is chiefly among gallied whales that this drugg is used. For then, more whales are close round you than you can possibly chase at one time. But sperm whales are not every day encountered; while you may, then, you must kill all you can. And if you cannot kill them all at once, you must wing them, so that they can be afterwards killed at your leisure. Hence it is, that at times like these the drugg comes into requisition. Our boat was furnished with three of them. The first and second were successfully darted, and we saw the whales staggeringly running off, fettered by the enormous sidelong resistance of the towing drugg. They were cramped like malefactors with the chain and ball. But upon flinging the third, in the act of tossing overboard the clumsy wooden block, it caught under one of the seats of the boat, and in an instant tore it out and carried it away, dropping the oarsman in the boat's bottom as the seat slid from under him. On both sides the sea came in at the wounded planks, but we stuffed two or three drawers and shirts in, and so stopped the leaks for the time.

It had been next to impossible to dart these drugged harpoons, were it not that as we advanced into the herd, our whale's way greatly diminished; moreover, that as we went still further and further from the circumference of commotion, the direful disorders seemed waning. So that when at last the jerking harpoon drew out, and the towing whale sideways vanished; then, with the tapering force of his parting momentum, we glided between two whales into the innermost heart of the shoal, as if from some mountain torrent we had slid into a serene valley lake. Here the storms in the roaring glens between the outermost whales, were heard but not felt. In this central expanse the sea presented that smooth satin-like surface, called a sleek, produced by the subtle moisture thrown off by the whale in his more quiet moods. Yes, we were now in that enchanted calm which they say lurks at the heart of every commotion. And still in the distracted distance we beheld the tumults of the outer concentric circles, and saw successive pods of whales, eight or ten in each, swiftly going round and round, like multiplied spans of horses in a ring; and so closely shoulder to shoulder, that a Titanic circus-rider might easily have over-arched the middle ones, and so have gone round on their backs. Owing to the density of the crowd of reposing whales, more immediately surrounding the embayed axis of the herd, no possible chance of escape was at present afforded us. We must watch for a breach in the living wall that hemmed us in; the wall that had only admitted us in order to shut us up. Keeping at the centre of the lake, we were occasionally visited by small tame cows and calves; the women and children of this routed host.

Now, inclusive of the occasional wide intervals between the revolving outer circles, and inclusive of the spaces between the various pods in any one of those circles, the entire area at this juncture, embraced by the whole multitude, must have contained at least two or three square miles. At any rate—though indeed such a test at such a time might be deceptive—spoutings might be discovered from our low boat that seemed playing up almost from the rim of the horizon. I mention this circumstance, because, as if the cows and calves had been purposely locked up in this innermost fold; and as if the wide extent of the herd had hitherto prevented them from learning the precise cause of its stopping; or, possibly, being so young, unsophisticated, and every way innocent and inexperienced; however it may have been, these smaller whales—now and then visiting our becalmed boat from the margin of the lake—evinced a wondrous fearlessness and confidence, or else a still, becharmed panic which it was impossible not to marvel at. Like household dogs they came snuffling round us, right up to our gunwales, and touching them; till it almost seemed that some spell had suddenly domesticated them. Queequeg patted their foreheads; Starbuck scratched their backs with his lance; but fearful of the consequences, for the time refrained from darting it.

But far beneath this wondrous world upon the surface, another and still stranger world met our eyes as we gazed over the side. For, suspended in those watery vaults, floated the forms of the nursing mothers of the whales, and those that by their enormous girth seemed shortly to become mothers. The lake, as I have hinted, was to a considerable depth exceedingly transparent; and as human infants while suckling will calmly and fixedly gaze away from the breast, as if leading two different lives at the time; and while yet drawing mortal nourishment, be still spiritually feasting upon some unearthly reminiscence;—even so did the young of these whales seem looking up towards us, but not at us, as if we were but a bit of Gulf-weed in their new-born sight. Floating on their sides, the mothers also seemed quietly eyeing us. One of these little infants, that from certain queer tokens seemed hardly a day old, might have measured some fourteen feet in length, and some six feet in girth. He was a little frisky; though as yet his body seemed scarce yet recovered from that irksome position it had so lately occupied in the maternal reticule; where, tail to head, and all ready for the final spring, the unborn whale lies bent like a Tartar's bow. The delicate side-fins, and the palms of his flukes, still freshly retained the plaited crumpled appearance of a baby's ears newly arrived from foreign parts.

'Line! line!' cried Queequeg, looking over the gunwale; 'him fast! him fast!—Who line him! Who struck?—Two whale; one big, one little!'

'What ails ye, man?' cried Starbuck.

'Look-e here,' said Queequeg pointing down.

As when the stricken whale, that from the tub has reeled out hundreds of fathoms of rope; as, after deep sounding, he floats up again, and shows the slackened curling line buoyantly rising and spiralling towards the air; so now, Starbuck saw long coils of the umbilical cord of Madame Leviathan, by which the young cub seemed still tethered to its dam. Not seldom in the rapid vicissitudes of the chase, this natural line, with the maternal end loose, becomes entangled with the hempen one, so that the cub is thereby trapped. Some of the subtlest secrets of the seas seemed divulged to us in this enchanted pond. We saw young Leviathan amours in the deep.*

And thus, though surrounded by circle upon circle of consternations and affrights, did these inscrutable creatures at the centre freely and fearlessly indulge in all peaceful concernments; yea, serenely revelled in dalliance and delight. But even so, amid the tornadoed Atlantic of my being, do I myself still for ever centrally disport in mute calm; and while ponderous planets of unwaning woe revolve round me, deep down and deep inland there I still bathe me in eternal mildness of joy.

---

* The sperm whale, as with all other species of the Leviathan, but unlike most other fish, breeds indifferently at all seasons; after a gestation which may probably be set down at nine months, producing but one at a time; though in some few known instances giving birth to an Esau and Jacob:—a contingency provided for in suckling by two teats, curiously situated, one on each side of the anus; but the breasts themselves extend upwards from that. When by chance these precious parts in a nursing whale are cut by the hunter's lance, the mother's pouring milk and blood rivallingly discolor the sea for rods. The milk is very sweet and rich; it has been tasted by man; it might do well with strawberries. When overflowing with mutual esteem, the whales salute *more hominum*.

Meanwhile, as we thus lay entranced, the occasional sudden frantic spectacles in the distance evinced the activity of the other boats, still engaged in drugging the whales on the frontier of the host; or possibly carrying on the war within the first circle, where abundance of room and some convenient retreats were afforded them. But the sight of the enraged drugged whales now and then blindly darting to and fro across the circles, was nothing to what at last met our eyes. It is sometimes the custom when fast to a whale more than commonly powerful and alert, to seek to hamstring him, as it were, by sundering or maiming his gigantic tail-tendon. It is done by darting a short-handled cutting-spade, to which is attached a rope for hauling it back again. A whale wounded (as we afterwards learned) in this part, but not effectually, as it seemed, had broken away from the boat, carrying along with him half of the harpoon line; and in the extraordinary agony of the wound, he was now dashing among the revolving circles like the lone mounted desperado Arnold, at the battle of Saratoga, carrying dismay wherever he went.

But agonizing as was the wound of this whale, and an appalling spectacle enough, any way; yet the peculiar horror with which he seemed to inspire the rest of the herd, was owing to a cause which at first the intervening distance obscured from us. But at length we perceived that by one of the unimaginable accidents of the fishery, this whale had become entangled in the harpoon-line that he towed; he had also run away with the cutting-spade in him; and while the free end of the rope attached to that weapon, had permanently caught in the coils of the harpoon-line round his tail, the cutting-spade itself had worked loose from his flesh. So that tormented to madness, he was now churning through the water, violently flailing with his flexible tail, and tossing the keen spade about him, wounding and murdering his own comrades.

This terrific object seemed to recall the whole herd from their stationary fright. First, the whales forming the margin of our lake began to crowd a little, and tumble against each other, as if lifted by half spent billows from afar; then the lake itself began faintly to heave and swell; the submarine bridal-chambers and nurseries vanished; in more and more contracting orbits the whales in the more central circles began to swim in thickening clusters. Yes, the long calm was departing. A low advancing hum was soon heard; and then like to the tumultuous masses of block-ice when the great river Hudson breaks up in Spring, the entire host of whales came tumbling upon their inner centre, as if to pile themselves up in one common mountain. Instantly Starbuck and Queequeg changed places; Starbuck taking the stern.

'Oars! Oars!' he intensely whispered, seizing the helm—'gripe your oars, and clutch your souls, now! My God, men, stand by! Shove him off, you Queequeg—the whale there!—prick him!—hit him! Stand up—stand up, and stay so! Spring, men—pull, men; never mind their backs—scrape them!—scrape away!'

The boat was now all but jammed between two vast black bulks, leaving a narrow Dardanelles between their long lengths. But by desperate endeavor we at last shot into a temporary opening; then giving way rapidly, and at the same time earnestly watching for another outlet. After many similar hair-breadth escapes, we at last swiftly glided into what had just been one of the outer circles, but now crossed by random whales, all violently making for one centre. This lucky salvation was cheaply purchased by the loss of Queequeg's hat, who, while standing in the bows to prick the fugitive whales, had his hat taken clean from his head by the air-eddy made by the sudden tossing of a pair of broad flukes close by.

Riotous and disordered as the universal commotion now was, it soon resolved itself into what seemed a systematic movement; for having clumped together at last in one dense body, they then renewed their onward flight with augmented fleetness. Further pursuit was useless; but the boats still lingered in their wake to pick up what drugged whales might be dropped astern, and likewise to secure one which Flask had killed and waifed. The waif is a pennoned pole, two or three of which are carried by every boat; and which, when additional game is at hand, are inserted upright into the floating body of a dead whale, both to mark its place on the sea, and also as token of prior possession, should the boats of any other ship draw near.

The result of this lowering was somewhat illustrative of that sagacious saying in the Fishery,—the more whales the less fish. Of all the drugged whales only one was captured. The rest contrived to escape for the time, but only to be taken, as will hereafter be seen, by some other craft than the Pequod.

88

SCHOOLS AND SCHOOLMASTERS

THE previous chapter gave account of an immense body or herd of Sperm Whales, and there was also then given the probable cause inducing those vast aggregations.

Now, though such great bodies are at times encountered, yet, as must have been seen, even at the present day, small detached bands are occasionally observed, embracing from twenty to fifty individuals each. Such bands are known as schools. They generally are of two sorts; those composed almost entirely of females, and those mustering none but young vigorous males, or bulls, as they are familiarly designated.

In cavalier attendance upon the school of females, you invariably see a male of full grown magnitude, but not old; who, upon any alarm, evinces his gallantry by falling in the rear and covering the flight of his ladies. In truth, this gentleman is a luxurious Ottoman, swimming about over the watery world, surroundingly accompanied by all the solaces and endearments of the harem. The contrast between this Ottoman and his concubines is striking; because, while he is always of the largest leviathanic proportions, the ladies, even at full growth, are not more than one third of the bulk of an average-sized male. They are comparatively delicate, indeed; I dare say, not to exceed half a dozen yards round the waist. Nevertheless, it cannot be denied, that upon the whole they are hereditarily entitled to *en bon point*.

It is very curious to watch this harem and its lord in their indolent ramblings. Like fashionables, they are for ever on the move in leisurely search of variety. You meet them on the Line in time for the full flower of the Equatorial feeding season, having just returned, perhaps, from spending the summer in the Northern seas, and so cheating summer of all unpleasant weariness and warmth. By the time they have lounged up and down the promenade of the Equator awhile, they start for the Oriental waters in anticipation of the cool season there, and so evade the other excessive temperature of the year.

When serenely advancing on one of these journeys, if any strange suspicious sights are seen, my lord whale keeps a wary eye on his interesting family. Should any unwarrantably pert young Leviathan

coming that way, presume to draw confidentially close to one of
the ladies, with what prodigious fury the Bashaw assails him, and
chases him away! High times, indeed, if unprincipled young rakes
like him are to be permitted to invade the sanctity of domestic
bliss; though do what the Bashaw will, he cannot keep the most
notorious Lothario out of his bed; for, alas! all fish bed in common.
As ashore, the ladies often cause the most terrible duels among
their rival admirers; just so with the whales, who sometimes come
to deadly battle, and all for love. They fence with their long lower
jaws, sometimes locking them together, and so striving for the
supremacy like elks that warringly interweave their antlers. Not a
few are captured having the deep scars of these encounters,—
furrowed heads, broken teeth, scolloped fins; and in some instances,
wrenched and dislocated mouths.

But supposing the invader of domestic bliss to betake himself
away at the first rush of the harem's lord, then is it very diverting
to watch that lord. Gently he insinuates his vast bulk among them
again and revels there awhile, still in tantalizing vicinity to young
Lothario, like pious Solomon devoutly worshipping among his
thousand concubines. Granting other whales to be in sight, the
fishermen will seldom give chase to one of these Grand Turks;
for these Grand Turks are too lavish of their strength, and hence
their unctuousness is small. As for the sons and the daughters
they beget, why, those sons and daughters must take care of
themselves; at least, with only the maternal help. For like certain
other omnivorous roving lovers that might be named, my Lord
Whale has no taste for the nursery, however much for the bower;
and so, being a great traveller, he leaves his anonymous babies
all over the world; every baby an exotic. In good time, nevertheless,
as the ardor of youth declines; as years and dumps increase; as
reflection lends her solemn pauses; in short, as a general lassitude
overtakes the sated Turk; then a love of ease and virtue supplants
the love for maidens; our Ottoman enters upon the impotent,
repentant, admonitory stage of life, forswears, disbands the harem,
and grown to an exemplary, sulky old soul, goes about all alone
among the meridians and parallels saying his prayers, and warning
each young Leviathan from his amorous errors.

Now, as the harem of whales is called by the fishermen a school,
so is the lord and master of that school technically known as the
schoolmaster. It is therefore not in strict character, however admirably satirical, that after going to school himself, he should then
go abroad inculcating not what he learned there, but the folly of
it. His title, schoolmaster, would very naturally seem derived from

the name bestowed upon the harem itself, but some have surmised that the man who first thus entitled this sort of Ottoman whale, must have read the memoirs of Vidocq, and informed himself what sort of a country-schoolmaster that famous Frenchman was in his younger days, and what was the nature of those occult lessons he inculcated into some of his pupils.

The same secludedness and isolation to which the schoolmaster whale betakes himself in his advancing years, is true of all aged Sperm Whales. Almost universally, a lone whale—as a solitary Leviathan is called—proves an ancient one. Like venerable moss-bearded Daniel Boone, he will have no one near him but Nature herself; and her he takes to wife in the wilderness of waters, and the best of wives she is, though she keeps so many moody secrets.

The schools composing none but young and vigorous males, previously mentioned, offer a strong contrast to the harem schools. For while those female whales are characteristically timid, the young males, or forty-barrel-bulls, as they call them, are by far the most pugnacious of all Leviathans, and proverbially the most dangerous to encounter; excepting those wondrous grey-headed, grizzled whales, sometimes met, and these will fight you like grim fiends exasperated by a penal gout.

The Forty-barrel-bull schools are larger than the harem schools. Like a mob of young collegians, they are full of fight, fun, and wickedness, tumbling round the world at such a reckless, rollicking rate, that no prudent underwriter would insure them any more than he would a riotous lad at Yale or Harvard. They soon relinquish this turbulence though, and when about three fourths grown, break up, and separately go about in quest of settlements, that is, harems.

Another point of difference between the male and female schools is still more characteristic of the sexes. Say you strike a Forty-barrel-bull—poor devil! all his comrades quit him. But strike a member of the harem school, and her companions swim around her with every token of concern, sometimes lingering so near her and so long, as themselves to fall a prey.

89

FAST-FISH AND LOOSE-FISH

THE allusion to the waifs and waif-poles in the last chapter but one, necessitates some account of the laws and regulations of the whale fishery, of which the waif may be deemed the grand symbol and badge.

It frequently happens that when several ships are cruising in company, a whale may be struck by one vessel, then escape, and be finally killed and captured by another vessel; and herein are indirectly comprised many minor contingencies, all partaking of this one grand feature. For example,—after a weary and perilous chase and capture of a whale, the body may get loose from the ship by reason of a violent storm; and drifting far away to leeward, be retaken by a second whaler, who, in a calm, snugly tows it alongside, without risk of life or line. Thus the most vexatious and violent disputes would often arise between the fishermen, were there not some written or unwritten, universal, undisputed law applicable to all cases.

Perhaps the only formal whaling code authorized by legislative enactment, was that of Holland. It was decreed by the States-General in A.D. 1695. But though no other nation has ever had any written whaling law, yet the American fishermen have been their own legislators and lawyers in this matter. They have provided a system which for terse comprehensiveness surpasses Justinian's Pandects and the By-laws of the Chinese Society for the Suppression of Meddling with other People's Business. Yes; these laws might be engraven on a Queen Anne's farthing, or the barb of a harpoon, and worn round the neck, so small are they.

I. A Fast Fish belongs to the party fast to it.

II. A Loose-Fish is fair game for anybody who can soonest catch it.

But what plays the mischief with this masterly code is the admirable brevity of it, which necessitates a vast volume of commentaries to expound it.

First. What is a Fast-Fish? Alive or dead a fish is technically fast, when it is connected with an occupied ship or boat, by any medium at all controllable by the occupant or occupants,—a mast, an oar, a nine-inch cable, a telegraph wire, or a strand of cobweb, it is all the same. Likewise a fish is technically fast when it bears a waif, or any other recognised symbol of possession; so long as the party waifing it plainly evince their ability at any time to take it alongside, as well as their intention so to do.

These are scientific commentaries; but the commentaries of the whalemen themselves sometimes consist in hard words and harder knocks—the Coke-upon-Littleton of the fist. True, among the more upright and honorable whalemen allowances are always made for peculiar cases, where it would be an outrageous moral injustice for one party to claim possession of a whale previously chased or killed by another party. But others are by no means so scrupulous.

Some fifty years ago there was a curious case of whaletrover litigated in England, wherein the plaintiffs set forth that after a hard chase of a whale in the Northern seas; and when indeed they (the plaintiffs) had succeeded in harpooning the fish; they were at last, through peril of their lives, obliged to forsake not only their lines, but their boat itself. Ultimately the defendants (the crew of another ship) came up with the whale, struck, killed, seized, and finally appropriated it before the very eyes of the plaintiffs. And when those defendants were remonstrated with, their captain snapped his fingers in the plaintiffs' teeth, and assured them that by way of doxology to the deed he had done, he would now retain their line, harpoons, and boat, which had remained attached to the whale at the time of the seizure. Wherefore the plaintiffs now sued for the recovery of the value of their whale, line, harpoons, and boat.

Mr Erskine was counsel for the defendants; Lord Ellenborough was the judge. In the course of the defence, the witty Erskine went on to illustrate his position, by alluding to a recent crim. con. case, wherein a gentleman, after in vain trying to bridle his wife's viciousness, had at last abandoned her upon the seas of life; but in the course of years, repenting of that step, he instituted an action to recover possession of her. Erskine was on the other side; and he then supported it by saying, that though the gentleman had originally harpooned the lady, and had once had her fast, and only by reason of the great stress of her plunging viciousness, had at last abandoned her; yet abandon her he did, so that she became a loose-fish; and therefore when a subsequent gentleman re-harpooned her, the lady then became that subsequent gentleman's property, along with whatever harpoon might have been found sticking in her.

Now in the present case Erskine contended that the examples of the whale and the lady were reciprocally illustrative of each other.

These pleadings, and the counter pleadings, being duly heard, the very learned judge in set terms decided, to wit,—That as for the boat, he awarded it to the plaintiffs, because they had merely abandoned it to save their lives; but that with regard to the controverted whale, harpoons, and line, they belonged to the defendants; the whale, because it was a Loose-Fish at the time of the final capture; and the harpoons and line because when the fish made off with them, it (the fish) acquired a property in those articles; and hence anybody who afterwards took the fish had a right to them. Now, the defendants afterwards took the fish; ergo, the aforesaid articles were theirs.

A common man looking at this decision of the very learned Judge, might possibly object to it. But ploughed up to the primary rock of the matter, the two great principles laid down in the twin whaling laws previously quoted, and applied and elucidated by Lord Ellenborough in the above cited case; these two laws touching Fast-Fish and Loose-Fish, I say, will, on reflection, be found the fundamentals of all human jurisprudence; for notwithstanding its complicated tracery of sculpture, the Temple of the Law, like the Temple of the Philistines, has but two props to stand on.

Is it not a saying in every one's mouth, Possession is half of the law: that is, regardless of how the thing came into possession? But often possession is the whole of the law. What are the sinews and souls of Russian serfs and Republican slaves but Fast-Fish, whereof possession is the whole of the law? What to the rapacious landlord is the widow's last mite but a Fast-Fish? What is yonder undetected villain's marble mansion with a door-plate for a waif; what is that but a Fast-Fish? What is the ruinous discount which Mordecai, the broker, gets from poor Woebegone, the bankrupt, on a loan to keep Woebegone's family from starvation; what is that ruinous discount but a Fast-Fish? What is the Archbishop of Savesoul's income of £100,000 seized from the scant bread and cheese of hundreds of thousands of broken backed laborers (all sure of heaven without any of Savesoul's help) what is that globular 100,000 but a Fast-Fish? What are the Duke of Dunder's hereditary towns and hamlets but Fast-Fish? What to that redoubted harpooneer, John Bull, is poor Ireland, but a Fast-Fish? What to that apostolic lancer, Brother Jonathan, is Texas but a Fast-Fish? And concerning all these, is not Possession the whole of the law?

But if the doctrine of Fast-Fish be pretty generally applicable, the kindred doctrine of Loose-Fish is still more widely so. That is internationally and universally applicable.

What was America in 1492 but a Loose-Fish, in which Columbus struck the Spanish standard by way of waifing it for his royal master and mistress? What was Poland to the Czar? What Greece to the Turk? What India to England? What at last will Mexico be to the United States? All Loose-Fish.

What are the Rights of Man and the Liberties of the World but Loose-Fish? What all men's minds and opinions but Loose-Fish? What is the principle of religious belief in them but a Loose-Fish? What to the ostentatious smuggling verbalists are the thoughts of thinkers but Loose-Fish? What is the great globe itself but a Loose-Fish? And what are you, reader, but a Loose-Fish and a Fast-Fish, too?

90

HEADS OR TAILS

De balena vero sufficit, si rex habeat caput, et regina caudam.
Bracton, l. 3, c. 3.

LATIN from the books of the Laws of England, which taken along with the context, means, that of all whales captured by anybody on the coast of that land, the King, as Honorary Grand Harpooneer, must have the head, and the Queen be respectfully presented with the tail. A division which, in the whale, is much like halving an apple; there is no intermediate remainder. Now as this law, under a modified form, is to this day in force in England; and as it offers in various respects a strange anomaly touching the general law of Fast and Loose-Fish, it is here treated of in a separate chapter, on the same courteous principle that prompts the English railways to be at the expense of a separate car, specially reserved for the accommodation of royalty. In the first place, in curious proof of the fact that the above-mentioned law is still in force, I proceed to lay before you a circumstance that happened within the last two years.

It seems that some honest mariners of Dover, or Sandwich, or some one of the Cinque Ports, had after a hard chase succeeded in killing and beaching a fine whale which they had originally descried afar off from the shore. Now the Cinque Ports are partially or somehow under the jurisdiction of a sort of policeman or beadle, called a Lord Warden. Holding the office directly from the crown, I believe, all the royal emoluments incident to the Cinque Port territories become by assignment his. By some writers this office is called a sinecure. But not so. Because the Lord Warden is busily employed at times in fobbing his perquisites; which are his chiefly by virtue of that same fobbing of them.

Now when these poor sun-burnt mariners, bare-footed, and with their trowsers rolled high up on their eely legs, had wearily hauled their fat fish high and dry, promising themselves a good £150 from the precious oil and bone; and in fantasy sipping rare tea

with their wives, and good ale with their cronies, upon the strength
of their respective shares; up steps a very learned and most
Christian and charitable gentleman, with a copy of Blackstone
under his arm; and laying it upon the whale's head, he says—
'Hands off! this fish, my masters, is a Fast-Fish. I seize it as the
Lord Warden's.' Upon this the poor mariners in their respectful
consternation—so truly English—knowing not what to say, fall to
vigorously scratching their heads all round; meanwhile ruefully
glancing from the whale to the stranger. But that did in nowise
mend the matter, or at all soften the hard heart of the learned
gentleman with the copy of Blackstone. At length one of them,
after long scratching about for his ideas, made bold to speak.

'Please, sir, who is the Lord Warden?'

'The Duke.'

'But the duke had nothing to do with taking this fish?'

'It is his.'

'We have been at great trouble, and peril, and some expense,
and is all that to go to the Duke's benefit; we getting nothing at
all for our pains but our blisters?'

'It is his.'

'Is the Duke so very poor as to be forced to this desperate mode
of getting a livelihood?'

'It is his.'

'I thought to relieve my old bed-ridden mother by part of my
share of this whale.'

'It is his.'

'Won't the Duke be content with a quarter or a half?'

'It is his.'

In a word, the whale was seized and sold, and his Grace the
Duke of Wellington received the money. Thinking that viewed in
some particular lights, the case might by a bare possibility in some
small degree be deemed, under the circumstances, a rather hard
one, an honest clergyman of the town respectfully addressed a
note to his Grace, begging him to take the case of those unfortunate
mariners into full consideration. To which my Lord Duke in
substance replied (both letters were published) that he had already
done so, and received the money, and would be obliged to the
reverend gentleman if for the future he (the reverend gentleman)
would decline meddling with other people's business. Is this the
still militant old man, standing at the corners of the three king-
doms, on all hands coercing alms of beggars?

It will readily be seen that in this case the alleged right of the
Duke to the whale was a delegated one from the Sovereign. We

must needs inquire then on what principle the Sovereign is originally invested with that right. The law itself has already been set
forth. But Plowdon gives us the reason for it. Says Plowdon, the
whale so caught belongs to the King and Queen, 'because of its
superior excellence.' And by the soundest commentators this has
ever been held a cogent argument in such matters.

But why should the King have the head, and the Queen the
tail? A reason for that, ye lawyers!

In his treatise on 'Queen-Gold,' or Queen-pinmoney, an old
King's Bench author, one William Prynne, thus discourseth: 'Y^e
tail is ye Queen's, that ye Queen's wardrobe may be supplied with
ye whalebone.' Now this was written at a time when the black
limber bone of the Greenland or Right whale was largely used in
ladies' bodices. But this same bone is not in the tail; it is in the
head, which is a sad mistake for a sagacious lawyer like Prynne.
But is the Queen a mermaid, to be presented with a tail? An
allegorical meaning may lurk here.

There are two royal fish so styled by the English law writers—
the whale and the sturgeon; both royal property under certain
limitations, and nominally supplying the tenth branch of the
crown's ordinary revenue. I know not that any other author has
hinted of the matter; but by inference it seems to me that the
sturgeon must be divided in the same way as the whale, the King
receiving the highly dense and elastic head peculiar to that fish,
which, symbolically regarded, may possibly be humorously grounded
upon some presumed congeniality. And thus there seems a reason
in all things, even in law.

91

THE PEQUOD MEETS THE ROSE-BUD

'In vain it was to rake for Ambergriese in the paunch of this Leviathan,
insufferable fetor denying that inquiry.'   *Sir T. Browne, V.E.*

IT was a week or two after the last whaling scene recounted, and
when we were slowly sailing over a sleepy, vapory, midday sea,
that the many noses on the Pequod's deck proved more vigilant
discoverers than the three pairs of eyes aloft. A peculiar and not
very pleasant smell was smelt in the sea.

'I will bet something now,' said Stubb, 'that somewhere here-

abouts are some of those drugged whales we tickled the other day.
I thought they would keel up before long.'

Presently, the vapors in advance slid aside; and there in the
distance lay a ship, whose furled sails betokened that some sort
of whale must be alongside. As we glided nearer, the stranger
showed French colors from his peak; and by the eddying cloud
of vulture sea-fowl that circled, and hovered, and swooped around
him, it was plain that the whale alongside must be what the
fishermen called a blasted whale, that is, a whale that has died
unmolested on the sea, and so floated an unappropriated corpse.
It may well be conceived, what an unsavory odor such a mass
must exhale; worse than an Assyrian city in the plague, when the
living are incompetent to bury the departed. So intolerable indeed
is it regarded by some, that no cupidity could persuade them to
moor alongside of it. Yet are there those who will still do it;
notwithstanding the fact that the oil obtained from such subjects
is of a very inferior quality, and by no means of the nature of
attar-of-rose.

Coming still nearer with the expiring breeze, we saw that the
Frenchmen had a second whale alongside; and this second whale
seemed even more of a nosegay than the first. In truth, it turned
out to be one of those problematical whales that seem to dry up
and die with a sort of prodigious dyspepsia, or indigestion; leaving
their defunct bodies almost entirely bankrupt of anything like oil.
Nevertheless, in the proper place we shall see that no knowing
fisherman will ever turn up his nose at such a whale as this,
however much he may shun blasted whales in general.

The Pequod had now swept so nigh to the stranger, that Stubb
vowed he recognized his cutting spade-pole entangled in the lines
that were knotted round the tail of one of these whales.

'There's a pretty fellow, now,' he banteringly laughed, standing
in the ship's bows, 'there's a jackal for ye! I well know that these
Crappoes of Frenchmen are but poor devils in the fishery; sometimes lowering their boats for breakers, mistaking them for Sperm
Whale spouts; yes, and sometimes sailing from their port with
their hold full of boxes of tallow candles, and cases of snuffers,
foreseeing that all the oil they will get won't be enough to dip
the Captain's wick into; aye, we all know these things; but look
ye, here's a Crappo that is content with our leavings, the drugged
whale there, I mean; aye, and is content too with scraping the
dry bones of that other precious fish he has there. Poor devil! I
say, pass round a hat, some one, and let's make him a present
of a little oil for dear charity's sake. For what oil he'll get from

that drugged whale there, wouldn't be fit to burn in a jail; no, not in a condemned cell. And as for the other whale, why, I'll agree to get more oil by chopping up and trying out these three masts of ours, than he'll get from that bundle of bones; though, now that I think of it, it may contain something worth a good deal more than oil; yes, ambergris. I wonder now if our old man has thought of that. It's worth trying. Yes, I'm in for it;' and so saying he started for the quarter-deck.

By this time the faint air had become a complete calm; so that whether or no, the Pequod was now fairly entrapped in the smell, with no hope of escaping except by its breezing up again. Issuing from the cabin, Stubb now called his boat's crew, and pulled off for the stranger. Drawing across her bow, he perceived that in accordance with the fanciful French taste, the upper part of her stem-piece was carved in the likeness of a huge drooping stalk, was painted green, and for thorns had copper spikes projecting from it here and there; the whole terminating in a symmetrical folded bulb of a bright red color. Upon her head boards, in large gilt letters, he read 'Bouton de Rose,'—Rose-button, or Rose-bud; and this was the romantic name of this aromatic ship.

Though Stubb did not understand the *Bouton* part of the inscription, yet the word *rose*, and the bulbous figure-head put together, sufficiently explained the whole to him.

'A wooden rose-bud, eh?' he cried with his hand to his nose, 'that will do very well; but how like all creation it smells!'

Now in order to hold direct communication with the people on deck, he had to pull round the bows to the starboard side, and thus come close to the blasted whale; and so talk over it.

Arrived then at this spot, with one hand still to his nose, he bawled—'Bouton-de-Rose, ahoy! are there any of you Bouton-de-Roses that speak English?'

'Yes,' rejoined a Guernsey-man from the bulwarks, who turned out to be the chief-mate.

'Well, then, my Bouton-de-Rose-bud, have you seen the White Whale?'

'*What* whale?'

'The *White* Whale—a Sperm Whale—Moby Dick, have ye seen him?'

'Never heard of such a whale. Cachalot Blanche? White Whale—no.'

'Very good, then; good bye now, and I'll call again in a minute.'

Then rapidly pulling back towards the Pequod, and seeing Ahab leaning over the quarter-deck rail awaiting his report, he moulded his two hands into a trumpet and shouted—'No, Sir! No!' Upon which Ahab retired, and Stubb returned to the Frenchman.

He now perceived that the Guernsey-man, who had just got into the chains, and was using a cutting-spade, had slung his nose in a sort of bag.

'What's the matter with your nose, there?' said Stubb. 'Broke it?'

'I wish it was broken, or that I didn't have any nose at all!' answered the Guernsey-man, who did not seem to relish the job he was at very much. 'But what are you holding *yours* for?'

'Oh, nothing! It's a wax nose; I have to hold it on. Fine day, aint it? Air rather gardenny, I should say; throw us a bunch of posies, will ye, Bouton-de-Rose?'

'What in the devil's name do you want here?' roared the Guernsey-man, flying into a sudden passion.

'Oh! keep cool—cool? yes, that's the word; why don't you pack those whales in ice while you're working at 'em? But joking aside, though; do you know, Rose-bud, that it's all nonsense trying to get any oil out of such whales? As for that dried up one, there, he hasn't a gill in his whole carcase.'

'I know that well enough; but, d'ye see, the Captain here won't believe it; this is his first voyage; he was a Cologne manufacturer before. But come aboard, and mayhap he'll believe you, if he won't me; and so I'll get out of this dirty scrape.'

'Anything to oblige ye, my sweet and pleasant fellow,' rejoined Stubb, and with that he soon mounted to the deck. There a queer scene presented itself. The sailors, in tasselled caps of red worsted, were getting the heavy tackles in readiness for the whales. But they worked rather slow and talked very fast, and seemed in anything but a good humor. All their noses upwardly projected from their faces like so many jib-booms. Now and then pairs of them would drop their work, and run up to the mast-head to get some fresh air. Some thinking they would catch the plague, dipped oakum in coal-tar, and at intervals held it to their nostrils. Others having broken the stems of their pipes almost short off at the bowl, were vigorously puffing tobacco-smoke, so that it constantly filled their olfactories.

Stubb was struck by a shower of outcries and anathemas proceeding from the Captain's round-house abaft; and looking in that direction saw a fiery face thrust from behind the door, which was held ajar from within. This was the tormented surgeon, who, after in vain remonstrating against the proceedings of the day, had betaken himself to the Captain's round-house (*cabinet* he called it) to avoid the pest; but still, could not help yelling out his entreaties and indignations at times.

Marking all this, Stubb argued well for his scheme, and turning to the Guernsey-man had a little chat with him, during which the stranger mate expressed his detestation of his Captain as a conceited ignoramus, who had brought them all into so unsavory and unprofitable a pickle. Sounding him carefully, Stubb further perceived that the Guernsey-man had not the slightest suspicion concerning the ambergris. He therefore held his peace on that head, but otherwise was quite frank and confidential with him, so that the two quickly concocted a little plan for both circumventing and satirizing the Captain, without his at all dreaming of distrusting their sincerity. According to this little plan of theirs, the Guernsey-man, under cover of an interpreter's office, was to tell the Captain what he pleased, but as coming from Stubb; and as for Stubb, he was to utter any nonsense that should come uppermost in him during the interview.

By this time their destined victim appeared from his cabin. He was a small and dark, but rather delicate looking man for a sea-captain, with large whiskers and moustache, however; and wore a red cotton velvet vest with watch-seals at his side. To this gentleman, Stubb was now politely introduced by the Guernsey-man, who at once ostentatiously put on the aspect of interpreting between them.

'What shall I say to him first?' said he.

'Why,' said Stubb, eyeing the velvet vest and the watch and seals, 'you may as well begin by telling him that he looks a sort of babyish to me, though I don't pretend to be a judge.'

'He says, Monsieur,' said the Guernsey-man, in French, turning to his captain, 'that only yesterday his ship spoke a vessel, whose captain, and chief-mate, with six sailors, had all died of a fever caught from a blasted whale they had brought alongside.'

Upon this the captain started, and eagerly desired to know more.

'What now?' said the Guernsey-man to Stubb.

'Why, since he takes it so easy, tell him that now I have eyed him carefully, I'm quite certain that he's no more fit to command a whale-ship than a St Jago monkey. In fact, tell him from me he's a baboon.'

'He vows and declares, Monsieur, that the other whale, the dried one, is far more deadly than the blasted one; in fine, Monsieur, he conjures us, as we value our lives, to cut loose from these fish.'

Instantly the captain ran forward, and in a loud voice commanded his crew to desist from hoisting the cutting-tackles, and at once cast loose the cables and chains confining the whales to the ship.

'What now?' said the Guernsey-man, when the captain had returned to them.

'Why, let me see; yes, you may as well tell him now that—that—in fact, tell him I've diddled him, and (aside to himself) perhaps somebody else.'

'He says, Monsieur, that he's very happy to have been of any service to us.'

Hearing this, the captain vowed that they were the grateful parties (meaning himself and mate) and concluded by inviting Stubb down into his cabin to drink a bottle of Bordeaux.

'He wants you to take a glass of wine with him,' said the interpreter.

'Thank him heartily; but tell him it's against my principles to drink with the man I've diddled. In fact, tell him I must go.'

'He says, Monsieur, that his principles won't admit of his drinking; but that if Monsieur wants to live another day to drink, then Monsieur had best drop all four boats, and pull the ship away from these whales, for it's so calm they won't drift.'

By this time Stubb was over the side, and getting into his boat, hailed the Guernsey-man to this effect,—that having a long tow-line in his boat, he would do what he could to help them, by pulling out the lighter whale of the two from the ship's side. While the Frenchman's boats, then, were engaged in towing the ship one way, Stubb benevolently towed away at his whale the other way, ostentatiously slacking out a most unusually long tow-line.

Presently a breeze sprang up; Stubb feigned to cast off from the whale; hoisting his boats, the Frenchman soon increased his distance, while the Pequod slid in between him and Stubb's whale, Whereupon Stubb quickly pulled to the floating body, and hailing the Pequod to give notice of his intentions, at once proceeded to reap the fruit of his unrighteous cunning. Seizing his sharp boat-spade, he commenced an excavation in the body, a little behind the side fin. You would almost have thought he was digging a cellar there in the sea; and when at length his spade struck against the gaunt ribs, it was like turning up old Roman tiles and pottery buried in fat English loam. His boat's crew were all in high excitement, eagerly helping their chief, and looking as anxious as gold-hunters.

And all the time numberless fowls were diving, and ducking, and screaming, and yelling, and fighting around them. Stubb was beginning to look disappointed, especially as the horrible nosegay increased, when suddenly from out of the very heart of this plague, there stole a faint stream of perfume, which flowed through the tide of bad smells without being absorbed by it, as one river will flow into and then along with another, without at all blending with it for a time.

'I have it, I have it,' cried Stubb, with delight, striking something in the subterranean regions, 'a purse! a purse!'

Dropping his spade, he thrust both hands in, and drew out handfuls of something that looked like ripe Windsor soap, or rich mottled old cheese; very unctuous and savory withal. You might easily dent it with your thumb; it is of a hue between yellow and ash color. And this, good friends, is ambergris, worth a gold guinea an ounce to any druggist. Some six handfuls were obtained; but more was unavoidably lost in the sea, and still more, perhaps, might have been secured were it not for impatient Ahab's loud command to Stubb to desist, and come on board, else the ship would bid them good bye.

92
AMBERGRIS

Now this ambergris is a very curious substance, and so important as an article of commerce, that in 1791 a certain Nantucket-born Captain Coffin was examined at the bar of the English house of Commons on that subject. For at that time, and indeed until a comparatively late day, the precise origin of ambergris remained, like amber itself, a problem to the learned. Though the word ambergris is but the French compound for grey amber, yet the two substances are quite distinct. For amber, though at times found on the sea-coast, is also dug up in some far inland soils, whereas ambergris is never found except upon the sea. Besides, amber is a hard, transparent, brittle, odorless substance, used for mouth-pieces to pipes, for beads and ornaments; but ambergris is soft, waxy, and so highly fragrant and spicy, that it is largely used in perfumery, in pastiles, precious candles, hair-powders, and pomatum. The Turks use it in cooking, and also carry it to Mecca, for the same purpose that frankincense is carried to St Peter's in Rome. Some wine merchants drop a few grains into claret, to flavor it.

Who would think, then, that such fine ladies and gentlemen should regale themselves with an essence found in the inglorious bowels of a sick whale! Yet so it is. By some, ambergris is supposed to be the cause, and by others the effect, of the dyspepsia in the whale. How to cure such a dyspepsia it were hard to say, unless by administering three or four boat loads of Brandreth's pills, and then running out of harm's way, as laborers do in blasting rocks.

I have forgotten to say that there were found in this ambergris, certain hard, round, bony plates, which at first Stubb thought might be sailors' trousers buttons; but it afterwards turned out that they were nothing more than pieces of small squid bones embalmed in that manner.

Now that the incorruption of this most fragrant ambergris should be found in the heart of such decay; is this nothing? Bethink thee of that saying of St Paul in Corinthians, about corruption and incorruption; how that we are sown in dishonor, but raised in glory. And likewise call to mind that saying of Paracelsus about what it is that maketh the best musk. Also forget not the strange fact that of all things of ill-savor, Cologne-water, in its rudimental manufacturing stages, is the worst.

I should like to conclude the chapter with the above appeal, but cannot, owing to my anxiety to repel a charge often made against whalemen, and which, in the estimation of some already biased minds, might be considered as indirectly substantiated by what has been said of the Frenchman's two whales. Elsewhere in this volume the slanderous aspersion had been disproved, that the vocation of whaling is throughout a slatternly, untidy business. But there is another thing to rebut. They hint that all whales always smell bad. Now how did this odious stigma originate?

I opine, that it is plainly traceable to the first arrival of the Greenland whaling ships in London, more than two centuries ago. Because those whalemen did not then, and do not now, try out their oil at sea as the Southern ships have always done; but cutting up the fresh blubber in small bits, thrust it through the bung holes of large casks, and carry it home in that manner; the shortness of the season in those Icy Seas, and the sudden and violent storms to which they are exposed, forbidding any other course. The consequence is, that upon breaking into the hold, and unloading one of these whale cemeteries, in the Greenland dock, a savor is given forth somewhat similar to that arising from excavating an old city grave-yard, for the foundations of a Lying-in Hospital.

I partly surmise also, that this wicked charge against whalers may be likewise imputed to the existence on the coast of Greenland, in former times, of a Dutch village called Schmerenburgh or Smeerenberg, which latter name is the one used by the learned Fogo Von Slack, in his great work on Smells, a textbook on that subject. As its name imports (smeer, fat; berg, to put up), this village was founded in order to afford a place for the blubber of the Dutch whale fleet to be tried out, without being taken home to Holland for that purpose. It was a collection of furnaces, fat-kettles, and oil sheds; and when the works were in full operation certainly gave forth no very pleasant savor. But all this is quite different with a South Sea Sperm Whaler; which in a voyage of four years perhaps, after completely filling her hold with oil, does not, perhaps, consume fifty days in the business of boiling out; and in the state that it is casked, the oil is nearly scentless. The truth is, that living or dead, if but decently treated, whales as a species are by no means creatures of ill odor; nor can whalemen be recognised, as the people of the middle ages affected to detect a Jew in the company, by the nose. Nor indeed can the whale possibly be otherwise than fragrant, when, as a general thing, he enjoys such high health; taking abundance of exercise; always out of doors; though, it is true, seldom in the open air. I say, that the motion of a Sperm Whale's flukes above water dispenses a perfume, as when a musk-scented lady rustles her dress in a warm parlor. What then shall I liken the Sperm Whale to for fragrance, considering his magnitude? Must it not be to that famous elephant, with jewelled tusks, and redolent with myrrh, which was led out of an Indian town to do honor to Alexander the Great?

93
THE CASTAWAY

IT was but some few days after encountering the Frenchman, that a most significant event befell the most insignificant of the Pequod's crew; an event most lamentable; and which ended in providing the sometimes madly merry and predestinated craft with a living and ever accompanying prophecy of whatever shattered sequel might prove her own.

Now, in the whale ship, it is not every one that goes in the boats. Some few hands are reserved called ship-keepers, whose province it is to work the vessel while the boats are pursuing the whale. As a general thing, these ship-keepers are as hardy fellows as the men comprising the boats' crews. But if there happen to be an unduly slender, clumsy, or timorous wight in the ship, that wight is certain to be made a ship-keeper. It was so in the Pequod with the little negro Pippin by nick-name, Pip by abbreviation. Poor Pip! ye have heard of him before; ye must remember his tambourine on that dramatic midnight, so gloomy-jolly.

In outer aspect, Pip and Dough-Boy made a match, like a black pony and a white one, of equal developments, though of dissimilar color, driven in one eccentric span. But while hapless Dough-Boy was by nature dull and torpid in his intellects, Pip, though over tender-hearted, was at bottom very bright, with that pleasant, genial, jolly brightness peculiar to his tribe; a tribe, which ever enjoy all holidays and festivities with finer, freer relish than any other race. For blacks, the year's calendar should show naught but three hundred and sixty-five Fourth of Julys and New Year's Days. Nor smile so, while I write that this little black was brilliant, for even blackness has its brilliancy; behold yon lustrous ebony, panelled in kings' cabinets. But Pip loved life, and all life's peaceable securities; so that the panic-striking business in which he had somehow unaccountably become entrapped, had most sadly blurred his brightness; though, as ere long will be seen, what was thus temporarily subdued in him, in the end was destined to be luridly illumined by strange wild fires, that fictitiously showed him off to ten times the natural lustre with which in his native Tolland County in Connecticut, he had once enlivened many a fiddler's frolic on the green; and at melodious even-tide, with his gay ha-ha! had turned the round horizon into one star-belled tambourine. So, though in the clear air of day, suspended against a blue-veined neck, the pure-watered diamond drop will healthful glow; yet, when the cunning jeweller would show you the diamond in its most impressive lustre, he lays it against a gloomy ground, and then lights it up, not by the sun, but by some unnatural gases. Then come out those fiery effulgences, infernally superb; then the evil-blazing diamond, once the divinest symbol of the crystal skies, looks like some crown-jewel stolen from the King of Hell. But let us to the story.

It came to pass, that in the ambergris affair Stubb's after-oarsman chanced so to sprain his hand, as for a time to become quite maimed; and, temporarily, Pip was put into his place.

The first time Stubb lowered with him, Pip evinced much nervousness; but happily, for that time, escaped close contact with the whale; and therefore came off not altogether discreditably; though Stubb observing him, took care, afterwards, to exhort him to cherish his courageousness to the utmost, for he might often find it needful.

Now upon the second lowering, the boat paddled upon the whale; and as the fish received the darted iron, it gave its customary rap, which happened, in this instance, to be right under poor Pip's seat. The involuntary consternation of the moment caused him to leap, paddle in hand, out of the boat; and in such a way, that part of the slack whale line coming against his chest, he breasted it overboard with him, so as to become entangled in it, when at last plumping into the water. That instant the stricken whale started on a fierce run, the line swiftly straightened; and presto! poor Pip came all foaming up to the chocks of the boat, remorselessly dragged there by the line, which had taken several turns around his chest and neck.

Tashtego stood in the bows. He was full of the fire of the hunt. He hated Pip for a poltroon. Snatching the boat-knife from its sheath, he suspended its sharp edge over the line, and turning towards Stubb, exclaimed interrogatively, 'Cut?' Meantime Pip's blue, choked face plainly looked, Do, for God's sake! All passed in a flash. In less than half a minute, this entire thing happened.

'Damn him, cut!' roared Stubb; and so the whale was lost and Pip was saved.

So soon as he recovered himself, the poor little negro was assailed by yells and execrations from the crew. Tranquilly permitted these irregular cursings to evaporate, Stubb then in a plain, business-like, but still half humorous manner, cursed Pip officially; and that done, unofficially gave him much wholesome advice. The substance was, Never jump from a boat, Pip, except—but all the rest was indefinite, as the soundest advice ever is. Now, in general, *Stick to the boat*, is your true motto in whaling; but cases will sometimes happen when *Leap from the boat*, is still better. Moreover, as if perceiving at last that if he should give undiluted conscientious advice to Pip, he would be leaving him too wide a margin to jump in for the future; Stubb suddenly dropped all advice, and concluded with a peremptory command, 'Stick to the boat, Pip, or by the Lord, I wont pick you up if you jump; mind that. We can't afford to lose whales by the likes of you; a whale would sell for thirty times what you would, Pip, in Alabama. Bear that in mind, and don't jump any more.' Hereby perhaps Stubb indirectly hinted, that though man loves his fellow, yet man is a money-making animal, which propensity too often interferes with his benevolence.

But we are all in the hands of the Gods; and Pip jumped again.

It was under very similar circumstances to the first performance; but this time he did not breast out the line; and hence, when the whale started to run, Pip was left behind on the sea, like a hurried traveller's trunk. Alas! Stubb was but too true to his word. It was a beautiful, bounteous, blue day; the spangled sea calm and cool, and flatly stretching away, all round, to the horizon, like gold-beater's skin hammered out to the extremest. Bobbing up and down in that sea, Pip's ebon head showed like a head of cloves. No boat-knife was lifted when he fell so rapidly astern. Stubb's inexorable back was turned upon him; and the whale was winged. In three minutes, a whole mile of shoreless ocean was between Pip and Stubb. Out from the centre of the sea, poor Pip turned his crisp, curling, black head to the sun, another lonely castaway, though the loftiest and the brightest.

Now, in calm weather, to swim in the open ocean is as easy to the practised swimmer as to ride in a spring-carriage ashore. But the awful lonesomeness is intolerable. The intense concentration of self in the middle of such a heartless immensity, my God! who can tell it? Mark, how when sailors in a dead calm bathe in the open sea—mark how closely they hug their ship and only coast along her sides.

But had Stubb really abandoned the poor little negro to his fate? No; he did not mean to, at least. Because there were two boats in his wake, and he supposed, no doubt, that they would of course come up to Pip very quickly, and pick him up; though, indeed, such considerateness towards oarsmen jeopardized through their own timidity, is not always manifested by the hunters in all similar instances; and such instances not unfrequently occur; almost invariably in the fishery, a coward, so called, is marked with the same ruthless detestation peculiar to military navies and armies.

But it so happened, that those boats, without seeing Pip, suddenly spying whales close to them on one side, turned, and gave chase; and Stubb's boat was now so far away, and he and all his crew so intent upon his fish, that Pip's ringed horizon began to expand around him miserably. By the merest chance the ship itself at last rescued him; but from that hour the little negro went about the deck an idiot; such, at least, they said he was. The sea had jeeringly kept his finite body up, but drowned the infinite of his soul. Not drowned entirely, though. Rather carried down alive to wondrous depths, where strange shapes of the unwarped primal world glided to and fro before his passive eyes; and the miser-merman, Wisdom, revealed his hoarded heaps; and among the joyous, heartless, ever-juvenile eternities, Pip saw the multitudinous, God-omnipresent, coral insects, that out of the firmament of waters heaved the colossal orbs. He saw God's foot upon the treadle of the loom, and spoke it; and therefore his shipmates called him mad. So man's insanity is heaven's sense; and wandering from all mortal reason, man comes at last to that celestial thought, which, to reason, is absurd and frantic; and weal or woe, feels then uncompromised, indifferent as his God.

For the rest, blame not Stubb too hardly. The thing is common in that fishery; and in the sequel of the narrative, it will then be seen what like abandonment befell myself.

94
A SQUEEZE OF THE HAND

THAT whale of Stubb's so dearly purchased, was duly brought to the Pequod's side, where all those cutting and hoisting operations previously detailed, were regularly gone through, even to the baling of the Heidelburgh Tun, or Case.

While some were occupied with this latter duty, others were employed in dragging away the larger tubs, so soon as filled with the sperm; and when the proper time arrived, this same sperm was carefully manipulated ere going to the try-works, of which anon.

It had cooled and crystallized to such a degree, that when, with several others, I sat down before a large Constantine's bath of it, I found it strangely concreted into lumps, here and there rolling about in the liquid part. It was our business to squeeze these lumps back into fluid. A sweet and unctuous duty! No wonder that in old times this sperm was such a favorite cosmetic. Such a clearer! such a sweetener! such a softener! such a delicious mollifier! After having my hands in it for only a few minutes, my fingers felt like eels, and began, as it were, to serpentine and spiralize.

As I sat there at my ease, cross-legged on the deck; after the bitter exertion at the windlass; under a blue tranquil sky; the ship under indolent sail, and gliding so serenely along; as I bathed my hands among those soft, gentle globules of infiltrated tissues, woven almost within the hour; as they richly broke to my fingers, and discharged all their opulence, like fully ripe grapes their wine; as I snuffed up that uncontaminated aroma,—literally and truly, like

the smell of spring violets; I declare to you, that for the time I
lived as in a musky meadow; I forgot all about our horrible oath;
in that inexpressible sperm, I washed my hands and my heart of
it; I almost began to credit the old Paracelsan superstition that
sperm is of rare virtue in allaying the heat of anger: while bathing
in that bath, I felt divinely free from all ill-will, or petulance, or
malice, of any sort whatsoever.

Squeeze! squeeze! squeeze! all the morning long; I squeezed that
sperm till I myself almost melted into it; I squeezed that sperm
till a strange sort of insanity came over me; and I found myself
unwittingly squeezing my co-laborers' hands in it, mistaking their
hands for the gentle globules. Such an abounding, affectionate,
friendly, loving feeling did this avocation beget; that at last I was
continually squeezing their hands, and looking up into their eyes
sentimentally; as much as to say,—Oh! my dear fellow beings,
why should we longer cherish any social acerbities, or know the
slightest ill-humor or envy! Come; let us squeeze hands all round;
nay, let us all squeeze ourselves into each other; let us squeeze
ourselves universally into the very milk and sperm of kindness.

Would that I could keep squeezing that sperm for ever! For
now, since by many prolonged, repeated experiences, I have perceived that in all cases man must eventually lower, or at least
shift, his conceit of attainable felicity; not placing it anywhere in
the intellect or the fancy; but in the wife, the heart, the bed, the
table, the saddle, the fire-side, the country; now that I have
perceived all this, I am ready to squeeze case eternally. In thoughts
of the visions of the night, I saw long rows of angels in paradise,
each with his hands in a jar of spermaceti.

Now, while discoursing of sperm, it behooves to speak of other
things akin to it, in the business of preparing the sperm whale
for the try-works.

First comes white-horse, so called, which is obtained from the
tapering part of the fish, and also from the thicker portions of
his flukes. It is tough with congealed tendons—a wad of muscle—
but still contains some oil. After being severed from the whale,
the white-horse is first cut into portable oblongs ere going to the
mincer. They look much like blocks of Berkshire marble.

Plum-pudding is the term bestowed upon certain fragmentary
parts of the whale's flesh, here and there adhering to the blanket
of blubber, and often participating to a considerable degree in its
unctuousness. It is a most refreshing, convivial, beautiful object

to behold. As its name imports, it is of an exceedingly rich, mottled tint, with a bestreaked snowy and golden ground, dotted with spots of the deepest crimson and purple. It is plums of rubies, in pictures of citron. Spite of reason, it is hard to keep yourself from eating it. I confess, that once I stole behind the foremast to try it. It tasted something as I should conceive a royal cutlet from the thigh of Louis le Gros might have tasted, supposing him to have been killed the first day after the venison season, and that particular venison season contemporary with an unusually fine vintage of the vineyards of Champagne.

There is another substance, and a very singular one, which turns up in the course of this business, but which I feel it to be very puzzling adequately to describe. It is called slobgollion; an appellation original with the whalemen, and even so is the nature of the substance. It is an ineffably oozy, stringy affair, most frequently found in the tubs of sperm, after a prolonged squeezing, and subsequent decanting. I hold it to be the wondrously thin, ruptured membranes of the case, coalescing.

Gurry, so called, is a term properly belonging to right whalemen, but sometimes incidentally used by the sperm fishermen. It designates the dark, glutinous substance which is scraped off the back of the Greenland or right whale, and much of which covers the decks of those inferior souls who hunt that ignoble Leviathan.

Nippers. Strictly this word is not indigenous to the whale's vocabulary. But as applied by whalemen, it becomes so. A whaleman's nipper is a short firm strip of tendinous stuff cut from the tapering part of Leviathan's tail: it averages an inch in thickness, and for the rest, is about the size of the iron part of a hoe. Edgewise moved along the oily deck, it operates like a leathern squilgee; and by nameless blandishments, as of magic, allures along with it all impurities.

But to learn all about these recondite matters, your best way is at once to descend into the blubber-room, and have a long talk with its inmates. This place has previously been mentioned as the receptacle for the blanket-pieces, when stript and hoisted from the whale. When the proper time arrives for cutting up its contents, this apartment is a scene of terror to all tyros, especially by night. On one side, lit by a dull lantern, a space has been left clear for the workmen. They generally go in pairs,—a pike-and-gaff-man and a spade-man. The whaling-pike is similar to a frigate's boarding-weapon of the same name. The gaff is something like a boat-hook. With his gaff, the gaffman hooks on to a sheet of blubber, and strives to hold it from slipping, as the ship pitches and lurches about. Meanwhile, the spade-man stands on the sheet itself, perpendicularly chopping it into the portable horse-pieces. This spade is sharp as hone can make it; the spademan's feet are shoeless; the thing he stands on will sometimes irresistibly slide away from him, like a sledge. If he cuts off one of his own toes, or one of his assistant's, would you be very much astonished? Toes are scarce among veteran blubber-room men.

95
THE CASSOCK

HAD you stepped on board the Pequod at a certain juncture of this post-mortemizing of the whale; and had you strolled forward nigh the windlass, pretty sure am I that you would have scanned with no small curiosity a very strange, enigmatical object, which you would have seen there, lying along lengthwise in the lee scuppers. Not the wondrous cistern in the whale's huge head; not the prodigy of his unhinged lower jaw; not the miracle of his symmetrical tail; none of these would so surprise you, as half a glimpse of that unaccountable cone,—longer than a Kentuckian is tall, nigh a foot in diameter at the base, and jet black as Yojo, the ebony idol of Queequeg. And an idol, indeed, it is; or, rather, in old times, its likeness was. Such an idol as that found in the secret groves of Queen Maachah in Judea; and for worshipping which, King Asa, her son, did depose her, and destroyed the idol, and burnt it for an abomination at the brook Kedron, as darkly set forth in the 15th chapter of the first book of Kings.

Look at the sailor, called the mincer, who now comes along, and assisted by two allies, heavily backs the grandissimus, as the mariners call it, and with bowed shoulders, staggers off with it as if he were a grenadier carrying a dead comrade from the field. Extending it upon the forecastle deck, he now proceeds cylindrically to remove its dark pelt, as an African hunter the pelt of a boa. This done he turns the pelt inside out, like a pantaloon leg; gives it a good stretching, so as almost to double its diameter; and at last hangs it, well spread, in the rigging, to dry. Ere long, it is taken down; when removing some three feet of it, towards the pointed extremity, and then cutting two slits for armholes at the other end, he lengthwise slips himself bodily into it. The mincer now stands before you invested in the full canonicals of his calling.

Immemorial to all his order, this investiture alone will adequately protect him, while employed in the peculiar functions of his office.

That office consists in mincing the horse-pieces of blubber for the pots; an operation which is conducted at a curious wooden horse, planted endwise against the bulwarks, and with a capacious tub beneath it, into which the minced pieces drop, fast as the sheets from a rapt orator's desk. Arrayed in decent black; occupying a conspicuous pulpit; intent on bible leaves; what a candidate for an archbishoprick, what a lad for a Pope were this mincer!*

96
THE TRY-WORKS

BESIDES her hoisted boats, an American whaler is outwardly distinguished by her try-works. She presents the curious anomaly of the most solid masonry joining with oak and hemp in constituting the completed ship. It is as if from the open field a brick-kiln were transported to her planks.

The try-works are planted between the foremast and main-mast, the most roomy part of the deck. The timbers beneath are of a peculiar strength, fitted to sustain the weight of an almost solid mass of brick and mortar, some ten feet by eight square, and five in height. The foundation does not penetrate the deck, but the masonry is firmly secured to the surface by ponderous knees of iron bracing it on all sides, and screwing it down to the timbers. On the flanks it is cased with wood, and at the top completely covered by a large, sloping, battened hatchway. Removing this hatch we expose the great try-pots, two in number, and each of several barrels' capacity. When not in use, they are kept remarkably clean. Sometimes they are polished with soapstone and sand, till they shine within like silver punch-bowls. During the night-watches some cynical old sailors will crawl into them and coil themselves away there for a nap. While employed in polishing them—one man in each pot, side by side—many confidential communications are carried on, over the iron lips. It is a place also for profound

---

* Bible leaves! Bible leaves! This is the invariable cry from the mates to the mincer. It enjoins him to be careful, and cut his work into as thin slices as possible, inasmuch as by so doing the business of boiling out the oil is much accelerated, and its quantity considerably increased, besides perhaps improving it in quality.

mathematical meditation. It was in the left hand try-pot of the Pequod, with the soapstone diligently circling round me, that I was first indirectly struck by the remarkable fact, that in geometry all bodies gliding along the cycloid, my soapstone for example, will descend from any point in precisely the same time.

Removing the fire-board from the front of the try-works, the bare masonry of that side is exposed, penetrated by the two iron mouths of the furnaces, directly underneath the pots. These mouths are fitted with heavy doors of iron. The intense heat of the fire is prevented from communicating itself to the deck, by means of a shallow reservoir extending under the entire inclosed surface of the works. By a tunnel inserted at the rear, this reservoir is kept replenished with water as fast as it evaporates. There are no external chimneys; they open direct from the rear wall. And here let us go back for a moment.

It was about nine o'clock at night that the Pequod's try-works were first started on this present voyage. It belonged to Stubb to oversee the business.

'All ready there? Off hatch, then, and start her. You cook, fire the works.' This was an easy thing, for the carpenter had been thrusting his shavings into the furnace throughout the passage. Here be it said that in a whaling voyage the first fire in the try-works has to be fed for a time with wood. After that no wood is used, except as a means of quick ignition to the staple fuel. In a word, after being tried out, the crisp, shrivelled blubber, now called scraps or fritters, still contains considerable of its unctuous properties. These fritters feed the flames. Like a plethoric burning martyr, or a self-consuming misanthrope, once ignited, the whale supplies his own fuel and burns by his own body. Would that he consumed his own smoke! for his smoke is horrible to inhale, and inhale it you must, and not only that, but you must live in it for the time. It has an unspeakable, wild, Hindoo odor about it, such as may lurk in the vicinity of funereal pyres. It smells like the left wing of the day of judgment; it is an argument for the pit.

By midnight the works were in full operation. We were clear from the carcase; sail had been made; the wind was freshening; the wild ocean darkness was intense. But that darkness was licked up by the fierce flames, which at intervals forked forth from the sooty flues, and illuminated every lofty rope in the rigging, as with the famed Greek fire. The burning ship drove on, as if remorselessly commissioned to some vengeful deed. So the pitch and sulphur-freighted brigs of the bold Hydriote, Canaris, issuing from their midnight harbors, with broad sheets of flame for sails,

bore down upon the Turkish frigates, and folded them in confla-
grations.

The hatch, removed from the top of the works, now afforded
a wide hearth in front of them. Standing on this were the Tartarean
shapes of the pagan harpooneers, always the whale-ship's stokers.
With huge pronged poles they pitched hissing masses of blubber
into the scalding pots, or stirred up the fires beneath, till the snaky
flames darted, curling, out of the doors to catch them by the feet.
The smoke rolled away in sullen heaps. To every pitch of the
ship there was a pitch of the boiling oil, which seemed all eagerness
to leap into their faces. Opposite the mouth of the works, on the
further side of the wide wooden hearth, was the windlass. This
served for a sea-sofa. Here lounged the watch, when not otherwise
employed, looking into the red heat of the fire, till their eyes felt
scorched in their heads. Their tawny features, now all begrimed
with smoke and sweat, their matted beards, and the contrasting
barbaric brilliancy of their teeth, all these were strangely revealed
in the capricious emblazonings of the works. As they narrated to
each other their unholy adventures, their tales of terror told in
words of mirth; as their uncivilized laughter forked upwards out
of them, like the flames from the furnace; as to and fro, in their
front, the harpooneers wildly gesticulated with their huge pronged
forks and dippers; as the wind howled on, and the sea leaped,
and the ship groaned and dived, and yet steadfastly shot her red
hell further and further into the blackness of the sea and the night,
and scornfully champed the white bone in her mouth, and viciously
spat round her on all sides; then the rushing Pequod, freighted
with savages, and laden with fire, and burning a corpse, and
plunging into that blackness of darkness, seemed the material
counterpart of her monomaniac commander's soul.

So it seemed it to me, as I stood at her helm, and for long
hours silently guided the way of this fire-ship on the sea. Wrapped,
for that interval, in darkness myself, I but the better saw the
redness, the madness, the ghastliness of others. The continual sight
of the fiend shapes before me, capering half in smoke and half
in fire, these at last begat kindred visions in my soul, so soon as
I began to yield to that unaccountable drowsiness which ever
would come over me at a midnight helm.

But that night, in particular, a strange (and ever since inexplicable) thing occurred to me. Starting from a brief standing sleep,
I was horribly conscious of something fatally wrong. The jaw-
bone tiller smote my side, which leaned against it; in my ears was
the low hum of sails, just beginning to shake in the wind; I thought

my eyes were open; I was half conscious of putting my fingers to the lids and mechanically stretching them still further apart. But, spite of all this, I could see no compass before me to steer by; though it seemed but a minute since I had been watching the card, by the steady binnacle lamp illuminating it. Nothing seemed before me but a jet gloom, now and then made ghastly by flashes of redness. Uppermost was the impression, that whatever swift, rushing thing I stood on was not so much bound to any haven ahead as rushing from all havens astern. A stark, bewildered feeling, as of death, came over me. Convulsively my hands grasped the tiller, but with the crazy conceit that the tiller was, somehow, in some enchanted way, inverted. My God! what is the matter with me? thought I. Lo! in my brief sleep I had turned myself about, and was fronting the ship's stern, with my back to her prow and the compass. In an instant I faced back, just in time to prevent the vessel from flying up into the wind, and very probably capsizing her. How glad and how grateful the relief from this unnatural hallucination of the night, and the fatal contingency of being brought by the lee!

Look not too long in the face of the fire, O man! Never dream with thy hand on the helm! Turn not thy back to the compass; accept the first hint of the hitching tiller; believe not the artificial fire, when its redness makes all things look ghastly. To-morrow, in the natural sun, the skies will be bright; those who glared like devils in the forking flames, the morn will show in far other, at least gentler, relief; the glorious, golden, glad sun, the only true lamp—all others but liars!

Nevertheless the sun hides not Virginia's Dismal Swamp, nor Rome's accursed Campagna, nor wide Sahara, nor all the millions of miles of deserts and of griefs beneath the moon. The sun hides not the ocean, which is the dark side of this earth, and which is two thirds of this earth. So, therefore, that mortal man who hath more of joy than sorrow in him, that mortal man cannot be true—not true, or undeveloped. With books the same. The truest of all men was the Man of Sorrows, and the truest of all books is Solomon's, and Ecclesiastes is the fine hammered steel of woe. 'All is vanity.' ALL. This wilful world hath not got hold of unchristian Solomon's wisdom yet. But he who dodges hospitals and jails, and walks fast crossing grave-yards, and would rather talk of operas than hell; calls Cowper, Young, Pascal, Rousseau, poor devils all of sick men; and throughout a care-free lifetime swears by Rabelais as passing wise, and therefore jolly;—not that man is fitted to sit down on tomb-stones, and break the green damp mould with unfathomably wondrous Solomon.

But even Solomon, he says, 'the man that wandereth out of
the way of understanding shall remain' (*i.e.* even while living) 'in
the congregation of the dead.' Give not thyself up, then, to fire,
lest it invert thee, deaden thee; as for the time it did me. There
is wisdom that is woe; but there is a woe that is madness. And
there is a Catskill eagle in some souls that can alike dive down
into the blackest gorges, and soar out of them again and become
invisible in the sunny spaces.

And even if he for ever flies within the gorge, that gorge is in
the mountains; so that even in his lowest swoop the mountain
eagle is still higher than other birds upon the plain, even though
they soar.

97
THE LAMP

HAD you descended from the Pequod's try-works to the Pequod's
forecastle, where the off duty watch were sleeping, for one single
moment you would have almost thought you were standing in
some illuminated shrine of canonized kings and counsellors. There
they lay in their triangular oaken vaults, each mariner a chiselled
muteness; a score of lamps flashing upon his hooded eyes.

In merchantmen, oil for the sailor is more scarce than the milk
of queens. To dress in the dark, and eat in the dark, and stumble
in darkness to his pallet, this is his usual lot. But the whaleman,
as he seeks the food of light, so he lives in light. He makes his
berth an Aladdin's lamp, and lays him down in it; so that in the
pitchiest night the ship's black hull still houses an illumination.

See with what entire freedom the whaleman takes his handful
of lamps—often but old bottles and vials, though—to the copper
cooler at the try-works, and replenishes them there, as mugs of
ale at a vat. He burns, too, the purest of oil, in its unmanufactured,
and, therefore, unvitiated state; a fluid unknown to solar, lunar,
or astral contrivances ashore. It is sweet as early grass butter in
April. He goes and hunts for his oil, so as to be sure of its freshness
and genuineness, even as the traveller on the prairie hunts up his
own supper of game.

98

STOWING DOWN AND CLEARING UP

ALREADY has it been related how the great leviathan is afar off descried from the mast-head; how he is chased over the watery moors, and slaughtered in the valleys of the deep; how he is then towed alongside and beheaded; and how (on the principle which entitled the headsman of old to the garments in which the beheaded was killed) his great padded surtout becomes the property of his executioner; how, in due time, he is condemned to the pots, and, like Shadrach, Meshach, and Abednego, his spermaceti, oil, and bone pass unscathed through the fire;—but now it remains to conclude the last chapter of this part of the description by rehearsing—singing, if I may—the romantic proceeding of decanting off his oil into the casks and striking them down into the hold, where once again leviathan returns to his native profundities, sliding along beneath the surface as before; but, alas! never more to rise and blow.

While still warm, the oil, like hot punch, is received into the six-barrel casks; and while, perhaps, the ship is pitching and rolling this way and that in the midnight sea, the enormous casks are slewed round and headed over, end for end, and sometimes perilously scoot across the slippery deck, like so many land slides, till at last man-handled and stayed in their course; and all round the hoops, rap, rap, go as many hammers as can play upon them, for now, *ex officio*, every sailor is a cooper.

At length, when the last pint is casked, and all is cool, then the great hatchways are unsealed, the bowels of the ship are thrown open, and down go the casks to their final rest in the sea. This done, the hatches are replaced, and hermetically closed, like a closet walled up.

In the sperm fishery, this is perhaps one of the most remarkable incidents in all the business of whaling. One day the planks stream with freshets of blood and oil; on the sacred quarter-deck enormous masses of the whale's head are profanely piled; great rusty casks lie about, as in a brewery yard; the smoke from the try-works has besooted all the bulwarks; the mariners go about suffused with unctuousness; the entire ship seems great leviathan himself; while on all hands the din is deafening.

But a day or two after, you look about you, and prick your
ears in this self-same ship; and were it not for the telltale boats
and try-works, you would all but swear you trod some silent
merchant vessel, with a most scrupulously neat commander. The
unmanufactured sperm oil possesses a singularly cleansing virtue.
This is the reason why the decks never look so white as just after
what they call an affair of oil. Besides, from the ashes of the
burned scraps of the whale, a potent ley is readily made; and
whenever any adhesiveness from the back of the whale remains
clinging to the side, that ley quickly exterminates it. Hands go
diligently along the bulwarks, and with buckets of water and rags
restore them to their full tidiness. The soot is brushed from the
lower rigging. All the numerous implements which have been in
use are likewise faithfully cleansed and put away. The great hatch
is scrubbed and placed upon the try-works, completely hiding the
pots; every cask is out of sight; all tackles are coiled in unseen
nooks; and when by the combined and simultaneous industry of
almost the entire ship's company, the whole of this conscientious
duty is at last concluded, then the crew themselves proceed to
their own ablutions; shift themselves from top to toe; and finally
issue to the immaculate deck, fresh and all aglow, as bridegrooms
new-leaped from out the daintiest Holland.

Now, with elated step, they pace the planks in twos and threes,
and humorously discourse of parlors, sofas, carpets, and fine
cambrics; propose to mat the deck; think of having hangings to
the top; object not to taking tea by moonlight on the piazza of
the forecastle. To hint to such musked mariners of oil, and bone,
and blubber, were little short of audacity. They know not the
thing you distantly allude to. Away, and bring us napkins!

But mark: aloft there, at the three mast heads, stand three men
intent on spying out more whales, which, if caught, infallibly will
again soil the old oaken furniture, and drop at least one small
grease-spot somewhere. Yes; and many is the time, when, after
the severest uninterrupted labors, which know no night; continuing
straight through for ninety-six hours; when from the boat, where
they have swelled their wrists with all day rowing on the Line,—
they only step to the deck to carry vast chains, and heave the
heavy windlass, and cut and slash, yea, and in their very sweatings
to be smoked and burned anew by the combined fires of the
equatorial sun and the equatorial try-works; when, on the heel of
all this, they have finally bestirred themselves to cleanse the ship,
and make a spotless dairy room of it; many is the time the poor
fellows, just buttoning the necks of their clean frocks, are startled

by the cry of 'There she blows!' and away they fly to fight another whale, and go through the whole weary thing again. Oh! my friends, but this is man-killing! Yet this is life. For hardly have we mortals by long toilings extracted from this world's vast bulk its small but valuable sperm; and then, with weary patience, cleansed ourselves from its defilements, and learned to live here in clean tabernacles of the soul; hardly is this done, when—*There she blows!*—the ghost is spouted up, and away we sail to fight some other world, and go through young life's old routine again.

Oh! the metempsychosis! Oh! Pythagoras, that in bright Greece, two thousand years ago, did die, so good, so wise, so mild; I sailed with thee along the Peruvian coast last voyage—and, foolish as I am, taught thee, a green simple boy, how to splice a rope!

99
THE DOUBLOON

ERE now it has been related how Ahab was wont to pace his quarter-deck, taking regular turns at either limit, the binnacle and mainmast; but in the multiplicity of other things requiring narration it has not been added how that sometimes in these walks, when most plunged in his mood, he was wont to pause in turn at each spot, and stand there strangely eyeing the particular object before him. When he halted before the binnacle, with his glance fastened on the pointed needle in the compass, that glance shot like a javelin with the pointed intensity of his purpose; and when resuming his walk he again paused before the mainmast, then, as the same riveted glance fastened upon the riveted gold coin there, he still wore the same aspect of nailed firmness, only dashed with a certain wild longing, if not hopefulness.

But one morning, turning to pass the doubloon, he seemed to be newly attracted by the strange figures and inscriptions stamped on it, as though now for the first time beginning to interpret for himself in some monomaniac way whatever significance might lurk in them. And some certain significance lurks in all things, else all things are little worth, and the round world itself but an empty cipher, except to sell by the cartload, as they do hills about Boston, to fill up some morass in the Milky Way.

Now this doubloon was of purest, virgin gold, raked somewhere out of the heart of gorgeous hills, whence, east and west, over golden sands, the head-waters of many a Pactolus flow. And though now nailed amidst all the rustiness of iron bolts and the verdigris of copper spikes, yet, untouchable and immaculate to any foulness, it still preserved its Quito glow. Nor, though placed amongst a ruthless crew and every hour passed by ruthless hands, and through the livelong nights shrouded with thick darkness which might cover any pilfering approach, nevertheless every sunrise found the doubloon where the sunset left it last. For it was set apart and sanctified to one awe-striking end; and however wanton in their sailor ways, one and all, the mariners revered it as the white whale's talisman. Sometimes they talked it over in the weary watch by night, wondering whose it was to be at last, and whether he would ever live to spend it.

Now these noble golden coins of South America are as medals of the sun and tropic token-pieces. Here palms, alpacas, and volcanoes; sun's disks and stars; ecliptics, horns-of-plenty, and rich banners waving, are in luxuriant profusion stamped; so that the precious gold seems almost to derive an added preciousness and enhancing glories, by passing through those fancy mints, so Spanishly poetic.

It so chanced that the doubloon of the Pequod was a most wealthy example of these things. On its round border it bore the letters, REPUBLICA DEL ECUADOR: QUITO. So this bright coin came from a country planted in the middle of the world, and beneath the great equator, and named after it; and it had been cast midway up the Andes, in the unwaning clime that knows no autumn. Zoned by those letters you saw the likeness of three Andes' summits; from one a flame; a tower on another; on the third a crowing cock; while arching over all was a segment of the partitioned zodiac, the signs all marked with their usual cabalistics, and the keystone sun entering the equinoctial point of Libra.

Before this equatorial coin, Ahab, not unobserved by others, was now pausing.

'There's something ever egotistical in mountain-tops and towers, and all other grand and lofty things; look here,—three peaks as proud as Lucifer. The firm tower, that is Ahab; the volcano, that is Ahab; the courageous, the undaunted, and victorious fowl, that, too, is Ahab; all are Ahab; and this round gold is but the image of the rounder globe, which, like a magician's glass, to each and every man in turn but mirrors back his own mysterious self. Great pains, small gains for those who ask the world to solve them; it cannot solve itself. Methinks now this coined sun wears a ruddy face; but see! aye, he enters the sign of storms, the equinox! and

but six months before he wheeled out of a former equinox at
Aries! From storm to storm! So be it, then. Born in throes, 'tis
fit that man should live in pains and die in pangs! So be it, then!
Here's stout stuff for woe to work on. So be it, then.'

'No fairy fingers can have pressed the gold, but devil's claws
must have left their mouldings there since yesterday,' murmured
Starbuck to himself, leaning against the bulwarks. 'The old man
seems to read Belshazzar's awful writing. I have never marked the
coin inspectingly. He goes below; let me read. A dark valley
between three mighty, heaven-abiding peaks, that almost seem the
Trinity, in some faint earthly symbol. So in this vale of Death,
God girds us round; and over all our gloom, the sun of Righteousness still shines a beacon and a hope. If we bend down our
eyes, the dark vale shows her mouldy soil; but if we lift them,
the bright sun meets our glance half way, to cheer. Yet, oh, the
great sun is no fixture; and if, at midnight, we would fain snatch
some sweet solace from him, we gaze for him in vain! This coin
speaks wisely, mildly, truly, but still sadly to me. I will quit it,
lest Truth shake me falsely.'

'There now's the old Mogul,' soliloquized Stubb by the try-
works, 'he's been twigging it; and there goes Starbuck from the
same, and both with faces which I should say might be somewhere
within nine fathoms long. And all from looking at a piece of gold,
which did I have it now on Negro Hill or in Corlaer's Hook, I'd
not look at it very long ere spending it. Humph! in my poor,
insignificant opinion, I regard this as queer. I have seen doubloons
before now in my voyagings; your doubloons of old Spain, your
doubloons of Peru, your doubloons of Chili, your doubloons of
Bolivia, your doubloons of Popayan; with plenty of gold moidores
and pistols, and joes, and half joes, and quarter joes. What then
should there be in this doubloon of the Equator that is so killing
wonderful? By Golconda! let me read it once. Halloa! here's signs
and wonders truly! That, now, is what old Bowditch in his Epitome
calls the zodiac, and what my almanack below calls ditto. I'll get
the almanack; and as I have heard devils can be raised with
Daboll's arithmetic, I'll try my hand at raising a meaning out of
these queer curvicues here with the Massachusetts calendar. Here's
the book. Let's see now. Signs and wonders; and the sun, he's
always among 'em. Hem, hem, hem; here they are—here they
go—all alive:—Aries, or the Ram; Taurus, or the Bull; and
Jimini! here's Gemini himself, or the Twins. Well; the sun he
wheels among 'em. Aye, here on the coin he's just crossing the
threshold between two of twelve sitting-rooms all in a ring. Book!

you lie there; the fact is, you books must know your places. You'll do to give us the bare words and facts, but we come in to supply the thoughts. That's my small experience, so far as the Massachusetts calendar, and Bowditch's navigator, and Daboll's arithmetic go. Signs and wonders, eh? Pity if there is nothing wonderful in signs, and significant in wonders! There's a clue somewhere; wait a bit; hist—hark! By Jove, I have it! Look you, Doubloon, your zodiac here is the life of man in one round chapter; and now I'll read it off, straight out of the book. Come, Almanack! To begin: there's Aries, or the Ram—lecherous dog, he begets us; then, Taurus, or the Bull—he bumps us the first thing; then Gemini, or the Twins—that is, Virtue and Vice; we try to reach Virtue, when lo! come Cancer the Crab, and drags us back; and here, going from Virtue, Leo, a roaring Lion, lies in the path— he gives a few fierce bites and surly dabs with his paw; we escape, and hail Virgo, the Virgin! that's our first love; we marry and think to be happy for aye, when pop comes Libra, or the Scales— happiness weighed and found wanting; and while we are very sad about that, Lord! how we suddenly jump, as Scorpio, or the Scorpion, stings us in rear; we are curing the wound, when whang come the arrows all around; Sagittarius, or the Archer, is amusing himself. As we pluck out the shafts, stand aside! here's the battering-ram, Capricornus, or the Goat; full tilt, he comes rushing, and head-long we are tossed; when Aquarius, or the Water-bearer, pours out his whole deluge and drowns us; and to wind up with Pisces, or the Fishes, we sleep. There's a sermon now, writ in high heaven, and the sun goes through it every year, and yet comes out of it all alive and hearty. Jollily, he, aloft there, wheels through toil and trouble; and so, alow here, does jolly Stubb. Oh, jolly's the word for aye! Adieu, Doubloon! But stop; here comes little King-Post; dodge round the try-works, now, and let's hear what he'll have to say. There; he's before it; he'll out with something presently. So, so; he's beginning.'

'I see nothing here, but a round thing made of gold, and whoever raises a certain whale, this round thing belongs to him. So, what's all this staring been about? It is worth sixteen dollars, that's true; and at two cents the cigar, that's nine hundred and sixty cigars. I wont smoke dirty pipes like Stubb, but I like cigars, and here's nine hundred and sixty of them; so here goes Flask aloft to spy 'em out.'

'Shall I call that wise or foolish, now; if it be really wise it has a foolish look to it; yet, if it be really foolish, then has it a sort of wiseish look to it. But, avast; here comes our old Manxman—

the old hearse-driver, he must have been, that is, before he took
to the sea. He luffs up before the doubloon; halloa, and goes
round on the other side of the mast; why, there's a horse-shoe
nailed on that side; and now he's back again; what does that
mean? Hark! he's muttering—voice like an old worn-out coffee-
mill. Prick ears, and listen!'

'If the White Whale be raised, it must be in a month and a
day, when the sun stands in some one of these signs. I've studied
signs, and know their marks; they were taught me two score years
ago, by the old witch in Copenhagen. Now, in what sign will the
sun then be? The horse-shoe sign; for there it is, right opposite
the gold. And what's the horse-shoe sign? The lion is the horse-
shoe sign—the roaring and devouring lion. Ship, old ship! my old
head shakes to think of thee.'

'There's another rendering now; but still one text. All sorts of
men in one kind of world, you see. Dodge again! here comes
Queequeg—all tattooing—looks like the signs of the Zodiac himself. What says the Cannibal? As I live he's comparing notes;
looking at his thigh bone; thinks the sun is in the thigh, or in
the calf, or in the bowels, I suppose, as the old women talk
Surgeon's Astronomy in the back country. And by Jove, he's
found something there in the vicinity of his thigh—I guess it's
Sagittarius, or the Archer. No: he don't know what to make of
the doubloon; he takes it for an old button off some king's trowsers.
But, aside again! here comes that ghost-devil, Fedallah; tail coiled
out of sight as usual, oakum in the toes of his pumps as usual.
What does he say, with that look of his? Ah, only makes a sign
to the sign and bows himself; there is a sun on the coin—fire
worshipper, depend upon it. Ho! more and more. This way comes
Pip—poor boy! would he had died, or I; he's half horrible to me.
He too has been watching all of these interpreters—myself included—and look now, he comes to read, with that unearthly
idiot face. Stand away again and hear him. Hark!'

'I look, you look, he looks; we look, ye look, they look.'

'Upon my soul, he's been studying Murray's Grammar! Improving his mind, poor fellow! But what's that he says now—
hist!'

'I look, you look, he looks; we look, ye look, they look.'

'Why, he's getting it by heart—hist! again.'

'I look, you look, he looks; we look, ye look, they look.'

'Well, that's funny.'

'And I, you, and he; and we, ye, and they, are all bats; and
I'm a crow, especially when I stand a'top of this pine tree here.

Caw! caw! caw! caw! caw! caw! Ain't I a crow? And where's the scare-crow? There he stands; two bones stuck into a pair of old trowsers, and two more poked into the sleeves of an old jacket.'

'Wonder if he means me?—complimentary!—poor lad!—I could go hang myself. Any way, for the present, I'll quit Pip's vicinity. I can stand the rest, for they have plain wits; but he's too crazy-witty for my sanity. So, so, I leave him muttering.'

'Here's the ship's navel, this doubloon here, and they are all on fire to unscrew it. But, unscrew your navel, and what's the consequence? Then again, if it stays here, that is ugly, too, for when aught's nailed to the mast it's a sign that things grow desperate. Ha, ha! old Ahab! the White Whale; he'll nail ye! This is a pine tree. My father, in old Tolland county, cut down a pine tree once, and found a silver ring grown over in it; some old darkey's wedding ring. How did it get there? And so they'll say in the resurrection, when they come to fish up this old mast, and find a doubloon lodged in it, with bedded oysters for the shaggy bark. Oh, the gold! the precious, precious gold!—the green miser 'll hoard ye soon! Hish! hish! God goes 'mong the worlds blackber-rying. Cook! ho, cook! and cook us! Jenny! hey, hey, hey, hey, hey, Jenny, Jenny! and get your hoecake done!'

100

LEG AND ARM

THE PEQUOD, OF NANTUCKET, MEETS THE SAMUEL ENDERBY, OF LONDON

'SHIP, ahoy! Hast seen the White Whale?'

So cried Ahab, once more hailing a ship showing English colors, bearing down under the stern. Trumpet to mouth, the old man was standing in his hoisted quarter-boat, his ivory leg plainly revealed to the stranger captain, who was carelessly reclining in his own boat's bow. He was a darkly-tanned, burly, good-natured, fine-looking man, of sixty or thereabouts, dressed in a spacious roundabout, that hung round him in festoons of blue pilot-cloth; and one empty arm of this jacket streamed behind him like the broidered arm of a huzzar's surcoat.

'Hast seen the White Whale?'

'See you this?' and withdrawing it from the folds that had hidden it, he held up a white arm of sperm whale bone, terminating in a wooden head like a mallet.

'Man my boat!' cried Ahab, impetuously, and tossing about the oars near him—'Stand by to lower!'

In less than a minute, without quitting his little craft, he and his crew were dropped to the water, and were soon alongside of the stranger. But here a curious difficulty presented itself. In the excitement of the moment, Ahab had forgotten that since the loss of his leg he had never once stepped on board of any vessel at sea but his own, and then it was always by an ingenious and very handy mechanical contrivance peculiar to the Pequod, and a thing not to be rigged and shipped in any other vessel at a moment's warning. Now, it is no very easy matter for anybody—except those who are almost hourly used to it, like whalemen—to clamber up a ship's side from a boat on the open sea; for the great swells now lift the boat high up towards the bulwarks, and then instantaneously drop it half way down to the kelson. So, deprived of one leg, and the strange ship of course being altogether unsupplied with the kindly invention, Ahab now found himself abjectly reduced to a clumsy landsman again; hopelessly eyeing the uncertain changeful height he could hardly hope to attain.

It has before been hinted, perhaps, that every little untoward circumstance that befell him, and which indirectly sprang from his luckless mishap, almost invariably irritated or exasperated Ahab. And in the present instance, all this was heightened by the sight of the two officers of the strange ship, leaning over the side, by the perpendicular ladder of nailed cleets there, and swinging towards him a pair of tastefully-ornamented man-ropes; for at first they did not seem to bethink them that a one-legged man must be too much of a cripple to use their sea bannisters. But this awkwardness only lasted a minute, because the strange captain, observing at a glance how affairs stood, cried out, 'I see, I see!—avast heaving there! Jump, boys, and swing over the cutting-tackle.'

As good luck would have it, they had had a whale alongside a day or two previous, and the great tackles were still aloft, and the massive curved blubber-hook, now clean and dry, was still attached to the end. This was quickly lowered to Ahab, who at once comprehending it all, slid his solitary thigh into the curve of the hook (it was like sitting in the fluke of an anchor, or the crotch of an apple tree), and then giving the word, held himself fast, and at the same time also helped to hoist his own weight, by pulling hand-over-hand upon one of the running parts of the tackle. Soon he was carefully swung inside the high bulwarks, and gently landed upon the capstan head. With his ivory arm frankly thrust forth

in welcome, the other captain advanced, and Ahab, putting out
his ivory leg, and crossing the ivory arm (like two sword-fish
blades) cried out in his walrus way, 'Aye, aye, hearty! let us shake
bones together!—an arm and a leg!—and arm that never can
shrink, d'ye see; and a leg that never can run. Where did'st thou
see the White Whale?—how long ago?'

'The White Whale,' said the Englishman, pointing his ivory arm
towards the East, and taking a rueful sight along it, as if it had
been a telescope; 'There I saw him, on the Line, last season.'

'And he took that arm off, did he?' asked Ahab, now sliding
down from the capstan, and resting on the Englishman's shoulder,
as he did so.

'Aye, he was the cause of it, at least; and that leg, too?'

'Spin me the yarn,' said Ahab; 'how was it?'

'It was the first time in my life that I ever cruised on the Line,'
began the Englishman. 'I was ignorant of the White Whale at that
time. Well, one day we lowered for a pod of four or five whales,
and my boat fastened to one of them; a regular circus horse he
was, too, that went milling and milling round so, that my boat's
crew could only trim dish, by sitting all their sterns on the outer
gunwale. Presently up breaches from the bottom of the sea a
bouncing great whale, with a milky-white head and hump, all
crows' feet and wrinkles.'

'It was he, it was he!' cried Ahab, suddenly letting out his
suspended breath.

'And harpoons sticking in near his starboard fin.'

'Aye, aye—they were mine—*my* irons,' cried Ahab, exultingly—
'but on!'

'Give me a chance, then,' said the Englishman, goodhumoredly.
'Well, this old great-grandfather, with the white head and hump,
runs all afoam into the pod, and goes to snapping furiously at
my fast-line.'

'Aye, I see!—wanted to part it; free the fast-fish—an old trick—
I know him.'

'How it was exactly,' continued the one-armed commander, 'I
do not know; but in biting the line, it got foul of his teeth, caught
there somehow; but we didn't know it then; so that when we
afterwards pulled on the line, bounce we came plump on to his
hump! instead of the other whale's that went off to windward, all
fluking. Seeing how matters stood, and what a noble great whale
it was—the noblest and biggest I ever saw, sir, in my life—I
resolved to capture him, spite of the boiling rage he seemed to
be in. And thinking the hap-hazard line would get loose, or the

tooth it was tangled to might draw (for I have a devil of a boat's
crew for a pull on a whale-line); seeing all this, I say, I jumped
into my first mate's boat—Mr Mounttop's here (by the way,
Captain—Mounttop; Mounttop—the captain);—as I was saying,
I jumped into Mounttop's boat, which, d'ye see, was gunwale and
gunwale with mine, then; and snatching the first harpoon, let this
old great-grandfather have it. But, Lord, look you, sir—hearts and
souls alive, man—the next instant, in a jiff, I was blind as a bat—
both eyes out—all befogged and bedeadened with black foam—
the whale's tail looming straight up out of it, perpendicular in the
air, like a marble steeple. No use sterning all, then; but as I was
groping at midday, with a blinding sun, all crown-jewels; as I was
groping, I say, after the second iron, to toss it overboard—down
comes the tail like a Lima tower, cutting my boat in two, leaving
each half in splinters; and, flukes first, the white hump backed
through the wreck, as though it was all chips. We all struck out.
To escape his terrible flailings, I seized hold of my harpoon-pole
sticking in him, and for a moment clung to that like a sucking
fish. But a combing sea dashed me off, and at the same instant,
the fish, taking one good dart forwards, went down like a flash;
and the barb of that cursed second iron towing along near me
caught me here' (clapping his hand just below his shoulders); 'yes,
caught me just here, I say, and bore me down to Hell's flames,
I was thinking; when, when, all of a sudden, thank the good God,
the barb ript its way along the flesh—clear along the whole length
of my arm—came out nigh my wrist, and up I floated;—and that
gentleman there will tell you the rest (by the way, captain—Dr
Bunger, ship's surgeon: Bunger, my lad,—the captain). Now, Bunger boy, spin your part of the yarn.'

The professional gentleman thus familiarly pointed out, had
been all the time standing near them, with nothing specific visible,
to denote his gentlemanly rank on board. His face was an exceedingly round but sober one; he was dressed in a faded blue
woollen frock or shirt, and patched trowsers; and had thus far
been dividing his attention between a marlingspike he held in one
hand, and a pill-box held in the other, occasionally casting a
critical glance at the ivory limbs of the two crippled captains. But,
at his superior's introduction of him to Ahab, he politely bowed,
and straightway went on to do his captain's bidding.

'It was a shocking bad wound,' began the whale-surgeon;
'and, taking my advice, Captain Boomer here, stood our old
Sammy—'

'Samuel Enderby is the name of my ship,' interrupted the one-armed captain, addressing Ahab; 'go on, boy.'

'Stood our old Sammy off to the northward, to get out of the blazing hot weather there on the Line. But it was no use—I did all I could; sat up with him nights; was very severe with him in the matter of diet—'

'Oh, very severe!' chimed in the patient himself; then suddenly altering his voice, 'Drinking hot rum toddies with me every night, till he couldn't see to put on the bandages; and sending me to bed, half seas over, about three o'clock in the morning. Oh, ye stars! he sat up with me indeed, and was very severe in my diet. Oh! a great watcher, and very dietetically severe, is Dr Bunger. (Bunger, you dog, laugh out! why don't ye? You know you're a precious jolly rascal.) But, heave ahead, boy, I'd rather be killed by you than kept alive by any other man.'

'My captain, you must have ere this perceived, respected sir'— said the imperturbable godly-looking Bunger, slightly bowing to Ahab—'is apt to be facetious at times; he spins us many clever things of that sort. But I may as well say—en passant, as the French remark—that I myself—that is to say, Jack Bunger, late of the reverend clergy—am a strict total abstinence man; I never drink—'

'Water!' cried the captain; 'he never drinks it; it's a sort of fits to him; fresh water throws him into the hydrophobia; but go on— go on with the arm story.'

'Yes, I may as well,' said the surgeon, coolly. 'I was about observing, sir, before Captain Boomer's facetious interruption, that spite of my best and severest endeavors, the wound kept getting worse and worse; the truth was, sir, it was as ugly gaping wound as surgeon ever saw; more than two feet and several inches long. I measured it with the lead line. In short, it grew black; I knew what was threatened, and off it came. But I had no hand in shipping that ivory arm there; that thing is against all rule'— pointing at it with the marlingspike—'that is the captain's work, not mine; he ordered the carpenter to make it; he had that clubhammer there put to the end, to knock some one's brains out with, I suppose, as he tried mine once. He flies into diabolical passions sometimes. Do ye see this dent, sir'—removing his hat, and brushing aside his hair, and exposing a bowl-like cavity in his skull, but which bore not the slightest scarry trace, or any token of ever having been a wound—'Well, the captain there will tell you how that came here; he knows.'

'No, I don't,' said the captain, 'but his mother did; he was born with it. Oh, you solemn rogue, you—you Bunger! was there ever

such another Bunger in the watery world? Bunger, when you die,
you ought to die in pickle, you dog; you should be preserved to
future ages, you rascal.'

'What became of the White Whale?' now cried Ahab, who thus
far had been impatiently listening to this bye-play between the
two Englishmen.

'Oh!' cried the one-armed captain, 'Oh, yes! Well; after he
sounded, we didn't see him again for some time; in fact, as I
before hinted, I didn't then know what whale it was that had
served me such a trick, till some time afterwards, when coming
back to the Line, we heard about Moby Dick—as some call him—
and then I knew it was he.'

'Did'st thou cross his wake again?'

'Twice.'

'But could not fasten?'

'Didn't want to try to: ain't one limb enough? What should I
do without this other arm? And I'm thinking Moby Dick doesn't
bite so much as he swallows.'

'Well, then,' interrupted Bunger, 'give him your left arm for
bait to get the right. Do you know, gentlemen'—very gravely and
mathematically bowing to each Captain in succession—'Do you
know, gentlemen, that the digestive organs of the whale are so
inscrutably constructed by Divine Providence, that it is quite
impossible for him to completely digest even a man's arm? And
he knows it too. So that what you take for the White Whale's
malice is only his awkwardness. For he never means to swallow
a single limb; he only thinks to terrify by feints. But sometimes
he is like the old juggling fellow, formerly a patient of mine in
Ceylon, that making believe swallow jack-knives, once upon a
time let one drop into him in good earnest, and there it stayed
for a twelvemonth or more; when I gave him an emetic, and he
heaved it up in small tacks, d'ye see. No possible way for him
to digest that jack-knife, and fully incorporate it into his general
bodily system. Yes, Captain Boomer, if you are quick enough
about it, and have a mind to pawn one arm for the sake of the
privilege of giving decent burial to the other, why in that case the
arm is yours; only let the whale have another chance at you
shortly, that's all.'

'No, thank ye, Bunger,' said the English Captain, 'he's welcome
to the arm he has, since I can't help it, and didn't know him
then; but not to another one. No more White Whales for me;
I've lowered for him once, and that has satisfied me. There would
be great glory in killing him, I know that; and there is a ship-

load of precious sperm in him, but, hark ye, he's best let alone;
don't you think so, Captain?'—glancing at the ivory leg.

'He is. But he will still be hunted, for all that. What is best let
alone, that accursed thing is not always what least allures. He's
all a magnet! How long since thou saw'st him last? Which way
heading?'

'Bless my soul, and curse the foul fiend's,' cried Bunger, stoop-
ingly walking round Ahab, and like a dog, strangely snuffing; 'this
man's blood—bring the thermometer;—it's at the boiling point!—
his pulse makes these planks beat!—sir!'—taking a lancet from
his pocket, and drawing near to Ahab's arm.

'Avast!' roared Ahab, dashing him against the bulwarks—'Man
the boat! Which way heading?'

'Good God!' cried the English Captain, to whom the question
was put. 'What's the matter? He was heading east, I think.—Is
your Captain crazy?' whispering Fedallah.

But Fedallah, putting a finger on his lip, slid over the bulwarks
to take the boat's steering oar, and Ahab, swinging the cutting-
tackle towards him, commanded the ship's sailors to stand by to
lower.

In a moment he was standing in the boat's stern, and the
Manilla men were springing to their oars. In vain the English
Captain hailed him. With back to the stranger ship, and face set
like a flint to his own, Ahab stood upright till alongside of the
Pequod.

101
THE DECANTER

ERE the English ship fades from sight, be it set down here, that
she hailed from London, and was named after the late Samuel
Enderby, merchant of that city, the original of the famous whaling
house of Enderby & Sons; a house which in my poor whaleman's
opinion, comes not far behind the united royal houses of the
Tudors and Bourbons, in point of real historical interest. How
long, prior to the year of our Lord 1775, this great whaling house
was in existence, my numerous fish-documents do not make plain;
but in that year (1775) it fitted out the first English ships that
ever regularly hunted the Sperm Whale; though for some score
of years previous (ever since 1726) our valiant Coffins and Maceys

of Nantucket and the Vineyard had in large fleets pursued that Leviathan, but only in the North and South Atlantic: not elsewhere. Be it distinctly recorded here, that the Nantucketers were the first among mankind to harpoon with civilized steel the great Sperm Whale; and that for half a century they were the only people of the whole globe who so harpooned him.

In 1778, a fine ship, the Amelia, fitted out for the express purpose, and at the sole charge of the vigorous Enderbys, boldly rounded Cape Horn, and was the first among the nations to lower a whale-boat of any sort in the great South Sea. The voyage was a skilful and lucky one; and returning to her berth with her hold full of the precious sperm, the Amelia's example was soon followed by other ships, English and American, and thus the vast Sperm Whale grounds of the Pacific were thrown open. But not content with this good deed, the indefatigable house again bestirred itself: Samuel and all his Sons—how many, their mother only knows— and under their immediate auspices, and partly, I think, at their expense, the British government was induced to send the sloop-of-war Rattler on a whaling voyage of discovery into the South Sea. Commanded by a naval Post-Captain, the Rattler made a rattling voyage of it, and did some service; how much does not appear. But this is not all. In 1819, the same house fitted out a discovery whale ship of their own, to go on a testing cruise to the remote waters of Japan. That ship—well called the 'Syren'— made a noble experimental cruise; and it was thus that the great Japanese Whaling Ground first became generally known. The Syren in this famous voyage was commanded by a Captain Coffin, a Nantucketer.

All honor to the Enderbies, therefore, whose house, I think, exists to the present day; though doubtless the original Samuel must long ago have slipped his cable for the great South Sea of the other world.

The ship named after him was worthy of the honor, being a very fast sailer and a noble craft every way. I boarded her once at midnight somewhere off the Patagonian coast, and drank good flip down in the forecastle. It was a fine gam we had, and they were all trumps—every soul on board. A short life to them, and a jolly death. And that fine gam I had—long, very long after old Ahab touched her planks with his ivory heel—it minds me of the noble, solid, Saxon hospitality of that ship; and may my parson forget me, and the devil remember me, if I ever lose sight of it. Flip? Did I say we had flip? Yes, and we flipped it at the rate of ten gallons the hour; and when the squall came (for it's squally off there by Patagonia), and all hands—visitors and all—were called to reef topsails, we were so top-heavy that we had to swing each other aloft in bowlines; and we ignorantly furled the skirts of our jackets into the sails, so that we hung there, reefed fast in the howling gale, a warning example to all drunken tars. However, the masts did not go overboard; and by and bye we scrambled down, so sober, that we had to pass the flip again, though the savage salt spray bursting down the forecastle scuttle, rather too much diluted and pickled it to my taste.

The beef was fine—tough, but with body in it. They said it was bull-beef; others, that it was dromedary beef; but I do not know, for certain, how that was. They had dumplings too; small, but substantial, symmetrically globular, and indestructible dumplings. I fancied that you could feel them, and roll them about in you after they were swallowed. If you stooped over too far forward, you risked their pitching out of you like billiard-balls. The bread— but that couldn't be helped; besides, it was an anti-scorbutic; in short, the bread contained the only fresh fare they had. But the forecastle was not very light, and it was very easy to step over into a dark corner when you ate it. But all in all, taking her from truck to helm, considering the dimensions of the cook's boilers, including his own live parchment boilers; fore and aft, I say, the Samuel Enderby was a jolly ship; of good fare and plenty; fine flip and strong; crack fellows all, and capital from boot heels to hat-band.

But why was it, think ye, that the Samuel Enderby, and some other English whalers I know of—not all though—were such famous, hospitable ships; that passed round the beef, and the bread, and the can, and the joke; and were not soon weary of eating, and drinking, and laughing? I will tell you. The abounding good cheer of these English whalers is matter for historical research. Nor have I been at all sparing of historical whale research, when it has seemed needed.

The English were preceded in the whale fishery by the Hollanders, Zealanders, and Danes; from whom they derived many terms still extant in the fishery; and what is yet more, their fat old fashions, touching plenty to eat and drink. For, as a general thing, the English merchant-ship scrimps her crew; but not so the English whaler. Hence, in the English, this thing of whaling good cheer is not normal and natural, but incidental and particular; and, therefore, must have some special origin, which is here pointed out, and will be still further elucidated.

During my researches in the Leviathanic histories, I stumbled

upon an ancient Dutch volume, which, by the musty whaling
smell of it, I knew must be about whalers. The title was, 'Dan
Coopman,' wherefore I concluded that this must be the invaluable
memoirs of some Amsterdam cooper in the fishery, as every whale
ship must carry its cooper. I was reinforced in this opinion by
seeing that it was the production of one 'Fitz Swackhammer.' But
my friend Dr Snodhead, a very learned man, professor of Low
Dutch and High German in the college of Santa Claus and St
Pott's, to whom I handed the work for translation, giving him a
box of sperm candles for his trouble—this same Dr Snodhead, so
soon as he spied the book, assured me that 'Dan Coopman' did
not mean 'The Cooper,' but 'The Merchant.' In short, this ancient
and learned Low Dutch book treated of the commerce of Holland;
and, among other subjects, contained a very interesting account
of its whale fishery. And in this chapter it was, headed 'Smeer,'
or 'Fat,' that I found a long detailed list of the outfits for the
larders and cellars of 180 sail of Dutch whalemen; from which
list, as translated by Dr Snodhead, I transcribe the following:

400,000 lbs. of beef.
 60,000 lbs. Friesland pork.
150,000 lbs. of stock fish.
550,000 lbs. of biscuit.
 72,000 lbs. of soft bread.
  2,800 firkins of butter.
 20,000 lbs. Texel & Leyden cheese.
144,000 lbs. cheese (probably an inferior article).
   550 ankers of Geneva.
 10,800 barrels of beer.

Most statistical tables are parchingly dry in the reading; not so
in the present case, however, where the reader is flooded with
whole pipes, barrels, quarts, and gills of good gin and good cheer.

At the time, I devoted three days to the studious digesting of
all this beer, beef, and bread, during which many profound thoughts
were incidentally suggested to me, capable of a transcendental and
Platonic application; and, furthermore, I compiled supplementary
tables of my own, touching the probable quantity of stock-fish,
&c., consumed by every Low Dutch harpooner in that ancient
Greenland and Spitzbergen whale fishery. In the first place, the
amount of butter, and Texel and Leyden cheese consumed, seems
amazing. I impute it, though, to their naturally unctuous natures,
being rendered still more unctuous by the nature of their vocation,
and especially by their pursuing their game in those frigid Polar

Seas, on the very coasts of that Esquimaux country where the convivial natives pledge each other in bumpers of train oil.

The quantity of beer, too, is very large, 10,800 barrels. Now, as those polar fisheries could only be prosecuted in the short summer of that climate, so that the whole cruise of one of these Dutch whalemen, including the short voyage to and from the Spitzbergen sea, did not much exceed three months, say, and reckoning 30 men to each of their fleet of 180 sail, we have 5,400 Low Dutch seamen in all; therefore, I say, we have precisely two barrels of beer per man, for a twelve weeks' allowance, exclusive of his fair proportion of that 550 ankers of gin. Now, whether these gin and beer harpooneers, so fuddled as one might fancy them to have been, were the right sort of men to stand up in a boat's head, and take good aim at flying whales; this would seem somewhat improbable. Yet they did aim at them, and hit them too. But this was very far North, be it remembered, where beer agrees well with the constitution; upon the Equator, in our southern fishery, beer would be apt to make the harpooneer sleepy at the mast-head and boozy in his boat; and grievous loss might ensure to Nantucket and New Bedford.

But no more; enough has been said to show that the old Dutch whalers of two or three centuries ago were high livers; and that the English whalers have not neglected so excellent an example. For, say they, when cruising in an empty ship, if you can get nothing better out of the world, get a good dinner out of it, at least. And this empties the decanter.

102

A BOWER IN THE ARSACIDES

HITHERTO, in descriptively treating of the Sperm Whale, I have chiefly dwelt upon the marvels of his outer aspect; or separately and in detail upon some few interior structural features. But to a large and thorough sweeping comprehension of him, it behoves me now to unbutton him still further, and untrussing the points of his hose, unbuckling his garters, and casting loose the hooks and the eyes of the joints of his innermost bones, set him before you in his ultimatum; that is to say, in his unconditional skeleton.

But how now, Ishmael? How is it, that you, a mere oarsman in the fishery, pretend to know aught about the subterranean parts of the whale? Did erudite Stubb, mounted upon your capstan, deliver lectures on the anatomy of the Cetacea; and by help of the windlass, hold up a specimen rib for exhibition? Explain thyself, Ishmael. Can you land a full-grown whale on your deck for examination, as a cook dishes a roast-pig? Surely not. A veritable witness have you hitherto been, Ishmael; but have a care how you seize the privilege of Jonah alone; the privilege of discoursing upon the joists and beams; the rafters, ridge-pole, sleepers, and under-pinnings, making up the frame-work of leviathan; and belike of the tallow-vats, dairy-rooms, butteries, and cheeseries in his bowels.

I confess, that since Jonah, few whalemen have penetrated very far beneath the skin of the adult whale; nevertheless, I have been blessed with an opportunity to dissect him in miniature. In a ship I belonged to, a small cub Sperm Whale was once bodily hoisted to the deck for his poke or bag, to make sheaths for the barbs of the harpoons, and for the heads of the lances. Think you I let that chance go, without using my boat-hatchet and jack-knife, and breaking the seal and reading all the contents of that young cub?

And as for my exact knowledge of the bones of the leviathan in their gigantic, full grown development, for that rare knowledge I am indebted to my late royal friend Tranquo, king of Tranque, one of the Arsacides. For being at Tranque, years ago, when attached to the trading-ship Dey of Algiers, I was invited to spend part of the Arsacidean holidays with the Lord of Tranque, at his retired palm villa at Pupella; a sea-side glen not very far distant from what our sailors called Bamboo-Town, his capital.

Among many other fine qualities, my royal friend Tranquo, being gifted with a devout love for all matters of barbaric vertù, had brought together in Pupella whatever rare things the more ingenious of his people could invent; chiefly carved woods of wonderful devices, chiselled shells, inlaid spears, costly paddles, aromatic canoes; and all these distributed among whatever natural wonders, the wonder-freighted, tribute-rendering waves had cast upon his shores.

Chief among these latter was a great Sperm Whale, which, after an unusually long raging gale, had been found dead and stranded, with his head against a cocoa-nut tree, whose plumage-like, tufted droopings seemed his verdant jet. When the vast body had at last been stripped of its fathom-deep enfoldings, and the bones become dust dry in the sun, then the skeleton was carefully transported up the Pupella glen, where a grand temple of lordly palms now sheltered it.

The ribs were hung with trophies; the vertebræ were carved with Arsacidean annals, in strange hieroglyphics; in the skull, the priests kept up an unextinguished aromatic flame, so that the mystic head again sent forth its vapory spout; while, suspended from a bough, the terrific lower jaw vibrated over all the devotees, like the hair-hung sword that so affrighted Damocles.

It was a wondrous sight. The wood was green as mosses of the Icy Glen; the trees stood high and haughty, feeling their living sap; the industrious earth beneath was as a weaver's loom, with a gorgeous carpet on it, whereof the ground-vine tendrils formed the warp and woof, and the living flowers the figures. All the trees, with all their laden branches; all shrubs, and ferns, and grasses; the message-carrying air; all these unceasingly were active. Through the lacings of the leaves, the great sun seemed a flying shuttle weaving the unwearied verdure. Oh, busy weaver! unseen weaver!—pause!—one word!—whither flows the fabric? what palace may it deck? wherefore all these ceaseless toilings? Speak, weaver!—stay thy hand!—but one single word with thee! Nay—the shuttle flies—the figures float from forth the loom; the freshet-rushing carpet for ever slides away. The weaver-god, he weaves; and by that weaving is he deafened, that he hears no mortal voice; and by the humming; we, too, who look on the loom are deafened; and only when we escape it shall we hear the thousand voices that speak through it. For even so it is in all material factories. The spoken words that are inaudible among the flying spindles; those same words are plainly heard without the walls, bursting from the opened casements. Thereby have villanies been detected. Ah, mortal! then, be heedful; for so, in all this din of the great world's loom, they subtlest thinkings may be overheard afar.

Now, amid the green, life-restless loom of that Arsacidean wood, the great, white, worshipped skeleton lay lounging—a gigantic idler! Yet, as the ever-woven verdant warp and woof intermixed and hummed around him, the mighty idler seemed the cunning weaver; himself all woven over with the vines; every month assuming greener, fresher verdure; but himself a skeleton. Life folded Death; Death trellised Life; the grim god wived with youthful Life, and begat him curly-headed glories.

Now, when with royal Tranquo I visited this wondrous whale, and saw the skull an altar, and the artificial smoke ascending from where the real jet had issued, I marvelled that the king should regard a chapel as an object of vertù. He laughed. But more I marvelled that the priests should swear that smoky jet of his was genuine. To and fro I paced before this skeleton—brushed the vines aside—broke through the ribs—and with a ball of Arsacidean twine, wandered, eddied long amid its many winding, shaded colonnades and arbors. But soon my line was out; and following it back, I emerged from the opening where I entered. I saw no living thing within; naught was there but bones.

Cutting me a green measuring-rod, I once more dived within the skeleton. From their arrow-slit in the skull, the priests perceived me taking the altitude of the final rib. 'How now!' they shouted; 'Dar'st thou measure this our god! That's for us.' 'Aye, priests—well, how long do ye make him, then?' But hereupon a fierce contest rose among them, concerning feet and inches; they cracked each other's sconces with their yard-sticks—the great skull echoed—and seizing that lucky chance, I quickly concluded my own admeasurements.

These admeasurements I now propose to set before you. But first, be it recorded, that, in this matter, I am not free to utter any fancied measurement I please. Because there are skeleton authorities you can refer to, to test my accuracy. There is a Leviathanic Museum, they tell me, in Hull, England, one of the whaling ports of the country, where they have some fine specimens of fin-backs and other whales. Likewise, I have heard that in the museum of Manchester, in New Hampshire, they have what the proprietors call 'the only perfect specimen of a Greenland or River Whale in the United States.' Moreover, at a place in Yorkshire, England, Burton Constable by name, a certain Sir Clifford Constable has in his possession the skeleton of a Sperm Whale, but of moderate size, by no means of the full-grown magnitude of my friend King Tranquo's.

In both cases, the stranded whales to which these two skeletons belonged, were originally claimed by their proprietors upon similar grounds. King Tranquo seizing his because he wanted it; and Sir Clifford, because he was lord of the seignories of those parts. Sir Clifford's whale has been articulated throughout; so that, like a great chest of drawers, you can open and shut him, in all his bony cavities—spread out his ribs like a gigantic fan—and swing all day upon his lower jaw. Locks are to be put upon some of his trap-doors and shutters; and a footman will show round future visitors with a bunch of keys at his side. Sir Clifford thinks of charging twopence for a peep at the whispering gallery in the spinal column; threepence to hear the echo in the hollow of his cerebellum; and sixpence for the unrivalled view from his forehead.

The skeleton dimensions I shall now proceed to set down are copied verbatim from my right arm, where I had them tattooed;

as in my wild wanderings at that period, there was no other secure way of preserving such valuable statistics. But as I was crowded for space, and wished the other parts of my body to remain a blank page for a poem I was then composing—at least, what untattooed parts might remain—I did not trouble myself with the odd inches; nor, indeed, should inches at all enter into a congenial admeasurement of the whale.

103
MEASUREMENT OF THE WHALE'S SKELETON

In the first place, I wish to lay before you a particular, plain statement, touching the living bulk of this leviathan, whose skeleton we are briefly to exhibit. Such a statement may prove useful here.

According to a careful calculation I have made, and which I partly base upon Captain Scoresby's estimate, of seventy tons for the largest sized Greenland whale of sixty feet in length; according to my careful calculation, I say, a Sperm Whale of the largest magnitude, between eighty-five and ninety feet in length, and something less than forty feet in its fullest circumference, such a whale will weigh at least ninety tons; so that, reckoning thirteen men to a ton, he would considerably outweigh the combined population of a whole village of one thousand one hundred inhabitants.

Think you not then that brains, like yoked cattle, should be put to this leviathan, to make him at all budge to any landsman's imagination?

Having already in various ways put before you his skull, spouthole, jaw, teeth, tail, forehead, fins, and divers other parts, I shall now simply point out what is most interesting in the general bulk of his unobstructed bones. But as the colossal skull embraces so very large a proportion of the entire extent of the skeleton; as it is by far the most complicated part; and as nothing is to be repeated concerning it in this chapter, you must not fail to carry it in your mind, or under your arm, as we proceed, otherwise you will not gain a complete notion of the general structure we are about to view.

In length, the Sperm Whale's skeleton at Tranque measured seventy-two feet; so that when fully invested and extended in life, he must have been ninety feet long; for in the whale, the skeleton loses about one fifth in length compared with the living body. Of this seventy-two feet, his skull and jaw comprised some twenty feet, leaving some fifty feet of plain back-bone. Attached to this back-bone, for something less than a third of its length, was the mighty circular basket of ribs which once enclosed his vitals.

To me this vast ivory-ribbed chest, with the long, unrelieved spine, extending far away from it in a straight line, not a little resembled the embryo hull of a great ship new-laid upon the stocks, when only some twenty of her naked bow-ribs are inserted, and the keel is otherwise, for the time, but a long, disconnected timber.

The ribs were ten on a side. The first, to begin from the neck, was nearly six feet long; the second, third, and fourth were each successively longer, till you came to the climax of the fifth, or one of the middle ribs, which measured eight feet and some inches. From that part, the remaining ribs diminished, till the tenth and last only spanned five feet and some inches. In general thickness, they all bore a seemly correspondence to their length. The middle ribs were the most arched. In some of the Arsacides they are used for beams whereon to lay foot-path bridges over small streams.

In considering these ribs, I could not but be struck anew with the circumstance, so variously repeated in this book, that the skeleton of the whale is by no means the mould of his invested form. The largest of the Tranque ribs, one of the middle ones, occupied that part of the fish which, in life, is greatest in depth. Now, the greatest depth of the invested body of this particular whale must have been at least sixteen feet; whereas, the corresponding rib measured but little more than eight feet. So that this rib only conveyed half of the true notion of the living magnitude of that part. Besides, for some way, where I now saw but a naked spine, all that had been once wrapped round with tons of added bulk in flesh, muscle, blood, and bowels. Still more, for the ample fins, I here saw but a few disordered joints; and in place of the weighty and majestic, but boneless flukes, an utter blank!

How vain and foolish, then, thought I, for timid untravelled man to try to comprehend aright this wondrous whale, by merely poring over his dead attenuated skeleton, stretched in this peaceful wood. No. Only in the heart of quickest perils; only when within the eddyings of his angry flukes; only on the profound unbounded sea, can the fully invested whale be truly and livingly found out.

But the spine. For that, the best way we can consider it is, with a crane, to pile its bones high up on end. No speedy enterprise. But now it's done, it looks much like Pompey's Pillar.

There are forty and odd vertebræ in all, which in the skeleton are not locked together. They mostly lie like the great knobbed blocks on a Gothic spire, forming solid courses of heavy masonry. The largest, a middle one, is in width something less than three feet, and in depth more than four. The smallest, where the spine tapers away into the tail, is only two inches in width, and looks something like a white billiard-ball. I was told that there were still smaller ones, but they had been lost by some little cannibal urchins, the priest's children, who had stolen them to play marbles with. Thus we see how that the spine of even the hugest of living things tapers off at last into simple child's play.

104

THE FOSSIL WHALE

FROM his mighty bulk the whale affords a most congenial theme whereon to enlarge, amplify, and generally expatiate. Would you, you could not compress him. By good rights he should only be treated of in imperial folio. Not to tell over again his furlongs from spiracle to tail, and the yards he measures about the waist; only think of the gigantic involutions of his intestines, where they lie in him like great cables and hausers coiled away in the subterranean orlop-deck of a line-of-battle-ship.

Since I have undertaken to manhandle this Leviathan, it behoves me to approve myself omnisciently exhaustive in the enterprise; not overlooking the minutest seminal germs of his blood, and spinning him out to the uttermost coil of his bowels. Having already described him in most of his present habitatory and anatomical peculiarities, it now remains to magnify him in an archæological, fossiliferous, and antediluvian point of view. Applied to any other creature than the Leviathan—to an ant or a flea— such portly terms might justly be deemed unwarrantably grandiloquent. But when Leviathan is the text, the case is altered. Fain am I to stagger to this emprise under the weightiest words of the dictionary. And here be it said, that whenever it has been convenient to consult one in the course of these dissertations, I have invariably used a huge quarto edition of Johnson, expressly purchased for that purpose; because that famous lexicographer's uncommon personal bulk more fitted him to compile a lexicon to be used by a whale author like me.

One often hears of writers that rise and swell with their subject, though it may seem but an ordinary one. How, then, with me, writing of this Leviathan? Unconsciously my chirography expands into placard capitals. Give me a condor's quill! Give me Vesuvius' crater for an inkstand! Friends, hold my arms! For in the mere act of penning my thoughts of the Leviathan, they weary me, and make me faint with their outreaching comprehensiveness of sweep, as if to include the whole circle of the sciences, and all the generations of whales, and men, and mastodons, past, present, and to come, with all the revolving panoramas of empire on earth, and throughout the whole universe, not excluding its suburbs. Such, and so magnifying, is the virtue of a large and liberal theme! We expand to its bulk. To produce a mighty book, you must choose a mighty theme. No great and enduring volume can ever be written on the flea, though many there be who have tried it.

Ere entering upon the subject of Fossil Whales, I present my credentials as a geologist, by stating that in my miscellaneous time I have been a stone-mason, and also a great digger of ditches, canals and wells, wine-vaults, cellars, and cisterns of all sorts. Likewise, by way of preliminary, I desire to remind the reader, that while in the earlier geological strata there are found the fossils of monsters now almost completely extinct; the subsequent relics discovered in what are called the Tertiary formations seem the connecting, or at any rate intercepted links, between the antechronical creatures, and those whose remote posterity are said to have entered the Ark; all the Fossil Whales hitherto discovered belong to the Tertiary period, which is the last preceding the superficial formations. And though none of them precisely answer to any known species of the present time, they are yet sufficiently akin to them in general respects, to justify their taking rank as Cetacean fossils.

Detached broken fossils of pre-adamite whales, fragments of their bones and skeletons, have within thirty years past, at various intervals, been found at the base of the Alps, in Lombardy, in France, in England, in Scotland, and in the States of Louisiana, Mississippi, and Alabama. Among the more curious of such remains is part of a skull, which in the year 1779 was disinterred in the Rue Dauphine in Paris, a short street opening almost directly upon the palace of the Tuileries; and bones disinterred in excavating the great docks of Antwerp, in Napoleon's time. Cuvier pronounced these fragments to have belonged to some utterly unknown Leviathanic species.

But by far the most wonderful of all cetacean relics was the almost complete vast skeleton of an extinct monster, found in the year 1842, on the plantation of Judge Creagh, in Alabama. The awe-stricken credulous slaves in the vicinity took it for the bones of one of the fallen angels. The Alabama doctors declared it a huge reptile, and bestowed upon it the name of Basilosaurus. But some specimen bones of it being taken across the sea to Owen, the English anatomist, it turned out that this alleged reptile was a whale, though of a departed species. A significant illustration of the fact, again and again repeated in this book, that the skeleton of the whale furnishes but little clue to the shape of his fully invested body. So Owen re-christened the monster Zeuglodon; and in his paper read before the London Geological Society, pronounced it, in substance, one of the most extraordinary creatures which the mutations of the globe have blotted out of existence.

When I stand among these mighty Leviathan skeletons, skulls, tusks, jaws, ribs, and vertebræ, all characterized by partial resemblances to the existing breeds of sea-monsters; but at the same time bearing on the other hand similar affinities to the annihilated ante-chronical Leviathans, their incalculable seniors; I am, by a flood, borne back to that wondrous period, ere time itself can be said to have begun; for time began with man. Here Saturn's grey chaos rolls over me, and I obtain dim, shuddering glimpses into those Polar eternities; when wedged bastions of ice pressed hard upon what are now the Tropics; and in all the 25,000 miles of this world's circumference, not an inhabitable hand's breadth of land was visible. Then the whole world was the whale's; and, king of creation, he left his wake along the present lines of the Andes and the Himmalehs. Who can show a pedigree like Leviathan? Ahab's harpoon had shed older blood than the Pharaohs'. Methuselah seems a school-boy. I look round to shake hands with Shem. I am horror-struck at this antemosaic, unsourced existence of the unspeakable terrors of the whale, which, having been before all time, must needs exist after all humane ages are over.

But not alone has this Leviathan left his pre-adamite traces in the stereotype plates of nature, and in limestone and marl bequeathed his ancient bust; but upon Egyptian tablets, whose antiquity seems to claim for them an almost fossiliferous character, we find the unmistakable print of his fin. In an apartment of the great temple of Denderah, some fifty years ago, there was discovered upon the granite ceiling a sculptured and painted planisphere, abounding in centaurs, griffins, and dolphins, similar to the grotesque figures on the celestial globe of the moderns. Gliding among them, old Leviathan swam as of yore; was there swimming in that planisphere, centuries before Solomon was cradled.

Nor must there be omitted another strange attestation of the antiquity of the whale, in his own osseous post-diluvian reality, as set down by the venerable John Leo, the old Barbary traveller.

'Not far from the Sea-side, they have a Temple, the Rafters and Beams of which are made of Whale-Bones; for Whales of a monstrous size are oftentimes cast up dead upon that shore. The Common People imagine, that by a secret Power bestowed by God upon the Temple, no Whale can pass it without immediate death. But the truth of the Matter is, that on either side of the Temple, there are Rocks that shoot two Miles into the Sea, and wound the Whales when they light upon 'em. They keep a Whale's Rib of an incredible length for a Miracle, which lying upon the Ground with its convex part uppermost, makes an Arch, the Head of which cannot be reached by a Man upon a Camel's Back. This Rib' (says John Leo) 'is said to have layn there a hundred Years before I saw it. Their Historians affirm, that a Prophet who prophesy'd of Mahomet, came from this Temple, and some do not stand to assert, that the Prophet Jonas was cast forth by the Whale at the Base of the Temple.'

In this Afric Temple of the Whale I leave you, reader, and if you be a Nantucketer, and a whaleman, you will silently worship here.

105

DOES THE WHALE'S MAGNITUDE DIMINISH?—WILL HE PERISH?

INASMUCH, then, as this Leviathan comes floundering down upon us from the head-waters of the Eternities, it may be fitly inquired, whether, in the long course of his generations, he has not degenerated from the original bulk of his sires.

But upon investigation we find, that not only are the whales of the present day superior in magnitude to those whose fossil remains are found in the Tertiary system (embracing a distinct geological period prior to man), but of the whales found in that Tertiary system, those belonging to its latter formations exceed in size those of its earlier ones.

Of all the pre-adamite whales yet exhumed, by far the largest is the Alabama one mentioned in the last chapter, and that was less than seventy feet in length in the skeleton. Whereas, we have already seen, that the tape-measure gives seventy-two feet for the skeleton of a large sized modern whale. And I have heard, on whalemen's authority, that Sperm Whales have been captured near a hundred feet long at the time of capture.

But may it not be, that while the whales of the present hour are an advance in magnitude upon those of all previous geological periods; may it not be, that since Adam's time they have degenerated?

Assuredly, we must conclude so, if we are to credit the accounts of such gentlemen as Pliny, and the ancient naturalists generally. For Pliny tells us of whales that embraced acres of living bulk, and Aldrovandus of others which measured eight hundred feet in length—Rope Walks and Thames Tunnels of Whales! And even in the days of Banks and Solander, Cooke's naturalists, we find a Danish member of the Academy of Sciences setting down certain Iceland Whales (reydan-siskur, or Wrinkled Bellies) at one hundred and twenty yards; that is, three hundred and sixty feet. And Lacépède, the French naturalist, in his elaborate history of whales, in the very beginning of his work (page 3), sets down the Right Whale at one hundred metres, three hundred and twenty-eight feet. And this work was published so late as A.D. 1825.

But will any whaleman believe these stories? No. The whale of to-day is as big as his ancestors in Pliny's time. And if ever I go where Pliny is, I, a whaleman (more than he was), will make bold to tell him so. Because I cannot understand how it is, that while the Egyptian mummies that were buried thousands of years before even Pliny was born, do not measure so much in their coffins as a modern Kentuckian in his socks; and while the cattle and other animals sculptured on the oldest Egyptian and Nineveh tablets, by the relative proportions in which they are drawn, just as plainly prove that the high-bred, stall-fed, prize cattle of Smithfield, not only equal, but far exceed in magnitiude the fattest of Pharaoh's fat kine; in the face of all this, I will not admit that of all animals the whale alone should be degenerated.

But still another inquiry remains; one often agitated by the more recondite Nantucketers. Whether owing to the almost omniscient look-outs at the mast-heads of the whale-ships, now penetrating even through Behring's straits, and into the remotest secret drawers and lockers of the world; and the thousand harpoons and lances darted along all continental coasts; the moot point is, whether Leviathan can long endure so wide a chase, and so remorseless a havoc; whether he must not at last be exterminated from the waters, and the last whale, like the last man, smoke his last pipe, and then himself evaporate in the final puff.

Comparing the humped herds of whales with the humped herds of buffalo, which, not forty years ago, overspread by tens of thousands the prairies of Illinois and Missouri, and shook their iron manes and scowled with their thunder-clotted brows upon the sites of populous river-capitals, where now the polite broker sells you land at a dollar an inch; in such a comparison an irresistible argument would seem furnished, to show that the hunted whale cannot now escape speedy extinction.

But you must look at this matter in every light. Though so short a period ago—not a good life-time—the census of the buffalo in Illinois exceeded the census of men now in London, and though at the present day not one horn or hoof of them remains in all that region; and though the cause of this wondrous extermination was the spear of man; yet the far different nature of the whale-hunt peremptorily forbids so inglorious an end to the Leviathan. Forty men in one ship hunting the Sperm Whale for forty-eight months think they have done extremely well, and thank God, if at last they carry home the oil of forty fish. Whereas, in the days of the old Canadian and Indian hunters and trappers of the West, when the far west (in whose sunset suns still rise) was a wilderness and a virgin, the same number of moccasined men, for the same number of months, mounted on horse instead of sailing in ships, would have slain not forty, but forty thousand and more buffaloes; a fact that, if need were, could be statistically stated.

Nor, considered aright, does it seem any argument in favor of the gradual extinction of the Sperm Whale, for example, that in former years (the latter part of the last century, say) these Leviathans, in small pods, were encountered much oftener than at present, and, in consequence, the voyages were not so prolonged, and were also much more remunerative. Because, as has been elsewhere noticed, those whales, influenced by some views to safety, now swim the seas in immense caravans, so that to a large degree the scattered solitaries, yokes, and pods, and schools of other days are now aggregated into vast but widely separated, unfrequent armies. That is all. And equally fallacious seems the conceit, that because the so-called whale-bone whales no longer haunt many grounds in former years abounding with them, hence that species also is declining. For they are only being driven from promontory to cape; and if one coast is no longer enlivened with their jets, then, be sure, some other and remoter stand has been very recently startled by the unfamiliar spectacle.

Furthermore: concerning these last mentioned Leviathans, they have two firm fortresses, which, in all human probability, will for ever remain impregnable. And as upon the invasion of their valleys, the frosty Swiss have retreated to their mountains; so, hunted from the savannas and glades of the middle seas, the whale-bone whales can at last resort to their Polar citadels, and diving under the ultimate glassy barriers and walls there, come up among icy fields and floes; and in a charmed circle of everlasting December, bid defiance to all pursuit from man.

But as perhaps fifty of these whale-bone whales are harpooned for one cachalot, some philosophers of the fore-castle have concluded that this positive havoc has already very seriously diminished their battalions. But though for some time past a number of these whales, not less than 13,000, have been annually slain on the nor' west coast by the Americans alone; yet there are considerations which render even this circumstance of little or no account as an opposing argument in this matter.

Natural as it is to be somewhat incredulous concerning the populousness of the more enormous creatures of the globe, yet what shall we say to Harto, the historian of Goa, when he tells us that at one hunting the King of Siam took 4000 elephants; that in those regions elephants are numerous as droves of cattle in the temperate climes. And there seems no reason to doubt that if these elephants, which have now been hunted for thousands of years, by Semiramis, by Porus, by Hannibal, and by all the successive monarchs of the East—if they still survive there in great numbers, much more may the great whale outlast all hunting, since he has a pasture to expatiate in, which is precisely twice as large as all Asia, both Americas, Europe and Africa, New Holland, and all the Isles of the sea combined.

Moreover: we are to consider, that from the presumed great longevity of whales, their probably attaining the age of a century and more, therefore at any one period of time, several distinct adult generations must be contemporary. And what that is, we may soon gain some idea of, by imagining all the grave-yards, cemeteries, and family vaults of creation yielding up the live bodies of all the men, women, and children who were alive seventy-five years ago; and adding this countless host to the present human population of the globe.

Wherefore, for all these things, we account the whale immortal in his species, however perishable in his individuality. He swam the seas before the continents broke water; he once swam over the site of Tuileries, and Windsor Castle, and the Kremlin. In Noah's flood he despised Noah's Ark; and if ever the world is to be again flooded, like the Netherlands, to kill off its rats, then the eternal whale will still survive, and rearing upon the top-most crest of the equatorial flood, spout his frothed defiance to the skies.

106
AHAB'S LEG

THE precipitating manner in which Captain Ahab had quitted the Samuel Enderby of London, had not been unattended with some small violence to his own person. He had lighted with such energy upon a thwart of his boat that his ivory leg had received a half-splintering shock. And when after gaining his own deck, and his own pivot-hole there, he so vehemently wheeled round with an urgent command to the steersman (it was, as ever, something about his not steering inflexibly enough); then, the already shaken ivory received such an additional twist and wrench, that though it still remained entire, and to all appearances lusty, yet Ahab did not deem it entirely trustworthy.

And, indeed, it seemed small matter for wonder, that for all his pervading, mad recklessness, Ahab did at times give careful heed to the condition of that dead bone upon which he partly stood. For it had not been very long prior to the Pequod's sailing from Nantucket, that he had been found one night lying prone upon the ground, and insensible; by some unknown, and seemingly inexplicable, unimaginable casualty, his ivory limb having been so violently displaced, that it had stake-wise smitten, and all but pierced his groin; nor was it without extreme difficulty that the agonizing wound was entirely cured.

Nor, at the time, had it failed to enter his monomaniac mind, that all the anguish of that then present suffering was but the direct issue of a former woe; and he too plainly seemed to see, that as the most poisonous reptile of the marsh perpetuates his

kind as inevitably as the sweetest songster of the grove; so, equally
with every felicity, all miserable events do naturally beget their
like. Yea, more than equally, thought Ahab; since both the ancestry
and posterity of Grief go further than the ancestry and posterity
of Joy. For, not to hint of this: that it is an inference from certain
canonic teachings, that while some natural enjoyments here shall
have no children born to them for the other world, but, on the
contrary, shall be followed by the joy-childlessness of all hell's
despair; whereas, some guilty mortal miseries shall still fertilely
beget to themselves an eternally progressive progeny of griefs
beyond the grave; not at all to hint of this, there still seems an
inequality in the deeper analysis of the thing. For, thought Ahab,
while even the highest earthly felicities ever have a certain unsig-
nifying pettiness lurking in them, but, at bottom, all heart-woes,
a mystic significance, and, in some men, an archangelic grandeur;
so do their diligent tracings-out not belie the obvious deduction.
To trail the genealogies of these high mortal miseries, carries us
at last among the sourceless primogenitures of the gods; so that,
in the face of all the glad, hay-making suns, and soft-cymballing,
round harvest-moons, we must needs give in to this: that the gods
themselves are not for ever glad. The ineffaceable, sad birth-mark
in the brow of man, is but the stamp of sorrow in the signers.

Unwittingly here a secret has been divulged, which perhaps
might more properly, in set way, have been disclosed before. With
many other particulars concerning Ahab, always had it remained
a mystery to some, why it was, that for a certain period, both
before and after the sailing of the Pequod, he had hidden himself
away with such Grand-Lama-like exclusiveness; and, for that one
interval, sought speechless refuge, as it were, among the marble
senate of the dead. Captain Peleg's bruited reason for this thing
appeared by no means adequate; though, indeed, as touching all
Ahab's deeper part, every revelation partook more of significant
darkness than of explanatory light. But, in the end, it all came
out; this one matter did, at least. The direful mishap was at the
bottom of his temporary recluseness. And not only this, but to
that ever-contracting, dropping circle ashore, who, for any reason,
possessed the privilege of a less banned approach to him; to that
timid circle the above hinted casualty—remaining, as it did, moodily unaccounted for by Ahab—invested itself with terrors, not
entirely underived from the land of spirits and of wails. So that,
through their zeal for him, they had all conspired, so far as in
them lay, to muffle up the knowledge of this thing from others;

and hence it was, that not till a considerable interval had elapsed, did it transpire upon the Pequod's decks.

But be all this as it may; let the unseen, ambiguous synod in the air, or the vindictive princes and potentates of fire, have to do or not with earthly Ahab, yet, in this present matter of his leg, he took plain practical procedures;—he called the carpenter.

And when that functionary appeared before him, he bade him without delay set about making a new leg, and directed the mates to see him supplied with all the studs and joists of jaw-ivory (Sperm Whale) which had thus far been accumulated on the voyage, in order that a careful selection of the stoutest, clearest-grained stuff might be secured. This done, the carpenter received orders to have the leg completed that night; and to provide all the fittings for it, independent of those pertaining to the distrusted one in use. Moreover, the ship's forge was ordered to be hoisted out of its temporary idleness in the hold; and, to accelerate the affair, the blacksmith was commanded to proceed at once to the forging of whatever iron contrivances might be needed.

107

THE CARPENTER

SEAT thyself sultanically among the moons of Saturn, and take high abstracted man alone; and he seems a wonder, a grandeur, and a woe. But from the same point, take mankind in mass, and for the most part, they seem a mob of unnecessary duplicates, both contemporary and hereditary. But most humble though he was, and far from furnishing an example of the high, humane abstraction; the Pequod's carpenter was no duplicate; hence, he now comes in person on this stage.

Like all sea-going ship carpenters, and more especially those belonging to whaling vessels, he was, to a certain off-handed, practical extent, alike experienced in numerous trades and callings collateral to his own; the carpenter's pursuit being the ancient and outbranching trunk of all numerous handicrafts which more or less have to do with wood as an auxiliary material. But, besides the application to him of the generic remark above, this carpenter of the Pequod was singularly efficient in those thousand nameless mechanical emergencies continually recurring in a large ship, upon a three or four years' voyage, in uncivilized and far-distant seas.

For not to speak of his readiness in ordinary duties:—repairing
stove boats, sprung spars, reforming the shape of clumsy-bladed
oars, inserting bull's eyes in the deck, or new tree-nails in the side
planks, and other miscellaneous matters more directly pertaining
to his special business; he was moreover unhesitatingly expert in
all manner of conflicting aptitudes, both useful and capricious.

The one grand stage where he enacted all his various parts so
manifold, was his vice-bench; a long rude ponderous table furnished with several vices, of different sizes, and both of iron and
of wood. At all times except when whales were alongside, this
bench was securely lashed athwartships against the rear of the
Try-works.

A belaying pin is found too large to be easily inserted into its
hole: the carpenter claps it into one of his ever-ready vices, and
straightway files it smaller. A lost land-bird of strange plumage
strays on board, and is made a captive: out of clean shaved rods
of right-whale bone, and cross-beams of sperm whale ivory, the
carpenter makes a pagoda-looking cage for it. An oarsman sprains
his wrist: the carpenter concocts a soothing lotion. Stubb longs
for vermillion stars to be painted upon the blade of his every oar:
screwing each oar in his big vice of wood, the carpenter symmetrically supplies the constellation. A sailor takes a fancy to wear
shark-bone ear-rings: the carpenter drills his ears. Another has the
toothache: the carpenter out pincers, and clapping one hand upon
his bench bids him be seated there; but the poor fellow unman-
ageably winces under the unconcluded operation; whirling round
the handle of this wooden vice, the carpenter signs him to clap
his jaw in that, if he would have him draw the tooth.

Thus, this carpenter was prepared at all points, and alike indifferent and without respect in all. Teeth he accounted bits of
ivory; heads he deemed but top-blocks; men themselves he lightly
held for capstans. But while now upon so wide a field thus variously
accomplished, and with such liveliness of expertness in him, too;
all this would seem to argue some uncommon vivacity of intelligence. But not precisely so. For nothing was this man more
remarkable, than for a certain impersonal stolidity as it were;
impersonal, I say; for it so shaded off into the surrounding infinite
of things, that it seemed one with the general stolidity discernible
in the whole visible world; which while pauselessly active in
uncounted modes, still eternally holds its peace, and ignores you,
though you dig foundations for cathedrals. Yet was this half-
horrible stolidity in him, involving, too, as it appeared, and all-
ramifying heartlessness;—yet was it oddly dashed at times, with

an old, crutch-like, antediluvian, wheezing humorousness, not unstreaked now and then with a certain grizzled wittiness; such as might have served to pass the time during the midnight watch on the bearded forecastle of Noah's ark. Was it that this old carpenter had been a life-long wanderer, whose much rolling, to and fro, not only had gathered no moss; but what is more, had rubbed off whatever small outward clingings might have originally pertained to him? He was a stript abstract; an unfractioned integral; uncompromised as a new-born babe; living without premeditated reference to this world or the next. You might almost say, that this strange uncompromisedness of him involved a sort of intelligence; for in his numerous trades, he did not seem to work so much by reason or by instinct, or simply because he had been tutored to it, or by any intermixture of all these, even or uneven; but merely by a kind of deaf and dumb, spontaneous literal process. He was a pure manipulator; his brain, if he had ever had one, must have early oozed along into the muscles of his fingers. He was like one of those unreasoning but still highly useful, *multum in parvo*, Sheffield contrivances, assuming the exterior—though a little swelled—of a common pocket knife; but containing, not only blades of various sizes, but also screw-drivers, cork-screws, tweezers, awls, pens, rulers, nail-filers, countersinkers. So, if his superiors wanted to use the carpenter for a screw-driver, all they had to do was to open that part of him, and the screw was fast: or if for tweezers, take him up by the legs, and there they were.

Yet, as previously hinted, this omnitooled, open-and-shut carpenter, was, after all, no mere machine of an automaton. If he did not have a common soul in him, he had a subtle something that somehow anomalously did its duty. What that was, whether essence of quicksilver, or a few drops of hartshorn, there is no telling. But there it was; and there it had abided for now some sixty years or more. And this it was, this same unaccountable, cunning life-principle in him; this it was, that kept him a great part of the time soliloquizing; but only like an unreasoning wheel, which also hummingly soliloquizes; or rather, his body was a sentry-box and this soliloquizer on guard there, and talking all the time to keep himself awake.

108

AHAB AND THE CARPENTER

THE DECK — FIRST NIGHT WATCH

(*Carpenter standing before his vice-bench, and by the light of two lanterns busily filing the ivory joist for the leg, which joist is firmly fixed in the vice. Slabs of ivory, leather straps, pads, screws, and various tools of all sorts lying about the bench. Forward, the red flame of the forge is seen, where the blacksmith is at work.*)

DRAT the file, and drat the bone! That is hard which should be soft, and that is soft which should be hard. So we go, who file old jaws and shinbones. Let's try another. Aye, now, this works better (*sneezes*). Halloa, this bone dust is (*sneezes*)—why it's (*sneezes*)—yes it's (*sneezes*)—bless my soul, it won't let me speak! This is what an old fellow gets now for working in dead lumber. Saw a live tree, and you don't get this dust; amputate a live bone, and you don't get it (*sneezes*). Come, come, you old Smut, there, bear a hand, and let's have that ferule and buckle-screw; I'll be ready for them presently. Lucky now (*sneezes*) there's no knee-joint to make; that might puzzle a little; but a mere shin-bone—why it's easy as making hop-poles; only I should like to put a good finish on. Time, time; if I but only had the time, I could turn him out as neat a leg now as ever (*sneezes*) scraped to a lady in a parlor. Those buckskin legs and calves of legs I've seen in shop windows wouldn't compare at all. They soak water, they do; and of course get rheumatic, and have to be doctored (*sneezes*) with washes and lotions, just like live legs. There; before I saw it off, now, I must call his old Mogulship, and see whether the length will be all right; too short, if anything, I guess. Ha! that's the heel; we are in luck; here he comes, or it's somebody else, that's certain.

AHAB (*advancing*).

(*During the ensuing scene, the carpenter continues sneezing at times.*)

Well, manmaker!

Just in time, sir. If the captain pleases, I will now mark the length. Let me measure, sir.

Measured for a leg! good. Well, it's not the first time. About it! There; keep thy finger on it. This is a cogent vice thou hast here, carpenter; let me feel its grip once. So, so; it does pinch some.

Oh, sir, it will break bones—beware, beware!

No fear; I like a good grip; I like to feel something in this slippery world that can hold, man. What's Prometheus about there?—the blacksmith, I mean—what's he about?

He must be forging the buckle-screw, sir, now.

Right. It's a partnership; he supplies the muscle part. He makes a fierce red flame there!

Aye, sir; he must have the white heat for this kind of fine work.

Um-m. So he must. I do deem it now a most meaning thing, that that old Greek, Prometheus, who made men, they say, should have been a blacksmith, and animated them with fire; for what's made in fire must properly belong to fire; and so hell's probable. How the soot flies! This must be the remainder the Greek made the Africans of. Carpenter, when he's through with that buckle, tell him to forge a pair of steel shoulder-blades; there's a pedlar aboard with a crushing pack.

Sir?

Hold; while Prometheus is about it, I'll order a complete man after a desirable pattern. Imprimis, fifty feet high in his socks; then, chest modelled after the Thames Tunnel; then, legs with roots to 'em, to stay in one place; then, arms three feet through the wrist; no heart at all, brass forehead, and about a quarter of an acre of fine brains; and let me see—shall I order eyes to see outwards? No, but put a sky-light on top of his head to illuminate inwards. There, take the order, and away.

Now, what's he speaking about, and who's he speaking to, I should like to know? Shall I keep standing here? (*aside*).

'Tis but indifferent architecture to make a blind dome; here's one. No, no, no; I must have a lantern.

Ho, ho! That's it, hey? Here are two, sir: one will serve my turn.

What are thou thrusting that thief-catcher into my face for, man? Thrusted light is worse than presented pistols.

I thought, sir, that you spoke to carpenter.

Carpenter? why that's—but no;—a very tidy, and, I may say, an extremely gentlemanlike sort of business thou art in here, carpenter;—or would'st thou rather work in clay?

Sir?—Clay? clay, sir? That's mud; we leave clay to ditches, sir.

The fellow's impious! What art thou sneezing about?

Bone is rather dusty, sir.

Take the hint, then; and when thou art dead, never bury thyself under living people's noses.

Sir?—oh! ah!—I guess so;—yes—oh, dear!

Look ye, carpenter, I dare say thou callest thyself a right good workmanlike workman, eh? Well, then, will it speak thoroughly well for thy work, if, when I come to mount this leg thou makest, I shall nevertheless feel another leg in the same identical place with it; that is, carpenter, my old lost leg; the flesh and blood one, I mean. Canst thou not drive that old Adam away?

Truly, sir. I begin to understand somewhat now. Yes, I have heard something curious on that score, sir; how that a dismasted man never entirely loses the feeling of his old spar, but it will be still pricking him at times. May I humbly ask if it be really so, sir?

It is, man. Look, put thy live leg in the place where mine once was; so, now, here is only one distinct leg to the eye, yet two to the soul. Where thou feelest tingling life; there, exactly there, there to a hair, do I. Is't a riddle?

I should humbly call it a poser, sir.

Hist, then. How dost thou know that some entire, living, thinking thing may not be invisibly and uninterpenatratingly standing precisely where thou now standest; aye, and standing there in thy spite? In thy most solitary hours, then, dost thou not fear eaves-droppers? Hold, don't speak! And if I still feel the smart of my crushed leg, though it be now so long dissolved; then, why mayst not thou, carpenter, feel the fiery pains of hell for ever, and without a body? Hah!

Good Lord! Truly, sir, if it comes to that, I must calculate over again; I think I didn't carry a small figure, sir.

Look ye, pudding-heads should never grant premises.—How long before the leg is done?

Perhaps an hour, sir.

Bungle away at it then, and bring it to me (*turns to go*). Oh, Life! Here I am, proud as Greek god, and yet standing debtor to this blockhead for a bone to stand on! Cursed be that mortal inter-indebtedness which will not do away with ledgers. I would be free as air; and I'm down in the whole world's books. I am so rich, I could have given bid for bid with the wealthiest Prætorians at the auction of the Roman empire (which was the world's); and yet I owe for the flesh in the tongue I brag with. By heavens! I'll get a crucible, and into it, and dissolve myself down to one small, compendious vertebra. So.

CARPENTER (*resuming his work*).

Well, well, well! Stubb knows him best of all, and Stubb always says he's queer; says nothing but that one sufficient little word queer; he's queer, says Stubb; he's queer—queer, queer; and keeps dinning it into Mr Starbuck all the time—queer, sir—queer, queer, very queer. And here's his leg! Yes, now that I think of it, here's his bedfellow! has a stick of whale's jaw-bone for a wife! And this is his leg; he'll stand on this. What was that now about one leg standing in three places, and all three places standing in one hell—how was that? Oh! I don't wonder he looked so scornful at me! I'm a sort of strange-thoughted sometimes, they say; but that's only haphazard-like. Then, a short, little old body like me, should never undertake to wade out into deep waters with tall, heron-built captains; the water chucks you under the chin pretty quick, and there's a great cry for life-boats. And here's the heron's leg! long and slim, sure enough! Now, for most folks one pair of legs lasts a lifetime, and that must be because they use them mercifully, as a tender-hearted old lady uses her roly-poly old coach-horses. But Ahab; oh he's a hard driver. Look, driven one leg to death, and spavined the other for life, and now wears out bone legs by the cord. Halloa, there, you Smut! bear a hand there with those screws, and let's finish it before the resurrection fellow comes a-calling with his horn for all legs, true or false, as brewery-men go round collecting old beer barrels, to fill 'em up again. What a leg this is! It looks like a real live leg, filed down to nothing but the core; he'll be standing on this to-morrow; he'll be taking altitudes on it. Halloa! I almost forgot the little oval slate, smoothed ivory, where he figures up the latitude. So, so; chisel, file, and sandpaper, now!

109
AHAB AND STARBUCK IN THE CABIN

ACCORDING to usage they were pumping the ship next morning; and lo! no inconsiderable oil came up with the water; the casks below must have sprung a bad leak. Much concern was shown; and Starbuck went down into the cabin to report this unfavorable affair.*

---

* In Sperm-whalemen with any considerable quantity of oil on board, it is a regular

Now, from the South and West the Pequod was drawing nigh to Formosa and the Bashee Isles between which lies one of the tropical outlets from the China waters into the Pacific. And so Starbuck found Ahab with a general chart of the oriental archipelagoes spread before him; and another separate one representing the long eastern coasts of the Japanese islands—Niphon, Matsmai, and Sikoke. With his snow-white new ivory leg braced against the screwed leg of his table, and with a long pruning-hook of a jack-knife in his hand, the wondrous old man, with his back to the gangway door, was wrinkling his brow, and tracing his old courses again.

'Who's there!' hearing the footstep at the door, but not turning round to it. 'On deck! Begone!'

'Captain Ahab mistakes; it is I. The oil in the hold is leaking, sir. We must up Burtons and break out.'

'Up Burtons and break out? Now that we are nearing Japan; heave-to here for a week to tinker a parcel of old hoops?'

'Either do that, sir, or waste in one day more oil than we may make good in a year. What we come twenty thousand miles to get is worth saving, sir.'

'So it is, so it is; if we get it.'

'I was speaking of the oil in the hold, sir.'

'And I was not speaking or thinking of that at all. Begone! Let it leak! I'm all aleak myself. Aye! leaks in leaks! not only full of leaky casks, but those leaky casks are in a leaky ship; and that's a far worse plight than the Pequod's, man. Yet I don't stop to plug my leak; for who can find it in the deep-loaded hull, or how hope to plug it, even if found, in this life's howling gale? Starbuck! I'll not have the Burtons hoisted.'

'What will the owners say, sir?'

'Let the owners stand on Nantucket beach and outyell the Typhoons. What cares Ahab? Owners, owners? Thou art always prating to me, Starbuck, about those miserly owners, as if the owners were my conscience. But look ye, the only real owner of anything is its commander; and hark ye, my conscience is in this ship's keel.—On deck!'

'Captain Ahab,' said the reddening mate, moving further into the cabin, with a daring so strangely respectful and cautious that

---

semi-weekly duty to conduct a hose into the hold, and drench the casks with sea-water; which afterwards, at varying intervals, is removed by the ship's pumps. Hereby the casks are sought to be kept damply tight; while by the changed character of the withdrawn water, the mariners readily detect any serious leakage in the precious cargo.

it almost seemed not only every way seeking to avoid the slightest outward manifestation of itself, but within also seemed more than half distrustful of itself; 'A better man than I might well pass over in thee what he would quickly enough resent in a younger man; aye, and in a happier, Captain Ahab.'

'Devils! Dost thou then so much as dare to critically think of me?—On deck!'

'Nay, sir, not yet; I do entreat. And I do dare, sir—to be forbearing! Shall we not understand each other better than hitherto, Captain Ahab?'

Ahab seized a loaded musket from the rack (forming part of most South-Sea-men's cabin furniture), and pointing it towards Starbuck, exclaimed: 'There is one God that is Lord over the earth, and one Captain that is lord over the Pequod.—On deck!'

For an instant in the flashing eyes of the mate, and his fiery cheeks, you would have almost thought that he had really received the blaze of the levelled tube. But, mastering his emotion, he half calmly rose, and as he quitted the cabin, paused for an instant and said: 'Thou hast outraged, not insulted me, sir; but for that I ask thee not to beware of Starbuck; thou wouldst but laugh; but let Ahab beware of Ahab; beware of thyself, old man.'

'He waxes brave, but nevertheless obeys; most careful bravery that!' murmured Ahab, as Starbuck disappeared. 'What's that he said—Ahab beware of Ahab—there's something there!' Then unconsciously using the musket for a staff, with an iron brow he paced to and fro in the little cabin; but presently the thick plaits of his forehead relaxed, and returning the gun to the rack, he went to the deck.

'Thou art but too good a fellow, Starbuck,' he said lowly to the mate; then raising his voice to the crew: 'Furl the t'gallant-sails and close-reef the top-sails, fore and aft; back the main-yard; up Burtons, and break out in the main-hold.'

It were perhaps vain to surmise exactly why it was, that as respecting Starbuck, Ahab thus acted. It may have been a flash of honesty in him; or mere prudential policy which, under the circumstances, imperiously forbade the slightest symptom of open disaffection, however transient, in the important chief officer of his ship. However it was, his orders were executed; and the Burtons were hoisted.

110

QUEEQUEG IN HIS COFFIN

UPON searching, it was found that the casks last struck into the hold were perfectly sound, and that the leak must be further off. So, it being calm weather, they broke out deeper and deeper, disturbing the slumbers of the huge ground-tier butts; and from that black midnight sending those gigantic moles into the daylight above. So deep did they go; and so ancient, and corroded, and weedy the aspect of the lowermost puncheons, that you almost looked next for some mouldy corner-stone cask containing coins of Captain Noah, with copies of the posted placards, vainly warning the infatuated old world from the flood. Tierce after tierce, too, of water, and bread, and beef, and shooks of staves, and iron bundles of hoops, were hoisted out, till at last the piled decks were hard to get about; and the hollow hull echoed under foot, as if you were treading over empty catacombs, and reeled and rolled in the sea like an air-freighted demijohn. Top-heavy was the ship as a dinnerless student with all Aristotle in his head. Well was it that the Typhoons did not visit them then.

Now, at this time it was that my poor pagan companion, and fast bosom-friend, Queequeg, was seized with a fever, which brought him nigh to his endless end.

Be it said, that in this vocation of whaling, sinecures are unknown; dignity and danger go hand and hand; till you get to be Captain, the higher you rise the harder you toil. So with poor Queequeg, who, as harpooneer, must not only face all the rage of the living whale, but—as we have elsewhere seen—mount his dead back in a rolling sea; and finally descend into the gloom of the hold, and bitterly sweating all day in that subterraneous confinement, resolutely manhandle the clumsiest casks and see to their stowage. To be short, among whalemen, the harpooneers are the holders, so called.

Poor Queequeg! when the ship was about half disembowelled, you should have stooped over the hatchway, and peered down upon him there; where, stripped to his woollen drawers, the tattooed savage was crawling about amid that dampness and slime, like a green spotted lizard at the bottom of a well. And a well, or an ice-house, it somehow proved to him, poor pagan; where, strange to say, for all the heat of his sweatings, he caught a terrible chill which lapsed into a fever; and at last, after some days' suffering, laid him in his hammock, close to the very sill of the door of death. How he wasted and wasted away in those few long-lingering days, till there seemed but little left of him but his frame and tattooing. But as all else in him thinned, and his cheek-bones grew sharper, his eyes, nevertheless, seemed growing fuller and fuller; they became of a strange softness of lustre; and mildly but deeply looked out at you there from his sickness, a wondrous testimony to the immortal health in him which could not die, or be weakened. And like circles on the water, which, as they grow fainter, expand; so his eyes seemed rounding and rounding, like the rings of Eternity. An awe that cannot be named would steal over you as you sat by the side of this waning savage, and saw as strange things in his face, as any beheld who were bystanders when Zoroaster died. For whatever is truly wondrous and fearful in man, never yet was put into words or books. And the drawing near of Death, which alike levels all, alike impresses all with a last revelation, which only an author from the dead could ade-quately tell. So that—let us say it again—no dying Chaldee or Greek had higher and holier thoughts than those, whose mysterious shades you saw creeping over the face of poor Queequeg, as he quietly lay in his swaying hammock, and the rolling sea seemed gently rocking him to his final rest, and the ocean's invisible flood-tide lifted him higher and higher towards his destined heaven.

Not a man of the crew but gave him up; and, as for Queequeg himself, what he thought of his case was forcibly shown by a curious favor he asked. He called one to him in the grey morning watch, when the day was just breaking, and taking his hand, said that while in Nantucket he had chanced to see certain little canoes of dark wood, like the rich war-wood of his native isle; and upon inquiry, he had learned that all whalemen who died in Nantucket, were laid in those same dark canoes, and that the fancy of being so laid had much pleased him; for it was not unlike the custom of his own race, who, after embalming a dead warrior, stretched him out in his canoe, and so left him to be floated away to the starry achipelagoes; for not only do they believe that the stars are isles, but that far beyond all visible horizons, their own mild, uncontinented seas, interflow with the blue heavens; and so form the white breakers of the milky way. He added, that he shuddered at the thought of being buried in his hammock, according to the usual sea-custom, tossed like something vile to the death-devouring sharks. No: he desired a canoe like those of Nantucket, all the

more congenial to him, being a whaleman, that like a whale-boat
these coffin-canoes were without a keel; though that involved but
uncertain steering and much lee-way adown the dim ages.

Now, when this stange circumstance was made known aft, the
carpenter was at once commanded to do Queequeg's bidding,
whatever it might include. There was some heathenish, coffin-
colored old lumber aboard, which, upon a long previous voyage,
had been cut from the aboriginal groves of the Lackaday islands,
and from these dark planks the coffin was recommended to be
made. No sooner was the carpenter apprised of the order, than
taking his rule, he forthwith with all the indifferent promptitude
of his character, proceeded into the forecastle and took Queequeg's
measure with great accuracy, regularly chalking Queequeg's person
as he shifted the rule.

'Ah! poor fellow! he'll have to die now,' ejaculated the Long
Island sailor.

Going to his vice-bench, the carpenter for convenience' sake
and general reference, now transferringly measured on it the exact
length the coffin was to be, and then made the transfer permanent
by cutting two notches at its extremities. This done, he marshalled
the planks and his tools, and to work.

When the last nail was driven, and the lid duly planed and
fitted, he lightly shouldered the coffin and went forward with it,
inquiring whether they were ready for it yet in that direction.

Overhearing the indignant but half-humorous cries with which
the people on deck began to drive the coffin away, Queequeg, to
every one's consternation, commanded that the thing should be
instantly brought to him, nor was there any denying him; seeing
that, of all mortals, some dying men are the most tyrannical; and
certainly, since they will shortly trouble us so little for evermore,
the poor fellows ought to be indulged.

Leaning over in his hammock, Queequeg long regarded the
coffin with an attentive eye. He then called for his harpoon, had
the wooden stock drawn from it, and then had the iron part
placed in the coffin along with one of the paddles of his boat.
All by his own request, also, biscuits were then ranged round the
sides within: a flask of fresh water was placed at the head, and a
small bag of woody earth scraped up in the hold at the foot; and
a piece of sailcloth being rolled up for a pillow, Queequeg now
entreated to be lifted into his final bed, that he might make trial
of its comforts, if any it had. He lay without moving a few
minutes, then told one to go to his bag and bring out his little
god, Yojo. Then crossing his arms on his breast with Yojo between,

he called for the coffin lid (hatch he called it) to be placed over him. The head part turned over with a leather hinge, and there lay Queequeg in his coffin with little but his composed countenance in view. 'Rarmai' (it will do; it is easy), he murmured at last, and signed to be replaced in his hammock.

But ere this was done, Pip, who had been slily hovering near by all this while, drew nigh to him where he lay, and with soft sobbings, took him by the hand; in the other, holding his tambourine.

'Poor rover! will ye never have done with all this weary roving? where go ye now? But if the currents carry ye to those sweet Antilles where the beaches are only beat with water-lilies, will ye do one little errand for me? Seek out one Pip, who's now been missing long: I think he's in those far Antilles. If ye find him, then comfort him; for he must be very sad; for look! he's left his tambourine behind;—I found it. Rig-a-dig, dig, dig! Now, Queequeg, die; and I'll beat ye your dying march.'

'I have heard,' murmured Starbuck, gazing down the scuttle, 'that in violent fevers, men, all ignorance, have talked in ancient tongues; and that when the mystery is probed, it turns out always that in their wholly forgotten childhood those ancient tongues had been really spoken in their hearing by some lofty scholars. So, to my fond faith, poor Pip, in this strange sweetness of his lunacy, brings heavenly vouchers of all our heavenly homes. Where learned he that, but there?—Hark! he speaks again: but more wildly now.'

'Form two and two! Let's make a General of him! Ho, where's his harpoon? Lay it across here.—Rig-a-dig, dig, dig! huzza! Oh for a game cock now to sit upon his head and crow! Queequeg dies game!—mind ye that; Queequeg dies game!—take ye good heed of that; Queequeg dies game! I say; game, game, game! but base little Pip, he died a coward; died all a'shiver;—out upon Pip! Hark ye; if ye find Pip, tell all the Antilles he's a runaway; a coward, a coward, a coward! Tell them he jumped from a whale-boat! I'd never beat my tambourine over base Pip, and hail him General, if he were once more dying here. No, no! shame upon all cowards—shame upon them! Let 'em go drown like Pip, that jumped from a whale-boat, Shame! shame!'

During all this, Queequeg lay with closed eyes, as if in a dream. Pip was led away, and the sick man was replaced in his hammock.

But now that he had apparently made every preparation for death; now that his coffin was proved a good fit, Queequeg suddenly rallied; soon there seemed no need of the carpenter's box; and thereupon, when some expressed their delighted surprise, he, in substance, said, that the cause of his sudden convalescence was this;—at a critical moment, he had just recalled a little duty ashore, which he was leaving undone; and therefore had changed his mind about dying: he could not die yet, he averred. They asked him, then, whether to live or die was a matter of his own sovereign will and pleasure. He answered, certainly. In a word, it was Queequeg's conceit, that if a man made up his mind to live, mere sickness could not kill him: nothing but a whale, or a gale, or some violent, ungovernable, unintelligent destroyer of that sort.

Now, there is this noteworthy difference between savage and civilized! that while a sick, civilized man may be six months convalescing, generally speaking, a sick savage is almost half-well again in a day. So, in good time my Queequeg gained strength; and at length after sitting on the windlass for a few indolent days (but eating with a vigorous appetite) he suddenly leaped to his feet, threw out arms and legs, gave himself a good stretching, yawned a little bit, and then springing into the head of his hoisted boat, and poising a harpoon, pronounced himself fit for a fight.

With a wild whimsiness, he now used his coffin for a sea-chest; and emptying into it his canvas bag of clothes, set them in order there. Many spare hours he spent, in carving the lid with all manner of grotesque figures and drawings; and it seemed that hereby he was striving, in his rude way, to copy parts of the twisted tattooing on his body. And this tattooing, had been the work of a departed prophet and seer of his island, who, by those hieroglyphic marks, had written out on his body a complete theory of the heavens and the earth, and a mystical treatise on the art of attaining truth; so that Queequeg in his own proper person was a riddle to unfold; a wondrous work in one volume; but whose mysteries not even himself could read, though his own live heart beat against them; and these mysteries were therefore destined in the end to moulder away with the living parchment whereon they were inscribed, and so be unsolved to the last. And this thought it must have been which suggested to Ahab that wild exclamation of his, when one morning turning away from surveying poor Queequeg—'Oh, devilish tantalization of the gods!'

111

THE PACIFIC

WHEN gliding by the Bashee isles we emerged at last upon the great South Sea; were it not for other things, I could have greeted my dear Pacific with uncounted thanks, for now the long supplication of my youth was answered; that serene ocean rolled eastwards from me a thousand leagues of blue.

There is, one knows not what sweet mystery about this sea, whose gently awful stirrings seem to speak of some hidden soul beneath; like those fabled undulations of the Ephesian sod over the buried Evangelist St John. And meet it is, that over these sea-pastures, wide-rolling watery prairies and Potter's Fields of all four continents, the waves should rise and fall, and ebb and flow unceasingly; for here, millions of mixed shades and shadows, drowned dreams, somnambulisms, reveries; all that we call lives and souls, lie dreaming, dreaming, still; tossing like slumberers in their beds; the ever-rolling waves but made so by their restlessness.

To any meditative Magian rover, this serene Pacific, once beheld, must ever after be the sea of his adoption. It rolls the midmost waters of the world, the Indian ocean and Atlantic being but its arms. The same waves wash the moles of the new-built Californian towns, but yesterday planted by the recentest race of men, and lave the faded but still gorgeous skirts of Asiatic lands, older than Abraham; while all between float milky-ways of coral isles, and low-lying, endless, unknown Archipelagoes, and impenetrable Japans. Thus this mysterious, divine Pacific zones the world's whole bulk about; makes all coasts one bay to it; seems the tide-beating heart of earth. Lifted by those eternal swells, you needs must own the seductive god, bowing your head to Pan.

But few thoughts of Pan stirred Ahab's brain, as standing like an iron statue at his accustomed place beside the mizen rigging, with one nostril he unthinkingly snuffed the sugary musk from the Bashee isles (in whose sweet woods mild lovers must be walking), and with the other consciously inhaled the salt breath of the new found sea; that sea in which the hated White Whale must even then be swimming. Launched at length upon these almost final waters, and gliding towards the Japanese cruising-ground, the old man's purpose intensified itself. His firm lips met like the lips of a vice; the Delta of his forehead's veins swelled like overladen brooks; in his very sleep, his ringing cry ran through the vaulted hull, 'Stern all! the White Whale spouts thick blood!'

112
THE BLACKSMITH

AVAILING himself of the mild, summer-cool weather that now reigned in these latitudes, and in preparation for the peculiarly active pursuits shortly to be anticipated, Perth, the begrimed, blistered old blacksmith, had not removed his portable forge to the hold again, after concluding his contributory work for Ahab's leg, but still retained it on deck, fast lashed to ringbolts by the foremast; being now almost incessantly invoked by the headsmen, and harpooneers, and bowsmen to do some little job for them; altering, or repairing, or new shaping their various weapons and boat furniture. Often he would be surrounded by an eager circle, all waiting to be served; holding boat-spades, pike-heads, harpoons, and lances, and jealously watching his every sooty movement, as he toiled. Nevertheless, this old man's was a patient hammer wielded by a patient arm. No murmur, no impatience, no petulance did come from him. Silent, slow, and solemn; bowing over still further his chronically broken back, he toiled away, as if toil were life itself, and the heavy beating of his hammer the heavy beating of his heart. And so it was.—Most miserable!

A peculiar walk in this old man, a certain slight but painful appearing yawing in his gait, had at an early period of the voyage excited the curiosity of the mariners. And to the importunity of their persisted questionings he had finally given in; and so it came to pass that every one now knew the shameful story of his wretched fate.

Belated, and not innocently, one bitter winter's midnight, on the road running between two country towns, the blacksmith half-stupidly felt the deadly numbness stealing over him, and sought refuge in a leaning, dilapidated barn. The issue was, the loss of the extremities of both feet. Out of this revelation, part by part, at last came out the four acts of the gladness, and the one long, and as yet uncatastrophied fifth act of the grief of his life's drama.

He was an old man, who at the age of nearly sixty, had postponedly encountered that thing in sorrow's technicals called

ruin. He had been an artisan of famed excellence, and with plenty
to do; owned a house and garden; embraced a youthful, daughter-
like, loving wife, and three blithe, ruddy children; every Sunday
went to a cheerful-looking church, planted in a grove. But one
night, under cover of darkness, and further concealed in a most
cunning disguisement, a desperate burglar slid into his happy home,
and robbed them all of everything. And darker yet to tell, the
blacksmith himself did ignorantly conduct this burglar into his
family's heart. It was the Bottle Conjuror! Upon the opening of
that fatal cork, forth flew the fiend, and shrivelled up his home.
Now, for prudent, most wise, and economic reasons the blacksmith's shop was in the basement of his dwelling, but with a
separate entrance to it; so that always had the young and loving
healthy wife listened with no unhappy nervousness, but with
vigorous pleasure, to the stout ringing of her young-armed old
husband's hammer; whose reverberations, muffled by passing
through the floors and walls, came up to her, not unsweetly, in
her nursery; and so, to stout Labor's iron lullaby the blacksmith's
infants were rocked to slumber.

Oh, woe on woe! Oh, Death, why canst thou not sometimes
be timely? Hadst thou taken this old blacksmith to thyself ere his
full ruin came upon him, then had the young widow had a delicious
grief, and her orphans a truly venerable, legendary sire to dream
of in their after years; and all of them a care-killing competency.
But Death plucked down some virtuous elder brother, on whose
whistling daily toil solely hung the responsibilities of some other
family, and left the worse than useless old man standing, till the
hideous rot of life should make him easier to harvest.

Why tell the whole? The blows of the basement hammer every
day grew more and more between; and each blow every day grew
fainter than the last; the wife sat frozen at the window, with
tearless eyes, glitteringly gazing into the weeping faces of her
children; the bellows fell; the forge choked up with cinders; the
house was sold; the mother dived down into the long church-yard
grass; her children twice followed her thither; and the houseless,
familyless old man staggered off a vagabond in crape; his every
woe unreverenced; his grey head a scorn to flaxen curls!

Death seems the only desirable sequel for a career like this; but
Death is only a launching into the region of the strange Untried;
it is but the first salutation to the possibilities of the immense
Remote, the Wild, the Watery, the Unshored; therefore, to the
death-longing eyes of such men, who still have left in them some
interior compunctions against suicide, does the all-contributed and

all-receptive ocean alluringly spread forth his whole plain of unimaginable, taking terrors, and wonderful, new-life adventures; and
from the hearts of infinite Pacifics, the thousand mermaids sing
to them—'Come hither, broken-hearted; here is another life without the guilt of intermediate death; here are wonders supernatural,
without dying for them. Come hither! bury thyself in a life which,
to your now equally abhorred and abhorring, landed world, is
more oblivious than death. Come hither! put up *thy* grave-stone,
too, within the churchyard, and come hither, till we marry thee!'

Hearkening to these voices, East and West, by early sunrise,
and by fall of eve, the blacksmith's soul responded, Aye, I come!
And so Perth went a-whaling.

113
THE FORGE

WITH matted beard, and swathed in a bristling shark-skin apron,
about midday, Perth was standing between his forge and anvil,
the latter placed upon an iron-wood log, with one hand holding
a pike-head in the coals, and with the other at his forge's lungs,
when Captain Ahab came along, carrying in his hand a small
rusty-looking leathern bag. While yet a little distance from the
forge, moody Ahab paused; till at last, Perth, withdrawing his iron
from the fire, began hammering it upon the anvil—the red mass
sending off the sparks in thick hovering flights, some of which
flew close to Ahab.

'Are these thy Mother Carey's chickens, Perth? they are always
flying in thy wake; birds of good omen, too, but not to all;—look
here, they burn; but thou—thou liv'st among them without a
scorch.'

'Because I am scorched all over, Captain Ahab,' answered Perth,
resting for a moment on his hammer; 'I am past scorching; not
easily can'st thou scorch a scar.'

'Well, well; no more. Thy shrunk voice sounds too calmly,
sanely woful to me. In no Paradise myself, I am impatient of all
misery in others that is not mad. Thou should'st go mad, blacksmith; say, why dost thou not go mad? How can'st thou endure
without being mad? Do the heavens yet hate thee, that thou can'st
not go mad?—What wert thou making there?'

'Welding an old pike-head, sir; there were seams and dents in it.'

'And can'st thou make it all smooth again, blacksmith, after such hard usage as it had?'

'I think so, sir.'

'And I suppose thou can'st smoothe almost any seams and dents; never mind how hard the metal, blacksmith?'

'Aye, sir, I think I can; all seams and dents but one.'

'Look ye here, then' cried Ahab, passionately advancing, and leaning with both hands on Perth's shoulders; 'look ye here—here—can you smoothe out a seam like this, blacksmith,' sweeping one hand across his ribbed brow; 'if thou could'st, blacksmith, glad enough would I lay my head upon thy anvil, and feel thy heaviest hammer between my eyes. Answer! Can'st thou smoothe this seam?'

'Oh! that is the one, sir! Said I not all seams and dents but one?'

'Aye, blacksmith, it is the one; aye, man, it is unsmoothable; for though thou only see'st it here in my flesh, it has worked down into the bone of my skull—*that* is all wrinkles! But, away with child's play; no more gaffs and pikes to-day. Look ye here!' jingling the leathern bag, as if it were full of gold coins. 'I, too, want a harpoon made; one that a thousand yoke of fiends could not part, Perth; something that will stick in a whale like his own fin-bone. There's the stuff,' flinging the pouch upon the anvil. 'Look ye, blacksmith, these are the gathered nail-stubs of the steel shoes of racing horses.'

'Horse-shoe stubbs, sir? Why, Captain Ahab, thou hast here, then, the best and stubbornest stuff we blacksmiths ever work.'

'I know it, old man; these stubbs will weld together like glue from the melted bones of murderers. Quick! forge me the harpoon. And forge me first, twelve rods for its shank; then wind, and twist, and hammer these twelve together like the yarns and strands of a tow-line. Quick! I'll blow the fire.'

When at last the twelve rods were made, Ahab tried them, one by one, by spiralling them, with his own hand, round a long, heavy iron bolt. 'A flaw!' rejecting the last one. 'Work that over again, Perth.'

This done, Perth was about to begin welding the twelve into one, when Ahab stayed his hand, and said he would weld his own iron. As, then, with regular, gasping hems, he hammered on the anvil, Perth passing to him the glowing rods, one after the other, and the hard pressed forge shooting up its intense straight flame, the Parsee passed silently, and bowing over his head towards the fire, seemed invoking some curse or some blessing on the toil. But, as Ahab looked up, he slid aside.

'What's that bunch of lucifers dodging about there for?' muttered Stubb, looking on from the forecastle. 'That Parsee smells fire like a fusee; and smells of it himself, like a hot musket's powder-pan.'

At last the shank, in one complete rod, received its final heat; and as Perth, to temper it, plunged it all hissing into the cask of water near by, the scalding steam shot up into Ahab's bent face.

'Would'st thou brand me, Perth?' wincing for a moment with the pain; 'have I been but forging my own branding-iron, then?'

'Pray God, not that; yet I fear something, Captain Ahab. Is not this harpoon for the White Whale?'

'For the white fiend! But now for the barbs; thou must make them thyself, man. Here are my razors—the best of steel; here, and make the barbs sharp as the needle-sleet of the Icy Sea.'

For a moment, the old blacksmith eyed the razors as though he would fain not use them.

'Take them, man, I have no need for them; for I now neither shave, sup, nor pray till—but here—to work!'

Fashioned at last into an arrowy shape, and welded by Perth to the shank, the steel soon pointed the end of the iron; and as the blacksmith was about giving the barbs their final heat, prior to tempering them, he cried to Ahab to place the water-cask near.

'No, no—no water for that; I want it of the true death-temper. Ahoy, there! Tashtego, Queequeg, Daggoo! What say ye, pagans! Will ye give me as much blood as will cover this barb? holding it high up. A cluster of dark nods replied, Yes. Three punctures were made in the heathen flesh, and the White Whale's barbs were then tempered.

'Ego non baptizo te in nomine patris, sed in nomine diaboli!' deliriously howled Ahab, as the malignant iron scorchingly devoured the baptismal blood.

Now, mustering the spare poles from below, and selecting one of hickory, with the bark still investing it, Ahab fitted the end to the socket of the iron. A coil of new tow-line was then unwound, and some fathoms of it taken to the windlass, and stretched to a great tension. Pressing his foot upon it, till the rope hummed like a harp-string, then eagerly bending over it, and seeing no strandings, Ahab exclaimed, 'Good! and now for the seizings.'

At one extremity the rope was unstranded, and the separate spread yarns were all braided and woven round the socket of the harpoon; the pole was then driven hard up into the socket; from the lower end the rope was traced half way along the pole's length, and firmly secured so, with intertwistings of twine. This done, pole, iron, and rope—like the Three Fates—remained inseparable, and Ahab moodily stalked away with the weapon; the sound of his ivory leg, and the sound of the hickory pole, both hollowly ringing along every plank. But ere he entered his cabin, a light, unnatural, half-bantering, yet most piteous sound was heard. Oh, Pip! thy wretched laugh, thy idle but unresting eye; all thy strange mummeries not unmeaningly blended with the black tragedy of the melancholy ship, and mocked it!

114
THE GILDER

PENETRATING further and further into the heart of the Japanese cruising ground, the Pequod was soon all astir in the fishery. Often, in mild, pleasant weather, for twelve, fifteen, eighteen, and twenty hours on the stretch, they were engaged in the boats, steadily pulling, or sailing, or paddling after the whales, or for an interlude of sixty or seventy minutes calmly awaiting their uprising; though with but small success for their pains.

At such times, under an abated sun; afloat all day upon smooth, slow heaving swells; seated in his boat, light as a birch canoe; and so sociably mixing with the soft waves themselves, that like hearth-stone cats they purr against the gunwale; these are the times of dreamy quietude, when beholding the tranquil beauty and brilliancy of the ocean's skin, one forgets the tiger heart that pants beneath it; and would not willingly remember, that this velvet paw but conceals a remorseless fang.

These are the times, when in his whale-boat the rover softly feels a certain filial, confident, land-like feeling towards the sea; that he regards it as so much flowery earth; and the distant ship revealing only the tops of her masts, seems struggling forward, not through high rolling waves, but through the tall grass of a rolling prairie: as when the western emigrants' horses only show their erected ears, while their hidden bodies widely wade through the amazing verdure.

The long-drawn virgin vales; the mild blue hill-sides; as over these there steals the hush, the hum; you almost swear that play-wearied children lie sleeping in these solitudes, in some glad May-

time, when the flowers of the woods are plucked. And all this
mixes with your most mystic mood; so that fact and fancy, half-
way meeting, interpenetrate, and form one seamless whole.

Nor did such soothing scenes, however temporary, fail of at
least as temporary an effect on Ahab. But if these secret golden
keys did seem to open in him his own secret golden treasuries,
yet did his breath upon them prove but tarnishing.

Oh, grassy glades! oh, ever vernal endless landscapes in the soul;
in ye,—though long parched by the dead drought of the earthy
life,—in ye, men yet may roll, like young horses in new morning
clover; and for some few fleeting moments, feel the cool dew of
the life immortal on them. Would to God these blessed calms
would last. But the mingled, mingling threads of life are woven
by warp and woof: calms crossed by storms, a storm for every
calm. There is no steady unretracing progress in this life; we do
not advance through fixed gradations, and at the last one pause:—
through infancy's unconscious spell, boyhood's thoughtless faith,
adolescence' doubt (the common doom), then scepticism, then
disbelief, resting at last in manhood's pondering repose of If. But
once gone through, we trace the round again; and are infants,
boys, and men, and Ifs eternally. Where lies the final harbor,
whence we unmoor no more? In what rapt ether sails the world,
of which the weariest will never weary? Where is the foundling's
father hidden? Our souls are like those orphans whose unwedded
mothers die in bearing them: the secret of our paternity lies in
their grave, and we must there to learn it.

And that same day, too, gazing far down from his boat's side
into that same golden sea, Starbuck lowly murmured:—

'Loveliness unfathomable, as ever lover saw in his young bride's
eye!— Tell me not of thy teeth-tiered sharks, and thy kidnapping
cannibal ways. Let faith oust fact; let fancy oust memory; I look
deep down and do believe.'

And Stubb, fish-like, with sparkling scales, leaped up in that
same golden light:—

'I am Stubb, and Stubb has his history; but here Stubb takes
oaths that he has always been jolly!'

115

THE PEQUOD MEETS THE BACHELOR

AND jolly enough were the sights and the sounds that came bearing down before the wind, some few weeks after Ahab's harpoon had been welded.

It was a Nantucket ship, the Bachelor, which had just wedged in her last cask of oil, and bolted down her bursting hatches; and now, in glad holiday apparel, was joyously, though somewhat vaingloriously, sailing round among the widely-separated ships on the ground, previous to pointing her prow for home.

The three men at her mast-head wore long streamers of narrow red bunting at their hats; from the stern, a whale-boat was suspended, bottom down; and hanging captive from the bowsprit was seen the long lower jaw of the last whale they had slain. Signals, ensigns, and jacks of all colors were flying from her rigging, on every side. Sideways lashed in each of her three basketed tops were two barrels of sperm; above which, in her top-mast crosstrees, you saw slender breakers of the same precious fluid; and nailed to her main truck was a brazen lamp.

As was afterwards learned, the Bachelor had met with the most surprising success; all the more wonderful, for that while cruising in the same seas numerous other vessels had gone entire months without securing a single fish. Not only had barrels of beef and bread been given away to make room for the far more valuable sperm, but additional supplemental casks had been bartered for, from the ships she had met; and these were stowed along the deck, and in the captain's and officer's state-rooms. Even the cabin table itself had been knocked into kindling-wood; and the cabin mess dined off the broad head of an oil-butt, lashed down to the floor for a centrepiece. In the forecastle, the sailors had actually caulked and pitched their chests, and filled them; it was humorously added, that the cook had clapped a head on his largest boiler, and filled it; that the steward had plugged his spare coffee-pot and filled it; that the harpooneers had headed the sockets of their irons and filled them; that indeed everything was filled with sperm, except the captain's pantaloons pockets, and those he reserved to thrust his hands into, in self-complacent testimony of his entire satisfaction.

As this glad ship of good luck bore down upon the moody Pequod, the barbarian sound of enormous drums came from her forecastle; and drawing still nearer, a crowd of her men were seen standing round her huge try-pots, which, covered with the parchment-like *poke* or stomach skin of the black fish, gave forth a loud roar to every stroke of the clenched hands of the crew. On the quarter-deck, the mates and harpooneers were dancing with the olive-hued girls who had eloped with them from the Polynesian Isles; while suspended in an ornamented boat, firmly secured aloft between the foremast and mainmast, three Long Island negroes, with glittering fiddle-bows of whale ivory, were presiding over the hilarious jig. Meanwhile, others of the ship's company were tumultuously busy at the masonry of the try-works, from which the huge pots had been removed. You would have almost thought they were pulling down the cursed Bastille, such wild cries they raised, as the now useless brick and mortar were being hurled into the sea.

Lord and master over all this scene, the captain stood erect on the ship's elevated quarter-deck, so that the whole rejoicing drama was full before him, and seemed merely contrived for his own individual diversion.

And Ahab, he too was standing on his quarter-deck, shaggy and black, with a stubborn gloom; and as the two ships crossed each other's wakes—one all jubilations for things passed, the other all forebodings as to things to come—their two captains in themselves impersonated the whole striking contrast of the scene.

'Come aboard, come aboard!' cried the gay Bachelor's commander, lifting a glass and a bottle in the air.

'Hast seen the White Whale?' gritted Ahab in reply.

'No; only heard of him; but don't believe in him at all,' said the other good-humoredly. 'Come aboard!'

'Thou art too damned jolly. Sail on. Hast lost any men?'

'Not enough to speak of—two islanders, that's all;—but come aboard, old hearty, come along. I'll soon take that black from your brow. Come along, will ye (merry's the play); a full ship and homeward-bound.'

'How wondrous familiar is a fool!' muttered Ahab; then aloud, 'Thou art a full ship and homeward bound, thou sayst; well, then, call me an empty ship, and outward-bound. So go thy ways, and I will mine. Forward there! Set all sail, and keep her to the wind!'

And thus, while the one ship went cheerily before the breeze, the other stubbornly fought against it; and so the two vessels parted; the crew of the Pequod looking with grave, lingering glances

towards the receding Bachelor; but the Bachelor's men never
heeding their gaze for the lively revelry they were in. And as Ahab,
leaning over the taffrail, eyed the homeward-bound craft, he took
from his pocket a small vial of sand, and then looking from the
ship to the vial, seemed thereby bringing two remote associations
together, for that vial was filled with Nantucket soundings.

116
THE DYING WHALE

NOT seldom in this life, when, on the right side, fortune's favorites
sail close by us, we, though all adroop before, catch somewhat of
the rushing breeze, and joyfully feel our bagging sails fill out. So
seemed it with the Pequod. For next day after encountering the
gay Bachelor, whales were seen and four were slain; and one of
them by Ahab.

It was far down the afternoon; and when all the spearings of
the crimson fight were done: and floating in the lovely sunset sea
and sky, sun and whale both stilly died together; then, such a
sweetness and such plaintiveness, such in-wreathing orisons curled
up in that rosy air, that it almost seemed as if far over from the
deep green convent valleys of the Manilla isles, the Spanish land-
breeze, wantonly turned sailor, had gone to sea, freighted with
these vesper hymns.

Soothed again, but only soothed to deeper gloom, Ahab, who
had sterned off from the whale, sat intently watching his final
wanings from the now tranquil boat. For that strange spectacle
observable in all sperm whales dying—the turning sunwards of
the head, and so expiring—that strange spectacle, beheld of such
a placid evening, somehow to Ahab conveyed a wondrousness
unknown before.

'He turns and turns him to it,—how slowly, but how steadfastly,
his homage-rendering and invoking brow, with his last dying
motions. He too worships fire; most faithful, broad, baronial vassal
of the sun!—Oh that these too-favoring eyes should see these too-
favoring sights. Look! here, far water-locked; beyond all hum of
human weal or woe; in these most candid and impartial seas;
where to traditions no rocks furnish tablets; where for long Chinese
ages, the billows have still rolled on speechless and unspoken to,
as stars that shine upon the Niger's unknown source; here, too,

life dies sunwards full of faith; but see! no sooner dead, than death whirls round the corpse, and it heads some other way.—

'Oh, thou dark Hindoo half of nature, who of drowned bones hast builded thy separate throne somewhere in the heart of these unverdured seas; thou art an infidel, thou queen, and too truly speakest to me in the wide-slaughtering Typhoon, and the hushed burial of its after calm. Nor has this thy whale sunwards turned his dying head, and then gone round again, without a lesson to me.

'Oh, trebly hooped and welded hip of power! Oh, high aspiring, rainbowed jet!—that one striveth, this one jetteth all in vain! In vain, oh whale, dost thou seek intercedings with yon all-quickening sun, that only calls forth life, but gives it not again. Yet dost thou, darker half, rock me with a prouder, if a darker faith. All thy unnamable imminglings float beneath me here; I am buoyed by breaths of once living things, exhaled as air, but water now.

'Then hail, for ever hail, O sea, in whose eternal tossings the wild fowl finds his only rest. Born of earth, yet suckled by the sea; though hill and valley mothered me, ye billows are my foster-brothers!'

117

THE WHALE WATCH

THE four whales slain that evening had died wide apart; one, far to windward; one, less distant, to leeward; one ahead; one astern. These last three were brought alongside ere nightfall; but the windward one could not be reached till morning; and the boat that had killed it lay by its side all night; and that boat was Ahab's.

The waif-pole was thrust upright into the dead whale's spout-hole; and the lantern hanging from its top, cast a troubled flickering glare upon the black, glossy back, and far out upon the midnight waves, which gently chafed the whale's broad flank, like soft surf upon a beach.

Ahab and all his boat's crew seemed asleep but the Parsee; who crouching in the bow, sat watching the sharks, that spectrally played round the whale, and tapped the light cedar planks with their tails. A sound like the moaning in squadrons over Asphaltites of unforgiven ghosts of Gomorrah, ran shuddering through the air.

Started from his slumbers, Ahab, face to face, saw the Parsee; and hooped round by the gloom of the night they seemed the last men in a flooded world. 'I have dreamed it again,' said he.

'Of the hearses? Have I not said, old man, that neither hearse nor coffin can be thine?'

'And who are hearsed that die on the sea?'

'But I said, old man, that ere thou couldst die on this voyage, two hearses must verily be seen by thee on the sea; the first not made by mortal hands; and the visible wood of the last one must be grown in America.'

'Aye, aye! a strange sight that, Parsee:—a hearse and its plumes floating over the ocean with the waves for the pall-bearers. Ha! Such a sight we shall not soon see.'

'Believe it or not, thou canst not die till it be seen, old man.'

'And what was that saying about thyself?'

'Though it come to the last, I shall still go before thee thy pilot.'

'And when thou art so gone before—if that ever befall—then ere I can follow, thou must still appear to me, to pilot me still?— Was it not so? Well, then, did I believe all ye say, oh my pilot! I have here two pledges that I shall yet slay Moby Dick and survive it.'

'Take another pledge, old man,' said the Parsee, as his eyes lighted up like fire-flies in the gloom—'Hemp only can kill thee.'

'The gallows, ye mean.—I am immortal then, on land and on sea,' cried Ahab with a laugh of derision;—'Immortal on land and on sea!'

Both were silent again, as one man. The grey dawn came on, and the slumbering crew arose from the boat's bottom, and ere noon the dead whale was brought to the ship.

118

THE QUADRANT

THE season for the Line at length drew near; and every day when Ahab, coming from his cabin, cast his eyes aloft, the vigilant helmsman would ostentatiously handle his spokes, and the eager mariners quickly run to the braces, and would stand there with all their eyes centrally fixed on the nailed doubloon; impatient for the order to point the ship's prow for the equator. In good time the order came. It was hard upon high noon; and Ahab, seated in the bows of his high-hoisted boat, was about taking his wonted daily observation of the sun to determine his latitude.

Now, in that Japanese sea, the days in summer are as freshets of effulgences. That unblinkingly vivid Japanese sun seems the blazing focus of the glassy ocean's immeasurable burning-glass. The sky looks lacquered; clouds there are none; the horizon floats; and this nakedness of unrelieved radiance is as the insufferable splendors of God's throne. Well that Ahab's quadrant was furnished with colored glasses, through which to take sight of that solar fire. So, swinging his seated form to the roll of the ship, and with his astrological-looking instrument placed to his eye, he remained in that posture for some moments to catch the precise instant when the sun should gain its precise meridian. Meantime while his whole attention was absorbed, the Parsee was kneeling beneath him on the ship's deck, and with face thrown up like Ahab's, was eyeing the same sun with him; only the lids of his eyes half hooded their orbs, and his wild face was subdued to an unearthly passionlessness. At length the desired observation was taken; and with his pencil upon his ivory leg, Ahab soon calculated what his latitude must be at that precise instant. Then falling into a moment's revery, he again looked up towards the sun and murmured to himself: 'Thou sea-mark! thou high and mighty Pilot! thou tellest me truly where I *am*—but canst thou cast the least hint where I *shall* be? Or canst thou tell where some other thing besides me is this moment living? Where is Moby Dick? This instant thou must be eyeing him. These eyes of mine look into the very eye that is even now beholding him; aye, and into the eye that is even now equally beholding the objects on the unknown, thither side of thee, thou sun!'

Then gazing at his quadrant, and handling, one after the other, its numerous cabalistical contrivances, he pondered again, and muttered: 'Foolish toy! babies' plaything of haughty Admirals, and Commodores, and Captains; the world brags of thee, of thy cunning and might; but what after all canst thou do, but tell the poor, pitiful point, where thou thyself happenest to be on this wide planet, and the hand that holds there: no! not one jot more! Thou canst not tell where one drop of water or one grain of sand will be to-morrow noon; and yet with thy impotence thou insultest the sun! Science! Curse thee, thou vain toy; and cursed be all the things that cast man's eyes aloft to that heaven, whose live vividness but scorches him, as these old eyes are even now scorched with thy light. O sun! Level by nature to this earth's horizon are the glances of man's eyes; not shot from the crown of his head, as if God had meant him to gaze on his firmament. Curse thee, thou quadrant!' dashing it to the deck, 'no longer will I guide my earthly way by thee; the level ship's compass, and the level dead-reckoning, by log and by line; *these* shall conduct me, and show me my place on the sea. Aye,' lighting from the boat to the deck, 'thus I trample on thee, thou paltry thing that feebly pointest on high; thus I split and destroy thee!'

As the frantic old man thus spoke and thus trampled with his live and dead feet, a sneering triumph that seemed meant for Ahab, and a fatalistic despair that seemed meant for himself— these passed over the mute, motionless Parsee's face. Unobserved he rose and glided away; while, awestruck by the aspect of their commander, the seamen clustered together on the forecastle, till Ahab, troubledly pacing the deck, shouted out—'To the braces! Up helm!—square in!'

In an instant the yards swung round; and as the ship half-wheeled upon her heel, her three firm-seated graceful masts erectly poised upon her long, ribbed hull, seemed as the three Horatii pirouetting on one sufficient steed.

Standing between the knight-heads, Starbuck watched the Pequod's tumultuous way, and Ahab's also, as he went lurching along the deck.

'I have sat before the dense coal fire and watched it all aglow, full of its tormented flaming life; and I have seen it wane at last, down, down, to dumbest dust. Old man of oceans! of all this fiery life of thine, what will at length remain but one little heap of ashes!'

'Aye,' cried Stubb, 'but sea-coal ashes—mind ye that, Mr Starbuck—sea-coal, not your common charcoal. Well, well; I heard Ahab mutter, "Here some one thrusts these cards into these old hands of mine; swears that I must play them, and no others." And damn me, Ahab, but thou actest right; live in the game, and die in it!'

119
THE CANDLES

WARMEST climes but nurse the cruellest fangs: the tiger of Bengal crouches in spiced groves of ceaseless verdure. Skies the most effulgent but basket the deadliest thunders: gorgeous Cuba knows tornadoes that never swept tame northern lands. So, too, it is, that in these resplendent Japanese seas the mariner encounters the direst of all storms, the Typhoon. It will sometimes burst from out that cloudless sky, like an exploding bomb upon a dazed and sleepy town.

Towards evening of that day, the Pequod was torn of her canvas, and bare-poled was left to fight a Typhoon which had struck her directly ahead. When darkness came on, sky and sea roared and split with the thunder, and blazed with the lightning, that showed the disabled masts fluttering here and there with the rags which the first fury of the tempest had left for its after sport.

Holding by a shroud, Starbuck was standing on the quarter-deck; at every flash of the lightning glancing aloft, to see what additional disaster might have befallen the intricate hamper there; while Stubb and Flask were directing the men in the higher hoisting and firmer lashing of the boats. But all their pains seemed naught. Though lifted to the very top of the cranes, the windward quarter boat (Ahab's) did not escape. A great rolling sea, dashing high up against the reeling ship's high tetering side, stove in the boat's bottom at the stern, and left it again, all dripping through like a sieve.

'Bad work, bad work! Mr Starbuck,' said Stubb, regarding the wreck, 'but the sea will have its way. Stubb, for one, can't fight it. You see, Mr Starbuck, a wave has such a great long start before it leaps, all round the world it runs, and then comes the spring! But as for me, all the start I have to meet it, is just across the deck here. But never mind; it's all in fun: so the old song says;'— (*sings.*)

> Oh! jolly is the gale,
> And a joker is the whale,
> A' flourishin' his tail,—
> Such a funny, sporty, gamy, jesty, joky, hoky-poky lad,
> is the Ocean, oh!

The scud all a flyin',
That's his flip only foamin';
When he stirs in the spicin',—
Such a funny, sporty, gamy, jesty, joky, hoky-poky lad,
is the Ocean, oh!

Thunder splits the ships,
But he only smacks his lips,
A tastin' of this flip,—
Such a funny, sporty, gamy, jesty, joky, hoky-poky lad,
is the Ocean, oh!

'Avast Stubb,' cried Starbuck, 'let the Typhoon sing, and strike his harp here in our rigging; but if thou are a brave man thou wilt hold thy peace.'

'But I am not a brave man; never said I was a brave man; I am a coward; and I sing to keep up my spirits. And I tell you what it is, Mr Starbuck, there's no way to stop my singing in this world but to cut my throat. And when that's done, ten to one I sing ye the doxology for a wind-up.'

'Madman! look through my eyes if thou hast none of thine own.'

'What! how can you see better of a dark night than anybody else, never mind how foolish?'

'Here!' cried Starbuck, seizing Stubb by the shoulder, and pointing his hand towards the weather bow, 'markest thou not that the gale comes from the eastward, the very course Ahab is to run for Moby Dick? the very course he swung to this day noon? now mark his boat there; where is that stove? In the stern-sheets, man; where he is wont to stand—his stand-point is stove, man! Now jump overboard, and sing away, if thou must!'

'I don't half understand ye: what's in the wind!'

'Yes, yes, round the Cape of Good Hope is the shortest way to Nantucket,' soliloquized Starbuck suddenly, heedless of Stubb's question. 'The gale that now hammers at us to stave us, we can turn it into a fair wind that will drive us towards home. Yonder, to windward, all is blackness of doom; but to leeward, homeward— I see it lightens up there; but not with the lightning.'

At that moment in one of the intervals of profound darkness, following the flashes, a voice was heard at his side; and almost at the same instant a volley of thunder peals rolled overhead.

'Who's there?'

'Old Thunder!' said Ahab, groping his way along the bulwarks to his pivot-hole; but suddenly finding his path made plain to him by elbowed lances of fire.

Now, as the lightning rod to a spire on shore is intended to carry off the perilous fluid into the soil; so the kindred rod which at sea some ships carry to each mast, is intended to conduct it into the water. But as this conductor must descend to considerable depth, that its end may avoid all contact with the hull; and as moreover, if kept constantly towing there, it would be liable to many mishaps, besides interfering not a little with some of the rigging, and more or less impeding the vessel's way in the water; because of all this, the lower parts of a ship's lightning-rods are not always overboard; but are generally made in long slender links, so as to be the more readily hauled up into the chains outside, or thrown down into the sea, as occasion may require.

'The rods! the rods!' cried Starbuck to the crew, suddenly admonished to vigilance by the vivid lightning that had just been darting flambeaux, to light Ahab to his post. 'Are they overboard? drop them over, fore and aft. Quick!'

'Avast!' cried Ahab; 'let's have fair play here, though we be the weaker side. Yet I'll contribute to raise rods on the Himmalehs and Andes, that all the world may be secured; but out on privileges! Let them be, sir.'

'Look aloft!' cried Starbuck. 'The corpusants! the corpusants!'

All the yard-arms were tipped with a pallid fire; and touched at each tri-pointed lightning-rod-end with three tapering white flames, each of the three tall masts was silently burning in that sulphurous air, like three gigantic wax tapers before an altar.

'Blast the boat! let it go!' cried Stubb at this instant, as a swashing sea heaved up under his own little craft, so that its gunwhale violently jammed his hand, as he was passing a lashing. 'Blast it!'—but slipping backward on the deck, his uplifted eyes caught the flames; and immediately shifting his tone, he cried— 'The corpusants have mercy on us all!'

To sailors, oaths are household words; they will swear in the trance of the calm, and in the teeth of the tempest; they will imprecate curses from the topsail-yard-arms, when most they teter over to a seething sea; but in all my voyagings, seldom have I heard a common oath when God's burning finger has been laid on the ship; when His 'Mene, Mene, Tekel, Upharsin' has been woven into the shrouds and the cordage.

While this pallidness was burning aloft, few words were heard from the enchanted crew; who in one thick cluster stood on the forecastle, all their eyes gleaming in that pale phosphorescence, like a far away constellation of stars. Relieved against the ghostly light, the gigantic jet negro, Daggoo, loomed up to thrice his real stature, and seemed the black cloud from which the thunder had come. The parted mouth of Tashtego revealed his shark-white teeth, which strangely gleamed as if they too had been tipped by corpusants; while lit up by the preternatural light, Queequeg's tattooing burned like Satanic blue flames on his body.

The tableau all waned at last with the pallidness aloft; and once more the Pequod and every soul on her decks were wrapped in a pall. A moment or two passed, when Starbuck, going forward, pushed against some one. It was Stubb. 'What thinkest thou now, man; I heard thy cry; it was not the same in the song.'

'No, no, it wasn't; I said the corpusants have mercy on us all; and I hope they will, still. But do they only have mercy on long faces?—have they no bowels for a laugh? And look ye, Mr Starbuck—but it's too dark to look. Hear me, then: I take that masthead flame we saw for a sign of good luck; for those masts are rooted in a hold that is going to be chock a'block with sperm-oil, d'ye see; and so, all that sperm will work up into the masts, like sap in a tree. Yes, our three masts will yet be as three spermaceti candles—that's the good promise we saw.'

At that moment Starbuck caught sight of Stubb's face slowly beginning to glimmer into sight. Glancing upwards, he cried: 'See! see!' and once more the high tapering flames were beheld with what seemed redoubled supernaturalness in their pallor.

'The corpusants have mercy on us all,' cried Stubb, again.

At the base of the mainmast, full beneath the doubloon and the flame, the Parsee was kneeling in Ahab's front, but with his head bowed away from him; while near by, from the arched and overhanging rigging, where they had just been engaged securing a spar, a number of the seamen, arrested by the glare, now cohered together, and hung pendulous, like a knot of numbed wasps from a drooping, orchard twig. In various enchanted attitudes, like the standing, or stepping, or running skeletons in Herculaneum, others remained rooted to the deck; but all their eyes upcast.

'Aye, aye, men!' cried Ahab. 'Look up at it; mark it well; the white flame but lights the way to the White Whale! Hand me those main-mast links there; I would fain feel this pulse, and let mine beat against it; blood against fire! So.'

Then turning—the last link held fast in his left hand, he put his foot upon the Parsee; and with fixed upward eye, and high-flung right arm, he stood erect before the lofty tri-pointed trinity of flames.

'Oh! thou clear spirit of clear fire, whom on these seas I as Persian once did worship, till in the sacramental act so burned by thee, that to this hour I bear the scar; I now know thee, thou clear spirit, and I now know that thy right worship is defiance. To neither love nor reverence wilt thou be kind; and e'en for hate thou canst but kill; and all are killed. No fearless fool now fronts thee. I own thy speechless, placeless power; but to the last gasp of my earthquake life will dispute its unconditional, unintegral mastery in me. In the midst of the personified impersonal, a personality stands here. Though but a point at best; whencesoe'er I came; wheresoe'er I go; yet while I earthly live, the queenly personality lives in me, and feels her royal rights. But war is pain, and hate is woe. Come in thy lowest form of love, and I will kneel and kiss thee; but at thy highest, come as mere supernal power; and though thou launchest navies of full-freighted worlds, there's that in here that still remains indifferent. Oh, thou clear spirit, of thy fire thou madest me, and like a true child of fire, I breathe it back to thee.'

[*Sudden, repeated flashes of lightning; the nine flames leap lengthwise to thrice their previous height; Ahab, with the rest, closes his eyes, his right hand pressed hard upon them.*]

'I own thy speechless, placeless power; said I not so? Nor was it wrung from me; nor do I now drop these links. Thou canst blind; but I can then grope. Thou canst consume; but I can then be ashes. Take the homage of these poor eyes, and shutter-hands. I would not take it. The lightning flashes through my skull; mine eye-balls ache and ache; my whole beaten brain seems as beheaded, and rolling on some stunning ground. Oh, oh! Yet blindfold, yet will I talk to thee. Light though thou be, thou leapest out of darkness; but I am darkness leaping out of light, leaping out of thee! The javelins cease; open eyes; see, or not? There burn the flames! Oh, thou magnanimous! now I do glory in my genealogy. But thou are but my fiery father; my sweet mother, I know not, Oh, cruel! what hast thou done with her? There lies my puzzle; but thine is greater. Thou knowest not how came ye; hence callest thyself unbegotten; certainly knowest not thy beginning, hence callest thyself unbegun. I know that of me, which thou knowest not of thyself, oh, thou omnipotent. There is some unsuffusing thing beyond thee, thou clear spirit, to whom all thy eternity is but time, all thy creativeness mechanical. Through thee, thy flaming self, my scorched eyes do dimly see it. Oh, thou foundling fire, thou hermit immemorial, thou too hast thy incommunicable rid-dle, thy unparticipated grief. Here again with haughty agony, I read my sire. Leap! leap up, and lick the sky! I leap with thee; I burn with thee; would fain be welded with thee, defyingly I worship thee!'

'The boat! the boat!' cried Starbuck, 'look at thy boat, old man!'

Ahab's harpoon, the one forged at Perth's fire, remained firmly lashed in its conspicuous crotch, so that it projected beyond his whale-boat's bow; but the sea that had stove its bottom had caused the loose leather sheath to drop off; and from the keen steel barb there now came a levelled flame of pale, forked fire. As the silent harpoon burned there like a serpent's tongue, Starbuck grasped Ahab by the arm—'God, God is against thee, old man; forbear! 'tis an ill voyage! ill begun, ill continued; let me square the yards, while we may, old man, and make a fair wind of it homewards, to go on a better voyage than this.'

Overhearing Starbuck, the panic-stricken crew instantly ran to the braces—though not a sail was left aloft. For the moment all the aghast mate's thoughts seemed theirs; they raised a half mutinous cry. But dashing the rattling lightning links to the deck, and snatching the burning harpoon, Ahab waved it like a torch among them; swearing to transfix with it the first sailor that but cast loose a rope's end. Petrified by his aspect, and still more shrinking from the fiery dart that he held, the men fell back in dismay, and Ahab spoke again:—

'All your oaths to hunt the White Whale are as binding as mine; and heart, soul, and body, lungs and life, old Ahab is bound. And that ye may know to what tune this heart beats; look ye here; thus I blow out the last fear!' And with one blast of his breath he extinguished the flame.

As in the hurricane that sweeps the plain, men fly the neighborhood of some lone, gigantic elm, whose very height and strength but render it so much the more unsafe, because so much the more a mark for thunderbolts; so at those last words of Ahab's many of the mariners did run from him in a terror of dismay.

120

THE DECK TOWARDS THE END OF
THE FIRST NIGHT WATCH

Ahab standing by the helm. Starbuck approaching him.

'WE must send down the main-top-sail yard, sir. The band is working loose, and the lee lift is half-stranded. Shall I strike it, sir?'

'Strike nothing; lash it. If I had sky-sail poles, I'd sway them up now.'

'Sir?—in God's name!—sir?'

'Well.'

'The anchors are working, sir. Shall I get them inboard?'

'Strike nothing, and stir nothing, but lash everything. The wind rises, but it has not got up to my table-lands yet. Quick, and see to it.—By masts and keels! he takes me for the hunch-backed skipper of some coasting smack. Send down my main-top-sail yard! Ho, gluepots! Loftiest trucks were made for wildest winds, and this brain-truck of mine now sails amid the cloud-scud. Shall I strike that? Oh, none but cowards send down their brain-trucks in tempest time. What a hooroosh aloft there! I would e'en take it for sublime, did I not know that the colic is a noisy malady. Oh, take medicine, take medicine!'

121

MIDNIGHT—THE FORECASTLE
BULWARKS

Stubb and Flask mounted on them, and passing additional lashings over the anchors there hanging.

'NO, Stubb; you may pound that knot there as much as you please, but you will never pound into me what you were just now saying. And how long ago is it since you said the very contrary? Didn't you once say that whatever ship Ahab sails in, that ship

should pay something extra on its insurance policy, just as though
it were loaded with powder barrels aft and boxes of lucifers forward?
Stop, now; didn't you say so?'

'Well, suppose I did? What then? I've part changed my flesh
since that time, why not my mind? Besides, supposing we *are*
loaded with powder barrels aft and lucifers forward; how the devil
could the lucifers get afire in this drenching spray here? Why, my
little man, you have pretty red hair, but you couldn't get afire
now. Shake yourself; you're Aquarius, or the water-bearer, Flask;
might fill pitchers at your coat collar. Don't you see, then, that
for these extra risks the Marine Insurance companies have extra
guarantees? Here are hydrants, Flask. But hark, again, and I'll
answer ye the other thing. First take your leg off from the crown
of the anchor here, though, so I can pass the rope; now listen.
What's the mighty difference between holding a mast's lightning-
rod in the storm, and standing close by a mast that hasn't got
any lightning-rod at all in a storm? Don't you see, you timber-
head, that no harm can come to the holder of the rod, unless the
mast is first struck? What are you talking about, then? Not one
ship in a hundred carries rods, and Ahab,—aye, man, and all of
us,—were in no more danger then, in my poor opinion, than all
the crews in ten thousand ships now sailing the seas. Why, you
King-Post, you, I suppose you would have every man in the world
go about with a small lightning-rod running up the corner of his
hat, like a militia officer's skewered feather, and trailing behind
like his sash. Why don't ye be sensible, Flask? it's easy to be
sensible; why don't ye, then? any man with half an eye can be
sensible.'

'I don't know that, Stubb. You sometimes find it rather hard.'

'Yes, when a fellow's soaked through, it's hard to be sensible,
that's a fact. And I am about drenched with this spray. Never
mind; catch the turn there, and pass it. Seems to me we are
lashing down these anchors now as if they were never going to
be used again. Tying these two anchors here, Flask, seems like
tying a man's hands behind him. And what big generous hands
they are, to be sure. These are your iron fists, hey? What a hold
they have, too! I wonder, Flask, whether the world is anchored
anywhere; if she is, she swings with an uncommon long cable,
though. There, hammer that knot down, and we've done. So; next
to touching land, lighting on deck is the most satisfactory. I say,
just wring out my jacket skirts, will ye? Thank ye. They laugh at
long-togs so, Flask; but seems to me, a long tailed coat ought
always to be worn in all storms afloat. The tails tapering down

that way, serve to carry off the water, d'ye see. Same with cocked
hats; the cocks form gable-end eave-troughs, Flask. No more
monkey-jackets and tarpaulins for me; I must mount a swallow-
tail, and drive down a beaver; so. Halloa! whew! there goes my
tarpaulin overboard; Lord, Lord, that the winds that come from
heaven should be so unmannerly! This is a nasty night, lad.'

122

MIDNIGHT ALOFT—THUNDER AND LIGHTNING

The Main-top-sail yard.—Tashtego passing new lashings around it.

'Um, um, um. Stop that thunder! Plenty too much thunder up
here. What's the use of thunder? Um, um, um. We don't want
thunder; we want rum; give us a glass of rum. Um, um, um!'

123

THE MUSKET

DURING the most violent shocks of the Typhoon, the man at the
Pequod's jaw-bone tiller had several times been reelingly hurled
to the deck by its spasmodic motions, even though preventer
tackles had been attached to it—for they were slack—because
some play to the tiller was indispensable.

In a severe gale like this, while the ship is but a tossed shuttlecock
to the blast, it is by no means uncommon to see the needles in
the compasses, at intervals, go round and round. It was thus with
the Pequod's; at almost every shock the helmsman had not failed
to notice the whirling velocity with which they revolved upon the
cards; it is a sight that hardly any one can behold without some
sort of unwonted emotion.

Some hours after midnight, the Typhoon abated so much, that
through the strenuous exertions of Starbuck and Stubb—one engaged forward and the other aft—the shivered remnants of the
jib and fore and main-top-sails were cut adrift from the spars,
and went eddying away to leeward, like the feathers of an albatross,

which sometimes are cast to the winds when that storm-tossed
bird is on the wing.

The three corresponding new sails were now bent and reefed,
and a storm-trysail was set further aft; so that the ship soon went
through the water with some precision again; and the course—
for the present, East-south-east—which he was to steer, if practicable, was once more given to the helmsman. For during the
violence of the gale, he had only steered according to its vicissitudes.
But as he was now bringing the ship as near her course as possible,
watching the compass meanwhile, lo! a good sign! the wind seemed
coming round astern; aye, the foul breeze became fair!

Instantly the yards were squared, to the lively song of '*Ho! the
fair wind! oh-he-yo, cheerly, men!*' the crew singing for joy, that
so promising an event should so soon have falsified the evil portents
preceding it.

In compliance with the standing order of his commander—to
report immediately, and at any one of the twenty-four hours any
decided change in the affairs of the deck,—Starbuck had no sooner
trimmed the yards to the breeze—however reluctantly and gloomily,—than he mechanically went below to apprise Captain Ahab
of the circumstance.

Ere knocking at his state-room, he involuntarily paused before
it a moment. The cabin lamp—taking long swings this way and
that—was burning fitfully, and casting fitful shadows upon the
old man's bolted door,—a thin one, with fixed blinds inserted, in
place of upper panels. The isolated subterraneousness of the cabin
made a certain humming silence to reign there, though it was
hooped round by all the roar of the elements. The loaded muskets
in the rack were shiningly revealed, as they stood upright against
the forward bulkhead. Starbuck was an honest, upright man; but
out of Starbuck's heart, at that instant when he saw the muskets,
there strangely evolved an evil thought; but so blent with its
neutral or good accompaniments that for the instant he hardly
knew it for itself.

'He would have shot me once,' he murmured, 'yes, there's the
very musket that he pointed at me;—that one with the studded
stock; let me touch it—lift it. Strange, that I, who have handled
so many deadly lances, strange, that I should shake so now.
Loaded? I must see. Aye, aye; and powder in the pan;—that's not
good. Best spill it?—wait. I'll cure myself of this. I'll hold the
musket boldly while I think.—I come to report a fair wind to
him. But how fair? Fair for death and doom,—*that's* fair for Moby
Dick. It's a fair wind that's only fair for that accursed fish.—The

very tube he pointed at me!—the very one; *this* one—I hold it
here; he would have killed me with the very thing I handle now.—
Aye and he would fain kill all his crew. Does he not say he will
not strike his spars to any gale? Has he not dashed his heavenly
quadrant? and in these same perilous seas, gropes he not his way
by mere dead reckoning of the error-abounding log? and in this
very Typhoon, did he not swear that he would have no lightning-
rods? But shall this crazed old man be tamely suffered to drag a
whole ship's company down to doom with him?—Yes, it would
make him the wilful murderer of thirty men and more, if this
ship come to any deadly harm; and come to deadly harm, my
soul swears this ship will, if Ahab have his way. If, then, he were
this instant—put aside, that crime would not be his. Ha! is he
muttering in his sleep? Yes, just there,—in there, he's sleeping.
Sleeping? aye, but still alive, and soon awake again. I can't withstand thee, then, old man. Not reasoning; not remonstrance; not
entreaty wilt thou hearken to; all this thou scornest. Flat obedience
to thy own flat commands, this is all thou breathest. Aye, and
say'st the men have vow'd thy vow; say'st all of us are Ahabs.
Great God forbid!—But is there no other way? no lawful way?—
Make him a prisoner to be taken home? What! hope to wrest this
old man's living power from his own living hands? Only a fool
would try it. Say he were pinioned even; knotted all over with
ropes and hawsers; chained down to ring-bolts on this cabin floor;
he would be more hideous than a caged tiger, then. I could not
endure the sight; could not possibly fly his howlings; all comfort,
sleep itself, inestimable reason would leave me on the long intolerable voyage. What, then, remains? The land is hundreds of
leagues away, and locked Japan the nearest. I stand alone here
upon an open sea, with two oceans and a whole continent between
me and law.—Aye, aye, 'tis so.—Is heaven a murderer when its
lightning strikes a would-be murderer in his bed, tindering sheets
and skin together?—And would I be a murderer, then, if—' and
slowly, stealthily, and half sideways looking, he placed the loaded
musket's end against the door.

'On this level, Ahab's hammock swings within; his head this
way. A touch, and Starbuck may survive to hug his wife and child
again.—Oh Mary! Mary!—boy! boy! boy!—But if I wake thee not
to death, old man, who can tell to what unsounded deeps Starbuck's body this day week may sink, with all the crew! Great
God, where art thou? Shall I? shall I?—The wind has gone down
and shifted, sir; the fore and main topsails are reefed and set; she
heads her course.'

'Stern all! Oh Moby Dick, I clutch thy heart at last!'

Such were the sounds that now came hurtling from out the old man's tormented sleep, as if Starbuck's voice had caused the long dumb dream to speak.

The yet levelled musket shook like a drunkard's arm against the panel; Starbuck seemed wrestling with an angel; but turning from the door, he placed the death-tube in its rack, and left the place.

'He's too sound asleep, Mr Stubb; go thou down, and wake him, and tell him. I must see to the deck here. Thou know'st what to say.'

124
THE NEEDLE

NEXT morning the not-yet-subsided sea rolled in long slow billows of mighty bulk, and striving in the Pequod's gurgling track, pushed her on like giants' palms outspread. The strong, unstaggering breeze abounded so, that sky and air seemed vast outbellying sails; the whole world boomed before the wind. Muffled in the full morning light, the invisible sun was only known by the spread intensity of his place; where his bayonet rays moved on in stacks. Emblazonings, as of crowned Babylonian kings and queens, reigned over everything. The sea was as a crucible of molten gold, that bubblingly leaps with light and heat.

Long maintaining an enchanted silence, Ahab stood apart; and every time the tetering ship loweringly pitched down her bowsprit, he turned to eye the bright sun's rays produced ahead; and when she profoundly settled by the stern, he turned behind, and saw the sun's rearward place, and how the same yellow rays were blending with his undeviating wake.

'Ha, ha, my ship! thou mightest well be taken now for the sea-chariot of the sun. Ho, ho! all ye nations before my prow, I bring the sun to ye! Yoke on the further billows; hallo! a tandem, I drive the sea!'

But suddenly reined back by some counter thought, he hurried towards the helm, huskily demanding how the ship was heading.

'East-sou-east, sir,' said the frightened steersman.

'Thou liest!' smiting him with his clenched fist. 'Heading East at this hour in the morning, and the sun astern?'

Upon this every soul was confounded; for the phenomenon just then observed by Ahab had unaccountably escaped every one else; but its very blinding palpableness must have been the cause.

Thrusting his head half way into the binnacle, Ahab caught one glimpse of the compasses; his uplifted arm slowly fell; for a moment he almost seemed to stagger. Standing behind him Starbuck looked, and lo! the two compasses pointed East, and the Pequod was as infallibly going West.

But ere the first wild alarm could get out abroad among the crew, the old man with a rigid laugh exclaimed, 'I have it! It has happened before. Mr Starbuck, last night's thunder turned our compasses—that's all. Thou hast before now heard of such a thing, I take it.'

'Aye; but never before has it happened to me, sir,' said the pale mate, gloomily.

Here, it must needs be said, that accidents like this have in more than one case occurred to ships in violent storms. The magnetic energy, as developed in the mariner's needle, is, as all know, essentially one with the electricity beheld in heaven; hence it is not to be much marvelled at, that such things should be. In instances where the lightning has actually struck the vessel, so as to smite down some of the spars and rigging, the effect upon the needle has at times been still more fatal; all its loadstone virtue being annihilated, so that the before magnetic steel was of no more use than an old wife's knitting needle. But in either case, the needle never again, of itself, recovers the original virtue thus marred or lost; and if the binnacle compasses be affected, the same fate reaches all the others that may be in the ship; even were the lowermost one inserted into the kelson.

Deliberately standing before the binnacle, and eyeing the transpointed compasses, the old man, with the sharp of his extended hand, now took the precise bearing of the sun, and satisfied that the needles were exactly inverted, shouted out his orders for the ship's course to be changed accordingly. The yards were braced hard up; and once more the Pequod thrust her undaunted bows into the opposing wind, for the supposed fair one had only been juggling her.

Meanwhile, whatever were his own secret thoughts, Starbuck said nothing, but quietly he issued all requisite orders; while Stubb and Flask—who in some small degree seemed then to be sharing his feelings—likewise unmurmuringly acquiesced. As for the men, though some of them lowly rumbled, their fear of Ahab was greater than their fear of Fate. But as ever before, the pagan harpooneers remained almost wholly unimpressed; or if impressed, it was only with a certain magnetism shot into their congenial hearts from inflexible Ahab's.

For a space the old man walked the deck in rolling reveries. But chancing to slip with his ivory heel, he saw the crushed copper sight-tubes of the quadrant he had the day before dashed to the deck.

'Thou poor, proud heaven-gazer and sun's pilot! yesterday I wrecked thee, and to-day the compasses would feign have wrecked me. So, so. But Ahab is lord over the level loadstone yet. Mr Starbuck—a lance without the pole; a top-maul, and the smallest of the sail-maker's needles. Quick!'

Accessory, perhaps, to the impulse dictating the thing he was now about to do, were certain prudential motives, whose object might have been to revive the spirits of his crew by a stroke of his subtle skill, in a matter so wondrous as that of the inverted compasses. Besides, the old man well knew that to steer by transpointed needles, though clumsily practicable, was not a thing to be passed over by superstitious sailors, without some shudderings and evil portents.

'Men,' said he, steadily turning upon the crew, as the mate handed him the things he had demanded, 'my men, the thunder turned old Ahab's needles; but out of this bit of steel Ahab can make one of his own, that will point as true as any.'

Abashed glances of servile wonder were exchanged by the sailors, as this was said; and with fascinated eyes they awaited whatever magic might follow. But Starbuck looked away.

With a blow from the top-maul Ahab knocked off the steel head of the lance, and then handing to the mate the long iron rod remaining, bade him hold it upright, without its touching the deck. Then, with the maul, after repeatedly smiting the upper end of this iron rod, he placed the blunted needle endwise on the top if it, and less strongly hammered that, several times, the mate still holding the rod as before. Then going through some small strange motions with it—whether indispensable to the magnetizing of the steel, or merely intended to augment the awe of the crew, is uncertain—he called for linen thread; and moving to the binnacle, slipped out the two reversed needles there, and horizontally suspended the sail-needle by its middle, over one of the compass-cards. At first, the steel went round and round, quivering and vibrating at either end; but at last it settled to its place, when Ahab, who had been intently watching for this result, stepped frankly back from the binnacle, and pointing his stretched arm towards it, exclaimed,—'Look ye, for yourselves, if Ahab be not lord of the level loadstone! The sun is East, and that compass swears it!'

One after another they peered in, for nothing but their own eyes could persuade such ignorance as theirs, and one after another they slunk away.

In his fiery eyes of scorn and triumph, you then saw Ahab in all his fatal pride.

125
THE LOG AND LINE

WHILE now the fated Pequod had been so long afloat this voyage, the log and line had but very seldom been in use. Owing to a confident reliance upon other means of determining the vessel's place, some merchantmen, and many whalemen, especially when cruising, wholly neglect to heave the log; though at the same time, and frequenlty more for form's sake than anything else, regularly putting down upon the customary slate the course steered by the ship, as well as the presumed average rate of progression every hour. It had been thus with the Pequod. The wooden reel and angular log attached hung, long untouched, just beneath the railing of the after bulwarks. Rains and spray had damped it; sun and wind had warped it; all the elements had combined to rot a thing that hung so idly. But heedless of all this, his mood seized Ahab, as he happened to glance upon the reel, not many hours after the magnet scene, and he remembered how his quadrant was no more, and recalled his frantic oath about the level log and line. The ship was sailing plungingly; astern the billows rolled in riots.

'Forward, there! Heave the log!'

Two seamen came. The golden-hued Tahitian and the grizzly Manxman. 'Take the reel, one of ye, I'll heave.'

They went towards the extreme stern, on the ship's lee side, where the deck, with the oblique energy of the wind, was now almost dipping into the creamy, sidelong-rushing sea.

The Manxman took the reel, and holding it high up, by the projecting handle-ends of the spindle, round which the spool of line revolved, so stood with the angular log hanging downwards, till Ahab advanced to him.

Ahab stood before him, and was lightly unwinding some thirty or forty turns to form a preliminary hand-coil to toss overboard, when the old Manxman, who was intently eyeing both him and the line, made bold to speak.

'Sir, I mistrust it; this line looks far gone, long heat and wet have spoiled it.'

' 'Twill hold, old gentleman. Long heat and wet, have they spoiled thee? Thou seem'st to hold. Or, truer perhaps, life holds thee; not thou it.'

'I hold the spool, sir. But just as my captain says. With these grey hairs of mine 'tis not worth while disputing, 'specially with a superior, who'll ne'er confess.'

'What's that? There now's a patched professor in Queen Nature's granite-founded College; but methinks he's too subservient. Where wert thou born?'

'In the little rocky Isle of Man, sir.'

'Excellent! Thou'st hit the world by that.'

'I know not, sir, but I was born there.'

'In the Isle of Man, hey? Well, the other way, it's good. Here's a man from Man; a man born in once independent Man, and now unmanned of Man; which is sucked in—by what? Up with the reel! The dead, blind wall butts all inquiring heads at last. Up with it! So.'

The log was heaved. The loose coils rapidly straightened out in a long dragging line astern, and then, instantly, the reel began to whirl. In turn, jerkingly raised and lowered by the rolling billows, the towing resistance of the log caused the old reelman to stagger strangely.

'Hold hard!'

Snap! the overstrained line sagged down in one long festoon; the tugging log was gone.

'I crush the quadrant, the thunder turns the needles, and now the mad sea parts the log-line. But Ahab can mend all. Haul in here, Tahitian; reel up, Manxman. And look ye, let the carpenter make another log, and mend thou the line. See to it.'

'There he goes now; to him nothing's happened; but to me, the skewer seems loosening out of the middle of the world. Haul in, haul in, Tahitian! These lines run whole, and whirling out: come in broken, and dragging slow. Ha, Pip? come to help; eh, Pip?'

'Pip? whom call ye Pip? Pip jumped from the whale-boat. Pip's missing. Let's see now if ye haven't fished him up here, fisherman. It drags hard; I guess he's holding on. Jerk him, Tahiti! Jerk him off; we haul in no cowards here. Ho! there's his arm just breaking water. A hatchet! a hatchet! cut it off—we haul in no cowards here. Captain Ahab! sir, sir! here's Pip, trying to get on board again.'

'Peace, thou crazy loon,' cried the Manxman, seizing him by the arm. 'Away from the quarter-deck!'

'The greater idiot ever scolds the lesser,' muttered Ahab, advancing. 'Hands off from that holiness! Where sayest thou Pip was, boy?'

'Astern there, sir, astern! Lo, lo!'

'And who are thou, boy? I see not my reflection in the vacant pupils of thy eyes. Oh God! that man should be a thing for immortal souls to sieve through! Who art thou, boy?'

'Bell-boy, sir; ship's-crier, ding, dong, ding! Pip! Pip! Pip! One hundred pounds of clay reward for Pip; five feet high—looks cowardly—quickest known by that! Ding, dong, ding! Who's seen Pip the coward?'

'There can be no hearts above the snow-line. Oh, ye frozen heavens! look down here. Ye did beget this luckless child, and have abandoned him, ye creative libertines. Here, boy; Ahab's cabin shall be Pip's home henceforth, while Ahab lives. Thou touchest my inmost centre, boy; thou art tied to me by cords woven of my heart-strings. Come, let's down.'

'What's this? here's velvet shark-skin,' intently gazing at Ahab's hand, and feeling it. 'Ah, now, had poor Pip but felt so kind a thing as this, perhaps he had ne'er been lost! This seems to me, sir, as a man-rope; something that weak souls may hold by. Oh, sir, let old Perth now come and rivet these two hands together; the black one with the white, for I will not let this go.'

'Oh, boy, nor will I thee, unless I should thereby drag thee to worse horrors than are here. Come, then, to my cabin. Lo! ye believers in gods all goodness, and in man all ill, lo you! see the omniscient gods oblivious of suffering man; and man, though idiotic, and knowing not what he does, yet full of the sweet things of love and gratitude. Come! I feel prouder leading thee by thy black hand, than though I grasped an Emperor's!'

'There go two daft ones now,' muttered the old Manxman. 'One daft with strength, the other daft with weakness. But here's the end of the rotten line—all dripping, too. Mend it, eh? I think we had best have a new line altogether. I'll see Mr Stubb about it.'

126

THE LIFE-BUOY

STEERING now south-eastward by Ahab's levelled steel, and her progress solely determined by Ahab's level log and line; the Pequod held on her path towards the Equator. Making so long a passage through such infrequented waters, descrying no ships, and ere long, sideways impelled by unvarying trade winds, over waves monotonously mild; all these seemed the strange calm things preluding some riotous and desperate scene.

At last, when the ship drew near to the outskirts, as it were, of the Equatorial fishing-ground, and in the deep darkness that goes before the dawn, was sailing by a cluster of rocky islets; the watch—then headed by Flask—was startled by a cry so plaintively wild and unearthly—like half-articulated wailings of the ghosts of all Herod's murdered Innocents—that one and all, they started from their reveries, and for the space of some moments stood, or sat, or leaned all transfixedly listening, like the carved Roman slave, while that wild cry remained within hearing. The Christian or civilized part of the crew said it was mermaids, and shuddered; but the pagan harpooneers remained unappalled. Yet the grey Manxman—the oldest mariner of all—declared that the wild thrilling sounds that were heard, were the voices of newly drowned men in the sea.

Below in his hammock, Ahab did not hear of this till grey dawn, when he came to the deck; it was then recounted to him by Flask, not unaccompanied with hinted dark meanings. He hollowly laughed, and thus explained the wonder.

Those rocky islands the ship had passed were the resort of great numbers of seals, and some young seals that had lost their dams, or some dams that had lost their cubs, must have risen nigh the ship and kept company with her, crying and sobbing with their human sort of wail. But this only the more affected some of them, because most mariners cherish a very superstitious feeling about seals, arising not only from their peculiar tones when in distress, but also from the human look of their round heads and semiintelligent faces, seen peeringly uprising from the water alongside. In the sea, under certain circumstances, seals have more than once been mistaken for men.

But the bodings of the crew were destined to receive a most plausible confirmation in the fate of one of their number that morning. At sun-rise this man went from his hammock to his mast-head at the fore; and whether it was that he was not yet half waked from his sleep (for sailors sometimes go aloft in a transition state), whether it was thus with the man, there is now no telling; but, be that as it may, he had not been long at his perch, when a cry was heard—a cry and a rushing—and looking up, they saw a falling phantom in the air; and looking down, a little tossed heap of white bubbles in the blue of the sea.

The life-buoy—a long slender cask—was dropped from the stern, where it always hung obedient to a cunning spring; but no hand rose to seize it, and the sun having long beat upon this cask it had shrunken, so that it slowly filled, and the parched wood also filled at its every pore; and the studded iron-bound cask followed the sailor to the bottom, as if to yield him his pillow, though in sooth but a hard one.

And thus the first man of the Pequod that mounted the mast to look out for the White Whale, on the White Whale's own peculiar ground; that man was swallowed up in the deep. But few, perhaps, thought of that at the time. Indeed, in some sort, they were not grieved at this event, at least as a portent; for they regarded it, not as a foreshadowing of evil in the future, but as the fulfilment of an evil already presaged. They declared that now they knew the reason of those wild shrieks they had heard the night before. But again the old Manxman said nay.

The lost life-buoy was now to be replaced; Starbuck was directed to see to it; but as no cask of sufficient lightness could be found, and as in the feverish eagerness of what seemed the approaching crisis of the voyage, all hands were impatient of any toil but what was directly connected with its final end, whatever that might prove to be; therefore, they were going to leave the ship's stern unprovided with a buoy, when by certain strange signs and in-nuendoes Queequeg hinted a hint concerning his coffin.

'A life-buoy of a coffin!' cried Starbuck, starting.

'Rather queer, that, I should say,' said Stubb.

'It will make a good enough one,' said Flask, 'the carpenter here can arrange it easily.'

'Bring it up; there's nothing else for it,' said Starbuck, after a melancholy pause. 'Rig it, carpenter; do not look at me so—the coffin, I mean. Dost thou hear me? Rig it.'

'And shall I nail down the lid, sir?' moving his hand as with a hammer.

'Aye.'

'And shall I caulk the seams, sir?' moving his hand as with a caulking-iron.

'Aye.'

'And shall I then pay over the same with pitch, sir?' moving his hand as with a pitch-pot.

'Away! what possesses thee to this? Make a life-buoy of the coffin, and no more.—Mr Stubb, Mr Flask, come forward with me.'

'He goes off in a huff. The whole he can endure; at the parts he baulks. Now I don't like this. I make a leg for Captain Ahab, and he wears it like a gentleman; but I make a bandbox for Queequeg, and he wont put his head into it. Are all my pains to go for nothing with that coffin? And now I'm ordered to make a life-buoy of it. It's like turning an old coat; going to bring the flesh on the other side now. I don't like this cobbling sort of business—I don't like it at all; it's undignified; it's not my place. Let tinkers' brats do tinkerings; we are their betters. I like to take in hand none but clean, virgin, fair-and-square mathematical jobs, something that regularly begins at the beginning, and is at the middle when midway, and comes to an end at the conclusion; not a cobbler's job, that's at an end in the middle, and at the beginning at the end. It's the old woman's tricks to be giving cobbling jobs. Lord! what an affection all old women have for tinkers. I know an old woman of sixty-five who ran away with a bald-headed young tinker once. And that's the reason I never would work for lonely widow old women ashore, when I kept my job-shop in the Vineyard; they might have taken it into their lonely old heads to run off with me. But heigh-ho! there are no caps at sea but snow-caps. Let me see. Nail down the lid; caulk the seams; pay over the same with pitch; batten them down tight, and hang it with the snap-spring over the ship's stern. Were ever such things done before with a coffin? Some superstitious old carpenters, now, would be tied up in the rigging, ere they would do the job. But I'm made of knotty Aroostook hemlock; I don't budge. Cruppered with a coffin! Sailing about with a grave-yard tray! But never mind. We workers in woods make bridal-bedsteads and card-tables, as well as coffins and hearses. We work by the month, or by the job, or by the profit; not for us to ask the why and wherefore of our work, unless it be too confounded cobbling, and then we stash it if we can. Hem! I'll do the job, now, tenderly. I'll have me—let's see—how many in the ship's company, all told? But I've forgotten. Any way, I'll have me thirty separate, Turk's-headed life-lines, each three feet long hanging all round to the coffin. Then, if the hull go down, there'll be thirty lively fellows all fighting for one coffin, a sight not seen very often beneath the sun! Come hammer, calking-iron, pitch-pot, and marling-spike! Let's to it.'

127
THE DECK

The coffin laid upon two line-tubs, between the vice-bench and the open hatchway; the Carpenter calking its seams; the string of twisted oakum slowly unwinding from a large roll of it placed in the bosom of his frock.—Ahab comes slowly from the cabin-gangway, and hears Pip following him.

'BACK, lad; I will be with ye again presently. He goes! Not this hand complies with my humor more genially than that boy.— Middle aisle of a church! What's here?'

'Life-buoy, sir. Mr Starbuck's orders. Oh, look, sir! Beware the hatchway!'

'Thank ye, man. Thy coffin lies handy to the vault.'

'Sir? The hatchway? oh! So it does, sir, so it does.'

'Art not thou the leg-maker? Look, did not this stump come from thy shop?'

'I believe it did, sir; does the ferrule stand, sir?'

'Well enough. But art thou not also the undertaker?'

'Aye, sir; I patched up this thing here as a coffin for Queequeg; but they've set me now to turning it into something else.'

'Then tell me; art thou not an arrant, all-grasping, intermeddling, monopolizing, heathenish old scamp, to be one day making legs, and the next day coffins to clap them in, and yet again life-buoys out of those same coffins? Thou art as unprincipled as the gods, and as much of a jack-of-all-trades.'

'But I do not mean anything, sir. I do as I do.'

'The gods again. Hark ye, dost thou not ever sing working about a coffin? The Titans, they say, hummed snatches when chipping out the craters for volcanoes; and the grave-digger in the play sings, spade in hand. Dost thou never?'

'Sing, sir. Do I sing? Oh, I'm indifferent enough, sir, for that; but the reason why the grave-digger made music must have been because there was none in his spade, sir. But the calking mallet is full of it. Hark to it.'

'Aye, and that's because the lid there's a sounding-board; and what in all things makes the sounding-board is this—there's naught beneath. And yet, a coffin with a body in it rings pretty much the same, Carpenter. Hast thou ever helped carry a bier, and heard the coffin knock against the churchyard gate, going in?'

'Faith, sir, I've—'

'Faith? What's that?'

'Why, faith, sir, it's only a sort of exclamation-like—that's all, sir.'

'Um, um; go on.'

'I was about to say, sir, that—'

'Art thou a silk-worm? Dost thou spin thy own shroud out of thyself? Look at thy bosom! Despatch! and get these traps out of sight.'

'He goes aft. That was sudden, now; but squalls come sudden in hot latitudes. I've heard that the Isle of Albemarle, one of the Gallipagos, is cut by the Equator right in the middle. Seems to me some sort of Equator cuts yon old man, too, right in his middle. He's always under the Line—fiery hot, I tell ye! He's looking this way—come, oakum; quick. Here we go again. This wooden mallet is the cork, and I'm the professor of musical glasses—tap, tap!'

(Ahab to himself.)

'There's a sight! There's a sound! The greyheaded woodpecker tapping the hollow tree! Blind and dumb might well be envied now. See! that thing rests on two line-tubs, full of tow-lines. A most malicious wag, that fellow. Rat-tat! So man's seconds tick! Oh! how immaterial are all materials! What things real are there, but imponderable thoughts? Here now's the very dreaded symbol of grim death, by a mere hap, made the expressive sign of the help and hope of most endangered life. A life-buoy of a coffin! Does it go further? Can it be that in some spiritual sense the coffin is, after all, but an immortality-preserver! I'll think of that. But no. So far gone am I in the dark side of earth, that its other side, the theoretic bright one, seems but uncertain twilight to me. Will ye never have done, Carpenter, with that accursed sound? I go below; let me not see that thing here when I return again. Now, then, Pip, we'll talk this over; I do suck most wondrous philosophies from thee! Some unknown conduits from the unknown worlds must empty into thee!'

128

THE PEQUOD MEETS THE RACHEL

NEXT day, a large ship, the Rachel, was descried, bearing directly down upon the Pequod, all her spars thickly clustering with men. At the time the Pequod was making good speed through the water; but as the broad-winged windward stranger shot nigh to her, the boastful sails all fell together as blank bladders that are burst, and all life fled from the smitten hull.

'Bad news; she brings bad news,' muttered the old Manxman. But ere her commander, who, with trumpet to mouth, stood up in his boat; ere he could hopefully hail, Ahab's voice was heard.

'Hast seen the White Whale?'

'Aye, yesterday. Have ye seen a whale-boat adrift?'

Throttling his joy, Ahab negatively answered this unexpected question; and would then have fain boarded the stranger, when the stranger captain himself, having stopped his vessel's way, was seen descending her side. A few keen pulls, and his boat-hook soon clinched the Pequod's main-chains, and he sprang to the deck. Immediately he was recognized by Ahab for a Nantucketer he knew. But no formal salutation was exchanged.

'Where was he?—not killed!—not killed!' cried Ahab, closely advancing. 'How was it?'

It seemed that somewhat late on the afternoon of the day previous, while three of the stranger's boats were engaged with a shoal of whales, which had led them some four or five miles from the ship; and while they were yet in swift chase to windward, the white hump and head of Moby Dick had suddenly loomed up out of the blue water, not very far to leeward; whereupon, the fourth rigged boat—a reserved one—had been instantly lowered in chase. After a keen sail before the wind, this fourth boat—the swiftest keeled of all—seemed to have succeeded in fastening—at least, as well as the man at the mast-head could tell anything about it. In the distance he saw the diminished dotted boat; and then a swift gleam of bubbling white water; and after that nothing more; whence it was concluded that the stricken whale must have indefinitely run away with his pursuers, as often happens. There was some apprehension, but no positive alarm, as yet. The recall signals were placed in the rigging; darkness came on; and forced to pick up her three far to windward boats—ere going in quest of the fourth one in the precisely opposite direction—the ship had not only been necessitated to leave that boat to its fate till near midnight, but, for the time, to increase her distance from it. But the rest of her crew being at last safe aboard, she crowded all sail—stunsail on stunsail—after the missing boat; kindling a fire in her try-pots for a beacon; and every other man aloft on the look-out. But though when she had thus sailed a sufficient distance to gain the presumed place of the absent ones when last seen; though she then paused to lower her spare boats to pull all around her; and not finding anything, had again dashed on; again paused, and lowered her boats; and though she had thus continued doing till day light; yet not the least glimpse of the missing keel had been seen.

The story told, the stranger Captain immediately went on to reveal his object in boarding the Pequod. He desired that ship to unite with his own in the search; by sailing over the sea some four or five miles apart, on parallel lines, and so sweeping a double horizon, as it were.

'I will wager something now,' whispered Stubb to Flask, 'that some one in that missing boat wore off that Captain's best coat; mayhap, his watch—he's so cursed anxious to get it back. Who ever heard of two pious whale-ships cruising after one missing whale-boat in the height of the whaling season? See, Flask, only see how pale he looks—pale in the very buttons of his eyes—look—it wasn't the coat—it must have been the—'

'My boy, my own boy is among them. For God's sake—I beg, I conjure'—here exclaimed the stranger Captain to Ahab, who thus far had but icily received his petition. 'For eight-and-forty hours let me charter your ship—I will gladly pay for it, and roundly pay for it if there be no other way—for eight-and-forty hours only—only that—you must, oh, you must, and you *shall* do this thing.'

'His son!' cried Stubb, 'oh, it's his son he's lost! I take back the coat and watch—what says Ahab? We must save that boy.'

'He's drowned with the rest on 'em, last night,' said the old Manx sailor standing behind them; 'I heard; all of ye heard their spirits.'

Now, as it shortly turned out, what made this incident of the Rachel's the more melancholy, was the circumstance, that not only was one of the Captain's sons among the number of the missing boat's crew; but among the number of the other boat's crews, at the same time, but on the other hand, separated from the ship during the dark vicissitudes of the chase, there had been still another son; as that for a time, the wretched father was plunged to the bottom of the cruellest perplexity; which was only solved for him by his chief mate's instinctively adopting the ordinary procedure of a whale-ship in such emergencies, that is, when placed between jeopardized but divided boats, always to pick up the majority first. But the captain, for some unknown constitutional reason, had refrained from mentioning all this, and not till forced to it by Ahab's iciness did he allude to his one yet missing boy; a little lad, but twelve years old, whose father with the earnest but unmisgiving hardihood of a Nantucketer's paternal love, had thus early sought to initiate him in the perils and wonders of a vocation almost immemorially the destiny of all his race. Nor does it unfrequently occur, that Nantucket captains will send a son of such tender age away from them, for a protracted three or four years' voyage in some other ship than their own; so that their first knowledge of a whaleman's career shall be unenervated by any chance display of a father's natural but untimely partiality, or undue apprehensiveness and concern.

Meantime, now the stranger was still beseeching his poor boon of Ahab; and Ahab still stood like an anvil, receiving every shock, but without the least quivering of his own.

'I will not go,' said the stranger, 'till you say *aye* to me. Do to me as you would have me do to you in the like case. For *you* too have a boy, Captain Ahab—though but a child, and nestling safely at home now—a child of your old age too—Yes, yes, you relent; I see it—run, run, men, now, and stand by to square in the yards.'

'Avast,' cried Ahab—'touch not a rope-yarn;' then in a voice that prolongingly moulded every word—'Captain Gardiner, I will not do it. Even now I lose time. Good bye, good bye. God bless ye, man, and may I forgive myself, but I must go. Mr Starbuck, look at the binnacle watch, and in three minutes from this present instant warn off all strangers: then brace forward again, and let the ship sail as before.'

Hurriedly turning, with averted face, he descended into his cabin, leaving the strange captain transfixed at this unconditional and utter rejection of his so earnest suit. But starting from his enchantment, Gardiner silently hurried to the side; more fell than stepped into his boat, and returned to his ship.

Soon the two ships diverged their wakes; and long as the strange vessel was in view, she was seen to yaw hither and thither at every dark spot, however small, on the sea. This way and that her yards were swung round; starboard and larboard, she continued to tack; now she beat against a head sea; and again it pushed her before it; while all the while, her masts and yards were thickly clustered with men, as three tall cherry trees, when the boys are cherrying among the boughs.

But by her still halting course and winding, woful way, you plainly saw that this ship that so wept with spray, still remained without comfort. She was Rachel, weeping for her children, because they were not.

129
THE CABIN

(Ahab moving to go on deck; Pip catches him by the hand to follow.)

'LAD, lad, I tell thee thou must not follow Ahab now. The hour is coming when Ahab would not scare thee from him, yet would not have thee by him. There is that in thee, poor lad, which I feel too curing to my malady. Like cures like; and for this hunt, my malady becomes my most desired health. Do thou abide below here, where they shall serve thee, as if thou wert the captain. Aye, lad, thou shalt sit here in my own screwed chair; another screw to it, thou must be.'

'No, no, no! ye have not a whole body, sir; do ye but use poor me for your one lost leg; only tread upon me, sir; I ask no more, so I remain a part of ye.'

'Oh! spite of million villains, this makes me a bigot in the fadeless fidelity of man!—and a black! and crazy!—but methinks like cures like applies to him too; he grows so sane again.'

'They tell me, sir, that Stubb did once desert poor little Pip, whose drowned bones now show white, for all the blackness of his living skin. But I will never desert ye, sir, as Stubb did him. Sir, I must go with ye.'

'If thou speakest thus to me much more, Ahab's purpose keels up in him. I tell thee no; it cannot be.'

'Oh good master, master, master!'

'Weep so, and I will murder thee! have a care, for Ahab too is mad. Listen, and thou wilt often hear my ivory foot upon the deck, and still know that I am there. And now I quit thee. Thy hand!—Met! True art thou, lad, as the circumference to its centre.

So: God for ever bless thee; and if it come to that,—God for ever save thee, let what will befall.'

(Ahab goes; Pip steps one step forward.)

'Here he this instant stood; I stand in his air,—but I'm alone. Now were even poor Pip here I could endure it, but he's missing. Pip! Pip! Ding, dong, ding! Who's seen Pip? He must be up here; let's try the door. What? neither lock, nor bolt, nor bar; and yet there's no opening it. It must be the spell; he told me to stay here: Aye, and told me this screwed chair was mine. Here, then, I'll seat me, against the transom, in the ship's full middle, all her keel and her three masts before me. Here, our old sailors say, in their black seventy-fours great admirals sometimes sit at table, and lord it over rows of captains and lieutenants. Ha! what's this? epaulets! epaulets! the epaulets all come crowding! Pass round the decanters; glad to see ye; fill up, monsieurs! What an odd feeling, now, when a black boy's host to white men with gold lace upon their coats!—Monsieurs, have ye seen one Pip?—a little negro lad, five feet high, hang-dog look, and cowardly! Jumped from a whale-boat once;—seen him? No! Well then, fill up again, captains, and let's drink shame upon all cowards! I name no names. Shame upon them! Put one foot upon the table. Shame upon all cowards.—Hist! above there, I hear ivory—Oh, master! master! I am indeed downhearted when you walk over me. But here I'll stay, though this stern strikes rocks; and they bulge through; and oysters come to join me.'

130
THE HAT

AND now that at the proper time and place, after so long and wide a preliminary cruise, Ahab,—all other whaling waters swept—seemed to have chased his foe into an ocean-fold, to slay him the more securely there; now, that he found himself hard by the very latitude and longitude where his tormenting wound had been inflicted; now that a vessel had been spoken which on the very day preceding had actually encountered Moby Dick;—and now that all his successive meetings with various ships contrastingly concurred to show the demoniac indifference with which the white whale tore his hunters, whether sinning or sinned against; now it was that there lurked a something in the old man's eyes, which it was hardly sufferable for feeble souls to see. As the unsetting polar star, which through the livelong, arctic, six months' night sustains its piercing, steady, central gaze; so Ahab's purpose now fixedly gleamed down upon the constant midnight of the gloomy crew. It domineered above them so, that all their bodings, doubts, misgivings, fears, were fain to hide beneath their souls, and not sprout forth a single spear or leaf.

In this foreshadowing interval, too, all humor, forced or natural, vanished. Stubb no more strove to raise a smile; Starbuck no more strove to check one. Alike, joy and sorrow, hope and fear, seemed ground to finest dust, and powdered, for the time, in the clamped mortar of Ahab's iron soul. Like machines, they dumbly moved about the deck, ever conscious that the old man's despot eye was on them.

But did you deeply scan him in his more secret confidential hours; when he thought no glance but one was on him; then you would have seen that even as Ahab's eyes so awed the crew's, the inscrutable Parsee's glance awed his; or somehow, at least, in some wild way, at times affected it. Such an added, gliding strangeness began to invest the thin Fedallah now; such ceaseless shudderings shook him; that the men looked dubious at him; half uncertain, as it seemed, whether indeed he were a mortal substance, or else a tremulous shadow cast upon the deck by some unseen being's body. And that shadow was always hovering there. For not by night, even, had Fedallah ever certainly been known to slumber, or go below. He would stand still for hours: but never sat or leaned; his wan but wondrous eyes did plainly say—We two watchmen never rest.

Nor, at any time, by night or day could the mariners now step up the deck, unless Ahab was before them; either standing in his pivot-hole, or exactly pacing the planks between two undeviating limits,—the main-mast and the mizen; or else they saw him standing in the cabin-scuttle,—his living foot advanced upon the deck, as if to step; his hat slouched heavily over his eyes; so that however motionless he stood, however the days and nights were added on, that he had not swung in his hammock; yet hidden beneath that slouching hat, they could never tell unerringly whether, for all this, his eyes were really closed at times: or whether he was still intently scanning them; no matter, though he stood so in the scuttle for a whole long hour on the stretch, and the unheeded night-damp gathered in beads of dew upon that stone-carved coat and hat. The clothes that the night had wet, the next

day's sunshine dried upon him; and so, day after day, and night
after night; he went no more beneath the planks; whatever he
wanted from the cabin that thing he sent for.

He ate in the same open air; that is, his two only meals,—
breakfast and dinner: supper he never touched; nor reaped his
beard; which darkly grew all gnarled, as unearthed roots of trees
blown over, which still grow idly on at naked base, though perished
in the upper verdure. But though his whole life was now become
one watch on deck; and though the Parsee's mystic watch was
without intermission as his own; yet these two never seemed to
speak—one man to the other—unless at long intervals some
passing unmomentous matter made it necessary. Though such a
potent spell seemed secretly to join the twain; openly, and to the
awe-struck crew, they seemed pole-like asunder. If by day they
chanced to speak one word; by night, dumb men were both, so
far as concerned the slightest verbal interchange. At times, for
longest hours, without a single hail, they stood far parted in the
starlight; Ahab in his scuttle, the Parsee by the main-mast; but
still fixedly gazing upon each other, as if in the Parsee Ahab saw
his forethrown shadow, in Ahab the Parsee his abandoned substance.

And yet, somehow, did Ahab—in his own proper self, as daily,
hourly, and every instant, commandingly revealed to his subordinates,—Ahab seemed an independent lord; the Parsee but his
slave. Still again both seemed yoked together, and an unseen tyrant
driving them; the lean shade siding the solid rib. For be this Parsee
what he may, all rib and keel was solid Ahab.

At the first faintest glimmering of the dawn, his iron voice was
heard from aft—'Man the mast-heads!'—and all through the day,
till after sunset and after twilight, the same voice every hour, at
the striking of the helmsman's bell, was heard—'What d'ye see?—
sharp! sharp!'

But when three or four days had slided by, after meeting the
children-seeking Rachel; and no spout had yet been seen; the
monomaniac old man seemed distrustful of his crew's fidelity; at
least, of nearly all except the Pagan harpooneers; he seemed to
doubt, even, whether Stubb and Flask might not willingly overlook
the sight he sought. But if these suspicions were really his, he
sagaciously refrained from verbally expressing them, however his
actions might seem to hint them.

'I will have the first sight of the whale myself,'—he said. 'Aye!
Ahab must have the doubloon!' and with his own hands he rigged
a nest of basketed bowlines; and sending a hand aloft, with a

single sheaved block, to secure to the main-mast head, he received
the two ends of the downward-reeved rope; and attaching one to
his basket prepared a pin for the other end, in order to fasten it
at the rail. This done, with that end yet in his hand and standing
beside the pin, he looked round upon his crew, sweeping from
one to the other; pausing his glance long upon Daggoo, Queequeg,
Tashtego; but shunning Fedallah; and then settling his firm relying
eye upon the chief mate, said,—'Take the rope, sir—I give it into
thy hands, Starbuck.' Then arranging his person in the basket, he
gave the word for them to hoist him to his perch, Starbuck being
the one who secured the rope at last; and afterwards stood near
it. And thus, with one hand clinging round the royal mast, Ahab
gazed abroad upon the sea for miles and miles,—ahead, astern,
this side, and that,—within the wide expanded circle commanded
at so great a height.

When in working with his hands at some lofty almost isolated
place in the rigging, which chances to afford no foothold, the
sailor at sea is hoisted up to that spot, and sustained there by the
rope; under these circumstances, its fastened end on deck is always
given in strict charge to some one man who has the special watch
of it. Because in such a wilderness of running rigging, whose
various different relations aloft cannot always be infallibly discerned
by what is seen of them at the deck; and when the deck-ends of
these ropes are being every few minutes cast down from the
fastenings, it would be but a natural fatality, if, unprovided with
a constant watchman, the hoisted sailor should by some careless-
ness of the crew be cast adrift and fall all swooping to the sea.
So Ahab's proceedings in this matter were not unusual; the only
strange thing about them seemed to be, that Starbuck, almost the
one only man who had ever ventured to oppose him with anything
in the slightest degree approaching to decison—one of those too,
whose faithfulness on the look-out he had seemed to doubt somewhat;—it was strange, that this was the very man he should select
for his watchman; freely giving his whole life into such an otherwise
distrusted person's hands.

Now for the first time Ahab was perched aloft; ere he had been
there ten minutes; one of those red-billed savage sea-hawks which
so often fly incommodiously close round the manned mast-heads
of whalemen in these latitudes; one of these birds came wheeling
and screaming round his head in a maze of untrackably swift
circlings. Then it darted a thousand feet straight up into the air;
then spiralized downwards, and went eddying again round his
head.

But with his gaze fixed upon the dim and distant horizon, Ahab seemed not to mark this wild bird; nor, indeed, would any one else have marked it much, it being no uncommon circumstance; only now almost the least heedful eye seemed to see some sort of cunning meaning in almost every sight.

'Your hat, your hat, sir!' suddenly cried the Sicilian seaman, who being posted at the mizen-mast-head, stood directly behind Ahab, though somewhat lower than his level, and with a deep gulf of air dividing them.

But already the sable wing was before the old man's eyes; the long hooked bill at his head: with a scream, the black hawk darted away with his prize.

An eagle flew thrice round Tarquin's head, removing his cap to replace it, and thereupon Tanaquil, his wife, declared that Tarquin would be king of Rome. But only by the replacing of the cap was that omen accounted good. Ahab's hat was never restored; the wild hawk flew on and on with it; far in advance of the prow: and at last disappeared; while from the point of that disappearance, a minute black spot was dimly discerned, falling from that vast height into the sea.

131
THE PEQUOD MEETS THE DELIGHT

THE intense Pequod sailed on; the rolling waves and days went by; the life-buoy-coffin still lightly swung; and another ship, most miserably misnamed the Delight, was descried. As she drew nigh, all eyes were fixed upon her broad beams, called shears, which, in some whale-ships, cross the quarter-deck at the height of eight or nine feet; serving to carry the spare, unrigged, or disabled boats.

Upon the stranger's shears were beheld the shattered, white ribs, and some few splintered planks, of what had once been a whale-boat; but you now saw through this wreck, as plainly as you see through the peeled, half-unhinged, and bleaching skeleton of a horse.

'Hast seen the White Whale?'

'Look!' replied the hollow-cheeked captain from his taffrail; and with his trumpet he pointed to the wreck.

'Hast killed him?'

'The harpoon is not yet forged that will ever do that,' answered the other, sadly glancing upon a rounded hammock on the deck, whose gathered sides some noiseless sailors were busy in sewing together.

'Not forged!' and snatching Perth's levelled iron from the crotch, Ahab held it out, exclaiming—'Look ye, Nantucketer; here in this hand I hold his death! Tempered in blood, and tempered by lightning are these barbs; and I swear to temper them triply in that hot place behind the fin, where the White Whale most feels his accursed life!'

'Then God keep thee, old man—see'st thou that'—pointing to the hammock—'I bury but one of five stout men, who were alive only yesterday; but were dead ere night. Only *that* one I bury; the rest were buried before they died; you sail upon their tomb.' Then turning to his crew—'Are ye ready there? place the plank then on the rail, and lift the body; so, then—Oh! God'—advancing towards the hammock with unlifted hands—'may the resurrection and the life—'

'Brace forward! Up helm!' cried Ahab like lightning to this men.

But the suddenly started Pequod was not quick enough to escape the sound of the splash that the corpse soon made as it struck the sea; not so quick, indeed, but that some of the flying bubbles might have sprinkled her hull with their ghostly baptism.

As Ahab now glided from the dejected Delight, the strange life-buoy hanging at the Pequod's stern came into conspicuous relief.

'Ha! yonder! look yonder, men!' cried a foreboding voice in her wake. 'In vain, oh, ye strangers, ye fly our sad burial; ye but turn us your taffrail to show us your coffin!'

132

THE SYMPHONY

IT was a clear steel-blue day. The firmaments of air and sea were hardly separable in that all-pervading azure; only, the pensive air was transparently pure and soft, with a woman's look, and the robust and man-like sea heaved with long, strong, lingering swells, as Samson's chest in his sleep.

Hither, and thither, on high, glided the snow-white wings of small, unspeckled birds; these were the gentle thoughts of the feminine air; but to and fro in the deeps, far down in the bottomless blue, rushed mighty leviathans, sword-fish, and sharks; and these

were the strong, troubled, murderous thinkings of the masculine
sea.

But though thus contrasting within, the contrast was only in
shades and shadows without; those two seemed one; it was only
the sex, as it were, that distinguished them.

Aloft, like a royal czar and king, the sun seemed giving this
gentle air to this bold and rolling sea; even as bride to groom.
And at the girdling line of the horizon, a soft and tremulous
motion—most seen here at the equator—denoted the fond, throbbing trust, the loving alarms, with which the poor bride gave her
bosom away.

Tied up and twisted; gnarled and knotted with wrinkles; hag-
gardly firm and unyielding; his eyes glowing like coals, that still
glow in the ashes of ruin; untottering Ahab stood forth in the
clearness of the morn; lifting his splintered helmet of a brow to
the fair girl's forehead of heaven.

Oh, immortal infancy, and innocency of the azure! Invisible
winged creatures that frolic all round us! Sweet childhood of air
and sky! how oblivious were ye of old Ahab's close-coiled woe!
But so have I seen little Miriam and Martha, laughing-eyed elves,
heedlessly gambol around their old sire; sporting with the circle
of singed locks which grew on the marge of that burnt-out crater
of his brain.

Slowly crossing the deck from the scuttle, Ahab leaned over the
side, and watched how his shadow in the water sank and sank to
his gaze, the more and the more that he strove to pierce the
profundity. But the lovely aromas in that enchanted air did at
last seem to dispel, for a moment, the cankerous thing in his soul.
That glad, happy air, that winsome sky, did at last stroke and
caress him; the step-mother world, so long cruel—forbidding—
now threw affectionate arms round his stubborn neck, and did
seem to joyously sob over him, as if over one, that however wilful
and erring, she could yet find it in her heart to save and to bless.
From beneath his slouched hat Ahab dropped a tear into the sea;
nor did all the Pacific contain such wealth as that one wee drop.

Starbuck saw the old man; saw him, how he heavily leaned
over the side; and he seemed to hear in his own true heart the
measureless sobbing that stole out of the centre of the serenity
around. Careful not to touch him, or be noticed by him, he yet
drew near to him, and stood there.

Ahab turned.

'Starbuck!'

'Sir.'

'Oh, Starbuck! it is a mild, mild wind, and a mild looking sky. On such a day—very much such a sweetness as this—I struck my first whale—a boy-harpooneer of eighteen! Forty—forty—forty years ago!—ago! Forty years of continual whaling! forty years of privation, and peril, and storm-time! forty years on the pitiless sea! for forty years has Ahab forsaken the peaceful land, for forty years to make war on the horrors of the deep! Aye and yes, Starbuck, out of those forty years I have not spent three ashore. When I think of this life I have led; the desolation of solitude it has been; the masoned, walled-town of a Captain's exclusiveness, which admits but small entrance to any sympathy from the green country without—oh, weariness, heaviness! Guinea-coast slavery of solitary command!—when I think of all this; only half-suspected, not so keenly known to me before—and how for forty years I have fed upon dry salted fare—fit emblem of the dry nourishment of my soul!—when the poorest landsman has had fresh fruit to his daily hand, and broken the world's fresh bread to my mouldy crusts—away, whole oceans away, from that young girl-wife I wedded past fifty, and sailed for Cape Horn the next day, leaving but one dent in my marriage pillow—wife? wife?—rather a widow with her husband alive! Aye, I widowed that poor girl when I married her, Starbuck; and then, the madness, the frenzy, the boiling blood and the smoking brow, with which, for a thousand lowerings old Ahab has furiously, foamingly chased his prey—more a demon than a man!—aye, aye! what a forty years' fool—fool—old fool, has old Ahab been! Why this strife of the chase? why weary, and palsy the arm at the oar, and the iron, and the lance? how the richer or better is Ahab now? Behold. Oh, Starbuck! is it not hard, that with this weary load I bear, one poor leg should have been snatched from under me? Here, brush this old hair aside; it blinds me, that I seem to weep. Locks so grey did never grow but from out some ashes! But do I look very old, so very, very old, Starbuck? I feel deadly faint, bowed, and humped, as though I were Adam, staggering beneath the piled centuries since Paradise. God! God! God!—crack my heart!—stave my brain!—mockery! mockery! bitter, biting mockery of grey hairs, have I lived enough joy to wear ye; and seem and feel thus intolerably old? Close! stand close to me, Starbuck; let me look into a human eye; it is better than to gaze into sea or sky; better than to gaze upon God. By the green land; by the bright hearth-stone! this is the magic glass, man; I see my wife and my child in thine eye. No, no; stay on board, on board!—lower not when I do; when branded Ahab gives chase to Moby Dick. That hazard shall not be thine. No, no! not with the far away home I see in that eye!'

'Oh, my Captain! my Captain! noble soul! grand old heart, after all! why should any one give chase to that hated fish! Away with me! let us fly these deadly waters! let us home! Wife and child, too, are Starbuck's—wife and child of his brotherly, sisterly, play-fellow youth; even as thine, sir, are the wife and child of thy loving, longing, paternal old age! Away! let us away!—this instant let me alter the course! How cheerily, how hilariously, O my Captain, would we bowl on our way to see old Nantucket again! I think, sir, they have some such mild blue days, even as this, in Nantucket.'

'They have, they have. I have seen them—some summer days in the morning. About this time—yes, it is his noon nap now—the boy vivaciously wakes; sits up in bed; and his mother tells him of me, of cannibal old me; how I am abroad upon the deep, but will yet come back to dance him again.'

' 'Tis my Mary, my Mary herself! She promised that my boy, every morning, should be carried to the hill to catch the first glimpse of his father's sail! Yes, yes! no more! it is done! we head for Nantucket! Come, my Captain, study out the course, and let us away! See, see! the boy's face from the window! the boy's hand on the hill!'

But Ahab's glance was averted; like a blighted fruit tree he shook, and cast his last, cindered apple to the soil.

'What is it, what nameless, inscrutable, unearthly thing is it; what cozzening, hidden lord and master, and cruel remorseless emperor commands me; that against all natural lovings and long-ings, I so keep pushing, and crowding, and jamming myself on all the time; recklessly making me ready to do what in my own proper, natural heart, I durst not so much as dare? Is Ahab, Ahab? Is it I, God, or who, that lifts this arm? But if the great sun move not of himself; but is as an errand-boy in heaven; nor one single star can revolve, but by some invisible power; how then can this one small heart beat; this one small brain think thoughts; unless God does that beating, does that thinking, does that living, and not I. By heaven, man, we are turned round and round in this world, like yonder windlass, and Fate is the handspike. And all the time, lo! that smiling sky, and this unsounded sea! Look! see yon Albicore! who put it into him to chase and fang that flying-fish? Where do murderers go, man! Who's to doom, when the judge himself is dragged to the bar? But it is a mild, mild wind, and a mild looking sky; and the air smells now, as if it blew from a far-away meadow; they have been making hay somewhere under the slopes of the Andes, Starbuck, and the mowers are sleeping among the new-mown hay. Sleeping? Aye, toil we how we may, we all sleep at last on the field. Sleep? Aye, and rust amid greenness; as last year's scythes flung down, and left in the half-cut swaths— Starbuck!'

But blanched to a corpse's hue with despair, the mate had stolen away.

Ahab crossed the deck to gaze over on the other side; but started at two reflected, fixed eyes in the water there. Fedallah was motionlessly leaning over the same rail.

133
THE CHASE—FIRST DAY

THAT night, in the mid-watch, when the old man—as his wont at intervals—stepped forth from the scuttle in which he leaned, and went to his pivot-hole, he suddenly thrust out his face fiercely, snuffing up the sea air as a sagacious ship's dog will, in drawing nigh to some barbarous isle. He declared that a whale must be near. Soon that peculiar odor, sometimes to a great distance given forth by the living sperm whale, was palpable to all the watch; nor was any mariner surprised when, after inspecting the compass, and then the dog-vane, and then ascertaining the precise bearing of the odor as nearly as possible, Ahab rapidly ordered the ship's course to be slightly altered, and the sail to be shortened.

The acute policy dictating these movements was sufficiently vindicated at daybreak, by the sight of a long sleek on the sea directly and lengthwise ahead, smooth as oil, and resembling in the pleated watery wrinkles bordering it, the polished metallic-like marks of some swift tide-rip, at the mouth of a deep, rapid stream.

'Man the mast-heads! Call all hands!'

Thundering with the butts of three clubbed handspikes on the forecastle deck, Daggoo roused the sleepers with such judgment claps that they seemed to exhale from the scuttle, so instantaneously did they appear with their clothes in their hands.

'What d'ye see?' cried Ahab, flattening his face to the sky.

'Nothing, nothing, sir!' was the sound hailing down in reply.

'T'gallant sails!—stunsails! alow and aloft, and on both sides!'

All sail being set, he now cast loose the life-line, reserved for

swaying him to the main royal-mast head; and in a few moments
they were hoisting him thither, when, while but two thirds of the
way aloft, and while peering ahead through the horizontal vacancy
between the main-top-sail and top-gallant-sail, he raised a gull-
like cry in the air, 'There she blows!—there she blows! A hump
like a snow-hill! It is Moby Dick!'

Fired by the cry which seemed simultaneously taken up by the
three look-outs, the men on deck rushed to the rigging to behold
the famous whale they had so long been pursuing. Ahab had now
gained his final perch, some feet above the other look-outs, Tashtego standing just beneath him on the cap of the top-gallant-mast,
so that the Indian's head was almost on a level with Ahab's heel.
From this height the whale was now seen some mile or so ahead,
at every roll of the sea revealing his high sparkling hump, and
regularly jetting his silent spout into the air. To the credulous
mariners it seemed the same silent spout they had so long ago
beheld in the moonlit Atlantic and Indian Oceans.

'And did none of ye see it before?' cried Ahab, hailing the
perched men all around him.

'I saw him almost that same instant, sir, that Captain Ahab
did, and I cried out,' said Tashtego.

'Not the same instant; not the same—no, the doubloon is mine,
Fate reserved the doubloon for me. *I* only; none of ye could have
raised the White Whale first. There she blows! there she blows!—
there she blows! There again!—there again!' he cried, in long-
drawn, lingering, methodic tones, attuned to the gradual prolong-
ings of the whale's visible jets. 'He's going to sound! In stunsails!
Down top-gallant-sails! Stand by three boats. Mr Starbuck, remember, stay on board, and keep the ship. Helm there! Luff, luff
a point! So; steady, man, steady! There go flukes! No, no; only
black water! All ready the boats there! Stand by, stand by! Lower
me, Mr Starbuck; lower, lower,—quick, quicker!' and he slid
through the air to the deck.

'He is heading straight to leeward, sir,' cried Stubb, 'right away
from us; cannot have seen the ship yet.'

'Be dumb, man! Stand by the braces! Hard down the helm!—
brace up! Shiver her!—shiver her! So; well that! Boats, boats!'

Soon all the boats but Starbuck's were dropped; all the boat-
sails set—all the paddles plying; with rippling swiftness, shooting
to leeward; and Ahab heading the onset. A pale, death-glimmer
lit up Fedallah's sunken eyes; a hideous motion gnawed his mouth.

Like noiseless nautilus shells, their light prows sped through the
sea; but only slowly they neared the foe. As they neared him, the

ocean grew still more smooth; seemed drawing a carpet over its waves; seemed a noon-meadow, so serenely it spread. At length the breathless hunter came so nigh his seemingly unsuspecting prey, that his entire dazzling hump was distinctly visible, sliding along the sea as if an isolated thing, and continually set in a revolving ring of finest, fleecy, greenish foam. He saw the vast, involved wrinkles of the slightly projecting head beyond. Before it, far out on the soft Turkish-rugged waters, went the glistening white shadow from his broad, milky forehead, a musical rippling playfully accompanying the shade; and behind, the blue waters interchangeably flowed over into the moving valley of his steady wake; and on either hand bright bubbles arose and danced by his side. But these were broken again by the light toes of hundreds of gay fowl softly feathering the sea, alternate with their fitful flight; and like to some flagstaff rising from the painted hull of an argosy, the tall but shattered pole of a recent lance projected from the white whale's back; and at intervals one of the cloud of soft-toed fowls hovering, and to and fro skimming like a canopy over the fish, silently perched and rocked on this pole, the long tail feathers streaming like pennons.

A gentle joyousness—a mighty mildness of repose in swiftness, invested the gliding whale. Not the white bull Jupiter swimming away with ravished Europa clinging to his graceful horns; his lovely, leering eyes sideways intent upon the maid; with smooth bewitching fleetness, rippling straight for the nuptial bower in Crete; not Jove, not that great majesty Supreme! did surpass the glorified White Whale as he so divinely swam.

On each soft side—coincident with the parted swell, that but once laving him, then flowed so wide away—on each bright side, the whale shed off enticings. No wonder there had been some among the hunters who namelessly transported and allured by all this serenity, had ventured to assail it; but had fatally found that quietude but the vesture of tornadoes. Yet calm, enticing calm, oh, whale! thou glidest on, to all who for the first time eye thee, no matter how many in that same way thou may'st have bejuggled and destroyed before.

And thus, through the serene tranquilities of the tropical sea, among waves whose hand-clappings were suspended by exceeding rapture, Moby Dick moved on, still withholding from sight the full terrors of his submerged trunk, entirely hiding the wrenched hideousness of his jaw. But soon the fore part of him slowly rose from the water; for an instant his whole marbleized body formed a high arch, like Virginia's Natural Bridge, and warningly waving his bannered flukes in the air, the grand god revealed himself, sounded, and went out of sight. Hoveringly halting, and dipping on the wing, the white sea-fowls longingly lingered over the agitated pool that he left.

With oars apeak, and paddles down, the sheets of their sails adrift, three boats now stilly floated, awaiting Moby Dick's reappearance.

'An hour,' said Ahab, standing rooted in his boat's stern; and he gazed beyond the whale's place, towards the dim blue spaces and wide wooing vacancies to leeward. It was only an instant; for again his eyes seemed whirling round in his head as he swept the watery circle. The breeze now freshened; the sea began to swell.

'The birds!—the birds!' cried Tashtego.

In long Indian file, as when herons take wing, the white birds were now all flying towards Ahab's boat; and when within a few yards began fluttering over the water there, wheeling round and round, with joyous expectant cries. Their vision was keener than man's; Ahab could discover no sign in the sea. But suddenly as he peered down and down into its depths, he profoundly saw a white living spot no bigger than a white weasel, with wonderful celerity uprising, and magnifying as it rose, till it turned, and then there were plainly revealed two long crooked rows of white, glistening teeth, floating up from the undiscoverable bottom. It was Moby Dick's open mouth and scrolled jaw; his vast, shadowed bulk still half blending with the blue of the sea. The glittering mouth yawned beneath the boat like an open-doored marble tomb; and giving one sidelong sweep with his steering oar, Ahab whirled the craft aside from this tremendous apparition. Then, calling upon Fedallah to change places with him, went forward to the bows, and seizing Perth's harpoon, commanded his crew to grasp their oars and stand by to stern.

Now, by reason of this timely spinning round the boat upon its axis, its bow, by anticipation, was made to face the whale's head while yet under water. But as if perceiving this strategem, Moby Dick, with that malicious intelligence ascribed to him, sidelingly transplanted himself, as it were, in an instant, shooting his pleated head lengthwise beneath the boat.

Through and through; through every plank and each rib, it thrilled for an instant, the whale obliquely lying on his back, in the manner of a biting shark, slowly and feelingly taking its bows full within his mouth, so that the long, narrow, scrolled lower jaw curled high up into the open air, and one of the teeth caught in a row-lock. The bluish pearl-white of the inside of the jaw was within six inches of Ahab's head, and reached higher than that. In this attitude the White Whale now shook the slight cedar as a mildly cruel cat her mouse. With unastonished eyes Fedallah gazed, and crossed his arms; but the tiger-yellow crew were tumbling over each other's heads to gain the uttermost stern.

And now, while both elastic gunwales were springing in and out, as the whale dallied with the doomed craft in this devilish way; and from his body being submerged beneath the boat, he could not be darted at from the bows, for the bows were almost inside of him, as it were; and while the other boats involuntarily paused, as before a quick crisis impossible to withstand, then it was that monomaniac Ahab, furious with this tantalizing vicinity of his foe, which placed him all alive and helpless in the very jaws he hated; frenzied with all this, he seized the long bone with his naked hands, and wildly strove to wrench it from its gripe. As now he thus vainly strove, the jaw slipped from him; the frail gunwales bent in, collapsed, and snapped, as both jaws, like an enormous shears, sliding further aft, bit the craft completely in twain, and locked themselves fast again in the sea, midway between the two floating wrecks. These floated aside, the broken ends drooping, the crew at the stern-wreck clinging to the gunwales, and striving to hold fast to the oars to lash them across.

At that preluding moment, ere the boat was yet snapped, Ahab, the first to perceive the whale's intent, by the crafty upraising of his head, a movement that loosed his hold for the time; at that moment his hand had made one final effort to push the boat out of the bite. But only slipping further into the whale's mouth, and tilting over sideways as it slipped, the boat had shaken off his hold on the jaw; spilled him out of it, as he leaned to the push; and so he fell flat-faced upon the sea.

Ripplingly withdrawing from his prey, Moby Dick now lay at a little distance, vertically thrusting his oblong white head up and down in the billows; and at the same time slowly revolving his whole spindled body; so that when his vast wrinkled forehead rose—some twenty or more feet out of the water—the now rising swells, with all their confluent waves, dazzlingly broke against it; vindictively tossing their shivered spray still higher into the air.* So, in a gale, the but half baffled Channel billows only recoil from

* This motion is peculiar to the sperm whale. It receives its designation (pitchpoling) from its being likened to that preliminary up-and-down poise of the whale-lance, in the exercise called pitch-poling, previously described. By this motion the whale must best and most comprehensively view whatever objects may be encircling him.

the base of the Eddystone, triumphantly to overleap its summit with their scud.

But soon resuming his horizontal attitude, Moby Dick swam swiftly round and round the wrecked crew; sideways churning the water in his vengeful wake, as if lashing himself up to still another and more deadly assault. The sight of the splintered boat seemed to madden him, as the blood of grapes and mulberries cast before Antiochus's elephants in the book of Maccabees. Meanwhile Ahab half smothered in the foam of the whale's insolent tail, and too much of a cripple to swim,—though he could still keep afloat, even in the heart of such a whirlpool as that; helpless Ahab's head was seen, like a tossed bubble which the least chance shock might burst. From the boat's fragmentary stern, Fedallah incuriously and mildly eyed him; the clinging crew, at the other drifting end, could not succor him; more than enough was it for them to look to themselves. For so revolvingly appalling was the White Whale's aspect, and so planetarily swift the ever-contracting circles he made, that he seemed horizontally swooping upon them. And though the other boats, unharmed, still hovered hard by; still they dared not pull into the eddy to strike, lest that should be the signal for the instant destruction of the jeopardized castaways, Ahab and all; nor in that case could they themselves hope to escape. With straining eyes, then, they remained on the outer edge of the direful zone, whose centre had now become the old man's head.

Meantime, from the beginning all this had been descried from the ship's mast heads; and squaring her yards, she had borne down upon the scene; and was now so nigh, that Ahab in the water hailed her;—'Sail on the'—but that moment a breaking sea dashed on him from Moby Dick, and whelmed him for the time. But struggling out of it again, and chancing to rise on a towering crest, he shouted,—'Sail on the whale!—Drive him off!'

The Pequod's prow was pointed; and breaking up the charmed circle, she effectually parted the white whale from his victim. As he sullenly swam off, the boats flew to the rescue.

Dragged into Stubb's boat with blood-shot, blinded eyes, the white brine caking in his wrinkles; the long tension of Ahab's bodily strength did crack, and helplessly he yielded to his body's doom: for a time, lying all crushed in the bottom of Stubb's boat, like one trodden under foot of herds of elephants. Far inland, nameless wails came from him, as desolate sounds from out ravines.

But this intensity of his physical prostration did but so much the more abbreviate it. In an instant's compass, great hearts sometimes condense to one deep pang, the sum total of those shallow pains kindly diffused through feebler men's whole lives. And so, such hearts, though summary in each one suffering; still, if the gods decree it, in their life-time aggregate a whole age of woe, wholly made up of instantaneous intensities; for even in their pointless centres, those noble natures contain the entire circumferences of inferior souls.

'The harpoon,' said Ahab, half way rising, and draggingly leaning on one bended arn—'is it safe?'

'Aye, sir, for it was not darted; this is it,' said Stubb, showing it.

'Lay it before me;—any missing men?'

'One, two, three, four, five;—there were five oars, sir, and here are five men.'

'That's good.—Help me, man; I wish to stand. So, so, I see him! there! there! going to leeward still; what a leaping spout!— Hands off from me! The eternal sap runs up in Ahab's bones again! Set the sail; out oars; the helm!'

It is often the case that when a boat is stove, its crew, being picked up by another boat, help to work that second boat; and the chase is thus continued with what is called double-banked oars. It was thus now. But the added power of the boat did not equal the added power of the whale, for he seemed to have treble-banked his every fin; swimming with a velocity which plainly showed, that if now, under these circumstances, pushed on, the chase would prove an indefinitely prolonged, if not a hopeless one; nor could any crew endure for so long a period, such an unintermitted, intense straining at the oar; a thing barely tolerable only in some one brief vicissitude. The ship itself, then, as it sometimes happens, offered the most promising intermediate means of overtaking the chase. Accordingly, the boats now made for her, and were soon swayed up to their cranes—the two parts of the wrecked boat having been previously secured by her—and then hoisting everything to her side, and stacking her canvas high up, and sideways outstretching it with stun-sails, like the double-jointed wings of an albatross; the Pequod bore down in the leeward wake of Moby Dick. At the well known, methodic intervals, the whale's glittering spout was regularly announced from the manned mast-heads; and when he would be reported as just gone down, Ahab would take the time, and then pacing the deck, binnacle-watch in hand, so soon as the last second of the allotted hour expired, his voice was heard.— 'Whose is the doubloon now? D'ye see him?' and if the reply was, No, sir! straightway he commanded them to lift him to his perch. In this way the day wore on; Ahab, now aloft and motionless; anon, unrestingly pacing the planks.

As he was thus walking, uttering no sound, except to hail the men aloft, or to bid them hoist a sail still higher, or to spread one to a still greater breadth—thus to and fro pacing, beneath his slouched hat, at every turn he passed his own wrecked boat, which had been dropped upon the quarter-deck, and lay there reversed; broken bow to shattered stern. At last he paused before it; and as in an already overclouded sky fresh troops of clouds will sometimes sail across, so over the old man's face there now stole some such added gloom as this.

Stubb saw him pause; and perhaps intending, not vainly, though, to evince his own unabated fortitude, and thus keep up a valiant place in his Captain's mind, he advanced, and eyeing the wreck exclaimed—'The thistle the ass refused; it pricked his mouth too keenly, sir; ha! ha!'

'What soulless thing is this that laughs before a wreck? Man, man! did I not know thee brave as fearless fire (and as mechanical) I could swear thou wert a poltroon. Groan nor laugh should be heard before a wreck.'

'Aye, sir,' said Starbuck drawing near, ' 'tis a solemn sight; an omen, and an ill one.'

'Omen? omen?—the dictionary! If the gods think to speak outright to man, they will honorably speak outright; not shake their heads, and give an old wives' darkling hint.—Begone! Ye two are the opposite poles of one thing; Starbuck is Stubb reversed, and Stubb is Starbuck; and ye two are all mankind; and Ahab stands alone among the millions of the peopled earth, nor gods nor men his neighbors! Cold, cold—I shiver!—How now? Aloft there? D'ye see him? Sing out for every spout, though he spout ten times a second!'

The day was nearly done; only the hem of his golden robe was rustling. Soon, it was almost dark, but the look-out men still remained unset.

'Can't see the spout now, sir;—too dark'—cried a voice from the air.

'How heading when last seen?'

'As before, sir,—straight to leeward.'

'Good! he will travel slower now 'tis night. Down royals and top-gallant stun-sails, Mr Starbuck. We must not run over him before morning; he's making a passage now, and may heave-to a while. Helm there! keep her full before the wind!—Aloft! come down!—Mr Stubb, send a fresh hand to the fore-mast head, and

see it manned till morning.'—Then advancing towards the doubloon in the main-mast—'Men, this gold is mine, for I earned it;
but I shall let it abide here till the White Whale is dead; and
then, whosoever of ye first raises him, upon the day he shall be
killed, this gold is that man's; and if on that day I shall again
raise him, then ten times its sum shall be divided among all of
ye! Away now!—the deck is thine, sir.'

And so saying, he placed himself half way within the scuttle,
and slouching his hat, stood there till dawn, except when at
intervals rousing himself to see how the night wore on.

134

THE CHASE—SECOND DAY

AT day-break, the three mast-heads were punctually manned afresh.

'D'ye see him?' cried Ahab, after allowing a little space for the
light to spread.

'See nothing, sir.'

'Turn up all hands and make sail! he travels faster than I thought
for;—the top-gallant sails!—aye, they should have been kept on
her all night. But no matter—'tis but resting for the rush.'

Here be it said, that this pertinacious pursuit of one particular
whale, continued through day into night, and through night into
day, is a thing by no means unprecedented in the South sea fishery.
For such is the wonderful skill, prescience of experience, and
invincible confidence acquired by some great natural geniuses
among the Nantucket commanders; that from the simple observation of a whale when last descried, they will, under certain given
circumstances, pretty accurately foretell both the direction in which
he will continue to swim for a time, while out of sight, as well
as his probable rate of progression during that period. And, in
these cases, somewhat as a pilot, when about losing sight of a
coast, whose general trending he well knows, and which he desires
shortly to return to again, but at some further point; like as this
pilot stands by his compass, and takes the precise bearing of the
cape at present visible, in order the more certainly to hit aright
the remote, unseen headland, eventually to be visited; so does the
fisherman, at his compass, with the whale; for after being chased,
and diligently marked, through several hours of daylight, then,
when night obscures the fish, the creature's future wake through

the darkness is almost as established to the sagacious mind of the hunter, as the pilot's coast is to him. So that to this hunter's wondrous skill, the proverbial evanescence of a thing writ in water, a wake, is to all desired purposes well nigh as reliable as the steadfast land. And as the mighty iron Leviathan of the modern railway is so familiarly known in its every pace, that, with watches in their hands, men time his rate as doctors that of a baby's pulse; and lightly say of it, the up train or the down train will reach such or such a spot, at such or such an hour; even so, almost, there are occasions when these Nantucketers time that other Leviathan of the deep, according to the observed humor of his speed; and say to themselves, so many hours hence this whale will have gone two hundred miles, will have about reached this or that degree of latitude or longitude. But to render this acuteness at all successful in the end, the wind and the sea must be the whaleman's allies; for of what present avail to the becalmed or windbound mariner is the skill that assures him he is exactly ninety-three leagues and a quarter from his port? Inferable from these statements, are many collateral subtile matters touching the chase of whales.

The ship tore on; leaving such a furrow in the sea as when a cannon-ball, missent, becomes a plough-share and turns up the level field.

'By salt and hemp!' cried Stubb, 'but this swift motion of the deck creeps up one's legs and tingles at the heart. This ship and I are two brave fellows!—Ha! ha! Some one take me up, and launch me, spine-wise, on the sea,—for by liveoaks! my spine's a keel. Ha, ha! we go the gait that leaves no dust behind!'

'There she blows—she blows!—she blows!—right ahead!' was now the mast-head cry.

'Aye, aye!' cried Stubb, 'I knew it—ye can't escape—blow on and split your spout, O whale! the mad fiend himself is after ye! blow your trump—blister your lungs!—Ahab will dam off your blood, as a miller shuts his water-gate upon the stream!'

And Stubb did but speak out for well nigh all that crew. The frenzies of the chase had by this time worked them bubblingly up, like old wine corked anew. Whatever pale fears and forebodings some of them might have felt before; these were not only now kept out of sight through the growing awe of Ahab, but they were broken up, and on all sides routed, as timid prairie hares that scatter before the bounding bison. The hand of Fate had snatched all their souls; and by the stirring perils of the previous day; the rack of the past night's suspense; the fixed, unfearing, blind, reckless way in which their wild craft went plunging towards its flying mark; by all these things, their hearts were bowled along. The wind that made great bellies of their sails, and rushed the vessel on by arms invisible as irresistible; this seemed the symbol of that unseen agency with so enslaved them to the race.

They were one man, not thirty. For as the one ship that held them all; though it was put together of all contrasting things— oak, and maple, and pine wood; iron, and pitch, and hemp—yet all these ran into each other in the one concrete hull, which shot on its way, both balanced and directed by the long central keel; even so, all the individualities of the crew, this man's valor, that man's fear; guilt and guiltiness, all varieties were welded into oneness, and were all directed to that fatal goal which Ahab their one lord and keel did point to.

The rigging lived. The mast-heads, like the tops of tall palms, were outspreadingly tufted with arms and legs. Clinging to a spar with one hand, some reached forth the other with impatient wavings; others, shading their eyes from the vivid sunlight, sat far out on the rocking yards; all the spars in full bearing of mortals, ready and ripe for their fate. Ah! how they still strove through that infinite blueness to seek out the thing that might destroy them!

'Why sing ye not out for him, if ye see him?' cried Ahab, when, after the lapse of some minutes since the first cry, no more had been heard. 'Sway me up, men; ye have been deceived; not Moby Dick casts one odd jet that way, and then disappears.'

It was even so; in their headlong eagerness, the men had mistaken some other thing for the whale-spout, as the event itself soon proved; for hardly had Ahab reached his perch; hardly was the rope belayed to its pin on deck, when he struck the key-note to an orchestra, that made the air vibrate as with the combined discharges of rifles. The triumphant halloo of thirty buckskin lungs was heard, as—much nearer to the ship than the place of the imaginary jet, less than a mile ahead—Moby Dick bodily burst into view! For not by any calm and indolent spoutings; not by the peaceable gush of that mystic fountain in his head, did the White Whale now reveal his vicinity; but by the far more wondrous phenomenon of breaching. Rising with his utmost velocity from the furthest depths, the Sperm Whale thus booms his entire bulk into the pure element of air, and piling up a mountain of dazzling foam, shows his place to the distance of seven miles and more. In those moments, the torn, enraged waves he shakes off, seem his mane; in some cases, this breaching is his act of defiance.

'There she breaches! there she breaches!' was the cry, as in his immeasurable bravadoes the White Whale tossed himself salmon-like to Heaven. So suddenly seen in the blue plain of the sea, and relieved against the still bluer margin of the sky, the spray that he raised, for the moment, intolerably glittered and glared like a glacier; and stood there gradually fading and fading away from its first sparkling intensity, to the dim mistiness of an advancing shower in a vale.

'Aye, breach your last to the sun, Moby Dick!' cried Ahab, 'thy hour and thy harpoon are at hand!—Down! down all of ye, but one man at the fore. The boats!—stand by!'

Unmindful of the tedious rope-ladders of the shrouds, the men, like shooting stars, slid to the deck, by the isolated backstays and halyards; while Ahab, less dartingly, but still rapidly was dropped from his perch.

'Lower away,' he cried, so soon as he had reached his boat— a spare one, rigged the afternoon previous. 'Mr Starbuck, the ship is thine—keep away from the boats, but keep near them. Lower, all!'

As if to strike a quick terror into them, by this time being the first assailant himself, Moby Dick had turned, and was now coming for the three crews. Ahab's boat was central; and cheering his men, he told them he would take the whale head-and-head,—that is, pull straight up to his forehead,—a not uncommon thing; for when within a certain limit, such a course excludes the coming onset from the whale's sidelong vision. But ere that close limit was gained, and while yet all three boats were plain as the ship's three masts to his eye; the White Whale churning himself into furious speed, almost in an instant as it were, rushing among the boats with open jaws, and a lashing tail, offered appalling battle on every side; and heedless of the irons darted at him from every boat, seemed only intent on annihilating each separate plank of which those boats were made. But skilfully manœuvred, incessantly wheeling like trained chargers in the field; the boats for a while eluded him; though, at times, but by a plank's breadth; while all the time, Ahab's unearthly slogan tore every other cry but his to shreds.

But at last in his untraceable evolutions, the White Whale so crossed and recrossed, and in a thousand ways entangled the slack of the three lines now fast to him, that they fore-shortened, and, of themselves, warped the devoted boats towards the planted irons in him; though now for a moment the whale drew aside a little, as if to rally for a more tremendous charge. Seizing that opportunity, Ahab first paid out more line: and then was rapidly hauling and jerking in upon it again—hoping that way to disencumber it of some snarls—when lo!—a sight more savage than the embattled teeth of sharks!

Caught and twisted—corkscrewed in the mazes of the line, loose harpoons and lances, with all their bristling barbs and points, came flashing and dripping up to the chocks in the bows of Ahab's boat. Only one thing could be done. Seizing the boat-knife, he critically reached within—through—and then, without—the rays of steel; dragged in the line beyond, passed it, inboard, to the bowsman, and then, twice sundering the rope near the chocks—dropped the intercepted fagot of steel into the sea; and was all fast again. That instant, the White Whale made a sudden rush among the remaining tangles of the other lines; by so doing, irresistibly dragged the more involved boats of Stubb and Flask towards his flukes; dashed them together like two rolling husks on a surf-beaten beach, and then, diving down into the sea, disappeared in a boiling maelstrom, in which, for a space, the odorous cedar chips of the wrecks danced round and round, like the grated nutmeg in a swiftly stirred bowl of punch.

While the two crews were yet circling in the waters, reaching out after the revolving line-tubs, oars, and other floating furniture, while aslope little Flask bobbed up and down like an empty vial, twitching his legs upwards to escape the dreaded jaws of sharks; and Stubb was lustily singing out for some one to ladle him up; and while the old man's line—now parting—admitted of his pulling into the creamy pool to rescue whom he could;—in that wild simultaneousness of a thousand concreted perils,—Ahab's yet unstricken boat seemed drawn up towards Heaven by invisible wires,— as, arrow-like, shooting perpendicularly from the sea, the White Whale dashed his broad forehead against its bottom, and sent it, turning over and over, into the air; till it fell again—gunwale downwards—and Ahab and his men struggled out from under it, like seals from a sea-side cave.

The first uprising momentum of the whale—modifying its direction as he struck the surface—involuntarily launched him along it, to a little distance from the centre of the destruction he had made; and with his back to it, he now lay for a moment slowly feeling with his flukes from side to side; and whenever a stray oar, bit of plank, the least chip or crumb of the boats touched his skin, his tail swiftly drew back, and came sideways smiting the sea. But soon, as if satisfied that his work for that time was done, he pushed his pleated forehead through the ocean, and trailing after him the intertangled lines, continued his leeward way at a traveller's methodic pace.

As before, the attentive ship having descried the whole fight, again came bearing down to the rescue, and dropping a boat, picked up the floating mariners, tubs, oars, and whatever else could be caught at, and safely landed them on her decks. Some sprained shoulders, wrists, and ankles; livid contusions; wrenched harpoons and lances; inextricable intricacies of rope; shattered oars and planks; all these were there; but no fatal or even serious ill seemed to have befallen any one. As with Fedallah the day before, so Ahab was now found grimly clinging to his boat's broken half, which afforded a comparatively easy float; nor did it so exhaust him as the previous day's mishap.

But when he was helped to the deck, all eyes were fastened upon him; as instead of standing by himself he still half-hung upon the shoulder of Starbuck, who had thus far been the foremost to assist him. His ivory leg had been snapped off, leaving but one short sharp splinter.

'Aye, aye, Starbuck, 'tis sweet to lean sometimes, be the leaner who he will; and would old Ahab had leaned oftener than he has.'

'The ferrule has not stood, sir,' said the carpenter, now coming up; 'I put good work into that leg.'

'But no bones broken, sir, I hope,' said Stubb with true concern.

'Aye! and all splintered to pieces, Stubb!—d'ye see it.—But even with a broken bone, old Ahab is untouched; and I account no living bone of mine one jot more me, than his dead one that's lost. Nor white whale, nor man, nor fiend, can so much as graze old Ahab in his own proper and inaccessible being. Can any lead touch yonder floor, any mast scrape yonder roof?—Aloft there! which way?'

'Dead to leeward, sir.'

'Up helm, then; pile on the sail again, ship keepers! down the rest of the spare boats and rig them—Mr Starbuck away, and muster the boats' crews.'

'Let me first help thee towards the bulwarks, sir.'

'Oh, oh, oh! how this spinter gores me now! Accursed fate! that the unconquerable captain in the soul should have such a craven mate!'

'Sir?'

'My body, man, not thee. Give me something for a cane— there, that shivered lance will do. Muster the men. Surely I have not seen him yet. By heaven it cannot be!—missing?—quick! call them all.'

The old man's hinted thought was true. Upon mustering the company, the Parsee was not there.

'The Parsee!' cried Stubb—'he must have been caught in—'

'The black vomit wrench thee!—run all of ye above, alow, cabin, forecastle—find him—not gone—not gone!'

But quickly they returned to him with the tidings that the Parsee was nowhere to be found.

'Aye, sir,' said Stubb—'caught among the tangles of your line—I thought I saw him dragging under.'

'*My* line! *my* line? Gone?—gone? What means that little word?—What death-knell rings in it, that old Ahab shakes as if here were the belfry. The harpoon, too!—toss over the litter there,—d'ye see it?—the forged iron, men, the white whale's—no, no, no,—blistered fool! this hand did dart it!—'tis in the fish!—Aloft there! Keep him nailed—Quick!—all hands to the rigging of the boats—collect the oars—harpooneers! the irons, the irons!—hoist the royals higher—a pull on all the sheets!—helm there! steady, steady for your life! I'll ten times girdle the unmeasured globe; yea and dive straight through it, but I'll slay him yet!'

'Great God! but for one single instant show thyself,' cried Starbuck; 'never, never wilt thou capture him, old man—In Jesus' name no more of this, that's worse than devil's madness. Two days chased; twice stove to splinters; thy very leg once more snatched from under thee; thy evil shadow gone—all good angels mobbing thee with warnings:—what more wouldst thou have?—Shall we keep chasing this murderous fish till he swamps the last man? Shall we be dragged by him to the bottom of the sea? Shall we be towed by him to the infernal world? Oh, oh,—Impiety and blasphemy to hunt him more!'

'Starbuck, of late I've felt strangely moved to thee; ever since that hour we both saw—thou know'st what, in one another's eyes. But in this matter of the whale, be the front of thy face to me as the palm of this hand—a lipless, unfeatured blank. Ahab is for ever Ahab, man. This whole act's immutably decreed. 'Twas rehearsed by thee and me a billion years before this ocean rolled. Fool! I am the Fates' lieutenant; I act under orders. Look thou, underling! that thou obeyest mine.—Stand round me, men. Ye see an old man cut down to the stump; leaning on a shivered lance; propped up on a lonely foot. 'Tis Ahab—his body's part; but Ahab's soul's a centipede, that moves upon a hundred legs. I feel strained, half stranded, as ropes that tow dismasted frigates in a gale; and I may look so. But ere I break, ye'll hear me crack; and till ye hear *that*, know that Ahab's hawser tows his purpose yet. Believe ye, men, in the things called omens? Then laugh aloud, and cry encore! For ere they drown, drowning things will twice rise to the surface; then rise again, to sink for evermore. So with Moby Dick—two days he's floated—to-morrow will be the third. Aye, men, he'll rise once more,—but only to spout his last! D'ye feel brave, men, brave?'

'As fearless fire,' cried Stubb.

'And as mechanical,' muttered Ahab. Then as the men went forward, he muttered on:—'The things called omens! And yesterday I talked the same to Starbuck there, concerning my broken boat. Ho! how valiantly I seek to drive out of others' hearts what's clinched so fast in mine!—The Parsee—the Parsee!—gone, gone? and he was to go before:—but still was to be seen again ere I could perish—How's that?—There's a riddle now might baffle all the lawyers backed by the ghosts of the whole line of judges:— like a hawk's beak it pecks my brain. *I'll, I'll* solve it, though!'

When dusk descended, the whale was still in sight to leeward.

So once more the sail was shortened, and everything passed nearly as on the previous night; only, the sound of hammers, and the hum of the grindstone was heard till nearly daylight, as the men toiled by lanterns in the complete and careful rigging of the spare boats and sharpening their fresh weapons for the morrow. Meantime, of the broken keel of Ahab's wrecked craft the carpenter made him another leg; while still as on the night before, slouched Ahab stood fixed within his scuttle; his hid, heliotrope glance anticipatingly gone backward on its dial; set due eastward for the earliest sun.

135

THE CHASE—THIRD DAY

THE morning of the third day dawned fair and fresh, and once more the solitary night-man at the fore-mast-head was relieved by crowds of the daylight look-outs, who dotted every mast and almost every spar.

'D'ye see him?' cried Ahab; but the whale was not yet in sight.

'In his infallible wake, though; but follow that wake, that's all. Helm there; steady, as thou goest, and hast been going. What a

lovely day again! were it a new-made world, and made for a
summer-house to the angels, and this morning the first of its
throwing open to them, a fairer day could not dawn upon that
world. Here's food for thought, had Ahab time to think; but Ahab
never thinks; he only feels, feels, feels; *that's* tingling enough for
mortal man! to think's audacity. God only has that right and
privilege. Thinking is, or ought to be, a coolness and a calmness;
and our poor hearts throb, and our poor brains beat too much
for that. And yet, I've sometimes thought my brain was very
calm—frozen calm, this old skull cracks so, like a glass in which
the contents turn to ice, and shiver it. And still this hair is growing
now; this moment growing, and heat must breed it; but no, it's
like that sort of common grass that will grow anywhere, between
the earthy clefts of Greenland ice or in Vesuvius' lava. How the
wild winds blow it; they whip it about me as the torn shreds of
split sails lash the tossed ship they cling to. A vile wind that has
no doubt blown ere this through prison corridors and cells, and
wards of hospitals, and ventilated them, and now comes blowing
hither as innocent as fleeces. Out upon it!—it's tainted. Were I
the wind, I'd blow no more on such a wicked, miserable world.
I'd crawl somewhere to a cave, and slink there. And yet, 'tis a
noble and heroic thing, the wind! who ever conquered it? In every
fight it has the last and bitterest blow. Run tilting at it, and you
but run through it. Ha! a coward wind that strikes stark naked
men, but will not stand to receive a single blow. Even Ahab is a
braver thing—a nobler thing than *that*. Would now the wind but
had a body; but all the things that most exasperate and outrage
mortal man, all these things are bodiless, but only bodiless as
objects, not as agents. There's a most special, a most cunning,
oh, a most malicious difference! And yet, I say again, and swear
it now, that there's something all glorious and gracious in the
wind. These warm Trade Winds, at least, that in the clear heavens
blow straight on, in strong and steadfast, vigorous mildness; and
veer not from their mark, however the baser currents of the sea
may turn and tack, and mightiest Mississippies of the land shift
and swerve about, uncertain where to go at last. And by the
eternal Poles! these same Trades that so directly blow my good
ship on; these Trades, or something like them—something so
unchangeable, and full as strong, blow my keeled soul along! To
it! Aloft there! What d'ye see?'

   'Nothing, sir.'

   'Nothing! and noon at hand! The doubloon goes a-begging! See
the sun! Aye, aye, it must be so. I've oversailed him. How, got

the start? Aye, he's chasing *me* now; not I, *him*—that's bad; I might have known it, too. Fool! the lines—the harpoons he's towing. Aye, aye, I have run him by last night. About! about! Come down, all of ye, but the regular look outs! Man the braces!'

Steering as she had done, the wind had been somewhat on the Pequod's quarter, so that now being pointed in the reverse direction, the braced ship sailed hard upon the breeze as she rechurned the cream in her own white wake.

'Against the wind he now steers for the open jaw,' murmured Starbuck to himself, as he coiled the new-hauled main-brace upon the rail. 'God keep us, but already my bones feel damp within me, and from the inside wet my flesh. I misdoubt me that I disobey my God in obeying him!'

'Stand by to sway me up!' cried Ahab, advancing to the hempen basket. 'We should meet him soon.'

'Aye, aye, sir,' and straightway Starbuck did Ahab's bidding, and once more Ahab swung on high.

A whole hour now passed; gold-beaten out to ages. Time itself now held long breaths with keen suspense. But at last, some three points off the weather bow, Ahab descried the spout again, and instantly from the three mast-heads three shrieks went up as if the tongues of fire had voiced it.

'Forehead to forehead I meet thee, this third time, Moby Dick! On deck there!—brace sharper up; crowd her into the wind's eye. He's too far off to lower yet, Mr Starbuck. The sails shake! Stand over that helmsman with a top-maul! So, so; he travels fast, and I must down. But let me have one more good round look aloft here at the sea; there's time for that. An old, old sight, and yet somehow so young; aye, and not changed a wink since I first saw it, a boy, from the sand-hills of Nantucket! The same!—the same!— the same to Noah as to me. There's a soft shower to leeward. Such lovely leewardings! They must lead somewhere—to something else than common land, more palmy than the palms. Leeward! the white whale goes that way; to look to windward, then; the better if the bitterer quarter. But good bye, good bye, old masthead! What's this?—green? aye, tiny mosses in these warped cracks. No such green weather stains on Ahab's head! There's the difference now between man's old age and matter's. But aye, old mast, we both grow old together; sound in our hulls, though, are we not, my ship? Aye, minus a leg, that's all. By heaven this dead wood has the better of my live flesh every way. I can't compare with it; and I've known some ships made of dead trees outlast the lives of men made of the most vital stuff of vital fathers. What's that he said? he should still go before me, my pilot; and yet to be seen again? But where? Will I have eyes at the bottom of the sea, supposing I descend those endless stairs? and all night I've been sailing from him, wherever he did sink to. Aye, aye, like many more thou told'st direful truth as touching thyself, O Parsee; but, Ahab, there thy shot fell short. Good by, mast-head—keep a good eye upon the whale, the while I'm gone. We'll talk to-morrow, nay, to-night, when the white whale lies down there, tied by head and tail.'

He gave the word; and still gazing round him, was steadily lowered through the cloven blue air to the deck.

In due time the boats were lowered; but as standing in his shallop's stern, Ahab just hovered upon the point of the descent, he waved to the mate,—who held one of the tackle-ropes on deck—and bade him pause.

'Starbuck!'

'Sir?'

'For the third time my soul's ship starts upon this voyage, Starbuck.'

'Aye, sir, thou wilt have it so.'

'Some ships sail from their ports, and ever afterwards are missing, Starbuck!'

'Truth, sir: saddest truth.'

'Some men die at ebb tide; some at low water; some at the full of the flood;—and I feel now like a billow that's all one crested comb, Starbuck. I am old;—shake hands with me, man.'

Their hands met; their eyes fastened; Starbuck's tears the glue.

'Oh, my captain, my captain!—noble heart—go not—go not!—see, it's a brave man that weeps; how great the agony of the persuasion then!'

'Lower away!'—cried Ahab, tossing the mate's arm from him. 'Stand by the crew!'

In an instant the boat was pulling round close under the stern.

'The sharks! the sharks!' cried a voice from the low cabin window there; 'O master, my master, come back!'

But Ahab heard nothing; for his own voice was high-lifted then; and the boat leaped on.

Yet the voice spake true; for scarce had he pushed from the ship, when numbers of sharks, seemingly rising from out the dark waters beneath the hull, maliciously snapped at the blades of the oars, every time they dipped in the water; and in this way accompanied the boat with their bites. It is a thing not uncommonly happening to the whale-boats in those swarming seas; the sharks

at times apparently following them in the same prescient way that
vultures hover over the banners of marching regiments in the east.
But these were the first sharks that had been observed by the
Pequod since the White Whale had been first descried; and whether
it was that Ahab's crew were all such tiger-yellow barbarians, and
therefore their flesh more musky to the senses of the sharks—a
matter sometimes well known to affect them,—however it was,
they seemed to follow that one boat without molesting the others.

'Heart of wrought steel!' murmured Starbuck gazing over the
side, and following with his eyes the receding boat—'canst thou
yet ring boldly to that sight?—lowering thy keel among ravening
sharks, and followed by them, open-mouthed to the chase; and
this the critical third day?—For when three days flow together in
one continuous intense pursuit; be sure the first is the morning,
the second the noon, and the third the evening and the end of
that thing—be that end what it may. Oh! my God! what is this
that shoots through me, and leaves me so deadly calm, yet expectant,—fixed at the top of a shudder! Future things swim before
me, as in empty outlines and skeletons; all the past is somehow
grown dim. Mary, girl! thou fadest in pale glories behind me; boy!
I seem to see but thy eyes grown wondrous blue. Strangest problems
of life seem clearing; but clouds sweep between—Is my journey's
end coming? My legs feel faint; like his who has footed it all day.
Feel thy heart,—beats it yet?—Stir thyself, Starbuck!—stave it
off—move, move! speak aloud!—Mast-head there! See ye my boy's
hand on the hill?—Crazed;—aloft there!—keep thy keenest eye
upon the boats:—mark well the whale!—Ho! again!—drive off that
hawk! see! he pecks—he tears the vane'—pointing to the red flag
flying at the main-truck—'Ha! he soars away with it!—Where's
the old man now? see'st thou that sight, oh Ahab!—shudder,
shudder!'

The boats had not gone very far, when by a signal from the
mast-heads—a downward pointed arm, Ahab knew that the whale
had sounded; but intending to be near him at the next rising, he
held on his way a little sideways from the vessel; the becharmed
crew maintaining the profoundest silence, as the head-beat waves
hammered and hammered against the opposing bow.

'Drive, drive in your nails, oh ye waves! to their uttermost heads
drive them in! ye but strike a thing without a lid; and no coffin
and no hearse can be mine:—and hemp only can kill me! Ha!
ha!'

Suddenly the waters around them slowly swelled in broad circles;
then quickly upheaved, as if sideways sliding from a submerged

berg of ice, swiftly rising to the surface. A low rumbling sound
was heard; a subterraneous hum; and then all held their breaths;
as bedraggled with trailing ropes, and harpoons, and lances, a vast
form shot lengthwise, but obliquely from the sea. Shrouded in a
thin drooping veil of mist, it hovered for a moment in the
rainbowed air; and then fell swamping back into the deep. Crushed
thirty feet upwards, the waters flashed for an instant like heaps
of fountains, then brokenly sank in a shower of flakes, leaving
the circling surface creamed like new milk round the marble trunk
of the whale.

'Give way!' cried Ahab to the oarsmen, and the boats darted
forward to the attack; but maddened by yesterday's fresh irons
that corroded in him, Moby Dick seemed combinedly possessed
by all the angels that fell from heaven. The wide tiers of welded
tendons overspreading his broad white forehead, beneath the transparent skin, looked knitted together; as head on, he came churning
his tail among the boats; and once more flailed them apart; spilling
out the irons and lances from the two mates' boats, and dashing
in one side of the upper part of their bows, but leaving Ahab's
almost without a scar.

While Daggoo and Queequeg were stopping the strained planks;
and as the whale swimming out from them, turned, and showed
one entire flank as he shot by them again; at that moment a
quick cry went up. Lashed round and round to the fish's back;
pinioned in the turns upon turns in which, during the past night,
the whale had reeled the involutions of the lines around him, the
half torn body of the Parsee was seen; his sable raiment frayed
to shreds; his distended eyes turned full upon old Ahab.

The harpoon dropped from his hand.

'Befooled, befooled!'—drawing in a long lean breath—'Aye, Parsee! I see thee again.—Aye, and thou goest before; and this, *this*
then is the hearse that thou didst promise. But I hold thee to the
last letter of thy word. Where is the second hearse? Away, mates,
to the ship! those boats are useless now; repair them if ye can in
time, and return to me; if not, Ahab is enough to die—Down,
men! for the first thing that but offers to jump from this boat I
stand in, that thing I harpoon. Ye are not other men, but my
arms and my legs; and so obey me.—Where's the whale? gone
down again?'

But he looked too nigh the boat; for as if bent upon escaping
with the corpse he bore, and as if the particular place of the last
encounter had been but a stage in his leeward voyage, Moby Dick
was now again steadily swimming forward; and had almost passed

the ship,—which thus far had been sailing in the contrary direction to him, though for the present her headway had been stopped. He seemed swimming with his utmost velocity, and now only intent upon pursuing his own straight path in the sea.

'Oh! Ahab,' cried Starbuck, 'not too late is it, even now, the third day, to desist. See! Moby Dick seeks thee not. It is thou, thou, that madly seekest him!'

Setting sail to the rising wind, the lonely boat was swiftly impelled to leeward, but both oars and canvas. And at last when Ahab was sliding by the vessel, so near as plainly to distinguish Starbuck's face as he leaned over the rail, he hailed him to turn the vessel about, and follow him, not too swiftly, at a judicious interval. Glancing upwards, he saw Tashtego, Queequeg, and Daggoo, eagerly mounting to the three mast-heads; while the oarsmen were rocking in the two staved boats which had just been hoisted to the side, and were busily at work in repairing them. One after the other, through the port-holes, as he sped, he also caught flying glimpses of Stubb and Flask, busying themselves on deck among bundles of new irons and lances. As he saw all this; as he heard the hammers in the broken boats; far other hammers seemed driving a nail into his heart. But he rallied. And now marking that the vane or flag was gone from the main-mast-head, he shouted to Tashtego, who had just gained that perch, to descend again for another flag, and a hammer and nails, and so nail it to the mast.

Whether fagged by the three days' running chase, and the resistance to his swimming in the knotted hamper he bore; or whether it was some latent deceitfulness and malice in him: whichever was true, the White Whale's way now began to abate, as it seemed, from the boat so rapidly nearing him once more; though indeed the whale's last start had not been so long a one as before. And still as Ahab glided over the waves the unpitying sharks accompanied him; and so pertinaciously stuck to the boat; and so continually bit at the plying oars, that the blades became jagged and crunched, and left small splinters in the sea, at almost every dip.

'Heed them not! those teeth but give new rowlocks to your oars. Pull on! 'tis the better rest, the shark's jaw than the yielding water.'

'But at every bite, sir, the thin blades grow smaller and smaller!'

'They will last long enough! pull on!—But who can tell'—he muttered—,'whether these sharks swim to feast on the whale or on Ahab?—But pull on! Aye, all alive, now—we near him. The helm! take the helm; let me pass,'—and so saying, two of the oarsmen helped him forward to the bows of the still flying boat.

At length as the craft was cast to one side, and ran ranging along with the White Whale's flank, he seemed strangely oblivious of its advance—as the whale sometimes will—and Ahab was fairly within the smoky mountain mist, which, thrown off from the whale's spout, curled round his great, Monadnock hump; he was even thus close to him; when, with body arched back, and both arms lengthwise highlifted to the poise, he darted his fierce iron, and his far fiercer curse into the hated whale. As both steel and curse sank to the socket, as if sucked into a morass, Moby Dick sideways writhed; spasmodically rolled his nigh flank against the bow, and, without staving a hole in it, so suddenly canted the boat over, that had it not been for the elevated part of the gunwale to which he then clung, Ahab would once more have been tossed into the sea. As it was, three of the oarsmen—who foreknew not the precise instant of the dart, and were therefore unprepared for its effects—these were flung out; but so fell, that, in an instant two of them clutched the gunwale again, and rising to its level on a combing wave, hurled themselves bodily inboard again; the third man helplessly dropping astern, but still afloat and swimming.

Almost simultaneously, with a mighty volition of ungraduated, instantaneous swiftness, the White Whale darted through the weltering sea. But when Ahab cried out to the steersman to take new turns with the line, and hold it so; and commanded the crew to turn round on their seats, and tow the boat up to the mark; the moment the treacherous line felt that double strain and tug, it snapped in the empty air!

'What breaks in me? Some sinew cracks!—'tis whole again; oars! oars! Burst in upon him!'

Hearing the tremendous rush of the sea-crashing boat, the whale wheeled round to present his blank forehead at bay; but in that evolution, catching sight of the nearing black hull of the ship; seemingly seeing in it the source of all his persecutions; bethinking it—it may be—a larger and nobler foe; of a sudden, he bore down upon its advancing prow, smiting his jaws amid fiery showers of foam.

Ahab staggered; his hand smote his forehead. 'I grow blind; hands! stretch out before me that I may yet grope my way. Is't night?'

'The whale! The ship!' cried the cringing oarsmen.

'Oars! oars! Slope downwards to thy depths, O sea, that ere it be for ever too late, Ahab may slide this last, last time upon his mark! I see: the ship! the ship! Dash on, my men! Will ye not save my ship?'

But as the oarsmen violently forced their boat through the sledge-hammering seas, the before whale-smitten bow-ends of two planks burst through, and in an instant almost, the temporarily disabled boat lay nearly level with the waves; its half-wading, splashing crew, trying hard to stop the gap and bale out the pouring water.

Meantime, for that one beholding instant, Tashtego's mast-head hammer remained suspended in his hand; and the red flag, half-wrapping him as with a plaid, then streamed itself straight out from him, as his own forward-flowing heart; while Starbuck and Stubb, standing upon the bowsprit beneath, caught sight of the down-coming monster just as soon as he.

'The whale, the whale! Up helm, up helm! Oh, all ye sweet powers of air, now hug me close! Let not Starbuck die, if die he must, in a woman's fainting fit. Up helm, I say—ye fools, the jaw! the jaw! Is this the end of all my bursting prayers? all my life-long fidelities? Oh, Ahab, Ahab, lo, thy work. Steady! helmsman, steady. Nay, nay! Up helm again! He turns to meet us! Oh, his unappeasable brow drives on towards one, whose duty tells him he cannot depart. My God, stand by me now!'

'Stand not by me, but stand under me, whoever you are that will now help Stubb; for Stubb, too, sticks here. I grin at thee, thou grinning whale! Who ever helped Stubb, or kept Stubb awake, but Stubb's own unwinking eye? And now poor Stubb goes to bed upon a mattress that is all too soft; would it were stuffed with brushwood! I grin at thee, thou grinning whale! Look ye, sun, moon, and stars! I call ye assassins of as good a fellow as ever spouted up his ghost. For all that, I would yet ring glasses with ye, would ye but hand the cup! Oh, oh! oh, oh! thou grinning whale, but there'll be plenty of gulping soon! Why fly ye not, O Ahab! For me, off shoes and jacket to it; let Stubb die in his drawers! A most mouldy and over salted death, though;—cherries! cherries! cherries! Oh, Flask, for one red cherry ere we die!'

'Cherries? I only wish that we were where they grow. Oh, Stubb, I hope my poor mother's drawn my part-pay ere this; if not, few coppers will now come to her, for the voyage is up.'

From the ship's bows, nearly all the seamen now hung inactive; hammers, bits of plank, lances, and harpoons, mechanically retained in their hands, just as they had darted from their various employments; all their enchanted eyes intent upon the whale, which from side to side strangely vibrating his predestinating head, sent a broad band of overspreading semicircular foam before him as he rushed. Retribution, swift vengeance, eternal malice were in his whole aspect, and spite of all that mortal man could do, the solid white buttress of his forehead smote the ship's starboard bow, till men and timbers reeled. Some fell flat upon their faces. Like dislodged trucks, the heads of the harpooneers aloft shook on their bull-like necks. Through the breach, they heard the waters pour, as mountain torrents down a flume.

'The ship! The hearse!—the second hearse!' cried Ahab from the boat; 'its wood could only be American!'

Diving beneath the settling ship, the whale ran quivering along its keel; but turning under water, swiftly shot to the surface again, far off the other bow, but within a few yards of Ahab's boat, where, for a time, he lay quiescent.

'I turn my body from the sun. What ho, Tashtego! let me hear thy hammer. Oh! ye three unsurrendered spires of mine; thou uncracked keel; and only god-bullied hull; thou firm deck, and haughty helm, and Pole-pointed prow,—death-glorious ship! must ye then perish, and without me? Am I cut off from the last fond pride of meanest ship-wrecked captains? Oh, lonely death on lonely life! Oh, now I feel my topmost greatness lies in my topmost grief. Ho, ho! from all your furthest bounds, pour ye now in, ye bold billows of my whole foregone life, and top this one piled comber of my death! Towards thee I roll, thou all-destroying but uncon-quering whale; to the last I grapple with thee; from hell's heart I stab at thee; for hate's sake I spit my last breath at thee. Sink all coffins and all hearses to one common pool! and since neither can be mine, let me then tow to pieces, while still chasing thee, though tied to thee, thou damned whale! *Thus*, I give up the spear!'

The harpoon was darted; the stricken whale flew forward; with igniting velocity the line ran through the groove;—ran foul. Ahab stooped to clear it; he did clear it; but the flying turn caught him round the neck, and voicelessly as Turkish mutes bowstring their victim, he was shot out of the boat, ere the crew knew he was gone. Next instant, the heavy eye-splice in the rope's final end flew out of the stark-empty tub, knocked down an oarsman, and smiting the sea, disappeared in its depths.

For an instant, the tranced boat's crew stood still; then turned. 'The ship? Great God, where is the ship?' Soon they through dim, bewildering mediums saw her sidelong fading phantom, as in the gaseous Fata Morgana; only the uppermost masts out of water; while fixed by infatuation, or fidelity, or fate, to their once lofty perches, the pagan harpooneers still maintained their sinking look-outs on the sea. And now, concentric circles seized the lone boat itself, and all its crew, and each floating oar, and every lance-pole, and spinning, animate and inanimate, all round and round in one vortex, carried the smallest chip of the Pequod out of sight.

But as the last whelmings intermixingly poured themselves over the sunken head of the Indian at the mainmast, leaving a few inches of the erect spar yet visible, together with long streaming yards of the flag, which calmly undulated, with ironical coincidings, over the destroying billows they almost touched;—at that instant, a red arm and a hammer hovered backwardly uplifted in the open air, in the act of nailing the flag faster and yet faster to the subsiding spar. A sky-hawk that tauntingly had followed the main-truck downwards from its natural home among the stars, pecking at the flag, and incommoding Tashtego there; this bird now chanced to intercept its broad fluttering wing between the hammer and the wood; and simultaneously feeling that etherial thrill, the sub-merged savage beneath, in his death-gasp, kept his hammer frozen there; and so the bird of heaven, with archangelic shrieks, and his imperial beak thrust upwards, and his whole captive form folded in the flag of Ahab, went down with his ship, which, like Satan, would not sink to hell till she had dragged a living part of heaven along with her, and helmeted herself with it.

Now small fowls flew screaming over the yet yawning gulf; a sullen white surf beat against its steep sides; then all collapsed, and the great shroud of the sea rolled on as it rolled five thousand years ago.

EPILOGUE

And I only am escaped alone to tell thee.
                                        Job

The drama's done. Why then here does any one step forth?—Because one did survive the wreck.

It so chanced, that after the Parsee's disappearance, I was he whom the Fates ordained to take the place of Ahab's bowsman, when that bowsman assumed the vacant post; the same, who, when on the last day the three men were tossed from out the rocking boat, was dropped astern. So, floating on the margin of the ensuing scene, and in full sight of it, when the half-spent suction of the sunk ship reached me, I was then, but slowly, drawn towards the closing vortex. When I reached it, it had subsided to a creamy pool. Round and round, then, and ever contracting towards the button-like black bubble at the axis of that slowly wheeling circle, like another Ixion I did revolve. Till, gaining that vital centre, the black bubble upward burst; and now, liberated by reason of its cunning spring, and, owing to its great buoyancy, rising with great force, the coffin life-buoy shot lengthwise from the sea, fell over, and floated by my side. Buoyed up by that coffin, for almost one whole day and night, I floated on a soft and dirge-like main. The unharming sharks, they glided by as if with padlocks on their mouths; the savage sea-hawks sailed with sheathed beaks. On the second day, a sail drew near, nearer, and picked me up at last. It was the devious-cruising Rachel, that in her retracing search after her missing children, only found another orphan.

FINIS.

BARTLEBY

I am a rather elderly man. The nature of my avocations, for the last thirty years, has brought me into more than ordinary contact with what would seem an interesting and somewhat singular set of men, of whom, as yet, nothing, that I know of, has ever been written—I mean, the law-copyists, or scriveners. I have known very many of them, professionally and privately, and, if I pleased, could relate divers histories, at which good-natured gentlemen might smile, and sentimental souls might weep. But I waive the biographies of all other scriveners, for a few passages in the life of Bartleby, who was a scrivener, the strangest I ever saw, or heard of. While, of other law-copyists, I might write the complete life, of Bartleby nothing of that sort can be done. I believe that no materials exist, for a full and satisfactory biography of this man. It is an irreparable loss to literature. Bartleby was one of those beings of whom nothing is ascertainable, except from the original sources, and, in his case, those are very small. What my own astonished eyes saw of Bartleby, *that* is all I know of him, except, indeed, one vague report, which will appear in the sequel.

Ere introducing the scrivener, as he first appeared to me, it is fit I make some mention of myself, my *employés,* my business, my chambers, and general surroundings; because some such description is indispensable to an adequate understanding of the chief character about to be presented. Imprimis: I am a man who, from his youth upwards, has been filled with a profound conviction that the easiest way of life is the best. Hence, though I belong to a profession proverbially energetic and nervous, even to turbulence, at times, yet nothing of that sort have I ever suffered to invade my peace. I am one of those unambitious lawyers who never addresses a jury, or in any way draws down public applause; but, in the cool tranquility of a snug retreat, do a snug business among rich men's bonds, and mortgages, and title-deeds. All who know me, consider me an eminently *safe* man. The late John Jacob Astor, a personage little given to poetic enthusiasm, had no hesitation in pronouncing my first grand point to be prudence; my next, method. I do not speak it in vanity, but simply record the fact, that I was not unemployed in my profession by the late John Jacob Astor; a name which, I admit, I love to repeat; for it hath a rounded and orbicular sound to it, and rings like unto bullion. I will freely add, that I was not insensible to the late John Jacob Astor's good opinion.

Some time prior to the period in which this little history begins, my avocations had been largely increased. The good old office, now extinct in the State of New York, of a Master of Chancery, had been conferred upon me. It was not a very arduous office, but very pleasantly remunerative. I seldom lose my temper; much more seldom indulge in dangerous indignation at wrongs and outrages; but, I must be permitted to be rash here, and declare, that I consider the sudden and violent abrogation of the office of Mastery in Chancery, by the new Constitution, as a——premature act; inasmuch as I had counted upon a life-lease of the profits, whereas I only received those of a few short years. But this is by the way.

My chambers were up stairs, at No.——Wall Street. At one end, they looked upon the white wall of the interior of a spacious sky-light shaft, penetrating the building from top to bottom.

This view might have been considered rather tame than otherwise, deficient in what landscape painters call 'life'. But, if so, the view from the other end of my chambers offered, at least, a contrast, if nothing more. In that direction, my windows commanded an unobstructed view of a lofty brick wall, black by age and everlasting shade; which wall required no spy-glass to bring out its lurking beauties, but, for the benefit of all near-sighted spectators, was pushed up to within ten feet of my window panes. Owing to the great height of the surrounding buildings, and my chambers being on the second floor, the interval between this wall and mine not a little resembled a huge square cistern.

At the period just preceding the advent of Bartleby, I had two persons as copyists in my employment, and a promising lad as an office-boy. First, Turkey; second, Nippers; third, Ginger Nut. These may seem names, the like of which are not usually found in the Directory. In truth, they were nicknames, mutually conferred upon each other by my three clerks, and were deemed expressive of their respective persons or characters. Turkey was a short, pursy Englishman, of about my own age—that is, somewhere not far

from sixty. In the morning, one might say, his face was of a fine
florid hue, but after twelve o'clock, meridian—his dinner hour—
it blazed like a grate full of Christmas coals; and continued
blazing—but, as it were, with a gradual wane—till six o'clock,
P.M., or thereabouts; after which, I saw no more of the proprietor
of the face, which, gaining its meridian with the sun, seemed to
set with it, to rise, culminate, and decline the following day, with
the like regularity and undiminished glory. There are many singular
coincidences I have known in the course of my life, not the least
among which was the fact, that, exactly when Turkey displayed
his fullest beams from his red and radiant countenance, just then,
too, at that critical moment, began the daily period when I
considered his business capacities as seriously disturbed for the
remainder of the twenty-four hours. Not that he was absolutely
idle, or averse to business, then; far from it. The difficulty was,
he was apt to be altogether too energetic. There was a strange,
inflamed, flurried, flighty recklessness of activity about him. He
would be incautious in dipping his pen into his inkstand. All his
blots upon my documents were dropped there after twelve o'clock,
meridian. Indeed, not only would he be reckless, and sadly given
to making blots in the afternoon, but, some days, he went further,
and was rather noisy. At such times, too, his face flamed with
augmented blazonry, as if cannel coal had been heaped on an-
thracite. He made an unpleasant racket with his chair; spilled his
sand-box; in mending his pens, impatiently split them all to pieces,
and threw them on the floor in a sudden passion; stood up, and
leaned over his table, boxing his papers about in a most indecorous
manner, very sad to behold in an elderly man like him. Nevertheless, as he was in many ways a most vauable person to me,
and all the time before twelve o'clock, meridian, was the quickest,
steadiest creature, too, accomplishing a great deal of work in a
style not easily to be matched—for these reasons, I was willing
to overlook his eccentricities, though, indeed, occasionally, I remonstrated with him. I did this very gently, however, because,
though the civilest, nay, the blandest and most reverential of men
in the morning, yet, in the afternoon, he was disposed, upon
provocation, to be slightly rash with his tongue—in fact insolent.
Now, valuing his morning services as I did, and resolved not to
lose them—yet, at the same time, made uncomfortable by his
inflamed ways after twelve o'clock—and being a man of peace,
unwilling by my admonitions to call forth unseemly retorts from
him, I took upon me, one Saturday noon (he was always worse
on Saturdays) to hint to him, very kindly, that, perhaps, now that

he was growing old, it might be well to abridge his labors; in short, he need not come to my chambers after twelve o'clock, but, dinner over, had best go home to his lodgings, and rest himself till tea-time. But no; he insisted upon his afternoon devotions. His countenance became intolerably fervid, as he oratorically assured me—gesticulating with a long ruler at the other end of the room—that if his services in the morning were useful, how indispensable, then, in the afternoon?

'With submission, sir,' said Turkey, on this occasion, 'I consider myself your right-hand man. In the morning I but marshal and deploy by columns; but in the afternoon I put myself at their head, and gallantly charge the foe, thus'—and he made a violent thrust with the ruler.

'But the blots, Turkey,' intimated I.

'True; but, with submission, sir, behold these hairs! I am getting old. Surely, sir, a blot or two of a warm afternoon is not to be severely urged against gray hairs. Old age—even if it blot the page—is honorable. With submission, sir, we *both* are getting old.'

This appeal to my fellow-feeling was hardly to be resisted. At all events, I saw that go he would not. So, I made up my mind to let him stay, resolving, nevertheless, to see to it that, during the afternoon, he had to do with my less important papers.

Nippers, the second on my list, was a whiskered, sallow, and, upon the whole, rather piratical-looking young man, of about five and twenty. I always deemed him the victim of two evil powers— ambition and indigestion. The ambition was envinced by a certain impatience of the duties of a mere copyist, an unwarrantable usurpation of strictly professional affairs, such as the original drawing up of legal documents. The indigestion seemed betokened in an occasional nervous testiness and grinning irritability, causing the teeth to audibly grind together over mistakes committed in copying; unnecessary maledictions, hissed, rather than spoken, in the heat of business; and especially by a continual discontent with the height of the table where he worked. Though of a very ingenious mechanical turn, Nippers could never get this table to suit him. He put chips under it, blocks of various sorts, bits of pasteboard, and at last went so far as to attempt an exquisite adjustment, by final pieces of folded blotting-paper. But no invention would answer. If, for the sake of easing his back, he brought the table lid at a sharp angle well up towards his chin, and wrote there like a man using the steep roof of a Dutch house for his desk, then he declared that it stopped the circulation in his arms. If now he lowered the table to his waistbands, and stooped over it in writing, then there was a sore aching in his back. In short, the truth of the matter was, Nippers knew not what he wanted. Or, if he wanted anything, it was to be rid of a scrivener's table altogether. Among the manifestations of his diseased ambition was a fondness he had for receiving visits from certain ambiguous-looking fellows in seedy coats, whom he called his clients. Indeed, I was aware that not only was he, at times, considerable of a ward-politician, but he occasionaly did a little business at the Justices' courts, and was not unknown on the steps of the Tombs. I have good reason to believe, however, that one individual who called upon him at my chambers, and who, with a grand air, he insisted was his client, was no other than a dun, and the alleged title-deed, a bill. But, with all his failings, and the annoyances he caused me, Nippers, like his compatriot Turkey, was a very useful man to me; wrote a neat, swift hand; and, when he chose, was not deficient in a gentlemanly sort of deportment. Added to this, he always dressed in a gentlemanly sort of way; and so, incidentally, reflected credit upon my chambers. Whereas, with respect to Turkey, I had much ado to keep him from being a reproach to me. His clothes were apt to look oily, and smell of eating-houses. He wore his pantaloons very loose and baggy in summer. His coats were execrable; his hat not to be handled. But while the hat was a thing of indifference to me, inasmuch as his natural civility and deference, as a dependent Englishman, always led him to doff it the moment he entered the room, yet his coat was another matter. Concerning his coats, I reasoned with him; but with no effect. The truth was, I suppose, that a man with so small an income could not afford to sport such a lustrous face and a lustrous coat at one and the same time. As Nippers once observed, Turkey's money went chiefly for red ink. One winter day, I presented Turkey with a highly respectable-looking coat of my own—a padded gray coat, of a most comfortable warmth, and which buttoned straight up from the knee to the neck. I thought Turkey would appreciate the favor, and abate his rashness and obstreperousness of afternoons. But no; I verily believe that buttoning himself up in so downy and blanket-like a coat had a pernicious effect upon him—upon the same principle that too much oats are bad for horses. In fact, precisely as a rash, restive horse is said to feel his oats, so Turkey felt his coat. It made him insolent. He was a man whom prosperity harmed.

Though, concerning the self-indulgent habits of Turkey, I had my own private surmises, yet, touching Nippers, I was well persuaded that, whatever might be his faults in other respects, he was, at least, a temperate young man. But, indeed nature herself seemed to have been his vintner, and, at his birth, charged him so thoroughly with an irritable, brandy-like disposition, that all subsequent potations were needless. When I consider how, amid the stillness of my chambers, Nippers would sometimes impatiently rise from his seat, and stooping over his table, spread his arms wide apart, seize the whole desk, and move it, and jerk it, with a grim, grinding motion on the floor, as if the table were a perverse voluntary agent, intent on thwarting and vexing him, I plainly perceive that, for Nippers, brandy-and-water were altogether superfluous.

It was fortunate for me that, owing to its peculiar cause—indigestion—the irritability and consequent nervousness of Nippers were mainly observable in the morning, while in the afternoon he was comparatively mild. So that, Turkey's paroxysms only coming on about twelve o'clock, I never had to do with their eccentricities at one time. Their fits relieved each other, like guards. When Nippers's was on, Turkey's was off; and *vice versa.* This was a good natural arrangement, under the circumstances.

Ginger Nut, the third on my list, was a lad, some twelve years old. His father was a car-man, ambitious of seeing his son on the bench instead of a cart, before he died. So he sent him to my office, as student at law, errand-boy, cleaner and sweeper, at the rate of one dollar a week. He had a little desk to himself, but he did not use it much. Upon inspection, the drawer exhibited a great array of the shells of various sorts of nuts. Indeed, to this quick-witted youth, the whole noble science of the law was contained in a nutshell. Not the least among the employments of Ginger Nut, as well as one which he discharged with the most alacrity, was his duty as cake and apple purveyor for Turkey and Nippers. Copying law-papers being proverbially a dry, husky sort of business, my two scriveners were fain to moisten their mouths very often with Spitzenbergs, to be had at the numerous stalls nigh the Custom House and Post Office. Also, they sent Ginger Nut very frequently for that perculiar cake—small, flat, round, and very spicy—after which he had been named by them. Of a cold morning, when business was but dull, Turkey would gobble up scores of these cakes, as if they were mere wafers—indeed, they sell them at the rate of six or eight for a penny—the scrape of his pen blending with the crunching of the crisp particles in his mouth. Of all the fiery afternoon blunders and flurried rashnesses of Turkey, was his once moistening a ginger-cake between his lips, and clapping it on to a mortgage, for a seal. I came

within an ace of dismissing him then. But he mollified me by
making an oriental bow, and saying—

'With submission, sir, it was generous of me to find you in
stationery on my own account.'

Now my original business—that of a conveyancer and title
hunter, and drawer-up of recondite documents of all sorts—was
considerably increased by receiving the master's office. There was
now great work for scriveners. Not only must I push the clerks
already with me, but I must have additional help.

In answer to my advertisement, a motionless young man one
morning stood upon my office threshold, the door being open,
for it was summer. I can see that figure now—pallidly neat, pitiably
respectable, incurably forlorn! It was Bartleby.

After a few words touching his qualifications, I engaged him,
glad to have among my corps of copyists a man of so singularly
sedate an aspect, which I thought might operate beneficially upon
the flighty temper of Turkey, and the fiery one of Nippers.

I should have stated before that ground glass folding-doors
divided my premises into two parts, one of which was occupied
by my scriveners, the other by myself. According to my humor,
I threw open these doors, or closed them. I resolved to assign
Bartleby a corner by the folding-doors, but on my side of them,
so as to have this quiet man within easy call, in case any trifling
thing was to be done. I placed his desk close up to a small side
window in that part of the room, a window which originally had
afforded a lateral view of certain grimy backyards and bricks, but
which, owing to subsequent erections, commanded at present no
view at all, though it gave some light. Within three feet of the
panes was a wall, and the light came down from far above, between
two lofty buildings, as from a very small opening in a dome. Still
further to a satisfactory arrangement, I procured a high green
folding screen, which might entirely isolate Bartleby from my sight,
though not remove him from my voice. And thus, in a manner,
privacy and society were conjoined.

At first, Bartleby did an extraordinary quantity of writing. As
if long famishing for something to copy, he seemed to gorge
himself on my documents. There was no pause for digestion. He
ran a day and night line, copying by sun-light and by candle-
light. I should have been quite delighted with his application, had
he been cheerfully industrious. But he wrote on silently, palely,
mechanically.

It is, of course, an indispensable part of a scrivener's business
to verify the accuracy of his copy, word by word. Where there

are two or more scriveners in an office, they assist each other in this examination, one reading from the copy, the other holding the original. It is a very dull, wearisome, and lethargic affair. I can readily imagine that, to some sanguine temperaments, it would be altogether intolerable. For example, I cannot credit that the mettlesome poet, Byron, would have contentedly sat down with Bartleby to examine a law document of, say five hundred pages, closely written in a crimpy hand.

Now and then, in the haste of business, it had been my habit to assist in comparing some brief document myself, calling Turkey or Nippers for this purpose. One object I had, in placing Bartleby so handy to me behind the screen, was, to avail myself of his services on such trivial occasions. It was on the third day, I think, of his being with me, and before any necessity had arisen for having his own writing examined, that, being much hurried to complete a small affair I had in hand, I abruptly called to Bartleby. In my haste and natural expectancy of instant compliance, I sat with my head bent over the original on my desk, and my right hand sideways, and somewhat nervously extended with the copy, so that, immediately upon emerging from his retreat, Bartleby might snatch it and proceed to business without the least delay.

In this very attitude did I sit when I called to him, rapidly stating what it was I wanted him to do—namely, to examine a small paper with me. Imagine my surprise, nay, my consternation, when, without moving from his privacy, Bartleby, in a singularly mild, firm voice, replied, 'I would prefer not to.'

I sat awhile in perfect silence, rallying my stunned faculties. Immediately it occurred to me that my ears had deceived me, or Bartleby had entirely misunderstood my meaning. I repeated my request in the clearest tone I could assume; but in quite as clear a one came the previous reply, 'I would prefer not to.'

'Prefer not to,' echoed I, rising in high excitement, and crossing the room with a stride. 'What do you mean? Are you moonstruck? I want you to help me compare this sheet here—take it,' and I thrust it towards him.

'I would prefer not to,' said he.

I looked at him steadfastly. His face was leanly composed; his gray eye dimly calm. Not a wrinkle of agitation rippled him. Had there been the least uneasiness, anger, impatience or impertinence in his manner; in other words, had there been any thing ordinarily human about him, doubtless I should have violently dismissed him from the premises. But as it was, I should have as soon thought of turning my pale plaster-of-paris bust of Cicero out of doors. I stood gazing at him awhile, as he went on with his own writing, and then reseated myself at my desk. This is very strange, thought I. What had one best do? But my business hurried me. I concluded to forget the matter for the present, reserving it for my future leisure. So calling Nippers from the other room, the paper was speedily examined.

A few days after this, Bartleby concluded four lengthy documents, being quadruplicates of a week's testimony taken before me in my High Court of Chancery. It became necessary to examine them. It was an important suit, and great accuracy was imperative. Having all things arranged, I called Turkey, Nippers, and Ginger Nut, from the next room, meaning to place the four copies in the hands of my four clerks, while I should read from the original. Accordingly, Turkey, Nippers, and Ginger Nut had taken their seats in a row, each with his document in his hand, when I called to Bartleby to join this interesting group.

'Bartleby! quick, I am waiting.'

I heard a slow scrape of his chair legs on the uncarpeted floor, and soon he appeared standing at the entrance of his hermitage.

'What is wanted?' said he, mildly.

'The copies, the copies,' said I hurriedly. 'We are going to examine them. There'—and I held towards him the fourth quadruplicate.

'I would prefer not to,' he said, and gently disappeared behind the screen.

For a few moments I was turned into a pillar of salt, standing at the head of my seated column of clerks. Recovering myself, I advanced towards the screen, and demanded the reason for such extraordinary conduct.

'*Why* do you refuse?'

'I would prefer not to.'

With any other man I should have flown outright into a dreadful passion, scorned all further words, and thrust him ignominiously from my presence. But there was something about Bartleby that not only strangely disarmed me, but, in a wonderful manner, touched and disconcerted me. I began to reason with him.

'These are your own copies we are about to examine. It is labor saving to you, because one examination will answer for your four papers. It is common usage. Every copyist is bound to help examine his copy. Is it not so? Will you not speak? Answer!'

'I prefer not to,' he replied in a flutelike tone. It seemed to me that, while I had been addressing him, he carefully revolved every statement that I made; fully comprehended the meaning; could not gainsay the irresistible conclusion; but, at the same time, some paramount consideration prevailed with him to reply as he did.

'You are decided, then, not to comply with my request—a request made according to common usage and common sense?'

He briefly gave me to understand, that on that point my judgment was sound. Yes: his decision was irreversible.

It is not seldom the case that, when a man is browbeaten in some unprecedented and violently unreasonable way, he begins to stagger in his own plainest faith. He begins, as it were, vaguely to surmise that, wonderful as it may be, all the justice and all the reason is on the other side. Accordingly, if any disinterested persons are present, he turns to them for some reinforcement of his own faltering mind.

'Turkey,' said I, 'what do you think of this? Am I not right?'

'With submission, sir,' said Turkey, in his blandest tone, 'I think that you are.'

'Nippers,' said I, 'what do *you* think of it?'

'I think I should kick him out of the office.'

(The reader, of nice perceptions, will here perceive that, it being morning, Turkey's answer is couched in polite and tranquil terms, but Nippers replies in ill-tempered ones. Or, to repeat a previous sentence, Nippers's ugly mood was on duty, and Turkey's off.)

'Ginger Nut,' said I, willing to enlist the smallest suffrage in my behalf, 'what do *you* think of it?'

'I think, sir, he's a little *luny*,' replied Ginger Nut, with a grin.

'You hear what they say,' said I, turning towards the screen, 'come forth and do your duty.'

But he vouchsafed no reply. I pondered a moment in sore perplexity. But once more business hurried me. I determined again to postpone the consideration of this dilemma to my future leisure. With a little trouble we made out to examine the papers without Bartleby, though at every page or two Turkey deferentially dropped his opinion, that this proceeding was quite out of the common; while Nippers, twitching in his chair with a dyspeptic nervousness, ground out, between his set teeth, occasional hissing maledictions against the stubborn oaf behind the screen. And for his (Nippers's) part, this was the first and the last time he would do another man's business without pay.

Meanwhile Bartleby sat in his hermitage, oblivious to everything but his own peculiar business there.

Some days passed, the scrivener being employed upon another lengthy work. His late remarkable conduct led me to regard his ways narrowly. I observed that he never went to dinner; indeed, that he never went anywhere. As yet I had never, of my personal knowledge, known him to be outside of my office. He was a perpetual sentry in the corner. At about eleven o'clock though, in the morning, I noticed that Ginger Nut would advance towards the opening in Bartleby's screen, as if silently beckoned thither by a gesture invisible to me where I sat. The boy would then leave the office, jingling a few pence, and reappear with a handful of ginger-nuts, which he delivered in the hermitage, receiving two of the cakes for his trouble.

He lives, then, on ginger-nuts, thought I; never eats a dinner, properly speaking; he must be a vegetarian, then; but no; he never eats even vegetables, he eats nothing but ginger-nuts. My mind then ran on in reveries concerning the probable effects upon the human constitution of living entirely on ginger-nuts. Ginger-nuts are so called, because they contain ginger as one of their peculiar constituents, and the final flavoring one. Now, what was ginger? A hot, spicy thing. Was Bartleby hot and spicy? Not at all. Ginger, then, had no effect upon Bartleby. Probably he preferred it should have none.

Nothing so aggravates an earnest person as a passive resistance. If the individual so resisted be of a not inhumane temper, and the resisting one perfectly harmless in his passivity, then, in the better moods of the former, he will endeavor charitably to construe to his imagination what proves impossible to be solved by his judgment. Even so, for the most part, I regarded Bartleby and his ways. Poor fellow! thought I, he means no mischief; it is plain he intends no insolence; his aspect sufficiently evinces that his eccentricities are involuntary. He is useful to me. I can get along with him. If I turn him away, the chances are he will fall in with some less-indulgent employer, and then he will be rudely treated, and perhaps driven forth miserably to starve. Yes. Here I can cheaply purchase a delicious self-approval. To befriend Bartleby; to humor him in his strange willfulness, will cost me little or nothing, while I lay up in my soul what will eventually prove a sweet morsel for my conscience. But this mood was not invariable with me. The passiveness of Bartleby sometimes irritated me. I felt strangely goaded on to encounter him in new opposition—to elicit some angry spark from him answerable to my own. But, indeed, I might as well have essayed to strike fire with my knuckles against a bit of Windsor soap. But one afternoon the evil impulse in me mastered me, and the following little scene ensued:

'Bartleby,' said I, 'when those papers are all copied, I will compare them with you.'

'I would prefer not to.'

'How? Surely you do not mean to persist in that mulish vagary?'
No answer.

I threw open the folding-doors near by, and, turning upon Turkey and Nippers, exclaimed:

'Bartleby a second time says, he won't examine his papers. What do you think of it, Turkey?'

It was afternoon, be it remembered. Turkey sat glowing like a brass boiler; his bald head steaming; his hands reeling among his blotted papers.

'Think of it?' roared Turkey; 'I think I'll just step behind his screen, and black his eyes for him!'

So saying, Turkey rose to his feet and threw his arms into a pugilistic position. He was hurrying away to make good his promise, when I detained him, alarmed at the effect of incautiously rousing Turkey's combativeness after dinner.

'Sit down, Turkey,' said I, 'and hear what Nippers has to say. What do you think of it, Nippers? Would I not be justified in immediately dismissing Bartleby?'

'Excuse me, that is for you to decide, sir. I think his conduct quite unusual, and, indeed, unjust, as regards Turkey and myself. But it may only be a passing whim.'

'Ah,' exclaimed I, 'you have strangely changed your mind, then—you speak very gently of him now.'

'All beer,' cried Turkey; 'gentleness is effects of beer—Nippers and I dined together to-day. You see how gentle *I* am, sir. Shall I go and black his eyes?'

'You refer to Bartleby, I suppose. No, not to-day, Turkey,' I replied; 'pray, put up your fists.'

I closed the doors, and again advanced towards Bartleby. I felt additional incentives tempting me to my fate. I burned to be rebelled against again. I remembered that Bartleby never left the office.

'Bartleby,' said I, 'Ginger Nut is away; just step around to the Post Office, won't you? (it was but a three minutes' walk), and see if there is anything for me.'

'I would prefer not to.'

'You *will* not?'

'I *prefer* not.'

I staggered to my desk, and sat there in a deep study. My blind inveteracy returned. Was there any other thing in which I could procure myself to be ignominiously repulsed by this lean, penniless wight?—my hired clerk? What added thing is there, perfectly reasonable, that he will be sure to refuse to do?

'Bartleby!'

No answer.

'Bartleby,' in a louder tone.

No answer.

'Bartleby,' I roared.

Like a very ghost, agreeably to the laws of magical invocation, at the third summons, he appeared at the entrance of his hermitage.

'Go to the next room, and tell Nippers to come to me.'

'I prefer not to,' he respectfully and slowly said, and mildly disappeared.

'Very good, Bartleby,' said I, in a quiet sort of serenely-severe self-possessed tone, intimating the unalterable purpose of some terrible retribution very close at hand. At the moment I half intended something of the kind. But upon the whole, as it was drawing towards my dinner-hour, I thought it best to put on my hat and walk home for the day, suffering much from perplexity and distress of mind.

Shall I acknowledge it? The conclusion of this whole business was, that it soon became a fixed fact of my chambers, that a pale young scrivener, by the name of Bartleby, had a desk there; that he copied for me at the usual rate of four cents a folio (one hundred words); but he was permanently exempt from examining the work done by him, that duty being transferred to Turkey and Nippers, out of compliment, doubtless, to their superior acuteness; moreover, said Bartleby was never, on any account, to be dispatched on the most trivial errand of any sort; and that even if entreated to take upon him such a matter, it was generally understood that he would 'prefer not to'—in other words, that he would refuse point-blank.

As days passed on, I became considerably reconciled to Bartleby. His steadiness, his freedom from all dissipation, his incessant industry (except when he chose to throw himself into a standing revery behind his screen), his great stillness, his unalterableness of demeanor under all circumstances, made him a valuable acquisition. One prime thing was this—*he was always there*—first in the morning, continually through the day, and the last at night. I had a singular confidence in his honesty. I felt my most precious papers perfectly safe in his hands. Sometimes, to be sure, I could not, for the very soul of me, avoid falling into sudden spasmodic passions with him. For it was exceeding difficult to bear in mind all the time those strange peculiarities, privileges, and unheard of exemptions, forming the tacit stipulations on Bartleby's part under

which he remained in my office. Now and then, in the eagerness
of dispatching pressing business, I would inadvertently summon
Bartleby, in a short, rapid tone, to put his finger, say, on the
incipient tie of a bit of red tape with which I was about compressing
some papers. Of course, from behind the screen the usual answer,
'I prefer not to,' was sure to come; and then, how could a human
creature, with the common infirmities of our nature, refrain from
bitterly exclaiming upon such perverseness—such unreasonable-
ness. However, every added repulse of this sort which I received
only tended to lessen the probability of my repeating the inadvertence.

Here it must be said, that according to the custom of most
legal gentlemen occupying chambers in densely-populated law
buildings, there were several keys to my door. One was kept by
a woman residing in the attic, which person weekly scrubbed and
daily swept and dusted my apartments. Another was kept by
Turkey for convenience sake. The third I sometimes carried in
my own pocket. The fourth I knew not who had.

Now, one Sunday morning I happened to go to Trinity Church,
to hear a celebrated preacher, and finding myself rather early on
the ground I thought I would walk around to my chambers for
a while. Luckily I had my key with me; but upon applying it to
the lock, I found it resisted by something inserted from the inside.
Quite surprised, I called out; when to my consternation a key was
turned from within; and thrusting his lean visage at me, and
holding the door ajar, the apparition of Bartleby appeared, in his
shirt sleeves, and otherwise in a strangely tattered deshabille, saying
quietly that he was sorry, but he was deeply engaged just then,
and—preferred not admitting me at present. In a brief word or
two, he moreover added, that perhaps I had better walk around
the block two or three times, and by that time he would probably
have concluded his affairs.

Now, the utterly unsurmised appearance of Bartleby, tenanting
my law-chambers of a Sunday morning, with his cadaverously
gentlemanly *nonchalance*, yet withal firm and self-possessed, had
such a strange effect upon me, that incontinently I slunk away
from my own door, and did as desired. But now without sundry
twinges of impotent rebellion against the mild effrontery of this
unaccountable scrivener. Indeed, it was his wonderful mildness
chiefly, which not only disarmed me, but unmanned me as it
were. For I consider that one, for the time, is a sort of unmanned
when he tranquilly permits his hired clerk to dictate to him, and
order him away from his own premises. Furthermore, I was full

of uneasiness as to what Bartleby would possibly be doing in my
office in his shirt sleeves, and in an otherwise dismantled condition
of a Sunday morning. Was anything amiss going on? Nay, that
was out of the question. It was not to be thought of for a moment
that Bartleby was an immoral person. But what could he be doing
there?—copying? Nay again, whatever might be his eccentricities,
Bartleby was an eminently decorous person. He would be the last
man to sit down to his desk in any state approaching to nudity.
Besides, it was Sunday; and there was something about Bartleby
that forbade the supposition that he would by any secular occupation violate the properties of the day.

Nevertheless, my mind was not pacified; and full of a restless
curiosity, at last I returned to the door. Without hindrance I
inserted my key, opened it, and entered. Bartleby was not to be
seen. I looked round anxiously, peeped behind his screen; but it
was very plain that he was gone. Upon more closely examining
the place, I surmised that for an indefinite period Bartleby must
have ate, dressed, and slept in my office, and that, too without
plate, mirror, or bed. The cushioned seat of a ricketty old sofa
in one corner bore the faint impress of a lean, reclining form.
Rolled away under his desk, I found a blanket; under the empty
grate, a blacking box and brush; on a chair, a tin basin, with soap
and a ragged towel; in a newspaper a few crumbs of ginger-nuts
and a morsel of cheese. Yes, thought I, it is evident enough that
Bartleby has been making his home here, keeping bachelor's hall
all by himself. Immediately then the thought came sweeping across
me, what miserable friendliness and loneliness are here revealed!
His poverty is great; but his solitude, how horrible! Think of it.
Of a Sunday, Wall Street is deserted as Petra; and every night of
every day it is an emptiness. This building, too, which of weekdays
hums with industry and life, at nightfall echoes with sheer vacancy,
and all through Sunday is forlorn. And here Bartleby makes his
home; sole spectator of a solitude which he has seen all populous—
a sort of innocent and transformed Marius brooding among the
ruins of Carthage!

For the first time in my life a feeling of over-powering stinging
melancholy seized me. Before, I had never experienced aught but
a not unpleasing sadness. The bond of a common humanity now
drew me irresistibly to gloom. A fraternal melancholy! For both
I and Bartleby were sons of Adam. I remembered the bright silks
and sparkling faces I had seen that day, in gala trim, swan-like
sailing down the Mississippi of Broadway; and I contrasted them
with the pallid copyist, and thought to myself, Ah, happiness

courts the light, so we deem the world is gay; but misery hides aloof, so we deem that misery there is none. These sad fancyings—chimeras, doubtless, of a sick and silly brain—led on to other and more special thoughts, concerning the eccentricities of Bartleby. Presentiments of strange discoveries hovered round me. The scrivener's pale form appeared to me laid out, among uncaring strangers, in its shivering winding sheet.

Suddenly I was attracted by Bartleby's closed desk, the key in open sight left in the lock.

I mean no mischief, seek the gratification of no heartless curiosity, thought I; besides, the desk is mine, and its contents, too, so I will make bold to look within. Everything was methodically arranged, the papers smoothly placed. The pigeon holes were deep, and removing the files of documents, I groped into their recesses. Presently I felt something there, and dragged it out. It was an old bandanna handkerchief, heavy and knotted. I opened it, and saw it was a saving's bank.

I now recalled all the quiet mysteries which I had noted in the man. I remembered that he never spoke but to answer; that, though at intervals he had considerable time to himself, yet I had never seen him reading—no, not even a newspaper; that for long periods he would stand looking out, at his pale window behind the screen, upon the dead brick wall; I was quite sure he never visited any refectory or eating house; while his pale face clearly indicated the he never drank beer like Turkey, or tea and coffee even, like other men; that he never went anywhere in particular that I could learn; never went out for a walk, unless, indeed, that was the case at present; that he had declined telling who he was, or whence he came, or whether he had any relatives in the world; that though so thin and pale, he never complained of ill health. And more than all, I remembered a certain unconscious air of pallid—how shall I call it?—of pallid haughtiness, say, or rather an austere reserve about him, which had positively awed me into my tame compliance with his eccentricities, when I had feared to ask him to do the slightest incidental thing for me, even though I might know, from his long-continued motionlessness, that behind his screen he must be standing in one of those dead-wall reveries of his.

Revolving all these things, and coupling them with the recently discovered fact, that he made my office his constant abiding place and home, and not forgetful of his morbid moodiness; revolving all these things, a prudential feeling began to steal over me. My first emotions had been those of pure melancholy and sincerest pity; but just in proportion as the forlornness of Bartleby grew and grew to my imagination, did that same melancholy merge into fear, that pity into repulsion. So true it is, and so terrible, too, that up to a certain point the thought or sight of misery enlists our best affections; but, in certain special cases, beyond that point it does not. They err who would assert that invariably this is owing to the inherent selfishness of the human heart. It rather proceeds from a certain hopelessness of remedying excessive and organic ill. To a sensitive being, pity is not seldom pain. And when at last it is perceived that such pity cannot lead to effectual succor, common sense bids the soul be rid of it. What I saw that morning persuaded me that the scrivener was the victim of innate and incurable disorder. I might give alms to his body; but his body did not pain him; it was his soul that suffered, and his soul I could not reach.

I did not accomplish the purpose of going to Trinity Church that morning. Somehow, the things I had seen disqualified me for the time from church-going. I walked homeward, thinking what I would do with Bartleby. Finally, I resolved upon this—I would put certain calm questions to him the next morning, touching his history, etc., and if he declined to answer them openly and unreservedly (and I supposed he would prefer not), then to give him a twenty dollar bill over and above whatever I might owe him, and tell him his services were no longer required; but that if in any other way I could assist him, I would be happy to do so, especially if he desired to return to his native place, wherever that might be, I would willingly help to defray the expenses. Moreover, if, after reaching home, he found himself at any time in want of aid, a letter from him would be sure of a reply.

The next morning came.

'Bartleby,' said I, gently calling to him behind his screen.

No reply.

'Bartleby,' said I, in a still gentler tone, 'come here; I am not going to ask you to do anything you would prefer not to do—I simply wish to speak to you.'

Upon this he noiselessly slid into view.

'Will you tell me, Bartleby, where you were born?'

'I would prefer not to.'

'Will you tell me *anything* about yourself?'

'I would prefer not to.'

'But what reasonable objection can you have to speak to me? I feel friendly towards you.'

He did not look at me while I spoke, but kept his glance fixed upon my bust of Cicero, which, as I then sat, was directly behind me, some six inches above my head.

'What is your answer, Bartleby,' said I, after waiting a considerable time for a reply, during which his countenance remained immovable, only there was the faintest conceivable tremor of the white attenuated mouth.

'At present I prefer to give no answer,' he said, and retired into his hermitage.

It was rather weak in me I confess, but his manner, on this occasion, nettled me. Not only did there seem to lurk in it a certain calm disdain, but his perverseness seemed ungrateful, considering the undeniable good usage and indulgence he had received from me.

Again I sat ruminating what I should do. Mortified as I was at his behavior, and resolved as I had been to dismiss him when I entered my office, nevertheless I strangely felt something superstitious knocking at my heart, and forbidding me to carry out my purpose, and denouncing me for a villain if I dared to breathe one bitter word against this forlornest of mankind. At last, familiarly drawing my chair behind his screen, I sat down and said: 'Bartleby, never mind, then, about revealing your history; but let me entreat you, as a friend, to comply as far as may be with the usages of this office. Say now, you will help to examine papers tomorrow or next day: in short, say now, that in a day or two you will begin to be a little reasonable:—say so, Bartleby.'

'At present I would prefer not to be a little reasonable,' was his mildly cadaverous reply.

Just then the folding doors opened, and Nippers approached. He seemed suffering from an unusually bad night's rest, induced by severer indigestion than common. He overheard those final words of Bartleby.

'*Prefer not,* eh?' gritted Nippers—'I'd *prefer* him, if I were you, sir,' addressing me—'I'd give him preferences, the stubborn mule! What is it, sir, pray, that he *prefers* not to do now?'

Bartleby moved not a limb.

'Mr. Nippers,' said I, 'I'd prefer that you would withdraw for the present.'

Somehow, of late, I had got into the way of involuntarily using the word 'prefer' upon all sorts of not exactly suitable occasions. And I trembled to think that my contact with the scrivener had already and seriously affected me in a mental way. And what further and deeper aberration might it not yet produce? This apprehension had not been without efficacy in determining me to summary measures.

As Nippers, looking very sour and sulky, was departing, Turkey blandly and deferentially approached.

'With submission, sir,' said he, 'yesterday I was thinking about Bartleby here, and I think that if he would but prefer to take a quart of good ale every day, it would do much towards mending him, and enabling him to assist in examining his papers.'

'So you have got the word, too,' said I, slightly excited.

'With submission, what word, sir,' asked Turkey, respectfully crowding himself into the contracted space behind the screen, and by so doing, making me jostle the scrivener. 'What word, sir?'

'I would prefer to be left alone here,' said Bartleby, as if offended at being mobbed in his privacy.

'*That's* the word, Turkey,' said I—'*that's* it.'

'Oh, *prefer*? oh yes—queer word. I never use it myself. But, sir, as I was saying, if he would but prefer—'

'Turkey,' interrupted I, 'you will please withdraw.'

'Oh, certainly, sir, if you prefer that I should.'

As he opened the folding-door to retire, Nippers at his desk caught a glimpse of me, and asked whether I would prefer to have a certain paper copied on blue paper or white. He did not in the least roguishly accent the word prefer. It was plain that it involuntarily rolled from his tongue. I thought to myself, surely I must get rid of a demented man, who already has in some degree turned the tongues, if not the heads of myself and clerks. But I thought it prudent not to break the dismission at once.

The next day I noticed that Bartleby did nothing but stand at his window in his dead-wall revery. Upon asking him why he did not write, he said that he had decided upon doing no more writing.

'Why, how now? what next?' exclaimed I, 'do no more writing?'

'No more.'

'And what is the reason?'

'Do you not see the reason for yourself?' he indifferently replied.

I looked steadfastly at him, and perceived that his eyes looked dull and glazed. Instantly it occurred to me, that his unexampled diligence in copying by his dim window for the first few weeks of his stay with me might have temporarily impaired his vision.

I was touched, I said something in condolence with him. I hinted that of course he did wisely in abstaining from writing for a while; and urged him to embrace that opportunity of taking wholesome exercise in the open air. This, however, he did not do. A few days after this, my other clerks being absent, and being in a great hurry to dispatch certain letters by the mail, I thought that, having nothing else earthly to do, Bartleby would surely be less inflexible than usual, and carry these letters to the postoffice. But he blankly declined. So, much to my inconvenience, I went myself.

Still added days went by. Whether Bartleby's eyes improved or not, I could not say. To all appearance, I thought they did. But when I asked him if they did, he vouchsafed no answer. At all events, he would do no copying. At last, in reply to my urgings, he informed me that he had permanently given up copying.

'What!' exclaimed I; 'suppose your eyes should get entirely well— better than ever before—would you not copy then?'

'I have given up copying,' he answered, and slid aside.

He remained as ever, a fixture in my chamber. Nay—if that were possible—he became still more of a fixture than before. What was to be done? He would do nothing in the office; why should he stay there? In plain fact, he had now become a millstone to me, not only useless as a necklace, but afflictive to bear. Yet I was sorry for him. I speak less than the truth when I say that, on his own account, he occasioned me uneasiness. If he would but have named a single relative or friend, I would instantly have written, and urged their taking the poor fellow away to some convenient retreat. But he seemed alone, absolutely alone in the universe. A bit of wreck in the mid Atlantic. At length, necessities connected with my business tyrannized over all other considerations. Decently as I could, I told Bartleby that in six days time he must unconditionally leave the office. I warned him to take measures, in the interval, for procuring some other abode. I offered to assist him in this endeavor, if he himself would but take the first step towards a removal. 'And when you finally quit me, Bartleby,' added I, 'I shall see that you go not away entirely unprovided. Six days from this hour, remember.'

At the expiration of that period, I peeped behind the screen, and lo! Bartleby was there.

I buttoned up my coat, balanced myself; advanced slowly towards him, touched his shoulder, and said, 'The time has come; you must quit this place; I am sorry for you; here is money; but you must go.'

'I would prefer not,' he replied, with his back still towards me.

'You *must*.'

He remained silent.

Now I had an unbounded confidence in this man's common honesty. He had frequently restored to me sixpences and shillings carelessly dropped upon the floor, for I am apt to be very reckless in such shirt-button affairs. The proceeding, then, which followed will not be deemed extraordinary.

'Bartleby,' said I, 'I owe you twelve dollars on account; here are thirty-two; the odd twenty are yours. Will you take it?' and I handed the bills towards him.

But he made no motion.

'I will leave them here, then,' putting them under a weight on the table. Then taking my hat and cane and going to the door, I tranquilly turned and added—'After you have removed your things from these offices, Bartleby, you will of course lock the door—since every one is now gone for the day but you—and if you please, slip your key underneath the mat, so that I may have it in the morning. I shall not see you again; so good-by to you. If, hereafter, in your new place of abode, I can be of any service to you, do not fail to advise me by letter. Good-by, Bartleby, and fare you well.'

But he answered not a word; like the last column of some ruined temple, he remained standing mute and solitary in the middle of the otherwise deserted room.

As I walked home in a pensive mood, my vanity got the better of my pity. I could not but highly plume myself on my masterly management in getting rid of Bartleby. Masterly I call it, and such it must appear to any dispassionate thinker. The beauty of my procedure seemed to consist of its perfect quietness. There was no vulgar bullying, no bravado of any sort, no choleric hectoring, and striding to and fro across the apartment, jerking out vehement commands for Bartleby to bundle himself off with his beggarly traps. Nothing of the kind. Without loudly bidding Bartleby depart—as an inferior genius might have done—I *assumed* the ground that depart he must; and upon that assumption built all I had to say. The more I thought over my procedure, the more I was charmed with it. Nevertheless, next morning, upon awakening, I had my doubts—I had somehow slept off the fumes of vanity. One of the coolest and wisest hours a man has, is just after he awakes in the morning. My procedure seemed as sagacious as ever—but only in theory. How it would prove in practice— there was the rub. It was truly a beautiful thought to have assumed Bartleby's departure; but, after all, that assumption was simply my own, and none of Bartleby's. The great point was, not whether I had assumed that he would quit me, but whether he would prefer to do so. He was more a man of preferences than assumptions.

After breakfast, I walked down town, arguing the probabilities *pro* and *con*. One moment I thought it would prove a miserable failure, and Bartleby would be found all alive at my office as usual; the next moment it seemed certain that I should find his chair empty. And so I kept veering about. At the corner of Broadway and Canal Street, I saw quite an excited group of people standing in earnest conversation.

'I'll take odds he doesn't,' said a voice as I passed.

'Doesn't go?—done!' said I, 'put up your money.'

I was instinctively putting my hand in my pocket to produce my own, when I remembered that this was an election day. The words I had overheard bore no reference to Bartleby, but to the success or non-success of some candidate for the mayoralty. In my intent frame of mind, I had, as it were, imagined that all Broadway shared in my excitement, and were debating the same question with me. I passed on, very thankful that the uproar of the street screened my momentary absentmindedness.

As I had intended, I was earlier than usual at my office door. I stood listening for a moment. All was still. He must be gone. I tried the knob. The door was locked. Yes, my procedure had worked to a charm; he indeed must be vanished. Yet a certain melancholy mixed with this: I was almost sorry for my brilliant success. I was fumbling under the door mat for the key, which Bartleby was to have left there for me, when accidentally my knee knocked against a panel, producing a summoning sound, and in response a voice came to me from within—'Not yet; I am occupied.'

It was Bartleby.

I was thunderstruck. For an instant I stood like the man who, pipe in mouth, was killed one cloudless afternoon long ago in Virginia, by summer lightning; at his own warm open window he was killed, and remained leaning out there upon the dreamy afternoon, till some one touched him, when he fell.

'Not gone!' I murmured at last. But again obeying that wondrous ascendancy which the inscrutable scrivener had over me, and from which ascendancy, for all my chafing, I could not completely escape, I slowly went down stairs and out into the street, and while walking round the block, considered what I should next do in this unheard-of perplexity. Turn the man out by an actual thrusting I could not; to drive him away by calling him hard names would not do; calling in the police was an unpleasant idea; and yet, permit him to enjoy his cadaverous triumph over me— this, too, I could not think of. What was to be done? or, if nothing could be done, was there anything further that I could *assume* in the matter? Yes, as before I had prospectively assumed that Bartleby would depart, so now I might retrospectively assume that departed he was. In the legitimate carrying out of this assumption, I might enter my office in a great hurry, and pretending not to see Bartleby at all, walk straight against him as if he were air. Such a proceeding would in a singular degree have the appearance of a home-thrust. It was hardly possible that Bartleby could withstand such an application of the doctrine of assumptions. But upon second thoughts the success of the plan seemed rather dubious. I resolved to argue the matter over with him again.

'Bartleby,' said I, entering the office, with a quietly severe expression, 'I am seriously displeased. I am pained, Bartleby. I had thought better of you. I had imagined you of such a gentlemanly organization, that in any delicate dilemma a slight hint would suffice—in short, an assumption. But it appears I am deceived. Why,' I added, unaffectedly starting, 'you have not even touched that money yet,' pointing to it, just where I had left it the evening previous.

He answered nothing.

'Will you, or will you not, quit me?' I now demanded in a sudden passion, advancing close to him.

'I would prefer *not* to quit you,' he replied, gently emphasizing the *not*.

'What earthly right have you to stay here? Do you pay any rent? Do you pay my taxes? Or is this property yours?'

He answered nothing.

'Are you ready to go on and write now? Are your eyes recovered? Could you copy a small paper for me this morning? or help examine a few lines? or step round to the post-office? In a word, will you do anything at all, to give a coloring to your refusal to depart the premises?'

He silently retired into his hermitage.

I was now in such a state of nervous resentment that I thought it but prudent to check myself as present from further demonstrations. Bartleby and I were alone. I remembered the tragedy of the unfortunate Adams and the still more unfortunate Colt in the solitary office of the latter; and how poor Colt, being dreadfully incensed by Adams, and imprudently permitting himself to get wildly excited, was at unawares hurried into his fatal act—an act which certainly no man could possibly deplore more than the actor himself. Often it had occurred to me in my ponderings upon the subject, that had that altercation taken place in the public

street, or at a private residence, it would not have terminated as
it did. It was the circumstance of being alone in a solitary office,
up stairs, of a building entirely unhallowed by humanizing domestic
associations—an uncarpeted office, doubtless, of a dusty, haggard
sort of appearance—this it must have been, which greatly helped
to enhance the irritable desperation of the hapless Colt.

But when this old Adam of resentment rose in me and tempted
me concerning Bartleby, I grappled him and threw him. How?
Why, simply by recalling the divine injunction: 'A new commandment give I unto you, that ye love one another.' Yes, this
it was that saved me. Aside from higher considerations, charity
often operates as a vastly wise and prudent principle—a great
safeguard to its possessor. Men have committed murder for jealousy's sake, and anger's sake, and hatred's sake, and selfishness'
sake, and spiritual pride's sake; but no man, that ever I heard of,
ever committed a diabolical murder for sweet charity's sake. Mere
self-interest, then, if no better motive can be enlisted, should,
especially with high-tempered men, prompt all beings to charity
and philanthropy. At any rate, upon the occasion in question, I
strove to drown my exasperated feelings towards the scrivener by
benevolently construing his conduct. Poor fellow, poor fellow!
thought I, he don't mean anything; and besides, he has seen hard
times, and ought to be indulged.

I endeavored, also, immediately to occupy myself, and at the
same time to comfort my despondency. I tried to fancy, that in
the course of the morning, at such time as might prove agreeable
to him, Bartleby, of his own free accord, would emerge from his
hermitage and take up some decided line of march in the direction
of the door. But no. Half-past twelve o'clock came; Turkey began
to glow in the face, overturn his inkstand, and become generally
obstreperous; Nippers abated down into quietude and courtesy;
Ginger Nut munched his noon apple; and Bartleby remained
standing at his window in one of his profoundest dead-wall reveries.
Will it be credited? Ought I to acknowledge it? That afternoon I
left the office without saying one further word to him.

Some days now passed, during which, at leisure intervals I
looked a little into 'Edwards on the Will,' and 'Priestley on
Necessity.' Under the circumstances, those books induced a salutary feeling. Gradually I slid into the persuasion that these troubles
of mine, touching the scrivener, had been all predestinated from
eternity, and Bartleby was billeted upon me for some mysterious
purpose of an allwise Providence, which it was not for a mere
mortal like me to fathom. Yes, Bartleby, stay there behind your

screen, thought I; I shall persecute you no more; you are harmless
and noiseless as any of these old chairs; in short, I never feel so
private as when I know you are here. At last I see it, I feel it; I
penetrate to the predestinated purpose of my life. I am content.
Others may have loftier parts to enact; but my mission in this
world, Bartleby, is to furnish you with office-room for such period
as you may see fit to remain.

I believe that this wise and blessed frame of mind would have
continued with me, had it not been for the unsolicited and
uncharitable remarks obtruded upon me by my professional friends
who visited the rooms. But thus it often is, that the constant
friction of illiberal minds wears out at last the best resolves of
the more generous. Though to be sure, when I reflected upon it,
it was not strange that people entering my office should be struck
by the peculiar aspect of the unaccountable Bartleby, and so be
tempted to throw out some sinister observations concerning him.
Sometimes an attorney, having business with me, and calling at
my office, and finding no one but the scrivener there, would
undertake to obtain some sort of precise information from him
touching my whereabouts; but without heeding his idle talk,
Bartleby would remain standing immovable in the middle of the
room. So after contemplating him in that position for a time, the
attorney would depart, no wiser than he came.

Also, when a reference was going on, and the room full of
lawyers and witnesses, and business driving fast, some deeply-
occupied legal gentleman present, seeing Bartleby wholly unemployed, would request him to run round to his (the legal gentleman's) office and fetch some papers for him. Thereupon, Bartleby
would tranquilly decline, and yet remain idle as before. Then the
lawyer would give a great stare, and turn to me. And what could
I say? At last I was made aware that all through the circle of my
professional acquaintance, a whisper of wonder was running round,
having reference to the strange creature I kept at my office. This
worried me very much. And as the idea came upon me of his
possibly turning out a long-lived man, and keep occupying my
chambers, and denying my authority; and perplexing my visitors;
and scandalizing my professional reputation; and casting a general
gloom over the premises; keeping soul and body together to the
last upon his savings (for doubtless he spent but half a dime a
day), and in the end perhaps outlive me, and claim possession of
my office by right of his perpetual occupancy: as all these dark
anticipations crowded upon me more and more, and my friends
continually intruded their relentless remarks upon the apparition

in my room; a great change was wrought in me. I resolved to gather all my faculties together, and forever rid me of this intolerable incubus.

Ere revolving any complicated project, however, adapted to this end, I first simply suggested to Bartleby the propriety of his permanent departure. In a calm and serious tone, I commended the idea to his careful and mature consideration. But, having taken three days to meditate upon it, he apprised me, that his original determination remained the same; in short, that he still preferred to abide with me.

What shall I do? I now said to myself, buttoning up my coat to the last button. What shall I do? what ought I to do? what does conscience say I *should* do with this man, or, rather, ghost. Rid myself of him, I must; go, he shall. But how? You will not thrust him, the poor, pale, passive mortal—you will not thrust such a helpless creature out of your door? you will not dishonor yourself by such cruelty? No, I will not, I cannot do that. Rather would I let him live and die here, and then mason up his remains in the wall. What, then, will you do? For all your coaxing, he will not budge. Bribes he leaves under your own paper-weight on your table; in short, it is quite plain that he prefers to cling to you.

Then something severe, something unusual must be done. What! surely you will not have him collared by a constable, and commit his innocent pallor to the common jail? And upon what ground could you procure such a thing to be done?—a vagrant, is he? What! he a vagrant, a wanderer, who refuses to budge? It is because he will *not* be a vagrant, then, that you seek to count him *as* a vagrant. That is too absurd. No visible means of support: there I have him. Wrong again: for indubitably he *does* support himself, and that is the only unanswerable proof that any man can show of his possessing the means so to do. No more, then. Since he will not quit me, I must quit him. I will change my offices; I will move elsewhere, and give him fair notice, that if I find him on my new premises I will then proceed against him as a common trespasser.

Acting accordingly, next day I thus addressed him: 'I find these chambers too far from the City Hall; the air is unwholesome. In a word, I propose to remove my offices next week, and shall no longer require your services. I tell you this now, in order that you may seek another place.'

He made no reply, and nothing more was said.

On the appointed day I engaged carts and men, proceeded to

my chambers, and, having but little furniture, everything was removed in a few hours. Throughout, the scrivener remained standing behind the screen, which I directed to be removed the last thing. It was withdrawn; and, being folded up like a huge folio, left him the motionless occupant of a naked room. I stood in the entry watching him a moment, while something from within me upbraided me.

I re-entered, with my hand in my pocket—and—and my heart in my mouth.

'Good-by, Bartleby; I am going—good-by, and God some way bless you; and take that,' slipping something in his hand. But it dropped upon the floor, and then—strange to say—I tore myself from him whom I had so longed to be rid of.

Established in my new quarters, for a day or two I kept the door locked, and started at every footfall in the passages. When I returned to my rooms, after any little absence, I would pause at the threshold for an instant, and attentively listen, ere applying my key. But these fears were needless. Bartleby never came nigh me.

I thought all was going well, when a perturbed-looking stranger visited me, inquiring whether I was the person who had recently occupied rooms at No.——Wall Street.

Full of forebodings, I replied that I was.

'Then, sir,' said the stranger, who proved a lawyer, 'you are responsible for the man you left there. He refuses to do any copying; he refuses to do anything, he says he prefers not to; and he refuses to quit the premises.'

'I am very sorry, sir,' said I, with assumed tranquillity, but an inward tremor, 'but, really, the man you allude to is nothing to me—he is no relation or apprentice of mine, that you should hold me responsible for him.'

'In mercy's name, who is he?'

'I certainly cannot inform you. I know nothing about him. Formerly I employed him as a copyist; but he has done nothing for me now for some time past.'

'I shall settle him, then—good morning, sir.'

Several days passed, and I heard nothing more; and, though I often felt a charitable prompting to call at the place and see poor Bartleby, yet a certain squeamishness, of I know not what, withheld me.

All is over with him, by this time, thought I, at last, when, through another week, no further intelligence reached me. But, coming to my room the day after, I found several persons waiting at my door in a high state of nervous excitement.

'That's the man—here he comes,' cried the foremost one, whom I recognized as the lawyer who had previously called upon me alone.

'You must take him away, sir, at once,' cried a portly person among them, advancing upon me, and whom I knew to be the landlord of No.—— Wall Street. 'These gentlemen, my tenants, cannot stand it any longer; Mr. B——,' pointing to the lawyer, 'has turned him out of his room, and he now persists in haunting the building generally, sitting upon the banisters of the stairs by day, and sleeping in the entry by night. Everybody is concerned; clients are leaving the offices; some fears are entertained of a mob; something you must do, and that without delay.'

Aghast at this torrent, I fell back before it, and would fain have locked myself in my new quarters. In vain I persisted that Bartleby was nothing to me—no more than to any one else. In vain—I was the last person known to have anything to do with him, and they held me to the terrible account. Fearful, then, of being exposed in the papers (as one person present obscurely threatened), I considered the matter, and, at length, said, that if the lawyer would give me a confidential interview with the scrivener, in his (the lawyer's) own room, I would, that afternoon, strive my best to rid them of the nuisance they complained of.

Going up stairs to my old haunt, there was Bartleby silently sitting upon the banister at the landing.

'What are you doing here, Bartleby?' said I.

'Sitting upon the banister,' he mildly replied.

I motioned him into the lawyer's room, who then left us.

'Bartleby,' said I, 'are you aware that you are the cause of great tribulation to me, by persisting in occupying the entry after being dismissed from the office?'

No answer.

'Now one of two things must take place. Either you must do something, or something must be done to you. Now what sort of business would you like to engage in? Would you like to re-engage in copying for some one?'

'No; I would prefer not to make any change.'

'Would you like a clerkship in a dry-goods store?'

'There is too much confinement about that. No, I would not like a clerkship; but I am not particular.'

'Too much confinement,' I cried, 'why you keep yourself confined all the time!'

'I would prefer not to take a clerkship,' he rejoined, as if to settle that little item at once.

'How would a bar-tender's business suit you? There is no trying of the eye-sight in that.'

'I would not like it at all; though, as I said before, I am not particular.'

His unwonted wordiness inspirited me. I returned to the charge.

'Well, then, would you like to travel through the country collecting bills for the merchants? That would improve your health.'

'No, I would prefer to be doing something else.'

'How, then, would going as a companion to Europe, to entertain some young gentleman with your conversation—how would that suit you?'

'Not at all. It does not strike me that there is anything definite about that. I like to be stationary. But I am not particular.'

'Stationary you shall be, then,' I cried, now losing all patience, and, for the first time in all my exasperating connection with him, fairly flying into a passion. 'If you do not go away from these premises before night, I shall feel bound—indeed, I *am* bound—to—to—to quit the premises myself!' I rather absurdly concluded, knowing not with what possible threat to try to frighten his immobility into compliance. Despairing of all further efforts, I was precipitately leaving him, when a final thought occurred to me—one which had not been wholly unindulged before.

'Bartleby,' said I, in the kindest tone I could assume under such exciting circumstances, 'will you go home with me now—not to my office, but my dwelling—and remain there till we can conclude upon some convenient arrangement for you at our leisure? Come, let us start now, right away.'

'No: at present I would prefer not to make any change at all.'

I answered nothing; but, effectually dodging every one by the suddenness and rapidity of my flight, rushed from the building, ran up Wall Street towards Broadway, and, jumping into the first omnibus, was soon removed from pursuit. As soon as tranquillity returned, I distinctly perceived that I had now done all that I possibly could, both in respect to the demands of the landlord and his tenants, and with regard to my own desire and sense of duty, to benefit Bartleby, and shield him from rude persecution. I now strove to be entirely care-free and quiescent; and my conscience justified me in the attempt; though, indeed, it was not so successful as I could have wished. So fearful was I of being again hunted out by the incensed landlord and his exasperated tenants, that, surrendering my business to Nippers, for a few days,

I drove about the upper part of the town and through the suburbs, in my rockaway; crossed over to Jersey City and Hoboken, and paid fugitive visits to Manhattanville and Astoria. In fact, I almost lived in my rockaway for the time.

When again I entered my office, lo, a note from the landlord lay upon the desk. I opened it with trembling hands. It informed me that the writer had sent to the police, and had Bartleby removed to the Tombs as a vagrant. Moreover, since I knew more about him than any one else, he wished me to appear at that place, and make a suitable statement of the facts. These tidings had a conflicting effect upon me. At first I was indignant; but, at last, almost approved. The landlord's energetic, summary disposition, had led him to adopt a procedure which I do not think I would have decided upon myself; and yet, as a last resort, under such peculiar circumstances, it seemed the only plan.

As I afterwards learned, the poor scrivener, when told that he must be conducted to the Tombs, offered not the slightest obstacle, but, in his pale, unmoving way, silently acquiesced.

Some of the compassionate and curious bystanders joined the party; and headed by one of the constables arm in arm with Bartleby, the silent procession filed its way through all the noise, and heat, and joy of the roaring thoroughfares at noon.

The same day I received the note, I went to the Tombs, or, to speak more properly, the Halls of Justice. Seeking the right officer, I stated the purpose of my call, and was informed that the individual I described was, indeed, within. I then assured the functionary that Bartleby was a perfectly honest man, and greatly to be compassionated, however unaccountably eccentric. I narrated all I knew, and closed by suggesting the idea of letting him remain in as indulgent confinement as possible, till something less harsh might be done—though, indeed, I hardly knew what. At all events, if nothing else could be decided upon, the alms-house must receive him. I then begged to have an interview.

Being under no disgraceful charge, and quite serene and harmless in all his ways, they had permitted him freely to wander about the prison, and, especially, in the inclosed grass-platted yards thereof. And so I found him there, standing all alone in the quietest of the yards, his face towards a high wall, while all around, from the narrow slits of the jail windows, I thought I saw peering out upon him the eyes of murderers and thieves.

'Bartleby!'

'I know you,' he said, without looking round—'and I want nothing to say to you.'

'It was not I that brought you here, Bartleby,' said I, keenly pained at his implied suspicion. 'And to you, this should not be so vile a place. Nothing reproachful attaches to you by being here. And see, it is not so sad a place as one might think. Look, there is the sky, and here is the grass.'

'I know where I am,' he replied, but would say nothing more, and so I left him.

As I entered the corridor again, a broad meat-like man, in an apron, accosted me, and, jerking his thumb over his shoulder, said—'Is that your friend?'

'Yes.'

'Does he want to starve? If he does, let him live on the prison fare, that's all.'

'Who are you?' asked I, not knowing what to make of such an unofficially speaking person in such a place.

'I am the grub-man. Such gentlemen as have friends here, hire me to provide them with something good to eat.'

'Is this so?' said I, turning to the turnkey.

He said it was.

'Well, then,' said I, slipping some silver into the grub-man's hands (for so they called him), 'I want you to give particular attention to my friend there; let him have the best dinner you can get. And you must be as polite to him as possible.'

'Introduce me, will you?' said the grub-man, looking at me with an expression which seemed to say he was all impatience for an opportunity to give a specimen of his breeding.

Thinking it would prove of benefit to the scrivener, I acquiesced; and, asking the grub-man his name, went up with him to Bartleby.

'Bartleby, this is a friend; you will find him very useful to you.'

'Your sarvant, sir, your sarvant,' said the grub-man, making a low salutation behind his apron. 'Hope you find it pleasant here, sir; nice grounds—cool apartments—hope you'll stay with us sometime—try to make it agreeable. What will you have for dinner to-day?'

'I prefer not to dine to-day,' said Bartleby, turning away. 'It would disagree with me; I am unused to dinners.' So saying, he slowly moved to the other side of the inclosure, and took up a position fronting the deadwall.

'How's this?' said the grub-man, addressing me with a stare of astonishment. 'He's odd, ain't he?'

'I think he is a little deranged,' said I, sadly.

'Deranged? deranged is it? Well, now, upon my word, I thought that friend of yourn was a gentleman forger; they are always pale

and genteel-like, them forgers. I can't help pity 'em—can't help
it, sir. Did you know Monroe Edwards?' he added, touchingly,
and paused. Then, laying his hand piteously on my shoulder,
sighed, 'he died of consumption at Sing-Sing. So you weren't
acquainted with Monroe?'

'No, I was never socially acquainted with any forgers. But I
cannot stop longer. Look to my friend yonder. You will not lose
by it. I will see you again.'

Some few days after this, I again obtained admission to the
Tombs, and went through the corridors in quest of Bartleby; but
without finding him.

'I saw him coming from his cell not long ago,' said a turnkey,
'may be he's gone to loiter in the yards.'

So I went in that direction.

'Are you looking for the silent man?' said another turnkey,
passing me. 'Yonder he lies—sleeping in the yard there. 'Tis not
twenty minutes since I saw him lie down.'

The yard was entirely quiet. It was not accessible to the common
prisoners. The surrounding walls, of amazing thickness, kept off
all sounds behind them. The Egyptian character of the masonry
weighed upon me with its gloom. But a soft imprisoned turf grew
under foot. The heart of the eternal pyramids, it seemed, wherein,
by some strange magic, through the clefts, grass-seed, dropped by
birds, had sprung.

Strangely huddled at the base of the wall, his knees drawn up,
and lying on his side, his head touching the cold stones, I saw
the wasted Bartleby. But nothing stirred. I paused; then went close
up to him; stooped over, and saw that his dim eyes were open;
otherwise he seemed profoundly sleeping. Something prompted
me to touch him. I felt his hand, when a tingling shiver ran up
my arm and down my spine to my feet.

The round face of the grub-man peered upon me now. 'His
dinner is ready. Won't he dine today, either? Or does he live
without dining?'

'Lives without dining,' said I, and closed the eyes.

'Eh!—He's asleep, ain't he?'

'With kings and counselors,' murmured I.

There would seem little need for proceeding further in this
history. Imagination will readily supply the meagre recital of poor
Bartleby's interment. But, ere parting with the reader, let me say,
that if this little narrative has sufficiently interested him, to awaken

curiosity as to who Bartleby was, and what manner of life he led prior to the present narrator's making his acquaintance, I can only reply, that in such curiosity I fully share, but am wholly unable to gratify it. Yet here I hardly know whether I should divulge one little item of rumor, which came to my ear a few months after the scrivener's decease. Upon what basis it rested, I could never ascertain; and hence, how true it is I cannot now tell. But, inasmuch as this vague report has not been without a certain suggestive interest to me, however said, it may prove the same with some others; and so I will briefly mention it. The report was this: that Bartleby had been a subordinate clerk in the Dead Letter Office at Washington, from which he had been suddenly removed by a change in the administration. When I think over this rumor, hardly can I express the emotions which seize me. Dead letters! does it not sound like dead men? Conceive a man by nature and misfortune prone to a pallid hopelessness, can any business seem more fitted to heighten it than that of continually handling these dead letters, and assorting them for the flames? For by the cart-load they are annually burned. Sometimes from out the folded paper the pale clerk takes a ring—the finger it was meant for, perhaps, moulders in the grave; a bank-note sent in swiftest charity— he whom it would relieve, nor eats nor hungers any more; pardon for those who died despairing; hope for those who died unhoping; good tidings for those who died stifled by unrelieved calamities. On errands of life, these letters speed to death.

Ah, Bartleby! Ah, humanity!

BENITO CERENO

In the year 1799, Captain Amasa Delano, of Duxbury, in Massachusetts, commanding a large sealer and general trader, lay at anchor with a valuable cargo, in the harbor of St Maria—a small, desert, uninhabited island toward the southern extremity of the long coast of Chili. There he had touched for water.

On the second day, not long after dawn, while lying in his berth, his mate came below, informing him that a strange sail was coming into the bay. Ships were then not so plenty in those waters as now. He rose, dressed, and went on deck.

The morning was one peculiar to that coast. Everything was mute and calm; everything gray. The sea, though undulated into long roods of swells, seemed fixed, and was sleeked at the surface like waved lead that has cooled and set in the smelter's mould. The sky seemed a gray surtout. Flights of troubled gray fowl, kith and kin with flights of troubled gray vapors among which they were mixed, skimmed low and fitfully over the waters, as swallows over meadows before storms. Shadows present, foreshadowing deeper shadows to come.

To Captain Delano's surprise, the stranger, viewed through the glass, showed no colors; though to do so upon entering a haven, however uninhabited in its shores, where but a single other ship might be lying, was the custom among peaceful seamen of all nations. Considering the lawlessness and loneliness of the spot, and the sort of stories, at that day, associated with those seas, Captain Delano's surprise might have deepened into some uneasiness had he not been a person of a singularly undistrustful good nature, not liable, except on extraordinary and repeated incentives, and hardly then, to indulge in personal alarms, any way involving the imputation of malign evil in man. Whether, in view of what humanity is capable, such a trait implies, along with a benevolent heart, more than ordinary quickness and accuracy of intellectual perception, may be left to the wise to determine.

But whatever misgivings might have obtruded on first seeing the stranger, would almost, in any seaman's mind, have been dissipated by observing that, the ship, in navigating into the harbor, was drawing too near the land; a sunken reef making out off her bow. This seemed to prove her a stranger, indeed, not only to the sealer, but the island; consequently, she could be no wonted freebooter on that ocean. With no small interest, Captain Delano continued to watch her—a proceeding not much facilitated by the vapors partly mantling the hull, through which the far matin light from her cabin streamed equivocally enough; much like the sun—by this time hemisphered on the rim of the horizon, and, apparently, in company with the strange ship entering the harbor—which, wimpled by the same low, creeping clouds, showed not unlike a Lima intriguante's one sinister eye peering across the Plaza from the Indian loop-hole of her dusk *saya-y-manta.*

It might have been but a deception of the vapors, but, the longer the stranger was watched the more singular appeared her manoeuvres. Ere long it seemed hard to decide whether she meant to come in or no—what she wanted, or what she was about. The wind, which had breezed up a little during the night, was now extremely light and baffling, which the more increased the apparent uncertainty of her movements.

Surmising, at last, that it might be a ship in distress, Captain Delano ordered his whale-boat to be dropped, and, much to the wary opposition of his mate, prepared to board her, and, at the least, pilot her in. On the night previous, a fishing-party of the seamen had gone a long distance to some detached rocks out of sight from the sealer, and, an hour or two before daybreak, had returned, having met with no small success. Presuming that the stranger might have been long off soundings, the good captain put several baskets of the fish, for presents, into his boat, and so pulled away. From her continuing too near the sunken reef, deeming her in danger, calling to his men, he made all haste to apprise those on board of their situation. But, some time ere the boat came up, the wind, light though it was, having shifted, had headed the vessel off, as well as partly broken the vapors from about her.

Upon gaining a less remote view, the ship, when made signally visible on the verge of the leaden-hued swells, with the shreds of fog here and there raggedly furring her, appeared like a whitewashed monastery after a thunderstorm, seen perched upon some dun cliff among the Pyrenees. But it was no purely fanciful resemblance which now, for a moment, almost led Captain Delano to think that nothing less than a ship-load of monks was before him. Peering over the bulwarks were what really seemed, in the hazy distance, throngs of dark cowls; while fitfully revealed through the open port-holes, other dark moving figures were dimly descried, as of Black Friars pacing the cloisters.

Upon a still nigher approach, this appearance was modified, and the true character of the vessel was plain—a Spanish merchantman of the first class, carrying negro slaves, amongst other valuable freight, from one colonial port to another. A very large, and, in its time, a very fine vessel, such as in those days were at intervals encountered along that main; sometimes superseded Acapulco treasure-ships, or retired frigates of the Spanish king's navy, which, like superannuated Italian palaces, still, under a decline of masters, preserved signs of former state.

As the whale-boat drew more and more nigh, the cause of the peculiar pipe-clayed aspect of the stranger was seen in the slovenly neglect pervading her. The spars, ropes and great part of the bulwarks, looked woolly, from long unacquaintance with the scraper, tar and the brush. Her keel seemed laid, her ribs put together, and she launched, from Ezekiel's Valley of Dry Bones.

In the present business in which she was engaged, the ship's general model and rig appeared to have undergone no material change from their original warlike and Froissart pattern. However, no guns were seen.

The tops were large, and were railed about with what had once been octagonal net-work, all now in sad disrepair. These tops hung overhead like three ruinous aviaries, in one of which was seen perched, on a ratlin, a white noddy, a strange fowl, so called from its lethargic, somnambulistic character, being frequently caught by hand at sea. Battered and mouldy, the castellated forecastle seemed some ancient turret, long ago taken by assault, and then left to decay. Toward the stern, two high-raised quarter galleries— the balustrades here and there covered with dry, tindery sea-moss— opening out from the unoccupied state-cabin, whose dead-lights, for all the mild weather, were hermetically closed and calked— these tenantless balconies hung over the sea as if it were the grand Venetian canal. But the principal relic of faded grandeur was the ample oval of the shield-like stern-piece, intricately carved with the arms of Castile and Leon, medallioned about by groups of mythological or symbolical devices; uppermost and central of which was a dark satyr in a mask, holding his foot on the prostrate neck of a writhing figure, likewise masked.

Whether the ship had a figure-head, or only a plain beak, was not quite certain, owing to canvas wrapped about that part, either to protect it while undergoing a re-furbishing, or else decently to hide its decay. Rudely painted or chalked, as in a sailor freak, along the forward side of a sort of pedestal below the canvas, was the sentence, *'Seguid vuestro jefe,'* (follow your leader); while upon the tarnished headboards, near by, appeared, in stately capitals, once gilt, the ship's name, 'SAN DOMINICK,' each letter streakingly corroded with tricklings of copper-spike rust; while, like mourning weeds, dark festoons of seagrass slimily swept to and fro over the name, with every hearse-like roll of the hull.

As, at last, the boat was hooked from the bow along toward the gangway amidship, its keel, while yet some inches separated from the hull, harshly grated as on a sunken coral reef. It proved a huge bunch of conglobated barnacles adhering below the water to the side like a wen—a token of baffling airs and long calms passed somewhere in those seas.

Climbing the side, the visitor was at once surrounded by a clamorous throng of whites and blacks, but the latter outnumbering the former more than could have been expected, negro transportation-ship as the stranger in port was. But, in one language, and as with one voice, all poured out a common tale of suffering; in which the negresses, of whom there were not a few, exceeded the others in their dolorous vehemence. The scurvy, together with the fever, had swept off a great part of their number, more especially the Spaniards. Off Cape Horn they had narrowly escaped shipwreck; then, for days together, they had lain tranced without wind; their provisions were low; their water next to none; their lips that moment were baked.

While Captain Delano was thus made the mark of all eager tongues, his one eager glance took in all faces, with every other object about him.

Always upon first boarding a large and populous ship at sea, especially a foreign one, with a nondescript crew such as Lascars or Manilla men, the impression varies in a peculiar way from that produced by first entering a strange house with strange inmates in a strange land. Both house and ship—the one by its walls and blinds, the other by its high bulwarks like ramparts—hoard from view their interiors till the last moment: but in the case of the ship there is this addition; that the living spectacle it contains, upon its sudden and complete disclosure, has, in contrast with the blank ocean which zones it, something of the effect of enchantment. The ship seems unreal; these strange costumes, gestures, and faces, but a shadowy tableau just emerged from the deep, which directly must receive back what it gave.

Perhaps it was some such influence, as above is attempted to be described, which, in Captain Delano's mind, heightened whatever, upon a staid scrutiny, might have seemed unusual; especially the conspicuous figures of four elderly grizzled negroes, their heads like black, doddered willow tops, who, in venerable contrast to the tumult below them, were couched, sphinx-like, one on the starboard cat-head, another on the larboard, and the remaining pair face to face on the opposite bulwarks above the main-chains. They each had bits of unstranded old junk in their hands, and, with a sort of stoical self-content, were picking the junk into oakum, a small heap of which lay by their sides. They accompanied the task with a continuous, low, monotonous chant; droning and druling away like so many gray-headed bag-pipers playing a funeral march.

The quarter-deck rose into an ample elevated poop, upon the forward verge of which, lifted, like the oakum-pickers, some eight feet above the general throng, sat along in a row, separated by regular spaces, the cross-legged figures of six other blacks; each with a rusty hatchet in his hand, which, with a bit of brick and a rag, he was engaged like a scullion in scouring; while between each two was a small stack of hatchets, their rusted edges turned forward awaiting a like operation. Though occasionally the four oakum-pickers would briefly address some person or persons in the crowd below, yet the six hatchet-polishers neither spoke to others, nor breathed a whisper among themselves, but sat intent upon their task, except at intervals, when, with the peculiar love in negroes of uniting industry with pastime, two and two they sideways clashed their hatchets together, like cymbals with a barbarous din. All six, unlike the generality, had the raw aspect of unsophisticated Africans.

But that first comprehensive glance which took in those ten figures, with scores less conspicuous, rested but an instant upon them, as, impatient of the hubbub of voices, the visitor turned in quest of whomsoever it might be that commanded the ship.

But as if not unwilling to let nature make known her own case among his suffering charge, or else in despair of restraining it for the time, the Spanish captain, a gentlemanly, reserved-looking, and rather young man to a stranger's eye, dressed with singular richness, but bearing plain traces of recent sleepless cares and disquietudes, stood passively by, leaning against the main-mast, at one moment casting a dreary, spiritless look upon his excited people, at the next an unhappy glance toward his visitor. By his side stood a black of small stature, in whose rude face, as occasionally, like a shepherd's dog, he mutely turned it up into the Spaniard's, sorrow and affection were equally blended.

Struggling through the throng, the American advanced to the Spaniard, assuring him of his sympathies, and offering to render whatever assistance might be in his power. To which the Spaniard returned for the present but grave and ceremonious acknowledgments, his national formality dusked by the saturnine mood of ill-health.

But losing no time in mere compliments, Captain Delano, returning to the gangway, had his basket of fish brought up; and as the wind still continued light, so that some hours at least must elapse ere the ship could be brought to the anchorage, he bade his men return to the sealer, and fetch back as much water as the whale-boat could carry, with whatever soft bread the steward might have, all the remaining pumpkins on board, with a box of sugar, and a dozen of his private bottles of cider.

Not many minutes after the boat's pushing off, to the vexation of all, the wind entirely died away, and the tide turning, began drifting back the ship helplessly seaward. But trusting this would not long last, Captain Delano sought, with good hopes, to cheer up the strangers, feeling no small satisfaction that, with persons in their condition, he could—thanks to his frequent voyages along the Spanish main—converse with some freedom in their native tongue.

While left alone with them, he was not long in observing some things tending to heighten his first impressions; but surprise was lost in pity, both for the Spaniards and blacks, alike evidently reduced from scarcity of water and provisions; while long-continued suffering seemed to have brought out the less good-natured qualities of the negroes, besides, at the same time, impairing the Spaniard's authority over them. But, under the circumstances, precisely this condition of things was to have been anticipated. In armies, navies, cities, or families, in nature herself, nothing more relaxes good order than misery. Still, Captain Delano was not without the idea, that had Benito Cereno been a man of greater energy, misrule would hardly have come to the present pass. But the debility, constitutional or induced by hardships, bodily and mental, of the Spanish captain, was too obvious to be overlooked. A prey to settled dejection, as if long mocked with hope he would not now indulge it, even when it had ceased to be a mock, the prospect of that day, or evening at furthest, lying at anchor, with plenty of water for his people, and a brother captain to counsel and befriend, seemed in no perceptible degree to encourage him. His mind appeared unstrung, if not still more seriously affected. Shut up in these oaken walls, chained to one dull round of command, whose unconditionality cloyed him, like some hypochondriac abbot he moved slowly about, at times suddenly pausing, starting, or staring, biting his lip, biting his finger-nail, flushing, paling, twitching his beard, with other symptoms of an absent or moody mind. This distempered spirit was lodged, as before hinted, in as distempered a frame. He was rather tall, but seemed never to have been robust, and now with nervous suffering was almost worn to a skeleton. A tendency to some pulmonary complaint appeared to have been lately confirmed. His voice was like that of one with lungs half gone—hoarsely suppressed, a husky whisper. No wonder that, as in this state he tottered about, his private servant apprehensively followed him. Sometimes the negro gave his master his arm, or took his handkerchief out of his pocket for him; performing these and similar offices with that affectionate zeal which transmutes into something filial or fraternal acts in themselves but menial; and which has gained for the negro the repute of making the most pleasing body-servant in the world; one, too, whom a master need be on no stiffly superior terms with, but may treat with familiar trust; less a servant than a devoted companion.

Marking the noisy indocility of the blacks in general, as well as what seemed the sullen inefficiency of the whites it was not without humane satisfaction that Captain Delano witnessed the steady good conduct of Babo.

But the good conduct of Babo, hardly more than the ill-behavior of others, seemed to withdraw the half-lunatic Don Benito from his cloudy languor. Not that such precisely was the impression made by the Spaniard on the mind of his visitor. The Spaniard's individual unrest was, for the present, but noted as a conspicuous feature in the ship's general affliction. Still, Captain Delano was not a little concerned at what he could not help taking for the time to be Don Benito's unfriendly indifference towards himself. The Spaniard's manner, too, conveyed a sort of sour and gloomy disdain, which he seemed at no pains to disguise. But this the American in charity ascribed to the harrassing effects of sickness, since, in former instances, he had noted that there are peculiar natures on whom prolonged physical suffering seems to cancel every social instinct of kindness; as if, forced to black bread themselves, they deemed it but equity that each person coming nigh them should, indirectly, by some slight or affront, be made to partake of their fare.

But ere long Captain Delano bethought him that, indulgent as he was at the first, in judging the Spaniard, he might not, after all, have exercised charity enough. At bottom it was Don Benito's reserve which displeased him; but the same reserve was shown towards all but his faithful personal attendant. Even the formal reports which, according to sea-usage, were, at stated times, made to him by some petty underling, either a white, mulatto or black, he hardly had patience enough to listen to without betraying contemptuous aversion. His manner upon such occasions was, in its degree, not unlike that which might be supposed to have been his imperial countryman's, Charles V., just previous to the anchoritish retirement of that monarch from the throne.

This splenetic disrelish of his place was evinced in almost every function pertaining to it. Proud as he was moody, he condescended to no personal mandate. Whatever special orders were necessary, their delivery was delegated to his body-servant, who in turn transferred them to their ultimate destination, through runners, alert Spanish boys or slave boys, like pages or pilot-fish within easy call continually hovering round Don Benito. So that to have beheld this undemonstrative invalid gliding about, apathetic and mute, no landsman could have dreamed that in him was lodged a dictatorship beyond which, while at sea, there was no earthly appeal.

Thus, the Spaniard, regarded in his reserve, seemed the involuntary victim of mental disorder. But, in fact, his reserve might, in some degree, have proceeded from design. If so, then here was evinced the unhealthy climax of that icy though conscientious policy, more or less adopted by all commanders of large ships, which, except in signal emergencies, obliterates alike the manifestation of sway with every trace of sociality; transforming the man into a block, or rather into a loaded cannon, which, until there is call for thunder, has nothing to say.

Viewing him in this light, it seemed but a natural token of the perverse habit induced by a long course of such hard self-restraint, that, notwithstanding the present condition of his ship, the Spaniard should still persist in a demeanor, which, however harmless, or, it may be, appropriate, in a well-appointed vessel, such as the *San Dominick* might have been at the outset of the voyage, was anything but judicious now. But the Spaniard, perhaps, thought that it was with captains as with gods: reserve, under all events, must still be their cue. But probably this appearance of slumbering dominion

might have been but an attempted disguise to conscious imbecility—not deep policy, but shallow device. But be all this as it
might, whether Don Benito's manner was designed or not, the
more Captain Delano noted its pervading reserve, the less he felt
uneasiness at any particular manifestation of that reserve towards
himself.

Neither were his thoughts taken up by the captain alone. Wonted
to the quiet orderliness of the sealer's comfortable family of a
crew, the noisy confusion of the *San Dominick's* suffering host
repeatedly challenged his eye. Some prominent breaches, not only
of discipline but of decency, were observed. These Captain Delano
could not but ascribe, in the main, to the absence of those
subordinate deck-officers to whom, along with higher duties, is
intrusted what may be styled the police department of a populous
ship. True, the old oakum-pickers appeared at times to act the
part of monitorial constables to their countrymen, the blacks; but
though occasionally succeeding in allaying trifling outbreaks now
and then between man and man, they could do little or nothing
toward establishing general quiet. The *San Dominick* was in the
condition of a transatlantic emigrant ship, among whose multitude
of living freight are some individuals, doubtless, as little troublesome as crates and bales; but the friendly remonstrances of such
with their ruder companions are of not so much avail as the
unfriendly arm of the mate. What the *San Dominick* wanted was,
what the emigrant ship has, stern superior officers. But on these
decks not so much as a fourth-mate was to be seen.

The visitor's curiosity was roused to learn the particulars of
those mishaps which had brought about such absenteeism, with
its consequences; because, though deriving some inkling of the
voyage from the wails which at the first moment had greeted him,
yet of the details no clear understanding had been had. The best
account would, doubtless, be given by the captain. Yet at first the
visitor was loth to ask it, unwilling to provoke some distant rebuff.
But plucking up courage, he at last accosted Don Benito, renewing
the expression of his benevolent interest, adding, that did he
(Captain Delano) but know the particulars of the ship's misfortunes, he would, perhaps, be better able in the end to relieve
them. Would Don Benito favor him with the whole story.

Don Benito faltered; then, like some somnambulist suddenly
interfered with, vacantly stared at his visitor, and ended by looking
down on the deck. He maintained this posture so long, that Captain
Delano, almost equally disconcerted, and involuntarily almost as
rude, turned suddenly from him, walking forward to accost one

of the Spanish seamen for the desired information. But he had
hardly gone five paces, when, with a sort of eagerness, Don Benito
invited him back, regretting his momentary absence of mind, and
professing readiness to gratify him.

While most part of the story was being given, the two captains
stood on the after part of the main-deck, a privileged spot, no
one being near but the servant.

'It is now a hundred and ninety days,' began the Spaniard, in
his husky whisper, 'that this ship, well officered and well manned,
with several cabin passengers—some fifty Spaniards in all—sailed
from Buenos Ayres bound to Lima, with a general cargo, hardware,
Paraguay tea and the like—and,' pointing forward, 'that parcel of
negroes, now not more than a hundred and fifty, as you see, but
then numbering over three hundred souls. Off Cape Horn we had
heavy gales. In one moment, by night, three of my best officers,
with fifteen sailors, were lost, with the main-yard; the spar snapping
under them in the slings, as they sought, with heavers, to beat
down the icy sail. To lighten the hull, the heavier sacks of mata
were thrown into the sea, with most of the water-pipes lashed on
deck at the time. And this last necessity it was, combined with
the prolonged detentions afterwards experienced, which eventually
brought about our chief causes of suffering. When—'

Here there was a sudden fainting attack of his cough, brought
on, no doubt, by his mental distress. His servant sustained him,
and drawing a cordial from his pocket placed it to his lips. He a
little revived. But unwilling to leave him unsupported while yet
imperfectly restored, the black with one arm still encircled his
master, at the same time keeping his eye fixed on his face, as if
to watch for the first sign of complete restoration, or relapse, as
the event might prove.

The Spaniard proceeded, but brokenly and obscurely, as one in
a dream.

—'Oh, my God! rather than pass through what I have, with
joy I would have hailed the most terrible gales; but—'

His cough returned and with increased violence; this subsiding,
with reddened lips and closed eyes he fell heavily against his
supporter.

'His mind wanders. He was thinking of the plague that followed
the gales,' plaintively sighed the servant; 'my poor, poor master!'
wringing one hand, and with the other wiping the mouth. 'But
be patient, Señor,' again turning to Captain Delano, 'these fits do
not last long; master will soon be himself.'

Don Benito reviving, went on; but as this portion of the story was very brokenly delivered, the substance only will here be set down.

It appeared that after the ship had been many days tossed in storms off the Cape, the scurvy broke out, carrying off numbers of the whites and blacks. When at last they had worked round into the Pacific, their spars and sails were so damaged, and so inadequately handled by the surviving mariners, most of whom were become invalids, that, unable to lay her northerly course by the wind, which was powerful, the unmanageable ship, for successive days and nights, was blown northwestward, where the breeze suddenly deserted her, in unknown waters, to sultry calms. The absence of the water-pipes now proved as fatal to life as before their presence had menaced it. Induced, or at least aggravated, by the more than scanty allowance of water, a malignant fever followed the scurvy; with the excessive heat of the lengthened calm, making such short work of it as to sweep away, as by billows, whole families of the Africans, and yet a larger number, proportionably, of the Spaniards, including, by a luckless fatality, every remaining officer on board. Consequently, in the smart west winds eventually following the calm, the already rent sails, having to be simply dropped, not furled, at need, had been gradually reduced to the beggars' rags they were now. To procure substitutes for his lost sailors, as well as supplies of water and sails, the captain, at the earliest opportunity, had made for Baldivia, the southernmost civilized port of Chili and South America; but upon nearing the coast the thick weather had prevented him from so much as sighting that harbor. Since which period, almost without a crew, and almost without canvas and almost without water, and, at intervals, giving its added dead to the sea, the *San Dominick* had been battledored about by contrary winds, inveigled by currents, or grown weedy in calms. Like a man lost in woods, more than once she had doubled upon her own track.

'But throughout these calamities,' huskily continued Don Benito, painfully turning in the half embrace of his servant, 'I have to thank those negroes you see, who, though to your inexperienced eyes appearing unruly, have, indeed, conducted themselves with less of restlessness than even their owner could have thought possible under such circumstances.'

Here he again fell faintly back. Again his mind wandered; but he rallied, and less obscurely proceeded.

'Yes, their owner was quite right in assuring me that no fetters would be needed with his blacks; so that while, as is wont in this transportation, those negroes have always remained upon deck—

not thrust below, as in the Guinea-men—they have, also, from the beginning, been freely permitted to range within given bounds at their pleasure.'

Once more the faintness returned—his mind roved—but, recovering, he resumed:

'But it is Babo here to whom, under God, I owe not only my own preservation, but likewise to him, chiefly, the merit is due, of pacifying his more ignorant brethren, when at intervals tempted to murmurings.'

'Ah, master,' sighed the black, bowing his face, 'don't speak of me; Babo is nothing; what Babo has done was but duty.'

'Faithful fellow!' cried Captain Delano. 'Don Benito, I envy you such a friend; slave I cannot call him.'

As master and man stood before him, the black upholding the white, Captain Delano could not but bethink him of the beauty of that relationship which could present such a spectacle of fidelity on the one hand and confidence on the other. The scene was heightened by the contrast in dress, denoting their relative positions. The Spaniard wore a loose Chili jacket of dark velvet; white small-clothes and stockings, with silver buckles at the knee and instep; a high-crowned sombrero, of fine grass; a slender sword, silver mounted, hung from a knot in his sash—the last being an almost invariable adjunct, more for utility than ornament, of a South American gentleman's dress to this hour. Excepting when his occasional nervous contortions brought about disarray, there was a certain precision in his attire curiously at variance with the unsightly disorder around; especially in the belittered Ghetto, forward of the mainmast, wholly occupied by the blacks.

The servant wore mothing but wide trowsers, apparently, from their coarseness and patches, made out of some old topsail; they were clean, and confined at the waist by a bit of unstranded rope, which, with his composed, deprecatory air at times, made him look something like a begging friar of St Francis.

However unsuitable for the time and place, at least in the blunt-thinking American's eyes, and however strangely surviving in the midst of all his afflictions, the toilette of Don Benito might not, in fashion at least, have gone beyond the style of the day among South Americans of his class. Though on the present voyage sailing from Buenos Ayres, he had avowed himself a native and resident of Chili, whose inhabitants had not so generally adopted the plain coat and once plebeian pantaloons; but, with a becoming modification, adhered to their provincial costume, picturesque as any in the world. Still, relatively to the pale history of the voyage,

and his own pale face, there seemed something so incongruous
in the Spaniard's apparel, as almost to suggest the image of an
invalid courtier tottering about London streets in the time of the
plague.

The portion of the narrative which, perhaps, most excited interest, as well as some surprise, considering the latitudes in question, was the long calms spoken of, and more particularly the
ship's so long drifting about. Without communicating the opinion,
of course, the American could not but impute at least part of the
detentions both to clumsy seamanship and faulty navigation. Eying
Don Benito's small, yellow hands, he easily inferred that the young
captain had not got into command at the hawsehole, but the
cabin-window; and if so, why wonder at incompetence, in youth,
sickness, and gentility united?

But drowning criticism in compassion, after a fresh repetition
of his sympathies, Captain Delano, having heard out his story,
not only engaged, as in the first place, to see Don Benito and his
people supplied in their immediate bodily needs, but, also, now
further promised to assist him in procuring a large permanent
supply of water, as well as some sails and rigging; and, though it
would involve no small embarrassment to himself, yet he would
spare three of his best seamen for temporary deck officers; so that
without delay the ship might proceed to Conception, there fully
to refit for Lima, her destined port.

Such generosity was not without its effect, even upon the invalid.
His face lighted up; eager and hectic, he met the honest glance
of his visitor. With gratitude he seemed overcome.

'This excitement is bad for master,' whispered the servant, taking
his arm, and with soothing words gently drawing him aside.

When Don Benito returned, the American was pained to observe
that his hopefulness, like the sudden kindling in his cheek, was
but febrile and transient.

Ere long, with a joyless mien, looking up towards the poop,
the host invited his guest to accompany him there, for the benefit
of what little breath of wind might be stirring.

As, during the telling of the story, Captain Delano had once or
twice started at the occasional cymballing of the hatchet-polishers,
wondering why such an interruption should be allowed, especially
in that part of the ship, and in the ears of an invalid; and moreover,
as the hatchets had anything but an attractive look, and the
handlers of them still less so, it was therefore, to tell the truth,
not without some lurking reluctance, or even shrinking, it may
be, that Captain Delano, with apparent complaisance, acquiesced

in his host's invitation. The more so, since, with an untimely caprice of punctilio, rendered distressing by his cadaverous aspect, Don Benito, with Castilian bows, solemnly insisted upon his guest's preceding him up the ladder leading to the elevation; where, one on each side of the last step, sat for armorial supporters and sentries two of the ominous file. Gingerly enough stepped good Captain Delano between them, and in the instant of leaving them behind, like one running the gauntlet, he felt an apprehensive twitch in the calves of his legs.

But when, facing about, he saw the whole file, like so many organ-grinders, still stupidly intent on their work, unmindful of everything beside, he could not but smile at his late fidgety panic.

Presently, while standing with his host, looking forward upon the decks below, he was struck by one of those instances of insubordination previously alluded to. Three black boys, with two Spanish boys, were sitting together on the hatches, scraping a rude wooden platter, in which some scanty mess had recently been cooked. Suddenly, one of the black boys, enraged at a word dropped by one of his white companions, seized the knife, and, though called to forbear by one of the oakum-pickers, struck the lad over the head, inflicting a gash from which blood flowed.

In amazement, Captain Delano inquired what this meant. To which the pale Don Benito dully muttered, that it was merely the sport of the lad.

'Pretty serious sport, truly,' rejoined Captain Delano. 'Had such a thing happened on board the *Bachelor's Delight*, instant punishment would have followed.'

At these words the Spaniard turned upon the American one of his sudden, staring, half-lunatic looks; then, relapsing into his torpor, answered, 'Doubtless, doubtless, Señor.'

It is, thought Captain Delano, that this hapless man is one of those paper captains I've known, who by policy wink at what by power they cannot put down? I know no sadder sight than a commander who has little of command but the name.

'I should think, Don Benito,' he now said, glancing towards the oakum-picker who had sought to interfere with the boys, 'that you would find it advantageous to keep all your blacks employed, especially the younger ones, no matter at what useless task, and no matter what happens to the ship. Why, even with my little band, I find such a course indispensable. I once kept a crew on my quarter-deck thrumming mats for my cabin, when, for three days, I had given up my ship—mats, men, and all—for a speedy loss, owing to the violence of a gale, in which we could do nothing but helplessly drive before it.'

'Doubtless, doubtless,' murmured Don Benito.

'But,' continued Captain Delano, again glancing upon the oakum-pickers and then at the hatchet-polishers, near by, 'I see you keep some, at least, of your host employed.'

'Yes,' was again the vacant response.

'Those old men there, shaking their pows from their pulpits,' continued Captain Delano, pointing to the oakum-pickers, 'seem to act the part of old dominies to the rest, little heeded as their admonitions are at times. Is this voluntary on their part, Don Benito, or have you appointed them shepherds to your flock of black sheep?'

'What posts they fill, I appointed them,' rejoined the Spaniard, in an acrid tone, as if resenting some supposed satiric reflection.

'And these others, these Ashantee conjurors here,' continued Captain Delano, rather uneasily eyeing the brandished steel of the hatchet-polishers, where, in spots, it had been brought to a shine, 'this seems a curious business they are at, Don Benito?'

'In the gales we met,' answered the Spaniard, 'what of our general cargo was not thrown overboard was much damaged by the brine. Since coming into calm weather, I have had several cases of knives and hatchets daily brought up for overhauling and cleaning.'

'A prudent idea, Don Benito. You are part owner of ship and cargo, I presume; but none of the slaves, perhaps?'

'I am owner of all you see,' impatiently returned Don Benito, 'except the main company of blacks, who belonged to my late friend, Alexandro Aranda.'

As he mentioned this name, his air was heart-broken; his knees shook; his servant supported him.

Thinking he divined the cause of such unusual emotion, to confirm his surmise, Captain Delano, after a pause, said: 'And may I ask, Don Benito, whether—since awhile ago you spoke of some cabin passengers—the friend, whose loss so afflicts you, at the outset of the voyage accompanied his blacks?'

'Yes.'

'But died of the fever?'

'Died of the fever. Oh, could I but—'

Again quivering, the Spaniard paused.

'Pardon me,' said Captain Delano, lowly, 'but I think that, by a sympathetic experience, I conjecture, Don Benito, what it is that gives the keener edge to your grief. It was once my hard fortune to lose, at sea, a dear friend, my own brother, then supercargo. Assured of the welfare of his spirit, its departure I could have borne like a man; but that honest eye, that honest hand—both of which had so often met mine—and that warm heart; all, all— like scraps to the dogs—to throw all to the sharks! It was then I vowed never to have for fellow-voyager a man I loved, unless, unbeknown to him, I had provided every requisite, in case of a fatality, for embalming his mortal part for interment on shore. Were your friend's remains now on board this ship, Don Benito, not thus strangely would the mention of his name affect you.'

'On board this ship?' echoed the Spaniard. Then, with horrified gestures, as directed against some spectre, he unconsciously fell into the ready arms of his attendant, who, with a silent appeal toward Captain Delano, seemed beseeching him not again to broach a theme so unspeakably distressing to his master.

This poor fellow now, thought the pained American, is the victim of that sad superstition which associates goblins with the deserted body of man, as ghosts with an abandoned house. How unlike are we made! What to me, in like case, would have been a solemn satisfaction, the bare suggestion, even, terrifies the Spaniard into this trance. Poor Alexandro Aranda! what would you say could you here see your friend—who, on former voyages, when you, for months, were left behind, has, I dare say, often longed, and longed, for one peep at you—now transported with terror at the least thought of having you anyway nigh him.

At this moment, with a dreary grave-yard toll, betokening a flaw, the ship's forecastle bell, smote by one of the grizzled oakum-pickers, proclaimed ten o'clock, through the leaden calm; when Captain Delano's attention was caught by the moving figure of a gigantic black, emerging from the general crowd below, and slowly advancing towards the elevated poop. An iron collar was about his neck, from which depended a chain, thrice wound round his body; the terminating links padlocked together at a broad band of iron, his girdle.

'How like a mute Atufal moves,' murmured the servant.

The black mounted the steps of the poop, and, like a brave prisoner, brought up to receive sentence, stood in unquailing muteness before Don Benito, now recovered from his attack.

At the first glimpse of his approach, Don Benito had started, a resentful shadow swept over his face; and, as with the sudden memory of bootless rage, his white lips glued together.

This is some mulish mutineer, thought Captain Delano, surveying, not without a mixture of admiration, the colossal form of the negro.

'See, he waits your question, master,' said the servant.

Thus reminded, Don Benito, nervously averting his glance, as if shunning, by anticipation, some rebellious response, in a disconcerted voice, thus spoke:—

'Atufal, will you ask my pardon, now?'

The black was silent.

'Again, master,' murmured the servant, with bitter upbraiding eyeing his countryman, 'Again, master; he will bend to master yet.'

'Answer,' said Don Benito, still averting his glance, 'say but the one word, *pardon*, and your chains shall be off.'

Upon this, the black, slowly raising both arms, let them lifelessly fall, his links clanking, his head bowed; as much as to say, 'no, I am content.'

'Go,' said Don Benito, with inkept and unknown emotion.

Deliberately as he had come, the black obeyed.

'Excuse me, Don Benito,' said Captain Delano, 'but this scene surprises me; what means it, pray?'

'It means that that negro alone, of all the band, has given me peculiar cause of offense, I have put him in chains; I—'

Here he paused; his hand to his head, as if there were a swimming there, or a sudden bewilderment of memory had come over him; but meeting his servant's kindly glance seemed reassured, and proceeded:—

'I could not scourge such a form. But I told him he must ask my pardon. As yet he has not. At my command, every two hours he stands before me.'

'And how long has this been?'

'Some sixty days.'

'And obedient in all else? And respectful?'

'Yes.'

'Upon my conscience, then,' exclaimed Captain Delano, impulsively, 'he has a royal spirit in him, this fellow.'

'He may have some right to it,' bitterly returned Don Benito, 'he says he was king in his own land.'

'Yes,' said the servant, entering a word, 'those slits in Atufal's ears once held wedges of gold; but poor Babo here, in his own land, was only a poor slave; a black man's slave was Babo, who now is the white's.'

Somewhat annoyed by the conversational familiarities Captain Delano turned curiously upon the attendant, then glanced inquiringly at his master; but as if long wonted to these little informalities, neither master nor man seemed to understand him.

'What, pray, was Atufal's offense, Don Benito?' asked Captain Delano; 'if it was not something very serious, take a fool's advice, and, in view of his general docility, as well as in some natural respect for his spirit, remit him his penalty.'

'No, no, master never will do that,' here murmured the servant to himself, 'proud Atufal must first ask master's pardon. The slave there carries the padlock, but master here carries the key.'

His attention thus directed, Captain Delano now noticed for the first, that, suspended by a slender silken cord, from Don Benito's neck, hung a key. At once, from the servant's muttered syllables, divining the key's purpose, he smiled and said:—'So, Don Benito—padlock and key—significant symbols, truly.'

Biting his lip, Don Benito faltered.

Though the remark of Captain Delano, a man of such native simplicity as to be incapable of satire or irony, had been dropped in playful allusion to the Spaniard's singularly evidenced lordship over the black; yet the hypochondriac seemed some way to have taken it as a malicious reflection upon his confessed inability thus far to break down, at least, on a verbal summons, the entrenched will of the slave. Deploring this supposed misconception, yet despairing of correcting it, Captain Delano shifted the subject; but finding his companion more than ever withdrawn, as if still sourly digesting the lees of the presumed affront abovementioned, by-and-by Captain Delano likewise became less talkative, oppressed, against his own will, by what seemed the secret vindictiveness of the morbidly sensitive Spaniard. But the good sailor, himself of a quite contrary disposition, refrained, on his part, alike from the appearance as from the feeling of resentment, and if silent, was only so from contagion.

Presently the Spaniard, assisted by his servant, somewhat discourteously crossed over from his guest; a procedure which, sensibly enough, might have been allowed to pass for idle caprice of ill-humor, had not the master and man, lingering round the corner of the elevated skylight, began whispering together in low voices. This was unpleasing. And more; the moody air of the Spaniard, which at times had not been without a sort of valetudinarian stateliness, now seemed anything but dignified; while the menial familiarity of the servant lost its original charm of simple-hearted attachment.

In his embarrassment, the visitor turned his face to the other side of the ship. By so doing, his glance accidentally fell on a young Spanish sailor, a coil of rope in his hand, just stepped from the deck to the first round of the mizzen-rigging. Perhaps the man would not have been particularly noticed, were it not that, during his ascent to one of the yards, he, with a sort of covert intentness, kept his eye fixed on Captain Delano, from whom, presently, it passed, as if by a natural sequence, to the two whisperers.

His own attention thus redirected to that quarter, Captain Delano gave a slight start. From something in Don Benito's manner just then, it seemed as if the visitor had, at least partly, been the subject of the withdrawn consultation going on—a conjecture as little agreeable to the guest as it was little flattering to the host.

The singular alternations of courtesy and ill-breeding in the Spanish captain were unaccountable, except on one of two suppositions—innocent lunacy, or wicked imposture.

But the first idea, though it might naturally have occurred to an indifferent observer, and, in some respect, had not hitherto been wholly a stranger to Captain Delano's mind, yet, now that, in an incipient way, he began to regard the stranger's conduct something in the light of an intentional affront, of course the idea of lunacy was virtually vacated. But if not a lunatic, what then? Under the circumstances, would a gentleman, nay, any honest boor, act the part now acted by his host? The man was an imposter. Some low-born adventurer, masquerading as an oceanic grandee; yet so ignorant of the first requisites of mere gentlemanhood as to be betrayed into the present remarkable indecorum. That strange ceremoniousness, too, at other times evinced, seemed not uncharacteristic of one playing a part above his real level. Benito Cereno—Don Benito Cereno—a sounding name. One, too, at that period, not unknown, in the surname, to supercargoes and sea captains trading along the Spanish Main, as belonging to one of the most enterprising and extensive mercantile families in all those provinces; several members of it having titles; a sort of Castilian Rothschild, with a noble brother, or cousin, in every great trading town in South America. The alleged Don Benito was in early manhood, about twenty-nine or thirty. To assume a sort of roving cadetship in the maritime affairs of such a house, what more likely scheme for a young knave of talent and spirit? But the Spaniard was a pale invalid. Never mind. For even to the degree of simulating mortal disease, the craft of some tricksters had been known to attain. To think that, under the aspect of infantile weakness, the most savage energies might be couched—those velvets of the Spaniard but the silky paw to his fangs.

From no train of thought did these fancies come; not from

within, but from without; suddenly, too, and in one throng, like hoar frost; yet as soon to vanish as the mild sun of Captain Delano's good-nature regained its meridian.

Glancing over once more towards his host—whose side-face, revealed above the skylight, was now turned towards him—he was struck by the profile, whose clearness of cut was refined by the thinness, incident to ill-health, as well as ennobled about the chin by the beard. Away with suspicion. He was a true off-shoot of a true hidalgo Cereno.

Relieved by these and other better thoughts, the visitor, lightly humming a tune, now began indifferently pacing the poop, so as not to betray to Don Benito that he had at all mistrusted incivility, much less duplicity; for such mistrust would yet be proved illusory, and by the event; though, for the present, the circumstance which had provoked that distrust remained unexplained. But when that little mystery should have been cleared up, Captain Delano thought he might extremely regret it, did he allow Don Benito to become aware that he had indulged in ungenerous surmises. In short, to the Spaniard's black-letter text, it was best, for awhile, to leave open margin.

Presently, his pale face twitching and overcast, the Spaniard, still supported by his attendant, moved over towards his guest, when, with even more than his usual embarrassment, and a strange sort of intriguing intonation in his husky whisper, the following conversation began:—

'Señor, may I ask how long you have lain at this isle?'

'Oh, but a day or two, Don Benito.'

'And from what port are you last?'

'Canton.'

'And there, Señor, you exchanged your sealskins for teas and silks, I think you said?'

'Yes, Silks, mostly.'

'And the balance you took in specie, perhaps?'

Captain Delano, fidgeting a little, answered—

'Yes; some silver; not a very great deal, though.'

'Ah—well. May I ask how many men have you, Señor?'

Captain Delano slightly startled, but answered—

'About five-and-twenty, all told.'

'And at present, Señor, all on board, I suppose?'

'All on board, Don Benito,' replied the Captain, now with satisfaction.

'And will be to-night, Señor?'

At this last question, following so many pertinacious ones, for

the soul of him, Captain Delano could not but look very earnestly
at the questioner, who, instead of meeting the glance, with every
token of craven discomposure dropped his eyes to the deck;
presenting an unworthy contrast to his servant, who, just then,
was kneeling at his feet, adjusting a loose shoe-buckle; his disengaged face meantime, with humble curiosity, turned openly up
into his master's downcast one.

The Spaniard, still with a guilty shuffle, repeated his question:
'And—and will be to-night, Señor?'

'Yes, for aught I know,' returned Captain Delano—'but nay,'
rallying himself into fearless truth, 'some of them talked of going
off on another fishing party about midnight.'

'Your ships generally go—go more or less armed, I believe,
Señor?'

'Oh, a six-pounder or two, in case of emergency,' was the
intrepidly indifferent reply, 'with a small stock of muskets, sealing-
spears, and cutlasses, you know.'

As he thus responded, Captain Delano again glanced at Don
Benito, but the latter's eyes were averted; while abruptly and
awkwardly shifting the subject, he made some peevish allusion to
the calm, and then, without apology, once more, with his attendant,
withdrew to the opposite bulwarks, where the whispering was
resumed.

At this moment, and ere Captain Delano could cast a cool
thought upon what had just passed, the young Spanish sailor,
before mentioned, was seen descending from the rigging. In act
of stooping over to spring inboard to the deck, his voluminous,
unconfined frock, or shirt, of coarse woolen, much spotted with
tar, opened out far down the chest revealing a soiled under garment
of what seemed the finest linen, edged, about the neck, with a
narrow blue ribbon, sadly faded and worn. At this moment the
young sailor's eye was again fixed on the whisperers, and Captain
Delano thought he observed a lurking significance in it, as if silent
signs, of some Freemason sort, had that instant been interchanged.

This once more impelled his own glance in the direction of
Don Benito, and, as before, he could not but infer that himself
formed the subject of the conference. He paused. The sound of
the hatchet-polishing fell on his ears. He cast another swift side-
look at the two. They had the air of conspirators. In connection
with the late questionings, and the incident of the young sailor,
these things now begat such return of involuntary suspicion, that
the singular guilelessness of the American could not endure it.
Plucking up a gay and humorous expression, he crossed over to

the two rapidly, saying:— 'Ha, Don Benito, your black here seems high in your trust; a sort of privy-counselor, in fact.'

Upon this, the servant looked up with a good-natured grin, but the master started as from a venomous bite. It was a moment or two before the Spaniard sufficiently recovered himself to reply; which he did, at last, with cold constraint:—'Yes, Señor, I have trust in Babo.'

Here Babo, changing his previous grin of mere animal humor into an intelligent smile, not ungratefully eyed his master.

Finding that the Spaniard now stood silent and reserved, as if involuntarily, or purposely giving hint that his guest's proximity was inconvenient just then, Captain Delano, unwilling to appear uncivil even to incivility itself, made some trivial remark and moved off; again and again turning over in his mind the mysterious demeanor of Don Benito Cereno.

He had descended from the poop, and, wrapped in thought, was passing near a dark hatchway, leading down into the steerage, when, perceiving motion there, he looked to see what moved. The same instant there was a sparkle in the shadowy hatchway, and he saw one of the Spanish sailors, prowling there, hurriedly placing his hand in the bosom of his frock, as if hiding something. Before the man could have been certain who it was that was passing, he slunk below out of sight. But enough was seen of him to make it sure that he was the same young sailor before noticed in the rigging.

What was that which so sparkled? thought Captain Delano. It was no lamp—no match—no live coal. Could it have been a jewel? But how come sailors with jewels?—or with silk-trimmed under-shirts either? Has he been robbing the trunks of the dead cabin-passengers? But if so, he would hardly wear one of the stolen articles on board ship here. Ah, ah—if, now, that was, indeed, a secret sign I saw passing between this suspicious fellow and his captain awhile since; if I could only be certain that, in my uneasiness, my senses did not deceive me, then—

Here, passing from one suspicious thing to another, his mind revolved the strange questions put to him concerning his ship.

By a curious coincidence, as each point was recalled, the black wizards of Ashantee would strike up with their hatchets, as in ominous comments on the white stranger's thoughts. Pressed by such enigmas and portents, it would have been almost against nature, had not, even into the least distrustful heart, some ugly misgivings obtruded.

Observing the ship, now helplessly fallen into a current, with enchanted sails, drifting with increased rapidity seaward; and noting that, from a lately intercepted projection of the land, the sealer was hidden, the stout mariner began to quake at thoughts which he barely durst confess to himself. Above all, he began to feel a ghostly dread of Don Benito. And yet, when he roused himself, dilated his chest, felt himself strong on his legs, and coolly considered it—what did all these phantoms amount to?

Had the Spaniard any sinister scheme, it must have reference not so much to him (Captain Delano) as to his ship (the *Bachelor's Delight*). Hence the present drifting away of the one ship from the other, instead of favoring any such possible scheme, was, for the time, at least, opposed to it. Clearly any suspicion, combining such contradictions, must need be delusive. Beside, was it not absurd to think of a vessel in distress—a vessel by sickness almost dismanned of her crew—a vessel whose inmates were parched for water—was it not a thousand times absurd that such a craft should, at present, be of a piratical character; or her commander, either for himself or those under him, cherish any desire but for speedy relief and refreshment? But then, might not general distress, and thirst in particular, be affected? And might not that same undiminished Spanish crew, alleged to have perished off to a remnant, be at that very moment lurking in the hold? On heart-broken pretense of entreating a cup of cold water, fiends in human form had got into lonely dwellings, nor retired until a dark deed had been done. And among the Malay pirates, it was no unusual thing to lure ships after them into their treacherous harbors, or entice boarders from a declared enemy at sea, by the spectacle of thinly manned or vacant decks, beneath which prowled a hundred spears with yellow arms ready to upthrust them through the mats. Not that Captain Delano had entirely credited such things. He had heard of them—and now, as stories, they recurred. The present destination of the ship was the anchorage. There she would be near his own vessel. Upon gaining that vicinity, might not the *San Dominick*, like a slumbering volcano, suddenly let loose energies now hid?

He recalled the Spaniard's manner while telling his story. There was a gloomy hesitancy and subterfuge about it. It was just the manner of one making up his tale for evil purposes, as he goes. But if that story was not true, what was the truth? That the ship had unlawfully come into the Spaniard's possession? But in many of its details, especially in reference to the more calamitous parts, such as the fatalities among the seamen, the consequent prolonged beating about, the past sufferings from obstinate calms, and still continued suffering from thirst; in all these points, as well as others, Don Benito's story had corroborated not only the wailing ejaculations of the indiscriminate multitude, white and black, but likewise—what seemed impossible to be counterfeit—by the very expression and play of every human feature, which Captain Delano saw. If Don Benito's story was, throughout, an invention, then every soul on board, down to the youngest negress, was his carefully drilled recruit in the plot: an incredible inference. And yet, if there was ground for mistrusting his veracity, that inference was a legitimate one.

But those questions of the Spaniard. There, indeed, one might pause. Did they not seem put with much the same object with which the burglar or assassin, by daytime, reconnoitres the walls of a house? But, with ill purposes, to solicit such information openly of the chief person endangered, and so, in effect, setting him on his guard; how unlikely a procedure was that? Absurd, then, to suppose that those questions had been prompted by evil designs. Thus, the same conduct, which, in this instance, had raised the alarm, served to dispel it. In short, scarce any suspicion or uneasiness, however apparently reasonable at the time, which was not now, with equal apparent reason, dismissed.

At last he began to laugh at his former forebodings; and laugh at the strange ship for, in its aspect, someway siding with them, as it were; and laugh, too, at the odd-looking blacks, particularly those old scissors-grinders, the Ashantees; and those bed-ridden old knitting women, the oakum-pickers; and almost at the dark Spaniard himself, the central hobgoblin of all.

For the rest, whatever in a serious way seemed enigmatical, was now good-naturedly explained away by the thought that, for the most part, the poor invalid scarcely knew what he was about; either sulking in black vapors, or putting idle questions without sense or object. Evidently, for the present, the man was not fit to be intrusted with the ship. On some benevolent plea withdrawing the command from him, Captain Delano would yet have to send her to Conception, in charge of his second mate, a worthy person and good navigator—a plan not more convenient for the *San Dominick* than for Don Benito; for, relieved from all anxiety, keeping wholly to his cabin, the sick man, under the good nursing of his servant, would, probably, by the end of the passage, be in a measure restored to health, and with that he should also be restored to authority.

Such were the American's thoughts. They were tranquilizing. There was a difference between the idea of Don Benito's darkly pre-ordaining Captain Delano's fate, and Captain Delano's lightly arranging Don Benito's. Nevertheless, it was not without something of relief that the good seaman presently perceived his whale-boat in the distance. Its absence had been prolonged by unexpected detention at the sealer's side, as well as its returning trip lengthened by the continual recession of the goal.

The advancing speck was observed by the blacks. Their shouts attracted the attention of Don Benito, who, with a return of courtesy, approaching Captain Delano, expressed satisfaction at the coming of some supplies, slight and temporary as they must necessarily prove.

Captain Delano responded; but while doing so, his attention was drawn to something passing on the deck below: among the crowd climbing the landward bulwarks, anxiously watching the coming boat, two blacks, to all appearances accidentally incommoded by one of the sailors, violently pushed him aside, which the sailor somewhat resenting, they dashed him to the deck, despite the earnest cries of the oakum-pickers.

'Don Benito,' said Captain Delano quickly, 'do you see what is going on there? Look!'

But, seized by his cough, the Spaniard staggered, with both hands to his face, on the point of falling. Captain Delano would have supported him, but the servant was more alert, who, with one hand sustaining his master, with the other applied the cordial. Don Benito restored, the black withdrew his support, slipping aside a little, but dutifully remaining within call of a whisper. Such discretion was here evinced as quite wiped away, in the visitor's eyes, any blemish of impropriety which might have attached to the attendant, from the indecorous conferences before mentioned; showing, too, that if the servant were to blame, it might be more the master's fault than his own, since, when left to himself, he could conduct thus well.

His glance called away from the spectacle of disorder to the more pleasing one before him, Captain Delano could not avoid again congratulating his host upon possessing such a servant, who, though perhaps a little too forward now and then, must upon the whole be invaluable to one in the invalid's situation.

'Tell me, Don Benito,' he added, with a smile—'I should like to have your man here, myself—what will you take for him? Would fifty doubloons be any object?'

'Master wouldn't part with Babo for a thousand doubloons,' murmured the black, overhearing the offer, and taking it in earnest, and, with the strange vanity of a faithful slave, appreciated by his master, scorning to hear so paltry a valuation put upon him by a stranger. But Don Benito, apparently hardly yet completely restored, and again interrupted by his cough, made but some broken reply.

Soon his physical distress became so great, affecting his mind, too, apparently, that, as if to screen the sad spectacle, the servant gently conducted his master below.

Left to himself, the American, to while away the time till his boat should arrive, would have pleasantly accosted some one of the few Spanish seamen he saw; but recalling something that Don Benito had said touching their ill conduct, he refrained; as a shipmaster indisposed to countenance cowardice or unfaithfulness in seamen.

While, with these thoughts, standing with eye directed forward towards that handful of sailors, suddenly he thought that one or two of them returned the glance and with a sort of meaning. He rubbed his eyes, and looked again; but again seemed to see the same thing. Under a new form, but more obscure than any previous one, the old suspicions recurred, but, in the absence of Don Benito, with less of panic than before. Despite the bad account given of the sailors, Captain Delano resolved forthwith to accost one of them. Descending the poop, he made his way through the blacks, his movement drawing a queer cry from the oakum-pickers, prompted by whom, the negroes, twitching each other aside, divided before him; but, as if curious to see what was the object of this deliberate visit to their Ghetto, closing in behind, in tolerable order, followed the white stranger up. His progress thus proclaimed as by mounted kings-at-arms, and escorted as by a Caffre guard of honor, Captain Delano, assuming a good-humored, offhanded air, continued to advance; now and then saying a blithe word to the negroes, and his eye curiously surveying the white faces, here and there sparsely mixed in with the blacks, like stray white pawns venturously involved in the ranks of the chess-men opposed.

While thinking which of them to select for his purpose, he chanced to observe a sailor seated on the deck engaged in tarring the strap of a large block, a circle of blacks squatted round him inquisitively eyeing the process.

The mean employment of the man was in contrast with something superior in his figure. His hand, black with continually thrusting it into the tar-pot held for him by a negro, seemed not naturally allied to his face, a face which would have been a very fine one but for its haggardness. Whether this haggardness had aught to do with criminality, could not be determined; since, as intense heat and cold, though unlike, produce like sensations, so innocence and guilt, when, through casual association with mental pain, stamping any visible impress, use one seal—a hacked one.

Not again that this reflection occurred to Captain Delano at the time, charitable man as he was. Rather another idea. Because observing so singular a haggardness combined with a dark eye, averted as in trouble and shame, and then again recalling Don Benito's confessed ill opinion of his crew, insensibly he was operated upon by certain general notions which, while disconnecting pain and abashment from virtue, invariably link them with vice.

If, indeed, there be any wickedness on board this ship, thought Captain Delano, be sure that man there has fouled his hand in it, even as now he fouls it in the pitch. I don't like to accost him. I will speak to this other, this old Jack here on the windlass.

He advanced to an old Barcelona tar, in ragged red breeches and dirty night-cap, cheeks trenched and bronzed, whiskers dense as thorn hedges. Seated between two sleepy-looking Africans, this mariner, like his younger shipmate, was employed upon some rigging—splicing a cable—the sleepy-looking blacks performing the inferior function of holding the outer parts of the ropes for him.

Upon Captain Delano's approach, the man at once hung his head below its previous level; the one necessary for business. It appeared as if he desired to be thought absorbed, with more than common fidelity, in his task. Being addressed, he glanced up, but with what seemed a furtive, diffident air, which sat strangely enough on his weather-beaten visage, much as if a grizzly bear, instead of growling and biting, should simper and cast sheep's eyes. He was asked several questions concerning the voyage—questions purposely referring to several particulars in Don Benito's narrative, not previously corroborated by those impulsive cries greeting the visitor on first coming on board. The questions were briefly answered, confirming all that remained to be confirmed of the story. The negroes about the windlass joined in with the old sailor; but, as they became talkative, he by degrees became mute, and at length quite glum, seemed morosely unwilling to answer more questions, and yet, all the while, this ursine air was somehow mixed with his sheepish one.

Despairing of getting into unembarrassed talk with such a centaur, Captain Delano, after glancing round for a more promising countenance, but seeing none, spoke pleasantly to the blacks to make way for him; and so, amid various grins and grimaces, returned to the poop, feeling a little strange at first, he could hardly tell why, but upon the whole with regained confidence in Benito Cereno.

How plainly, thought he, did that old whiskerando yonder betray a consciousness of ill desert. No doubt, when he saw me coming, he dreaded lest I, apprised by his Captain of the crew's general misbehaviour, came with sharp words for him, and so down with his head. And yet—and yet, now that I think of it, that very old fellow, if I err not, was one of those who seemed so earnestly eyeing me here awhile since. Ah, these currents spin one's head round almost as much as they do the ship. Ha, there now's a pleasant sort of sunny sight; quite sociable, too.

His attention had been drawn to a slumbering negress, partly disclosed through the lace-work of some rigging, lying, with youthful limbs carelessly disposed, under the lee of the bulwarks, like a doe in the shade of a woodland rock. Sprawling at her lapped breasts, was her wide-awake fawn, stark naked, its black little body half lifted from the deck, crosswise with its dam's; its hands, like two paws, clambering upon her; its mouth and nose ineffectually rooting to get at the mark; and meantime giving a vexatious half-grunt, blending with the composed snore of the negress.

The uncommon vigor of the child at length roused the mother. She started up, at a distance facing Captain Delano. But as if not at all concerned at the attitude in which she had been caught, delightedly she caught the child up, with maternal transports, covering it with kisses.

There's naked nature, now; pure tendernes and love, thought Captain Delano, well pleased.

This incident prompted him to remark the other negresses more particularly than before. He was gratified with their manners: like most uncivilized women, they seemed at once tender of heart and tough of constitution; equally ready to die for their infants or fight for them. Unsophisticated as leopardesses; loving as doves. Ah! thought Captain Delano, these, perhaps, are some of the very women whom Ledyard saw in Africa, and gave such a noble account of.

These natural sights somehow insensibly deepened his confidence and ease. At last he looked to see how his boat was getting on; but it was still pretty remote. He turned to see if Don Benito had returned; but he had not.

To change the scene, as well as to please himself with a leisurely observation of the coming boat, stepping over into the mizzen-chains, he clambered his way into the starboard quarter-gallery— one of those abandoned Venetian-looking water-balconies previ-

ously mentioned—retreats cut off from the deck. As his foot pressed
the half-damp, half-dry sea-mosses matting the place, and a chance
phantom cat's-paw—an islet of breeze, unheralded, unfollowed—
as this ghostly cat's-paw came fanning his cheek; as his glance fell
upon the row of small, round dead-lights—all closed like coppered
eyes of the coffined—and the state-cabin door, once connecting
with the gallery, even as the dead-lights had once looked out upon
it, but now calked fast like a sarcophagus lid; and to a purple-
black tarred-over panel, threshold, and post; and he bethought
him of the time, when that state-cabin and this state-balcony had
heard the voices of the Spanish king's officers, and the forms of
the Lima viceroy's daughters had perhaps leaned where he stood—
as these and other images flitted through his mind, as the cat's-
paw through the calm, gradually he felt rising a dreamy inquietude,
like that of one who alone on the prairie feels unrest from the
repose of the noon.

He leaned against the carved balustrade, again looking off toward
his boat; but found his eye falling upon the ribbon grass, trailing
along the ship's water-line, straight as a border of green box; and
parterres of sea-weed, broad ovals and crescents, floating nigh and
far, with what seemed long formal alleys between, crossing the
terraces of swells, and sweeping round as if leading to the grottoes
below. And overhanging all was the balustrade by his arm, which,
partly stained with pitch and partly embossed with moss, seemed
the charred ruin of some summer-house in a grand garden long
running to waste.

Trying to break one charm, he was but becharmed anew. Though
upon the wide sea, he seemed in some far inland country; prisoner
in some deserted château, left to stare at empty grounds, and peer
out at vague roads, where never wagon or wayfarer passed.

But these enchantments were a little disenchanted as his eye
fell on the corroded main-chains. Of an ancient style, massy and
rusty in link, shackle and bolt, they seemed even more fit for the
ship's present business than the one for which she had been built.

Presently he thought something moved nigh the chains. He
rubbed his eyes, and looked hard. Groves of rigging were about
the chains; and there, peering from behind a great stay, like an
Indian from behind a hemlock, a Spanish sailor, a marlingspike
in his hand, was seen, who made what seemed an imperfect gesture
towards the balcony, but immediately, as if alarmed by some
advancing step along the deck within, vanished into the recesses
of the hempen forest, like a poacher.

What meant this? Something the man had sought to commu-

nicate, unbeknown to any one, even to his captain. Did the secret
involve aught unfavorable to his captain? Were those previous
misgivings of Captain Delano's about to be verified? Or, in his
haunted mood at the moment, had some random, unintentional
motion of the man, while busy with the stay, as if repairing it,
been mistaken for a significant beckoning?

Not unbewildered, again he gazed off for his boat. But it was
temporarily hidden by a rocky spur of the isle. As with some
eagerness he bent forward, watching for the first shooting view of
its beak, the balustrade gave way before him like charcoal. Had
he not clutched an out-reaching rope he would have fallen into
the sea. The crash, though feeble, and the fall, though hollow, of
the rotten fragments, must have been overheard. He glanced up.
With sober curiosity peering down upon him was one of the old
oakum-pickers, slipped from his perch to an outside boom; while
below the old negro, and, invisible to him, reconnoitering from
a port-hole like a fox from the mouth of its den, crouched the
Spanish sailor again. From something suddenly suggested by the
man's air, the mad idea now darted into Captain Delano's mind,
that Don Benito's plea of indisposition, in withdrawing below,
was but a pretense: that he was engaged there maturing his plot,
of which the sailor, by some means gaining an inkling, had a
mind to warn the stranger against; incited, it may be, by gratitude
for a kind word on first boarding the ship. Was it from foreseeing
some possible interference like this, that Don Benito had, beforehand, given such a bad character of his sailors, whie praising the
negroes; though, indeed, the former seemed as docile as the latter
the contrary? The whites, too, by nature, were the shrewder race.
A man with some evil design, would he not be likely to speak
well of that stupidity which was blind to his depravity, and malign
that intelligence from which it might not be hidden? Not unlikely,
perhaps. But if the whites had dark secrets concerning Don Benito,
could then Don Benito be any way in complicity with the blacks?
But they were too stupid. Besides, who ever heard of a white so
far a renegade as to apostatize from his very species almost, by
leaguing in against it with negroes? These difficulties recalled former
ones. Lost in their mazes, Captain Delano, who had now regained
the deck, was uneasily advancing along it, when he observed a
new face; an aged sailor seated cross-legged near the main hatchway. His skin was shrunk up with wrinkles like a pelican's empty
pouch; his hair frosted; his countenance grave and composed. His
hands were full of ropes, which he was working into a large knot.
Some blacks were about him obligingly dipping the strands for

him, here and there, as the exigencies of the operation demanded.

Captain Delano crossed over to him, and stood in silence surveying the knot; his mind, by a not uncongenial transition, passing from its own entanglements to those of the hemp. For intricacy, such a knot he had never seen in an American ship, nor indeed any other. The old man looked like an Egyptian priest, making Gordian knots for the temple of Ammon. The knot seemed a combination of double-bowline-knot, treble-crown-knot, back-handed-well-knot, knot-in-and-out-knot, and jamming-knot.

At last, puzzled to comprehend the meaning of such a knot, Captain Delano addressed the knotter:—

'What are you knotting there, my man?'

'The knot,' was the brief reply, without looking up.

'So it seems; but what is it for?'

'For some one else to undo,' muttered back the old man, plying his fingers harder than ever, the knot being now nearly completed.

While Captain Delano stood watching him, suddenly the old man threw the knot towards him, saying in broken English—the first heard in the ship—something to this effect: 'Undo it, cut it, quick.' It was said lowly, but with such condensation of rapidity, that the long, slow words in Spanish, which had preceded and followed, almost operated as covers to the brief English between.

For a moment, knot in hand, and knot in head, Captain Delano stood mute; while, without further heeding him, the old man was now intent upon other ropes. Presently there was a slight stir behind Captain Delano. Turning, he saw the chained negro, Atufal, standing quietly there. The next moment the old sailor rose, muttering, and, followed by his subordinate negroes, removed to the forward part of the ship, where in the crowd he disappeared.

An elderly negro, in a clout like an infant's, and with a pepper and salt head, and a kind of attorney air, now approached Captain Delano. In tolerable Spanish, and with a good-natured, knowing wink, he informed him that the old knotter was simple-witted, but harmless; often playing his odd tricks. The negro concluded by begging the knot, for of course the stranger would not care to be troubled with it. Unconsciously, it was handed to him. With a sort of congé, the negro received it, and, turning his back, ferreted into it like a detective customhouse officer after smuggled laces. Soon, with some African word, equivalent to pshaw, he tossed the knot overboard.

All this is very queer now, thought Captain Delano, with a qualmish sort of emotion; but, as one feeling incipient seasickness, he strove, by ignoring the symptoms, to get rid of the malady.

Once more he looked off for his boat. To his delight, it was now again in view, leaving the rocky spur astern.

The sensation here experienced, after at first relieving his uneasiness, with unforseen efficacy soon began to remove it. The less distant sight of that well-known boat—showing it, not as before, half blended with the haze, but with outline defined, so that its individuality, like a man's, was manifest; that boat, *Rover* by name, which, though now in strange seas, had often pressed the beach of Captain Delano's home, and, brought to its threshold for repairs, had familiarly lain there, as a Newfoundland dog; the sight of that household boat evoked a thousand trustful associations, which, contrasted with previous suspicions, filled him not only with lightsome confidence, but somehow with half humorous self-reproaches at his former lack of it.

'What, I, Amasa Delano—Jack of the Beach, as they called me when a lad—I, Amasa; the same that, duck-satchel in hand, used to paddle along the water-side to the school-house made from the old hulk—I, little Jack of the Beach, that used to go berrying with cousin Nat and the rest; I to be murdered here at the ends of the earth, on board a haunted pirate-ship by a horrible Spaniard? Too nonsensical to think of! Who would murder Amasa Delano? His conscience is clean. There is some one above. Fie, fie, Jack of the Beach! you are a child indeed; a child of the second childhood, old boy; you are beginning to dote and drule, I'm afraid.'

Light of heart and foot, he stepped aft, and there was met by Don Benito's servant, who, with a pleasing expression, responsive to his own present feelings, informed him that his master had recovered from the effects of his coughing fit, and had just ordered him to go present his compliments to his good quest, Don Amasa, and say that he (Don Benito) would soon have the happiness to rejoin him.

There now, do you mark that? again thought Captain Delano, walking the poop. What a donkey I was. This kind gentleman who here sends me his kind compliments, he, but ten minutes ago, dark-lantern in hand, was dodging round some old grindstone in the hold, sharpening a hatchet for me, I thought. Well, well; these long calms have a morbid effect on the mind, I've often heard, though I never believed it before. Ha! glancing towards the boat; there's *Rover*; good dog; a white bone in her mouth. A pretty big bone though, seems to me.—What? Yes, she has fallen afoul of the bubbling tide-rip there. It sets her the other way, too, for the time. Patience.

It was now about noon, though, from the grayness of everything, it seemed to be getting towards dusk.

The calm was confirmed. In the far distance, away from the influence of land, the leaden ocean seemed laid out and leaded up, its course finished, soul gone, defunct. But the current from landward, where the ship was, increased; silently sweeping her further and further towards the tranced waters beyond.

Still, from his knowledge of those latitudes, cherishing hopes of a breeze, and a fair and fresh one, at any moment, Captain Delano, despite present prospects, buoyantly counted upon bringing the *San Dominick* safely to anchor ere night. The distance swept over was nothing; since, with a good wind, ten minutes' sailing would retrace more than sixty minutes' drifting. Meantime, one moment turning to mark *Rover* fighting the tide-rip, and the next to see Don Benito approaching, he continued walking the poop.

Gradually he felt a vexation arising from the delay of his boat; this soon merged into uneasiness; and at last—his eye falling continually, as from a stage-box into the pit, upon the strange crowd before and below him, and, by-and-by, recognizing there the face—now composed to indifference—of the Spanish sailor who had seemed to beckon from the main-chains—something of his old trepidations returned.

Ah, thought he—gravely enough—this is like the ague: because it went off, it follows not that it won't come back.

Though ashamed of the relapse, he could not altogether subdue it; and so, exerting his good-nature to the utmost, insensibly he came to a compromise.

Yes, this is a strange craft; a strange history, too, and strange folks on board. But—nothing more.

By way of keeping his mind out of mischief till the boat should arrive, he tried to occupy it with turning over and over, in a purely speculative sort of way, some lesser peculiarities of the captain and crew. Among others, four curious points recurred:

First, the affair of the Spanish lad assailed with a knife by the slave boy; an act winked at by Don Benito. Second, the tyranny in Don Benito's treatment of Atufal, the black; as if a child should lead a bull of the Nile by the ring in his nose. Third, the trampling of the sailor by the two negroes; a piece of insolence passed over without so much as a reprimand. Fourth, the cringing submission to their master of all the ship's underlings, mostly blacks; as if by the least inadvertence they feared to draw down his despotic displeasure.

Coupling these points, they seemed somewhat contradictory. But what then, thought Captain Delano, glancing towards his now nearing boat—what then? Why, Don Benito is a very capricious commander. But he is not the first of the sort I have seen; though it's true he rather exceeds any other. But as a nation—continued he in his reveries—these Spaniards are all an odd set; the very word Spaniard has a curious, conspirator, Guy-Fawkish twang to it. And yet, I dare say, Spaniards in the main are as good folks as any in Duxbury, Massachusetts. Ah good! At last *Rover* has come.

As, with its welcome freight, the boat touched the side, the oakum-pickers, with venerable gestures, sought to restrain the blacks, who, at the sight of three gurried water-casks in its bottom, and a pile of wilted pumpkins in its bow, hung over the bulwarks in disorderly raptures.

Don Benito, with his servant, now appeared; his coming, perhaps, hastened by hearing the noise. Of him Captain Delano sought permission to serve out the water, so that all might share alike, and none injure themselves by unfair excess. But sensible, and, on Don Benito's account, kind as this offer was, it was received with what seemed impatience; as if aware that he lacked energy as a commander, Don Benito, with the true jealousy of weakness, resented as an affront any interference. So, at least, Captain Delano inferred.

In another moment the casks were being hoisted in, when some of the eager negroes accidentally jostled Captain Delano, where he stood by the gangway; so that, unmindful of Don Benito, yielding to the impulse of the moment, with good-natured authority he bade the blacks stand back; to enforce his words making use of a half-mirthful, half-menacing gesture. Instantly the blacks paused, just where they were, each negro and negress suspended in his or her posture, exactly as the world had found them—for a few seconds continuing so—while, as between the responsive posts of a telegraph, an unknown syllable ran from man to man among the perched oakum-pickers. While the visitor's attention was fixed by this scene, suddenly the hatchet-polishers half rose, and a rapid cry came from Don Benito.

Thinking that at the signal of the Spaniard he was about to be massacred, Captain Delano would have sprung for his boat, but paused, as the oakum-pickers, dropping down into the crowd with earnest exclamations, forced every white and every negro back, at the same moment, with gestures friendly and familiar, almost jocose, bidding him, in substance, not be a fool. Simultaneously the hatchet-polishers resumed their seats, quietly as so many tailors, and at once, as if nothing had happened, the work of hoisting in the casks was resumed, whites and blacks singing at the tackle.

Captain Delano glanced towards Don Benito. As he saw his meagre form in the act of recovering itself from reclining in the servant's arms, into which the agitated invalid had fallen, he could not but marvel at the panic by which himself had been surprised, on the darting supposition that such a commander, who, upon a legitimate occasion, so trivial, too, as it now appeared, could lose all self-command, was, with energetic iniquity, going to bring about his murder.

The casks being on deck, Captain Delano was handed a number of jars and cups by one of the steward's aids, who, in the name of his captain, entreated him to do as he had proposed—dole out the water. He complied, with republican impartiality as to this republican element, which always seeks one level, serving the oldest white no better than the youngest black; excepting, indeed, poor Don Benito, whose condition, if not rank, demanded an extra allowance. To him, in the first place, Captain Delano presented a fair pitcher of the fluid; but, thirsting as he was for it, the Spaniard quaffed not a drop until after several grave bows and salutes. A reciprocation of courtesies which the sight-loving Africans hailed with clapping of hands.

Two of the less wilted pumpkins being reserved for the cabin table, the residue were minced up on the spot for the general regalement. But the soft bread, sugar, and bottled cider, Captain Delano would have given the whites alone, and in chief Don Benito; but the latter objected; which disinterestedness not a little pleased the American; and so mouthfuls all around were given alike to whites and blacks; excepting one bottle of cider, which Babo insisted upon setting aside for his master.

Here it may be observed that as, on the first visit of the boat, the American had not permitted his men to board the ship, neither did he now; being unwilling to add to the confusion of the decks.

Not uninfluenced by the peculiar good-humor at present prevailing, and for the time oblivious of any but benevolent thoughts, Captain Delano, who, from recent indications, counted upon a breeze within an hour or two at furthest, dispatched the boat back to the sealer, with orders for all the hands that could be spared immediately to set about rafting casks to the watering-place and filling them. Likewise he bade word be carried to his chief officer, that if, against present expectation, the ship was not brought to anchor by sunset, he need be under no concern; for as there was to be a full moon that night, he (Captain Delano) would remain on board ready to play the pilot, come the wind soon or late.

As the two Captains stood together, observing the departing boat—the servant, as it happened, having just spied a spot on his master's velvet sleeve, and silently engaged in rubbing it out—the American expressed his regrets that the *San Dominick* had no boats; none, at least, but the unseaworthy old hulk of the long-boat, which, warped as a camel's skeleton in the desert, and almost as bleached, lay pot-wise inverted amidships, one side a little tipped, furnishing a subterranean sort of den for family groups of the blacks, mostly women and small children; who, squatting on old mats below, or perched above in the dark dome, on the elevated seats, were descried, some distance within, like a social circle of bats, sheltering in some friendly cave; at intervals, ebon flights of naked boys and girls, three or four years old, darting in and out of the den's mouth.

'Had you three or four boats now, Don Benito,' said Captain Delano, 'I think that, by tugging at the oars, your negroes here might help along matters some. Did you sail from port without boats, Don Benito?'

'They were stove in the gales, Señor.'

'That was bad. Many men, too, you lost then. Boats and men. Those must have been hard gales, Don Benito.'

'Past all speech,' cringed the Spaniard.

'Tell me, Don Benito,' continued his companion with increased interest, 'tell me, were these gales immediately off the pitch of Cape Horn?'

'Cape Horn?—who spoke of Cape Horn?'

'Yourself did, when giving me an account of your voyage,' answered Captain Delano, with almost equal astonishment at this eating of his own words, even as he ever seemed eating his own heart, on the part of the Spaniard. 'You yourself, Don Benito, spoke of Cape Horn,' he emphatically repeated.

The Spaniard turned, in a sort of stooping posture, pausing an instant, as one about to make a plunging exchange of elements, as from air to water.

At this moment a messenger-boy, a white, hurried by, in the regular performance of his function carrying the last expired half hour forward to the forecastle, from the cabin time-piece, to have it struck at the ship's large bell.

'Master,' said the servant, discontinuing his work on the coat sleeve, and addressing the rapt Spaniard with a sort of timid apprehensiveness, as one charged with a duty, the discharge of which, it was foreseen, would prove irksome to the very person who had imposed it, and for whose benefit it was intended, 'master told me never mind where he was, or how engaged, always to remind him, to a minute, when shaving-time comes. Miguel has gone to strike the half-hour afternoon. It is *now* master. Will master go into the cuddy?'

'Ah—yes,' answered the Spaniard, starting, as from dreams into realities; then turning upon Captain Delano, he said that ere long he would resume the conversation.

'Then if master means to talk more to Don Amasa,' said the servant, 'why not let Don Amasa sit by master in the cuddy, and master can talk, and Don Amasa can listen, while Babo here lathers and strops.'

'Yes,' said Captain Delano, not unpleased with this social plan, 'yes, Don Benito, unless you had rather not, I will go with you.'

'Be it so, Señor.'

As the three passed aft, the American could not but think it another strange instance of his host's capriciousness, this being shaved with such uncommon punctuality in the middle of the day. But he deemed it more than likely that the servant's anxious fidelity had something to do with the matter; inasmuch as the timely interruption served to rally his master from the mood which had evidently been coming upon him.

The place called the cuddy was a light deck-cabin formed by the poop, a sort of attic to the large cabin below. Part of it had formerly been the quarters of the officers; but since their death all the partitionings had been thrown down, and the whole interior converted into one spacious and airy marine hall, for absence of fine furniture and picturesque disarray of odd appurtenances, somewhat answering to the wide, cluttered hall of some eccentric bachelor-squire in the country, who hangs his shooting-jacket and tobacco-pouch on deer antlers, and keeps his fishing-rod, tongs, and walking-stick in the same corner.

The similitude was heightened, if not originally suggested, by glimpses of the surrounding sea; since, in one aspect, the country and the ocean seem cousins-german.

The floor of the cuddy was matted. Overhead, four or five old muskets were stuck into horizontal holes along the beams. On one side was a claw-footed old table lashed to the deck; a thumbed missal on it, and over it a small, meagre crucifix attached to the bulk-head. Under the table lay a dented cutlass or two, with a hacked harpoon, among some melancholy old rigging, like a heap of poor friars' girdles. There were also two long, sharp-ribbed settees of Malacca cane, black with age, and uncomfortable to look at as inquisitors' racks, with a large, misshapen arm-chair, which, furnished with a rude barber's crotch at the back, working with a screw, seemed some grotesque engine of torment. A flag locker was in one corner, open, exposing various colored bunting, some rolled up, others half unrolled, still others tumbled. Opposite was a cumbrous washstand, of black mahogany, all of one block, with a pedestal, like a font, and over it a railed shelf, containing combs, brushes, and other implements of the toilet. A torn hammock of stained grass swung near; the sheets tossed, and the pillow wrinkled up like a brow, as if whoever slept here slept but illy, with alternate visitations of sad thoughts and bad dreams.

The further extremity of the cuddy, overhanging the ship's stern, was pierced with three openings, windows or port-holes, according as men or cannon might peer, socially or unsocially, out of them. At present neither men nor cannon were seen, though huge ringbolts and other rusty iron fixtures of the wood-work hinted of twenty-four-pounders.

Glancing towards the hammock as he entered, Captain Delano said, 'You sleep here, Don Benito?'

'Yes, Señor, since we got into mild weather.'

'This seems a sort of dormitory, sitting-room, sail-loft, chapel, armory, and private closet all together, Don Benito,' added Captain Delano, looking round.

'Yes, Señor; events have not been favorable to much order in my arrangements.'

Here the servant, napkin on arm, made a motion as if waiting his master's good pleasure. Don Benito signified his readiness, when, seating him in the Malacca armchair, and for the guest's convenience drawing opposite one of the settees, the servant commenced operations by throwing back his master's collar and loosening his cravat.

There is something in the negro which, in a peculiar way, fits him for avocations about one's person. Most negroes are natural valets and hair-dressers; taking to the comb and brush congenially as to the castinets, and flourishing them apparently with almost equal satisfaction. There is, too, a smooth tact about them in this employment, with a marvelous, noiseless, gliding briskness, not ungraceful in its way, singularly pleasing to behold, and still more so to be the manipulated subject of. And above all is the great gift of good-humor. Not the mere grin or laugh is here meant. Those were unsuitable. But a certain easy cheerfulness, harmonious in every glance and gesture; as though God had set the whole negro to some pleasant tune.

When to this is added the docility arising from the unaspiring contentment of a limited mind, and that susceptibility of bland attachment sometimes inhering in indisputable inferiors, one readily perceives why those hypochondriacs, Johnson and Byron—it may be, something like the hypochondriac Benito Cereno—took to their hearts, almost to the exclusion of the entire white race, their serving men, the negroes, Barber and Fletcher. But if there be that in the negro which exempts him from the inflicted sourness of the morbid or cynical mind, how, in his most prepossessing aspects, must he appear to a benevolent one? When at ease with respect to exterior things, Captain Delano's nature was not only benign, but familiarly and humorously so. At home, he had often taken rare satisfaction in sitting in his door, watching some free man of color at his work or play. If on a voyage he chanced to have a black sailor, invariably he was on chatty and half-gamesome terms with him. In fact, like most men of a good, blithe heart, Captain Delano took to negroes, not philanthropically, but genially, just as other men to Newfoundland dogs.

Hitherto, the circumstances in which he found the *San Dominick* had repressed the tendency. But in the cuddy, relieved from his former uneasiness, and, for various reasons, more sociably inclined than at any previous period of the day, and seeing the colored servant, napkin on arm, so debonair about his master, in a business so familiar as that of shaving, too, all his old weakness for negroes returned.

Among other things, he was amused with an odd instance of the African love of bright colors and fine shows, in the black's informally taking from the flag-locker a great piece of bunting of all hues, and lavishly tucking it under his master's chin for an apron.

The mode of shaving among the Spaniards is a little different from what it is with other nations. They have a basin, specifically called a barber's basin, which on one side is scooped out, so as accurately to receive the chin, against which it is closely held in lathering; which is done, not with a brush, but with soap dipped in the water of the basin and rubbed on the face.

In the present instance salt-water was used for lack of better; and the parts lathered were only the upper lip, and low down under the throat, all the rest being cultivated beard.

The preliminaries being somewhat novel to Captain Delano, he sat curiously eyeing them, so that no conversation took place, nor, for the present, did Don Benito appear disposed to renew any.

Setting down his basin, the negro searched among the razors, as for the sharpest, and having found it, gave it an additional edge by expertly strapping it on the firm, smooth, oily skin of his open palm; he then made a gesture as if to begin, but midway stood suspended for an instant, one hand elevating the razor, the other professionally dabbling among the bubbling suds on the Spaniard's lank neck. Not unaffected by the close sight of the gleaming steel, Don Benito nervously shuddered; his usual ghastliness was heightened by the lather, which lather, again, was intensified in its hue by the contrasting sootiness of the negro's body. Altogether the scene was somewhat peculiar, at least to Captain Delano, nor, as he saw the two thus postured, could he resist the vagary, that in the black he saw a headsman, and in the white a man at the block. But this was one of those antic conceits, appearing and vanishing in a breath, from which, perhaps, the best regulated mind is not aways free.

Meantime the agitation of the Spaniard had a little loosened the bunting from around him, so that one broad fold swept curtain-like over the chair-arm to the floor, revealing, amid a profusion of armorial bars and ground-colors—black, blue, and yellow—a closed castle in a blood-red field diagonal with a lion rampant in a white.

'The castle and the lion,' exclaimed Captain Delano—'why, Don Benito, this is the flag of Spain you use here. It's well it's only I, and not the King, that sees this,' he added, with a smile, 'but'—turning towards the black—'it's all one, I suppose, so the colors be gay;' which playful remark did not fail somewhat to tickle the negro.

'Now, master,' he said, readjusting the flag, and pressing the head gently further back into the crotch of the chair; 'now, master,' and the steel glanced nigh the throat.

Again Don Benito faintly shuddered.

'You must not shake so, master. See, Don Amasa, master always shakes when I shave him. And yet master knows I never yet have drawn blood, though it's true, if master will shake so, I may some of these times. Now master,' he continued. 'And now, Don Amasa, please go on with your talk about the gale, and all that; master can hear, and, between times, master can answer.'

'Ah yes, these gales,' said Captain Delano; 'but the more I think of your voyage, Don Benito, the more I wonder, not at the gales, terrible as they must have been, but at the disastrous interval following them. For here, by your account, have you been these two months and more getting from Cape Horn to St Maria, a distance which I myself, with a good wind, have sailed in a few days. True, you had calms, and long ones, but to be becalmed for two months, that is, at least, unusual. Why, Don Benito, had almost any other gentleman told me such a story, I should have been half disposed to a little incredulity.'

Here an involuntary expression came over the Spaniard, similar to that just before on the deck, and whether it was the start he gave, or a sudden gawky roll of the hull in the calm, or a momentary unsteadiness of the servant's hand, however it was, just then the razor drew blood, spots of which stained the creamy lather under the throat; immediately the black barber drew back his steel, and, remaining in his professional attitude, back to Captain Delano, and face to Don Benito, held up the trickling razor, saying, with a sort of half humorous sorrow, 'See, master—you shook so—here's Babo's first blood.'

No sword drawn before James the First of England, no assassination in that timid King's presence, could have produced a more terrified aspect than was now presented by Don Benito.

Poor fellow, thought Captain Delano, so nervous he can't even bear the sight of barber's blood; and this unstrung, sick man, is it credible that I should have imagined he meant to spill all my blood, who can't endure the sight of one little drop of his own? Surely, Amasa Delano, you have been beside yourself this day. Tell it not when you get home, sappy Amasa. Well, well, he looks like a murderer, doesn't he? More like as if himself were to be done for. Well, well, this day's experience shall be a good lesson.

Meantime, while these things were running through the honest seaman's mind, the servant had taken the napkin from his arm, and to Don Benito he said—,'But answer Don Amasa, please, master, while I wipe this ugly stuff off the razor, and strop it again.'

As he said the words, his face was turned half round, so as to be alike visible to the Spaniard and the American, and seemed, by its expression, to hint, that he was desirous, by getting his master to go on with the conversation, considerately to withdraw his attention from the recent annoying accident. As if glad to snatch the offered relief, Don Benito resumed to Captain Delano, that not only were the calms of unusual duration, but the ship had fallen in with obstinate currents; and other things he added, some of which were but repetitions of former statements, to explain how it came to pass that the passage from Cape Horn to St Maria had been so exceedingly long; now and then mingling with his words, incidental praises, less qualified than before, to the blacks, for their general good conduct. These particulars were not given consecutively, the servant, at convenient times, using his razor, and so, between the intervals of shaving, the story and panegyric went on with more than usual huskiness.

To Captain Delano's imagination, now again not wholly at rest, there was something so hollow in the Spaniard's manner, with apparently some reciprocal hollowness in the servant's dusky comment of silence, that the idea flashed across him, that possibly master and man, for some unknown purpose, were acting out, both in word and deed, nay, to the very tremor of Don Benito's limbs, some juggling play before him. Neither did the suspicion of collusion lack apparent support, from the fact of those whispered conferences before mentioned. But then, what could be the object of enacting this play of the barber before him? At last, regarding the notion as a whimsy, insensibly suggested, perhaps, by the theatrical aspect of Don Benito in his harlequin ensign, Captain Delano speedily banished it.

The shaving over, the servant bestirred himself with a small bottle of scented waters, pouring a few drops on the head, and then diligently rubbing; the vehemence of the exercise causing the muscles of his face to twitch rather strangely.

His next operation was with comb, scissors, and brush; going round and round, smoothing a curl here, cliping an unruly whisker-hair there, giving a graceful sweep to the temple-lock, with other impromptu touches evincing the hand of a master; while, like any resigned gentleman in barber's hands, Don Benito bore all, much less uneasily, at least, than he had done the razoring; indeed, he sat so pale and rigid now, that the negro seemed a Nubian sculptor finishing off a white statue-head.

All being over at last, the standard of Spain removed, tumbled over, and tossed back into the flag-locker, the negro's warm breath blowing away any stray hair which might have lodged down his master's neck; collar and cravat readjusted; a speck of lint whisked off the velvet lapel; all this being done; backing off a little space, and pausing with an expression of subdued self-complacency, the servant for a moment surveyed his master, as, in toilet at least, the creature of his own tasteful hands.

Captain Delano playfully complimented him upon his achievement; at the same time congratulating Don Benito.

But neither sweet waters, nor shampooing, nor fidelity, nor sociality, delighted the Spaniard. Seeing him relapsing into forbidding gloom, and still remaining seated, Captain Delano, thinking that his presence was undesired just then, withdrew, on pretense of seeing whether, as he had prophesied, any signs of a breeze were visible.

Walking forward to the main-mast, he stood awhile thinking over the scene, and not without some undefined misgivings, when he heard a noise near the cuddy, and turning, saw the negro, his hand to his cheek. Advancing, Captain Delano perceived that the cheek was bleeding. He was about to ask the cause, when the negro's wailing soliloquy enlightened him.

'Ah, when will master get better from his sickness; only the sour heart that sour sickness breeds made him serve Babo so; cutting Babo with the razor, because, only by accident, Babo had given master one little scratch; and for the first time in so many a day, too. Ah, ah, ah,' holding his hand to his face.

Is it possible, thought Captain Delano; was it to wreak in private his Spanish spite against this poor friend of his, that Don Benito, by his sullen manner, impelled me to withdraw? Ah, this slavery breeds ugly passions in man.—Poor fellow!

He was about to speak in sympathy to the negro, but with a timid reluctance he now re-entered the cuddy.

Presently master and man came forth; Don Benito leaning on his servant as if nothing had happened.

But a sort of love-quarrel, after all, thought Captain Delano.

He accosted Don Benito, and they slowly walked together. They had gone but a few paces, when the steward—a tall, rajah-looking mulatto, orientally set off with a pagoda turban formed by three or four Madras handkerchiefs wound about his head, tier on tier—approaching with a saalam, announced lunch in the cabin.

On their way thither, the two captains were preceded by the mulatto, who, turning round as he advanced, with continual smiles and bows, ushered them on, a display of elegance which quite completed the insignificance of the small bare-headed Babo, who, as if not unconscious of inferiority, eyed askance the graceful steward. But in part, Captain Delano imputed his jealous watchfulness to that peculiar feeling which the full-blooded African entertains for the adulterated one. As for the steward, his manner, if not bespeaking much dignity or self-respect, yet evidenced his extreme desire to please; which is doubly meritorious, as at once Christian and Chesterfieldian.

Captain Delano observed with interest that while the complexion of the mulatto was hybrid, his physiognomy was European—classically so.

'Don Benito,' whispered he, 'I am glad to see this usher-of-the-golden-rod of yours; the sight refutes an ugly remark once made to me by a Barbadoes planter; that when a mulatto has a regular European face, look out for him; he is a devil. But see, your steward here has features more regular than King George's of England; and yet there he nods, and bows, and smiles; a king, indeed—the king of kind hearts and polite fellows. What a pleasant voice he has, too?'

'He has, Señor.'

'But tell me, has he not, so far as you have known him, always proved a good, worthy fellow?' said Captain Delano, pausing, while with a final genuflexion the steward disappeared into the cabin; 'come, for the reason just mentioned, I am curious to know.'

'Francesco is a good man,' a sort of sluggishly responded Don Benito, like a phlegmatic appreciator, who would neither find fault nor flatter.

'Ah, I thought so. For it were strange, indeed, and not very creditable to us white-skins, if a little of our blood mixed with the African's, should, far from improving the latter's quality, have the sad effect of pouring vitriolic acid into black broth; improving the hue, perhaps, but not the wholesomeness.'

'Doubtless, doubtless, Señor, but'—glancing at Babo—'not to speak of negroes, your planter's remark I have heard applied to the Spanish and Indian intermixtures in our provinces. But I know nothing about the matter,' he listlessly added.

And here they entered the cabin.

The lunch was a frugal one. Some of Captain Delano's fresh fish and pumpkins, biscuit and salt beef, the reserved bottle of cider, and the *San Dominick's* last bottle of Canary.

As they entered, Francesco, with two or three colored aids, was hovering over the table giving the last adjustments. Upon perceiving their master they withdrew, Francesco making a smiling congé, and the Spaniard, without condescending to notice it, fastidiously remarking to his companion that he relished not superfluous attendance.

Without companions, host and guest sat down, like a childless married couple, at opposite ends of the table, Don Benito waving Captain Delano to his place, and, weak as he was, insisting upon that gentleman being seated before himself.

The negro placed a rug under Don Benito's feet, and a cushion behind his back, and then stood behind, not his master's chair, but Captain Delano's. At first, this a little surprised the latter. But it was soon evident that, in taking his position, the black was still true to his master; since by facing him he could the more readily anticipate his slightest want.

'This is an uncommonly intelligent fellow of yours, Don Benito,' whispered Captain Delano across the table.

'You say true, Señor.'

During the repast, the guest again reverted to parts of Don Benito's story, begging further particulars here and there. He inquired how it was that the scurvy and fever should have committed such wholesale havoc upon the whites, while destroying less than half of the blacks. As if this question reproduced the whole scene of plague before the Spaniard's eyes, miserably reminding him of his solitude in a cabin where before he had had so many friends and officers round him, his hand shook, his face became hueless, broken words escaped; but directly the sane memory of the past seemed replaced by insane terrors of the present. With starting eyes he stared before him at vacancy. For nothing was to be seen but the hand of his servant pushing the Canary over towards him. At length a few sips served partially to restore him. He made random reference to the different constitution of races, enabling one to offer more resistance to certain maladies than another. The thought was new to his companion.

Presently Captain Delano, intending to say something to his host concerning the pecuniary part of the business he had undertaken for him, especially—since he was strictly accountable to his owners—with reference to the new suit of sails, and other things of that sort; and naturally preferring to conduct such affairs in private, was desirous that the servant should withdraw; imagining that Don Benito for a few minutes could dispense with his attendance. He, however, waited awhile; thinking that, as the conversation proceeded, Don Benito, without being prompted, would perceive the propriety of the step.

But it was otherwise. At last catching his host's eye, Captain Delano, with a slight backward gesture of his thumb, whispered, 'Don Benito, pardon me, but there is an interference with the full expression of what I have to say to you.'

Upon this the Spaniard changed countenance; which was imputed to his resenting the hint, as in some way a reflection upon his servant. After a moment's pause, he assured his guest that the black's remaining with them could be of no disservice; because since losing his officers he had made Babo (whose original office, it now appeared, had been captain of the slaves) not only his constant attendant and companion, but in all things his confidant.

After this, nothing more could be said; though, indeed, Captain

Delano could hardly avoid some little tinge of irritation upon being left ungratified in so inconsiderable a wish, by one, too, for whom he intended such solid services. But it is only his querulousness, thought he; and so filling his glass he proceeded to business.

The price of the sails and other matters was fixed upon. But while this was being done, the American observed that, though his original offer of assistance had been hailed with hectic animation, yet now when it was reduced to a business transaction, indifference and apathy were betrayed. Don Benito, in fact, appeared to submit to hearing the details more out of regard to common propriety, than from any impression that weighty benefit to himself and his voyage was involved.

Soon, his manner became still more reserved. The effort was vain to seek to draw him into social talk. Gnawed by his splenetic mood, he sat twitching his beard, while to little purpose the hand of his servant, mute as that on the wall, slowly pushed over the Canary.

Lunch being over, they sat down on the cushioned transom; the servant placing a pillow behind his master. The long continuance of the calm had now affected the atmosphere. Don Benito sighed heavily, as if for breath.

'Why not adjourn to the cuddy,' said Catain Delano; 'there is more air there.' But the host sat silent and motionless.

Meantime his servant knelt before him, with a large fan of feathers. And Francesco coming in on tiptoes, handed the negro a little cup of aromatic waters, with which at intervals he chafed his master's brow; smoothing the hair along the temples as a nurse does a child's. He spoke no word. He only rested his eye on his master's, as if, amid all Don Benito's distress, a little to refresh his spirit by the silent sight of fidelity.

Presently the ship's bell sounded two o'clock; and through the cabin windows a slight rippling of the sea was discerned; and from the desired direction.

'There,' exclaimed Captain Delano, 'I told you so, Don Benito, look!'

He had risen to his feet, speaking in a very animated tone, with a view the more to rouse his companion. But though the crimson curtain of the stern window near him that moment fluttered against his pale cheek, Don Benito seemed to have even less welcome for the breeze than the calm.

Poor fellow, thought Captain Delano, bitter experience has taught him that one ripple does not make a wind, any more than one

~~~~~~

swallow a summer. But he is mistaken for once. I will get his ship in for him, and prove it.

Briefly alluding to his weak condition, he urged his host to remain quietly where he was, since he (Captain Delano) would with pleasure take upon himself the responsibility of making the best use of the wind.

Upon gaining the deck, Captain Delano started at the unexpected figure of Atufal, monumentally fixed at the threshold, like one of those sculptured porters of black marble guarding the porches of Egyptian tombs.

But this time the start was, perhaps, purely physical. Atufal's presence, singularly attesting docility even in sullenness, was contrasted with that of the hatchet-polishers, who in practice evinced their industry; while both spectacles showed, that lax as Don Benito's general authority might be, still, whenever he chose to exert it, no man so savage or colossal but must, more or less, bow.

Snatching a trumpet which hung from the bulwarks, with a free step Captain Delano advanced to the forward edge of the poop, issuing his orders in his best Spanish. The few sailors and many negroes, all equally pleased, obediently set about heading the ship towards the harbor.

While giving some directions about setting a lower stu'n'sail, suddenly Captain Delano heard a voice faithfully repeating his orders. Turning, he saw Babo, now for the time acting, under the pilot, his original part of captain of the slaves. This assistance proved valuable. Tattered sails and warped yards were soon brought into some trim. And no brace or halyard was pulled but to the blithe songs of the inspired negroes.

Good fellows, thought Captain Delano, a little training would make fine sailors of them. Why see, the very women pull and sing too. These must be some of those Ashantee negresses that make such capital soldiers, I've heard. But who's at the helm. I must have a good hand there.

He went to see.

The *San Dominick* steered with a cumbrous tiller, with large horizontal pullies attached. At each pully-end stood a subordinate black, and between them, at the tiller-head, the responsible post, a Spanish seaman, whose countenance evinced his due share in the general hopefulness and confidence at the coming of the breeze.

He proved the same man who had behaved with so shame-faced an air on the windlass.

'Ah—it is you, my man,' exclaimed Captain Delano—'well, no

more sheep's-eyes now;—look straight forward and keep the ship so. Good hand, I trust? And want to get into the harbor, don't you?'

The man assented with an inward chuckle, grasping the tiller-head firmly. Upon this, unperceived by the American, the two blacks eyed the sailor intently.

Finding all right at the helm, the pilot went forward to the forecastle, to see how matters stood there.

The ship now had way enough to breast the current. With the approach of evening, the breeze would be sure to freshen.

Having done all that was needed for the present, Captain Delano, giving his last orders to the sailors, turned aft to report affairs to Don Benito in the cabin; perhaps additionally incited to rejoin him by the hope of snatching a moment's private chat while the servant was engaged upon deck.

From opposite sides, there were, beneath the poop, two approaches to the cabin; one further forward than the other, and consequently communicating with a longer passage. Marking the servant still above, Captain Delano, taking the nighest entrance— the one last named, and at whose porch Atufal still stood—hurried on his way, till, arrived at the cabin threshold, he paused an instant, a little to recover from his eagerness. Then, with the words of his intended business upon his lips, he entered. As he advanced toward the seated Spaniard, he heard another footstep, keeping time with his. From the opposite door, a slaver in hand, the servant was likewise advancing.

'Confound the faithful fellow,' thought Captain Delano; 'what a vexatious coincidence.'

Possibly, the vexation might have been something different, were it not for the brisk confidence inspired by the breeze. But even as it was, he felt a slight twinge, from a sudden indefinite association in his mind of Babo with Atufal.

'Don Benito,' said he, 'I give you joy; the breeze will hold, and will increase. By the way, your tall man and time-piece, Atufal, stands without. By your order, of course?'

Don Benito recoiled, as if at some bland satirical touch, delivered with such adroit garnish of apparent good breeding as to present no handle for retort.'

He is like one flayed alive, thought Captain Delano; where may one touch him without causing a shrink?

The servant moved before his master, adjusting a cushion; recalled to civility, the Spaniard stiffly replied: 'You are right. The slave appears where you saw him, according to my command;

which is, that if at the given hour I am below, he must take his stand and abide my coming.'

'Ah now, pardon me, but that is treating the poor fellow like an ex-king indeed. Ah, Don Benito,' smiling, 'for all the license you permit in some things, I fear lest, at bottom, you are a bitter hard master.'

Again, Don Benito shrank; and this time, as the good sailor thought, from a genuine twinge of his conscience.

Again conversation became constrained. In vain Captain Delano called attention to the now perceptible motion of the keel gently cleaving the sea; with lack-lustre eye, Don Benito returned words few and reserved.

By-and-by, the wind having steadily risen, and still blowing right into the harbor, bore the *San Dominick* swiftly on. Rounding a point of land, the sealer at distance came into open view.

Meantime Captain Delano had again repaired to the deck, remaining there sometime. Having at last altered the ship's course, so as to give the reef a wide berth, he returned for a few moments below.

I will cheer up my poor friend, this time, thought he.

'Better and better, Don Benito,' he cried as he blithely re-entered: 'there will soon be an end to your cares, at least for awhile. For when, after a long, sad voyage, you know, the anchor drops into the haven, all its vast weight seems lifted from the captain's heart. We are getting on famously, Don Benito. My ship is in sight. Look through this side-light here; there she is; all a-taunt-o! The *Bachelor's Delight*, my good friend. Ah, how this wind braces one up. Come, you must take a cup of coffee with me this evening. My old steward will give you as fine a cup as ever any sultan tasted. What say you, Don Benito, will you?'

At first, the Spaniard glanced feverishly up, casting a longing look towards the sealer, while with mute concern his servant gazed into his face. Suddenly the old ague of coldness returned, and dropping back to his cushions he was silent.

'You do not answer. Come, all day you have been my host; would you have hospitality all on one side?'

'I cannot go,' was the response.

'What? it will not fatigue you. The ships will lie together as near as they can, without swinging foul. It will be little more than stepping from deck to deck; which is but as from room to room. Come, come, you must not refuse me.'

'I cannot go,' decisively and repulsively repeated Don Benito.

Renouncing all but the last appearance of courtesy, with a sort of cadaverous sullenness, and biting his thin nails to the quick, he glanced, almost glared, at his guest, as if impatient that a stranger's presence should interfere with the full indulgence of his morbid hour. Meantime the sound of the parted waters came more and more gurglingly and merrily in at the windows; as reproaching him for his dark spleen; as telling him that, sulk as he might, and go mad with it, nature cared not a jot; since, whose fault was it, pray?

But the foul mood was now at its depth, as the fair wind at its height.

There was something in the man so far beyond any mere unsociality or sourness previously evinced, that even the forbearing good-nature of his guest could no longer endure it. Wholly at a loss to account for such demeanor, and deeming sickness with eccentricity, however extreme, no adequate excuse, well satisfied, too, that nothing in his own conduct could justify it, Captain Delano's pride began to be roused. Himself became reserved. But all seemed one to the Spaniard. Quitting him, therefore, Captain Delano once more went to the deck.

The ship was now within less than two miles of the sealer. The whale-boat was seen darting over the interval.

To be brief, the two vessels, thanks to the pilot's skill, ere long in neighborly style lay anchored together.

Before returning to his own vessel, Captain Delano had intended communicating to Don Benito the smaller details of the proposed services to be rendered. But, as it was, unwilling anew to subject himself to rebuffs, he resolved, now that he had seen the *San Dominick* safely moored, immediately to quit her, without further allusion to hospitality or business. Indefinitely postponing his ulterior plans, he would regulate his future actions according to future circumstances. His boat was ready to receive him; but his host still tarried below. Well, thought Captain Delano, if he has little breeding, the more need to show mine. He descended to the cabin to bid a ceremonious, and, it may be, tacitly rebukeful adieu. But to his great satisfaction, Don Benito, as if he began to feel the weight of that treatment with which his slighted guest had, not indecorously, retaliated upon him, now supported by his servant, rose to his feet, and grasping Captain Delano's hand, stood tremulous; too much agitated to speak. But the good augury hence drawn was suddenly dashed, by his resuming all his previous reserve, with augmented gloom, as, with half-averted eyes, he silently reseated himself on his cushions. With a corresponding return of his own chilled feelings, Captain Delano bowed and withdrew.

He was hardly midway in the narrow corridor, dim as a tunnel, leading from the cabin to the stairs, when a sound, as of the tolling for execution in some jail-yard, fell on his ears. It was the echo of the ship's flawed bell, striking the hour, drearily reverberated in this subterranean vault. Instantly, by a fatality not to be withstood, his mind, responsive to the portent, swarmed with superstitious suspicions. He paused. In images far swifter than these sentences, the minutest details of all his former distrusts swept through him.

Hitherto, credulous good-nature had been too ready to furnish excuses for reasonable fears. Why was the Spaniard, so superfluously punctilious at times, now heedless of common propriety in not accompanying to the side his departing guest? Did indisposition forbid? Indisposition had not forbidden more irksome exertion that day. His last equivocal demeanor recurred. He had risen to his feet, grasped his guest's hand, motioned toward his hat; then, in an instant, all was eclipsed in sinister muteness and gloom. Did this imply one brief, repentant relenting at the final moment, from some iniquitous plot, followed by remorseless return to it? His last glance seemed to express a calamitous, yet acquiescent farewell to Captain Delano forever. Why decline the invitation to visit the sealer that evening? Or was the Spaniard less hardened than the Jew, who refrained not from supping at the board of him whom the same night he meant to betray? What imported all those day-long enigmas and contradictions, except they were intended to mystify, preliminary to some stealthy blow? Atufal, the pretended rebel, but punctual shadow, that moment lurked by the threshold without. He seemed a sentry, and more. Who, by his own confession, had stationed him there? Was the negro now lying in wait?

The Spaniard behind—his creature before: to rush from darkness to light was the involuntary choice.

The next moment, with clenched jaw and hand, he passed Atufal, and stood unharmed in the light. As he saw his trim ship lying peacefully at anchor, and almost within ordinary call; as he saw his household boat, with familiar faces in it, patiently rising and falling on the short waves by the *San Dominick*'s side; and then, glancing about the decks where he stood, saw the oakum-pickers still gravely plying their fingers; and heard the low buzzing whistle and industrious hum of the hatchet-polishers, still bestirring themselves over their endless occupation; and more than all, as he saw the benign aspect of nature, taking her innocent repose in the evening; the screened sun in the quiet camp of the west shining out like the mild light from Abraham's tent; as charmed eye and ear took in all these, with the chained figure of the black, clenched jaw and hand relaxed. Once again he smiled at the phantoms which had mocked him, and felt something like a tinge of remorse, that, by harboring them even for a moment, he should by implication, have betrayed an atheist doubt of the ever-watchful Providence above.

There was a few minutes' delay, while, in obedience to his orders, the boat was being hooked along to the gangway. During this interval, a sort of saddened satisfaction stole over Captain Delano, at thinking of the kindly offices he had that day discharged for a stranger. Ah, thought he, after good actions one's conscience is never ungrateful, however much so the benefited party may be.

Presently, his foot, in the first act of descent into the boat, pressed the first round of the side-ladder, his face presented inward upon the deck. In the same moment, he heard his name courteously sounded; and, to his pleased surprise, saw Don Benito advancing— an unwonted energy in his air, as if, at the last moment, intent upon making amends for his recent discourtesy. With instinctive good feeling, Captain Delano, withdrawing his foot, turned and reciprocally advanced. As he did so, the Spaniard's nervous eagerness increased, but his vital energy failed; so that, the better to support him, the servant, placing his master's hand on his naked shoulder, and gently holding it there, formed himself into a sort of crutch.

When the two captains met, the Spaniard again fervently took the hand of the American, at the same time casting an earnest glance into his eyes, but, as before, too much overcome to speak.

I have done him wrong, self-reproachfully thought Captain Delano; his apparent coldness has deceived me; in no instance has he meant to offend.

Meantime, as if fearful that the continuance of the scene might too much unstring his master, the servant seemed anxious to terminate it. And so, still presenting himself as a crutch, and walking between the two captains, he advanced with them towards the gangway; while still, as if full of kindly contrition, Don Benito would not let go the hand of Captain Delano, but retained it in his, across the black's body.

Soon they were standing by the side, looking over into the boat, whose crew turned up their curious eyes. Waiting a moment for the Spaniard to relinquish his hold, the now embarrassed Captain

Delano lifted his foot, to overstep the threshold of the open gangway; but still Don Benito would not let go his hand. And yet, with an agitated tone, he said, 'I can go no further; here I must bid you adieu. Adieu, my dear, dear Don Amasa. Go—go!' suddenly tearing his hand loose, 'go, and God guard you better than me, my best friend.'

Not unaffected, Captain Delano would now have lingered; but catching the meekly admonitory eye of the servant, with a hasty farewell he descended into his boat, followed by the continual adieus of Don Benito, standing rooted in the gangway.

Seating himself in the stern, Captain Delano, making a last salute, ordered the boat shoved off. The crew had their oars on end. The bowsmen pushed the boat a sufficient distance for the oars to be lengthwise dropped. The instant that was done, Don Benito sprang over the bulwarks, falling at the feet of Captain Delano; at the same time calling towards his ship, but in tones so frenzied, that none in the boat could understand him. But, as if not equally obtuse, three sailors, from three different and distant parts of the ship, splashed into the sea, swimming after their captain, as if intent upon his rescue.

The dismayed officer of the boat eagerly asked what this meant. To which, Captain Delano, turning a disdainful smile upon the unaccountable Spaniard, answered that, for his part, he neither knew nor cared; but it seemed as if Don Benito had taken it into his head to produce the impression among his people that the boat wanted to kidnap him. 'Or else—give way for your lives,' he wildly added, starting at a clattering hubbub in the ship, above which rang the tocsin of the hatchet-polishers; and seizing Don Benito by the throat he added, 'this plotting pirate means murder!' Here, in apparent verification of the words, the servant, a dagger in his hand, was seen on the rail overhead, poised, in the act of leaping, as if with desperate fidelity to befriend his master to the last; while, seemingly to aid the black, the three white sailors were trying to clamber into the hampered bow. Meantime, the whole host of negroes, as if inflamed at the sight of their jeopardized captain, impended in one sooty avalanche over the bulwarks.

All this, with what preceded, and what followed, occurred with such involutions of rapidity, that past, present, and future seemed one.

Seeing the negro coming, Captain Delano had flung the Spaniard aside, almost in the very act of clutching him, and, by the unconscious recoil, shifting his place, with arms thrown up, so promptly grappled the servant in his descent, that with dagger presented at Captain Delano's heart, the black seemed of purpose to have leaped there as to his mark. But the weapon was wrenched away, and the assailant dashed down into the bottom of the boat, which now, with disentangled oars, began to speed through the sea.

At this juncture, the left hand of Captain Delano, on one side, again clutched the half-reclined Don Benito, heedless that he was in a speechless faint, while his right foot, on the other side, ground the prostrate negro; and his right arm pressed for added speed on the after oar, his eye bent forward, encouraging his men to their utmost.

But here, the officer of the boat, who had at last succeeded in beating off the towing sailors and was now, with face turned aft, assisting the bowsman at his oar, suddenly called to Captain Delano, to see what the black was about; while a Portuguese oarsman shouted to him to give heed to what the Spaniard was saying.

Glancing down at his feet, Captain Delano saw the freed hand of the servant aiming with a second dagger—a small one, before concealed in his wool—with this he was snakishly writhing up from the boat's bottom, at the heart of his master, his countenance lividly vindictive, expressing the centred purpose of his soul; while the Spaniard, half-choked, was vainly shrinking away, with husky words, incoherent to all but the Portuguese.

That moment, across the long-benighted mind of Captain Delano, a flash of revelation swept, illuminating, in unanticipated clearness, his host's whole mysterious demeanor, with every enigmatic event of the day, as well as the entire past voyage of the *San Dominick*. He smote Babo's hand down, but his own heart smote him harder. With infinite pity he withdrew his hold from Don Benito. Not Captain Delano, but Don Benito, the black, in leaping into the boat, had intended to stab.

Both the black's hands were held, as, glancing up towards the *San Dominick*, Captain Delano, now with scales dropped from his eyes, saw the negroes, not in misrule, not in tumult, not as if frantically concerned for Don Benito, but with mask torn away, flourishing hatchets and knives, in ferocious piratical revolt. Like delirious black dervishes, the six Ashantees danced on the poop. Prevented by their foes from springing into the water, the Spanish boys were hurrying up to the topmost spars, while such of the few Spanish sailors, not already in the sea, less alert, were descried, helplessly mixed in, on deck, with the blacks.

Meantime Captain Delano hailed his own vessel, ordering the

ports up, and the guns run out. But by this time the cable of the
San Dominick had been cut; and the fag-end, in lashing out,
whipped away the canvas shroud about the beak, suddenly revealing, as the bleached hull swung round towards the open ocean,
death for the figurehead, in a human skeleton; chalky comment
on the chalked words below, *'Follow your leader.'*

At the sight, Don Benito, covering his face, wailed out: ' 'Tis
he, Aranda! my murdered, unburied friend!'

Upon reaching the sealer, calling for ropes, Captain Delano
bound the negro, who made no resistance, and had him hoisted
to the deck. He would then have assisted the now almost helpless
Don Benito up the side; but Don Benito, wan as he was, refused
to move, or be moved, until the negro should have been first put
below out of view. When, presently assured that it was done, he
no more shrank from the ascent.

The boat was immediately dispatched back to pick up the three
swimming sailors. Meantime, the guns were in readiness, though,
owing to the *San Dominick* having glided somewhat astern of the
sealer, only the aftermost one could be brought to bear. With this,
they fired six times; thinking to cripple the fugitive ship by bringing
down her spars. But only a few inconsiderable ropes were shot
away. Soon the ship was beyond the gun's range, steering broad
out of the bay; the blacks thickly clustering round the bowsprit,
one moment with taunting cries towards the whites, the next with
upthrown gestures hailing the now dusky moors of ocean—cawing
crows escaped from the hand of the fowler.

The first impulse was to slip the cables and give chase. But,
upon second thoughts, to pursue with whale-boat and yawl seemed
more promising.

Upon inquiring of Don Benito what fire-arms they had on board
the *San Dominick*, Captain Delano was answered that they had
none that could be used; because, in the earlier stages of the
mutiny, a cabin-passenger, since dead, had secretly put out of
order the locks of what few muskets there were. But with all his
remaining strength, Don Benito entreated the American not to
give chase, either with ship or boat; for the negroes had already
proved themselves such desperadoes, that, in case of a present
assault, nothing but a total massacre of the whites could be looked
for. But, regarding this warning as coming from one whose spirit
had been crushed by misery the American did not give up his
design.

The boats were got ready and armed. Captain Delano ordered

his men into them. He was going himself when Don Benito grasped his arm.

'What! have you saved my life, Señor, and are you now going to throw away your own?'

The officers also, for reasons connected with their interests and those of the voyage, and a duty owing to the owners, strongly objected against their commander's going. Weighing their remonstrances a moment, Captain Delano felt bound to remain; appointing his chief mate—an athletic and resolute man, who had been a privateer's-man—to head the party. The more to encourage the sailors, they were told that the Spanish captain considered his ship good as lost; that she and her cargo, including some gold and silver, were worth more than a thousand doubloons. Take her, and no small part should be theirs. The sailors replied with a shout.

The fugitives had now almost gained an offing. It was nearly night; but the moon was rising. After hard, prolonged pulling, the boats came up on the ship's quarters, at a suitable distance laying upon their oars to discharge their muskets. Having no bullets to return, the negroes sent their yells. But, upon the second volley, Indian-like, they hurtled their hatchets. One took off a sailor's fingers. Another struck the whale-boat's bow, cutting off the rope there, and remaining stuck in the gunwale like a woodman's axe. Snatching it, quivering from its lodgment, the mate hurled it back. The returned gauntlet now stuck in the ship's broken quarter-gallery, and so remained.

The negroes giving too hot a reception, the whites kept a more respectful distance. Hovering now just out of reach of the hurtling hatchets, they, with a view to the close encounter which must soon come, sought to decoy the blacks into entirely disarming themselves of their most murderous weapons in a hand-to-hand fight, by foolishly flinging them, as missiles, short of the mark, into the sea. But, ere long, perceiving the stratagem, the negroes desisted, though not before many of them had to replace their lost hatchets with handspikes; an exchange which, as counted upon, proved, in the end, favorable to the assailants.

Meantime, with a strong wind, the ship still clove the water; the boats alternately falling behind, and pulling up, to discharge fresh volleys.

The fire was mostly directed towards the stern, since there, chiefly, the negroes, at present, were clustering. But to kill or maim the negroes was not the object. To take them, with the ship, was the object. To do it, the ship must be boarded; which could not be done by boats while she was sailing so fast.

A thought now struck the mate. Observing the Spanish boys still aloft, high as they could get, he called to them to descend to the yards, and cut adrift the sails. It was done. About this time, owing to causes hereafter to be shown, two Spaniards, in the dress of sailors, and conspicuously showing themselves, were killed; not by volleys, but by deliberate marksman's shots; while, as it afterwards appeared, by one of the general discharges, Atufal, the black, and the Spaniard at the helm likewise were killed. What now, with the loss of the sails, and loss of leaders, the ship became unmanageable to the negroes.

With creaking masts, she came heavily round to the wind; the prow slowly swinging into view of the boats, its skeleton gleaming in the horizontal moonlight, and casting a gigantic ribbed shadow upon the water. One extended arm of the ghost seemed beckoning the whites to avenge it.

'Follow your leader!' cried the mate; and, one on each bow, the boats boarded. Sealing-spears and cutlasses crossed hatchets and hand-spikes. Huddled upon the long-boat amidships, the negresses raised a wailing chant, whose chorus was the clash of the steel.

For a time, the attack wavered; the negroes wedging themselves to beat it back; the half-repelled sailors, as yet unable to gain a footing, fighting as troopers in the saddle, one leg sideways flung over the bulwarks, and one without, plying their cutlasses like carters' whips. But in vain. They were almost overborne, when, rallying themselves into a squad as one man, with a huzza, they sprang inboard, where, entangled, they involuntarily separated again. For a few breaths' space, there was a vague, muffled, inner sound, as of submerged sword-fish rushing hither and thither through shoals of black-fish. Soon, in a reunited band, and joined by the Spanish seamen, the whites came to the surface, irresistibly driving the negroes towards the stern. But a barricade of casks and sacks, from side to side, had been thrown up by the mainmast. Here the negroes faced about, and though scorning peace or truce, yet fain would have had respite. But, without pause, overleaping the barrier, the unflagging sailors again closed. Exhausted, the blacks now fought in despair. Their red tongues lolled, wolf-like, from their black mouths. But the pale sailors' teeth were set; not a word was spoken; and, in five minutes more, the ship was won.

Nearly a score of the negroes were killed. Exclusive of those by the balls, many were mangled; their wounds—mostly inflicted by the long-edged sealing spears, resembling those shaven ones of the

English at Preston Pans, made by the poled scythes of the Highlanders. On the other side, none were killed, though several were wounded; some severely, including the mate. The surviving negroes were temporarily secured, and the ship, towed back into the harbor at midnight, once more lay anchored.

Omitting the incidents and arrangements ensuing, suffice it that, after two days spent in refitting, the ships sailed in company for Conception, in Chili, and thence for Lima, in Peru; where, before the vice-regal courts, the whole affair, from the beginning, underwent investigation.

Though, midway on the passage, the ill-fated Spaniard, relaxed from constraint, showed some signs of regaining health with freewill; yet, agreeably to his own foreboding, shortly before arriving at Lima, he relapsed, finally becoming so reduced as to be carried ashore in arms. Hearing of his story and plight, one of the many religious institutions, of the City of Kings opened an hospitable refuge to him, where both physician and priest were his nurses, and a member of the order volunteered to be his one special guardian and consoler, by night and by day.

The following extracts, translated from one of the official Spanish documents, will, it is hoped, shed light on the preceding narrative, as well as, in the first place, reveal the true port of departure and true history of the *San Dominick*'s voyage, down to the time of her touching at the island of St Maria.

But, ere the extracts come, it may be well to preface them with a remark.

The document selected, from among many others, for partial translation, contains the deposition of Benito Cereno; the first taken in the case. Some disclosures therein were, at the time, held dubious for both learned and natural reasons. The tribunal inclined to the opinion that the deponent, not undisturbed in his mind by recent events, raved of some things which could never have happened. But subsequent depositions of the surviving sailors, bearing out the revelations of their captain in several of the strangest particulars, gave credence to the rest. So that the tribunal, in its final decision, rested its capital sentences upon statements which, had they lacked confirmation, it would have deemed it but duty to reject.

I, DON JOSÉ DE ABOS AND PADILLA, His Majesty's Notary for the Royal Revenue, and Register of this Province, and Notary Public of the Holy Crusade of this Bishopric, etc.

Do certify and declare, as much as is requisite in law, that, in the criminal cause commenced the twenty-fourth of the month of September, in the year seventeen hundred and ninety-nine, against the negroes of the ship *San Dominick*, the following declaration before me was made:

Declaration of the first witness, DON BENITO CERENO.

The same day, and month, and year, His Honor, Doctor Juan Martinez de Rozas, Councilor of the Royal Audience of this Kingdom, and learned in the law of this Intendency, ordered the captain of the ship *San Dominick*, Don Benito Cereno, to appear; which he did in his litter, attended by the monk Infelez; of whom he received the oath, which he took by God, our Lord, and a sign of the Cross; under which he promised to tell the truth of whatever he should know and should be asked;—and being interrogated agreeably to the tenor of the act commencing the process, he said, that on the twentieth of May last, he set sail with his ship from the port of Valparaiso, bound to that of Callao; loaded with the produce of the country beside thirty cases of hardware and one hundred and sixty blacks, of both sexes, mostly belonging to Don Alexandro Aranda, gentleman, of the city of Mendoza; that the crew of the ship consisted of thirty-six men, beside the persons who went as passengers; that the negroes were in part as follows:

[*Here, in the original, follows a list of some fifty names, descriptions, and ages, compiled from certain recovered documents of Aranda's, and also from recollections of the deponent, from which portions only are extracted.*]

—One, from about eighteen to nineteen years, named José, and this was the man that waited upon his master, Don Alexandro, and who speaks well the Spanish, having served him four or five years; * * * a mulatto, named Francesco, the cabin steward, of a good person and voice, having sung in the Valparaiso churches, native of the province of Buenos Ayres, aged about thirty-five years. * * * A smart negro, named Dago, who had been for many years a grave-digger among the Spaniards, aged forty-six years. * * * Four old negroes, born in Africa, from sixty to seventy, but sound, calkers by trade, whose names are as follows:—the first was named Muri, and he was killed (as was also his son named Diamelo); the second, Nacta; the third, Yola, likewise killed; the fourth, Ghofan; and six full-grown negroes, aged from thirty to forty-five, all raw, and born among the Ashantees—Matiluqui,

Yan, Lecbe, Mapenda, Yambaio, Akim; four of whom were killed;
* * * a powerful negro named Atufal, who being supposed to
have been a chief in Africa, his owner set great store by him.
* * * And a small negro of Senegal, but some years among the
Spaniards, aged about thirty, which negro's name was Babo; * * *
that he does not remember the names of the others, but that still
expecting the residue of Don Alexandro's papers will be found,
will then take due account of them all, and remit to the court;
* * * and thirty-nine women and children of all ages.

[*The catalogue over, the deposition goes on.*]

* * * That all the negroes slept upon deck, as is customary in
this navigation, and none wore fetters, because the owner, his
friend Aranda, told him that they were all tractable; * * * that
on the seventh day after leaving port, at three o'clock in the
morning, all the Spaniards being asleep except the two officers on
the watch, who were the boatswain, Juan Robles, and the carpenter,
Juan Bautista Gayete, and the helmsman and his boy, the negroes
revolted suddenly, wounded dangerously the boatswain and the
carpenter, and successively killed eighteen men of those who were
sleeping upon deck, some with hand-spikes and hatchets, and
others by throwing them alive overboard, after tying them; that
of the Spaniards upon deck, they left about seven, as he thinks,
alive and tied, to manoeuvre the ship, and three or four more,
who hid themselves, remained also alive. Although in the act of
revolt the negroes made themselves masters of the hatchway, six
or seven wounded went through it to the cockpit, without any
hindrance on their part; that during the act of revolt, the mate
and another person, whose name he does not recollect, attempted
to come up through the hatchway, but being quickly wounded,
were obliged to return to the cabin; that the deponent resolved
at break of day to come up the companionway, where the negro
Babo was, being the ringleader, and Atufal, who assisted him, and
having spoken to them, exhorted them to cease committing such
atrocities, asking them, at the same time, what they wanted and
intended to do, offering, himself, to obey their commands; that
notwithstanding this, they threw, in his presence, three men, alive
and tied, overboard; that they told the deponent to come up, and
that they would not kill him; which having done, the negro Babo
asked him whether there were in those seas any negro countries
where they might be carried, and he answered them, No; that the
negro Babo afterwards told him to carry them to Senegal, or to
the neighboring islands of St Nicholas; and he answered, that this

was impossible, on account of the great distance, the necessity involved of rounding Cape Horn, the bad condition of the vessel, the want of provisions, sails, and water; but that the negro Babo replied to him he must carry them in any way; that they would do and conform themselves to everything the deponent should require as to eating and drinking; that after a long conference, being absolutely compelled to please them, for they threatened to kill all the whites if they were not, at all events, carried to Senegal, he told them that what was most wanting for the voyage was water; that they would go near the coast to take it, and thence they would proceed on their course; that the negro Babo agreed to it; and the deponent steered towards the intermediate ports, hoping to meet some Spanish or foreign vessel that would save them; that within ten or eleven days they saw the land, and continued their course by it in the vicinity of Nasca; that the deponent observed that the negroes were now restless and mutinous, because he did not effect the taking in of water, the negro Babo having required, with threats, that it should be done, without fail, the following day; he told him he saw plainly that the coast was steep, and the rivers designated in the maps were not to be found, with other reasons suitable to the circumstances; that the best way would be to go to the island of Santa Maria, where they might water easily, it being a solitary island, as the foreigners did; that the deponent did not go to Pisco, that was near, nor make any other port of the coast, because the negro Babo had intimated to him several times, that he would kill all the whites the very moment he should perceive any city, town, or settlement of any kind on the shores to which they should be carried: that having determined to go to the island of Santa Maria, as the deponent had planned, for the purpose of trying whether, on the passage or near the island itself, they could find any vessel that should favor them, or whether he could escape from it in a boat to the neighboring coast of Arruco, to adopt the necessary means he immediately changed his course, steering for the island; that the negroes Babo and Atufal held daily conferences, in which they discussed what was necessary for their design of returning to Senegal, whether they were to kill all the Spaniards, and particularly the deponent; that eight days after parting from the coast of Nasca, the deponent being on the watch a little after day-break, and soon after the negroes had their meeting, the negro Babo came to the place where the deponent was, and told him that he had determined to kill his master, Don Alexandro Aranda, both because he and his companions could not otherwise be sure of their liberty, and that to keep the seamen in subjection, he wanted to prepare a warning of what road they should be made to take did they or any of them oppose him; and that, by means of the death of Don Alexandro, that warning would best be given; but, that what this last meant, the deponent did not at the time comprehend, nor could not, further than that the death of Don Alexandro was intended; and moreover the negro Babo proposed to the deponent to call the mate Raneds, who was sleeping in the cabin, before the thing was done, for fear, as the deponent understood it, that the mate, who was a good navigator, should be killed with Don Alexandro and the rest; that the deponent, who was the friend, from youth, of Don Alexandro, prayed and conjured, but all was useless; for the negro Babo answered him that the thing could not be prevented, and that all the Spaniards risked their death if they should attempt to frustrate his will in this matter, or any other; that, in this conflict, the deponent called the mate, Raneds, who was forced to go apart, and immediately the negro Babo commanded the Ashantee Martinqui and the Ashantee Lecbe to go and commit the murder; that those two went down with hatchets to the berth of Don Alexandro; that, yet half alive and mangled, they dragged him on deck; that they were going to throw him overboard in that state, but the negro Babo stopped them, bidding the murder be completed on the deck before him, which was done, when, by his orders, the body was carried below, forward; that nothing more was seen of it by the deponent for three days; * * * that Don Alonzo Sidonia, an old man, long resident at Valparaiso, and lately appointed to a civil office in Peru, whither he had taken passage, was at the time sleeping in the berth opposite Don Alexandro's; that awakening at his cries, surprised by them, and at the sight of the negroes with their bloody hatchets in their hands, he threw himself into the sea through a window which was near him, and was drowned, without it being in the power of the deponent to assist or take him up; * * * that a short time after killing Aranda, they brought upon deck his german-cousin, of middle-age, Don Francisco Masa, of Mendoza, and the young Don Joaquin, Marques de Aramboalaza, then lately from Spain, with his Spanish servant Ponce, and the three young clerks of Aranda, José Mozairi, Lorenzo Bargas, and Hermenegildo Gandix, all of Cadiz; that Don Joaquin and Hermenegildo Gandix, the negro Babo, for purposes hereafter to appear, preserved alive; but Don Francisco Masa, José Mozairi, and Lorenzo Bargas, with Ponce the servant, beside the boatswain, Juan Robles, the boatswain's mates, Manuel Viscaya and Roderigo Hurta, and four of the sailors, the negro Babo ordered to be thrown alive into the sea, although they made no resistance, nor begged for anything else but mercy; that the boatswain, Juan Robles, who knew how to swim, kept the longest above water, making acts of contrition, and, in the last words he uttered, charged this deponent to cause mass to be said for his soul to our Lady of Succor: * * * that, during the three days which followed, the deponent, uncertain what fate had befallen the remains of Don Alexandro, frequently asked the negro Babo where they were, and, if still on board, whether they were to be preserved for interment ashore, entreating him so to order it; that the negro Babo answered nothing till the fourth day, when at sunrise, the deponent coming on deck, the negro Babo showed him a skeleton, which had been substituted for the ship's proper figure-head—the image of Christopher Colon, the discoverer of the New World; that the negro Babo asked him whose skeleton that was, and whether, from its whiteness, he should not think it a white's; that, upon discovering his face, the negro Babo, coming close, said words to this effect: 'Keep faith with the blacks from here to Senegal, or you shall in spirit, as now in body, follow your leader,' pointing to the prow; * * * that the same morning the negro Babo took by succession each Spaniard forward, and asked him whose skeleton that was, and whether, from its whiteness, he should not think it a white's; that each Spaniard covered his face; that then to each the negro repeated the words in the first place said to the deponent; * * * that they (the Spaniards), being then assembled aft, the negro Babo harangued them, saying that he had now done all; that the deponent (as navigator for the negroes) might pursue his course, warning him and all of them that they should, soul and body, go the way of Don Alexandro, if he saw them (the Spaniards) speak or plot anything against them (the negroes)—a threat which was repeated every day; that, before the events last mentioned, they had tied the cook to throw him overboard, for it is not known what thing they heard him speak, but finally the negro Babo spared his life, at the request of the deponent; that a few days after, the deponent, endeavoring not to omit any means to preserve the lives of the remaining whites, spoke to the negroes of peace and tranquillity, and agreed to draw up a paper, signed by the deponent and the sailors who could write, as also by the negro Babo, for himself and all the blacks, in which the deponent obliged himself to carry them to Senegal, and they not to kill any more, and he formally to make over to them the ship, with the cargo, with which they were for that time satisfied and quieted. * * * But the next day,

the more surely to guard against the sailors' escape, the negro
Babo commanded all the boats to be destroyed but the long-boat,
which was unseaworthy, and another, a cutter in good condition,
which knowing it would yet be wanted for towing the water casks,
he had it lowered down into the hold.

———

[*Various particulars of the prolonged and perplexed navigation
ensuing here follow, with incidents of a calamitous calm, from
which portion one passage is extracted, to wit:*]
—That on the fifth day of the calm, all on board suffering much
from the heat, and want of water, and five having died in fits,
and mad, the negroes became irritable, and for a chance gesture,
which they deemed suspicious—though it was harmless—made by
the mate, Raneds, to the deponent in the act of handing a quadrant,
they killed him; but that for this they afterwards were sorry, the
mate being the only remaining navigator on board, except the
deponent.

———

—That omitting other events, which daily happened, and which
can only serve uselessly to recall past misfortunes and conflicts,
after seventy-three days' navigation, reckoned from the time they
sailed from Nasca, during which they navigated under a scanty
allowance of water, and were afflicted with the calms before
mentioned, they at last arrived at the island of Santa Maria, on
the seventeenth of the month of August, at about six o'clock in
the afternoon, at which hour they cast anchor very near the
American ship, *Bachelor's Delight*, which lay in the same bay,
commanded by the generous Captain Amasa Delano; but at six
o'clock in the morning, they had already descried the port, and
the negroes became uneasy, as soon as at distance they saw the
ship, not having expected to see one there; that the negro Babo
pacified them, assuring them that no fear need be had; that
straightway he ordered the figure on the bow to be covered with
canvas, as for repairs, and had the decks a little set in order; that
for a time the negro Babo and the negro Atufal conferred; that
the negro Atufal was for sailing away, but the negro Babo would
not, and, by himself, cast about what to do; that at last he came
to the deponent, proposing to him to say and do all that the
deponent declares to have said and done to the American captain;

—or that the negro Babo warned him that if he varied in the
least, or uttered any word, or gave any look that should give the

least intimation of the past events or present state, he would instantly kill him, with all his companions, showing a dagger, which he carried hid, saying something which, as he understood it, meant that that dagger would be alert as his eye; that the negro Babo then announced the plan to all his companions, which pleased them; that he then, the better to disguise the truth, devised many expedients, in some of them uniting deceit and defense; that of this sort was the device of the six Ashantees before named, who were his bravoes; that them he stationed on the break of the poop, as if to clean certain hatchets (in cases, which were part of the cargo), but in reality to use them, and distribute them at need, and at a given word he told them; that, among other devices, was the device of presenting Atufal, his right hand man, as chained, though in a moment the chains could be dropped; that in every particular he informed the deponent what part he was expected to enact in every device, and what story he was to tell on every occasion, always threatening him with instant death if he varied in the least: that, conscious that many of the negroes would be turbulent, the negro Babo appointed the four aged negroes, who were calkers, to keep what domestic order they could on the decks; that again and again he harangued the Spaniards and his companions, informing them of his intent, and of his devices, and of the invented story that this deponent was to tell; charging them lest any of them varied from that story; that these arrangements were made and matured during the interval of two or three hours, between their first sighting the ship and the arrival on board of Captain Amasa Delano; that this happened about half-past seven o'clock in the morning, Captain Amasa Delano coming in his boat, and all gladly receiving him; that the deponent, as well as he could force himself, acting then the part of principal owner, and a free captain of the ship, told Captain Amasa Delano, when called upon, that he came from Buenos Ayres, bound to Lima, with three hundred negroes; that off Cape Horn, and in a subsequent fever, many negroes had died; that also, by similar casualties, all the sea officers and the greatest part of the crew had died.

———

[And so the deposition goes on, circumstantially recounting the fictitious story dictated to the deponent by Babo, and through the deponent imposed upon Captain Delano; and also recounting the friendly offers of Captain Delano, with other things, but all of

which is here omitted. After the fictitious story, etc. the deposition proceeds:]

———

—That the generous Captain Amasa Delano remained on board all the day, till he left the ship anchored at six o'clock in the evening, deponent speaking to him always of his pretended misfortunes, under the fore-mentioned principals, without having had it in his power to tell a single word, or give him the least hint, that he might know the truth and state of things; because the negro Babo, performing the office of an officious servant with all the appearance of submission of the humble slave, did not leave the deponent one moment; that this was in order to observe the deponent's actions and words, for the negro Babo understands well the Spanish; and besides, there were thereabout some others who were constantly on the watch, and likewise understood the Spanish; * * * that upon one occasion, while deponent was standing on the deck conversing with Amasa Delano, by a secret sign the negro Babo drew him (the deponent) aside, the act appearing as if originating with the deponent; that then, he being drawn aside, the negro Babo proposed to him to gain from Amasa Delano full particulars about his ship, and crew, and arms; that the deponent asked 'For what?' that the negro Babo answered he might conceive; that, grieved at the prospect of what might overtake the generous Captain Amasa Delano, the deponent at first refused to ask the desired questions, and used every argument to induce the negro Babo to give up this new design; that the negro Babo showed the point of his dagger; that, after the information had been obtained the negro Babo again drew him aside, telling him that that very night he (the deponent) would be captain of two ships, instead of one, for that, great part of the American's ship's crew being to be absent fishing, the six Ashantees, without any one else, would easily take it; that at this time he said other things to the same purpose; that no entreaties availed; that, before Amasa Delano's coming on board, no hint had been given touching the capture of the American ship: that to prevent this project the deponent was powerless; * * *—that in some things his memory is confused, he cannot distinctly recall every event; * * *—that as soon as they had cast anchor at six of the clock in the evening, as has before been stated, the American Captain took leave, to return to his vessel; that upon a sudden impulse, which the deponent believes to have come from God and his angels, he, after the farewell had been said, followed the generous Captain

Amasa Delano as far as the gunwale, where he stayed, under
pretense of taking leave, until Amasa Delano should have been
seated in his boat; that on shoving off, the deponent sprang from
the gunwale into the boat, and fell into it, he knows not how,
God, guarding him; that—

*[Here, in the original, follows the account of what further happened
at the escape, and how the San Dominick was retaken, and of
the passage to the coast; including in the recital many expressions
of 'eternal gratitude' to the 'generous Captain Amasa Delano.' The
deposition then proceeds with recapitulatory remarks, and a partial
renumeration of the negroes, making record of their individual part
in the past events, with a view to furnishing, according to command
of the court, the data whereon to found the criminal sentences to
be pronounced. From this portion is the following;]*

—That he believes that all the negroes, though not in the first
place knowing to the design of revolt, when it was accomplished,
approved it. * * * That the negro, José, eighteen years old, and
in the personal service of Don Alexandro, was the one who
communicated the information to the negro Babo, about the state
of things in the cabin, before the revolt; that this is known, because,
in the preceding midnight, he used to come from his berth, which
was under his master's, in the cabin, to the deck where the
ringleader and his associates were, and had secret conversations
with the negro Babo, in which he was several times seen by the
mate; that, one night, the mate drove him away twice; * * * that
this same negro José was the one who, without being commanded
to do so by the negro Babo, as Lecbe and Martinqui were, stabbed
his master, Don Alexandro, after he had been dragged half-lifeless
to the deck; * * * that the mulatto steward, Francesco, was of
the first band of revolters, that he was, in all things, the creature
and tool of the negro Babo; that, to make his court, he, just before
a repast in the cabin, proposed, to the negro Babo, poisoning a
dish for the generous Captain Amasa Delano; this is known and
believed, because the negroes have said it; but that the negro
Babo, having another design, forbade Francesco; * * * that the
Ashantee Lecbe was one of the worst of them; for that, on the
day the ship was retaken, he assisted in the defense of her, with
a hatchet in each hand, with one of which he wounded, in the
breast, the chief mate of Amasa Delano, in the first act of boarding;
this all knew; that, in sight of the deponent, Lecbe struck, with

a hatchet, Don Francisco Masa, when, by the negro Babo's orders, he was carrying him to throw him overboard, alive, beside participating in the murder, before mentioned, of Don Alexandro Aranda, and others of the cabin-passengers; that, owing to the fury with which the Ashantees fought in the engagement with the boats, but this Lecbe and Yan survived; that Yan was bad as Lecbe; that Yan was the man who, by Babo's command, willingly prepared the skeleton of Don Alexandro, in a way the negroes afterwards told the deponent, but which he, so long as reason is left him, can never divulge; that Yan and Lecbe were the two who, in a calm by night, riveted the skeleton to the bow; this also the negroes told him; that the negro Babo was he who traced the inscription below it; that the negro Babo was the plotter from first to last; he ordered every murder, and was the helm and keel of the revolt; that Atufal was his lieutenant in all; but Atufal, with his own hand, committed no murder; nor did the negro Babo; * * * that Atufal was shot, being killed in the fight with the boats, ere boarding; * * * that the negresses, of age, were knowing to the revolt, and testified themselves satisfied at the death of their master, Don Alexandro; that, had the negroes not restrained them, they would have tortured to death, instead of simply killing, the Spaniards slain by command of the negro Babo; that the negresses used their utmost influence to have the deponent made away with; that, in the various acts of murder, they sang songs and danced—not gaily, but solemnly; and before the engagement with the boats, as well as during the action, they sang melancholy songs to the negroes, and that this melancholy tone was more inflaming than a different one would have been, and was so intended; that all this is believed, because the negroes have said it.

—that of the thirty-six men of the crew, exclusive of the passengers (all of whom are now dead), which the deponent had knowledge of, six only remained alive, with four cabin-boys and ship-boys, not included with the crew; * * *

—that the negroes broke an arm of one of the cabin-boys and gave him strokes with hatchets.

[*Then follow various random disclosures referring to various periods of time. The following are extracted;*]

—That during the presence of Captain Amasa Delano on board, some attempts were made by the sailors, and one by Hermenegildo Gandix, to convey hints to him of the true state of affairs; but that these attempts were ineffectual, owing to fear of incurring

death, and, furthermore, owing to the devices which offered contradictions to the true state of affairs, as well as owing to the
generosity and piety of Amasa Delano incapable of sounding such
wickedness; * * * that Luys Galgo, a sailor about sixty years of
age, and formerly of the king's navy, was one of those who sought
to convey tokens to Captain Amasa Delano; but his intent, though
undiscovered, being suspected, he was, on a pretense, made to
retire out of sight, and at last into the hold, and there was made
away with. This the negroes have since said; * * * that one of
the ship-boys feeling, from Captain Amasa Delano's presence,
some hopes of release, and not having enough prudence, dropped
some chance-word respecting his expectations, which being overheard and understood by a slave-boy with whom he was eating
at the time, the latter struck him on the head with a knife,
inflicting a bad wound, but of which the boy is now healing; that
likewise, not long before the ship was brought to anchor, one of
the seamen, steering at the time, endangered himself by letting
the blacks remark some expression in his countenance, arising
from a cause similar to the above; but this sailor, by his heedful
after conduct, escaped; * * * that these statements are made to
show the court that from the beginning to the end of the revolt,
it was impossible for the deponent and his men to act otherwise
than they did; * * *—that the third clerk, Hermenegildo Gandix,
who before had been forced to live among the seamen, wearing
a seaman's habit, and in all respects appearing to be one for the
time; he, Gandix, was killed by a musket ball fired through mistake
from the boats before boarding; having in his fright run up the
mizzen-rigging, calling to the boats—'don't board,' lest upon their
boarding the negroes should kill him; that this inducing the Americans to believe he some way favored the cause of the negroes,
they fired two balls at him, so that he fell wounded from the
rigging, and was drowned in the sea; * * *—that the young Don
Joaquin, Marques de Aramboalaza, like Hermenegildo Gandix,
the third clerk, was degraded to the office and appearance of a
common seaman; that upon one occasion when Don Joaquin
shrank, the negro Babo commanded the Ashantee Lecbe to take
tar and heat it, and pour it upon Don Joaquin's hands; * * *—
that Don Joaquin was killed owing to another mistake of the
Americans, but one impossible to be avoided, as upon the approach
of the boats, Don Joaquin, with a hatchet tied edge out and
upright to his hand, was made by the negroes to appear on the
bulwarks; whereupon, seen with arms in his hands and in a
questionable attitude, he was shot for a renegade seaman; * * *—

that on the person of Don Joaquin was found secreted a jewel, which, by papers that were discovered, proved to have been meant for the shrine of our Lady of Mercy in Lima; a votive offering, beforehand prepared and guarded, to attest his gratitude, when he should have landed in Peru, his last destination, for the safe conclusion of his entire voyage from Spain; * * *—that the jewel, with the other effects of the late Don Joaquin, is in the custody of the brethren of the Hospital de Sacerdotes, awaiting the disposition of the honorable court; * * *—that, owing to the condition of the deponent, as well as the haste in which the boats departed for the attack, the Americans were not forewarned that there were, among the apparent crew, a passenger and one of the clerks disguised by the negro Babo; * * *—that, beside the negroes killed in the action, some were killed after the capture and reanchoring at night, when shackled to the ring-bolts on deck; that these deaths were committed by the sailors, ere they could be prevented. That so soon as informed of it, Captain Amasa Delano used all his authority, and, in particular with his own hand, struck down Martinez Gola, who, having found a razor in the pocket of an old jacket of his, which one of the shackled negroes had on, was aiming it at the negro's throat; that the noble Captain Amasa Delano also wrenched from the hand of Bartholomew Barlo a dagger, secreted at the time of the massacre of the whites, with which he was in the act of stabbing a shackled negro, who, the same day, with another negro, had thrown him down and jumped upon him; * * *—that, for all the events, befalling through so long a time, during which the ship was in the hands of the negro Babo, he cannot here give account; but that, what he has said is the most substantial of what occurs to him at present, and is the truth under the oath which he has taken; which declaration he affirmed and ratified, after hearing it read to him.

He said that he is twenty-nine years of age, and broken in body and mind; that when finally dismissed by the court, he shall not return home to Chili, but betake himself to the monastery on Mount Agonia without; and signed with his honor, and crossed himself, and, for the time, departed as he came, in his litter, with the monk Infelez, to the Hospital de Sacerdotes.

BENITO CERENO.

DOCTOR ROZAS.

If the Deposition have served as the key to fit into the lock of the complications which precede it, then, as a vault whose door has been flung back, the *San Dominick*'s hull lies open to-day.

Hitherto the nature of this narrative, besides rendering the intricacies in the beginning unavoidable, has more or less required that many things, instead of being set down in the order of occurrence, should be retrospectively, or irregularly given; this last is the case with the following passages, which will conclude the account:

During the long, mild voyage to Lima, there was, as before hinted, a period during which the sufferer a little recovered his health, or, at least in some degree, his tranquillity. Ere the decided relapse which came, the two captains had many cordial conversations—their fraternal unreserve in singular contrast with former withdrawments.

Again and again it was repeated, how hard it had been to enact the part forced on the Spaniard by Babo.

'Ah, my dear friend,' Don Benito once said, 'at those very times when you thought me so morose and ungrateful, nay, when, as you now admit, you half thought me plotting your murder, at those very times my heart was frozen; I could not look at you, thinking of what, both on board this ship and your own, hung, from other hands, over my kind benefactor. And as God lives, Don Amasa, I know not whether desire for my own safety alone could have nerved me to that leap into your boat, had it not been for the thought that, did you, unenlightened, return to your ship, you, my best friend, with all who might be with you, stolen upon, that night, in your hammocks, would never in this world have wakened again. Do but think how you walked this deck, how you sat in this cabin, every inch of ground mined into honey-combs under you. Had I dropped the least hint, made the least advance towards an understanding between us, death, explosive death— yours as mine—would have ended the scene.'

'True, true,' cried Captain Delano, starting, 'you have saved my life, Don Benito, more than I yours; saved it, too, against my knowledge and will.'

'Nay, my friend,' rejoined the Spaniard, courteous even to the point of religion, 'God charmed your life, but you saved mine. To think of some things you did—those smilings and chattings, rash pointings and gesturings. For less than these, they slew my mate, Raneds, but you had the Prince of Heaven's safe-conduct through all ambuscades.'

'Yes, all is owing to Providence, I know: but the temper of my mind that morning was more than commonly pleasant, while the sight of so much suffering, more apparent than real, added to my good-nature, compassion, and charity, happily interweaving the three. Had it been otherwise, doubtless, as you hint, some of my interferences might have ended unhappily enough. Besides, those feelings I spoke of enabled me to get the better of momentary distrust, at times when acuteness might have cost me my life, without saving another's. Only at the end did my suspicions get the better of me, and you know how wide of the mark they then proved.'

'Wide, indeed,' said Don Benito, sadly; 'you were with me all day; stood with me, sat with me, talked with me, looked at me, ate with me, drank with me; and yet, your last act was to clutch for a monster, not only an innocent man, but the most pitiable of all men. To such degree may malign machinations and deceptions impose. So far may even the best man err, in judging the conduct of one with the recesses of whose condition he is not acquainted. But you were forced to it; and you were in time undeceived. Would that, in both respects, it was so ever, and with all men.'

'You generalize, Don Benito; and mournfully enough. But the past is passed; why moralize upon it? Forget it. See, yon bright sun has forgotten it all, and the blue sea, and the blue sky; these have turned over new leaves.'

'Because they have no memory,' he dejectedly replied; 'because they are not human.'

'But these mild trades that now fan your cheek, do they not come with a human-like healing to you? Warm friends, steadfast friends are the trades.'

'With their steadfastness they but waft me to my tomb, Señor,' was the foreboding response.

'You are saved,' cried Captain Delano, more and more astonished and pained; 'you are saved: what has cast such a shadow upon you?'

'The negro.'

There was silence, while the moody man sat, slowly and unconsciously gathering his mantle about him, as if it were a pall.

There was no more conversation that day.

But if the Spaniard's melancholy sometimes ended in muteness upon topics like the above, there were others upon which he never spoke at all; on which, indeed, all his old reserves were piled. Pass over the worst, and, only to elucidate, let an item or two of these be cited. The dress, so precise and costly, worn by him on the day whose events have been narrated, had not willingly been put on. And that silver-mounted sword, apparent symbol of despotic command, was not, indeed, a sword, but the ghost of one. The scabbard, artificially stiffened, was empty.

As for the black—whose brain, not body, had schemed and led the revolt, with the plot—his slight frame, inadequate to that which it held, had at once yielded to the superior muscular strength of his captor, in the boat. Seeing all was over, he uttered no sound, and could not be forced to. His aspect seemed to say, since I cannot do deeds, I will not speak words. Put in irons in the hold, with the rest, he was carried to Lima. During the passage, Don Benito did not visit him. Nor then, nor at any time after, would he look at him. Before the tribunal he refused. When pressed by the judges he fainted. On the testimony of the sailors alone rested the legal identity of Babo.

Some months after, dragged to the gibbet at the tail of a mule, the black met his voiceless end. The body was burned to ashes; but for many days, the head, that hive of subtlety, fixed on a pole in the Plaza, met, unabashed, the gaze of the whites; and across the Plaza looked towards St Bartholomew's church, in whose vaults slept then, as now, the recovered bones of Aranda: and across the Rimac bridge looked towards the monastery, on Mount Agonia without; where, three months after being dismissed by the court, Benito Cereno, borne on the bier, did, indeed, follow his leader.

THE PARADISE OF BACHELORS AND THE TARTARUS OF MAIDS

1
THE PARADISE OF BACHELORS

IT lies not far from Temple Bar.

Going to it, by the usual way, is like stealing from a heated plain into some cool, deep glen, shady among harboring hills.

Sick with the din and soiled with the mud of Fleet Street—where the Benedick tradesmen are hurrying by, with ledger-lines ruled along their brows, thinking upon rise of bread and fall of babies—you adroitly turn a mystic corner—not a street—glide down a dim, monastic way, flanked by dark, sedate, and solemn piles, and still wending on, give the whole care-worn world the slip, and, disentangled, stand beneath the quiet cloisters of the Paradise of Bachelors.

Sweet are the oases in Sahara; charming the isle groves of August prairies; delectable pure faith amidst a thousand perfidies; but sweeter, still more charming, most delectable, the dreamy Paradise of Bachelors, found in the stony heart of stunning London.

In mild meditation pace the cloisters; take your pleasure, sip your leisure, in the garden waterward; go linger in the ancient library; go worship in the sculptured chapel; but little have you seen, just nothing do you know, not the sweet kernel have you tasted, till you dine among the banded Bachelors, and see their convivial eyes and glasses sparkle. Not dine in bustling commons, during term-time, in the hall; but tranquilly, by private hint, at a private table; some fine Templar's hospitably invited guest.

Templar? That's a romantic name. Let me see. Brian de Bois-Guilbert was a Templar, I believe. Do we understand you to insinuate that those famous Templars still survive in modern London? May the ring of their armed heels be heard, and the rattle of their shields, as in mailed prayer the monk-knights kneel before the consecrated Host? Surely a monk-knight were a curious sight picking his way along the Strand, his gleaming corselet and snowy surcoat spattered by an omnibus. Long-bearded, too, according to his order's rule; his face fuzzy as a pard's; how would the grim ghost look among the crop-haired, close-shaven citizens? We know indeed—sad history recounts it—that a moral blight tainted at last this sacred Brotherhood. Though no sworded foe might outskill them in the fence, yet the worm of luxury crawled beneath their guard, gnawing the core of knightly troth, nibbling the monastic vow, till at last the monk's austerity relaxed to wassailing, and the sworn knights-bachelors grew to be but hypocrites and rakes.

But for all this, quite unprepared were we to learn that Knights-Templars (if at all in being) were so entirely secularized as to be reduced from carving out immortal fame in glorious battling for the Holy Land, to the carving of roast-mutton at a dinner-board. Like Anacreon, do these degenerate Templars now think it sweeter far to fall in banquet than in war? Or, indeed, how can there be any survival of that famous order? Templars in modern London! Templars in their red-cross mantles smoking cigars at the Divan! Templars crowded in a railway train, till, stacked with steel helmet, spear, and shield, the whole train looks like one elongated locomotive!

No. The genuine Templar is long since departed. Go view the wondrous tombs in the Temple Church; see there the rigidly-haughty forms stretched out, with crossed arms upon their silly hearts, in everlasting and undreaming rest. Like the years before the flood, the bold Knights Templars are no more. Nevertheless, the name remains, and the nominal society, and the ancient grounds, and some of the ancient edifices. But the iron heel is changed to a boot of patent-leather; the long two-handed sword to a one-handed quill; the monk-giver of gratuitous ghostly counsel now counsels for a fee; the defender of the sarcophagus (if in good practice with his weapon) now has more than one case to defend; the vowed opener and clearer of all highways leading to the Holy Sepulchre, now has it in particular charge to check, to clog, to hinder, and embarrass all the courts and avenues of Law; the knight-combatant of the Saracen, breasting spear-points at Acre, now fights law-points in Westminster Hall. The helmet is a wig. Struck by Time's enchanter's wand, the Templar is to-day a Lawyer.

But, like many others tumbled from proud glory's height—like the apple, hard on the bough but mellow on the ground—the Templar's fall has but made him all the finer fellow.

I dare say those old warrior-priests were but gruff and grouty at the best; cased in Birmingham hardware, how could their crimped arms give yours or mine a hearty shake? Their proud, ambitious, monkish souls clasped shut, like horn-book missals; their very faces clapped in bomb-shells; what sort of genial men were these? But best of comrades, most affable of hosts, capital diner is the modern Templar. His wit and wine are both of sparkling brands.

The church and cloisters, courts and vaults, lanes and passages, banquet-halls, refectories, libraries, terraces, gardens, broad walks, domiciles, and dessert-rooms, covering a very large space of ground, and all grouped in central neighborhood, and quite sequestered from the old city's surrounding din; and everything about the place being kept in most bachelor-like particularity, no part of London offers to a quiet wight so agreeable a refuge.

The Temple is, indeed, a city by itself. A city with all the best appurtenances, as the above enumeration shows. A city with a park to it, and flower-beds, and a riverside—the Thames flowing by as openly, in one part, as by Eden's primal garden flowed the mild Euphrates. In what is now the Temple Garden the old Crusaders used to exercise their steeds and lances; the modern Templars now lounge on the benches beneath the trees, and switching their patent-leather boots, in gay discourse exercise at repartee.

Long lines of stately portraits in the banquet-halls, show what great men of mark—famous nobles, judges, and Lord Chancellors—have in their time been Templars. But all Templars are not known to universal fame; though, if the having warm hearts and warmer welcomes, full minds and fuller cellars, and giving good advice and glorious dinners, spiced with rare divertissements of fun and fancy, merit immortal mention, set down, ye muses, the names of R. F. C. and his imperial brother.

Though to be a Templar, in the one true sense, you must needs be a lawyer, or a student at the law, and be ceremoniously enrolled as member of the order, yet as many such, though Templars, do not reside within the Temple's precincts, though they may have their offices there, just so, on the other hand, there are many residents of the hoary old domiciles who are not admitted Templars. If being, say, a lounging gentleman and bachelor, or a quiet, unmarried, literary man, charmed with the soft seclusion of the spot, you much desire to pitch your shady tent among the rest in this serene encampment, then you must make some special friend among the order, and procure him to rent, in his name but at your charge, whatever vacant chamber you may find to suit.

Thus, I suppose, did Dr. Johnson, that nominal Benedick and widower but virtual bachelor, when for a space he resided here. So, too, did that undoubted bachelor and rare good soul, Charles Lamb. And hundreds more, of sterling spirits, Brethren of the Order of Celibacy, from time to time have dined, and slept, and tabernacled here. Indeed, the place is all a honey-comb of offices and domiciles. Like any cheese, it is quite perforated through and through in all directions with the snug cells of bachelors. Dear, delightful spot! Ah! when I bethink me of the sweet hours there passed, enjoying such genial hospitalities beneath those time-honored roofs, my heart only finds due utterance through poety; and, with a sigh, I softly sing, 'Carry me back to old Virginny!'

Such then, at large, is the Paradise of Bachelors. And such I found it one pleasant afternoon in the smiling month of May, when, sallying from my hotel in Trafalgar Square, I went to keep my dinner-appointment with that fine Barrister, Bachelor, and Bencher, R. F. C. (he *is* the first and second and *should be* the third; I hereby nominate him), whose card I kept fast pinched between my gloved forefinger and thumb, and every now and then snatched still another look at the pleasant address inscribed beneath the name, 'No.——, Elm Court, Temple.'

At the core he was a right bluff, care-free, right comfortable, and most companionable Englishman. If on a first aquaintance he seemed reserved, quite icy in his air—patience; this Champagne will thaw. And if it never do, better frozen Champagne than liquid vinegar.

There were nine gentlemen, all bachelors, at the dinner. One was from 'No.——, King's Beach Walk, Temple'; a second, third, and fourth, and fifth, from various courts or passages christened with some similarly rich resounding syllables. It was, indeed, a sort of Senate of the Bachelors, sent to this dinner from widely scattered districts, to represent the general celibacy of the Temple. Nay, it was, by representation, a Grand Parliament of the best Bachelors in universal London; several of those present being from distant quarters of the town, noted immemorial seats of lawyers and unmarried men—Lincoln's Inn, Furnival's Inn; and one gentleman, upon whom I looked with a sort of collateral awe, hailed from the spot where Lord Verulam once abode a bachelor—Gray's Inn.

The apartment was well up toward heaven. I know not how many strange old stairs I climbed to get to it. But a good dinner, with famous company, should be well earned. No doubt our host had his dining-room so high with a view to secure the prior exercise necessary to the due relishing and digesting of it.

The furniture was wonderfully unpretending, old and snug. No new shining mahogany, sticky with undried varnish; no uncomfortably luxurious ottomans, and sofas too fine to use, vexed you in this sedate apartment. It is a thing which every sensible American should learn from every sensible Englishman, that glare and glitter, gimcracks and gewgaws, are not indispensable to domestic solacement. The American Benedick snatches, down-town, a tough chop in a gilded show-box; the English bachelor leisurely dines at home on that incomparable South Down of his, off a plain deal board.

The ceiling of the room was low. Who wants to dine under the dome of St. Peter's? High ceilings! If that is your demand, and the higher the better, and you be so very tall, then go dine out with the topping giraffe in the open air.

In good time the nine gentlemen sat down to nine covers, and soon were fairly under way.

If I remember right, ox-tail soup inaugurated the affair. Of a rich russet hue, is aggeeable flavor dissipated my first confounding of its main ingredient with teamsters' gads and the raw-hides of ushers. (By way of interlude, we here drank a little claret.) Neptune's was the next tribute rendered—turbot coming second; snow-white, flaky, and just gelatinous enough, not too turtleish in its unctuousness.

(At this point we refreshed ourselves with a glass of sherry.) After these light skirmishers had vanished, the heavy artillery of the feast marched in, led by that well-known English generalissimo, roast beef. For aides-de-camp we had a saddle of mutton, a fat turkey, a chicken-pie, and endless other savory things; while for avant-couriers came nine silver flagons of humming ale. This heavy ordnance having departed on the track of the light skirmishers, a picked brigade of game-foul encamped upon the board, their camp-fires lit by the ruddiest of decanters.

Tarts and puddings followed, with innumerable niceties; then cheese and crackers. (By way of ceremony, simply, only to keep up good old fashions, we here each drank a glass of good old port.)

The cloth was now removed; and, like Blucher's army coming in at the death on the field of Waterloo, in marched a fresh detachment of bottles, dusty with their hurried march.

All these manoeuvrings of the forces were superintended by a surprising old field-marshal (I can not school myself to call him by the inglorious name of waiter), with snowy hair and napkin, and a head like Socrates. Amidst all the hilarity of the feast, intent on important business, he disdained to smile. Venerable man!

I have above endeavored to give some slight schedule of the general plan of operations. But any one knows that a good, genial dinner is a sort of pell-mell, indiscriminate affair, quite baffling to detail in all particulars. Thus, I spoke of taking a glass of claret, and a glass of sherry, and a glass of port, and a mug of ale—all at certain specific periods and times. But those were merely the state bumpers, so to speak. Innumerable impromptu glasses were drained between the periods of those grand imposing ones.

The nine bachelors seemed to have the most tender concern for each other's health. All the time, in flowing wine, they most earnestly expressed their sincerest wishes for the entire well-being and lasting hygiene of the gentleman on the right and on the left. I noticed that when one of these kind bachelors desired a little more wine (just for his stomach's sake, like Timothy), he would not help himself to it unless some other bachelor would join him. It seemed held something indelicate, selfish, and unfraternal, to be seen taking a lonely, unparticipated glass. Meantime, as the wine ran apace, the spirits of the company grew more and more to perfect genialness and unconstraint. They related all sorts of pleasant stories. Choice experiences in their private lives were now brought out, like choice brands of Moselle or Rhenish, only kept for particular company. One told us how mellowly he lived when a student at Oxford; with various spicy anecdotes of most frank-hearted noble lords, his liberal companions. Another bachelor, a gray-headed man, with a sunny face, who, by his own account, embraced every opportunity of leisure to cross over into the Low Countries, on sudden tours of inspection of the fine old Flemish architecture there—this learned, white-haired, sunny-faced old bachelor excelled in his descriptions of the elaborate splendors of those old guild-halls, town-halls, and stadthold-houses, to be seen in the land of the ancient Flemings. A third was a great frequenter of the British Museum, and knew all about scores of wonderful antiquities, of Oriental manuscripts, and costly books without a duplicate. A fourth had lately returned from a trip to Old Granada, and, of course, was full of Saracenic scenery. A fifth had a funny case in law to tell. A sixth was erudite in wines. A seventh had a strange characteristic anecdote of the private life of the Iron Duke, never printed, and never before announced in any public or private company. An eighth had lately been amusing his evenings, now and then, with translating a comic poem of Pulci's. He quoted for us the more amusing passages.

And so the evening slipped along, the hours told, not by a water-clock, like King Alfred's, but a wine-chronometer. Meantime the table seemed a sort of Epsom Heath; a regular ring, where the decanters galloped round. For fear one decanter should not with sufficient speed reach his destination, another was sent express after him to hurry him; and then a third to hurry the second; and so on with a fourth and fifth. And throughout all this nothing loud, nothing unmannerly, nothing turbulent. I am quite sure, from the scrupulous gravity and austerity of his air, that had Socrates, the field-marshal, perceived aught of indecorum in the company he served, he would have forthwith departed without giving warning. I afterward learned that, during the repast, an invalid bachelor in an adjoining chamber enjoyed his first sound refreshing slumber in three long, weary weeks.

It was the very perfection of quiet absorption of good living, good drinking, good feeling, and good talk. We were a band of brothers. Comfort—fraternal, household comfort, was the grand trait of the affair. Also, you could plainly see that these easy-hearted men had no wives or children to give an anxious thought. Almost all of them were travelers, too; for bachelors alone can travel freely, and without any twinges of their consciences touching desertion of the fireside.

The thing called pain, the bugbear styled trouble—those two legends seemed preposterous to their bachelor imaginations. How could men of liberal sense, ripe scholarship in the world, and capacious philosophical and convivial understandings—how could they suffer themselves to be imposed upon by such monkish fables? Pain! Trouble! As well talk of Catholic miracles. No such thing.— Pass the sherry, sir.—Pooh, pooh! Can't be!—The port, sir, if you please. Nonsense; don't tell me so.—The decanter stops with you, sir, I believe.

And so it went.

Not long after the cloth was drawn our host glanced significantly upon Socrates, who, solemnly stepping to a stand, returned with an immense convolved horn, a regular Jericho horn, mounted with polished silver, and otherwise chased and curiously enriched; not omitting two life-like goats' heads, with four more horns of solid silver, projecting from opposite sides of the mouth of the noble main horn.

Not having heard that our host was a performer on the bugle, I was surprised to see him lift this horn from the table, as if he were about to blow an inspiring blast. But I was relieved from this, and set quite right as touching the purposes of the horn, by

his now inserting his thumb and forefinger into its mouth; whereupon a slight aroma was stirred up, and my nostrils were greeted
with the smell of some choice Rappee. It was a mull of snuff. It
went the rounds. Capital idea this, thought I, of taking snuff about
this juncture. This goodly fashion must be introduced among my
countrymen at home, further ruminated I.

The remarkable decorum of the nine bachelors—a decorum not
to be affected by any quantity of wine—a decorum unassailable
by any degree of mirthfulness—this was again set in a forcible
light to me, by now observing that, though they took snuff very
freely, yet not a man so far violated the proprieties, or so far
molested the invalid bachelor in the adjoining room as to indulge
himself in a sneeze. The snuff was snuffed silently, as if it had
been some fine innoxious powder brushed off the wings of butterflies.

But fine though they be, bachelors' dinners, like bachelors' lives,
can not endure forever. The time came for breaking up. One by
one the bachelors took their hats, and two by two, and arm-in-
arm they descended, still conversing, to the flagging of the court;
some going to their neighboring chambers to turn over the *De-
cameron* ere retiring for the night; some to smoke a cigar, prom-
enading in the garden on the cool river-side; some to make for
the street, call a hack, and be driven snugly to their distant lodgings.

I was the last lingerer.

'Well,' said my smiling host, 'what do you think of the Temple
here, and the sort of life we bachelors make out to live in it?'

'Sir,' said I, with a burst of admiring candor—'Sir, this is the
very Paradise of Bachelors!'

2

THE TARTARUS OF MAIDS

It lies not far from Woedolor Mountain in New England. Turning
to the East, right out from among bright farms and sunny meadows,
nodding in early June with odorous grasses, you enter ascendingly
among bleak hills. These gradually close in upon a dusky pass,
which, from the violent Gulf Stream of air unceasingly driving
between its cloven walls of haggard rock, as well as from the
tradition of a crazy spinster's hut having long ago stood somewhere
hereabouts, is called the Mad Maid's Bellows-pipe.

Winding along at the bottom of the gorge is a dangerously narrow wheel-road, occupying the bed of a former torrent. Following this road to its highest point, you stand as within a Dantean gateway. From the steepness of the walls here, their strangely ebon hue, and the sudden contraction of the gorge, this particular point is called the Black Notch. The ravine now expandingly descends into a great, purple, hopper-shaped hollow, far sunk among many Plutonian, shaggy-wooded mountains. By the country people this hollow is called the Devil's Dungeon. Sounds of torrents fall on all sides upon the ear. These rapid waters unite at last in one turbid brick-colored stream, boiling through a flume among enormous boulders. They call this strange-colored torrent Blood River. Gaining a dark precipice it wheels suddenly to the West, and makes one maniac spring of sixty feet into the arms of a stunted wood of gray-haired pines, between which it thence edies on its further way down to the invisible low-lands.

Conspicuously crowning a rocky bluff high to one side, at the cataract's verge, is the ruin of an old saw-mill, built in those primitive times when vast pines and hemlocks super-abounded throughout the neighboring region. The black-mossed bulk of those immense, rough-hewn, and spike-knotted logs, here and there tumbled all together, in long abandonment and decay, or left in solitary, perilous projection over the cataract's gloomy brink, impart to this rude wooden ruin not only much of the aspect of one of rough-quarried stone, but also a sort of feudal, Rhineland, and Thurmberg look, derived from the pinnacled wildness of the neighboring scenery.

Not far from the bottom of the Dungeon stands a large white-washed building, relieved, like some great whited sepulchre, against the sullen background of mountainside firs, and other hardy ever-greens, inaccessibly rising in grim terraces for some two thousand feet.

The building is a paper-mill.

Having embarked on a large scale in the seedsman's business (so extensively and broadcast, indeed, that at length my seeds were distributed through all the Eastern and Northern States, and even fell into the far soil of Missouri and the Carolinas), the demand for paper at my place became so great, that the expenditure soon amounted to a most important item in the general account. It need hardly be hinted how paper comes into use with seedsmen, as envelopes. These are mostly made of yellowish paper, folded square; and when filled, are all but flat, and being stamped, and superscribed with the nature of the seeds contained, assume not

a little the appearance of business-letters ready for the mail. Of
these small envelopes I used an incredible quantity—several
hundreds of thousands in a year. For a time I had purchased my
paper from the wholesale dealers in a neighboring town. For
economy's sake, and partly for the adventure of the trip, I now
resolved to cross the mountains, some sixty miles, and order my
future paper at the Devil's Dungeon paper-mill.

The sleighing being uncommonly fine toward the end of January,
and promising to hold so for no small period, in spite of the bitter
cold I started one gray Friday noon in my pung, well fitted with
buffalo and wolf robes; and, spending one night on the road, next
noon came in sight of Woedolor Mountain.

The far summit fairly smoked with frost; white vapors curled
up from its white-wooded top, as from a chimney. The intense
congelation made the whole country look like one petrifaction.
The steel shoes of my pung craunched and gritted over the vitreous,
chippy snow, as if it had been broken glass. The forests here and
there skirting the route, feeling the same all-stiffening influence,
their inmost fibres penetrated with the cold, strangely groaned—
not in the swaying branches merely, but likewise in the vertical
trunk—as the fitful gusts remorselessly swept through them. Brittle
with excessive frost, many colossal tough-grained maples, snapped
in twain like pipe-stems, cumbered the unfeeling earth.

Flaked all over with frozen sweat, white as a milky ram, his
nostrils at each breath sending forth two horn-shaped shoots of
heated respiration, Black, my good horse, but six years old, started
at a sudden turn, where, right across the track—not ten minutes
fallen—an old distorted hemlock lay, darkly undulatory as an
anaconda.

Gaining the Bellows-pipe, the violent blast, dead from behind,
all but shoved my high-backed pung up-hill. The gust shrieked
through the shivered pass, as if laden with lost spirits bound to
the unhappy world. Ere gaining the summit, Black, my horse, as
if exasperated by the cutting wind, slung out with his strong hind
legs, tore the light pung straight up-hill, and sweeping grazingly
through the narrow notch, sped downward madly past the ruined
saw-mill. Into the Devil's Dungeon horse and cataract rushed
together.

With might and main, quitting my seat and robes, and standing
backward, with one foot braced against the dashboard, I rasped
and churned the bit, and stopped him just in time to avoid
collision, at a turn, with the bleak nozzle of a rock, couchant like
a lion in the way—a roadside rock.

At first I could not discover the paper-mill.

The whole hollow gleamed with the white, except, here and there, where a pinnacle of granite showed one windswept angle bare. The mountains stood pinned in shrouds—a pass of Alpine corpses. Where stands the mill? Suddenly a whirring, humming sound broke upon my ear. I looked, and there, like an arrested avalanche, lay the large whitewashed factory. It was subordinately surrounded by a cluster of other and smaller buildings, some of which, from their cheap, blank air, great length, gregarious windows, and comfortless expression, no doubt were boarding-houses of the operatives. A snow-white hamlet amidst the snows. Various rude, irregular squares and courts resulted from the somewhat picturesque clusterings of these buildings, owing to the broken, rocky nature of the ground, which forbade all method in their relative arrangement. Several narrow lanes and alleys, too, partly blocked with snow fallen from the roof, cut up the hamlet in all directions.

When, turning from the traveled highway, jingling with bells of numerous farmers—who, availing themselves of the fine sleighing, were dragging their wood to market—and frequently diversified with swift cutters dashing from inn to inn of the scattered villages— when, I say, turning from that bustling main-road, I by degrees wound into the Mad-Maid's Bellows-pipe, and saw the grim Black Notch beyond, then something latent, as well as something obvious in the time and scene, strangely brought back to my mind my first sight of dark and grimy Temple Bar. And when Black, my horse, went darting through the Notch, perilously grazing its rocky wall, I remembered being in a runaway London omnibus, which in much the same sort of style, though by no means at an equal rate, dashed through the ancient arch of Wren. Though the two objects did by no means completely correspond, yet this partial inadequacy but served to tinge the similitude not less with the vividness than the disorder of a dream. So that, when upon reining up at the protruding rock I at last caught sight of the quaint groupings of the factory-buildings, and with the traveled highway and the Notch behind, found myself all alone, silently and privily stealing through deep-cloven passages into this sequestered spot, and saw the long, high-gabled main factory edifice, with a rude tower for hoisting heavy boxes—at one end, standing among its crowded outbuildings and boarding-houses, as the Temple Church amidst the surrounding offices and dormitories, and when the marvelous retirement of this mysterious nook fastened its whole spell upon me, then, what memory lacked, all tributary imagination

furnished, and I said to myself, 'This is the very counterpart of
the Paradise of Bachelors, but snowed upon, and frost-painted to
a sepulchre.'

Dismounting and warily picking my way down the dangerous
declivity—horse and man both sliding now and then upon the
icy ledges—at length I drove, or the blast drove me, into the
largest square, before one side of the main edifice. Piercingly and
shrilly the shotted blast blew by the corner; and redly and de-
moniacally boiled Blood River at one side. A long wood-pile, of
many scores of cords, all glittering in mail of crusted ice, stood
crosswise in the square. A row of horseposts, their north sides
plastered with adhesive snow, flanked the factory wall. The bleak
frost packed and paved the square as with some ringing metal.

The inverted similitude recurred—'The sweet, tranquil Temple
garden, with the Thames bordering its green beds,' strangely meditated I.

But where are the gay bachelors?

Then, as I and my horse stood shivering in the windspray, a
girl ran from a neighboring dormitory door, and throwing her
thin apron over her bare head, made for the opposite building.

'One moment, my girl; is there no shed hereabouts which I
may drive into?'

Pausing, she turned upon me a face pale with work, and blue
with cold; an eye supernatural with unrelated misery.

'Nay,' faltered I, 'I mistook you. Go on; I want nothing.'

Leading my horse close to the door from which she had come,
I knocked. Another pale, blue girl appeared, shivering in the
doorway as, to prevent the blast, she jealously held the door ajar.

'Nay, I mistake again. In God's name shut the door. But hold,
is there no man about?'

That moment a dark-complexioned, well-wrapped personage
passed, making for the factory door, and spying him coming, the
girl rapidly closed the other one.

'Is there no horse-shed here, sir?'

'Yonder, to the wood-shed,' he replied, and disappeared inside
the factory.

With much ado I managed to wedge in horse and pung between
the scattered piles of wood all sawn and split. Then, blanketing
my horse, and piling my buffalo on the blanket's top, and tucking
in its edges well around the breast-band and breeching, so that
the wind might not strip him bare, I tied him fast, and ran lamely
for the factory door, stiff with frost, and cumbered with my driver's
dread-naught.

Immediately I found myself standing in a spacious place, intolerably lighted by long rows of windows, focusing inward the snowy scene without.

At rows of blank-looking counters sat rows of blank-looking girls, with blank, white folders in their blank hands, all blankly folding blank paper.

In one corner stood some huge frame of ponderous iron, with a vertical thing like a piston periodically rising and falling upon a heavy wooden block. Before it—its tame minister—stood a tall girl, feeding the iron animal with half-quires of rose-hued note-paper which, at every downward dab of the piston-like machine, received in the corner the impress of a wreath of roses. I looked from the rosy paper to the pallid cheek, but said nothing.

Seated before a long apparatus, strung with long, slender strings like any harp, another girl was feeding it with foolscap sheets which, so soon as they curiously traveled from her on the cords, were withdrawn at the opposite end of the machine by a second girl. They came to the first girl blank; they went to the second girl ruled.

I looked upon the first girl's brow, and saw it was young and fair; I looked upon the second girl's brow, and saw it was ruled and wrinkled. Then, as I still looked, the two—for some small variety to the monotony—changed places; and where had stood the young, fair brow, now stood the ruled and wrinkled one.

Perched high upon a narrow platform, and still higher upon a high stool crowning it, sat another figure serving some other iron animal; while below the platform sat her mate in some sort of reciprocal attendance.

Not a syllable was breathed. Nothing was heard but the low, steady overruling hum of the iron animals. The human voice was banished from the spot. Machinery—the vaunted slave of humanity—here stood menially served by human beings, who served mutely and cringingly as the slave serves the Sultan. The girls did not so much seem accessory wheels to the general machinery as mere cogs to the wheels.

All this scene around me was instantaneously taken in at one sweeping glance—even before I had proceeded to unwind the heavy fur tippet from around my neck. But as soon as this fell from me, the dark-complexioned man, standing close by, raised a sudden cry, and seizing my arm, dragged me out into the open air, and without pausing for a word instantly caught up some congealed snow and began rubbing both my cheeks.

'Two white spots like the whites of your eyes,' he said; 'man, your cheeks are frozen.'

'That may well be,' muttered I; ' 'tis some wonder the frost of the Devil's Dungeon strikes in no deeper. Rub away.'

Soon a horrible, tearing pain caught at my reviving cheeks. Two gaunt blood-hounds, one on each side, seemed mumbling them. I seemed Actaeon.

Presently, when all was over, I re-entered the factory, made known my business, concluded it satisfactorily, and then begged to be conducted throughout the place to view it.

'Cupid is the boy for that,' said the dark-complexioned man. 'Cupid!' and by this odd fancy-name calling a dimpled, red-cheeked, spirited-looking forward little fellow, who was rather impudently, I thought, gliding about among the passive-looking girls—like a gold-fish through hueless waves—yet doing nothing in particular that I could see, the man bade him lead the stranger through the edifice.

'Come first and see the water-wheel,' said this lively lad, with the air of boyishly-brisk importance.

Quitting the folding-room, we crossed some damp, cold boards, and stood beneath a great wet shed, incessantly showering with foam, like the green barnacled bow of some East Indiaman in a gale. Round and round here went the enormous revolutions of the dark colossal water-wheel, grim with its one immutable purpose.

'This sets our whole machinery a-going, sir; in every part of all these buildings; where the girls work and all.'

I looked, and saw that the turbid waters of Blood River had not changed their hue by coming under the use of man.

'You make only blank paper; no printing of any sort, I suppose? All blank paper, don't you?'

'Certainly; what else should a paper-factory make?'

The lad here looked at me as if suspicious of my common-sense.

'Oh, to be sure!' said I, confused and stammering; 'it only struck me as so strange that red waters should turn out pale chee—paper, I mean.'

He took me up a wet and rickety stair to a great light room, furnished with no visible thing but rude, manger-like receptacles running all around its sides: and up to these mangers, like so many mares haltered to the rack, stood rows of girls. Before each was vertically thrust up a long, glittering scythe, immovably fixed at bottom to the manger-edge. The curve of the scythe, and its

having no snath to it, made it look exactly like a sword. To and
fro, across the sharp edge, the girls forever dragged long strips of
rags, washed white, picked from baskets at one side; thus ripping
asunder every seam, and converting the tatters almost into lint.
The air swam with the fine, poisonous particles, which from all
sides darted, subtilely, as motes in sunbeams, into the lungs.

'This is the rag-room,' coughed the boy.

'You find it rather stifling here,' coughed I, in answer; 'but the
girls don't cough.'

'Oh, they are used to it.'

'Where do you get such hosts of rags?' picking up a handful
from a basket.

'Some from the country round about; some from far over sea—
Leghorn and London.'

'Tis not unlikely, then,' murmured I, 'that among thcsc hcaps
of rags there may be some old shirts, gathered from the dormitories
of the Paradise of Bachelors. But the buttons are all dropped off.
Pray, my lad, do you ever find any bachelors' buttons hereabouts?'

'None grow in this part of the country. The Devil's Dungeon
is no place for flowers.'

'Oh! you mean the *flowers* so called—the Bachelor's Buttons?'

'And was not that what you asked about? Or did you mean
the gold bosom-buttons of our boss, Old Bach, as our whispering
girls all call him?'

'The man, then, I saw below is a bachelor, is he?'

'Oh, yes, he's a Bach,'

'The edges of those swords, they are turned outward from the
girls, if I see right; but their rags and fingers fly so, I can not
distinctly see.'

'Turned outward.'

Yes, murmured I to myself; I see it now; turned outward; and
each erected sword is so borne, edge-outward before each girl. If
my reading fails me not, just so, of old, condemned state-prisoners
went from the hall of judgment to their doom: an officer before,
bearing a sword, its edge turned outward, in significance of their
fatal sentence. So, through consumptive pallors of this blank, raggy
life, go these white girls to death.

'Those scythes look very sharp,' again turning toward the boy.

'Yes; they have to keep them so. Look!'

That moment two of the girls, dropping their rags, plied each
a whet-stone up and down the sword-blade. My unaccustomed
blood curdled at the sharp shriek of the tormented steel.

Their own executioners; themselves whetting the very swords that slay them; meditated I.

'What makes those girls so sheet-white, my lad?'

'Why—with a roguish twinkle, pure ignorant drollery, not knowing heartlessness—'I suppose the handling of such white bits of sheets all the time makes them so sheety.'

'Let us leave the rag-room now, my lad.'

More tragical and more inscutably mysterious than any mystic sight, human or machine, throughout the factory, was the strange innocence of cruel-heartedness in this usage-hardened boy.

'And now,' said he cheerily, 'I suppose you want to see our great machine, which cost us twelve thousand dollars only last autumn. That's the machine that makes the paper, too. This way, sir.'

Following him, I crossed a large, bespattered place, with two great round vats in it, full of a white, wet, woolly-looking stuff, not unlike the albuminous part of an egg, soft-boiled.

'There,' said Cupid, tapping the vats carelessly, 'these are the first beginnings of the paper, this white pulp you see. Look how it swims bubbling round and round, moved by the paddle here. From hence it pours from both vats into that one common channel yonder, and so goes, mixed up and leisurely, to the great machine. And now for that.'

He led me into a room, stifling with a strange, blood-like, abdominal heat, as if here, true enough, were being finally developed the germinous particles lately seen.

Before me, rolled out like some long Eastern manuscript, lay stretched one continuous length of iron frame-work—multitudinous and mystical, with all sorts of rollers, wheels, and cylinders, in slowly-measured and unceasing motion.

'Here first comes the pulp now,' said Cupid, pointing to the highest end of the machine. 'See; first it pours out and spreads itself upon this wide, sloping board; and then—look—slides, thin and quivering, beneath the first roller there. Follow on now, and see it as it slides from under that to the next cylinder. There; see how it has become just a very little less pulpy now. One step more, and it grows still more to some slight consistence. Still another cylinder, and it is so knitted—through as yet mere dragonfly wing—that it forms an air-bridge here, like a suspended cobweb, between two more separated rollers; and flowing over the last one, and under again, and doubling about there out of sight for a minute among all those mixed cylinders you indistinctly see, it reappears here, looking now at last a little less like pulp and more

like paper, but still quite delicate and defective yet awhile. But—
a little further onward, sir, if you please—here now, at this further
point, it puts on something of a real look, as if it might turn out
to be something you might possibly handle in the end. But it's
not yet done, sir. Good way to travel yet, and plenty more of
cylinders must roll it.'

'Bless my soul!' said I, amazed at the elongation, interminable
convolutions, and deliberate slowness of the machine; 'it must
take a long time for the pulp to pass from end to end, and come
out paper.'

'Oh! not so long,' smiled the precious lad, with a superior and
partonizing air; 'only nine minutes. But look; you may try it for
yourself. Have you a bit of paper? Ah! here's a bit on the floor.
Now mark that with any word you please, and let me dab it on
here, and we'll see how long before it comes out at the other
end.'

'Well, let me see,' said I, taking out my pencil; 'come, I'll mark
it with your name.'

Bidding me take out my watch, Cupid adroitly dropped the
inscribed slip on an exposed part of the incipient mass.

Instantly my eye marked the second-hand on my dial-plate.

Slowly I followed the slip, inch by inch; sometimes pausing for
full half a minute as it disappeared beneath inscrutable groups of
the lower cylinders, but only gradually to emerge again, and so,
on, and on, and on—inch by inch; now in open sight, sliding
along like a freckle on the quivering sheet; and then again wholly
vanished; and so, on, and on, and on—inch by inch; all the time
the main sheet growing more and more to final firmness—when,
suddenly, I saw a sort of paper-fall, not wholly unlike a water-
fall; a scissory sound smote my ear, as of some cord being snapped;
and down dropped an unfolded sheet of perfect foolscap, with my
'Cupid' half faded out of it, and still moist and warm.

My travels were at an end, for here was the end of the machine.

'Well, how long was it? said Cupid.

'Nine minutes to a second,' replied I, watch in hand.

'I told you so.'

For a moment a curious emotion filled me, not wholly unlike
that which one might experience at the fulfillment of some mysterious prophecy. But how absurd, thought I again; the thing is
a mere machine, the essence of which is unvarying punctuality
and precision.

Previously absorbed by the wheels and cylinders, my attention
was now directed to a sad-looking woman standing by.

'That is rather an elderly person so silently tending the machine-end here. She would not seem wholly used to it either.'

'Oh,' knowingly whispered Cupid, through the din, 'she only came last week. She was a nurse formerly. But the business is poor in these parts, and she's left it. But look at the paper she is piling there.'

'Aye, foolscap,' handling the piles of moist, warm sheets, which continually were being delivered into the woman's waiting hands. 'Don't you turn out anything but foolscap at this machine?'

'Oh, sometimes, but not often, we turn out finer work—cream-laid and royal sheets, we call them. But foolscap being in chief demand, we turn out foolscap most.'

It was very curious. Looking at that blank paper continually dropping, dropping, dropping, my mind ran on in wonderings of those strange uses to which those thousand sheets eventually would be put. All sorts of writings would be writ on those now vacant things—sermons, lawyers' briefs, physicians' prescriptions, love-letters, marriage certificates, bills of divorce, registers of births, death-warrants, and so on, without end. Then, recurring back to them as they here lay all blank, I could not but bethink me of that celebrated comparison of John Locke, who, in demonstration of his theory that man had no innate ideas, compared the human mind at birth to a sheet of blank paper; something destined to be scribbled on, but what sort of characters no soul might tell.

Pacing slowly to and fro along the involved machine, still humming with its play, I was struck as well by the inevitability as the evolvement-power in all its motions.

'Does that thin cobweb there,' said I, pointing to the sheet in its more imperfect stage, 'does that never tear or break? It is marvelous fragile, and yet this machine it passes through is so mighty.'

'It never is known to tear a hair's point.'

'Does it never stop—get clogged?'

'No, It *must* go. The machinery makes it go just *so*; just that very way, and that very pace you there plainly *see* it go. The pulp can't help going.'

Something of awe now stole over me, as I gazed upon this inflexible iron animal. Always, more or less, machinery of this ponderous, elaborate sort strikes, in some moods, strange dread into the human heart, as some living, panting Behemoth might. But what made the thing I saw so specially terrible to me was the metallic necessity, the unbudging fatality which governed it. Though, here and there, I could not follow the thin, gauzy vail of pulp in the course of its more mysterious or entirely invisible advance, yet it was indubitable that, at those points where it eluded me, it still marched on in unvarying docility to the autocratic cunning of the machine. A fascination fastened on me. I stood spell-bound and wandering in my soul. Before my eyes—there, passing in slow procession along the wheeling cylinders, I seemed to see, glued to the pallid incipience of the pulp, the yet more pallid faces of all the pallid girls I had eyed that heavy day. Slowly, mournfully, beseechingly, yet unresistingly, they gleamed along, their agony dimly outlined on the imperfect paper, like the print of the tormented face on the handkerchief of Saint Veronica.

'Halloa! the heat of the room is too much for you,' cried Cupid, staring at me.

'No—I am rather chill, if anything.'

'Come out, sir—out—out,' and, with the protecting air of a careful father, the precocious lad hurried me outside.

In a few moments, feeling revived a little, I went into the folding-room—the first room I had entered, and where the desk for transacting business stood, surrounded by the blank counters and blank girls engaged at them.

'Cupid here has led me a strange tour,' said I to the dark-complexioned man before mentioned, whom I had ere this discovered not only to be an old bachelor, but also the principal proprietor. 'Yours is a most wonderful factory. Your great machine is a miracle of inscrutable intricacy.'

'Yes, all our visitors think it so. But we don't have many. We are in a very out-of-the-way corner here. Few inhabitants, too. Most of our girls come from far-off villages.'

'The girls,' echoed I, glancing round at their silent forms. 'Why is it, sir, that in most factories, female operatives, of whatever age, are indiscriminately called girls, never women?'

'Oh! as to that—why, I suppose, the fact of their being generally unmarried—that's the reason, I should think. But it never struck me before. For our factory here, we will not have married women; they are apt to be off-and-on too much. We want none but steady workers: twelve hours to the day, day after day, through the three hundred and sixty-five days, excepting Sundays, Thanksgiving, and Fast-days. That's our rule. And so, having no married women, what females we have are rightly enough called girls.'

'Then these are all maids,' said I, while some pained homage to their pale virginity made me involuntarily bow.

'All maids.'

Again the strange emotion filled me.

'Your cheeks look whitish yet, sir,' said the man, gazing at me narrowly. 'You must be careful going home. Do they pain you at all now? It's a bad sign, if they do.'

'No doubt, sir,' answered I, 'when once I have got out of the Devil's Dungeon, I shall feel them mending.'

'Ah, yes; the winter air in valleys, or gorges, or any sunken place, is far colder and more bitter than elsewhere. You would hardly believe it now, but it is colder here than at the top of Woedolor Mountain.'

'I dare say it is, sir. But time presses me; I must depart.'

With that, remuffling myself in dread-naught and tippet, thrusting my hands into my huge seal-skin mittens, I sallied out into the nipping air, and found poor Black, my horse, all cringing and doubled up with the cold.

Soon, wrapped in furs and meditations, I ascended from the Devils's Dungeon.

At the Black Notch I paused, and once more bethought me of Temple Bar. Then, shooting through the pass, all alone with inscrutable nature, I exclaimed—Oh! Paradise of Bachelors! and oh! Tartarus of Maids!

BILLY BUDD, SAILOR

DEDICATED

TO

JACK CHASE

ENGLISHMAN

Wherever that great heart may now be
Here on Earth or harbored in Paradise

CAPTAIN OF THE MAINTOP

IN THE YEAR 1843

IN THE U.S. FRIGATE

UNITED STATES

1

IN the time before steamships, or then more frequently than now, a stroller along the docks of any considerable seaport would occasionally have his attention arrested by a group of bronzed mariners, man-of-war's men or merchant sailors in holiday attire, ashore on liberty. In certain instances they would flank, or like a bodyguard quite surround, some superior figure of their own class, moving along with them like Aldebaran among the lesser lights of his constellation. That signal object was the 'Handsome Sailor' of the less prosaic time alike of the military and merchant navies. With no perceptible trace of the vainglorious about him, rather with the offhand unaffectedness of natural regality, he seemed to accept the spontaneous homage of his shipmates.

A somewhat remarkable instance recurs to me. In Liverpool, now half a century ago, I saw under the shadow of the great dingy street-wall of Prince's Dock (an obstruction long since removed) a common sailor so intensely black that he must needs have been a native African of the unadulterate blood of Ham—a symmetric figure much above the average height. The two ends of a gay silk handkerchief thrown loose about the neck danced upon the displayed ebony of his chest, in his ears were big hoops of gold, and a Highland bonnet with a tartan band set off his shapely head. It was a hot noon in July; and his face, lustrous with perspiration, beamed with barbaric good humor. In jovial sallies right and left, his white teeth flashing into view, he rollicked along, the center of a company of his shipmates. These were made up of such an assortment of tribes and complexions as would have well fitted them to be marched up by Anacharsis Cloots before the bar of the first French Assembly as Representatives of the Human Race. At each spontaneous tribute rendered by the wayfarers to this black pagod of a fellow—the tribute of a pause and stare, and less frequently an exclamation—the motley retinue showed that they took that sort of pride in the evoker of it which the Assyrian priests doubtless showed for their grand sculptured Bull when the faithful prostrated themselves.

To return. If in some cases a bit of a nautical Murat in setting forth his person ashore, the Handsome Sailor of the period in question evinced nothing of the dandified Billy-be-Dam, an amusing character all but extinct now, but occasionally to be encountered, and in a form yet more amusing than the original, at the tiller of the boats on the tempestuous Erie Canal or, more likely, vaporing in the groggeries along the towpath. Invariably a proficient in his perilous calling, he was also more or less of a mighty boxer or wrestler. It was strength and beauty. Tales of his prowess were recited. Ashore he was the champion; afloat the spokesman; on every suitable occasion always foremost. Close-reefing topsails in a gale, there he was, astride the weather yardarm-end, foot in the Flemish horse as stirrup, both hands tugging at the earing as at a bridle, in very much the attitude of young Alexander curbing the fiery Bucephalus. A superb figure, tossed up as by the horns of Taurus against the thunderous sky, cheerily hallooing to the strenuous file along the spar.

The moral nature was seldom out of keeping with the physical make. Indeed, except as toned by the former, the comeliness and power, always attractive in masculine conjunction, hardly could have drawn the sort of honest homage the Handsome Sailor in some examples received from his less gifted associates.

Such a cynosure, at least in aspect, and something such too in nature, though with important variations made apparent as the story proceeds, was welkin-eyed Billy Budd—or Baby Budd, as more familiarly, under circumstances hereafter to be given, he at last came to be called—aged twenty-one, a foretopman of the British fleet toward the close of the last decade of the eighteenth century. It was not very long prior to the time of the narration that follows that he had entered the King's service, having been impressed on the Narrow Seas from a homeward-bound English merchantman into a seventy-four outward bound, H.M.S. *Bellipotent*; which ship, as was not unusual in those hurried days, having been obliged to put to sea short of her proper complement of men. Plumb upon Billy at first sight in the gangway the boarding officer, Lieutenant Ratcliffe, pounced, even before the merchantman's crew was formally mustered on the quarter-deck for his deliberate inspection. And him only he elected. For whether it was because the other men when ranged before him showed to ill advantage after Billy, or whether he had some scruples in view of the merchantman's being rather short-handed, however it might be, the officer contented himself with his first spontaneous choice. To the surprise of the ship's company, though much to the lieutenant's satisfaction, Billy made no demur. But, indeed, any demur would have been as idle as the protest of a goldfinch popped into a cage.

Noting this uncomplaining acquiescence, all but cheerful, one might say, the shipmaster turned a surprised glance of silent reproach at the sailor. The shipmaster was one of those worthy mortals found in every vocation, even the humbler ones—the sort of person whom everybody agrees in calling 'a respectable man.' And—nor so strange to report as it may appear to be—though a ploughman of the troubled waters, lifelong contending with the intractable elements, there was nothing this honest soul at heart loved better than simple peace and quiet. For the rest, he was fifty or thereabouts, a little inclined to corpulence, a prepossessing face, unwhiskered, and of an agreeable color—or rather full face, humanely intelligent in expression. On a fair day with a fair wind and all going well, a certain musical chime in his voice seemed to be the veritable unobstructed outcome of the innermost man. He had much prudence, much conscientiousness, and there were occasions when these virtues were the cause of overmuch disquietude in him. On a passage, so long as his craft was in any proximity to land, no sleep for Captain Graveling. He took to heart those serious responsibilities not so heavily borne by some shipmasters.

Now while Billy Budd was down in the forecastle getting his kit together, the *Bellipotent*'s lieutenant, burly and bluff, nowise disconcerted by Captain Graveling's omitting to proffer the customary hospitalities on an occasion so unwelcome to him, an omission simply caused by preoccupation of thought, unceremoniously invited himself into the cabin, and also to a flask from the spirit locker, a receptacle which his experienced eye instantly discovered. In fact he was one of those sea dogs in whom all the hardship and peril of naval life in the great prolonged wars of his time never impaired the natural instinct for sensuous enjoyment. His duty he always faithfully did; but duty is sometimes a dry obligation, and he was for irrigating its aridity, whensoever possible, with a fertilizing decoction of strong waters. For the cabin's proprietor there was nothing left but to play the part of the enforced host with whatever grace and alacrity were practicable. As necessary adjuncts to the flask, he silently placed tumbler and water jug before the irrepressible guest. But excusing himself from partaking

just then, he dismally watched the unembarrassed officer deliberately diluting his grog a little, then tossing it off in three swallows,
pushing the empty tumbler away, yet not so far as to be beyond
easy reach, at the same time settling himself in his seat and
smacking his lips with high satisfaction, looking straight at the
host.

These proceedings over, the master broke the silence; and there
lurked a rueful reproach in the tone of his voice; 'Lieutenant, you
are going to take my best man from me, the jewel of 'em.'

'Yes, I know,' rejoined the other, immediately drawing back
the tumbler preliminary to a replenishing. 'Yes, I know. Sorry.'

'Beg pardon, but you don't understand, Lieutenant. See here,
now. Before I shipped that young fellow, my forecastle was a rat-
pit of quarrels. It was black times, I tell you, aboard the *Rights*
here. I was worried to that degree my pipe had no comfort for
me. But Billy came; and it was like a Catholic priest striking peace
in an Irish shindy. Not that he preached to them or said or did
anything in particular; but a virtue went out of him, sugaring the
sour ones. They took to him like hornets to treacle; but all the
buffer of the gang, the big shaggy chap with the fire-red whiskers.
He indeed, out of envy, perhaps, of the new comer, and thinking
such a 'sweet and pleasant fellow,' as he mockingly designated
him to the others, could hardly have the spirit of a gamecock,
must needs bestir himself in trying to get up an ugly row with
him. Billy forebore with him and reasoned with him in a pleasant
way—he is something like myself, Lieutenant, to whom aught like
a quarrel is hateful—but nothing served. So, in the second dogwatch one day, the Red Whiskers in presence of the others, under
pretense of showing Billy just whence a sirloin steak was cut—
for the fellow had once been a butcher—insultingly gave him a
dig under the ribs. Quick as lightening Billy let fly his arm. I dare
say he never meant to do quite so much as he did, but anyhow
he gave the burly fool a terrible drubbing. It took about half a
minute, I should think. And lord bless you, the lubber was astonished at the celerity. And will you believe it, Lieutenant, the
Red Whiskers now really loves Billy—loves him, or is the biggest
hypocrite that ever I heard of. But they all love him. Some of
'em do his washing, darn his old trousers for him; the carpenter
is at odd times making a pretty little chest of drawers for him.
Anybody will do anything for Billy Budd; and it's the happy family
here. But now, Lieutenant, if that young fellow goes—I know how
it will be aboard the *Rights*. Not again very soon shall I, coming
up from dinner, lean over the capstan smoking a quiet pipe—no,

not very soon again, I think. Ay, Lieutenant, you are going to take away the jewel of 'em; you are going to take away my peacemaker!' And with that the good soul had really some ado in checking a rising sob.

'Well,' said the lieutenant, who had listened with amused interest to all this and now was waxing merry with his tipple: 'well, blessed are the peacemakers, especially the fighting peacemakers. And such are the seventy-four beauties some of which you see poking their noses out of the portholes of yonder warship lying to for me,' pointing through the cabin window at the *Bellipotent*. 'But courage! Don't look so downhearted, man. Why, I pledge you in advance the royal approbation. Rest assured that His Majesty will be delighted to know that in a time when his hardtack is not sought for by sailors with such avidity as should be, a time also when some shipmasters privily resent the borrowing from them a tar or two for the service; His Majesty, I say, will be delighted to learn that *one* shipmaster at least cheerfully surrenders to the King the flower of his flock, a sailor who with equal loyalty makes no dissent.—But where's my beauty? Ah,' looking through the cabin's open door, 'here he comes; and, by Jove, lugging along his chest— Apollo with his portmanteau!—My man,' stepping out to him, 'you can't take that big box aboard a warship. The boxes there are mostly shot boxes. Put your duds in a bag, lad. Boot and saddle for the cavalryman, bag and hammock for the man-of-war's man.'

The transfer from chest to bag was made. And, after seeing his man into the cutter and then following him down, the lieutenant pushed off from the *Rights-of-Man*. That was the merchant ship's name, though by her master and crew abbreviated in sailor fashion into the *Rights*. The hardheaded Dundee owner was a staunch admirer of Thomas Paine, whose book in rejoinder to Burke's arraignment of the French Revolution had then been published for some time and had gone everywhere. In christening his vessel after the title of Paine's volume the man of Dundee was something like his contemporary ship-owner, Stephen Girard of Philadelphia, whose sympathies, alike with this native land and its liberal philosophers, he evinced by naming his ships after Voltaire, Diderot, and so forth.

But now, when the boat swept under the merchantman's stern, and officer and oarsmen were noting—some bitterly and others with a grin—the name emblazoned there; just then it was that the new recruit jumped up from the bow where the coxswain had directed him to sit, and waving hat to his silent shipmates sorrowfully looking over at him from the taffrail, bade the lads a genial good-bye. Then, making a salutation as to the ship herself, 'And good-bye to you too, old *Rights-of-Man*.'

'Down sir!' roared the lieutenant, instantly assuming all the rigor of his rank, though with difficulty repressing a smile.

To be sure, Billy's action was a terrible breach of naval decorum. But in that decorum he had never been instructed; in consideration of which the lieutenant would hardly have been so energetic in reproof but for the concluding farewell to the ship. This he rather took as meant to convey a covert sally on the new recruit's part, a sly slur at impressment in general, and that of himself in especial. And yet, more likely, if satire it was in effect, it was hardly so by intention, for Billy, though happily endowed with the gaiety of high health, youth, and a free heart, was yet by no means of a satirical turn. The will to it and the sinister dexterity were alike wanting. To deal in double meanings and insinuations of any sort was quite foreign to his nature.

As to his enforced enlistment, that he seemed to take pretty much as he was wont to take any vicissitude of weather. Like the animals, though no philosopher, he was, without knowing it, practically a fatalist. And it may be that he rather liked this adventurous turn in his affairs, which promised an opening into novel scenes and martial excitements.

Aboard the *Bellipotent* our merchant sailor was forthwith rated as an able seaman and assigned to the starboard watch of the foretop. He was soon at home in the service, not at all disliked for his unpretentious good looks and a sort of genial happy-go-lucky air. No merrier man in his mess: in marked contrast to certain other individuals included like himself among the impressed portion of the ship's company; for these when not actively employed were sometimes, and more particularly in the last dogwatch when the drawing near of twilight induced revery, apt to fall into a saddish mood which in some partook of sullenness. But they were not so young as our foretopman, and no few of them must have known a hearth of some sort, others may have had wives and children left, too probably, in uncertain circumstances, and hardly any but must have had acknowledged kith and kin, while for Billy, as will shortly be seen, his entire family was practically invested in himself.

2

THOUGH our new-made foretopman was well received in the top and on the gun decks, hardly here was he that cynosure he had previously been among those minor ship's companies of the merchant marine, with which companies only had he hitherto consorted.

He was young; and despite his all but fully developed frame, in aspect looked even younger than he really was, owing to a lingering adolescent expression in the as yet smooth face all but feminine in purity of natural complexion but where, thanks to his seagoing, the lily was quite suppressed and the rose had some ado visibly to flush through the tan.

To one essentially such a novice in the complexities of factitious life, the abrupt transition from his former and simpler sphere to the ampler and more knowing world of a great warship; this might well have abashed him had there been any conceit or vanity in his composition. Among her miscellaneous multitude, the *Bellipotent* mustered several individuals who however inferior in grade were of no common natural stamp, sailors more signally susceptive of that air which continuous martial discipline and repeated presence in battle can in some degree impart even to the average man. As the Handsome Sailor, Billy Budd's position aboard the seventy-four was something analogous to that of a rustic beauty transplanted from the provinces and brought into competition with the high-born dames of the court. But this change of circumstances he scarce noted. As little did he observe that something about him provoked an ambiguous smile in one or two harder faces among the bluejackets. Nor less unaware was he of the peculiar favorable effect his person and demeanor had upon the more intelligent gentlemen of the quarter-deck. Nor could this well have been otherwise. Cast in a mold peculiar to the finest physical examples of those Englishmen in whom the Saxon strain would seem not at all to partake of any Norman or other admixture, he showed in face that humane look of reposeful good nature which the Greek sculptor in some instances gave to his heroic strong man, Hercules. But this again was subtly modified by another and pervasive quality. The ear, small and shapely, the arch of the foot, the curve in mouth and nostril, even the indurated hand dyed to the orange-tawny of the toucan's bill, a hand telling alike of the halyards and tar bucket; but, above all, something in the mobile expression, and every chance attitude and movement, something suggestive of a mother eminently favored by Love and the Graces; all this strangely indicated lineage in direct contradiction to his lot. The mysteriousness here became less mysterious through a matter of fact elicited when Billy at the capstan was being formally mustered into the service. Asked by the officer, a small, brisk little gentleman as it chanced, among other questions, his place of birth, he replied, 'Please, sir, I don't know.'

'Don't know where you were born? Who was your father?'

'God knows, sir.'

Struck by the straightforward simplicity of these replies, the officer next asked, Do you know anything about your beginning?'

'No, sir. But I have heard that I was found in a pretty silk-lined basket hanging one morning from the knocker of a good man's door in Bristol.'

'*Found*, say you? Well,' throwing back his head and looking up and down the new recruit; 'well, it turns out to have been a pretty good find. Hope they'll find some more like you, my man; the fleet sadly needs them.'

Yes, Billy Budd was a foundling, a presumable by-blow, and, evidently, no ignoble one. Noble descent was as evident in him as in a blood horse.

For the rest, with little or no sharpness of faculty or any trace of the wisdom of the serpent, nor yet quite a dove, he possessed that kind and degree of intelligence going along with the unconventional rectitude of a sound human creature, one to whom not yet has been proffered the questionable apple of knowledge. He was illiterate; he could not read, but he could sing, and like the illiterate nightingale was sometimes the composer of his own song.

Of self-consciousness he seemed to have little or none, or about as much as we may reasonably impute to a dog of Saint Bernard's breed.

Habitually living with the elements and knowing little more of the land than as a beach, or, rather, that portion of the terraqueous globe providentially set apart for dance-houses, doxies, and tapsters, in short what sailors call a 'fiddler's green,' his simple nature remained unsophisticated by those moral obliquities which are not in every case incompatible with that manufacturable thing known as respectability. But are sailors, frequenters of fiddler's greens, without vices? No; but less often than with landsmen do their vices, so called, partake of crookedness of heart, seeming less to proceed from viciousness than exuberance of vitality after long constraint: frank manifestations in accordance with natural law. By his original constitution aided by the co-operating influences of his lot, Billy in many respects was little more than a sort of upright barbarian, much such perhaps as Adam presumably might have been ere the urbane Serpent wriggled himself into his company.

And here be it submitted that apparently going to corroborate the doctrine of man's Fall, a doctrine now popularly ignored, it is observable that where certain virtues pristine and unadulterate peculiarly characterize anybody in the external uniform of civilization, they will upon scrutiny seem not to be derived from custom or convention, but rather to be out of keeping with these, as if indeed exceptionally transmitted from a period prior to Cain's city and citified man. The character marked by such qualities has to an unvitiated taste an untampered-with flavor like that of berries, while the man thoroughly civilized, even in a fair specimen of the breed, has to the same moral palate a questionable smack as of a compounded wine. To any stray inheritor of these primitive qualities found, like Caspar Hauser, wandering dazed in any Christian capital of our time, the good-natured poet's famous invocation, near two thousand years ago, of the good rustic out of his latitude in the Rome of the Caesars, still appropriately holds:

> Honest and poor, faithful in word and thought,
> What hath thee, Fabian, to the city brought?

Though our Handsome Sailor had as much of masculine beauty as one can expect anywhere to see; nevertheless, like the beautiful woman in one of Hawthorne's minor tales, there was just one thing amiss in him. No visible blemish indeed, as with the lady; no, but an occasional liability to a vocal defect. Though in the hour of elemental uproar or peril he was everything that a sailor should be, yet under sudden provocation of strong heart-feeling his voice, otherwise singularly musical, as if expressive of the harmony within, was apt to develop an organic hesitancy, in fact more or less of a stutter of even worse. In this particular Billy was a striking instance that the arch interferer, the envious marplot of Eden, still has more or less to do with every human consignment to this planet of Earth. In every case, one way or another he is sure to slip in his little card, as much as to remind us—I too have a hand here.

The avowal of such an imperfection in the Handsome Sailor should be evidence not alone that he is not presented as a conventional hero, but also that the story in which he is the main figure is no romance.

3

AT the time of Billy Budd's arbitrary enlistment into the *Bellipotent* that ship was on her way to join the Mediterranean fleet. No long time elapsed before the junction was effected. As one of that fleet the seventy-four participated in its movements, though at times on account of her superior sailing qualities, in the absence of frigates, dispatched on separate duty as a scout and at times on less temporary service. But with all this the story has little concernment, restricted as it is to the inner life of one particular ship and the career of an individual sailor.

It was the summer of 1797. In the April of that year had occurred the commotion at Spithead followed in May by a second and yet more serious outbreak in the fleet at the Nore. The latter is known, and without exaggeration in the epithet, as 'the Great Mutiny.' It was indeed a demonstration more menacing to England than the contemporary manifestoes and conquering and proselyting armies of the French Directory. To the British Empire the Nore Mutiny was what a strike in the fire brigade would be to London threatened by general arson. In a crisis when the kingdom might well have anticipated the famous signal that some years later published along the naval line of battle what it was that upon occasion England expected of Englishmen; *that* was the time when at the mastheads of the three-deckers and seventy-fours moored in her own roadstead—a fleet the right arm of a Power then all but the sole free conservative one of the Old World—the bluejackets, to be numbered by thousands, ran up with huzzas the British colors with the union and cross wiped out; by that cancellation transmuting the flag of founded law and freedom defined, into the enemy's red meteor of unbridled and unbounded revolt. Reasonable discontent growing out of practical grievances in the fleet had been ignited into irrational combustion as by live cinders blown across the Channel from France in flames.

The event converted into irony for a time those spirited strains of Dibdin—as a song-writer no mean auxiliary to the English government at that European conjuncture—strains celebrating, among other things, the patriotic devotion of the British tar: 'And as for my life, 'tis the King's!'

Such an episode in the Island's grand naval story her naval historians naturally abridge, one of them (William James) candidly acknowledging that fain would he pass it over did not 'impartiality forbid fastidiousness.' And yet his mention is less a narration than a reference, having to do hardly at all with details. Nor are these readily to be found in the libraries. Like some other events in every age befalling states everywhere, including America, the Great Mutiny was of such character that national pride along with views of policy would fain shade it off into the historical background. Such events cannot be ignored, but there is a considerate way of historically treating them. If a well-constituted individual refrains from blazoning aught amiss or calamitous in his family, a nation in the like circumstance may without reproach be equally discreet.

Though after parleyings between government and the ringleaders, and concessions by the former as to some glaring abuses, the first uprising—that at Spithead—with difficulty was put down, or matters for the time pacified; yet at the Nore the unforeseen renewal of insurrection on a yet larger scale, and emphasized in the conferences that ensued by demands deemed by the authorities not only inadmissible but aggressively insolent, indicated—if the Red Flag did not sufficiently do so—what was the spirit animating the men. Final suppression, however, there was; but only made possible perhaps by the unswerving loyalty of the marine corps and a voluntary resumption of loyalty among influential sections of the crews.

To some extent the Nore Mutiny may be regarded as analogous to the distempering irruption of contagious fever in a frame constitutionally sound, and which anon throws it off.

At all events, of these thousands of mutineers were some of the tars who not so very long afterwards—whether wholly prompted thereto by patriotism, or pugnacious instinct, or by both—helped to win a coronet for Nelson at the Nile, and the naval crown of crowns for him at Trafalgar. To the mutineers, those battles and especially Trafalgar were a plenary absolution and a grand one. For all that goes to make up scenic naval display and heroic magnificence in arms, those battles, especially Trafalgar, stand unmatched in human annals.

4

In this matter of writing, resolve as one may to keep to the main road, some bypaths have an enticement not readily to be withstood. I am going to err into such a bypath. If the reader will keep me company I shall be glad. At the least, we can promise ourselves that pleasure which is wickedly said to be in sinning, for a literary sin the divergence will be.

Very likely it is no new remark that the inventions of our time have at last brought about a change in sea warfare in degree corresponding to the revolution in all warfare effected by the original introduction from China into Europe of gunpowder. The first European firearm, a clumsy contrivance, was, as is well known, scouted by no few of the knights as a base implement, good enough peradventure for weavers too craven to stand up crossing steel with steel in frank fight. But as ashore knightly valor, though shorn of its blazonry, did not cease with the knights, neither on the seas—though nowadays in encounters there a certain kind of displayed gallantry be fallen out of date as hardly applicable under changed circumstances—did the nobler qualities of such naval magnates as Don John of Austria, Doria, Van Tromp, Jean Bart, the long line of British admirals, and the American Decaturs of 1812 become obsolete with their wooden walls.

Nevertheless, to anybody who can hold the Present at its worth without being inappreciative of the Past, it may be forgiven, if to such an one the solitary old hulk at Portsmouth, Nelson's *Victory*, seems to float there, not alone as the decaying monument of a fame incorruptible, but also as a poetic reproach, softened by its picturesqueness, to the *Monitors* and yet mightier hulls of the European ironclads. And this not altogether because such craft are unsightly, unavoidably lacking the symmetry and grand lines of the old battleships, but equally for other reasons.

There are some, perhaps, who while not altogether inaccessible to that poetic reproach just alluded to, may yet on behalf of the new order be disposed to parry it; and this to the extent of iconoclasm, if need be. For example, prompted by the sight of the star inserted in the *Victory's* quarter-deck designating the spot where the Great Sailor fell, these martial utilitarians may suggest considerations implying that Nelson's ornate publication of his person in battle was not only unneccessary, but not military, nay, savored of foolhardiness and vanity. They may add, too, that at Trafalgar it was in effect nothing less than a challenge to death; and death came; and that but for his bravado the victorious admiral might possibly have survived the battle, and so, instead of having his sagacious dying injunctions overruled by his immediate successor in command, he himself when the contest was decided might have brought his shattered fleet to anchor, a proceeding which might have averted the deplorable loss of life by shipwreck in the elemental tempest that followed the martial one.

Well, should we set aside the more than disputable point whether for various reasons it was possible to anchor the fleet, then plausibly enough the Benthamites of war may urge the above. But the *might-have-been* is but boggy ground to build on. And, certainly, in foresight as to the larger issue of an encounter, and anxious preparations for it—buoying the deadly way and mapping it out, as at Copenhagen—few commanders have been so painstakingly circumspect as this same reckless declarer of his person in fight.

Personal prudence, even when dictated by quite other than selfish considerations, surely is no special virtue in a military man; while an excessive love of glory, impassioning a less burning impulse, the honest sense of duty, is the first. If the name *Wellington* is not so much of a trumpet to the blood as the simpler name *Nelson*, the reason for this may perhaps be inferred from the above. Alfred in his funeral ode on the victor of Waterloo ventures not to call him the greatest soldier of all time, though in the same ode he invokes Nelson as 'the greatest sailor since our world began.'

At Trafalgar Nelson on the brink of opening the fight sat down and wrote his last brief will and testament. If under the presentiment of the most magnificent of all victories to be crowned by his own glorious death, a sort of priestly motive led him to dress his person in the jewelled vouchers of his own shining deeds; if thus to have adorned himself for the altar and the sacrifice were indeed vainglory, then affectation and fustian is each more heroic line in the great epics and dramas, since in such lines the poet but embodies in verse those exaltations of sentiment that a nature like Nelson, the opportunity being given, vitalizes into acts.

5

YES, the outbreak at the Nore was put down. But not every grievance was redressed. If the contractors, for example, were no longer permitted to ply some practices peculiar to their tribe everywhere, such as providing shoddy cloth, rations not sound, or false in the measure; not the less impressment, for one thing, went on. By custom sanctioned for centuries, and judicially maintained by a Lord Chancellor as late as Mansfield, that mode of manning the fleet, a mode now fallen into a sort of abeyance but never formally renounced, it was not practicable to give up in those years. Its abrogation would have crippled the indispensable fleet, one wholly under canvas, no steam power, in innumerable sails and thousands of cannon, everything in short, worked by muscle alone; a fleet the more insatiate in demand for men, because then multiplying its ships of all grades against contingencies present and to come of the convulsed Continent.

Discontent foreran the Two Mutinies, and more or less it lurkingly survived them. Hence it was not unreasonable to apprehend some return of trouble sporadic or general. One instance of such apprehensions: In the same year with this story, Nelson, then Rear Admiral Sir Horatio, being with the fleet off the Spanish coast, was directed by the admiral in command to shift his pennant from the *Captain* to the *Theseus*; and for this reason: that the latter ship having newly arrived on the station from home, where it had taken part in the Great Mutiny, danger was apprehended from the temper of the men; and it was thought that an officer like Nelson was the one, not indeed to terrorize the crew into base subjection, but to win them, by force of his mere presence and heroic personality, back to an allegiance if not as enthusiastic as his own yet as true.

So it was that for a time, on more than one quarter-deck, anxiety did exist. At sea, precautionary vigilance was strained against relapse. At short notice an engagement might come on. When it did, the lieutenants assigned to batteries felt it incumbent on them, in some instances, to stand with drawn swords behind the men working the guns.

658

6

BUT on board the seventy-four in which Billy now swung his hammock, very little in the manner of the men and nothing obvious in the demeanor of the officers would have suggested to an ordinary observer that the Great Mutiny was a recent event. In their general bearing and conduct the commissioned officers of a warship naturally take their tone from the commander, that is if he have that ascendancy of character that ought to be his.

Captain the Honorable Edward Fairfax Vere, to give his full title, was a bachelor of forty or thereabouts, a sailor of distinction even in a time prolific of renowned seamen. Though allied to the higher nobility, his advancement had not been altogether owing to influences connected with that circumstance. He had seen much service, been in various engagements, always acquitting himself as an officer mindful of the welfare of his men, but never tolerating an infraction of discipline; thoroughly versed in the science of his profession, and intrepid to the verge of temerity, though never injudiciously so. For his gallantry in the West Indian waters as flag lieutenant under Rodney in that admiral's crowning victory over De Grasse, he was made a post captain.

Ashore, in the garb of a civilian, scarce anyone would have taken him for a sailor, more especially that he never garnished unprofessional talk with nautical terms, and grave in his bearing, evinced little appreciation of mere humor. It was not out of keeping with these traits that on a passage when nothing demanded his paramount action, he was the most undemonstrative of men. Any landsman observing this gentleman not conspicuous by his stature and wearing no pronounced insignia, emerging from his cabin to the open deck, and noting the silent deference of the officers retiring to leeward, might have taken him for the King's guest, a civilian aboard the King's ship, some highly honorable discreet envoy on his way to an important post. But in fact this unobtrusiveness of demeanor may have proceeded from a certain unaffected modesty of manhood sometimes accompanying a resolute nature, a modesty evinced at all times not calling for pronounced action, which shown in any rank of life suggests a virtue aristocratic in kind. As with some others engaged in various departments of the world's more heroic activities, Captain Vere though practical enough upon occasion would at times betray a certain dreaminess of mood. Standing alone on the weather side of the quarter-deck, one hand holding by the rigging, he would absently gaze off at the blank sea. At the presentation to him then of some minor matter interrupting the current of his thoughts, he would show more or less irascibility; but instantly he would control it.

In the navy he was popularly known by the appellation 'Starry Vere.' How such a designation happened to fall upon one who whatever his sterling qualities was without any brilliant ones, was in this wise: A favorite kinsman, Lord Denton, a freehearted fellow, had been the first to meet and congratulate him upon his return to England from his West Indian cruise; and but the day previous turning over a copy of Andrew Marvell's poems had lighted, not for the first time, however, upon the lines entitled 'Appleton House,' the name of one of the seats of their common ancestor, a hero in the German wars of the seventeenth century, in which poem occur the lines:

> This 'tis to have been from the first
> In a domestic heaven nursed,
> Under the discipline severe
> Of Fairfax and the starry Vere.

And so, upon embracing his cousin fresh from Rodney's great victory wherein he had played so gallant a part, brimming over with just family pride in the sailor of their house, he exuberantly exclaimed, 'Give ye joy, Ed; give ye joy, my starry Vere!' This got currency, and the novel prefix serving a familiar parlance readily to distinguish the *Bellipotent*'s captain from another Vere his senior, a distant relative, an officer of like rank in the navy, it remained permanently attached to the surname.

7

In view of the part that the commander of the *Bellipotent* plays in scenes shortly to follow, it may be well to fill out that sketch of him outlined in the previous chapter.

Aside from his qualities as a sea officer Captain Vere was an exceptional character. Unlike no few of England's renowned sailors, long and arduous service with signal devotion to it had not resulted in absorbing and *salting* the entire man. He had a marked leaning toward everything intellectual. He loved books, never going to sea without a newly replenished library, compact but of the best. The isolated leisure, in some cases so wearisome, falling at intervals to commanders even during a war cruise, never was tedious to Captain Vere. With nothing of that literary taste which less heeds the thing conveyed than the vehicle, his bias was toward those books to which every serious mind of superior order occupying any active post of authority in the world naturally inclines: books treating of actual men and events no matter of what era—history, biography, and unconventional writers like Montaigne, who, free from cant and convention, honestly and in the spirit of common sense philosophize upon realities. In this line of reading he found confirmation of his own more reserved thoughts—confirmation which he had vainly sought in social converse, so that as touching most fundamental topics, there had got to be established in him some positive convictions which he forefelt would abide in him essentially unmodified so long as his intelligent part remained unimpaired. In view of the troubled period in which his lot was cast, this was well for him. His settled convictions were as a dike against those invading waters of novel opinion social, political, and otherwise, which carried away as in a torrent no few minds in those days, minds by nature not inferior to his own. While other members of that aristocracy to which by birth he belonged were incensed in the innovators mainly because their theories were inimical to the privileged classes, Captain Vere disinterestedly opposed them not alone because they seemed to him insusceptible of embodiment in lasting institutions, but at war with the peace of the world and the true welfare of mankind.

With minds less stored than his and less earnest, some officers of this rank, with whom at times he would necessarily consort, found him lacking in the companionable quality, a dry and bookish gentleman, as they deemed. Upon any chance withdrawal from their company one would be apt to say to another something like this: 'Vere is a noble fellow, Starry Vere. 'Spite the gazettes, Sir Horatio' (meaning him who became Lord Nelson) 'is at bottom scarce a better seaman or fighter. But between you and me now, don't you think there is a queer streak of the pedantic running through him? Yes, like the King's yarn in a coil of navy rope?'

Some apparent ground there was for this sort of confidential criticism; since not only did the captain's discourse never fall into the jocosely familiar, but in illustrating of any point touching the stirring personages and events of the time he would be as apt to cite some historic character or incident of antiquity as he would be to cite from the moderns. He seemed unmindful of the circumstance that to his bluff company such remote allusions, however pertinent they might really be, were altogether alien to men whose reading was mainly confined to the journals. But considerateness in such matters is not easy to natures constituted like Captain Vere's. Their honesty prescribes to them directness, sometimes far-reaching like that of a migratory fowl that in its flight never heeds when it crosses a frontier.

8

THE lieutenants and other commissioned gentlemen forming Captin Vere's staff it is not necessary here to particularize, nor needs it to make any mention of any of the warrant officers. But among the petty officers was one who, having much to do with the story, may as well be forthwith introduced. His portrait I essay, but shall never hit it. This was John Claggart, the master-at-arms. But that sea title may to landsmen seem somewhat equivocal. Originally, doubtless, that petty officer's function was the instruction of the men in the use of arms, sword or cutlass. But very long ago, owing to the advance in gunnery making hand-to-hand encounters less frequent and giving to niter and sulphur the pre-eminence over steel, that function ceased; the master-at-arms of a great warship becoming a sort of chief of police charged among other matters with the duty of preserving order on the populous lower gun decks.

Claggart was a man about five-and-thirty, somewhat spare and tall, yet of no ill figure upon the whole. His hand was too small and shapely to have been accustomed to hard toil. The face was a notable one, the features all except the chin cleanly cut as those on a Greek medallion; yet the chin, beardless as Tecumseh's, had something of strange protuberant broadness in its make that recalled the prints of the Reverend Dr Titus Oates, the historic deponent with the clerical drawl in the time of Charles II and the fraud of the alleged Popish Plot. It served Claggart in his office that his eye could cast a tutoring glance. His brow was of the sort phrenologically associated with more than average intellect; silken jet curls partly clustering over it, making a foil to the pallor below, a pallor tinged with a faint shade of amber akin to the hue of time-tinted marbles of old. This complexion, singularly contrasting with the red or deeply bronzed visages of the sailors, and in part the result of his official seclusion from the sunlight, though it was not exactly displeasing, nevertheless seemed to hint of something defective or abnormal in the constitution and blood. But his general aspect and manner were so suggestive of an education and career incongruous with his naval function that when not actively engaged in it he looked like a man of high quality, social and moral, who for reasons of his own was keeping incog. Nothing was known of his former life. It might be that he was an Englishman; and yet there lurked a bit of accent in his speech suggesting that possibly he was not such by birth, but through naturalization in early childhood. Among certain grizzled sea gossips of the gun decks and forecastle went a rumor perdue that the master-at-arms was a *chevalier* who had volunteered into the King's navy by way of compounding for some mysterious swindle whereof he had been arraigned at the King's Bench. The fact that nobody could substantiate this report was, of course, nothing against its secret currency. Such a rumor once started on the gun decks in reference to almost anyone below the rank of a commissioned officer would, during the period assigned to this narrative, have seemed not altogether wanting in credibility to the tarry old wise-acres of a man-of-war crew. And indeed a man of Claggart's accomplishments, without prior nautical experience entering the navy at mature life, as he did, and necessarily allotted at the start to the lowest grade in it; a man too who never made allusion to his previous life ashore; these were circumstances which in the earth of exact knowledge as to his true antecedents opened to the invidious a vague field for unfavorable surmise.

But the sailors' dogwatch gossip concerning him derived a vague plausibility from the fact that now for some period the British navy could so little afford to be squeamish in the matter of keeping up the muster rolls, that not only were press gangs notoriously abroad both afloat and ashore, but there was little or no secret about another matter, namely, that the London police were at liberty to capture any able-bodied suspect, any questionable fellow at large, and summarily ship him to the dockyard or fleet. Furthermore, even among voluntary enlistments there were instances where the motive thereto partook neither of patriotic impulse nor yet of a random desire to experience a bit of sea life and martial adventure. Insolvent debtors of minor grade, together with the promiscuous lame ducks of morality, found in the navy a convenient and secure refuge, secure because, once enlisted aboard a King's ship, they were as much in sanctuary as the transgressor of the Middle Ages harboring himself under the shadow of the altar. Such sanctioned irregularities, which for obvious reasons the government would hardly think to parade at the time and which consequently, and as affecting the least influential class of mankind, have all but dropped into oblivion, lend color to something for the truth whereof I do not vouch, and hence have some scruple in stating; something I remember having seen in print though the book I cannot recall; but the same thing was personally communicated to me now more than forty years ago by an old pensioner in a cocked hat with whom I had a most interesting talk on the terrace at Greenwich, a Baltimore Negro, a Trafalgar man. It was to this effect: In the case of a warship short of hands whose speedy sailing was imperative, the deficient quota, in lack of any other way of making it good, would be eked out by drafts culled direct from the jails. For reasons previously suggested it would not perhaps be easy at the present day directly to prove or disprove the allegation. But allowed as a verity, how significant would it be of England's straits at the time confronted by those wars which like a flight of harpies rose shrieking from the din and dust of the fallen Bastille. That era appears measurably clear to us who look back at it, and but read of it. But to the grandfathers of us graybeards, the more thoughtful of them, the genius of it presented an aspect like that of Camoëns' Spirit of the Cape, an eclipsing menace mysterious and prodigious. Not America was exempt from apprehension. At the height of Napoleon's unexampled conquests, there were Americans who had fought at Bunker Hill who looked forward to the possibility that the Atlantic might prove no barrier against the ultimate schemes of this French portentous upstart from the revolutionary chaos who seemed in act of fulfilling judgment prefigured in the Apocalypse.

But the less credence was to be given to the gun-deck talk touching Claggart, seeing that no man holding his office in a man-of-war can ever hope to be popular with the crew. Besides, in derogatory comments upon anyone against whom they have a grudge, or for any reason or no reason mislike, sailors are much like landsmen: they are apt to exaggerate or romance it.

About as much was really known to the *Bellipotent*'s tars of the master-at-arms' career before entering the service as an astronomer knows about a comet's travels prior to its first observable appearance in the sky. The verdict of the sea quidnuncs has been cited only by way of showing what sort of moral impression the man made upon rude uncultivated natures whose conceptions of human wickedness were necessarily of the narrowest, limited to ideas of vulgar rascality—a thief among the swinging hammocks during a night watch, or the man-brokers and land-sharks of the seaports.

It was no gossip, however, but fact that though, as before hinted, Claggart upon his entrance into the navy was, as a novice, assigned to the least honorable section of a man-of-war's crew, embracing the drudgery, he did not long remain there. The superior capacity he immediately evinced, his constitutional sobriety, an ingratiating deference to superiors, together with a peculiar ferreting genius manifested on a singular occasion; all this, capped by a certain austere patriotism, abruptly advanced him to the position of master-at-arms.

Of this maritime chief of police the ship's corporals, so called, were the immediate subordinates, and compliant ones; and this, as is to be noted in some business departments ashore, almost to a degree inconsistent with entire moral volition. His place put various converging wires of underground influence under the chief's control, capable when astutely worked through his understrappers of operating to the mysterious discomfort, if nothing worse, of any of the sea commonalty.

9

LIFE in the foretop well agreed with Billy Budd. There, when not actually engaged on the yards yet higher aloft, the topmen, who as such had been picked out for youth and activity, constituted and aerial club lounging at ease against the smaller stun'sails rolled up into cushions, spinning yarns like the lazy gods, and frequently amused with what was going on in the busy world of the decks below. No wonder then that a young fellow of Billy's disposition was well content in such society. Giving no cause of offense to anybody, he was always alert at a call. So in the merchant service it had been with him. But now such a punctiliousness in duty was shown that his topmates would sometimes good-naturedly laugh at him for it. This heightened alacrity had its cause, namely, the impression made upon him by the first formal gangway-punishment he had ever witnessed, which befell the day following his impressment. It had been incurred by a little fellow, young, a novice afterguardsman absent from his assigned post when the ship was being put about; a dereliction resulting in a rather serious hitch to that maneuver, one demanding instantaneous promptitude in letting go and making fast. When Billy saw the culprit's naked back under the scourge, gridironed with red welts and worse, when he marked the dire expression in the liberated man's face as with his woolen shirt flung over him by the executioner he rushed forward from the spot to bury himself in the crowd, Billy was horrified. He resolved that never through remissness would he make himself liable to such a visitation or do or omit aught that might merit even verbal reproof. What then was his surprise and concern when ultimately he found himself getting into petty trouble occasionally about such matters as the stowage of his bag or something amiss in his hammock, matters under the police over-sight of the ship's corporals of the lower decks, and which brought down on him a vague threat from one of them.

So heedful in all things as he was, how could this be? He could not understand it, and it more than vexed him. When he spoke to his young topmates about it they were either lightly incredulous or found something comical in his unconcealed anxiety. 'Is it your bag, Billy?' said one. 'Well, sew yourself up in it, bully boy, and then you'll be sure to know if anybody meddles with it.'

Now there was a veteran aboard who because his years began to disqualify him for more active work had been recently assigned duty as mainmastman in his watch, looking to the gear belayed at the rail roundabout that great spar near the deck. At off-times the foretopman had picked up some acquaintance with him, and now in his trouble it occurred to him that he might be the sort of person to go to for wise counsel. He was an old Dansker long anglicized in the service, of few words, many wrinkles, and some honorable scars. His wizened face, time-tinted and weather-stained to the complexion of an antique parchment, was her and there peppered blue by the chance explosion of a gun cartridge in action.

He was an *Agamemnon* man, some two years prior to the time of this story having served under Nelson when still captain in that ship immortal in naval memory, which dismantled and in part broken up to her bare ribs is seen a grand skeleton in Haden's etching. As one of a boarding party from the *Agamemnon* he had received a cut slantwise along one temple and cheek leaving a long pale scar like a streak of dawn's light falling athwart the dark visage. It was on account of that scar and the affair in which it was known that he had received it, as well as from his blue-peppered complexion, that the Dansker went among the *Bellipotent*'s crew by the name of 'Board-Her-in-the-Smoke.'

Now the first time that his small weasel eyes happened to light on Billy Budd, a certain grim internal merriment set all his ancient wrinkles into antic play. Was it that his eccentric unsentimental old sapience, primitive in its kind, saw or thought it saw something which in contrast with the warship's environment looked oddly incongruous in the Handsome Sailor? But after slyly studying him at intervals, the old Merlin's equivocal merriment was modified; for now when the twain would meet, it would start in his face a quizzing sort of look, but it would be but momentary and sometimes replaced by an expression of speculative query as to what might eventually befall a nature like that, dropped into a world not without some mantraps and against whose subtleties simple courage lacking experience and address, and without any touch of defensive ugliness, is of little avail; and where such innocence as man is capable of does yet in a moral emergency not always sharpen the faculties or enlighten the will.

However it was, the Dansker in his ascetic way rather took to Billy. Nor was this only because of a certain philosophic interest in such a character. There was another cause. While the old man's eccentricities, sometimes bordering on the ursine, repelled the juniors, Billy, undeterred thereby, revering him as a salt hero, would make advances, never passing the old *Agamemnon* man without a salutation marked by that respect which is seldom lost on the aged, however crabbed at times or whatever their station in life.

There was a vein of dry humor, or what not, in the mastman; and, whether in freak of patriarchal irony touching Billy's youth and athletic frame, or for some other and more recondite reason, from the first in addressing him he always substituted *Baby* for Billy, the Dansker in fact being the originator of the name by which the foretopman eventually became known aboard ship.

Well then, in his mysterious little difficulty going in quest of the wrinkled one, Billy found him off duty in a dogwatch ruminating by himself, seated on a shot box of the upper gun deck, now and then surveying with a somewhat cynical regard certain of the more swaggering promenaders there. Billy recounted his trouble, again wondering how it all happened. The salt seer attentively listened, accompanying the foretopman's recital with queer twitchings of his wrinkles and problematical little sparkles of his small ferret eyes. Making an end of his story, the foretopman asked, 'And now, Dansker, do tell me what you think of it.'

The old man, shoving up the front of his tarpaulin and deliberately rubbing the long slant scar at the point where it entered the thin hair, laconically said, 'Baby Budd, *Jemmy Legs*' (meaning the master-at-arms) 'is down on you.'

'*Jemmy Legs!*' ejaculated Billy, his welkin eyes expanding. 'What for? Why, he calls me "the sweet and pleasant young fellow," they tell me.'

'Does he so?' grinned the grizzled one; then said, 'Ay, Baby lad, a sweet voice has Jemmy Legs.'

'No, not always. But to me he has. I seldom pass him but there cones a pleasant word.'

'And that's because he's down upon you, Baby Budd.'

Such reiteration, along with the manner of it, incomprehensible to a novice, disturbed Billy almost as much as the mystery for which he had sought explanation. Something less unpleasingly oracular he tried to extract; but the old sea Chiron, thinking perhaps that for the nonce he had sufficiently instructed his young Achilles, pursed his lips, gathered all his wrinkles together, and would commit himself to nothing further.

Years, and those experiences which befall certain shrewder men subordinated lifelong to the will of superiors, all this had developed in the Dansker the pithy guarded cynicism that was his leading characteristic.

10

THE next day an incident served to confirm Billy Budd in his incredulity as to the Dansker's strange summing up of the case submitted. The ship at noon, going large before the wind, was rolling on her course, and he below at dinner and engaged in some sportful talk with the members of his mess, chanced in a sudden lurch to spill the entire contents of his soup pan upon the new-scrubbed deck. Claggart, the master-at-arms, official rattan in hand, happened to be passing along the battery in a bay of which the mess was lodged, and the greasy liquid streamed just across his path. Stepping over it, he was proceeding on his way without comment, since the matter was nothing to take notice of

under the circumstances, when he happened to observe who it
was that had done the spilling. His countenance changed. Pausing,
he was about to ejaculate something hasty at the sailor, but checked
himself, and pointing down to the streaming soup, playfully tapped
him from behind with his rattan, saying in a low musical voice
peculiar to him at times, 'Handsomely done, my lad! And handsome is as handsome did it, too!' And with that passed on. Not
noted by Billy as not coming within his view was the involuntary
smile, or rather grimace, that accompanied Claggart's equivocal
words. Aridly it drew down the thin corners of his shapely mouth.
But everybody taking his remark as meant for humorous, and at
which therefore as coming from a superior they were bound to
laugh 'with counterfeited glee,' acted accordingly; and Billy, tickled,
it may be, by the allusion to his being the Handsome Sailor,
merrily joined in; then addressing his messmates exclaimed, 'There
now, who says that Jemmy Legs is down on me!'
      'And who said he was, Beauty?' demanded one Donald with
some surprise. Whereat the foretopman looked a little foolish,
recalling that it was only one person, Board-Her-in-the-Smoke,
who had suggested what to him was the smoky idea that this
master-at-arms was in any peculiar way hostile to him. Meantime
that functionary, resuming his path, must have momentarily worn
some expression less guarded than that of the bitter smile, usurping
the face from the heart—some distorting expression perhaps, for
a drummer-boy heedlessly frolicking along from the opposite direction and chancing to come into light collision with his person
was strangely disconcerted by his aspect. Nor was the impression
lessened when the official, impetuously giving him a sharp cut
with the rattan, vehemently exclaimed, 'Look where you go!'

11

WHAT was the matter with the master-at-arms? And, be the matter
what it might, how could it have direct relation to Billy Budd,
with whom prior to the affair of the spilled soup he had never
come into any special contact official or otherwise? What indeed
could the trouble have to do with one so little inclined to give
offense as the merchantship's 'peacemaker,' even him who in
Claggart's own phrase was 'the sweet and pleasant young fellow'?

Yes, why should Jemmy Legs, to borrow the Dansker's expression, be 'down' on the Handsome Sailor? But, at heart and not for nothing, as the late chance encounter may indicate to the discerning, down on him, secretly down on him, he assuredly was.

Now to invent something touching the more private career of Claggart, something involving Billy Budd, of which something the latter should be wholly ignorant, some romantic incident implying that Claggart's knowledge of the young bluejacket began at some period anterior to catching sight of him on board the seventy-four—all this, not so difficult to do, might avail in a way more or less interesting to account for whatever of enigma may appear to lurk in the case. But in fact there was nothing of the sort. And yet the cause necessarily to be assumed as the sole one assignable is in its very realism as much charged with that prime element of Radcliffian romance, the mysterious, as any that the ingenuity of the author of *The Mysteries of Udolpho* could devise. For what can more partake of the mysterious than an antipathy spontaneous and profound such as is evoked in certain exceptional mortals by the mere aspect of some other mortal, however harmless he may be, if not called forth by this very harmlessness itself?

Now there can exist no irritating juxtaposition of dissimilar personalities comparable to that which is possible aboard a great warship fully manned and at sea. There, every day among all ranks, almost every man comes into more or less of contact with almost every other man. Wholly there to avoid even the sight of an aggravating object one must needs give it Jonah's toss or jump overboard himself. Imagine how all this might eventually operate on some peculiar human creature the direct reverse of a saint!

But for the adequate comprehending of Claggart by a normal nature these hints are insufficient. To pass from a normal nature to him one must cross 'the deadly space between.' And this is best done by indirection.

Long ago an honest scholar, my senior, said to me in reference to one who like himself is now no more, a man so unimpeachably respectable that against him nothing was ever openly said though among the few something was whispered, 'Yes, X—— is a nut not to be cracked by the tap of a lady's fan. You are aware that I am the adherent of no organized religion, much less of any philosophy built into a system. Well, for all that, I think that to try and get into X——, enter his labyrinth and get out again, without a clue derived from some source other than what is known as "knowledge of the world"—that were hardly possible, at least for me.'

'Why,' said I, 'X——, however singular a study to some, is yet human, and knowledge of the world assuredly implies the knowledge of human nature, and in most of its varieties.'

'Yes, but a superficial knowledge of it, serving ordinary purposes. But for anything deeper, I am not certain whether to know the world and to know human nature be not two distinct branches of knowledge, which while they may coexist in the same heart, yet either may exist with little or nothing of the other. Nay, in an average man of the world, his constant rubbing with it blunts that finer spiritual insight indispensable to the understanding of the essential in certain exceptional characters, whether evil ones or good. In a matter of some importance I have seen a girl wind an old lawyer about her little finger. Nor was it the dotage of senile love. Nothing of the sort. But he knew law better than he knew the girl's heart. Coke and Blackstone hardly shed so much light into obscure spiritual places as the Hebrew prophets. And who were they? Mostly recluses.'

At the time, my inexperience was such that I did not quite see the drift of all this. It may be that I see it now. And, indeed, if that lexicon which is based on Holy Writ were any longer popular, one might with less difficulty define and denominate certain phenomenal men. As it is, one must turn to some authority not liable to the charge of being tinctured with the biblical element.

In a list of definitions included in the authentic translation of Plato, a list attributed to him, occurs this: 'Natural Depravity: a depravity according to nature,' a definition which, though savoring of Calvinism, by no means involves Calvin's dogma as to total mankind. Evidently its intent makes it applicable but to individuals. Not many are the examples of this depravity which the gallows and jail supply. At any rate, for notable instances, since these have no vulgar alloy of the brute in them, but invariably are dominated by intellectuality, one must go elsewhere. Civilization, especially if of the austerer sort, is auspicious to it. It folds itself in the mantle of respectability. It has certain negative virtues serving as silent auxiliaries. It never allows wine to get within its guard. It is not going too far to say that it is without vices or small sins. There is a phenomenal pride in it that excludes them. It is never mercenary or avaricious. In short, the depravity here meant partakes nothing of the sordid or sensual. It is serious, but free from acerbity. Though no flatterer of mankind it never speaks ill of it.

But the thing which in eminent instances signalizes so exceptional a nature is this: Though the man's even temper and discreet bearing would seem to intimate a mind peculiarly subject to the law of reason, not the less in heart he would seem to riot in complete exemption from that law, having apparently little to do with reason further than to employ it as an ambidexter implement for effecting the irrational. That is to say: Toward the accomplishment of an aim which in wantonness of atrocity would seem to partake of the insane, he will direct a cool judgment sagacious and sound. These men are madmen, and of the most dangerous sort, for their lunacy is not continuous, but occasional, evoked by some special object; it is protectively secretive, which is as much as to say it is self-contained, so that when, moreover, most active it is to the average mind not distinguishable from sanity, and for the reason above suggested: that whatever its aims may be—and the aim is never declared—the method and the outward proceeding are always perfectly rational.

Now something such an one was Claggart, in whom was the mania of an evil nature, not engendered by vicious training or corrupting books or licentious living, but born with him and innate, in short 'a depravity according to nature.'

Dark sayings are these, some will say. But why? Is it because they somewhat savor of Holy Writ in its phrase 'mystery of iniquity'? If they do, such savor was far enough from being intended, for little will it commend these pages to many a reader of today.

The point of the present story turning on the hidden nature of the master-at-arms has necessitated this chapter. With an added hint or two in connection with the incident at the mess, the resumed narrative must be left to vindicate, as it may, its own credibility.

12

THAT Claggart's figure was not amiss, and his face, save the chin, well molded, has already been said. Of these favorable points he seemed not insensible, for he was not only neat but careful in his dress. But the form of Billy Budd was heroic; and if his face was without the intellectual look of the pallid Claggart's, not the less was it lit, like his, from within, though from a different source. The bonfire in his heart made luminous the rose-tan in his cheek.

In view of the marked contrast between the persons of the twain, it is more than probable that when the master-at-arms in the scene last given applied to the sailor the proverb 'Handsome is as handsome does,' he there let escape an ironic inkling, not caught by the young sailors who heard it, as to what it was that had first moved him against Billy, namely, his significant personal beauty.

Now envy and antipathy, passions irreconcilable in reason, nevertheless in fact may spring conjoined like Chang and Eng in one birth. Is Envy then such a monster? Well, though many an arraigned mortal has in hopes of mitigated penalty pleaded guilty to horrible actions, did ever anybody seriously confess to envy? Something there is in it universally felt to be more shameful than even felonious crime. And not only does everybody disown it, but the better sort are inclined to incredulity when it is in earnest imputed to an intelligent man. But since its lodgment is in the heart not the brain, no degree of intellect supplies a guarantee against it. But Claggart's was no vulgar form of the passion. Nor, as directed toward Billy Budd, did it partake of that streak of apprehensive jealousy that marred Saul's visage perturbedly brooding on the comely young David. Claggart's envy struck deeper. If askance he eyed the good looks, cheery health, and frank enjoyment of young life in Billy Budd, it was because these went along with a nature that, as Claggart magnetically felt, had in its simplicity never willed malice or experienced the reactionary bite of that serpent. To him, the spirit lodged within Billy, and looking out from his welkin eyes as from windows, that ineffability it was which made the dimple in his dyed cheek, suppled his joints, and dancing in his yellow curls made him preeminently the Handsome Sailor. One person excepted, the master-at-arms was perhaps the only man in the ship intellectually capable of adequately appreciating the moral phenomenon presented in Billy Budd. And the insight but intensified his passion, which assuming various secret forms within him, at times assumed that of cynic disdain, disdain of innocence—to be nothing more than innocent! Yet in an aesthetic way he saw the charm of it, the courageous free-and-easy temper of it, and fain would have shared it, but he despaired of it.

With no power to annul the elemental evil in him, though readily enough he could hide it; apprehending the good, but powerless to be it; a nature like Claggart's, surcharged with energy as such natures almost invariably are, what recourse is left to it but to recoil upon itself and, like the scorpion for which the

Creator alone is responsible, act out to the end the part allotted it.

13

PASSION, and passion in its profoundest, is not a thing demanding a palatial stage whereon to play its part. Down among the ground-lings, among the beggars and rakers of the garbage, profound passion is enacted. And the circumstances that provoke it, however trivial or mean, are no measure of its power. In the present instance the stage is a scrubbed gun deck, and one of the external provocations a man-of-war's man's spilled soup.

Now when the master-at-arms noticed whence came that greasy fluid streaming before his feet, he must have taken it—to some extent wilfully, perhaps—not for the mere accident it assuredly was, but for the sly escape of a spontaneous feeling on Billy's part more or less answering to the antipathy on his own. In effect a foolish demonstration, he must have thought, and very harmless, like the futile kick of a heifer, which yet were the heifer a shod stallion would not be so harmless. Even so was it that into the gall of Claggart's envy he infused the vitriol of his contempt. But the incident confirmed to him certain telltale reports purveyed to his ear by 'Squeak,' one of his more cunning corporals, a grizzled little man, so nicknamed by the sailors on account of his squeaky voice and sharp visage ferreting about the dark corners of the lower decks after interlopers, satirically suggesting to them the idea of a rat in a cellar.

From his chief's employing him as an implicit tool in laying little traps for the worriment of the foretopman—for it was from the master-at-arms that the petty persecutions heretofore adverted to had proceeded—the corporal, having naturally enough con-cluded that his master could have no love for the sailor, made it his business, faithful understrapper that he was, to foment the ill blood by perverting to his chief certain innocent frolics of the good-natured foretopman, besides inventing for his mouth sundry contumelious epithets he claimed to have overheard him let fall. The master-at-arms never suspected the veracity of these reports, more especially as to the epithets, for he well knew how secretly unpopular may become a master-at-arms, at least a master-at-arms of those days, zealous in his function, and how the bluejackets shoot at him in private their raillery and wit; the nickname by which he goes among them (Jemmy Legs) implying under the form of merriment their cherished disrespect and dislike. But in view of the greediness of hate for pabulum it hardly needed a purveyor to feed Claggart's passion.

An uncommon prudence is habitual with the subtler depravity, for it has everything to hide. And in case of an injury but suspected, its secretiveness voluntarily cuts it off from enlightenment or disillusion; and, not unreluctantly, action is taken upon surmise as upon certainty. And the retaliation is apt to be in monstrous disproportion to the supposed offense; for when in anybody was revenge in its exactions aught else but an inordinate usurer? But how with Claggart's conscience? For though consciences are unlike as foreheads, every intelligence, not excluding the scriptural devils who 'believe and tremble,' has one. But Claggart's conscience being but the lawyer to his will, made ogres of trifles, probably arguing that the motive imputed to Billy in spilling the soup just when he did, together with the epithets alleged, these, if nothing more, made a strong case against him; nay, justified animosity into a sort of retributive righteousness. The Pharisee is the Guy Fawkes prowling in the hid chambers underlying some natures like Claggart's. And they can really form no conception of an unreciprocated malice. Probably the master-at-arms' clandestine persecution of Billy was started to try the temper of the man; but it had not developed any quality in him that enmity could make official use of or even pervert into plausible self-justification; so that the occurrence at the mess, petty if it were, was a welcome one to that peculiar conscience assigned to be the private mentor of Claggart; and, for the rest, not improbably it put him upon new experiments.

14

NOT many days after the last incident narrated, something befell Billy Budd that more graveled him than aught that had previously occurred.

It was a warm night for the latitude; and the foretopman, whose watch at the time was properly below, was dozing on the uppermost

deck whither he had ascended from his hot hammock, one of
hundreds suspended so closely wedged together over a lower gun
deck that there was little or no swing to them. He lay as in the
shadow of a hillside, stretched under the lee of the booms, a piled
ridge of spare spars amidships between foremast and mainmast
among which the ship's largest boat, the launch, was stowed.
Alongside of three other slumberers from below, he lay near that
end of the booms which approaches the foremast; his station aloft
on duty as a foretopman being just over the deck-station of the
forecastlemen, entitling him according to usage to make himself
more or less at home in that neighborhood.

Presently he was stirred into semiconsciousness by somebody,
who must have previously sounded the sleep of the others, touching
his shoulder, and then, as the foretopman raised his head, breathing
into his ear in a quick whisper, 'Slip into the lee forechains, Billy;
there is something in the wind. Don't speak. Quick, I will meet
you there,' and disappearing.

Now Billy, like sundry other essentially good-natured ones, had
some of the weaknesses inseparable from essential good nature;
and among these was a reluctance, almost an incapacity of plumply
saying *no* to an abrupt proposition not obviously absurd on the
face of it, nor obviously unfriendly, nor iniquitous. And being of
warm blood, he had not the phlegm tacitly to negative any
proposition by unresponsive inaction. Like his sense of fear, his
apprehension as to aught outside of the honest and natural was
seldom very quick. Besides, upon the present occasion, the drowse
from his sleep still hung upon him.

However it was, he mechanically rose and, sleepily wondering
what could be in the wind, betook himself to the designated place,
a narrow platform, one of six, outside of the high bulwarks and
screened by the great deadeyes and multiple columned lanyards
of the shrouds and backstays; and, in a great warship of that time,
of dimensions commensurate to the hull's magnitude; a tarry
balcony in short, overhanging the sea, and so secluded that one
mariner of the *Bellipotent*, a Nonconformist old tar of a serious
turn, made it even in daytime his private oratory.

In this retired nook the stranger soon joined Billy Budd. There
was no moon as yet; a haze obscured the starlight. He could not
distinctly see the stranger's face. Yet from something in the outline
and carriage, Billy took him, and correctly, for one of the afterguard.

'Hist! Billy,' said the man, in the same quick cautionary whisper
as before. 'You were impressed, weren't you? Well, so was I'; and

he paused, as to mark the effect. But Billy, not knowing exactly what to make of this, said nothing. Then the other: 'We are not the only impressed ones, Billy. There's a gang of us.—Couldn't you—help—at a pinch?'

'What do you mean?' demanded Billy, here thoroughly shaking off his drowse.

'Hist, hist!' the hurried whisper now growing husky. 'See here,' and the man held up two small objects faintly twinkling in the night-light; 'see, they are yours, Billy, if you'll only—'

But Billy broke in, and in his resentful eagerness to deliver himself his vocal infirmity somewhat intruded. 'D—d—damme, I don't know what you are d—d—driving at, or what you mean, but you had better g—g—go where you belong!' For the moment the fellow, as confounded, did not stir; and Billy, springing to his feet, said, 'If you d—don't start, I'll t—t—toss you back over the r—rail!' There was no mistaking this, and the mysterious emissary decamped, disappearing in the direction of the main-mast in the shadow of the booms.

'Hallo, what's the matter?' here came growling from a forecastleman awakened from his deck-doze by Billy's raised voice. And as the foretopman reappeared and was recognized by him: 'Ah, Beauty, is it you? Well, something must have been the matter, for you st—st—stuttered.'

'Oh,' rejoined Billy, now mastering the impediment, 'I found an afterguardsman in our part of the ship here, and I bid him be off where he belongs.'

'And is that all you did about it, Foretopman?' gruffly demanded another, an irascible old fellow of brick-colored visage and hair who was known to his associate forecastlemen as 'Red Pepper.' 'Such sneaks I should like to marry to the gunner's daughter!'— by that expression meaning that he would like to subject them to disciplinary castigation over a gun.

However, Billy's rendering of the matter satisfactorily accounted to these inquirers for the brief commotion, since of all the sections of a ship's company the forecastlemen, veterans for the most part and bigoted in their sea prejudices, are the most jealous in resenting territorial encroachments, especially on the part of any of the afterguard, of whom they have but a sorry opinion—chiefly landsmen, never going aloft except to reef or furl the mainsail, and in no wise competent to handle a marlin-spike or turn in a deadeye, say.

15

THIS incident sorely puzzled Billy Budd. It was an entirely new experience, the first time in his life that he had ever been personally approached in underhand intriguing fashion. Prior to this encounter he had known nothing of the afterguardsman, the two men being stationed wide apart, one forward and aloft during his watch, the other on deck and aft.

What could it mean? And could they really be guineas, those two glittering objects the interloper had held up to his (Billy's) eyes? Where could the fellow get guineas? Why, even spare buttons are not so plentiful at sea. The more he turned the matter over, the more he was nonplussed, and made uneasy and discomfited. In his disgustful recoil from an overture which, though he but ill comprehended, he instinctively knew must involve evil of some sort, Billy Budd was like a young horse fresh from the pasture suddenly inhaling a vile whiff from some chemical factory, and by repeated snortings trying to get it out of his nostrils and lungs. This frame of mind barred all desire of holding farther parley with the fellow, even were it but for the purpose of gaining some enlightenment as to his design in approaching him. And yet he was not without natural curiosity to see how such a visitor in the dark would look in broad day.

He espied him the following afternoon in his first dogwatch below, one of the smokers on that forward part of the upper gun deck allotted to the pipe. He recognized him by his general cut and build more than by his round freckled face and glassy eyes of pale blue, veiled with lashes all but white. And yet Billy was a bit uncertain whether indeed it were he—yonder chap about his own age chatting and laughing in freehearted way, leaning against a gun; a genial young fellow enough to look at, and something of a rattle-brain, to all appearance. Rather chubby too for a sailor, even an afterguardsman. In short, the last man in the world, one would think, to be over-burdened with thoughts, especially those perilous thoughts that must needs belong to a conspirator in any serious project, or even to the underling of such a conspirator.

Although Billy was not aware of it, the fellow, with a sidelong watchful glance, had perceived Billy first, and then noting that Billy was looking at him, thereupon nodded a familiar sort of friendly recognition as to an old acquaintance, without interrupting the talk he was engaged in with the group of smokers. A day or two afterwards, chancing in the evening promenade on a gun deck to pass Billy, he offered a flying word of goodfellowship, as it were, which by its unexpectedness, and equivocalness under the circumstances, so embarrassed Billy that he knew not how to respond to it, and let it go unnoticed.

Billy was now left more at a loss than before. The ineffectual speculations into which he was led were so disturbingly alien to him that he did his best to smother them. It never entered his mind that here was a matter which, from its extreme question-ableness, it was his duty as a loyal bluejacket to report in the proper quarter. And, probably, had such a step been suggested to him, he would have been deterred from taking it by the thought, one of novice magnanimity, that it would savor overmuch of the dirty work of a telltale. He kept the thing to himself. Yet upon one occasion he could not forbear a little disburdening himself to the old Dansker, tempted thereto perhaps by the influence of a balmy night when the ship lay becalmed; the twain, silent for the most part, sitting together on the deck, their heads propped against the bulwarks. But it was only a partial and anonymous account that Billy gave, the unfounded scruples above referred to preventing full disclosure to anybody. Upon hearing Billy's version, the sage Dansker seemed to divine more than he was told; and after a little meditation, during which his wrinkles were pursed as into a point, quite effacing for the time that quizzing expression his face sometimes wore: 'Didn't I say so, Baby Budd?'

'Say what?' demanded Billy.

'Why, *Jemmy Legs* is *down* on you.'

'And what,' rejoined Billy in amazement, 'has *Jemmy Legs* to do with that cracked afterguardsman?'

'Ho, it was an afterguardsman, then. A cat's-paw, a cat's-paw!' And with that exclamation, whether it had reference to a light pufff of air just then coming over the calm sea, or a subtler relation to the afterguardsman, there is no telling, the old Merlin gave a twisting wrench with his black teeth at his plug of tobacco, vouch-safing no reply to Billy's impetuous question, though now repeated, for it was his wont to relapse into grim silence when interrogated in skeptical sort as to any of his sententious oracles, not always very clear ones, rather partaking of that obscurity which invests most Delphic deliverances from any quarter.

Long experience had very likely brought his old man to that bitter prudence which never interferes in aught and never gives advice.

16

YES, despite the Dansker's pithy insistence as to the master-at-arms being at the bottom of these strange experiences of Billy on board the *Bellipotent*, the young sailor was ready to ascribe them to almost anybody but the man who, to use Billy's own expression, 'always had a pleasant word for him.' This is to be wondered at. Yet not so much to be wondered at. In certain matters, some sailors even in mature life remain unsophisticated enough. But a young seafarer of the disposition of our athletic foretopman is much of a child-man. And yet a child's utter innocence is but its blank ignorance, and the innocence more or less wanes as intelligence waxes. But in Billy Budd intelligence, such as it was, had advanced while yet his simple-mindedness remained for the most part unaffected. Experience is a teacher indeed; yet did Billy's years make his experience small. Besides, he had none of that intuitive knowledge of the bad which in natures not good or incompletely so foreruns experience, and therefore may pertain, as in some instances it too clearly does pertain, even to youth.

And what could Billy know of man except of man as a mere sailor? And the old-fashioned sailor, the veritable man before the mast, the sailor from boyhood up, he, though indeed of the same species as a landsman, is in some respects singularly distinct from him. The sailor is frankness, the landsman is finesse. Life is not a game with the sailor, demanding the long head—no intricate games of chess where few moves are made in straight-forwardness and ends are attained by indirection, an oblique, tedious, barren game hardly worth that poor candle burnt out in playing it.

Yes, as a class, sailors are in character a juvenile race. Even their deviations are marked by juvenility, this more especially holding true with the sailors of Billy's time. Then too, certain things which apply to all sailors do more pointedly operate here and there upon the junior one. Every sailor, too, is accustomed to obey orders without debating them; his life afloat is externally ruled for him; he is not brought into that promiscuous commerce

with mankind where unobstructed free agency on equal terms—
equal superficially, at least—soon teaches one that unless upon
occasion he exercise a distrust keen in proportion to the fairness
of the appearance, some foul turn may be served him. A ruled
undemonstrative distrustfulness is so habitual, not with business-
men so much as with men who know their kind in less shallow
relations than business, namely, certain men of the world, that
they come to at last to employ it all but unconsciously; and some
of them would very likely feel real surprise at being charged with
it as one of their general characteristics.

17

BUT after the little matter at the mess Billy Budd no more found
himself in strange trouble at times about his hammock or his
clothes bag or what not. As to that smile that occasionally sunned
him, and the pleasant passing word, these were, if not more
frequent, yet if anything more pronounced than before.

But for all that, there were certain other demonstrations now.
When Claggart's unobserved glance happened to light on belted
Billy rolling along the upper gun deck in the leisure of the second
dogwatch, exchanging passing broadsides of fun with other young
promenaders in the crowd, that glance would follow the cheerful
sea Hyperion with a settled meditative and melancholy expression,
his eyes strangely suffused with incipient feverish tears. Then would
Claggart look like the man of sorrows. Yes, and sometimes the
melancholy expression would have in it a touch of soft yearning,
as if Claggart could even have loved Billy but for fate and ban.
But this was an evanescence, and quickly repented of, as it were,
by an immitigable look, pinching and shriveling the visage into
the momentary semblance of a wrinkled walnut. But sometimes
catching sight in advance of the foretopman coming in his direction, he would, upon their nearing, step aside a little to let him
pass, dwelling upon Billy for the moment with the glittering dental
satire of a Guise. But upon any abrupt unforeseen encounter a
red light would flash forth from his eye like a spark from an anvil
in a dusk smithy. That quick, fierce light was a strange one, darted
from orbs which in repose were of a color nearest approaching a
deeper violet, the softest of shades.

Though some of these caprices of the pit could not but be observed by their object, yet were they beyond the construing of such a nature. And the thews of Billy were hardly compatible with that sort of sensitive spiritual organization which in some cases instinctively conveys to ignorant innocence an admonition of the proximity of the malign. He thought the master-at-arms acted in a manner rather queer at times. That was all. But the occasional frank air and pleasant word went for what they purported to be, the young sailor never having heard as yet of the 'too fair-spoken man.'

Had the foretopman been conscious of having done or said anything to provoke the ill will of the official, it would have been different with him, and his sight might have been purged if not sharpened. As it was, innocence was his blinder.

So was it with him in yet another matter. Two minor officers, the armorer and captain of the hold, with whom he had never exchanged a word, his position in the ship not bringing him into contact with them, these men now for the first began to cast upon Billy, when they chanced to encounter him, that peculiar glance which evidences that the man from whom it comes has been some way tampered with, and to the prejudice of him upon whom the glance lights. Never did it occur to Billy as a thing to be noted or a thing suspicious, though he well knew the fact, that the armorer and captain of the hold, with the ship's yeoman, apothecary, and others of that grade, were by naval usage messmates of the master-at-arms, men with ears convenient to his confidential tongue.

But the general popularity that came from our Handsome Sailor's manly forwardness upon occasion and irresistible good nature, indicating no mental superiority tending to excite an invidious feeling, this good will on the part of most of his shipmates made him the less to concern himself about such mute aspects toward him as those whereto allusion has just been made, aspects he could not so fathom as to infer their whole import.

As to the afterguardsman, though Billy for reasons already given necessarily saw little of him, yet when the two did happen to meet, invariably came the fellow's offhand cheerful recognition, sometimes accompanied by a passing pleasant word or two. Whatever that equivocal young person's original design may really have been, or the design of which he might have been the deputy, certain it was from his manner upon these occasions that he had wholly dropped it.

It was as if his precocity of crookedness (and every vulgar villain is precocious) had for once deceived him, and the man he had sought to entrap as a simpleton had through his very simplicity ignominiously baffled him.

But shrewd ones may opine that it was hardly possible for Billy to refrain from going up to the afterguardsman and bluntly demanding to know his purpose in the initial interview so abruptly closed in the forechains. Shrewd ones may also think it but natural in Billy to set about sounding some of the other impressed men of the ship in order to discover what basis, if any, there was for the emissary's obscure suggestions as to plotting disaffection aboard. Yes, shrewd ones may so think. But something more, or rather something else than mere shrewdness is perhaps needful for the due understanding of such a character as Bully Budd's.

As to Claggart, the monomania in the man—if that indeed it were—as involuntarily disclosed by starts in the manifestations detailed, yet in general covered over by his self-contained and rational demeanor; this, like a subterranean fire, was eating its way deeper and deeper in him. Something decisive must come of it.

18

AFTER the mysterious interview in the forechains, the one so abruptly ended there by Billy, nothing especially germane to the story occurred until the events now about to be narrated.

Elsewhere it has been said that in the lack of frigates (of course better sailers than line-of-battle ships) in the English squadron up the Straits at that period, the *Bellipotent 74* was occasionally employed not only as an available substitute for a scout, but at times on detached service of more important kind. This was not alone because of her sailing qualities, not common in a ship of her rate, but quite as much, probably, that the character of her commander, it was thought, specially adapted him for any duty where under unforeseen difficulties a prompt initiative might have to be taken in some matter demanding knowledge and ability in addition to those qualities implied in good seamanship. It was on an expedition of the latter sort, a somewhat distant one, and when the *Bellipotent* was almost at her furthest remove from the fleet, that in the latter part of an afternoon watch she unexpectedly came in sight of a ship of the enemy. It proved to be a frigate. The latter, perceiving through the glass that the weight of men and metal would be heavily against her, invoking her light heels crowded sail to get away. After a chase urged almost against hope and lasting until about the middle of the first dogwatch, she signally succeeded in effecting her escape.

Not long after the pursuit had been given up, and ere the excitement incident thereto had altogether waned away, the master-at-arms, ascending from his cavernous sphere, made his appearance cap in hand by the mainmast respectfully waiting the notice of Captain Vere, then solitary walking the weather side of the quarter-deck, doubtless somewhat chafed at the failure of the pursuit. The spot where Claggart stood was the place allotted to men of lesser grades seeking some more particular interview either with the officer of the deck or the captain himself. But from the latter it was not often that a sailor or petty officer of those days would seek a hearing; only some exceptional cause would, according to established custom, have warranted that.

Presently, just as the commander, absorbed in his reflections, was on the point of turning aft in his promenade, he became sensible of Claggart's presence, and saw the doffed cap held in deferential expectancy. Here be it said that Captain Vere's personal knowledge of this petty officer had only begun at the time of the ship's last sailing from home, Claggart then for the first, in transfer from a ship detained for repairs, supplying on board the *Bellipotent* the place of a previous master-at-arms disabled and ashore.

No sooner did the commander observe who it was that now deferentially stood awaiting his notice than a peculiar expression came over him. It was not unlike that which uncontrollably will flit across the countenance of one at unawares encountering a person who, though known to him indeed, has hardly been long enough known for thorough knowledge, but something in whose aspect nevertheless now for the first provokes a vaguely repellent distaste. But coming to a stand and resuming much of his wonted official manner, save that a sort of impatience lurked in the intonation of the opening word, he said 'Well? What is it, Master-at-arms?'

With the air of a subordinate grieved at the necessity of being a messenger of ill tidings, and while conscientiously determined to be frank yet equally resolved upon shunning overstatement, Claggart at this invitation, or rather summons to disburden, spoke up. What he said, conveyed in the language of no uneducated man, was to the effect following, if not altogether in these words, namely, that during the chase and preparations for the possible encounter he had seen enough to convince him that at least one sailor aboard was a dangerous character in a ship mustering some who not only had taken a guilty part in the late serious troubles, but others also who, like the man in question, had entered His Majesty's service under another form than enlistment.

At this point Captain Vere with some impatience interrupted him: 'Be direct, man; say *impressed men*.'

Claggart made a gesture of subservience, and proceeded. Quite lately he (Claggart) had begun to suspect that on the gun decks some sort of movement prompted by the sailor in question was covertly going on, but he had not thought himself warranted in reporting the suspicion so long as it remained indistinct. But from what he had that afternoon observed in the man referred to, the suspicion of something clandestine going on had advanced to a point less removed from certainty. He deeply felt, he added, the serious responsibility assumed in making a report involving such possible consequences to the individual mainly concerned, besides tending to augment those natural anxieties which every naval commander must feel in view of extraordinary outbreaks so recent as those which, he sorrowfully said it, it needed not to name.

Now at the first broaching of the matter Captain Vere, taken by surprise, could not wholly dissemble his disquietude. But as Claggart went on, the former's aspect changed into restiveness under something in the testifier's manner in giving his testimony. However, he refrained from interrupting him. And Claggart, continuing, concluded with this: 'God forbid, your honor, that the *Bellipotent*'s should be the experience of the—'

'Never mind that!' here peremptorily broke in the superior, his face altering with anger, instinctively divining the ship that the other was about to name, one in which the Nore Mutiny had assumed a singularly tragical character that for a time jeopardized the life of its commander. Under the circumstances he was indignant at the purposed allusion. When the commissioned officers themselves were on all occasions very heedful how they referred to the recent events in the fleet, for a petty officer unnecessarily to allude to them in the presence of his captain, this struck him as a most immodest presumption. Besides, to his quick sense of self-respect it even looked under the circumstances something like an attempt to alarm him. Nor at first was he without some surprise that one who so far as he had hitherto come under his notice had shown considerable tact in his function should in this particular evince such lack of it.

But these thoughts and kindred dubious ones flitting across his mind were suddenly replaced by an intuitional surmise which, though as yet obscure in form, served practically to affect his reception of the ill tidings. Certain it is that, long versed in everything pertaining to the complicated gun-deck life, which like every other form of life has its secret mines and dubious side, the side popularly disclaimed, Captain Vere did not permit himself to be unduly disturbed by the general tenor of his subordinate's report.

Furthermore, if in view of recent events prompt action should be taken at the first palpable sign of recurring insubordination, for all that, not judicious would it be, he thought, to keep the idea of lingering disaffection alive by undue forwardness in crediting an informer, even if his own subordinate and charged among other things with police surveillance of the crew. This feeling would not perhaps have so prevailed with him were it not that upon a prior occasion the patriotic zeal officially evinced by Claggart had somewhat irritated him as appearing rather supersensible and strained. Furthermore, something even in the official's self-possessed and somewhat ostentatious manner in making his specifications strangely reminded him of a bandsman, a perjurious witness in a capital case before a court-martial ashore of which when a lieutenant he (Captain Vere) had been a member.

Now the peremptory check given to Claggart in the matter of the arrested allusion was quickly followed up by this: 'You say that there is at least one dangerous man aboard. Name him.'

'William Budd, a foretopman, your honor.'

'William Budd!' repeated Captain Vere with unfeigned astonishment. 'And mean you the man that Lieutenant Ratcliffe took from the merchantman not very long ago, the young fellow who seems to be so popular with the men—Billy the Handsome Sailor, as they call him?'

'The same your honor; but for all his youth and good looks, a deep one. Not for nothing does he insinuate himself into the good will of his shipmates, since at the least they will at a pinch say— all hands will—a good word for him, and at all hazards. Did Lieutenant Ratcliffe happen to tell your honor of that adroit fling of Budd's, jumping up in the cutter's bow under the merchantman's stern when he was being taken off? It is even masked by that sort of good-humored air that at heart he resents his impressment. You have but noted his fair cheek. A mantrap may be under the ruddy-tipped daisies.'

Now the Handsome Sailor as a signal figure among the crew

had naturally enough attracted the captain's attention from the first. Though in general not very demonstrative to his officers, he had congratulated Lieutenant Ratcliffe upon his good fortune in lighting on such a fine specimen of the *genus homo*, who in the nude might have posed for a statue of a young Adam before the Fall. As to Billy's adieu to the ship *Rights-of-Man*, which the boarding lieutenant had indeed reported to him, but, in a deferential way, more as a good story than aught else, Captain Vere, though mistakenly understanding it as a satiric sally, had but thought so much the better of the impressed man for it; as a military sailor, admiring the spirit that could take an arbitrary enlistment so merrily and sensibly. The foretopman's conduct, too, so far as it had fallen under the captain's notice, had confirmed the first happy augury, while the new recruit's qualities as a 'sailorman' seemed to be such that he had thought of recommending him to the exicutive officer for promotion to a place that would more frequently bring him under his own observation, namely, the captaincy of the mizzentop, replacing there in the starboard watch a man not so young whom partly for that reason he deemed less fitted for the post. Be it parenthesized here that since the mizzentopmen have not to handle such breadths of heavy canvas as the lower sails on the mainmast and foremast, a young man if of the right stuff not only seems best adapted to duty there, but in fact is generally selected for the captaincy of that top, and the company under him are light hands and often but striplings. In sum, Captain Vere had from the beginning deemed Billy Budd to be what in the naval parlance of the time was called a 'King's bargain': that is to say, for His Britannic Majesty's navy a capital investment at small outlay or none at all.

After a brief pause, during which the reminiscences above mentioned passed vividly through his mind and he weighed the import of Claggart's last suggestion conveyed in the phrase 'mantrap under the daisies,' and the more he weighed it the less reliance he felt in the informer's good faith, suddenly he turned upon him and in a low voice demanded: 'Do you come to me, Master-at-arms, with so foggy a tale? As to Budd, cite me an act or spoken word of his confirmatory of what you in general charge against him. Stay,' drawing nearer to him; 'heed what you speak. Just now, and in a case like this, there is a yardarm-end for the false witness.'

'Ah, your honor!' sighed Claggart, mildly shaking his shapely head as in sad deprecation of such unmerited severity of tone. Then, bridling—erecting himself as in virtuous self-assertion—he circumstantially alleged certain words and acts which collectively, if credited, led to presumptions mortally inculpating Budd. And for some of these averments, he added, substantiating proof was not far.

With gray eyes impatient and distrustful essaying to fathom to the bottom Claggart's calm violet ones, Captain Vere again heard him out; then for the moment stood ruminating. The mood he evinced, Claggart—himself for the time liberated from the other's scrutiny—steadily regarded with a look difficult to render: a look curious of the operation of his tactics, a look such as might have been that of the spokesman of the envious children of Jacob deceptively imposing upon the troubled patriarch the blood-dyed coat of young Joseph.

Though something exceptional in the moral quality of Captain Vere made him, in earnest encounter with a fellow man, a veritable touchstone of that man's essential nature, yet now as to Claggart and what was really going on in him his feeling partook less of intuitional conviction than of strong suspicion clogged by strange dubieties. The perplexity he evinced proceeded less from aught touching the man informed against—as Claggart doubtless opined—than from considerations how best to act in regard to the informer. At first, indeed, he was naturally for summoning that substantiation of his allegations which Claggart said was at hand. But such a proceeding would result in the matter at once getting abroad, which in the present stage of it, he thought, might undesirably affect the ship's company. If Claggart was a false witness—that closed the affair. And therefore, before trying the accusation, he would first practically test the accuser; and he thought this could be done in a quiet, undemonstrative way.

The measure he determined upon involved a shifting of the scene, a transfer to a place less exposed to observation than the broad quarter-deck. For although the few gun-room officers there at the time had, in due observance of naval etiquette, withdrawn to leeward the moment Captain Vere had begun his promenade on the deck's weather side; and though during the colloquy with Claggart they of course ventured not to diminish the distance; and though throughout the interview Captain Vere's voice was far from him, and Claggart's silvery and low; and the wind in the cordage and the wash of the sea helped the more to put them beyond earshot; nevertheless, the interview's continuance already had attracted observation from some topmen aloft and other sailors in the waist or further forward.

Having determined upon his measures, Captain Vere forthwith

took action. Abruptly truning to Claggart, he asked, 'Master-at-arms, is it now Budd's watch aloft?'

'No, your honor.'

Whereupon, 'Mr Wilkes!' summoning the nearest midshipman. 'Tell Albert to come to me.' Albert was the captain's hammock-boy, a sort of sea valet in whose discretion and fidelity his master had much confidence. The lad appeared.

'You know Budd, the foretopman?'

'I do, sir.'

'Go find him. It is his watch off. Manage to tell him out of earshot that he is wanted aft. Contrive it that he speaks to nobody. Keep him in talk yourself. And not till you get well aft here, not till then let him know that the place where he is wanted is my cabin. You understand. Go.—Master-at-arms, show yourself on the decks below, and when you think it time for Albert to be coming with his man, stand by quietly to follow the sailor in.'

19

Now when the foretopman found himself in the cabin, closeted there, as it were, with the captain and Claggart, he was surprised enough. But it was a surprise unaccompanied by apprehension or distrust. To an immature nature essentially honest and humane, forewarning intimations of subtler danger from one's kind come tardily if at all. The only thing that took shape in the young sailor's mind was this: Yes, the captain, I have always thought, looks kindly upon me. Wonder if he's going to make me his coxswain. I should like that. And may be now he is going to ask the master-at-arms about me.

'Shut the door there, sentry,' said the commander; 'stand without, and let nobody come in.—Now, Master-at-arms, tell this man to his face what you told of him to me,' and stood prepared to scrutinize the mutually confronting visages.

With the measured step and calm collected air of an asylum physician approaching in the public hall some patient beginning to show indications of a coming paroxysm, Claggart deliberately advanced within short range of Billy and, mesmerically looking him in the eye, briefly recapitulated the accusation.

Not at first did Billy take it in. When he did, the rosetan of

his cheek looked struck as by white leprosy. He stood like one
impaled and gagged. Meanwhile the accuser's eyes, removing not
as yet from the blue dilated ones, underwent a phenomenal change,
their wonted rich violet color blurring into a muddy purple. Those
lights of human intelligence, losing human expression, were gelidly
protruding like the alien eyes of certain uncatalogued creatures of
the deep. The first mesmeristic glance was one of serpent fascination; the last was the paralyzing lurch of the torpedo fish.

'Speak, man!' said Captain Vere to the transfixed one, struck
by his aspect even more than by Claggart's. 'Speak! Defend yourself!' Which appeal caused but a strange dumb gesturing and
gurgling in Billy; amazement at such an accusation so suddenly
sprung on inexperienced nonage; this, and, it may be, horror of
the accuser's eyes, serving to bring out his lurking defect and in
this instance for the time intensifying it into a convulsed tongue-
tie; while the intent head and entire form straining forward in an
agony of ineffectual eagerness to obey the injunction to speak and
defend himself, gave an expression to the face like that of a
condemned vestal priestess in the moment of being buried alive,
and in the first struggle against suffocation.

Though at the time Captain Vere was quite ignorant of Billy's
liability to vocal impediment, he now immediately divined it, since
vividly Billy's aspect recalled to him that of a bright young school-
mate of his whom he had once seen struck by much the same
startling impotence in the act of eagerly rising in the class to be
foremost in response to a testing question put to it by the master.
Going close up to the young sailor, and laying a soothing hand
on his shoulder, he said, 'There is no hurry, my boy. Take your
time, take your time.' Contrary to the effect intended, these words
so fatherly in tone, doubtless touching Billy's heart to the quick,
prompted yet more violent efforts at utterance—efforts soon ending
for the time in confirming the paralysis, and bringing to his face
an expression which was as a crucifixion to behold. The next
instant, quick as the flame from a discharged cannon at night,
his right arm shot out, and Claggart dropped to the deck. Whether
intentionally or but owing to the young athlete's superior height,
the blow had taken effect full upon the forehead, so shapely and
intellectual-looking a feature in the master-at-arms; so that the
body fell over lengthwise, like a heavy plank tilted from erectness.
A gasp or two, and he lay motionless.

'Fated boy,' breathed Captain Vere in tone so low as to be
almost a whisper, 'what have you done! But here, help me.'

The twain raised the felled one from the loins up into a sitting position. The spare form flexibly acquiesced, but inertly. It was like handling a dead snake. They lowered it back. Regaining erectness, Captain Vere with one hand covering his face stood to all appearance as impassive as the object at his feet. Was he absorbed in taking in all the bearings of the event and what was best not only now at once to be done, but also in the sequel? Slowly he uncovered his face; and the effect was as if the moon emerging from eclipse should reappear with quite another aspect than that which had gone into hiding. The father in him, manifested towards Billy thus far in the scene, was replaced by the military disciplinarian. In his official tone he bade the foretopman retire to a stateroom aft (pointing it out), and there remain till thence summoned. This order Billy in silence mechanically obeyed. Then going to the cabin door where it opened on the quarter-deck, Captain Vere said to the sentry without, 'Tell somebody to send Albert here.' When the lad appeared, his master so contrived it that he should not catch sight of the prone one. 'Albert,' he said to him, 'tell the surgeon I wish to see him. You need not come back till called.'

When the surgeon entered—a self-poised character of that grave sense and experience that hardly anything could take him aback—Captain Vere advanced to meet him, thus unconsciously intercepting his view of Claggart, and, interrupting the other's wonted ceremonious salutation, said, 'Nay. Tell me how it is with yonder man,' directing his attention to the prostrate one.

The surgeon looked, and for all his self-command somewhat started at the abrupt revelation. On Claggart's always pallid complexion, thick black blood was now oozing from nostil and ear. To the gazer's professional eye it was unmistakably no living man that he saw.

'Is it so, then?' said Captain Vere, intently watching him. 'I thought it. But verify it.' Whereupon the customary tests confirmed the surgeon's first glance, who now, looking up in unfeigned concern, cast a look of intense inquisitiveness upon his superior. But Captain Vere, with one hand to his brow, was standing motionless. Suddenly, catching the surgeon's arm convulsively, he exclaimed, pointing down to the body, 'It is the divine judgment on Ananias! Look!'

Disturbed by the excited manner he had never before observed in the *Bellipotent*'s captain, and as yet wholly ignorant of the affair, the prudent surgeon nevertheless held his peace, only again looking an earnest interrogatory as to what it was that had resulted in such a tragedy.

But Captain Vere was now again motionless, standing absorbed in thought. Again starting, he vehemently exclaimed, 'Struck dead by an angel of God! Yet the angel must hang!'

At these passionate interjections, mere incoherences to the listener as yet unapprised of the antecedents, the surgeon was profoundly discomposed. But now, as recollecting himself, Captain Vere in less passionate tone briefly related the circumstances leading up to the event. 'But come; we must dispatch,' he added. 'Help me to remove him' (meaning the body) 'to yonder compartment,' designating one opposite that where the foretopman remained immured. Anew disturbed by a request that, as implying a desire for secrecy, seemed unaccountably strange to him, there was nothing for the subordinate to do but comply.

'Go now,' said Captain Vere with something of his wonted manner. 'Go now. I presently shall call a drumhead court. Tell the lieutenants what has happened, and tell Mr Mordant' (meaning the captain of marines), 'and charge them to keep the matter to themselves.'

20

FULL of disquietude and misgiving, the surgeon left the cabin. Was Captain Vere suddenly affected in his mind, or was it but a transient excitement, brought about by so strange and extraordinary a tragedy? As to the drumhead court, it struck the surgeon as impolitic, if nothing more. The thing to do, he thought, was to place Billy Budd in confinement, and in a way dictated by usage, and postpone further action in so extraordinary a case to such time as they should rejoin the squadron, and then refer it to the admiral. He recalled the unwonted agitation of Captian Vere and his excited exclamations, so at variance with his normal manner. Was he unhinged?

But assuming that he is, it is not so susceptible of proof. What then can the surgeon do? No more trying situation is conceivable than that of an officer subordinate under a captain whom he suspects to be not mad, indeed, but yet not quite unaffected in his intellects. To argue his order to him would be insolence. To resist him would be mutiny.

In obedience to Captain Vere, he communicated what had

happened to the lieutenants and captain of marines, saying nothing as to the captain's state. They fully shared his own surprise and concern. Like him too, they seemed to think that such a matter should be referred to the admiral.

21

WHO in the rainbow can draw the line where the violet tint ends and the orange tint begins? Distinctly we see the difference of the colors, but where exactly does the one first blendingly enter into the other? So with sanity and insanity. In pronounced cases there is no question about them. But in some supposed cases, in various degrees supposedly less pronounced, to draw the exact line of demarcation few will undertake, though for a fee becoming considerate some professional experts will. There is nothing nameable but that some men will, or undertake to, do it for pay.

Whether Captain Vere, as the surgeon professionally and privately surmised, was really the sudden victim of any degree of aberration, every one must determine for himself by such light as this narrative may afford.

That the unhappy event which has been narrated could not have happened at a worse juncture was but too true. For it was close on the heel of the suppressed insurrections, an aftertime very critical to naval authority, demanding from every English sea commander two qualities not readily interfusable—prudence and rigor. Moreover, there was something crucial in the case.

In the jugglery of circumstances preceding and attending the event on board the *Bellipotent*, and in the light of that martial code whereby it was formally to be judged, innocence and guilt personified in Claggart and Budd in effect changed places. In a legal view the apparent victim of the tragedy was he who had sought to victimize a man blameless; and the indisputable deed of the latter, navally regarded, constituted the most heinous of military crimes. Yet more. The essential right and wrong involved in the matter, the clearer that might be, so much the worse for the responsibility of a loyal sea commander, inasmuch as he was not authorized to determine the matter on that primitive basis.

Small wonder then that the *Bellipotent*'s captain, though in general a man of rapid decision, felt that circumspectness not less than promptitude was necessary. Until he could decide upon his course, and in each detail; and not only so, but until the concluding measure was upon the point of being enacted, he deemed it advisable, in view of all the circumstances, to guard as much as possible against publicity. Here he may or may not have erred. Certain it is, however, that subsequently in the confidential talk of more than one or two gun rooms and cabins he was not a little criticized by some officers, a fact imputed by his friends and vehemently by his cousin Jack Denton to professional jealousy of Starry Vere. Some imaginative ground for invidious comment there was. The maintenance of secrecy in the matter, the confining all knowledge of it for a time to the place where the homicide occurred, the quarter-deck cabin; in these particulars lurked some resemblance to the policy adopted in those tragedies of the palace which have occurred more than once in the capital founded by Peter the Barbarian.

The case indeed was such that fain would the *Bellipotent*'s captain have deferred taking any action whatever respecting it further than to keep the foretopman a close prisoner till the ship rejoined the squadron and then submitting the matter to the judgment of his admiral.

But a true military officer is in one particular like a true monk. Not with more of self-abnegation will the latter keep his vows of monastic obedience than the former his vows of allegiance to martial duty.

Feeling that unless quick action was taken on it, the deed of the foretopman, so soon as it should be known on the gun decks, would tend to awaken any slumbering embers of the Nore among the crew, a sense of the urgency of the case overruled in Captain Vere every other consideration. But though a conscientious disciplinarian, he was no lover of authority for mere authority's sake. Very far was he from embracing opportunities for monopolizing to himself the perils of moral responsibility, none at least that could properly be referred to an official superior of shared with him by his official equals or even subordinates. So thinking, he was glad it would not be at variance with usage to turn the matter over to a summary court of his own officers, reserving to himself, as the one on whom the ultimate accountability would rest, the right of maintaining a supervision of it, or formally or informally interposing at need. Accordingly a drumhead court was summarily convened, he electing the individuals composing it: the first lieutenant, the captain of marines, and the sailing master.

In associating an officer of marines with the sea lieutenant and the sailing master in a case having to do with a sailor, the commander perhaps deviated from general custom. He was prompted thereto by the circumstance that he took that soldier to be a judicious person, thoughtful, and not altogether incapable of grappling with a difficult case unprecedented in his prior experience. Yet even as to him he was not without some latent misgiving, for withal he was an extremely good-natured man, an enjoyer of his dinner, a sound sleeper, and inclined to obesity—a man who though he would always maintain his manhood in battle might not prove altogether reliable in a moral dilemma involving aught of the tragic. As to the first lieutenant and the sailing master, Captain Vere could not but be aware that though honest natures, of approved gallantry upon occasion, their intelligence was mostly confined to the matter of active seamanship and the fighting demands of their profession.

The court was held in the same cabin where the unfortunate affair had taken place. This cabin, the commander's, embraced the entire area under the poop deck. Aft, and on either side, was a small stateroom, the one now temporarily a jail and the other a dead-house, and a yet smaller compartment, leaving a space between expanding forward into a goodly oblong of length coinciding with the ship's beam. A skylight of moderate dimension was overhead, and at each end of the oblong space were two sashed porthole windows easily convertible back into embrasures for short carronades.

All being quickly in readiness, Billy Budd was arraigned, Captain Vere necessarily appearing as the sole witness in the case, and as such temporarily sinking his rank, though singularly maintaining it in a matter apparently trivial, namely, that he testified from the ship's weather side, with that object having caused the court to sit on the lee side. Concisely he narrated all that had led up to the catastrophe, omitting nothing in Claggart's accusation and deposing as to the manner in which the prisoner had received it. At this testimony the three officers glanced with no little surprise at Billy Budd, the last man they would have suspected either of the mutinous design alleged by Claggart or the undeniable deed he himself had done. The first lieutenant, taking judicial primacy and turning toward the prisoner, said, 'Captain Vere has spoken. Is it or is it not as Captain Vere says?'

In response came syllables not so much impeded in the utterance as might have been anticipated. They were these: 'Captain Vere tells the truth. It is just as Captain Vere says, but it is not as the master-at-arms said. I have eaten the King's bread and I am true to the King.'

'I believe you, my man,' said the witness, his voice indicating a suppressed emotion not otherwise betrayed.

'God will bless you for that, your honor!' not without stammering said Billy, and all but broke down. But immediately he was recalled to self-control by another question, to which with the same emotional difficulty of utterance he said, 'No, there was no malice between us. I never bore malice against the master-at-arms. I am sorry that he is dead. I did not mean to kill him. Could I have used my tongue I would not have struck him. But he foully lied to my face and in presence of my captain, and I had to say something, and I could only say it with a blow, God help me!'

In the impulsive aboveboard manner of the frank one the court saw confirmed all that was implied in words that just previously had perplexed them, coming as they did from the testifier to the tragedy and promptly following Billy's impassioned disclaimer of mutinous intent—Captain Vere's words, 'I believe you, my man.'

Next it was asked of him whether he knew of or suspected aught savoring of incipient trouble (meaning mutiny, though the explicit term was avoided) going on in any section of the ship's company.

The reply lingered. This was naturally imputed by the court to the same vocal embarrassment which had retarded or obstructed previous answers. But in main it was otherwise here, the question immediately recalling to Billy's mind the interview with the afterguardsman in the forechains. But in innate repugnance to playing a part at all approaching that of an informer against one's own shipmates—the same erring sense of uninstructed honor which had stood in the way of his reporting the matter at the time, though as a loyal man-of-war's man it was incumbent on him, and failure so to do, if charged against him and proven, would have subjected him to the heaviest of penalties; this, with the blind feeling now his that nothing really was being hatched, prevailed with him. When the answer came it was a negative.

'One question more,' said the officer of marines, now first speaking and with a troubled earnestness. 'You tell us that what the master-at-arms said against you was a lie. Now why should he have so lied, so maliciously lied, since you declare there was no malice between you?'

At that question, unintentionally touching on a spiritual sphere wholly obscure to Billy's thoughts, he was nonplussed, evincing a confusion indeed that some observers, such as can readily be imagined, would have construed into involuntary evidence of hidden guilt. Nevertheless, he strove some way to answer, but all at once relinquished the vain endeavor, at the same time turning an appealing glance towards Captain Vere as deeming him his best helper and friend. Captain Vere, who had been seated for a time, rose to his feet, addressing the interrogator. 'The question you put to him comes naturally enough. But how can he rightly answer it?—or anybody else, unless indeed it be he who lies within there,' designating the compartment where lay the corpse. 'But the prone one there will not rise to our summons. In effect, though, as it seems to me, the point you make is hardly material. Quite aside from any conceivable motive actuating the master-at-arms, and irrespective of the provocation to the blow, a martial court must needs in the present case confine its attention to the blow's consequence, which consequence justly is to be deemed not otherwise than as the striker's deed.'

This utterance, the full significance of which it was not at all likely that Billy took in, nevertheless caused him to turn a wistful interrogative look toward the speaker, a look in its dumb expressiveness not unlike that which a dog of generous breed might turn upon his master, seeking in his face some elucidation of a previous gesture ambiguous to the canine intelligence. Nor was the same utterance without marked effect upon the three officers, more especially the soldier. Couched in it seemed to them a meaning unanticipated, involving a prejudgment on the speaker's part. It served to augment a mental disturbance previously evident enough.

The soldier once more spoke, in a tone of suggestive dubiety addressing at once his associates and Captain Vere: 'Nobody is present—none of the ship's company, I mean—who might shed lateral light, if any is to be had, upon what remains mysterious in this matter.'

'That is thoughtfully put,' said Captain Vere; 'I see your drift. Ay, there is a mystery; but, to use a scriptural phrase, it is a "mystery of iniquity," a matter for psychologic theologians to discuss. But what has a military court to do with it? Not to add that for us any possible investigation of it is cut off by the lasting tongue-tie of—him—in yonder,' again designating the mortuary stateroom. 'The prisoner's deed—with that alone we have to do.'

To this, and particularly the closing reiteration, the marine soldier, knowing not how aptly to reply, sadly abstained from saying aught. The first lieutenant, who at the outset had not unnaturally assumed primacy in the court, now overrulingly in-

structed by a glance from Captain Vere, a glance more effective
than words, resumed that primacy. Turning to the prisoner, 'Budd,'
he said, and scarce in equable tones, 'Budd, if you have aught
further to say for yourself, say it now.'

Upon this the young sailor turned another quick glance toward
Captain Vere; then, as taking a hint from that aspect, a hint
confirming his own instinct that silence was now best, replied to
the lieutenant, 'I have said all, sir.'

The marine—the same who had been the sentinel without the
cabin door at the time that the foretopman, followed by the
master-at-arms, entered it—he, standing by the sailor throughout
these judicial proceedings, was now directed to take him back to
the after compartment originally assigned to the prisoner and his
custodian. As the twain disappeared from view, the three officers,
as partially liberated from some inward constraint associated with
Billy's mere presence, simultaneously stirred in their seats. They
exchanged looks of troubled indecision, yet feeling that decide
they must and without long delay. For Captain Vere, he for the
time stood—unconsciously with his back toward them, apparently
in one of his absent fits—gazing out from a sashed porthole to
windward upon the monotonous blank of the twilight sea. But
the court's silence continuing, broken only at moments by brief
consultations, in low earnest tones, this served to arouse him and
energize him. Turning, he to-and-fro paced the cabin athwart; in
the returning ascent to windward climbing the slant deck in the
ship's lee roll, without knowing it symbolizing thus in his action
a mind resolute to surmount difficulties even if against primitive
instincts strong as the wind and the sea. Presently he came to a
stand before the three. After scanning their faces he stood less as
mustering his thoughts for expression than as one inly deliberating
how best to put them to well-meaning men not intellectually
mature, men with whom it was necessary to demonstrate certain
principles that were axioms to himself. Similar impatience as to
talking is perhaps one reason that deters some minds from addressing any popular assemblies.

When speak he did, something, both in the substance of what
he said and his manner of saying it, showed the influence of
unshared studies modifying and tempering the practical training
of an active career. This, along with his phraseology, now and
then was suggestive of the grounds whereon rested that imputation
of a certain pedantry socially alleged against him by certain naval
men of wholly practical cast, captains who nevertheless would

frankly concede that His Majesty's navy mustered no more efficient officer of their grade than Starry Vere.

What he said was to this effect: 'Hitherto I have been but the witness, little more; and I should hardly think now to take another tone, that of your coadjutor for the time, did I not perceive in you—at the crisis too—a troubled hesitancy, proceeding, I doubt not, from the clash of military duty with moral scruple—scruple vitalized by compassion. For the compassion, how can I otherwise than share it? But, mindful of paramount obligations, I strive against scruples that may tend to enervate decision. Not, gentlemen, that I hide from myself that the case is an exceptional one. Speculatively regarded, it well might be referred to a jury of casuists. But for us here, acting not as casuists or moralists, it is a case practical, and under martial law practically to be dealt with.

'But your scruples: do they move as in a dusk? Challenge them. Make them advance and declare themselves. Come now; do they import something like this: If, mindless of palliating circumstances, we are bound to regard the death of the master-at-arms as the prisoner's deed, then does that deed constitute a capital crime whereof the penalty is a mortal one. But in natural justice is nothing but the prisoner's overt act to be considered? How can we adjudge to summary and shameful death a fellow creature innocent before God, and whom we feel to be so?—Does that state it aright? You sign sad assent. Well, I too feel that, the full force of that. It is Nature. But do these buttons that we wear attest that our allegiance is to Nature? No, to the King. Though the ocean, which is inviolate nature primeval, though this be the element where we move and have our being as sailors, yet as the King's officers lies our duty in a sphere correspondingly natural? So little is that true, that in receiving our commissions we in the most important regards ceased to be natural free agents. When war is declared are we the commissioned fighters previously consulted? We fight at command. If our judgments approve the war, that is but coincidence. So in other particulars. So now. For suppose condemnation to follow these present proceedings. Would it be so much we ourselves that would condemn as it would be martial law operating through us? For that law and the rigor of it, we are not responsible. Our vowed responsibility is in this: That however pitilessly that law may operate in any instances, we nevertheless adhere to it and administer it.

'But the exceptional in the matter moves the hearts within you. Even so too is mine moved. But let not warm hearts betray heads that should be cool. Ashore in a criminal case, will an upright judge allow himself off the bench to be waylaid by some tender kinswoman of the accused seeking to touch him with her tearful plea? Well, the heart here, sometimes the feminine in man, is as that piteous woman, and hard though it be, she must here be ruled out.'

He paused, earnestly studying them for a moment; then resumed.

'But something in your aspect seems to urge that it is not solely the heart that moves in you, but also the conscience, the private conscience. But tell me whether or not, occupying the position we do, private conscience should not yield to that imperial one formulated in the code under which alone we officially proceed?'

Here the three men moved in their seats, less convinced than agitated by the course of an argument troubling but the more the spontaneous conflict within.

Perceiving which, the speaker paused for a moment; then abruptly changing his tone, went on.

'To steady us a bit, let us recur to the facts.—In wartime at sea a man-of-war's man strikes his superior in grade, and the blow kills. Apart from its effect the blow itself is, according to the Articles of War, a capital crime. Furthermore—'

'Ay, sir,' emotionally broke in the officer of marines, 'in one sense it was. But surely Budd proposed neither mutiny nor homicide.'

'Surely not, my good man. And before a court less arbitrary and more merciful than a martial one, that plea would largely extenuate. At the Last Assizes it shall accquit. But how here? We proceed under the law of the Mutiny Act. In feature no child can resemble his father more than that Act resembles in spirit the thing from which it derives—War. In His Majesty's service—in this ship, indeed—there are Englishmen forced to fight for the King against their will. Against their conscience, for aught we know. Though as their fellow creatures some of us may appreciate their position, yet as navy officers what reck we of it? Still less recks the enemy. Our impressed men he would fain cut down in the same swath with our volunteers. As regards the enemy's naval conscripts, some of whom may even share our own abhorrence of the regicidal French Directory, it is the same on our side. War looks but to the frontage, the appearance. And the Mutiny Act, War's child, takes after the father. Budd's intent or non-intent is nothing to the purpose.

'But while, put to it by those anxieties in you which I cannot but respect, I only repeat myself—while thus strangely we prolong proceedings that should be summary—the enemy may be sighted and an engagement result. We must do; and one of two things must we do—condemn or let go.'

'Can we not convict and yet mitigate the penalty?' asked the sailing master, here speaking, and falteringly, for the first.

'Gentlemen, were that clearly lawful for us under the circumstances, consider the consequences of such clemency. The people' (meaning the ship's company) 'have native sense; most of them are familiar with our naval usage and tradition; and how would they take it? Even could you explain to them—which our official position forbids—they, long molded by arbitrary discipline, have not that kind of intelligent responsiveness that might qualify them to comprehend and discriminate. No, to the people the foretopman's deed, however it be worded in the announcement, will be plain homicide committed in a flagrant act of mutiny. What penalty for that should follow, they know. But it does not follow. *Why?* they will ruminate. You know what sailors are. Will they not revert to the recent outbreak at the Nore? Ay. They know the well-founded alarm—the panic it struck throughout England. Your clement sentence they would account pusillanimous. They would think that we flinch, that we are afraid of them—afraid of practicing a lawful rigor singularly demanded at this juncture, lest it should provoke new troubles. What shame to us such a conjecture on their part, and how deadly to discipline. You see then, whither, prompted by duty and the law, I steadfastly drive. But I beseech you, my friends, do not take me amiss. I feel as you do for this unfortunate boy. But did he know our hearts, I take him to be of that generous nature that he would feel even for us on whom in this military necessity so heavy a compulsion is laid.'

With that, crossing the deck he resumed his place by the sashed porthole, tacitly leaving the three to come to a decision. On the cabin's opposite side the troubled court sat silent. Loyal lieges, plain and practical, though at bottom they dissented from some points Captain Vere had put to them, they were without the faculty, hardly had the inclination, to gainsay one whom they felt to be an earnest man, one too not less their superior in mind than in naval rank. But it is not improbable that even such of his words as were not without influence over them, less came home to them than his closing appeal to their instinct as sea officers: in the forethought he threw out as to the practical consequences to discipline, considering the unconfirmed tone of the fleet at the time, should a man-of-war's man's violent killing at sea of a superior in grade be allowed to pass for aught else than a capital crime demanding prompt infliction of the penalty.

Not unlikely they were brought to something more or less akin to that harassed frame of mind which in the year 1842 actuated the commander of the U.S. brig-of-war *Somers* to resolve, under the so-called Articles of War, Articles modeled upon the English Mutiny Act, to resolve upon the execution at sea of a midshipman and two sailors as mutineers designing the seizure of the brig. Which resolution was carried out though in a time of peace and within not many days' sail of home. An act vindicated by a naval court of inquiry subsequently convened ashore. History, and here cited without comment. True, the circumstances on board the *Somers* were different from those on board the *Bellipotent*. But the urgency felt, well-warranted or otherwise, was much the same.

Says a writer whom few know, 'Forty years after a battle it is easy for a noncombatant to reason about how it ought to have been fought. It is another thing personally and under fire to have to direct the fighting while involved in the obscuring smoke of it. Much so with respect to other emergencies involving considerations both practical and moral, and when it is imperative promptly to act. The greater the fog the more it imperils the steamer, and speed is put on though at the hazard of running somebody down. Little ween the snug card players in the cabin of the responsibilities of the sleepless man on the bridge.'

In brief, Billy Budd was formally convicted and sentenced to be hung at the yardarm in the early morning watch, it being now night. Otherwise, as is customary in such cases, the sentence would forthwith have been carried out. In wartime on the field or in the fleet, a mortal punishment decreed by a drumhead court—on the field sometimes decreed by but a nod from the general—follows without delay on the heel of conviction, without appeal.

22

IT was Captain Vere himself who of his own motion communicated the finding of the court to the prisoner, for that purpose going to the compartment where he was in custody and bidding the marine there to withdraw for the time.

Beyond the communication of the sentence, what took place at this interview was never known. But in view of the character of the twain briefly closeted in that stateroom, each radically sharing in the rarer qualities of our nature—so rare indeed as to be all but incredible to average minds however much cultivated—some conjectures may be ventured.

It would have been in consonance with the spirit of Captain Vere should he on this occasion have concealed nothing from the condemned one—should he indeed have frankly disclosed to him the part he himself had played in bringing about the decision, at the same time revealing his actuating motives. On Billy's side it is not improbable that such a confession would have been received in much the same spirit that prompted it. Not without a sort of joy, indeed, he might have appreciated the brave opinion of him implied in his captain's making such a confidant of him. Nor, as to the sentence itself, could he have been insensible that it was imparted to him as to one not afraid to die. Even more may have been. Captain Vere in end may have developed the passion sometimes latent under an exterior stoical or indifferent. He was old enough to have been Billy's father. The austere devotee of military duty, letting himself melt back into what remains primeval in our formalized humanity, may in end have caught Billy to his heart, even as Abraham may have caught young Isaac on the brink of resolutely offering him up in obedience to the exacting behest. But there is no telling the sacrament, seldom if in any case revealed to the gadding world, wherever under circumstances at all akin to those here attempted to be set forth two of great Nature's nobler order embrace. There is privacy at the time, inviolable to the survivor; and holy oblivion, the sequel to each diviner magnanimity, providentially covers all at last.

The first to encounter Captain Vere in act of leaving the compartment was the senior lieutenant. The face he beheld, for the moment one expressive of the agony of the strong, was to that officer, though a man of fifty, a startling revelation. That the condemned one suffered less than he who mainly had effected the condemnation was apparently indicated by the former's exclamation in the scene soon perforce to be touched upon.

23

OF a series of incidents with a brief term rapidly following each other, the adequate narration may take up a term less brief,

especially if explanation or comment here and there seem requisite
to the better understanding of such incidents. Between the entrance
into the cabin of him who never left it alive, and him who when
he did leave it left it as one condemned to die; between this and
the closeted interview just given, less than an hour and a half had
elapsed. It was an interval long enough, however, to awaken
speculations among no few of the ship's company as to what it
was that could be detaining in the cabin the master-at-arms and
the sailor; for a rumor that both of them had been seen to enter
it and neither of them had been seen to emerge, this rumor had
got abroad upon the gun decks and in the tops, the people of a
great warship being in one respect like villagers, taking microscopic
note of every outward movement or non-movement going on.
When therefore, in weather not at all tempestuous, all hands were
called in the second dogwatch, a summons under such circumstances not usual in those hours, the crew were not wholly unprepared for some announcement extraordinary, one having connection too with the continued absence of the two men from their
wonted haunts.

There was a moderate sea at the time; and the moon, newly
risen and near to being at its full, silvered the white spar deck
wherever not blotted by the clear-cut shadows horizontally thrown
of fixtures and moving men. On either side the quarter-deck the
marine guard under arms was drawn up; and Captain Vere,
standing in his place surrounded by all the wardroom officers,
addressed his men. In so doing, his manner showed neither more
nor less than that properly pertaining to his supreme position
aboard his own ship. In clear terms and concise he told them
what had taken place in the cabin: that the master-at-arms was
dead, that he who had killed him had been already tried by a
summary court and condemned to death, and that the execution
would take place in the early morning watch. The word *mutiny*
was not named in what he said. He refrained too from making
the occasion an opportunity for any preachment as to the maintenance of discipline, thinking perhaps that under existing circumstances in the navy the consequence of violating discipline should
be made to speak for itself.

Their captain's announcement was listened to by the throng of
standing sailors in a dumbness like that of a seated congregation
of believers in hell listening to the clergyman's announcement of
his Calvinistic text.

At the close, however, a confused murmur went up. It began
to wax. All but instantly, then, at a sign, it was pierced and

suppressed by shrill whistles of the boatswain and his mates. The word was given to about ship.

To be prepared for burial Claggart's body was delivered to certain petty officers of his mess. And here, not to clog the sequel with lateral matters, it may be added that at a suitable hour, the master-at-arms was committed to the sea with every funeral honor properly belonging to his naval grade.

In this proceeding as in every public one growing out of the tragedy strict adherence to usage was observed. Nor in any point could it have been at all deviated from, either with respect to Claggart or Billy Budd, without begetting undesirable speculations in the ship's company, sailors, and more particularly men-of-war's men, being of all men the greatest sticklers for usage. For similar cause, all communication between Captain Vere and the condemned one ended with the closeted interview already given, the latter being now surrendered to the ordinary routine preliminary to the end. His transfer under guard from the captain's quarters was effected without unusual precautions—at least no visible ones. If possible, not to let the men so much as surmise that their officers anticipate aught amiss from them is the tacit rule in a military ship. And the more that some sort of trouble should really be apprehended, the more do the officers keep that apprehension to themselves, though not the less unostentatious vigilance may be augmented. In the present instance, the sentry placed over the prisoner had strict orders to let no one have communication with him but the chaplain. And certain unobtrusive measures were taken absolutely to insure this point.

24

IN a seventy-four of the old order the deck known as the upper gun deck was the one covered over by the spar deck, which last, though not without its armament, was for the most part exposed to the weather. In general it was at all hours free from hammocks; those of the crew swinging on the lower gun deck and berth deck, the latter being not only a dormitory but also the place for the stowing of the sailors' bags, and on both sides lined with the large chests or movable pantries of the many messes of the men.

On the starboard side of the *Bellipotent*'s upper gun deck, behold

Billy Budd under sentry lying prone in irons in one of the bays formed by the regular spacing of the guns comprising the batteries on either side. All these pieces were of the heavier caliber of that period. Mounted on lumbering wooden carriages, they were hampered with cumbersome harness of breeching and strong sidetackles for running them out. Guns and carriages, together with the long rammers and shorter linstocks lodged in loops overhead—all these, as customary, were painted black; and the heavy hempen breechings, tarred to the same tint, wore the like livery of the undertakers. In contrast with the funeral hue of these surroundings, the prone sailor's exterior apparel, white jumper and white duck trousers, each more or less soiled, dimly glimmered in the obscure light of the bay like a patch of dicolored snow in early April lingering at some upland cave's black mouth. In effect he is already in his shroud, or the garments that shall serve him in lieu of one. Over him but scarce illuminating him, two battle lanterns swing from two massive beams of the deck above. Fed with the oil supplied by the war contractors (whose gains, honest or otherwise, are in every land an anticipated portion of the harvest of death), with flickering splashes of dirty yellow light they pollute the pale moonshine all but ineffectually struggling in obstructed flecks through the open ports from which the tampioned cannon protrude. Other lanterns at intervals serve but to bring out somewhat the obscurer bays which, like small confessionals or side-chapels in a cathedral, branch from the long dim-vistaed broad aisle between the two batteries of that covered tier.

Such was the deck where now lay the Handsome Sailor. Through the rose-tan of his complexion no pallor could have shown. It would have taken days of sequestration from the winds and the sun to have brought about the effacement of that. But the skeleton in the cheekbone at the point of its angle was just beginning delicately to be defined under the warm-tinted skin. In fervid hearts self-contained, some brief experiences devour our human tissue as secret fire in a ship's hold consumes cotton in the bale.

But now lying between the two guns, as nipped in the vice of fate, Billy's agony, mainly proceeding from a generous young heart's virgin experience of the diabolical incarnate and effective in some men—the tension of that agony was over now. It survived not the something healing in the closeted interview with Captain Vere. Without movement, he lay as in a trance, that adolescent expression previously noted as his taking on something akin to the look of a slumbering child in the cradle when the warm hearthglow of the still chamber at night plays on the dimples that at whiles mysteriously form in the cheek, silently coming and going there. For now and then in the gyved one's trance a serene happy light born of some wandering reminiscence or dream would diffuse itself over his face, and then wane away only anew to return.

The chaplain, coming to see him and finding him thus, and perceiving no sign that he was conscious of his presence, attentively regarded him for a space, then slipping aside, withdrew for the time, peradventure feeling that even he, the minister of Christ though receiving his stipend from Mars, had no consolation to proffer which could result in a peace transcending that which he beheld. But in the small hours he came again. And the prisoner, now awake to his surroundings, noticed his approach, and civilly, all but cheerfully, welcomed him. But it was to little purpose that in the interview following, the good man sought to bring Billy Budd to some godly understanding that he must die, and at dawn. True, Billy himself freely referred to his death as a thing close at hand; but it was something in the way that children will refer to death in general, who yet among their other sports will play a funeral with hearse and mourners.

Not that like children Billy was incapable of conceiving what death really is. No, but he was wholly without irrational fear of it, a fear more prevalent in highly civilized communities than those so-called barbarous ones which in all respects stand nearer to unadulterate Nature. And, as elsewhere said, a barbarian Billy radically was—as much so, for all the costume, as his countrymen the British captives, living trophies, made to march in the Roman triumph of Germanicus. Quite as much so as those later barbarians, young men probably, and picked specimens among the earlier British converts to Christianity, at least nominally such, taken to Rome (as today converts from lesser isles of the sea may be taken to London), of whom the Pope at that time, admiring the strangeness of their personal beauty so unlike the Italian stamp, their clear ruddy complexion and curled flaxen locks, exclaimed, 'Angles' (meaning *English*, the modern derivative), 'Angles, do you call them? And is it because they look so like angels?' Had it been later in time, one would think that the Pope had in mind Fra Angelico's seraphs, some of whom, plucking apples in gardens of the Hesperides, have the faint rosebud complexion of the more beautiful English girls.

If in vain the good chaplain sought to impress the young barbarian with ideas of death akin to those conveyed in the skull, dial and crossbones on old tombstones, equally futile to all appearance were his efforts to bring home to him the thought of salvation and Savior. Billy listened, but less out of awe or reverence, perhaps, than from a certain natural politeness, doubtless a bottom regarding all that in much the same way that most mariners of his class take any discourse abstract or out of the common tone of the workaday world. And this sailor way of taking clerical discourse is not wholly unlike the way in which the primer of Christianity, full of transcendent miracles, was received long ago on tropic isles by any superior *savage*, so called—a Tahitian, say, of Captain Cook's time or shortly after that time. Out of natural courtesy he received, but did not appropriate. It was like a gift placed in the palm of an outreached hand upon which the fingers do not close.

But the *Bellipotent*'s chaplain was a discreet man possessing the good sense of a good heart. So he insisted not in his vocation here. At the instance of Captain Vere, a lieutenant had apprised him of pretty much everything as to Billy; and since he felt that innocence was even a better thing than religion wherewith to go to Judgment, he reluctantly withdrew; but in his emotion not without first performing an act strange enough in an Englishman, and under the circumstances yet more so in any regular priest. Stooping over, he kissed on the fair cheek his fellow man, a felon in martial law, one whom though on the confines of death he felt he could never convert to a dogma; nor for all that did he fear for his future.

Marvel not that having been made acquainted with the young sailor's essential innocence the worthy man lifted not a finger to avert the doom of such a martyr to martial discipline. So to do would not only have been as idle as invoking the desert, but would also have been an audacious transgression of the bounds of his function, one as exactly prescribed to him by military law as that of the boatswain or any other naval officer. Bluntly put, a chaplain is the minister of the Prince of Peace serving in the host of the God of War—Mars. As such, he is as incongruous as a musket would be on the altar at Christmas. Why, then, is he there? Because he indirectly subserves the purpose attested by the cannon; because too he lends the sanction of the religion of the meek to that which practically is the abrogation of everything but brute Force.

25

THE night so luminous on the spar deck, but otherwise on the cavernous ones below, levels so like the tiered galleries in a coal mine—the luminous night passed away. But like the prophet in the chariot disappearing in heaven and dropping his mantle to Elisha, the withdrawing night transferred its pale robe to the breaking day. A meek, shy light appeared in the East, where stretched a diaphanous fleece of white furrowed vapor. That light slowly waxed. Suddenly *eight bells* was struck aft, responded to by one louder metallic stroke from forward. It was four o'clock in the morning. Instantly the silver whistles were heard summoning all hands to witness punishment. Up through the great hatchways rimmed with racks of heavy shot the watch below came pouring, overspreading with the watch already on deck the space between the mainmast and foremast including that occupied by the capacious launch and the black booms tiered on either side of it, boat and booms making a summit of observation for the powder-boys and younger tars. A different group comprising one watch of topmen leaned over the rail of that sea balcony, no small one in a seventy-four, looking down on the crowd below, Man or boy, none spake but in whisper, and few spake at all. Captain Vere— as before, the central figure among the assembled commissioned officers—stood nigh the break of the poop deck facing forward. Just below him on the quarter-deck the marines in full equipment were drawn up much as at the scene of the promulgated sentence.

At sea in the old time, the execution by halter of a military sailor was generally from the foreyard. In the present instance, for special reasons the mainyard was assigned. Under an arm of that yard the prisoner was presently brought up, the chaplain attending him. It was noted at the time, and remarked upon afterwards, that in this final scene the good man evinced little or nothing of the perfunctory. Brief speech indeed he had with the condemned one, but the genuine Gospel was less on his tongue than in his aspect and manner towards him. The final preparations personal to the latter being speedily brought to an end by two boatswain's mates, the consummation impended. Billy stood facing aft. At the penultimate moment, his words, his only ones, words wholly unobstructed in the utterance, were these: 'God bless Captain Vere!' Syllables so unanticipated coming from one with the ignominious hemp about his neck—a conventional felon's benediction directed aft towards the quarters of honor; syllables too delivered in the clear melody of a singing bird on the point of launching from the twig—had a phenomenal effect, not unenhanced by the rare personal beauty of the young sailor, spiritualized now through late experiences so poignantly profound.

Without volition, as it were, as if indeed the ship's populace were but the vehicles of some vocal current electric, with one voice from alow and aloft came a resonant sympathetic echo: 'God bless Captain Vere!' And yet at that instant Billy alone must have been in their hearts, even as in their eyes.

At the pronounced words and the spontaneous echo that voluminously rebounded them, Captain Vere, either through stoic self-control or a sort of momentary paralysis induced by emotional shock, stood erectly rigid as a musket in the ship-armorer's rack.

The hull, deliberately recovering from the periodic roll to leeward, was just regaining an even keel when the last signal, a preconcerted dumb one, was given. At the same moment it chanced that the vapory fleece hanging low in the East was shot through with a soft glory as of the fleece of the Lamb of God seen in mystical vision, and simultaneously therewith, watched by the wedged mass of upturned faces, Billy ascended; and, ascending, took the full rose of the dawn.

In the pinioned figure arrived at the yard-end, to the wonder of all no motion was apparent, none save that created by the slow roll of the hull in moderate weather, so majestic in a great ship ponderously cannoned.

26

WHEN some days afterwards, in reference to the singularity just mentioned, the purser, a rather ruddy, rotund person more accurate as an accountant than profound as a philosopher, said at mess to the surgeon, 'What testimony to the force lodged in will power,' the latter, saturnine, spare, and tall, one in whom a discreet causticity went along with a manner less genial than polite, replied, 'Your pardon, Mr Purser. In a hanging scientifically conducted—

and under special orders I myself directed how Budd's was to be effected—any movement following the completed suspension and originating in the body suspended, such movement indicates mechanical spasm in the muscular system. Hence the absence of that is no more attributable to will power, as you call it, than to horsepower—begging your pardon.'

'But this muscular spasm you speak of, is not that in a degree more or less invariable in these cases?'

'Assuredly so, Mr Purser.'

'How then, my good sir, do you account for its absence in this instance?'

'Mr Purser, it is clear that your sense of the singularity in this matter equals not mine. You account for it by what you call will power—a term not yet included in the lexicon of science. For me, I do not, with my present knowledge, pretend to account for it at all. Even should we assume the hypothesis that at the first touch of the halyards the action of Budd's heart, intensified by extraordinary emotion at its climax, abruptly stopped—much like a watch when in carelessly winding it up you strain at the finish, thus snapping the chain—even under that hypothesis how account for the phenomenon that followed?'

'You admit, then, that the absence of spasmodic movement was phenomenal.'

'It was phenomenal, Mr Purser, in the sense that it was an appearance the cause of which is not immediately to be assigned.'

'But tell me, my dear sir,' pertinaciously continued the other, 'was the man's death effected by the halter, or was it a species of euthanasia?'

'*Euthanasia*, Mr Purser, is something like your *will power*. I doubt its authenticity as a scientific term—begging your pardon again. It is at once imaginative and metaphysical—in short, Greek.— But,' abruptly changing his tone, 'there is a case in the sick bay that I do not care to leave to my assistants. Beg your pardon, but excuse me.' And rising from the mess he formally withdrew.

27

THE silence at the moment of execution and for a moment or two continuing thereafter, a silence but emphasized by the regular wash of the sea against the hull or the flutter of a sail caused by the helmsman's eyes being tempted astray, this emphasized silence was gradually disturbed by a sound not easily to be verbally rendered. Whoever has heard the freshet-wave of a torrent suddenly swelled by pouting showers in tropical mountains, showers not shared by the plain; whoever has heard the first muffled murmur of its sloping advance through precipitous woods may form some conception of the sound now heard. The seeming remoteness of its source was because of its murmurous indistinctness, since it came from close by, even from the men passed on the ship's open deck. Being inarticulate, it was dubious in significance further than it seemed to indicate some capricious revulsion of thought or feeling such as mobs ashore are liable to, in the present instance possibly implying a sullen revocation on the men's part of their involuntary echoing of Billy's benediction. But ere the murmur had time to wax into clamor it was met by a strategic command, the more telling that it came with abrupt unexpectedness: 'Pipe down the starboard watch, Boatswain, and see that they go.'

Shrill as the shriek of the sea hawk, the silver whistles of the boatswain and his mates pierced that ominous low sound, dissipating it; and yielding to the mechanism of discipline the throng was thinned by one-half. For the remainder, most of them were set to temporary employments connected with trimming the yards and so forth, business readily to be got up to serve occasion by any officer of the deck.

Now each proceeding that follows a mortal sentence pronounced at sea by a drumhead court is characterized by promptitude not perceptibly merging into hurry, though bordering that. The hammock, the one which had been Billy's bed when alive, having already been ballasted with shot and otherwise prepared to serve for his canvas coffin, the last offices of the sea undertakers, the sailmaker's mates, were now speedily completed. When everything was in readiness a second call for all hands, made necessary by the strategic movement before mentioned, was sounded, now to witness burial.

The details of this closing formality it needs not to give. But when the tilted plank let slide its freight into the sea, a second strange human murmur was heard, blended now with another inarticulate sound proceeding from certain larger seafowl who, their attention having been attracted by the peculiar commotion in the water resulting from the heavy sloped dive of the shotted hammock into the sea, flew screaming to the spot. So near the hull did they come, that the stridor or bony creak of their gaunt double-jointed pinions was audible. As the ship under light airs passed on, leaving the burial spot astern, they still kept circling it low down with the moving shadow of their outstretched wings and the croaked requiem of their cries.

Upon sailors as superstitious as those of the age preceding ours, men-of-war's men too who had just beheld the prodigy of repose in the form suspended in air, and now foundering in the deeps; to such mariners the action of the seafowl, though dictated by mere animal greed for prey, was big with no prosaic significance. An uncertain movement began among them, in which some encroachment was made. It was tolerated but for a moment. For suddenly the drum beat to quarters, which familiar sound happening at least twice every day, had upon the present occasion a signal peremptoriness in it. True martial discipline long continued superinduces in average man a sort of impulse whose operation at the official word of command much resembles in its promptitude the effect of an instinct.

The drumbeat dissolved the multitude, distributing most of them along the batteries of the two covered gun decks. There, as wonted, the guns' crews stood by their respective cannon erect and silent. In due course the first officer, sword under arm and standing in his place on the quarter-deck, formally received the successive reports of the sworded lieutenants commanding the sections of batteries below; the last of which reports being made, the summed report he delivered with the customary salute to the commander. All this occupied time, which in the present case was the object in beating to quarters at an hour prior to the customary one. That such variance from usage was authorized by an officer like Captain Vere, a martinet as some deemed him, was evidence of the necessity for unusual action implied in what he deemed to be temporarily the mood of his men: 'With mankind,' he would say, 'forms, measured forms, are everything; and this is the import couched in the story of Orpheus with his lyre spellbinding the wild denizens of the wood.' And this he once applied to the disruption of forms going on across the Channel and the consequences thereof.

At this unwonted muster at quarters, all proceeded as at the regular hour. The band on the quarter-deck played a sacred air, after which the chaplain went through the customary morning service. That done, the drum beat the retreat; and toned by music and religious rites subserving the discipline and purposes of war, the men in their wonted orderly manner dispersed to the places allotted them when not at the guns.

And now it was full day. The fleece of low-hanging vapor had vanished, licked up by the sun that late had so glorified it. And the circumambient air in the clearness of its serenity was like smooth white marble in the polished block not yet removed from the marble-dealer's yard.

28

THE symmetry of form attainable in pure fiction cannot so readily be achieved in a narration essentially having less to do with fable than with fact. Truth uncompromisingly told will always have its ragged edges; hence the conclusion of such a narration is apt to be less finished than an architectural finial.

How it fared with the Handsome Sailor during the year of the Great Mutiny has been faithfully given. But though properly the story ends with his life, something in way of sequel will not be amiss. Three brief chapters will suffice.

In the general rechristening under the Directory of the craft originally forming the navy of the French monarchy, the *St Louis* line-of-battle ship was named the *Athée* (the *Atheist*). Such a name, like some other substituted ones in the Revolutionary fleet, while proclaiming the infidel audacity of the ruling power, was yet, though no so intended to be the aptest name, if one consider it, ever given to a warship; far more so indeed than the *Devastation*, the *Erebus* (the *Hell*), and similar names bestowed upon fighting ships.

On the return passage to the English fleet from the detached cruise during which occurred the events already recorded, the *Bellipotent* fell in with the *Athée*. An engagement ensued, during which Captain Vere, in the act of putting his ship alongside the enemy with a view of throwing his boarders across her bulwarks, was hit by a musket ball from a porthole of the enemy's main cabin. More than disabled, he dropped to the deck and was carried below to the same cockpit where some of his men already lay. The senior lieutenant took command. Under him the enemy was finally captured, and though much crippled was by rare good fortune successfully taken into Gibraltar, and English port not very distant from the scene of the fight. There, Captain Vere with the rest of the wounded was put ashore. He lingered for some days, but the end came. Unhappily he was cut off too early for the Nile and Trafalgar. The spirit that 'spite its philosophic austerity may yet have indulged in the most secret of all passions, ambition, never attained to the fulness of fame.

Not long before death, while lying under the influence of that magical drug which, soothing the physical frame, mysteriously operates on the subtler element in man, he was heard to murmur words inexplicable to his attendant: 'Billy Budd, Billy Budd.' That these were not the accents of remorse would seem clear from what the attendant said to the *Bellipotent*'s senior officer of marines, who, as the most reluctant to condemn of the members of the drumhead court, too well knew, though here he kept the knowledge to himself, who Billy Budd was.

29

SOME few weeks after the execution, among other matters under the head of 'News from the Mediterranean,' there appeared in a naval chronicle of the time, an authorized weekly publication, an account of the affair. It was doubtless for the most part written in good faith, though the medium, partly rumor, through which the facts must have reached the writer served to deflect and in part falsify them. The account was as follows:

'On the tenth of the last month a deplorable occurrence took place on board H.M.S. *Bellipotent*. John Claggart, the ship's master-at-arms, discovering that some sort of plot was incipient among an inferior section of the ship's company, and that the ringleader was one William Budd; he, Claggart, in the act of arraigning the man before the captain, was vindictively stabbed to the heart by the suddenly drawn sheath knife of Budd.

'The deed and the implement employed sufficiently suggest that though mustered into the service under an English name the assassin was no Englishman, but one of those aliens adopting English cognomens whom the present extraordinary necessities of the service have caused to be admitted into it in considerable numbers.

'The enormity of the crime and the extreme depravity of the criminal appear the greater in view of the character of the victim, a middle-aged man respectable and discreet, belonging to that minor official grade, the petty officers, upon whom, as none know better than the commissioned gentlemen, the efficiency of His Majesty's navy so largely depends. His function was a responsible one, at once onerous and thankless; and his fidelity in it the greater because of his strong patriotic impulse. In this instance as in so many other instances in these days, the character of this unfortunate man signally refutes, if refutation were needed, that peevish saying attributed to the late Dr Johnson, that patriotism is the last refuge of a scoundrel.

'The criminal paid the penalty of his crime. The promptitude of the punishment has proved salutary. Nothing amiss is now apprehended aboard H.M.S. *Bellipotent.*'

The above, appearing in a publication now long ago superannuated and forgotten, is all that hitherto has stood in human record to attest what manner of men respectively were John Claggart and Billy Budd.

30

EVERYTHING is for a term venerated in navies. Any tangible object associated with some striking incident of the service is converted into a monument. The spar from which the foretopman was suspended was for some few years kept trace of by the bluejackets. Their knowledges followed it from ship to dockyard and again from dockyard to ship, still pursuing it even when at last reduced to a mere dockyard boom. To them a chip of it was as a piece of the Cross. Ignorant though they were of the secret facts of the tragedy, and not thinking but that the penalty was somehow unavoidably inflicted from the naval point of view, for all that, they instinctively felt that Billy was a sort of man as incapable of mutiny as of wilful murder. They recalled the fresh young image of the Handsome Sailor, that face never deformed by a sneer or subtler vile freak of the heart within. This impression of him was doubtless deepened by the fact that he was gone, and in a measure mysteriously gone. On the gun decks of the *Bellipotent* the general estimate of his nature and its unconscious simplicity eventually found rude utterance from another foretopman, one of his own watch, gifted, as some sailors are, with an artless *poetic* temperament. The tarry hand made some lines which, after circulating among the shipboard crews for a while, finally got rudely

printed at Portsmouth as a ballad. The title given to it was the
sailor's.

BILLY IN THE DARBIES

Good of the chaplain to enter Lone Bay
And down on his marrowbones here and pray
For the likes just o' me, Billy Budd.—But, look·
Through the port comes the moonshine astray!
It tips the guard's cutlass and silver this nook;
But 'twill die in the dawning to Billy's last day.
A jewel-block they'll make of me tomorrow,
Pendant pearl from the yardarm-end
Like the eardrop I gave to Bristol Molly—
O, 'tis me, not the sentence they'll suspend.
Ay, ay, all is up; and I must up too,
Early in the morning, aloft from alow.
On an empty stomach now never it would do.
They'll give me a nibble—bit o' biscuit ere I go.
Sure, a messmate will reach me the last parting cup;
But, turning heads away from the hoist and the belay,
Heaven knows who will have the running of me up!
No pipe to those halyards.—But aren't it all sham?
A blur's in my eyes; it is dreaming that I am.
A hatchet to my hawser? All adrift to go?
The drum roll to grog, and Billy never know?
But Donald he has promised to stand by the plank;
So I'll shake a friendly hand ere I sink.
But—no! It is dead then I'll be, come to think.
I remember Taff the Welshman when he sank.
And his cheek it was like the budding pink.
But me they'll lash in hammock, drop me deep.
Fathoms down, fathoms down, how I'll dream fast asleep.
I feel it stealing now. Sentry, are you there?
Just ease these darbies at the wrist,
And roll me over fair!
I am sleepy, and the oozy weeds about me twist.

ABOUT THE AUTHOR

~~~~~~

HERMAN MELVILLE was born in 1819 in New York City. As a
young man, he signed aboard as a crewman on several whaling
ships and frigates. His experiences at sea provided him with the
material for much of his fiction, including *Typee, Moby Dick,* and
Billy Budd, Sailor. Now recognized as one of the great American
writers, his innovative prose and natural gift as a storyteller were
largely neglected by the reading public in his own lifetime. He
died in obscurity in 1891, having published nothing in nearly
thirty years.